EIMI

By E. E. Cummings

POETRY

Tulips & Chimneys

& [And]

is 5

W [ViVa]

No Thanks

22 and 50 Poems

1 X 1 [One Times One]

XAIPE

95 Poems

73 Poems

Uncollected Poems 1910–1962

Etcetera: The Unpublished Poems

Selected Poems

Complete Poems 1942–1962

AnOther Cummings

PROSE

The Enormous Room

Eimi

Fairy Tales

EIMI

A Journey Through Soviet Russia

E. E. CUMMINGS

Edited by George J. Firmage
Preface by Madison Smartt Bell
Afterword by Norman Friedman

LIVERIGHT
New York London

Copyright © 1933, 1961 by the E. E. Cummings Trust
Copyright © 2007 by Liveright Publishing Corporation
Preface by Madison Smartt Bell copyright © 2007 by Madison Smartt Bell

All rights reserved
Printed in the United States of America

For information about special discounts for bulk purchases, please contact
W. W. Norton Special Sales at specialsales@wwnorton.com or 800-233-4830

Manufacturing by The Haddon Craftsmen, Inc.

Library of Congress Cataloging-in-Publication Data

Cummings, E. E. (Edward Estlin), 1894–1962.
Eimi : a journey through Soviet Russia / E. E. Cummings ; preface
by Madison Smartt Bell. — 4th ed.
p. cm.
ISBN 978-0-87140-652-1 (pbk.)
1. Travel—Fiction. 2. Soviet Union—Description and travel. I. Title.
PS3505.U334E5 2007
813'.52—dc22   2007024004

Liveright Publishing Corporation
500 Fifth Avenue, New York, N.Y. 10110
www.wwnorton.com

W. W. Norton & Company Ltd.
Castle House, 75/76 Wells Street, London W1T 3QT

1 2 3 4 5 6 7 8 9 0

Contents

Preface

by
Madison Smartt Bell

Best remembered for his innovative style in poetry, E. E. Cummings was a jack of many artistic trades: poet, painter, draftsman, playwright, and (on two occasions) a writer of extended prose. *The Enormous Room* is his first full length prose narrative. *Eimi* is the second and the last. Both of these books were published as novels, but neither quite meets that standard definition. Both are closely based on Cummings's own experience and both feature a protagonist closely similar to himself. Cummings was too much the lyric poet to project casts of invented characters into a wholly invented narrative. What sets his long prose works apart from simple memoir is an artistic shaping accomplished by Cummings's eye, ear and hand.

As a visual artist, Cummings has not been much remembered, though he had a quick eye and a clever touch. Two of his wives had been (among other things) fashion models, and Cummings made the most of their beauty in portraits—his images of Marion Morehouse add up to a small but respectable opus all on their own. As a representational painter he was influenced by Matisse, and as an abstractionist he was affected by Picasso in his Cubist phase and by other Cubists with a softer palette, such as Juan Gris. He was a handy sketch artist, who could capture an image quickly if lines seemed more efficient than words, and sometimes he used the two together, as in a pictorial note to Miss Morehouse: an elephant drawn in the words of the message, the word love cunningly positioned as the penis.[1]

Cummings's considerable skill as a visual artist colors his work as a writer. He used the typewriter as a graphic instrument and was particularly interested in the position of words on a page. Often crucial in his poetry, visual arrangement can be just as important in prose works like *Eimi*, especially in passages that cannot be easily grasped in the more conventional way:

> Parcours:(heart my suddenly)FRANCE(paused)
>   BON pour:GOOD for
>   UN PREMIER DEJEUNER
>   ONE MEAT BREAKFAST(politely he murmurs)
> and here's your passport with all the necessary visas
>   (handing whom dollars)I can(7)scarce(90)ly believe it
>   ninety-(gentil Mr. Wagons)seven(-Lits taking my)
> dollars(dollars politely murmurs)
>
> . . . incr
>   (oya
>   bl
>   )e . . .
> O
> re
> mus
>
> just inside hugENess,a poet is praying.
>   I feel that he is blind[2]

Eimi is based on a visit to Russia that Cummings made in May and June of 1931. In this period between the first and second World Wars (well before the atrocities of Stalin's regime were unmasked), the Communist experiment was seen by many in Cummings's circle—the Stateside politically progressive sector overlapping with an artistic avant-garde—as a Utopia in the making, and perhaps even the inevitable "future of mankind,"[3] (a term which Cummings himself, however, uses only ironically). Individualistic to a point near anarchy, Cummings was presciently suspicious of the Soviet regime, whose insistence on collectivism struck him as repressive, even by report. But he wanted to see for himself.

> "Five . . . The redfox leans toward me. Why do you wish
> to go to Russia?
>   because I've never been there.

(He slumps,recovers). You are interested in economic and sociological problems?

. no.

Perhaps you are aware that there has been a change of government in recent years?

yes(I say without being able to suppress a smile).

And your sympathies are not with socialism?

may I be perfectly frank?

Please!

I know almost nothing about these important matters and care even less.

(His eyes appreciate my answer). For what do you care?

my work.

Which is writing?

and painting.

What kind of writing?

chiefly v erse;some prose.

Then you wish to go to Russia as a writer and painter? Is that it?

no;I wish to go as myself.

(An almost smile). Do you realize that to go as what you call Yourself will cost a great deal?

I've been told so.

Let me earnestly warn you(says the sandyhaired spokesman for the Soviet Embassy in Paris)that such is the case. Visiting Russia as you intend would be futile from every point of view.[4]

This gloomy prognostication proves in many ways to be true. Cummings kept a diary during his trip, not without trepidation; since he had jumped the tourist rails from the day he first arrived in Moscow, he was shadowed by the state secret police (then known as the GPU) and regarded, at least potentially, as a spy. (One wonders what Stalin's enforcers would have made of Cummings's highly unusual prose style if they ever had confiscated the diary.) Once he emerged, he worked the diary into the published version of *Eimi*, retaining the day-by-day, date-lined structure of the original.

The journey is presented as a passage through the underworld. *The Enormous Room* (based on Cummings's three-month confinement during

World War I in a French internment camp where he had been sent for the absolutely ridiculous reason that he refused to declare that he hated Germans) has a similar limbo-like quality. In a preface to *Eimi*'s second edition (published twenty-five years after the first) Cummings puts the matter frankly:

> ... I enter "a world of Was"(p. 8)—the subhuman communist superstate, where men are shadows & women are nonmen;the preindividual marxist unworld. This unworld is Hell.[5]

The tour of Hell is modeled (though very loosely) on Dante's *Inferno*. At the outset, as Cummings does his all to escape from the overpriced official Intourist Hotel Metropole in Moscow, the Cummings character is adopted by a guide, variously addressed as "mentor," "ex-mentor," or "Virgil"—in reality the American scholar Henry Wadsworth Longfellow Dana, who was then a great admirer of the Soviet social enterprise. Soon, however, Cummings shakes off this guidance and moves in with (in reality) the American journalist Charles Malamuth and his wife, Jack London's daughter Joan (variously addressed in the text as "Beatrice" or "Turkess").

At the same time that he invents these highly idiosyncratic appellations for his companions on the way, the Cummings figure projects (or is compelled by circumstance to project) other avatars of himself: not only Cummings (the foreigner traveling Russia in conspicuous want of an agenda), but also Comrade Kemminkz (an alter-ego properly susceptible to the dubious blandishments of the Soviet state), and Peesahtel (Writer) or Hoodozhnik (Painter)—these last two being shell identities Cummings was obliged to assume in his several quasi-official encounters with his Russian *compères* in literature and the arts.

Naturally quick with languages, Cummings picked up a smattering of Russian during his stay, and he already spoke passable French, which was convenient at a time when this language was spoken by many survivors of the Russian upper classes. Still, Cummings, Kemminkz, Peesahtel, and Hoodozhnik could not navigate very far on their own, but required the assistance of others more fluent in Russian, and (perhaps more importantly) better experienced in the perverse vagaries of the so-called system. In none of his guises did Cummings see anything that would really interest a spy, though he ate a lot of bad food, saw a lot of bad art and bad theater, and felt (and resisted) the weight of a vast hierarchy bent on stamping his experience into its mold. His way out of Russia (from Moscow via Kiev to Odessa by train, by ship to Istanbul and to Paris on the Orient Express) is presented as a journey from darkness toward light.

In the "unworld," where all being is expressed as its negation, our protagonist often refers to himself as the "heroless hero." But within the matrioshka shells of Cummings, Kemminkz, Peesahtel, Hoodozhnik, and heroless there persists the ultimate Cummings lowercase i—a letter which stands up twice for itself in the title. "the word eimi,pronounced 'a-ME', stands for the Greek word ειμι=am," Cummings explains in the 1958 preface. "To devotees of the Old Testament,this may suggest Exodus III,14—'I AM THAT I AM' ".[6] Yet Cummings's i has little of YAHWEH's bombast. i is small, usually inconspicuous, but nimble and resilient and completely committed to its liberty. It runs around inside the wainscots of Soviet Russia like the mouse in a *Tom and Jerry* cartoon. All the overwhelming pressures of Stalinist totalitarianism cannot crush it.

For its extravagance in language, *Eimi* has sometimes been compared to *Finnegans Wake*, but (though the special sort of popularity Joyce had won in the thirties may have helped to enable *Eimi*'s first publication) it does not set out to batter the reader with difficulty. To all that Soviet Russia can marshal against him, Cummings opposes his own very frolicsome idea of free speech. He gives us a language completely unfettered, romping through episodes of fair a nd faithful figuration, cubistic fracturing of the episode and scene, flights of pidgin Russian and utterly unorthodox French, phonetic renditions of dialect that would spin the head of Mark Twain—and more. Cummings had a hell of a good time writing this book, and the reader is meant to have that good time too.

[1.] Reproduced on p. 40 of *Dreams in the Mirror*, a biography of Cummings by Richard S. Kennedy (Liveright, 1980).

[2.] *Eimi* p. 424.

[3.] *Eimi* p. 129.

[4.] *Eimi* p. 15–16.

[5.] *Eimi* p. xv.

[6.] *Eimi* p. xv.

Sketch for a Preface
(1958 edition)

title

the word eimi,pronounced "a-ME",stands for the Greek word ειμι=am.
To devotees of the Old Testament,this may suggest Exodus III,14—"I
AM THAT I AM". If someone should have encountered a small book
entitled i(six nonlectures),he or she will perhaps recall the quotation(p
63)concerning "an IS". See also my introduction to the Modern Library
edition of The Enormous Room

subject

eimi,first published in 1933,is the diary(May 10-June 14 1931)which I
kept during most of a trip from Paris to Russia,thence to Turkey,& back
to Paris. When my diary opens,I'm on a train bound for the Polish-
Russian border. At N(Negoreloe)I enter "a world of Was"(p 8)—the
subhuman communist superstate,where men are shadows & women are
nonmen;the preindividual marxist unworld. This unworld is Hell. In Hell
I visit Moscow,Kiev,Odessa. From Hell an unship takes me to Istanbul
(Constantinople)where I reenter the World(pp 393–403)—returning to
France by train

structure

my journey falls in 9 parts,paged as follows
Paris-Warsaw-N,& N-Moscow,by train. . .1–11
Moscow. . .12–264
Moscow-Kiev train. . .264–271
Kiev. . .271–287
Kiev-Odessa train. . .287–297

furthermore,the Moscow section(more than half eimi)divides itself into
an earlier(12–130)& a later(133–266)period. During the earlier,my
address is the Hotel Metropole & my guide is VIRGIL. During the
later,I am the guest of BEATRICE & TURK;chez Chinesey

characters

thanks to a maker's congenital fondness for metaphor—heightened by
Russia's immemorially merciless(once tzarist,now socialist)Gay-Pay-
Oo or Secret Police—the persons described in eimi are masked with
nicknames. A single person may have many nicknames:thus,during my
first Moscow day(May 12)"1 ultrabenevolent denizen of Cambridge
mass(who hibernates half of each year in Russia,spinning meanwhile an
opus on the theatre)" becomes Mr. Spinner & mentor & the benefactor
of benefactors & Virgil & Sibyl & benevolence & wc(walking corpse)&
the 3rd good Cantabrigian & our guardian angel & Dante's cicerone &
the recorder. As VIRGIL,he is one of eimi's chief characters. Another
is Lack Dungeon's daughter(from the standpoint of the marxists;who've
canonized her moderately popular father as a Great i.e. Proletarian
Writer)alias BEATRICE(in relation to VIRGIL)alias Turkess or Harem
with respect to chief character number three—who's the TURK,sometimes
called Assyrian or that bourgeois face or Charlie. Then comes the NOO
INGLUNDUR of Odessa,or otherwise known as defunct & mentor &
Noo. Last we have tovarich(comrade)peesahtel y hoodozhnik(writer
& painter)Kem-min-kz(Russian for Cummings)alias I or C or K,alias
Poietes(Greek ποιητηζ=maker=poet). Item:the church of St Basil in
atheist Moscow is also masked—first(p 25)appearing as "Something
Fabulous";later(91)as "sheer barberpolemiracle-pineappleprodigy",&
still later(106)as "the Arabian Nights cathedral" abbreviated(110)to
"Arabian Nights"

synopsis(chief characters are capitalized when they first appear.
"R"=Russia,Russian. Italics indicate a keypassage. Compare pp 248–251
with my Caedmon recording)

May 10

a twoberth 2ndclass compartment of the train from Paris to "N". Finical votary of Somerset Maugham(2)gets out;hearty exwarrior with mustachios,seen off by an equally hearty pal,gets in—*"change,that's all"*(2–4)

May 11

wake to find mustachios gone(5). Lunch with excited Swiss who boasts he's everywhere met. Train crosses PolishRussian border. Customs-shed at "N"—Swiss is bringing in a lot of tools over which a mirror's smashed(7)—all the junk I'm bringing in on behalf of A's wife's sister is passed—have my first sight of roubles—buy ticket to Moscow. And enter *"a world of Was"*(8). Swiss is met by a R who immediately separates us(8). Antique train & fantastic diningcar(9). R compartment-mate & I discuss America via gestures & picturepostcards

May 12

breakfast in diningcar(11). Arrive Moscow. Am not met by a great R poet & novelist(12). VIRGIL appears at Hotel Metropole(17)—introduces shy young American(19)—M deskman finds me a room. Stroll:guided by Virgil,experience a socialist bank(21–22)& meet distinguished R censor with hole in forehead(24)& sample uneatable proletarian lunch(25)—glimpse Marxist slogan(*religion is opium* etc)plus Lenin's mausoleum plus Something Fabulous(church of St Basil,now an antireligious museum). Virgil retires with bellyache;I manage to send telegram—elevator surprise(26). Virgil(recovered)walks me upstairs to meet young American couple,but they're out—descending,we encounter them;plus livid R military tactician(27)who's helping them move to cheaper quarters in some suburb. Virgil takes me chez fanatical Cambridge Mass convert(Mary)to communism(28–29)—then introduces me to genial president of Writers' Club(31)& later to his own "interpreter"(31–32) with whom we witness a propagenda play called Necktie(33–34)

May 13

waked by request for passportphotos—breakfast with Virgil—
enter(35)livid R(29)who's shopping for shy American(19). The
foodhunt(36)—Torgsin fakery(37–38). Underground lunch with
Virgil(39). Glimpse of Grand Hotel(40). We tram:call on Duranty,who's
out(41)—visit sick friend of Virgil. . .oo-Borneye-ah(42). Tram back
to Metropole & meet Virgil's "other secretary",lame(43)—we three
start for theatre:he(unaware of her lameness)causes transportation
crisis(44–45)—prapaganda play The West Is Nervous(45). He
& I visit pseudonightclub—my *tirade* against collectivity attracts
GPUs(47–50)

May 14

breakfast chez Virgil;sick youth(now better)present. *Argument*
(51–53)Q(Virgil)vs A(Kem-min-kz). We visit chief R publisher,who's
out(53)& revisit(55)Torgsin(37)where Chinesey warns Virgil in
vain(56). The *GPU* parade. Lunch at Writers'. A park peepshow(57).
A propaganda melodrama(58–59)called Roar China(162)—& a
row(59–60). I visit St Basil

May 15

Madame Potiphar(sister of Mme A)phones,inviting me to lunch(61)—
breakfast with Virgil,who kindly maps my way. His young friend
guides me to bank(in vain)& Intourist(62)—pass a sleepingdictionary
correspondent. A godlike voice. Laden with junk,start for
Madame's(64)—arrive(64)& receive cordial welcome—*"shining things"*
(66)—she phones & gives me address which may get me cheaper
room(66). Enter husband—& a hero of work(66–67)—banquet(67–
68). Enter & exeunt a GPU & his nonman. Madame's husband,left
alone with me,delivers speech of *indoctrination*(69)—takes me to Hotel
in taxi(72–73). Virgil says dayaftertomorrow we dine with charming
daughter of much by Rs admired American writer(Lack Dungeon)plus
the R who didn't(12)meet my train

May 16

my R permis de séjour appears(74). Breakfast chez Virgil,who tells me how to reach address(of Revolutionary Literature Bureau)given by Madame(66)—there I find fat & lean nonmen;also a cadaverous he(75)who invites me to dine with him & fat(76)—enter the female member(Scratch)of American couple(27)followed by male(Grouch);& carrotheaded(Clara Bow)Englishman,offering me half a room with old lady sans plumbing & giving me a translation to look over(77). We 3 Americans go to my hotel,where she persuades deskman to give me cheaper room(77–78)then we visit market(79–82)—I tram with them to see a still cheaper room chez eux(80)& meet proprietor(81). Alone,experience socialist hosing & atheist emanation. . .(81–82)—keep my dinner-date with fat & cadaverous(Jill & Jack)—banquet(83–84)with a *reminiscence of Dos*—am shown R books;deliver message from EP—receive a 3hour speech of *indoctrination* by cadaverous(85–89)—*The Verb*(89–90). Learn how to order breakfast myself—walk miles & buy matches

May 17

waked by omelet(91)—venture inside St Basil:a nonman is lecturing to comrades—the madonna of the string(92). Visit Revolutionary Literature Bureau;make acquaintance of Otto Can't(93)who says husband of Lack Dungeon's daughter has a bourgeois face. Virgil & I go to Chinesey's house where daughter & husband live—I meet her(BEATRICE)& him(TURK)& the missing(94)great R poet & novelist & a great R dramatist(romp)& an American newsman plus wife(94)—delicious meal(95)—Virgil,furious,rushes off to be in time for propaganda play based on tale by Beatrice's father(96). We follow later;tram overcrowded,I jump through window. After infantile play(97)during which I learn about roubles(98)we try(99)to locate romp's domicile(he having disappeared to prepare a party for us chez lui)—en route,Turk tells enlightening *story of a R scientist* who refused to "volunteer"—finally we arrive(101). Romp gives us bootleg champagne;then everyone adjourns to the Savoy(102). Romp wants me to accompany him to a model factorytown in country;all expenses paid—encouraged by

Turk,I riposte(103)—*afraid to be afraid.* Find myself on top of a ladder outdoors. Assure romp I'm a family man(104)

May 18

hangover & sore foot. Virgil's very feeble. Writers' Club President finds me seat for this evening at art theatre(105–106)—lunch with great R poet & novelist(we glimpse romp:he stares)who tells me tzarist tale about St Basil. And buys flowers—(K)*there is an I Feel*(107). At Revolutionary Literature Bureau,Otto Can't soothes 2 angry comrades(107–108)then insists on strolling with me. A gaga street-sprinkler(108). Otto warns me that flowerbuyer is a mere fellow-traveler(109)and relates marxist tale about St Basil(110). On Metropole's 5th floor,encounter the sleepingdictionary correspondent(111)—he shows me his room(111)— "*the woman's touch*". At theatre am given 2 frontrow seats—run into Virgil & interpreter(112)& exchange seats with him(112). After propaganda play,Virgil & I visit pseudojoint with ancient jazz(113–114)whence a drunk is expelled(115)—"*work*" & "*slave*"—I tell Virgil story of me & Mr. X(116)—we shake a GPU(117)

May 19

an honest chambermaid(118). I seek Art Museum—not a boobyhatch nor a planetarium—sans success(118–119). Virgil invisible. Go alone to Chinesey's—he's with 2 deathlydull American hes—says my mentor's expected soon—a 3rd compatriot joins us(120). Enter Virgil—then Turkess & Turk—later I glimpse 2 nonmen & a pianoplaying someone(121). Uncomfortable meal with also R actor,making 9. Turk & Turkess & I leave together—they're bound for opera—he wangles me a ticket(121–122). Bolshoy theatre;Turk points out Gorky—Prince Igor well presented(123)—a doctor & wife & child appear. During final intermission am invited by Turk via Turkess to be their guest as long as I remain in Moscow. Child bedded at Grand Hotel;we 5 go dancing(124)—Turk enlightens doctor's wife re R(127)"*a total stranger*".   I go home with Turk & Turkess—she finds a cheering cablegram(129). The wolfboy accepts pyjamas(130)

May 20

handorgan with cockatoo—breakfast(131). A hot bath(133)—& a latchkey. Turk's halfR-halfEnglish secretary(Nat). Nobody at Writer's Club—no mail at Intourist(134). Visit Metropole Hotel—livid R tactician(134)helps me pack. Call on flowerbuying(135)R poet & novelist(135–136). Return to Hotel,ask deskman(Foxy Grandpa)for bill—financial transaction via abacus—eventually taxi arrives(139)—I taxi with baggage to Chinesey's. Turk & Turkess's maid(wooden alias ogress)says nobody's home—Turk & Turkess enter with bundles—a chess-set(139). I work at translation of A's "Red Front"—Turk takes me out for a drink(140)*"the real reason"*. Meet the AP man(god)who battles Turk(*"the idea's right"*)re R(141–144)

May 21

worry over absence of mail. Turkess talks of her father. A's poem(145)*analyzed*. Turk introduces unhappy nongal(not Nat) secretary(146). Young Englishman calls. I walk to Intourist(shut)& then to Metropole:no mail(148). President of Writers' Club arranges rendezvous with famous theatre director(Something)tomorrow— delicious meal(149). Wonderful party chez flowerbuyer(150)with Turk & Turkess(151)—la lune

May 22

Turk,Turkess,Nat & I(153)—joined(154)at Volks by Grouch & Scratch(76, 77)—visit a socialist jail(154–161)—the R captain,the radio question—*"personal issue does not exist"*. I return to Chinesey's & shave—locate Something,director of Roar China(162),& family(163). Party at god's—Mammy Sunshine (165–167)—god's Indian(168). Soviet movie,Don(168). A passport crisis

May 23

wagon-jaunt(170)with Turk for packingcases—Mr. Electriclight & icechest—American hay,American nailpuller(171)—*"we Rs can only*

TALK"(172). Turk & I walk back. Turkess & I tram,bearing food to non-volunteering(173)scientist—*a man,a human being*—& wife(173–174). A knock—enter a tovarich—questions the priest of the microscope—exit:we relax. Flowers. I visit(175)Intourist & Hotel:no mail. Turk & Turkess & I go to a Soviet circus;whose elephant is antisocialist(175–178). Accident(178–179). Good news re my passport

May 24

visit Revolutionary Literature Bureau & give Clara Bow(180)my translation(145–146) of A's hymn of hate(180). Breakfast chez god & Mammy(180). Look in at Something(161)'s showhouse(181). Meet Turk & Turkess at art theatre—also exVirgil(182)—3 Gorky dramatizations(183). Turk & I inspect Lenin institute;he puts on phonograph record. We plus Turkess dine chez scientist & wife,with their child & his wife's sister(185–186)—"*the only reason*" bells don't ring. K & T re an *idea* vs its *application.* Alone,I have a close call(187–188)

May 25

Turkess depressed—Nat hurt(189). Diagram given me by scientist leads to miraculous Museum Of Western Art—Picasso & Matisse(190). Sobbing of a nonman chez Chinesey(191). Boris—& bells! Turk & I visit pseudojoint. *We of whom Is partakes*

May 26

catch glimpse of unknown boyface;hear sobbing of nonman. Story of *a frameup*(194). Kremlin tour cancelled. Intourist—& a letter for me!(195). No luck at Turkish consulate(196). Writers' Club ditto. Torgsin,dolls—& exmentor:who pales on hearing that livid R tactician(197)is a GPU. A cross between a pawnshop & a picturegallery(198). At Something(165)'s theatre,a propaganda play called The Last Decisive(199–201). Homing,pass a Gay-Pay & see a domestic crisis;& hear a girl singing! Tremendous party with Turk & Turkess chez an exsaloniste—R *heart* vs *head*—with ravishing Polish blonde & marvellously alive cricket(202–206)

May 27

everyone halfdead—except Nat,who'll deal with my exit visa(207). I(bearing gifts)visit socialist family which includes le citoyen russe(208–210). Then present my 2nd letter of introduction—the nonman's at work. Turk re Nat—"*Never trust a R*"—I discuss war with Turkess(211–212). Peruse article re Americans(213). 2 nonmen—one(eyes)I saw chez Chinesey;the other(plumper)is harder—& Harem & I stroll to Turk's office;he's with young Englishman(148)& another man(213)—we 7 stroll—other man & Englishman leave us—we 5 go to god's. Chez god a tremendous party;with Chinesey & the very distinguished R censor(24)& Nat(214). Nat & I dance;then nonman(eyes)whose exiled husband translated some of my poems,& I. Gypsy songs—a briefly luscious she—more songs—Mammy takes a header(216). Speech by Dum,who's one of the deadly chez Chinesey Americans(215),in rhyme;re a man named Wood(216–217). I don't meet Duranty. Tell-off a she-reporter(218–219)—"*I AM a little boy*"

May 28

phonecall:dinner invitation for tomorrow. Go with Turk & Harem to the Bolshoy—music("Pickwick")—Rborn English conductor—my seat collapses twice(220–221)—house enthusiastic. Feel depressed—find letter at Intourist,telling of R's suicide. No president at Writers'. A delightful outdoor photography establishment. Discover conductor snoring chez Turk,guarded by private secretary(222). Dinner given by Chinesey: nonmen plump & eyes(223),conductor & private secretary,Turk & Turkess,myself—conductor in raptures re Moscow(223). We go to a musical burlesk—whose cast twice visits our box in honour of Pickwick. Female correspondent(yellow)joins us (224)—Turk phones censor:no news. Chez Turkess,I converse with "dame russe"(friend of eyes,but differs with her re flowerbuyer)about Rs & Americans(225–226). Turk elucidates *deviation*(226–227). Kittens(227)

May 29

Turk explains what *poet* means under socialism. No mail. I go to Metropole,ask about Lenin's tomb;nobody agrees—investigate premises(228)& learn it's open daily at 7 PM(229). Run into Grouch(229)at Intourist—no service—he recommends another ticket agency,but that's shut;so return—an American's ahead of me—eventually pay for "soft" to Kiev & get information re Odessa & Constantinople— must come back tomorrow at 3:30. Torgsin—watch a teakettle being wrapped(231)& buy toys(232)—accused by(dark bozo)salesman of capitalism. I laugh;"*no artist ever is a capitalist*"(233)—now feel am really going out of the unworld!(234). Get myself photographed at outdoor place(234);photographer speaks German(234–235). Chez Turk,meet lofty Jewess. *To govern or be governed?* Mr Electriclight & refrigerator(236)'s father versus god—son warns me to get my exit visa in Moscow(236). Dine with socialist family(237–238)—doll & frau & citoyen russe & boy(237–238)leave bearing their gifts. *Noone can learn growing*—granddaughter of Tolstoy & R's foremost prosewriter's wife(238)

May 30

visit the drycleaners with Nat(239)—then she helps me get my exit visa(240)—Rose Marie—too much love—& a photograph(242). No mail. Collect my toys—& buy dark bozo(243)food with valuta,taking his roubles in exchange(244). Forgetmenots. Turk's American social secretary (trustworthy)guides me chez yellow(245)—they talk,gossip;we eat;I tell of *the R who touched Turkess's eveningdress*—hear of omnivorous *censorship* & implacable *propaganda*—define *thinking*(247). Darksmoothlyestishful (247)& husband(247)to dinner—something 's gone completely wrong:she's terrified. Extraordinary procession entering Lenin's tomb—I say I'm an American newsman & am put at head of line—I descend,behold,arise:*again false noun* (248–251). Untheatre,with Turk & Turkess & blonde(251)'s husband(hal)—who describes agonies of *socialist railroading*(252–253). Turk re *happiness*

May 31

R history per me(255),Torgsin(bozo 255)with Turk:I buy presents. He demands & gets my exit visa(256). We visit Turkish consulate: closed,& consul out(257). Attend a church service—priest,mother & baby,flowers—"*it's TRUE!*"(258). *The tragedy of life*,per Assyrian(258).

Cummings & Kem-min-kz. My ticket!(260). On the way to farewelling St Basil,run into exmentor with 2 unyouths—finally I escape(261). Enter a ghost—the former toolbringer(261);wants dollars & a cigarette—a comrade takes him away(262). Hunchback(262). Tolstoy's granddaughter dines with us—*Russians;artists*—won't let Turk photograph her. Turk & Turkess & I & baggage tram to station— nomads—my baggage is boosted into stinking car(264). T says he'll wire a Kiev hotel to reserve room for me—away I go,waving(264). In my car is a gentle Jew,enthusiastic over R;we exchange food—also an angry industrial hero who vainly tries to take this-for-everyone-candle(266). I sit,writing,in the aisle(266)

June 1

hop down from upper shelf—chocolate with Gentle—his story:3 armies,misery & pogroms(268–269)but now all's well;yet he's depressed(269). 2 GPUs board chattering train—*total terror & absolute silence*:passengers & baggage searched—cops vanish(270). Kiev:untaxi to hotel(271)—a chair floors me—(272). Sweet air—I stroll—oldmen on hilltop. Marvellous starry churches—*here the lone star of socialism dies*—I attend a service(273). Magnificent sunset. I go to bed dinnerless

June 2

breakfast(276)—Intourist:pay for "soft" to Odessa;ticket will be given me at station(276)—don't get back passport—pack(277)pay hotel bill & am given passport(278)—buy postcards—Torgsin—arrange for departure(280)—walk to monastery & return(281)—no taxi;wait;with bum—whirlwind ride to station(282)—bum tells me to sit:wait & wait(284)train lost(285)—train not lost:beers with bum—enter weasellike,says no ticket. Pause. He rushes me to GPU;where am finally given an order for a "hard" ticket—ticket is at last procured(286–287)—& am stopped at gate to train. Speak 3 words—the gate opens(287)—baggage & self squeezed aboard train. Am examined by group of fellow-passengers(289–291)—an artist draws me a picture(291)—am brought food—one of examiners *insists I take his bunk*,with linen sheets;refuses chocolate,suggests I give some to scared nearby kids(293)—exhausted I doze(293)—waked by a GPU—who vanishes(293–294)

June 3

cogitation(295)—slight catastrophy(296). Odessa—Ocean!(297). A Ritzy hotel—its Intourist urges me to return to Kiev. *A bidet in hell*—bathe,sketch,stroll(298–299). Proud-erect(299)ly headwaiter—garden—& the NOO INGLUNDUR (300)who orders me food,raves against Intourist(300) reserves cheaper room for me & arranges my meals(302)says boat for Istanbul leaves Monday,gives me anti-Intourist booklet & loans me volume by Edgar Wallace(302). I stroll—lunch—note Torgsin blonde & child. Night:actually girls & boys,young!(303–304). And a bootblack

June 4

Noo(defunct)Inglundur gives me telegram—reserves my boat ticket & gets me a Turkish visa(305). Real beer. Noo presents dwarfish individual (stunned)& we 3 lunch(306). Stunned's story—"*Il ME FAUT Travailler!*"(308). Potemkin(309)stairs. Buy food & drink with defunct(309). He shows me where I'll take boat(311). We debate(312)dangerous visit to mother of my Paris R teacher(12,241,101). I meet defunct's daughter & wife. He says he'll give me a letter to benevolent American wife of the American builder of Stalingrad tractorplant. Their son & daughter attend Roberts College in Constantinople & will show me all the sights(313–314). Defunct & I make dangerous visit;am left alone with Head:rain(314–317). Back to hotel—my new cheaper room. Mentor(Noo)re nude bathing,the *"noo ruhligion"* of communism,*money* ,his Noo Haven father,*prostitution,*his family(318–319)& *"Karl Marx's wiskus"*(319–320). Stunned's case improved. A wink from proud-erectly(322)headwaitering dignity(322). Find in my pocket a draft of an already sent telegram(323)

June 5

my lastnight's wash almost dry—donning merely moist shirt,descend to shawdan(jardin)mentor(Noo)presents a grumbling American leonine chipmunk(325)who inveighs against Intourist & Americans(325–327). Mentor & I hunt vainly a shoestring(328)—am guided to a beach(Arcadia)by a R comrade & wife. Stroll,alone;noting 1 attractive nude(330). Children—the Potemkin stairs(331)—stunned re fascism. Defunct has bad news for stunned:I translate;he understands(333). "Shine"(bootblack)& my shoes—*fine weather & nothing to eat*"(334–335). A gruesome pair

June 6

tall tales by Noo mentor—grumbling(336)is skeptical(336–338). After vainly visiting a bank,grumbling reveals himself as a musician(339). I buy food & drink. More bad news—hotel manager will throw stunned out. Noo wangles reprieve from commissariat of work(340)—takes mushyoo(monsieur i.e.,stunned)& me to see mudbathing:Noo & I swim(341–343). Back to hotel—stunned won't enter diningroom unless manager invites him—manager will allow stunned 3 days more,but won't feed him(344)stunned collapses—we get him to my room:he won't accept a loan;goes to his own room. I lunch with Noo;we visit the thankful wife(345). Later:knock—stunned enters my room,calmer now. An unlucky fairy(346)

June 7

tomorrow,departure! Noo & stunned & I visit a beach—I swim;then collect stones & shells—three reactions to a soft drink(347–348). My twicedropped watch stops. Back at hotel,stunned gives in—& from dignity(348)we order a feast(348). Mentor recommends movie called Morale—stunned & I,waiting for it to begin,are properly gypped at "Cafe Restaurant". In theatre's foyer,stunned finds his consul;who encourages him. Am amazed by *shadow-pictures* of reality,of Germany,of *the world* (351). An *African* American—in panic(352). From the Hotel's garden comes LAUGHTER—stunned & I investigate—behold capitalist drunks shouting for service at(dignity having vanished)comrade(GPU) waiters(352–354)

June 8

K(em-min-kz)& C(ummings):a dialogue(355). Thanks to socialism, 2ndhand $1 watch would cost me $55—cost of repairing my watch would be 1 lb butter in open market(356). Stunned's consul has given him 2 more days but he must go to commissariat of labour—he & Noo & I go:it's shut. Noo returns to Hotel,stunned & I visit eatery;then rejoin mentor—who's jubilant:says everything OK but don't tell him yet(358)—we revisit commissariat:where stunned is examined(in French)re matters electric & tells what he knows—& *"je Vais TRAVAILLER!"*(359). I give Noo imitation-razorblades & present my holey socks to "shine";pay my bill;lunch with jovial Noo & amazed stunned;dignity(322,348)himself shakes hands with me—off go Noo & stunned & I plus my baggage(359–360). Have slipped Noo all my remaining roubles—no trouble with R officials—goodbye to stunned—go aboard with Noo:he unlocks an empty cabin,inserts baggage;relocks. Wave to stunned(362). Noo's goodbye(362–363). Boat seems to be named "French Marine":why? Make acquaintance of a dude(364). Dinner—dude summons me to entertain 2 tablemates: Palestine bound Americans,unfemale(pop)& nonmale(spouse)—they lecture about R glories(*"a man here don't have to worry"*)—pop's in drugstore business(364–369). Dude produces phonograph,plays jazz. Out boat can't start because of engine-trouble —its name is really "Franz Mering"(370). Dude & spouse dance;then he puts on Turkish record,which pop prefers. Since dude has 3 cabinmates & I'm solo,I offer him a bunk chez moi(372)

June 9

our ship hasn't moved an inch(373). After breakfast,lecture by pop(374–376). Ship moves,but in a circle because(a man with a boy tells dude)captain's trying-out compass:we're soon back at Odessa(376). Finally voyage begins—while pop lectures(377–379). Dude suggests tea—man with boy joins us—I learn that dude's an Afghanistanian(fuzzy-wuzzy);boy-man knows Chinesey,Turk, Beatrice,also flowerbuyer(380);asks why I chose Odessa—I can't say it was in order to see the mother(314–317)of my Paris R teacher(12,102)—suddenly realize I forgot to bring earth. Dude & boyman & I discuss R(381)—Mr. boyman reminds me of grumbling (324)the musician(339). Don(dude)Juan re R economics(381). Pop's name is Sam. Portrait of(Horseface comrade 382)Forsooth,a friendly

R seaman(381–82). Notice a youth sawing a bootsole from a piece of wood(383). Superb sunset(383)—plus Sam

June 10

fine weather. Boyman explains *how a communist ship functions*(385). Pop lectures(385–387). At lunch,his spouse suddenly reveals cause of their mutual enthusiasm re R—& the R 2ndmate(388)halfsmiles. More lecturing(388). The World's coast appears(391). Harbour—horseface(391)assembles passengers—passport inspection by Turkish caviarspurning officials(391). Mirror magic(391). Thanks to Forsooth,my passport's okd;i.e. shall go ashore this evening. A Parisienne phantom. Stars & lights—*O,now everything begins*(391–392). Dude warns me to keep near him(394). Ship anchors—confusion;boats & boatmen;wailing—dude introduces his Eddie Cantorish brother. My baggage is grabbed by somebody & rushed down gangplank into a boat—dude yells that I must get into his-&-Eddie's boat—many voices tell me(in French)to get into boat where my baggage is & my friends will follow;but as soon as I'm in this boat,its 2 boatmen push off & start rowing away from ship—dude yells for me to return—I(poietes)command boatmen to stop;they merely row harder:I promise to kill them(396)—immediately they turn around & row back to ship. Grabbing my bags I transfer to dude-&-Eddie's boat. As we move shoreward in darkness,Eddie insists I'd have been slain(397). *Terra firma*(397). Customs-shed:weeping mother,idiotic son(398),cheerful baby,boy & sobbing girl—father,dude says,tried to stow away on R ship & was caught. Dude's tin trunk provokes amazing scene(399–400). He & Eddie & I squeeze into taxi—my baggage tied on or hanging from car. Moonrocket ride to a hotel—where my pals deposit me(403). Room—my baggage appears:I lean out of open window—*not by un deceived any more*

June 11

morning:view from a window(405–406). Am guided by genial hotelkeeper's boy down Pera to ticketoffice—kindly youth takes my passport for visas:everything will be ready tomorrow;changes my money:telephones Roberts College & discovers whereabout of Noo's guardianangel(407). I buy watch named Tosca(407)firsthand & inexpensive. Taxi—find guardianangel's daughter(408)—we taxi to shore & she hails her brother who's out sailing with a friend(freckles)of his—taxi runs over sister's suitcase—I join the boys in sailboat(409)—am warned that Kemal has ruined Constantinople(410)—we land—I meet son's other sister & mom—American family meal(411–412). Goodnatured boys taxi me to town—I behold Saint Sophia(414)& Blue Mosque(415)& Gate & Bazaar—street of silks;of jewels;of weapons:freckles buys old pistol(416)—Hill Of Wonders & Bridge Of Boats over the Golden Horn—train to Pera;& finally delicious beers(417). Back at hotel solo—knock:dude—we visit taxim:he lauds Kemal & science & progress—religion everywhere dying(418–419)—buys me Turkish records—after dinner we visit a Dancing on *The street*,where we see R dancers & are joined by a dressy youth—drunk,am TALKING,even LAUGHING(420–422). Eddie in taxi Cantor(422)

June 12

collect my train ticket(423–424). Revisit Saint Sophia:*the blind poet*,children,an oldman,birds(424–426). Now am sitting at a piano(426)—after wrestling with Sophia's licelike guides & buying postcards & entering(alone)the Blue Mosque(SpiReingA 426)& losing myself looking for the Gate & Bazaar,& presenting fuzzy-wuzzy(dude)'s drunkenly last night scribbled address to a gentle taximan & violently arriving at this diplomatic mansion & finally being admitted(427). Dude leads me upstairs,disappears to shave & bathe:I read Turkish history. Coffee(fragrantly-smokingly)served. Lunch? But somebody on official business arrives—& am smuggled out(428). Pera. Memories of childhood(429–430)& youth(430)—death & rebirth: *we have arisen.* Now am en route to Paris via the Simplon Orient Express—it's incredibly hot;but my 2ndclass compartment-mate is a jolly French travellingsalesman who hates Syrians. And I remember leaving my hotel(431)& taxiing to station & seeing my train come in & boarding it(as did 2 shes suggesting an Oriental bathing-beauty contest winner plus her aunt). Sunset—*not hell's Red* —but I can remember hell(432)

June 13

W.C. crisis(433–434). The Balkans. Am reminded of a piece of string(435)—
my Tosca(407) still functions(436). Memories(268,318,363) of hell(432).
I stroll out to see our locomotive,& address it in terms of *prophecy*(436–
437). And *revelation*(437). One American(the money we have)vs our
conductor(439–440). I recall my Odessa Hotel's garden(jardin,shawdan,
440)with its unfunctioning fountain & serious comrades;then girls &
boys(441)who are young(442). Our first parent

June 14

memories of Paris:Luxembourg Gardens(balloons,toyboats,donkey-
& goat-cars,a punch&judy show)& Trees(443)times Valery(443)re
God(443). Again crisis. Recapitulation(443–444). We enter Italy.
Memories & Venice & lunch & heat & memories & heat & dinner(447)&
mountains & memories & Switzerland & coolness. Recapitulation
continued(448). French border—jolly(450)vs the customs(450–451).
Recapitulation concluded:from SHUT(1)to OPENS(452)

R words
(their pronunciation imitated, & their meaning)

AhdEEn—one
americANitz—American
ARbat—nightclub section, Moscow
beel-yET—ticket
boyshOY—big
boo-mAH-gah—paper
boo-tEN-kah—shoes
byez-par-tEEnee—sans political affiliations
chEH-loh-vek—man
cheye—tea
   "   hatEEtyeh?—do you wish tea?
chOR-nee-yeh—black
correspondENt—newspaperman
da—yes
dAHs-vee-dAHn-yah—goodbye
dOHmah—at home
dvah—two
dyES-itch—ten
gAHl-stook—necktie
gOR-od—town
hAH-rah-shOH—good
hOHda nyET—no passing through
hoo-dOZh-nik—painter
IZ-ven-EE-cheh—pardon, excuse me
kAHk vee-pah-sheh vEYE-tyeh—how are you?
kOFF-yeh—coffee
klOOtch—kety
kOM-nah-tah—room
kOO-shat nyET—nothing to eat
Kras-EE-vah pa-gOHda—fine weather
kwass—a soft drink
lOZh-ka—spoon
nah-zAHn—mineral water

nEE-cheh-vOH—no matter, never mind
nyEH gah-voo-rEET—(he) doesn't speak
nyET—no, not
nyEZ nEYE-oo—(I) don't know
oo-BOR-neye-ah—toilet
oo-mehn-yAH mAHla d-yEH-nik—I haven't much money
pa-gOH-da—weather
pAHn-yee-mEYE-oo—(I) understand
pah-jAHl-stah—please
pap-eer-OH-sa—cigarette
pay-rOOk-mah-care—barber
pee-sAH-tel—writer
pEE-voh—beer
per-OSH-kee—meat pies
plOK-oh—bad
pOCH-eh-mOO—why
pOS-leh—after
     "   zAHf-trah—day after tomorrow
pota-mOOsh-toh—because
pyATch—fifth
rab—slave
rAB-oh-tAH—work
rOO-kah—hand
sah-bAH-kah—dog
schlAH-pah—hat
sesh—six
shtOH—what
sh-chOT—(hotel) bill
skOIl-koh—how much
soo-dAH—hither
SOR-ok syEM—47
spas-EE-bah—thank you
spEEch-kih—matches
syeh-vOHd-nyeh—today
tAHk—so
tAHm—there
tovARich—comrade

val-OO-tah—foreign money (vs roubles)
vAH-shez-darOHv-yah—your health
yah—I
"   nyeh hah-chOO—I don't wish
"   "   mag-OO—I can't
yEStch—there is
zAHf-trah—tomorrow
zdyES—here

EIMI

SHUT seems to be The Verb:gent of lower("ça ne vous fait rien si je me déshabille?")whose baggage strangles a sickly neatness of deuxième coffin Shut the window(don't you think we'll have too much smoke?)and tactfully funeral director,upon glimpsing milord today drowsing after cakes & ale by mister mome,Shut our door(this morning I was thoroughly amazed:met,en route to breakfast,Fresh Air!—in a troisième common grave)

and lunch was more Shut than a cemetery:4 separate corpses collectively illatease:no ghost of conversation. Ponderous grub;because(last night,Shut in a breathless box with a grunting doll)I rushed sidewise into Germany(but that swirling tomb of horizontality was less Shut than the emptiest rightangledness which called itself "essen")

lowering weather through SHUTnesses—dank dark fields,smutted towns.
Enlivened by
    (1)a trainmaster(or whatever)in colours remembering how those children who are our ancestors would emblazon images of hourglass-ladies-fair(displayed,with other touching nonsense,on quais)
    (2)Das Magazine—at least 2 really delicious allbutetc. girlies
    (3)astonishingly armears of windmill poking over a brief worldedge
    (4),,OO"
    (5)hugest(andtoadreamstreamlined)locomotive-nakedly-floating-most-lazily-who(throughhanoverstation)slid-whispering-extinction
    and framed with
                    nie wychylaá sie
                    omwieraá drzwia
                    podczas biegu pociagu

. . . Bahnhof Zoo(swirling bells(church we knew(park I walked in)))

at a pause:horridly roboty child smothered by ferocious Blau,swinging a ditto balloon at end of wire and guarded by fallenarches mother. Enter hairless father dragging a scooter by its neck;gestures:wearily . . . but life,life!—they've detached the inert poisonous ball and are batting it foolishly among themselves.

A stop—cakes & ale disappears("so,goodbye" to me)and kissed 2 arminarm appearing friends,of whom 1(erect,worldly;mustachios)inherits my erstwhile Shutter's lower.

"The thing is,to make room" he said,wondering toward the ceiling.

"Because there's plenty of everything else" I agree.

"Y-e-s."

"The compartments are small" I dare to assume.

"They are. But this—" indicating a gilded bump occurring for ornamental unreasons "used to stick out more."

His crony(big,cleanshaven;mutilated mouth)temporarily garnished our cubbyhole with the majesty of a waterspout. He too has English: wherein explains that yearns to go gunning in a certain now fabulous land . . .

"I went to the place and everyone was very polite and a girl told me It's all right It's all right because you're a Polish citizen. But the expense!"

"how much would a little hunting trip in Russia cost?" I ask

"she told me twentyfive dollars. I said Preposterous. Then she said But it's being reduced to seventeen. That's still preposterous."

"Twen-ty . . . five . . . dol-lars?" the mustachios protested vaguely.

"Twentyfivedollarsaday."

"O,a day—hm. Well,I think you'd surprise them,coming there with your guns and butlers and everything" he winked at me and shook à la Deerslayer. "With your butlers! As you used to do it! That would be funny,eh? Something new to them!"

"the funnier it would be,the better" said the waterspout genially. "I should make it as funny as could be. Why not? —This your first time?" he asks myself.

"Absolutely."

"O well . . . but we who've seen Russia before—they can't fool us!"(foot never exterminated cigarette with more premeditated violence)

"I fought the bolsheviks twice and I'd fight 'em again"(says mustachios,the exterminator having departed)"once as a White Russian officer and once in the Polish army." And learning that my own visit is quite negligibly pacific "why I think they ought to be more afraid of you than of me"(chuckling horribly)"—I'm all through with 'em;but writing's . . . dangerous."

Twilight—a wet rolling land of gentle infinite darkness . . . a little silhouette with a lantern,himself dissolved in universal . . . a bird,reading the air . . . (what spirits go & come?curiously into Whom are we all unpossibly melting?)
Mustachios,comfortably bedded with a colossal tome,utters Deutsch:apologises("it's difficult to—to . . . shift")and proceeds "I should think Duranty could help you. I know him. He's a terrible bolshevik."
"Really?"
"nonono;we just call him that. But he thinks the five year plan will succeed and I don't."
The Perfect Spread For Bread. "Does he think it will spread?"
"I'm not talking about that:if it succeeds,of course it will spread."
"Really?"
"he doesn't think so but I do." Then he shaded childeyes with a woman's hand and asked "are you English or American?—I thought so. Good night"

no objection as I open window!

the train reels. "I've seen all sorts of revolutions" he remarks "and I've come to the conclusion that people are idiots. It doesn't make a darn"(sic)"bit of difference what the government is—because the secret of the trouble is somewhere else. I was radical when I was young(and I'm still young). They told me A republic is the only form of government because it's cheaper." Reel. "But a republic is a thousand times more expensive than a monarchy because in a republic there are so many people to pay." Reel. "Now if Spain had become communistic,that would be something worth while;but republic—! It's idiotic." He upsquirmed. "All governments are good when they're young,but later on they all break to pieces;because there's something in everybody that breaks to pieces." And portentously "change,that's all."

11 o'clock:timid customsofficial salutingly intrudes & extrudes. Is this indeed Stench or merely Poland? The mustachios orders a

bottle of water("I ordered water—she doesn't bring it")which finally arrives("there:she brings it"):we discuss abolition of passports("could be done tomorrow")and of customsofficials("very difficult—even worse in the middle ages"). Presently "why don't you undress and go to bed?" Eventually "why don't you go out and look at the new station,since it's the first time you've been here?"—which I do;'tis quite the model American bathroom.

Wake alone—he got out at 6(Warsaw)while I was chez the gentleman from Vienna;but for some unconscious reason there's rather less room than before(perhaps compartments made of elastic nonspace,which contracts automatically when something is put into it and automatically expands when something is taken out)

seek the diner,semiexpecting(thanks to my American-procommunists-living-in-Paris—The Horrors Of Capitalist Poland)to be brutally cheated;if not softly knocked down and simply robbed. Frank E. Campbell turns me round with a word of his own,supposed to be "wagon restaurant": march tipsily back through train,past living corpses hit with Fresh Air and luxuriously outstretched on authentic wood. Promptly and courteously I'm supplied with excellent coffee butter bread and cheese:at nearby table,a plutocrat,insisting that the only waiter(who's obviously Robinson Crusoe)accept one entire American dollar;R.C. obliges with footprint-in-the-sand reflex—my own(less immodest)generosity provokes the more hysterical thanks of 5 languages.

Windmills! Reeling up–&-over-behind villages or standing soishly among sunful skies. An everywhere of fields,spattered with animals,pricked with beings. Big holes of air & crude blocks of land(I can almost smell this world). When the savage beings wear colours,the colours are hard red and tight blue. The gruesome faces of the tiny beings come at me immediately, genuinely,through Shutness. And(look)pinetrees are,whose here Thelike together creates an Aful leaning;and(there)specks(and look)browse all forming one direction. Rhythm:organic Is—neither fillable nor emptyable;actually(how clumsily)alive.

Pause:Unser Gott still effective;beer at 60pf and Berlin newspapers at 30. Across the way something flutters:a woman? Not a woman;woman: immensely crouched beside grey pond she rubs 1 by 1 black pots. Ducks patrol,geese survey. And the coarse fierce earth spouts dandelions. This(who's shoving a bottle to someone in 3rd)has dainty legs but her thick face roosts on a tough neck and she grins(unable to smile? Can noone smile in Poland?) Here's a sickly youth;grabbing into himself a soiled child clumsily who waves,waves,as our drowsy train stumbles away—he smiles,an idiot's distant rare smile

after vainly more than suggesting that 100 mark notes must sooner or later disintegrate,friend Robinson cheerfully announces "dé jeuner ready." I sit opposite

the greater
HOTEL ST. REGIS
new york
where Fifth Avenue is Smrtest

on rear of a menu murderfully wielded by wildish ignorantlooking bozo with a palpably fixed look,who(hearing my commande)timidly indicates through his own Shutness a "petite cheval." The houses hereabouts,hints he,are "tout neuf." (A Swiss. Going to Moscow upon some mission which I cannot understand;will be met—everywhere he travels he's met.) Proudly points to a kind of shield on his lapel:I distinguish 3 rays. From his upper right vest pocket produces a larger version of kind of:I observe 3 lightningflashes,emanating from 3 phallic protuberances labelled "dynamo magneto starter." Below is stamped a mystic word. He flashes a pocketbook—stamped with the same word;and reaches into his upper left vest pocket:appears a metal pencil,with the word again. Points to lapel;the word is on the kind of. I comprehend nothing—"pourquoi?" "Instructeur." Slightly above the kind of,a scarlet ladybug. We arrive at N,says he,at 4.30 and noone will get back anyone's passport and everyone will be emptied out of the train and made to undress;and "you smoke camel." Adding,sadly,that all the country about us(all the country from Varsovie on)used to be Russian(while I glare at ravages of portable sawmills)

actual crossing of borderofborders occurred so quickly and so gently not to say softly I didn't know what had happened until glimpsed a lot of jumping off Polish uniforms & some redflags on an unfinished building & a man in a 2dug ditch looking at his bandaged 1stfinger

tipped,tactful orchestrator of mourning peeps through Shutness at descending me. Almost child(these porters are almost children)beckons.

We enter barndancelike structure:YMCAish,crammed full of limp stink and interminability;upon one end wall,beaucoup bunting frames the coloured photograph of Lenin. Beside me,at bar of judgment,my Swiss. I help him close his big bright valises:containing at least a dozen blankets,some food,and a flock of occult tools—over nearly everything a mirror has been broken. He,ere vanishing,translates a few sentences of Russian German. What are these?am languidly asked. Magazines I truthfully reply. They will be examined by the political censor murmurs my questioner,an overgrown schoolboy. Time yawns. The magazines listlessly are inspected by an imperturbable roundish shaveless chap;are casually returned to the overgrown schoolboy,lazily who pushes them at myself. Your passport? Here(with,under "Visas",the carefully pencilled forgot to erase them Russian equivalents for WC and sonofabitch). This is? A typewriter. (Somebody makes a note of the typewriter's existence). Time sighs. What have you here? Coffee. Etcetera,ad infin.,time goes to sleep. Eventually somebody gently says something about money. Much pointing. Pass beneath SantaClausred banners to investigate a microscopic slit in a newly boarded wall;behind slit sways somebody's occasionally shouting face:French and German and Polish unwealth disappears,appears a scribbled bit of paper and some dirty oblongs and a few mysterious disks(now Marx grant that the scribbling is a receipt and that the receipt is what my Paris-American-procommunists lectured me anent—Horrors Of Not Getting,Or Of Losing,Statement Certifying That Somuch Capital Came In With You—better ask). I ask,even in Russian,and a kindly little man reassures with slowed-up-movie wavings. Shouldn't one present one's traveller's cheques?I threaten. —Nonononono he reassures torpidly. And nothing,even and,happens. But glance at what appeared with the scribble:how tired—asleep,almost . . . what tried,almost asleep,moneyless money! Certainly these ruglike oblongs don't take themselves seriously? Upon this tinsel disk a hammer and a sickle contentedly embracing. Almost child nudges;evidently I'm off:but he doesn't pick up baggage. "Par ici?" I whisper at the suddenly unvanishing Swiss. Go somewhere and do something my excited fellowsufferer complains in several languages simultaneously. Something?—ah,the ticket,from here to Moscow:I go and I do:but what a ticketless ticket! So,in dream moving,preceded by trifles,through very gate of

7

inexorably has a magic wand been waved;miraculously did reality disintegrate:where am I?

in a world of Was—everything shoddy;everywhere dirt and cracked fingernails—guarded by 1 helplessly handsome implausibly immaculate soldier. Look! A rickety train,centuries BC. Tiny rednosed genial antique wasman,swallowed by outfit of patches,nods almost merrily as I climb cautiously aboard. My suitcase knapsack typewriter gradually are heaved(each by each)into a lofty alcove;leaving this massive barrenness of compartment much more than merely empty(a kissing sickle and hammer sink in heaver's palm,almost child trickles away). Dizzily myself seeks Fresh Air. Genially(with an "I'd be naughty if I took it" shrug)the antique wasman refuses a cigarette. Wildly my Swiss greets me— gestures—"train internationale!"(positively ecstatic;has quite forgotten about his mirror). Well,I too have that for which to be thankful:all my gifts came through,even the perfume(after weighing)and the coffee(after spilling)—and ye censor evidently approves of erotica . . . Suddenly,realize that palpitator is now plural;that the knight of the mystic word has been met. And I further notice(or seem to notice)a none too arcane connection between this plurality and Sir Ladybug's now wondrously reduplicated enthusiasm. . . . But tell,O tell me:where are we? Who lives? Who has died? Is there space or time or both for e.g. a drink?—Yes? Glowingly the lord of the broken mirror asserts that both there is,that he and his noble "camarade" are drinkward bound,that I may join(if am so inclined)their fundamentally most worshipful—(exeunt Swiss and Swissmeeter;the former propelled,the latter propelling:and was that by any chance a scowl which I had from the comrade?) Careful . . . Reenter Swissmeeter and Swiss;the former activating,the latter activated by,a bottle—Everyone Here Is So Young!our toolbringer declaims frenziedly. What about passports?drinklessly I inquire. He asks the noble comrade;who states(in crisp Russian German)that all passports will be examined on board— delicately,in kowtowing français,tender my eternal gratitude . . .

reentering formerly-morethanemptiness,find a tall blond stranger simultaneously muttering Russian and tearing at a Shut:he gives up and runs down corridor(leaving ticket and money on a species of tableshelf)as anyhow trainless train hobbles Whereward. Enter the dilapidated wasman:he bobs,leers,dances and makes the sleepsign;I bob,leer,dance and make the sleepsign;both of us bob,leer,dance and make the sleepsign—then I hear "dyenghee." Then I give him something. Then he gives me something. Then we give each other something and I faintly stagger down the trainless train

behind,blundering,2 Americans(And How). 1—"this smells like a stable."

Diner:outmiracling of miracle. Deer in snow(a painting). Pink plant(real?) Customer without necktie(real). 3 roubles for 2 boot-air-broat(a half of a ham- and a half of a cheese-sandwich)1 bottle(vile)beer(but I was warned—Horrors Of Making The Mistake Of Expecting To Find In Russia What You Elsewhere Find Without Expecting)& 1 glass tea. Round bit of Austrian sits opposite;we talk finance,in Goethe which am beginning to remember. And where(O,where)may I be?—and the headwaiter(no less,probably more)has a bandaged 1stfinger. The tea,however,is good. The headwaiter sits,sullenly reading a perfectly blank piece of paper. The deer are in the snow,a painting;and everywhere exist motheaten flyspecked unnecessaries of ultraornamentation(if only everywhere did smell like a stable,or something smelled like a stable;but something and everywhere distinctly don't)and nobody seems anything except lonesome;hideously lonesome in hideousness,in rundownness,in outatheelness,in neglected-ness,in strictly omnipotent whichnessandwhatness. Ah well,the tea is excellent. But everybody's actually elsewhere(I thou he she or it we you they don't have to be told they you we it or she he thou I am elsewhere because nothing if not elsewhere possibly is possible). Elsewhere being where? Perhaps in Russia—for obviously this whateveritis or defunct-Ritz-on-square-wheels isn't anywhere or anything,isn't Russia,isn't a diningcar,isn't(incredibly enough)Isn't. Never hath been begotten,never shall be conceived,such head- and such waiter;such Deer and such In Snow:such nonlife and such undeath and such grim prolifically cruel most infraSuch

a doll's hand captures a pourboire;a speechless face vaguely goes away.

Barrenness now harbours shutnesswrestler;is at ease,his valuables have disappeared. Begins itself conversation. Russian equals English equals square root of minus 1. French he has not;German do I forget. But of gesture we both(fortunately)are made(and quite unmitigatedly is my companion gentil—incidentally,knows several thousand times more about America than I know,or will ever). Expresses not merely approbation of the home of the slave. Especially was lifted by its "lakes" and moved by its "mountains". Also beheld,during a month and a half,innumerable great cities—ungreat picturepostcards whereof he with not merely alacrity produces(we are now communicating in the aisle,while wasman dumps a linen sheet and a stunted blanket upon each of the compartment's sleepshelves)via purely prodigious portfolio. Feel(with not merely relief)in this mind,and coming out of this mind,utterly natural seriousness;gentle:distinct;eager:he is—,quite like a child and totally unlike a childish person—comprised by,composed of,amazingly complex simplicity. (And

seated on the terrace of the maggots,announce "je vais faire un petit voyage en Russie" . . . Larionov rolls back-and-sideways—"Voo?" . . . "Moi" . . . His eyes tighten;quizzically his big face lunges:spinning pours tumbling sounds at Gontcharova,who starts;stares—"Vous?" . . . "Moi" . . . Pain heaps quickly itself up in her eyes;caving(memory)surges outward as wish . . . relaxing,her life how very much more than quietly affirms,You are right:Spring is nowhere else.) —And

unlight from smashed lantern totters slowly over filth,over a("see")picturepostcard of Topeka(over a strolling hard nonmale dirtily whom with a notold tired male adjoining barrenness swallows)over slenderly gesturing scarcely hands. The nontrain shudders slowly. A final cigarette: and America returns to its portfolio. "Change,that's all." I have the lower,for a change. It's cold(even through Shutness)just for a change.

Tues.

Alive?arrive? Whenwhere? —O it's not too late for breakfast(cries,cheer
fully tottering beside his meeter and beaming at scrubby cosmos of field
and forest,Swiss)for we're "un heure de retard." I hasten toward deer in
snow(perforating a frighteningly sanitary sleepwagon full of Americans)and
presently am confronted by black shirt,tieless;soiled dull suit:hair back in a
mane—dead ringer for Trotsky. Also noisefully eating are twain apparently
Cambridge Mass really USSR dames,with horse teeth and dishevelled
cavaliers;this unpretty little group actually seems almost more than
mechanically animated(O say,does la régime soviétique hand all singularly
ugly nonmales a break?) And tea is good.

Quite after considerable imprisonment(in beforementioned highly
polished 1st class slumbermachine—both ends were locked with
mighty keys,on account of a station's dangerous proximity;and
natty German was trying to get in at 1 even harder than was I to
get out)"good morning" says my picturepostcard Russian pleasantly.
"Good morning" say I . . . "Besetzt" Russian admonishes(as try for
the Nth time)whereupon wasman—more power to him—seizes my
shoulders,dances me to further end of car,points,bobs,weaves,winks,
and elsewheres . . . By the bye,Mr. Swiss has a most important
correction to make:he was unpardonably mistaken:it appears that
our unquestionably innocent and undeniably excellent train isn't late
after all(how could it be,comrade?). No;winter time's done for(which
explains hitherto odd fact that round Austrian dinnermate compelled
me to set my watch 2 hours ahead). "Pays magnifique,n'est-ce pas?"
cries the met. To speak truth,I cynically respond,it reminds me
of—he is gone:his meeter has corralled him again . . . evidently I
smell bourgeois

train's. train's Trainlessness. train's trainlessness Expanding. train's
trainlessness expanding To. train's trainlessness expanding to Infinity.
Train's Trainlessness Expanding To Infinity vanishes!

moscow?

"Dadada" from electrified picture-postcard—vividly(look)exit Swiss-in-tow(alas,without even a farewell nod.) The alcove yields its prey. I typewriter knapsack valise fall all over each other,collectively attaining our individual freedoms per not altogether large(but far from peculiarly small)station. Now wouldn't I be in a nice fix if he didn't take it into his unknown head to show up,that prominent Russian writer;the comrade for whom have a gaudy box of chocolates—the fellow to whom obediently I sent a telegram written and signed by that prominent Russian-in-Paris novelist(to whom was introduced by what's her name,the beauteous lady for whose farfamed sister am bringing all those nifty magazines and all that gudjus perfume)? Suppose he simply wasn't here to welcome his brother in literature,alias me? Such would indeed be droll. But something else would be droller! Suppose he did show up,and neither of us recognized the other(it seems,when I stop to think,considerably possible;for both of us haven't the slightest idea what either of us looks like). However,dogs will be dogs and Pavlov,with the aid of lampposts,may have discovered a brand-new recognition reflex;meanwhile,lampposts being unhandy,our hero may just as well ask certain distinguishedlooking comrades whether or no they happen to coincide with the anonymous celebrity who's to direct my very not unerring footsteps(if only everybody didn't look so equally distinguished,to put it mildly!). I approach jittery dude who's a little taller than the divine average

Excuse me:are you Soandso?

hardly,although he farts with an eyebrow. (That was my best Russian,too). Try next the little chap who's just fallen out of an observation balloon into a glass of sour milk

Pardon me:are you SoandSo?

emphatically nyet. Once again—for luck. And this time I choose a comparatively undistinguished comrade;who may or may not be asleep,feebleminded,or both

Forgive me:are you SoandSo?

he doesn't seem to understand. I reiterate my query;nothing doing. I soar into Heine—and a light dawns;the face opens,contracts,and in perfect American says

Nn-nn.

Then he turns his socalled back.

arrives a mystic word—a word not out of a lapel but out of a past;out
of a dingy hole,into which mystically are crushed a stove and 4 chairs
and 3 pedigreed dogs and a tall smashed woman(who's trying to teach
me an unlearnable language)and,very last and most least,my muddled
completely self—the Word,opening myself's mouth,escapes:presto!my
baggage and I find one another escorted through x,and confronted by y
which might easily be mistaken for a fiacre crossed with a catastrophe.
Generously amid which monstrosity buried a monotonous whine sprouts
softly;and(oddly enough)I understand what the sprout is whining. He wants
10. That's what he wants and he can't and won't want anything else. Life
is a mystery and 10 is his favorite flower and not 9 and not 11 and why
not. A shaggy imitation of insanity weaves and wallows before me,tying
and untying itself in willbes and havebeens of frantic affirmation:a looney
Santa Claus,whose 8 tiny reindeer consist of something very(very)distantly
resembling a horse—something whose restless front- and rear-ends are
continually readjusting,but without the smallest success or as if their
hidden protagonists quite vainly were suppressing a natural inclination
to separate and become(as it was in the beginning)a horse's before and
a horse's behind. "Dyesyatdyesyatdyesyatdyesyatdyesyat . . . " From
far and wide,but chiefly wide,at least a dozen other proprietors of
wonderful one hoss shays tune in. All(willbes)weave and(hasbeens)
wallow:a centripetal moan explodes—. Desperate,begin shouting
categorical imperatives at subjunctively unexisting phantom who hugs my
baggage:assure him and mankind that a different concept now possesses
me,that there are new worlds for old and may long live whatsoever might
impermanently serve as a refuge for possessions temporal. The phantom
nods:we advance towards an outhouse. Glimpse(left)of little poorish
square;many human(presumably)beings,disguised as incidents and
accidents,are busily walking(walking overearnestly;walking as if they were
bent on proving to someone their almost if not quite aliveness). —Find
within outhouse(which isn't an outhouse) myself,beside,and partly
atop,Teutonic Beau Brummel who's exchanging with an emaciated Slavic
nonmale something slipshod and otherwise suggestive of the American
language. By timid interpolation the non- isn't a whit alarmed(although
I must smell more than ever bourgeois)—nay,non- volunteers to guide

me,together with Brummel,unto most very wonderfulest oasis entitled "intourist";but first check your baggage,comrade. I,comrade,check my comrade baggage. And now,comrade,give somuch to the comrade. Embellish the phantom(who shows no sign of joy)and greedily our comrade 3some advances toward the poorish little square. Hearseburstingly outrumbles what once was bus—the non- and non-'s charges(and socialism only knows how many less or more comrades)being more or less(but chiefly less)inside. Amen. Pray humbly permission to pay for 3 and politely am permitted to pay for 2 and am gently prevented from offering an enormous banknote to a quiet seamstresslike woman who functions as faretaker and Beau remarks that he has been in India which "I like;very much." So do I. One of our 11 closest neighbours,a comrade with a full pack and no hair,yields to early swerve,knocking kittycornered half a dozen comrades(including So do I). And beyond immemorially mildewed Shutnesses many things which might(or might not)be comrades seem to be leaping for what might not(or might)be lives,thumphurlingly while we hurlbump all(bumphurlthump)along

                            . . . suddenly the whole universe stops—

            recovering,trio disentangles self from extraneous legs and arms;to(lumpishly)jut,into a street.

Non- points:sign INTOURIST

again:an alarmingly ample structure,possibly a crematory? "And this is the Hotel Metropole."

"Very expensive" I feebly protest,as(with a flipperwiggle of adieu)BB floats toward oasis.

"O-no,not in valyootah—well,goodbye:and what is your name? Kem-min-kz?" and gave me a nice smile

my fearingly eyes explore "the Hotel Metropole"(never,in America,has this comrade stopped at a really "first class" robbinghouse. Studiously,in Europe,did he avoid the triplestar of Herr Baedeker . . . and now?) "Change,that's all." O plutocracy,O socialism—gird we up our loins: forward,into paradox . . .

At the sight of a flight of marble-or-something steps framed by boundlessly flowering plants we verily tremble:is(impossibly)the

14

candle worth the game? And just as if to answer said unsaidness,down something-or-marble vista visionary with vegetation waddles 1 prodigiously pompous,quite supernaturally unlovely,infratrollop with far(far)too golden locks;gotup rather than arrayed in ultraerstwhile vividly various whathaveyous;assertingly(if not pugnaciously)puffing a gigantic cigarette;vaguely but unmistakably clutching,to this more hulking than that mammiform appendage,a brutally battered skeleton of immense milkcan. ("And they talk of Swinburne's women" myself comfortingly quoted,floating meanwhile briskly upward and inward). A not imposing counter. Behind it,a ½bald notimposing clerk wailing DAs into a notimposing telephone. Above,around,unbelievable emanation of ex-;incredible apotheosis of isn't. Thither,hauntingly hither,glide a few uncouth ghosts. Near,lounge crepuscularly 2 comehithering poules(alive?) At my left elbow,anyone(with the air of having been someone and who is now merely patient and helpless)and for whom the ½bald is telephoning or pretending to telephone or probably both. In vain—patiently he abandons the instrument to its fate:regards my neighbour helplessly,boosting eyebrowless eyebrows;the regarded helplessly comrade patiently shrugs,copiously meanders. "Have you any rooms?" I said.

"Yes"(not at all disagreeably).

"How much are they?"

"five dollars. But that includes breakfast."

"Five . . . The redfox leans toward me. Why do you wish to go to Russia?

because I've never been there.

(He slumps,recovers). You are interested in economic and sociological problems?

no.

Perhaps you are aware that there has been a change of government in recent years?

yes(I say without being able to suppress a smile).

And your sympathies are not with socialism?

may I be perfectly frank?

Please!

I know almost nothing about these important matters and care even less.

(His eyes appreciate my answer). For what do you care?

my work.
Which is writing?
and painting.
What kind of writing?
chiefly verse;some prose.
Then you wish to go to Russia as a writer and painter? Is that it?
no;I wish to go as myself.
(An almost smile). Do you realize that to go as what you call Yourself
will cost a great deal?
I've been told so.
Let me earnestly warn you(says the sandyhaired spokesman for the
Soviet Embassy in Paris)that such is the case. Visiting Russia as you
intend would be futile from every point of view. The best way for you
to go would be as a member of some organization—
but,so far as I know,I'm not a member of any organization.
In that case you should go as a tourist. And I'm speaking not only
from the financial standpoint:do you realize that without some sort of
guidance you will not see anything,let alone understand?
I realize what you mean. But—
yes?(he encourages).
Again frankly—
Well?
I'm ready to take my chances . . . Dollars?"
"a day."
"O,a day. Hm."
"But you have valyootah"(that serious disease).
"Perhaps" darkly suggested Scotch descent "it would be worth while
. . . what's the name of that—Volks:they might know of something
cheaper there."
"Perhaps."
"Could you give me the address?"
"Yes." Consults a species of encyclopaedia:finding,laboriously
translates something upon iota of paper and hands to me. A streetname
—unfamiliar . . . why? Because,at Mayo's Marine Bar,1 ultrabenevolent
denizen of Cambridge Mass(who hibernates half of each and every
year in Russia,spinning meanwhile an opus on the theatre)gave me his
visitingcard,having first adorned its backside with the name(Volks)and
address(which I don't think is what I now hold in my hand)of Moscow's

foremost Society For The Prevention of Misguidance To Foreigners.
—Our fumbling through pockets hero finally exhumes Mr. Spinner's
gift,remarking "there's an American who lives here:don't know whether
he's here now . . . "

"please" the clerk said,taking(before I have time to compare addresses)
the card and turning it over. "Yes" he said,having read benevolent's
cognomen "I think he lives here."

"?"(my Here had meant USSR;his means the Hotel Metropole).

"Shall I telephone?"

"of course"(nothing short of nonplussed)

" . . . he will be right down." And time moans in time's sleep . . . and a
professorial voice almost pettishly inquires "well why don't you recognize
me?" immediately adding "I thought you were Russian:it's the cap—how
did you know that everyone here wears them? Yes,of course,Lenin began
it. Are you alone? Dear me,there seem to be a great many wives parked
in Paris—by the way,I'm so sorry I didn't realize that the charming lady
. . . you missed the first of May? Odear. But how in the world did
you discover my address? No,not really! Well! Isn't it extraordinary
how things happen. Come come:we must have a talk—let's not wait
for the elevator:you'll notice"(greying his tone)"that the standard of
efficiency is somewhat . . . not that they haven't done wonders!"(together
mounting a group of slightly less marble-or-something)"Do you see
that sign—pair,rook,mah,care? It means Barber. He's an excellent
barber,incidentally,if you should want your hair cut. But what was I
going to say—O yes,you'll notice a great many words,borrowed from
other languages;Russian is full of them—"

a sunlitness highceilinged. "Quite luxurious for me. Yes,that's a radio:
there's one in every room;the programs are mostly propaganda,but very
interesting. On this wall you behold my indispensable theatre map—it
gives the names dates and locations of all the plays. Of course I shouldn't
dream of living like this anywhere else:the point is,what you spend here
enriches the government instead of some private individual who has a
great deal too much already—and it's really not expensive;they give you an
excellent breakfast with real coffee(you probably don't realize that coffee is
a tremendous luxury!—not that things aren't getting better every day;it's
really nothing short of miraculous,what they've done). Mymymymymy.
How I envy you. Seeing Moscow for the first time. . . . O,I meant to ask:

have you had breakfast? Then do let me order you something! Eggs?and jam? Not at all:if you knew how glad I was to see you;it's no trouble,I merely telephone the restaurant—you'll soon discover that it's a pleasure to telephone in Moscow,the service is so efficient;not at all like Paris—"

a few terrifying words directed at invisibility

"—they'll be right up with it. Yes indeed. The service here is really excellent. And while we're waiting,let's step out on the balcony(which isn't very good syntax,but you'll forgive me!)" opening a Shutness,through which we crawl "as you see,I'm pretty centrally situated. That big thing over there is the Bolshoy theatre—Bolshoy means Big—and this over here . . . morgen!"(bowing to a pale overapparelled youth who,with a very handsome thoroughly European lass,graces the continuation of our(precarious perch)"you've heard of him,of course:a leader of the left wing of the German cinema—she's quite attractive,isn't she . . . but what was I saying? O,before I forget:let me warn you particularly against newspaper correspondents." And,in an almost whisper "a terrible thing happened the other day—you know Gene Tunney?well,Tunney—who's really a nice fellow,perfectly honest at heart and of course a Roman Catholic—came here;and the officials opened their arms to him and he was much impressed by everything and went everywhere and showed a genuine understanding of the basic principles on which this workers' republic is founded. Really. Yes. But some of the newspapermen,who are always doing mischievous things—I assure you,they'll poison your mind if they possibly can;you really must take care!—these mischievous correspondents(at least the Russians are honest thieves)got hold of poor Gene Tunney and they took him to a place where ecclesiastical refuse of one sort and another was being burnt—not the really good things,of course:the good ones are carefully preserved by the government,it's extraordinary what they've done,really extraordinary—by the way,this is a dead secret:I'm interested in ikons,myself,but from a purely business standpoint,you understand—even my worst enemies can't accuse me of being religious! . . . Now I've lost the—O:well,and the correspondents arranged it so that,just as poor brother Tunney came walking in,a lifesize statue of Our Lord Jesus Christ rolled right out of the flames clear to Gene's most Catholic feet." Giggle. "At least that's the story. Tunney,of course,was horribly shocked—it spoiled his entire Russian trip—now I wonder if we shouldn't go inside;your breakfast ought to arrive shortly—"(in we crawl)"—ah,here it is"(and a respectful waiter respectfully deposits the tastefully arranged trayful of delicate dainties)"Dada Da—SPASEEBA"(exit respectfully the respectful)"please sit down. Isn't it good. Yes. I suggest that you make the Metropole your headquarters—that is,if there should happen to be a vacancy,and provided you think you can afford it. Of course one can always comfort one's self— I always do—with the reflection that what you pay here goes directly to the state,instead of enriching some dreadful plutocrat. Odear. I suddenly remember something:I must go to the bank and get money for my hotel—would you like to come along? It might be a good thing for you to know where the bank is. And that reminds me of something else:I really must pay brother What'shisname;it was such a good party and I practically invited myself . . . but how can I possibly persuade brother What'shisname to take it?that's the question. Hm. Ah!—I shall fold up a bill and put it in this envelope"(suiting action to word)"and I shan't tell the good brother how much it is;I really want to pay my share—yes. Well,shall we start? Nonono;finish your cup of coffee,by all means:there's no telling when you'll get another—I'm exaggerating,of course;as a matter of fact people live well here. And excuse me,please,for rushing you this way,but if we don't leave immediately the bank will be closed;besides,I really must exonerate myself before brother What'shisname . . . so you think you'll stop here,if you can find a room? For a few days,perhaps—hm. I think that's a very sound idea;not to mention the pleasure it would give me . . . I know personally several of the people to whom you have letters. Yes. It's almost as though one were seeing Russia with virgin eyes,one'sself. Quite,in fact. HAH-RAH-SHOH!"

right turn:at end of hall "here's his door"(tapping gingerly)"let's not go in,he might be with—O,how do you do! No,we can't stay:well,only for a moment—let me present brother Cummings." A shy young American, surrounded by bachelorneatness,shakes my hand. "Excuse us for intruding:it's about that excellent party to which I invited myself—but I did!—nono,really we mustn't,you see we're on our way to the bank,but my conscience troubled me so much:please be merciful and let me pay my share!" "Your share was practically nothing" objects shy. "Well anyway"(most mysteriously passing him the envelope)"do let me give you this. And thank you so much for the party—not at all,my dear fellow—by the way,won't you come to lunch? Well,another time,then:

DAHS-VEE-DAHN-YAH!" We hurry up the hall. "Charming,isn't he(I wanted to leave before he opened it). One of the few really nice—did I warn you against correspondents in general? Good. And now we'll go right down stairs . . . O,what about your baggage?"

to ½bald my mentor speaks wingless words—promptly I exchange still sinful(why can't I remember to erase those 2)credentials for a(by some miraculous accident unoccupied)sanctuary,situated on floor 1 of the Hotel Metropole,Moscow,USSR("you're really terribly lucky. To my certain knowledge there hasn't been a vacancy here for months—of course you've heard of the housing problem;people really do marry to get a room. O don't worry about your passport—it's the custom:they'll give it back later. Incidentally,the room you're getting isn't as large as mine,of course;but on the other hand it's nearer certain indispensable conveniences(did you bring some with you?Odear)and I'm not at all sure that your view isn't even better than my own"). Collecting what I,comrade,checked in the comrade outhouse will cost—the comrade clerk seems cautious on this point—about 10 roubles("is that all the izvostchik at the station wanted? I'm surprised! But you were probably right to come by bus;the fact is,it's almost impossible to find a taxi.— Now where is my . . . don't tell me I've forgotten to take that pill! I have. Excuse me,I'll just run upstairs and be right down—how perfectly stupid and ridiculous!") Time stirs;whispering,relaxes . . . until,armed with all things unnecessary and necessary(including a twice forgotten letter of credit and a violent attack of indigestion)the benefactor of benefactors announces "—we're off!" and descending comrade visionary vista we comrades emerge:into

Fresh Air,burgeoning with amorphous beings:sunlight,tucked with swarming closeups of oldfashioned streetcars("don't they remind you of Harvard Square" the Sibyl mused,whimsically). "I was just thinking how somehow Athens-Of-America everything seems" agreed(dimly)Æneas;who never(no,not even in Bosting)beheld so frank a flaunting of optical atrocities. Eheu fugaces . . . posthumously the mostly becapped men wear anything;the nonmen(especially those who are of maternal construction)show an indubitable preference for kiddie-frocks(reaching less than ½way to the knee)and socklets;as a result,only comrade God can make a tree—but even comrade Kem-min-kz knows that the sum total would be not quite ½worse if women were present

"I like it here so much!" lyrically exclaims Virgil "have you noticed a particular feeling in the air—a tension?"

"Have I!"

and Dante has. Apparently one cubic inch of Moscow is to all the metropolis of New York—so far as "tension" goes—as all the metropolis of New York is to tensionless Silver Lake,New Hampshire:around,through,under, behind, over myself do amazingly not physical vibrations contract,expand,collide, mesh,and murderfully procreate:each fraction,every particle,of the atmosphere in which moving moves,of my moving,of me,of cityless city,of peopleless people,actually is charged to a literally prodigious degree with what might faintly be described as compulsory psychic promiscuity. Whereby(if in no other respect)Moscow of the inexorably obsessing mentality,and merely mad New York(not to mention most complacent Cambridge Mass and proudly peaceful New Hampshire)belong to different universes . . . verily,verily have I entered a new realm,whose inhabitants are made of each other;proudly I swear that they shall not fail to note my shadow and the moving of the leaves.

A singularly unbanklike bank:outside,mildly imposing mansion; inside,hugely promiscuous hideousness—not the impeccable sanitary ordered and efficient hideousness of American or imitation-American banks,but a strictly ubiquitous whenwhere of casual filth and aimless commotion and profound hoping inefficiency. We both give groundless ground before a Herculean nonman(from whom Cerberus himself might shrink)and carom off several ½asleep youthless youths. Dreamily in rags a greenskinned hunchback passes,picking his teeth;and in rags repasses,rubbing one dreamily larger than the other ear—back and strollingly forth many emptyfaced uniforms clumsily are leading nowhere guns—a pregnancy on kneehigh boots totes everywhere a ½untied bundle of something angrily. Amid which phantasmal picnic are windows,arguments,transactions, prayers:more particularly a little Jew baffles himself against fate— proclaiming in various lingos that he cannot wait longer having stood in line 3 days;that tomorrow he must be somewhere else,that his desperate business could easily be consummated in 2 shakes of a

lamb's—"Be Patient" booms westernly thick middleaged businessman—
"look at Me!" Virgil and I obey. "I'm General Electric" boom adds
sumptuously;pushing(in the puss)a comrade who would sacrifice the
rights of man to human wishes "and I spend just ninety-three percent of
my time here trying to get money,although everything's supposed to have
been arranged beforehand;but you know how it is." "Of course it will be
better soon" Virgil coos "in fact it's getting better every day." "WHAT'S
getting better." "Why the standard of effic—." GE snorts;then grins
"listen. Don't make a big mistake. It's easy for the correspondents;they
see things from the outside:but we"(with a gesture which commingles
London Paris and New York)"are IN it."

"But I've got to go away!" shrieks the little Jew disastrously.

"Nothing of the sort" booms GE.

"Whaddahyahmeen?" deliriously martyr screams.

"I mean" ponderously retorts big business "that there's no Got To
here except Wait!"

poor Sibyl is quivering and sweating with a combination of stomachache,suppressed critical faculty,and not unnatural fatigue—vainly does he
implore Russianly,vainly assert his ineradicable loyalty to Labour;we are
merely sent to another window whose protagonist sends us back to the
1st,whose protagonist sends us again to the 2nd,whence we are directed to a
3rd and a 4th;finding ourselves(at the end of 20 promiscuous minutes)once
more at number 1—where(without the slightest warning)something
happens;my guardian's woes are heard,his letter of credit is inspected and
his credentials approved . . . we relax).

"You know" I(dazed)whisper "what strikes me most is that all these
inefficient officials appear to be perfectly honest."

"But I've got to go—" the Jew sobs.

All will be well(Virgil now tranquilly soothes)just keepcalm . . .
then,starting—"my God!"

"what's up?"

GE laughs heartily(than hearty laughter at that bankless bank a
3legged moose bearing in its silver beak 5 orange kittens would be
slightly less startling);Virgil furiously blushes:peering,among heads
cropped and uncropped,I perceive that the comrade who(almost)was
in the very act of sealing my illstarred angel's fate has indelibly ceased to
function . . . also,that over the comrade is now bending a nonman(are

they in consultation? Not exactly—he merely is being taught, at this critical juncture, to run an addingmachine)

"I told you!" moans GE mopping mirthtears "can you beat it?" Apparently nobody but itself can beat it—for from a totally strange window out bounces letter of credit with requisite moneyless money: and, fleeing, I glimpse(with a corner of confused eye)the little Jew wrestling crazily with GE and a filthy big baby stealthily creeping(under what may have been a table)toward what has served as(among many other thingless things)a wastebasket

"such" muses mentor "are the evils of bureaucracy; not that—" and we dodge a tumbledown exRolls(driven at 40 mph by something in ½ a uniform for benefit of hatbox clasped by a somethingelse in sporty new suit of winter underwear) "but of course it's simply unbelievable what they've accomplished" he resumes. "Was it worse?" lightly I ask. "Unbelievable" says the Sibyl "—that is, what they've done of course. O it was much worse. Yes indeed. But I always feel that we haven't any right to criticise: the point is, you are now in a workers' republic which is bound to make mistakes like anything else; but the mistakes are being rectified as quickly as possible—and after all, the ideal is what counts, isn't it!" "I shouldn't wonder if life is what—" (plucking him from a careening upholsteryless Daimler) "counts" (and shoving him past a leaping recent Ford) "—was that a taxicab?" I ask. "Thank you, I didn't see the Jehu: yes, that was a taxicab, and we're going to have a great many of them soon. My dear fellow, let me beg you most earnestly not to make the ridiculous mistake of judging by appearances; the thing to realize is, that here people run themselves: they are truly—for the first time in human history—free . . . now where am I going: yes. Our next stop is a very important personage: all the dispatches which are sent out by newspapermen have to pass through him; he might be immensely valuable to you. I'll tell him you're America's leading—." "Pah-zhahloostah." "Well well well, I thought you said you didn't speak Russian!" "I don't." "What a pity; you ought to find yourself a teacher, a nice attractive young teacher; that's what everyone does: it's so much easier to learn from the pillow, you know(and it won't cost you much, in fact practically nothing)—after five or six months you'll be able to understand a surprising amount. How?—you can't afford to stay—O but the Revolutionary Literature

Bureau will be glad to have you do something for them,and they pay well—in roubles of course,but you can live on roubles. Nobody really ought to live as I do,at a foreigner's hotel where roubles aren't accepted: in fact,my only excuse is that I have a little money,and I enjoy spending it here where every penny goes to help the workers—what a pity you couldn't arrive for the first of May!—now for a pass"(soldier;conversation: a species of affidavit is made out by benevolence:we climb chewed stairs in a mouldy building;enter a neat dentistlike reception room). "The man whom you're going to meet" in a whisper "is very cultured:yes;he knows what's going on in artistic circles all over the world—I want you to compare him with the American equivalent:O—how do you do!"(bowing to a plump nonman who smiles agreeably,converses briefly in stilted English,bowingly departs)"—that was one of my secretaries. Very intelligent girl. Attractive,don't you think? Well of course they can afford to dress better—besides,it's more or less in their line of business . . . do sit down;he's preposterously busy,we may have to—" an ornate wallslice opens:appears Tallness crowned with Skull

"please—come in"

a voice modulated,a smile orchestrated;the strictly organic dignity of that subtle gracious(and possibly mythical)creature "a gentleman" . . . look,feeling myriad impacts of focussed carefulness;talk,dissected by daintily strenuous tentacles of appraisal;listen,always confronted with(high in the glistening volume of forehead)a healed hole . . .

"please—come again."

Down chewed stairs plunging,resume clumsily the how merely nervous street,the mercilessly general more aggressive vibration,the unskilfully less infinite obsession. "Do please have lunch with me! We can stroll around afterwards and I'll show you the old and new Gay-Pay-Oo buildings—of course you know what the 'three letters' stand for;O not at all,quite the contrary;the Gay-Pay-Oo is a most benevolent organization,all those rumors which one hears are sheer nonsense:I tell you,quite the most intelligent and delightful people I know are in the Gay-Pay-Oo;you'll see for yourself when you meet them—the whole idea is entirely different,my dear fellow:all members of the Gay-Pay-Oo are persons of the highest calibre,especially chosen for their idealism;it's an honour,you understand: nonono,they're not police at all,they're guardians of the proletariat,and quite the most splendid organization in Soviet Russia—altogether noble

and unselfish—why, I've been accused of being in the Gay-Pay-Oo myself
. . . but what were we talking about:yes. Well if you like, we'll go to a
really Russian place;except that I'm afraid you won't be able to stand
it—the smell is pretty bad. I took a couple of American friends there
recently, and they didn't seem to appreciate the food—"

lunch(underground)at circa 2 roubles per head
  fair soup
  sweetly dreadful "macaroni" and unmeat(the latter could not be cut
      either by me or by mentor:when hammered for several minutes
      it split)
  fearful perfume-beverage
  not quite right dessert
a truly magnificent stink("they should give clothespins here" says
Virgil, nipping his nose)being the one and only redeeming feature of
this otherwise merely Very Bad Childs'. "Odear, I must go back to the
hotel and take a pill—my stomach isn't what it used to be:afraid I gave
you a very bad introduction to Moscow;you shouldn't have been taken
here—well just to make up for this, I'll show you Lenin's mausoleum"

Seeing The Sights
  the Slogan Of Slogans
      itself disconcertingly illpresented, occurs near an enticing gate via
      which we're bumped by a most wonderfully refreshing lump of
      nearly comradeless space:on one edge of this lump sits
  L's M
      a rigid pyramidal composition of blocks;an impurely mathematical
      game of edges:not quite cruelly a cubic cerebration—equally
      glamourless and emphatic, withal childish . . . perhaps the
      architectural equivalent for "boo!—I scared you that time!"(hard
      by are buried martyrs)
  the lump ends at Something Fabulous
      a frenzy of writhing hues—clusteringly not possible whirls together
      grinding into one savage squirtlike ecstasy:a crazed Thinglike dream
      solemnly shouting out of timespace, a gesture fatal, acrobatic(goring
      tomorrow's lunge with bright beyondness of yesterday)—utterly a
      Self, catastrophic;distinct, unearthly and without fear.

The tearing of mere me and this miracle from each other demands effort on part of failing benevolence("yes,it's impressive—but you should see the inside,which has been turned into a Revolutionary Museum:really I must get back to the hotel,please don't desert me now;I wonder if I've been poisoned—Odear,you can look at that any time:there are so many much more important things")who increasingly resembles a walking corpse. If combining the best(I murmur)elements of barberpole and pineapple be opium,more power to it. We cringes,palm over belly. "Where can I send a telegram?" I wonder;inconsiderately adding "—to my wife." He starts:staggers "O yes—of course:a devoted husband . . . " "From the hotel?" I devotedly persist. "Yes,but the clerk wouldn't know how much to charge—you'd better go directly to the postoffice just around the corner;there's a charming woman who speaks French and German and(I think)a little English—ow!—well,we're almost back,thank Heaven!" "Don't be uneasy;I shall not inform the republic of your heresy" I promise:at which Virgil recovers sufficiently to gasp "what is that proverb . . . the devil is sick,the devil a monk—Odear!" "Now you're talking:incidentally,has the proletariat any particular commerce with psychology?" "Psychology? Why,don't you know Pavlov's work? One of the monumental—" "Or as Pope Watson has it,you ring a snake and show your bell a child. But what of Our Lord Sigmund Freud?" "Odear,are you one of those people? You aren't going to analyse me,are you? Please!"

"charming woman"(50ish)speaks only Russian and German,latter to such an extent that decide I'll dilate my daily wrestlings with yah nyeh hahchoo. Purely for practice,lisp in numbers to a grinning comrade at keycounter;heartened,await lift and further progress. Hereupon occurs a curious phenomenon:many obviously native citizens are also expecting the elevator—in fact,there's a small multitude—but when that far from mighty machine arrives,its deus very rudely excludes a number of worthy compatriots while,very politely,accepting the mere foreigner myself(who was lurking on the outskirts and doesn't believe that the last shall be first;just a good democrat). Sanctuary,not overample,sufficiently sunlit,appears as haven of refuge—but knock:Sibyl's himself again,wants me to help him call on 2 "young people" upstairs . . . something about having received a note from them,impossibility of their lunching with him;must arrange something. We climb(on foot,at my request)flights

of less and less marble-or-something-or-marble and exhaustedly arrive
before an open door through which the birds have flown. On foot(by
request)we descend to the foyer's cigarettecounter—and vaguely I observe
an adolescent pair of uncouths emanating awkwardly nonhappiness.
"You are being signalled" I hint. "Odear,there they are!"(he rushes
forward:instantly parts of the pair begin fallingdown revealing a 3rd
uncouth;who's also full of bundles—a livid pigmy with a sharp face,which
upon making my acquaintance almost swallows its cigarette)"we were
just looking for you!" It seems that the pair,pimply American stripling
embarrassed in a Russian blouse and his somewhat starved decidedly
Radcliffe helpmate,are on the verge of deserting the Hotel Metropole
for a less sumptuous life. I gather that the livid is assisting. Blouse
hasn't enough valyootah to patronize "fleet" of Ford taxis outside—the
Metropole's modest contribution to proletarian cause;you,capitalist,pay
in advance at the desk—and unattached taxis are scarcer than hen's
teeth and,in short,death is stingless. But Virgil will have none of
that—cheerfully he shoulders bundles(bidding me do likewise):merrily
our quintet attains the sidewalk;blithely the blouse departs in search of
conveyance,gaily his spouse spurns further aid and every cloud has a silver
lining(and the 3rd uncouth bows to the bottom of a ruined raincoat
and waves courtierlike a sweatsoiled sombrero,pronouncing in Queen's
English the word Tomorrow). "They're awfully nice—her husband
teaches English:of course you've read his distinguished father,whom
the Russians consider one of America's great writers although you may
not—that little man helping them is an authority on military tactics"
then,beaming upon my greatly perplexed self "three good Cantabrigians
should meet today. Come!"

long gently rising street. A priest passes,motheaten—Virgil gloats
"they're few and far between,now:O not at all,that persecution story
is ridiculous my dear fellow;the point is,anyone who still wants to
serve The Lord can do so,but The Lord's servant must have a useful
occupation or starve;people have awakened to the fact that religion is
opium:in a worker's republic there's no place for parasites . . . excuse
me." Halting,peeps cautiously into his shirt;resumes "a false alarm.
Yes,religion is inextricably bound up with the family;and since the safety
of the state depends on the abolition of the family,religion must go.
Of course it's hard for some of us who've been educated according to

bourgeois traditions;but if we're intelligent we see that there's no other way—not that I miss my religion,quite the contrary. Odear,you really must stay at least six months;there are so many things to understand,so many thrilling aspects of this new world—" we enter a gloomful dwelling. "I admire Mary more than any girl I've ever met" Virgil states enthusiastically. "—Mary?" "Yes indeed,a splendid person—notice this hotel"(as he spoke,a mean reek of rancid food drifted over us)"how I love it! In this hotel I have lived longer than in any other. Yes. I feel about it almost as a wandering mariner feels about his beloved home—not really,of course;my own bourgeois tendencies are pretty well stifled,thank—well,here we are." Corridor pitchdark;glimpse of several buxom nonmen,attired as maids,respectfully who recoil as Virgil gropes toward something . . . knocks. Crack of light—sharp hysterical squeal "you can't come in! You can't!"—tiny door opens—"you mustn't! The room's in such a mess!" and I'm bowing to a worn doll with naked emaciated arms,vast feet,sunken eyes,mop of colourless hair,crazed jumpy laugh,and 2 stockingless laths protruding from ultraabbreviated kiddiefrock.

"Sitdownsitdownsitdownsitdown" the 3rd good Cantabrigian's mangled voice chatters foolishly "can you imagine it,can you imagine what she's done now?the bitch!"

"Mary!" admonishes Virgil,with mock gravity "is that the way to refer to your female progenitor?"

"she is,she is;mother is a bitch—excuse me,I suppose I shouldn't be so frank before a guest . . . "

"what has mother done now?" the benefactor of benefactors inquires with a helpful smile.

"Done? What has she done? She's gotten what she calls pneumonia! That's the latest excuse."

"Perhaps you ought to explain the circumstances" says mentor "I'm sure our guest will be interested."

"Very much" I corroborate.

"Well you see"(twisting her gnarled skinnyness)"I was once a fool—do you understand? No? He doesn't understand!"

"you mean that you got married" the Sibyl slyly interprets.

"Married. Yes. How lovely. I married a man. Nice pretty ceremony. You know. Flowers! Bless you my children and all that sort of nonsense—well,he wasn't a man because he was a beast,a beast!"

"you don't spare your enemies,Mary" our guardian angel comments admiringly.

"Why should I? They don't spare me! Do they? You know me;do they?"

"you're going to win,my dear" encourages the spinner "I'm sure of that."

"I'll win" the doll's voice snapped,to open in a sob "—hun! Yes,I'll win. —Well,ten years ago I was born. Do you know what that means? I became a communist. And I wanted to come to Soviet Russia where a child can grow up to be free;and the beast went to a judge,to the courts of the fair state of Ohio,and the old judge made a great speech giving what he called my Husband the custody of the child—on what grounds? On what grounds do you suppose?—Tell him on what grounds!"

"You tell him" invites benevolence.

"On . . . the . . . grounds . . . "(with a deeply gradual writhe beginning in empty eyes and ending in famished hips)"That A Woman Who Puts Her Political Ideas Before Her Family Is Unfit To Be A Mother. HAHAHAHAHA!"—the sawdust body exploded in paroxysms of coughing;a snapshot,stuck in mirroredge,slips slightly.

"There is really something unique about the cruelty of what millions call Justice" mentor murmured. A microscopic room quivered with coughing;tranquilly from flimsy wall glared at the smallest bed one fatfaced child . . . "There there,dear Mary:you'll win!"(and coughing subsides).

"So the question was,how to get him here—I asked all my friends,but none of them could manage it—"

"she asked even me" giggles angel,making a wry face "but I somehow couldn't see myself successfully abducting a baby boy from the bosom of his bourgeois family and placing him in the hands of his communist mother in Moscow!—just an old bachelor."

"Bless you,dear friend,for your counsel" the puppet whimpered "if it hadn't been for such encouragement . . . well,finally my mother agreed to do it—My Mother—haha! At the last moment,I get a cable from her,saying my child can't be moved because he's got to have an appendicitis operation! Can you imagine? Can you?—she had one breast cut off for cancer and thought nothing of it;but just because a kid has a scratch on his belly he's to stay quiet for three weeks! Ugh! —And now she's delayed it a second time,to give herself what she calls A close call . . . Pneumonia! What will that creature do next?"

"you must fight on" cooed benevolence "and you're a great little fighter. I often wonder,Mary,where you got your own fighting spirit."

"Not from her!" the marionette snarled "mother has no strength of character:mother and father never got on since I can remember,but she keeps going back to him—why mother couldn't live without him" words skidding in how much more contempt than a human voice possibly could extrude "—no,really."

"I believe it" said I,seriously.

"Wonderful girl . . . simply extraordinary . . . a perfect trump" Virgil mused "when I think of her I'm almost proud of Cambridge." We turn a corner;embark upon a long muddy treeful boulevard,clogged with overhurrying nonmen and men. "This is one of our main streets,it divides the inner Moscow from the outer—very much like the Ring in Vienna,if you know Vienna . . . lovely tranquil town:but of course I prefer Moscow." "The police were charging when I was in Wien" our hero gently remarks "and the horses were trying not to step on women;and beggars stood just inside cafés,never moving,with holes in their faces for eyes;and it rained a great deal." "Really?" he surveyed me with a mixture of respect and alarm "you were there during the rioting? They smashed the Bristol,didn't they?" "It had been mended when I arrived. O well,I imagine Russia was a most interesting place during the revolution . . . " "You mean that what you've seen so far doesn't interest you?" "I didn't mean that. I did mean,how different something moving is from something won." "O but nothing's really won—that is,of course the revolution's victorious and the future of humanity firmly established,but Russia is still fighting,you know;her triumph can't possibly be complete until the rest of the world comes to its senses,until the proletariat asserts its rights everywhere and capitalism bows its bloody head"(he sighed;adding)"how nice the colour is:do you see that girl with her red scarf? It means she's a young communist . . . there are thousands of fine healthy lassies like her." "Where are we going,if I may ask?" "Why I thought I'd take you to see the president of the Writers' Club:a charming person;you'll like him particularly because he speaks French—not that I don't wish I could speak French well myself;however,I take comfort in the fact that I've really mastered a little Russian;the accent is what bothers me most;but my teachers tell me I'm improving every day(I do hope it isn't mere politeness!)"

An authentic chaos of unhuman smells,a joyous anarchy of noises which are not words,a merciful complexity of illogical shapes and irrational colours,an alive mad intricately free feel of tree and rock,of movingness and earth,welcome my lonely nostrils ears eyes flesh spirit. Wandering carefully among carpenters masons ditchdiggers(and similar comrades disguised as workmen)we walk the plank to a speakeasylike door—and collide with dismally cheerful citizen who promptly reveals himself as personal friend of that prominent Russian-in-Paris novelist whose(by me personally sent)telegram did not scare up a brother in literature. And now I achieve my first bad break;now,asked the prominent's address,I spontaneously reply Don't know but he's always at the Coupole—words better left un-(said John Boyle)return to create ample sorrow when we consider them comfortably defunct

    —nevertheless if not however,am soon speaking with someone whom I immediately liked,someone who perhaps likes me and who certainly enjoys talking French,someone who invites me to a few minutes' conversation quite as if conversation were a perfectly recognized form of derring do;and Virgil,to his eternal credit I record this,shoves me almost brutally at the conversationally inclined comrade("see you later: be at my room about six;we'll go to Gahlstook—that means Necktie—" and capping the climax "à bientôt!")

    What chiefly interests you?the diminutive president('tis himself,not a picture)quietly asks,asks almost peacefully. A not big untidy room remarkably buntingless(but Lenin's bust listens just outside). Miscellaneous whisper of implements,how unlike generic machine thunder,seeps through Unshutness. —Would you like to see the vast industrial plants by which Russia is trying to get her place in the world? Russia is striving;a whole race,a vast part of earth . . . —I understand: you are interested in the cultural side. More especially drama? Let me know whenever you want to see a play;I'd be only too delighted to telephone for you,the theatre reserves your seats gladly—and it will cost you nothing. Tomorrow our great writer,Gorky,arrives:may I suggest that you visit the club next day and meet him? Now let me show you our club—as a writer,you're more than welcome here

    (and,astonished,behold—hidden away under ground—positively not depressing rathskeller;nay,an almost gay . . . with several almost lively looking customers engaged in almost luxurious gastronomics . . . and someone almost who might be an actress,perhaps because herself wears what might have been(almost and long since)stylish garments,or is it that this comrade doesn't seem to be exactly carrying the woes of a sinful world upon shoulders precisely which were never made for unpleasure . . . and withal an atmosphere of semitranquility,of notuneasiness,almost of something approximating that blessedly aesthetic phenomenon: relaxation)

which bountiful crop of almosts dignifies a not quite terrifying perspective;myself begins-to-begin to almost conjecture that possibly comrade Kem-min-kz has an impossible place in the impossibly possible USSR. Also,how sweet(how proudly purely sweet)is the mother of imagination;courtesy

—Probably that telegram never arrived:I know most of the comrades on this list of yours and I'm sure they'll do everything they can for you. "Venez ici déjeuner,c'est le centre des écrivains" our food is good,the beer I can vouch for. Cigarettes? Of course;over here—

Peacefully returning(proudly,without error)through streetless streets (tranquilly among peopleless people moving)surprise Dante's cicerone in the very act of consulting his mural theatreschedule. Unpresently present is faded Interpreter,who very distinctly wears That Elsewhere Look—times pathetic habit of shifting stance whenever viewed;as if avoiding a wellaimed blow—probably an erstwhile member of the longlost wellborns;anyhow inwardly ashamed of current occupation(whatever it may be). And this dodger 'phones Proletcult,where The Necktie's displayed(Virgil must see The Necktie tonight because he must,because The Necktie won't be shown again,and finally because Virgil's opus requires liberal documentation re proletarian histrionics)winning 3 places(the 3rd,I almost understand,for a distinguished American painter and writer who— luckily for Russia—happens to be in town). Selah. The distinguished, allowed 15 minutes' freedom,hastens to pump $\frac{1}{2}$baldness anent my not yet arrived wordly goods—hb promises(Russianly,am beginning to understand)profound action;he will even interrogate a highly responsible comrade who departed this hotel in the direction of the outhouseless outhouse at 11 A.M. and is expected back in something very like $\frac{1}{2}$ an hour,comrade weather permitting . . . ("Can you beat it?") . . . but no sooner am semidesperately upstairs than out respectfully rushes a not quite cheerfulness,crying Luggage?and pocketing 35 comrade kopecks almost without a comrade murmur. (Horrors Of Trying To Tip A

Comrade). Acci- or inci-(or both)dentally my poor old suitcase sprung one noble leak but("honest thieves")regurgitated nothing;no,not even the means of enjoying singularly painful shave and equally appropriate scrub—therefore,at 6:45 punctually,do I present burnished arms chez Sibyl & Interpreter Inc.

A ponderiferously(And How)YMCA atmosphere,strongly suggesting N(holy image of Ulianov much in evidence)pervades the radiatingly EDuCAtional promenoir replete with sundry and various And How uplifting exhibits(models of bombing planes,tractors,whatnot;around which cluster curiously silent folk,bigeyed patient clumsy beholders,awed childlike beings) . . . everywhere a mysterious sense of behaving,of housebrokenness,of watch-your-stepism. No Smoking. Benevolently our delegation graces the 2nd row of a rustic rendezvous wriggling with children (including 1 spontaneous and charming and otherwise noteworthy comrade of 8 or 10)for whom The Necktie might well have been composed—for it's all "funnies",slapstick,hocuspocus(example: a bookcase full of ancient tomes and priceless knickknacks receives a good push;whereupon the whole contraption homogeneously disappears to magically become flat wall)and it culminates in 1 suh-wel Universal Cataclysm Finale(with someobody rushing up the aisle and everything and you know what I mean and Tah-de-de-ahhh!)—indeed,circa X through this hugely long foolery,begin to suspect that all the grownupless grownups in Russia are children . . .

Item:during the 1st of numberless entr'actes we invade(by special request)an atomic spicandspanness,more than miraculously into which—at the bidding of a flannelshirted necktieless almost jolly comrade manager(?)and a similarly bedecked modestly straightforward comradedirector(?)—are forced delicious tea and luscious sweetmeats. Our hosts(brisk but courteous,efficient but sympathetic,in short:fine fellows both)beg us to partake of the good cheer and with nothing short of incredible patience answer Virgil's innumer-able(sic)questions(the numerable answers being recorded in a Harvard Coöperative Society Harvard Square Cambridge Mass notebook). The recorder is adopted,at intermission number 3,by an Hebraically extracted Little Girl With A Big Heart,who not unrecently left her native New York with the May Day Unit of radicals,never(she announces)to return(Tah-de-de-ahhh!)—viciously almost whose(almost but,alas,not quite sublimated via propaganda)corporeality responds to sundry and various settingupexercises in which members of the cast very frequently indulge:a hungrily dreadful specimen,on the whole—and guzzles 4 cakes to dodger's 1 and seems to know more than is good for any 6 comrades(our hosts' dum & dee faces betray no secrets,but their eyes actually smile when comrade mentor,statisticsward bound,checks comrade Unit's illimitable exposition)

—of this particular proletarian fable the Moral,as explained(a)by dodger to angel(b)by angel to me(c)by Unit to dodger,oddly coincides with my ignorant own interpretation,viz. It's not things that matters,comrade,it's how you make use of things that matters:thus even a necktie,that symbol of bourgeois idiocy,may end as nothing less than a proletarian banner waving from loyal matchlock of Comrade Righto while all Our Boys(and Girls AND HOW)go forth to make the whole world 1 big family. Perhaps—only perhaps—to imagine Life deliberately lifting Itself,by that hypothetical guiltsense which equals Its own bootstraps,out of fatally stupendous unconsciousness into the(how comfortably measurable)tinyness of "humanity"—into a "scientific" infrared-ultraviolet illusion-of-a-future,into an omne-vivum-e-vivo ABC "reality",into a vicariously infantile Kingdom of Slogan—softly is not to misunderstand the message of Proletcult per(come all ye traumdeutungs!)Necktie.

With an especially dodgeless dodge comrade Interpreter abandons us for comrade streetcar(tactfully thereby allowing comrade Unit unmitigated access to benevolence over the 2 Good Comrades Together or tastes-in-common route). As for I,announce low craving for brightlights—whereupon 2 Good Comrades Together emit mild astonishment and(wrapped in loftier than trivial matters)manoeuvre me several murderful miles to the deathsmelling portals of Hotel Metropole . . .

"well,I suppose you're tired—I'll take the comrade home . . . don't mention it my dear chap! Let's have breakfast in my room tomorrow—I like so much to breakfast in my pyjamas. But not before ten,eh? Just give me a knock. Gahlstook was wonderful,wasn't it;we'll see The West Is Nervous next. Goodnight,tovarich! —O,remember about correspondents, and—something else I wanted to say . . . well,never mind,I can't seem to think;see you tomorrow!"

Away walked one of earth's queerest couples.

jump from(BongbangS hinting ogre)sleep;stand . . . opening upon a
mere ducklike visitor(grinning)who
   Good morning sir,how are
(all in quack German)
   sorry to disturb;will you give us two photographs?
   For what?
   For your Russian passport sir;you have been decided to be a person
who must possess a Russian passport—thank you thank you very much
thank you very

appearing in(thank you)the(very) same figment of space where you laid
you down to disappear is strange;more than strange is appearing in particle
of Hotel Extraordinary of capitalless capital of huge ultrasomething like
$1/6$ of the singing ball which a moon forgot to remember. Strangely
unstrange,these("9:30" & Pay To The Order Of)measures whispering
and whisperless under unpillow which have survived night—and,how
immeasurably beyond strangest,myself!not of wealth who dreamed,not
of poverty;not of space:not of time . . . isfully who was,like a tree(never
which and always sleeps)always and which never moves

"yes" com(through lather)fort with goodmorningness "'ll be right
over for breakfast" the wistful with pale guardian pink angel pyjamas.
Mirrored who utters "I have a waiter at my door,but never mind;we'll
order anon,don't hurry—Odear" a cry,dismal "you'll cut yourself!" (And
would the Soviets thereupon collapse? Would millions of dark millions
of sleeping faces laugh?) And would wings fly straight up into the sky
further almost than tomorrow?

Dressed(less wistful)the master—playing the man with cheery
difficulty—farsounds 2 regalements;playing with unnatural ease the
master,tells comrade respectfully respectful that comrade Kem-min-kz's
breakfast must grace comrade Kem-min-kz's bill("I'm afraid of being
charged with graft" to my greatly relieved self). Then and hence and
therefore eat we and drink we and be merry we for(a mighty swoop

of sweatsoiled sombrero)here's lividly sir ruined raincoat,our socalled military tactician,bowing to imaginary everywhere plaudits without count or reckoning—"I have the foodbook!"

"foodbook?" Whose(say)book,whose food? Shy young bachelor neatness American's . . . Note that a worker in a workers' republic has the "right" to work and that,workers being eaters,a worker has the "right" to eat and that,given the millenium,all god's chillun forcibly will be(not to mention collectively)fed through the factory etc.—meanwhile,certain proletarians should and must content themselves with the "foodbook",or individual rationing,system of noncompulsory feeding. Note that,even in a workers' republic,those monsters the "correspondents" possess privileges;for instance,comrade shy has a foodbook(merely capitalistically speaking,shy finds it fantastically cheaper to obtain raw materials and cook them himself than to patronize a restaurant ready made for capitalists: he'd die young if he ate at a Very Bad Childs'). So far,so comrade. Now Russian being not precisely "communication" in the East Maxman(reel critical)sense—nor are My ways thy ways saith the Lord—our livid tactician Russianly performs our American correspondent's shopping,and acci- or incidentally profiteth. Note that today comrade shy has lent his foodbook and his livid to comrade Virgil;meaning that Virgil(against the dictates of Virgil's conscience)may acquire the fruits of labour for a so to speak song and dance . . . Flourish without;enter consubstantially the foodhunt,that ultraconfusing most socialist phenomenon

not(perhaps)least confusing isn't the factless fact that(after walking long distances and waiting large moments)we've attained nothing,and is the puissant impression that a great many more deserving(sic)than ourselves comrades fare much worse. But,only thanks to Virgilless Virgil,our livider lividest shopper's military disposition survives,until a peculiarly dirty passageway manifests innumerable nonmen(all Elsewhere Looking,some stoically nursing fretful offspring). Here I,comrade,witness comrade fireworks:3 times cleverly having tried to dispense with the lazily(alert beside doorless door)lolling comrade who gradually examines all hungry comers,good comrade shy's comrade shopper's comrade curdled pride ragefully disintegrates:provoking several bovine stares,a few pitying leers . . . between frustration and disappointment,Carybdis and Scylla,T.S.Waistline and the Eliot(this almost and almost that)resounds our disintegrator's love of rus—his hate of manmade urbs "take with me,one day,the train and we'll go outside:there's country, hills and valleys and animals and sweet air to breathe. Not like"(fiercely spitting)"here."

"Shall we step into the Torgsin" nervously suggests Virgil "and soothe our weary spirits?—I really must talk with the comrade who promised me a new one;simply a beauty,he said . . . hm! It must be stupendous if it's better than the ones I've picked out already."

Livid curled sneerfully—"ikons!"

"now my dear fellow,you shouldn't criticise;it's not as if I had a religious interest in such things,quite the contrary—of course" he modestly added "I appreciate their aesthetic value;but business is business:ikons are going up this winter,I'm anxious to make a good investment,the government of workers and peasants need my dollars,I need their treasures,each of us can do the other a good—"

"Dead" snapped livid.

Virgil jumped. "What?"

"They are Dead" the sombrero maintained sullenly

. . . in vain;for lo!a luxuriously obsequious uninvitingness:presto!our wayworn triad treads red carpets,glimpses gilt gewgaws,and(with some difficulty)overcomes the odourless odour of lofty junk basking amid nearly fatal quietude. To leftward rising and to rightward,Englishspeaking nonmen caparisoned as women Orientally make obeisance before lord Virgil,crusaderlike who leads his(by multiple smokeeaten masterpieces undaunted)minions up sumptuously silent stairs and:ah!a wee museum,nicely enveloped in its own sanctity,skilfully from filth shut and turmoil and all human misery;carefully(clear to ceilingless ceiling)cluttered with occasionally profane but chiefly ecclesiastical pseudos.

"This"($\frac{1}{2}$sings carefully a dark voice)"comes from the bedroom of the last Tzar."

"Y-e-s?"(around cornerless corner peeping I spot y-e-s:a pseudofemale;unfair,40ish,American).

"Really." (Also the realist:a particularly unsvelte nonman-in-disguise languidly and O so Asiatically whose eyes consult the spiritless spirit of their idiot prey).

"I want" prey pompously insists:wagging loose chins "something" (these were once words)"small and not too heavy,with a sentiment attached . . ."

"This?" eyeing,the unsvelte lifts a plaque.

"No—er,something daintier . . ."

"This?" murderfully another lifting:eyeing.

"That's better . . ." pause "—it seems"(and you could hear a fly love at that momentless moment)"like ikons are the thing we really ought to take home from Moscow!"

(Eyefully)"yes"(the dark singing agrees)"they're typically Russian—"

"but I'm travelling alone" period. (Coyly)"you know;not taking much baggage . . ."

looking,merely "yes?"

And at small distance Virgil,clutching a palpably improvised antique,bubbles raptures at earnestly scholarful gentlemansalesman,while "this" drones 40ish "morning I was so tired" plus intimately "I didn't wake up until t-e-n o'clock!"

and livid,motionless,inspects a highhung moreandmore bathing lessandless comrade;and not(from street below)1 whisper . . . Blossoms hereupon abundantly the conviction that,of all sacred or profane fakeunfakeness,nothing matters

chuckle. And(pointing toward more-or-less a prurient professorial digit)"there's our friend's taste" snickers comrade gleeful benevolence,shrewdly.

"YES!" whirls raincoat:spins sombrero—I(instantaneously)catch (somewhere behind seethingly mask)1 transient ghost or momentary spectre of a man. . . ("And They're Better Than Ikons" resuming,the stare growls wickedly).

"But let's be serious—what do you,brother Cummings,advise? This is the new one(magnificent,isn't it)and over there you'll find three which I've already picked out—now I simply can't afford all four . . . yet each of them is so fine in its way!"(languidly eyes of Asia,gentlemanly earnest scholarsalesman eyes,for my most buried thoughts begin searchpartying).

Unflourish flourish:the hunt is o'er . . . Enter John Benet's Body,comrades;or Success At Loss or They Want What They Didn't or Too Much Is Enough Of A Feast. Livid(oscillating under bundled purchases—his own and shy's and Virgil's)and mentor and(marvelling)myself dare that muckmaze of treacherous tramtracks past which lies visionary vista of something-or-marble. Yes;I recall having(for the tactician squirms with every teasing of the ikonist)soothingly stated that life was a few valleys and animals and several fairsized mountains—eagerly at which striking,bundlesmothered broaches allday tomorrow heandI excursion;whereupon benevolence flung something jealous if not positively méchante(and for no,or some,reason I saw with my mindless mind 2 buildings,1 new,1 old;both Gay-Pay-Oo)

—bountifully a voice:becoming un-;becoming voice unknown,boiled—up;to:scream.

Virgil(ghastly)—"what?"

"I said:in the days of the Tzar,a Russian's soul was his passport;now"(medium shot of rattler,its back broken by small rock,spiralling)"his soul belongs to the government." Then,bundlejuggling,our naturelover sways:spins;totters—and a marvellously feeble comrade with a very much bandaged 1stfinger floated distinctly by . . .

"—You?" the greyjowled mentor of mentors chokes

"and would a communist" cautiously rock lifting from rattler(rapidly who seems to be turning into somethingelse)"ever say a thing like that?" I ask.

It,he,stiffened;seizing me with big eyes on which tears burn,gasps "we FEEL it;there's nothing to say."

3 comrades moved. "Why don't you lunch in your rooms" livid's familiar voice tantrumlessly suggests. "Come on!"

"I think" Virgil parries,looking remarkably like an O'Jean Euneil heroine "I rather think we'd prefer that nice quiet little restaurant over there. Its beer(if I'm not mistaken;and I doubt if I am)is excellent. Will you be so very kind as to deposit my purchases with brother SoandSo?—thanks. And I'll call for them later"

underground

—with nothing more incredible than sunlight!

food much less improbable than at Very Bad Childs';edible almost(some birdless bird;for desert "plum" sternly insists,against awful odds,my pocketdictionary). And mentor,unprompted,rings for another round of drinks which almost might be beer and which anyhow are drinkable. "I find I enjoy alcohol—that is,occasionally:the communist party is of course perfectly right in objecting that a worker's efficiency is reduced(so much more sensible than trying to combat drunkenness with a lot of silly moral slogans,the Demon Rum and so forth) . . . it's truly extraordinary what they've done;especially when you realise that for centuries vodka was the curse of Russia—not that I'm a fanatic,if my friends like to drink I don't mind in the least:Odear no. I'm rather pleased. Yes . . . hm. It's the abuse of alcohol that's deplorable after all,isn't it."

"Is it?"

"you don't think? —But surely you're not in favor of a man's disgracing himself and letting his defenceless wife and children starve and lowering his own vitality and possibly contracting a serious social disease because he can't exercise a little honest healthy selfcontrol! Well—what if prohibition Is a failure in America? That's the fault of America's social system:the burdens imposed upon a worker by capitalistic society are enough to weaken anyone's character!"

"but assuming I like the kick—"

"now that's perverse:you're trying to live down your New England heritage" and he unreally smiled. "How did the ancient Greeks put it? Mayden ah-ghan? But I suppose you'll bring up Dionysian festivals against me"(this is unbelievable;Virgil's almost gay)

"one more,Apollo—my treat?"

"nonono,I mustn't" with the wasman's shrug at N "why,I'm really befuddled already!"(and,naughtily)"it Is pleasant,Isn't it . . . what a pity the effects are so injurious! Hm . . . Now why don't you" he muses mellowly "come over the river with me in a few minutes:I'm visiting a sick friend there. It won't take long;and you might like to call on the great Duranty—did you know he had a wooden leg?who(by some extraordinary coincidence)lives just across the street from this poor sick fellow . . . besides,a suburb of Moscow is worth seeing for its own sake—"

"Lead,kindly light."

"Er,yes. Let's walk a little:I want to show you the Grand Hotel—"

upon entering which(slightly less than ye Metropole)capitalistic monument to absurdity and luxe am threatened with 2 amazingly jocular stuffed bears;but recover. "Very nice,eh?" as out we go

"the view is really superb"(and the tram is so comradey that nobody can see anything except somebody else;but while shimmying over a little bridge)"look!" and I jeopardise life if not limb to discern towers; dreamlike,wonderfully floundering upon noon(whispers of another world:unborn of this dayless day;obsolete exquisitely trembling

metaphors) . . . "now" he gasps "we'd better begin moving ahead."
"Pochehmoo?"grunt—with reason;since ourselves infinitely are nearer
the bellowing vehicle's hinder end—I. "Because it's the law"(worming).
"Law?"(we're thrown for a loss). "—That you must leave by the front
end"(and his schlyahpah disappears)"Odear!" "But already I've seen
three comrades use the back way"—and enter hat,horribly distorted;at
which instant a temporarily nonbalanced neighbour dislocates my own
Leninbonnet. "Have you?" "Yes I have." "Are you perfectly sure?" "I
am perfectly sure." "Hm." "—And that's how this comrade is getting
off,law or no law." Virgil's mask,scared and sad,moans "you're really
going to risk it?" "In the name of humanity" I challenge. "Well . . . I
suppose you shouldn't be allowed to take such a chance alone:here we
are—quick!"

an emptily toppling court. At its end squats vacantlooking
structure("there's the great man's—but I'll stop making fun of him;he's
an excellent person,not at all like your average newspaper scribe—in
fact,proSoviet at heart")Sibyl,plumbing deftly obscurity,painfully
locates a smallish door;knocks. Very sleepfully thereat emerges young
woman;yes,not a nonman(no,not unRussian—by her dazedness,and
styleless style,and movingless moving,a subjectless subject of Old kingless
King Karl)
    "he is out"
and That Elsewhere Look shifts as("may I present the" etc.)her hand
hands me itself
    "he will return"
—listlessly(with vast miraculous resignation)her mind minds,obediently
while I scribble the etc.'s name on back of a kindly provided by mentor
visitingcard;and she(taking) 2smiles,
    "I will say you are here"
. . . sunless erect sliver of too roomlike room diminishes;gently the(dis
solves)herself;small 1 enlargingly closes:door.
    "Attractive,eh"

& appears greedily a tumblingness,newly constructed for this(tell duh
carpuntuz tuh get busy un dat slum set)picture;quietly and which
distinctly,under kliegday,emanates AngelPenguin(the filliping of upjump
cane;selfthehim,The Homeless One:imperiously flutterwobbling the)

41

a refuseridden yard. 6 lazily or 7 men-and-nonmen ½slowlyfully semi(cinematographically)strolling . . . Virgil request:all look,pause. The common gesture,ungesturing,waves commonly him and me into hallfilth;ecco—an almost child(blond,big;with highboots,belted blouse)

"I want you to meet a real Russian"
who from sincere palest blue grins(after limply jerking at my hand)eyes— pivoting,beckons:Darkness. And then a dim hollow cube—3 unbeds,1 untable over which blonder—perhaps realler?—Russian shavingly crouches,mansmell,a Shutness,a broken chair,silence,a homemade radio. Shaver(down laying atom of smashed mirror)straightens:bows;grins. Virgil glides

"kahk veepahzheh veye-tyeh . . ."
& 1 un-(the)opens(darkest)-bed to upyearn humanly this youthless what,smiling to me which gives(mumbling)its wet hand

"observe the,er,decorations;they are all Russian."
Over whom watches an almost but not quite(tits will be tits)colourless Salome backed by a dead sprig of pine;picturepostcards;that(for noone else ever to be mistaken)Tzar,with his dying

"murdered by his father's hand"
son . . . Bowingly I am offered the broken chair. Kindly(yes)Virgil sitting beside youthless chatters;exit unvisibly comrade-perhaps-realler . . .

so now urge. Now peevoh speaks—serene,implacable;immense, mightier than gods and men. (That word,that word ensconced in passportsplendour? Not sonofabitch;the other . . . timidly bend toward murmuring mentor—he graciously responds

"oo-Bor-neye-ah").
Belted(heartily laughing but soundlessly)slips-off-the-untable; grinning,beckons:we waft though Dark;reenter hallfilth;he points. Nor by my well of loneliness burst out of the devil's unimagination such nonlight,in fact 8 matches barely show that altar clogged with travellers' pious offerings(ah,notebookpage,faithful even unto dissolution!) . . . and madly out—more blind than any bull gushing into fatal sunlight of the arena;lurching more very sightlessly—comes drunkening my(into Aria)self,Aria Fresca! Breathe lungs! Breathe;and breathe deep! (But soft—soft . . . is this the door which led through Dark to dim,through emptiness to windowed cubic woe & vice versa?) Nothing like trying—

I,on lintel of Dark frozen,contemplate twain utterly immobile perfectly horizontal completely objectlike human shapes

 . . . corpses?

But how did corpses get here? Not corpses? (Perhaps asleep?)

 —and why didn't I trip over perhaps asleep on my previous wanderings through the Dark? Or is our heroless possibly hero gone suddenly cuckoo? —But look:they're only asleep,not corpses. They are 2 men,perfectly both asleep(utterly tired,who inhabit elsewhere;only their semblances remain). For some,or no,reason feeling like a child who imagines(and quite without believing)death cautiously myself tiptoes past the 2;to(blundering against wall)fumble—then fall into a silence-of-Shutness-sweat-unbeds-untable-chair-blond-radio-doctorVirgil-and-the-youthlessness(gently whose unearthly salutation welcomes me,comrade myself,to bedless bedside

"he's reading Tolstoy in English:see?"

Almost(dimness)grinning,lifts;War:And;Peace. The Sibyl scolds

"he spends thirty roubles out of fifty every month for cigarettes!"

"Hah-rah-Shoh" I encourage. And dim smiles—suddenly:unknotting forehead(untieing a bright raw rash). And Virgil,relenting(leaning toward dim)whispers syllables of comfort . . . tactfully the booted-and-belted drifts toward Shutness:at untable I join him:we pleasantly proceed for some moments by signs;then—inspiration!

"Radio"

stooping,grinning wondrously,he tests the earpieces. Nn-nn. And again. Neechehvoh-nyet. Nothing is happening . . . no,not even nothing

(by jammed tram's front end lawfully tumble 2 comrade ghosts). Glooms hotelless comrade Metropole:ghost 3. (A portal). A flight of marble-or-something. A vista(stairless stair by visionary stair). A not very imposing counter,behind which a ½bald not very imposing clerk is wailing DAs into a not very imposing telephone—.

"Look:there she is!"

(buried in isn't;no ghost:an almost pretty nonman)

"my other secretary"

and Gertie,quitting onceplush in deference to her pupilmaster-man,bestows upon my ghostly gaze dissimilar feet:a dainty and a huge.

"I want you to meet the distinguished American" etc.etc.etc. Childface lights.

"Yes . . . er—well,now I guess we'd better go to my room,hadn't we,and telephone the theatre. See you anon,comrade!" away indefatigably hurries ghost Virgil,the comrade childface cleverly limping alongside. (Sluggard,your conjugations!dullness,your declensions! Arise,thou Bloom—and that speedily:for peevoh,mightier than gods or men,uplifts his once more dim inexorable) . . .

—Taking,en route,a potshot at ½bald

can you perhaps tell me(hurriedly I beg)something about the SuchandSuch museum—

"yes" ghost number 4 impenetrably responds "it has moved."

What? ready? in 5 minutes? Pyaht? Absolutely.

The West may be Nervous,but Virgil's more:nobody apparently knows which tram goes where;that childface inquires of this nothingdoing group of doingnothing comrades,all these of those whom give those these different answers—up here doingly and comes a nothingish there beggar,perhaps he she it knows?and these all those interrupt that this discussion and 1st she nyets him soundly and 2nd the group soundly nyets him and 3rd Virgil(not to be outdone)nyets soundly him and 4th soundlessly he nothingish doingly goes therehereing away nyetted,and all these those comrades resume their this that and now the question isn't which tram goes where and is where do we board which tram?not here(say the donothings)over there(they say)and we over there and all of we squeeze all of selvesour into an allish muddle of allful comrades and allfulishly the muddle flows Ogroaning aboard tinflimflamtram . . . ("will you lend me that map,comrade?" bellows mentor "I have a feeling we're—.") "Certainly,comrade" I yell . . . he(reelingly)consults numbers,names;bawls—"my god! It's the right car and the wrong direction:quick . . . push ahead:we'll be late—we've got to get off!"(and the tram sighs)a sigh of comradely gladness(as out we)comrades fall(all 3 but)Virgil skips promptly in(front of an oncoming comrade other tram;he)lurches—leaping,boards(it and also I'd have but stop in air at child her screamface It's Forbidden)and he beckon-,wink-ing; shouting to us "hurry!come on!run!"(Run?—but she can't run!) though gallop she does;lumpishly,but at a fair clip;I trotting alongside to "—hurryhurry!"(and fainterest)"q-u-i-c-k!"(what the hell,is he mad?)off skip-he-hops;glaring at us,who keep galtrotloping(on past

which what cops,who cry out!and to whom she cries out!and who what
nod grinning which make way—and meanallwhile all tram ½ has up
slowed there here down:Virgil,and glaring,and shouting,reboards)it(our
galloptrotting downup duet heaves alongside she)grabs—I(boost;
he)glareshouts giggling . . . away(tram andfully)staggers on with(them
all inside and)out ½all me ½hopped(all up meansidewhile behind . . .
saved!hurrah!tree times tree!)

A little grandma is faretaker. Little nonman grandma is aflutter. What
do you mean(she,furiously fluttering)boarding my tram when my tram
was all in flight? —Stupendous argument(and the grandma shudders
scowls chatters wriggles mutters;and the cripple gestures insists denies
shrugs expatiates)and 3 neighbouring comrades add their voiceless(yesno
rightwrong whybecause)voices:and Virgil gloatglares and I,panting,pull
together my ½self. Hubbub horrible . . . ending,if you please,with
everyone beginningly grinning,nodding,heartily congratulating everyone.
(Childface turns to me;smiles:remarks,in English,that she has a pull
with the police—which fact grandma didn't understand). But grandma
understands now! Assuredly we could now buy the moon if the moon
were grinning grandma's to sell:not that we now want the moon . . . there's
enough to do now on this earth;it seems that The West Is Nervous

only just which has begun. A very crazy bubbling angular tiny personage
unjustly won't leave his only seat(which isn't his and is 1 of our 3:Virgil's
whisper tells me through darkness to move in,I do;no place—childface,to
me:Sit down . . . and limps patiently back up the aisle into unvisibility).
Ahead,via technique of Bigger And Better Constructivism,occurs
meanderingly Our Team Wins,or Capitalists Wear Silkhats. Da—and I
gather that all American women wear low(fore & aft)cut gowns day and
night(and not ever for any reason,such as to sleep,stop charlestoning)and
incessantly demand ropes(and more ropes)of priceless pearls(and more
perpetually diamonds)and live on flattery alcohol and cigarette salad
with liprouge dressing(and always shamelessly flirt with everybody and
especially anybody)and it's obvious to him who runs may read that all
American men puff cigars get drunk are idiots. (The unvisible audience
seems rather mildly,almost wearily,amused). But visible Virgil's ecstatic
And How . . . Here's the tail you chase,he prods and That's what
liquor does,he nudges and Where's your answer to this?he snickers.
Then—mask suddenly(as scene 1 ends)tragiking—

"I tried to make you hurry. Why didn't you?"

"—hurry?"

"if you two had hurried we wouldn't have arrived late?"

"do you mean, why didn't your secretary and I hurry when all of us changed cars?"

"of course! Didn't either of you see me beckoning and hear me shouting?"(angular the bubbling tinily verying crazy stumbles over these our those knees;bubbling tinily,reels;angularly very crazying disappears) "you must have realised we had no time to lose" Virgil sourly added,with a toss of his brains.

"Yes" I said "but having noticed her foot I didn't feel like urging—"

"foot?"

"her foot."

"Whose foot?"

"whose? Why,your charming little secretary's."

Spraying me with complete blankness—"what's the matter with my little secretary's foot?"

this questionless question,simply and for a blind moment,was not to be quite believed(and how it should it be?or anything;particularly everything?)then,hauling literally credulity into me "it's deformed" I answer.

His face—or to whatever these words were spoken—leaps:probably I shall never again meet so much horror and astonishment—"well!" Virgil smirked foolishly "that shows how observing I am . . . never noticed it!"

. . . dizzied,thereupon seek hastily solitude(sound of scuffling proletarian feet in upstairs lobby)and I find amid a multitude loneliness;I buy 1 cracker and 1 strange thing for 2 roubles and some kopeks;I watch and wonder;rushing out into daylight,smoke a cigarette;I stand and marvel;dizzier,but less nervous,resume The West.

Not unshortly after said blague has come to wellearned silence,Virgil tells childface to go boldly behind the scenes and find her idol of idols(who happens to be The West's hero—a spiritualized warrior appearing once,at the very end). Childface blushes . . . You'll have to come and ask questions about the play as an excuse,she suggests;therefore(Virgil promising)we wind among tunnels. Presently am shaking hands with a courteous businesslike comrade secretary(whose welcome causes twin comrade guards such wideeyedness that I tread the dark stage,examine at leisure its revolving mostly metal set . . .) He told me,childface confides(meaning the secretary)that my hero wasn't interesting—at which Virgil hazards that my hero might not be interesting mentally and might still be interesting physically(and comrade Kem-min-kz hears himself think "in other words,girlie,interesting")

but mentor pauses—"the nominative would be . . ." (Behind us strut limp feet). "—Don't tell" he pleads with childface;then,frowning at this affiche(which unto starless night heralds this coming of Russia's Greatest Proletarian Writer)tries bravely—

Not at all!(slumpily beside me alights total and cadaverous stranger). You're wrong(who wobbles;an amiable scarecrow). It would be(and a wild dull shriek informs us at forever's length what it would be and a thick will cackles foreverfully over that nominative and a loosely stuffed suggestion of head waves its crumpled eyes and wags its crumbling ears over all nominatives,any nominative,The nominative . . . (suddenly)night takes:voice head stance hungriness(away)

"don't think he's crazy,do you?" Virgil inquires.

"He might be drunk" I wonder "or both."

And she nods.

"O I don't see how he could be drunk" my guardian objects "—you never see drunkards in Moscow any more." 3 comrades move . . .

she comrade smiles,waves;hunches into a comrade tram:which— hobbles,whinnying;nightward:

"now there's my cursed stupidity again" benevolence eventually complains. "Why didn't we take that car to the Writers' Club?—you'd see nightlife there,perhaps. —O well;let's walk a little further:I know of one place;with music,at any rate."

Largeness;welllighted,clean. (Tense struggling against relaxed:many and white tablecloths,mended and few patrons). A pompous how small orchestra.

"It's frightfully dear,isn't it."

That it is—if menu knows.

"And what may I serve you gentlemen?"

(heartily if briefly demands erect,grey,bearlike almost noble headwaiter). We order hair of the dog that alias beers,and a dish of mushrooms.

The best unbeer yet. Music(strenuously trying to be gay)sounds somewhat shocking but(there)sitting(and here)patrons stare dully at merely us;don't,can't,heed music . . . And—possibly thanks to omnipotent peevoh—out now came(from mindless me)10,000 copiously embroidered oathprayers times circa 50,000,000 stumbling pocketthunderbolts

"b-b-b-but" angel registers incredulity "what are you saying?"

"I'm saying:by God Christ and Ghost,by a prick in the rose,by three(by cheers You Es Ay blind mice Gay-Pay-Oo and speeds forward)—never,never,never,has that(immaculately goosed by a moonbeam) unmitigated rectum The Socalled Human Mind conceived quite so centrifugally superconstipated a calamity as poisons with what hyperlugubrious(I Ask You)logic the airless air we(quotes)breathe. I'm saying:by You Es Es Are,by four(finite but unbounded)—if-and-unless I go loonier than any young sixfingered thimble,may god help it,I'll beg borrow steal and convey—even to innocently absolute immensity to wit a small sheet of paper—each speck and each spot of sadistic nonsubstance which secretly is,or is otherwise,harboured by ineradicably this distinctly unimpeachable system of meretricious murderfully(Allow Me)masochism. Get it? Long live Is! Up—in the holy name of uncommon NonSense! Viva!"

he leered,indulgently. Sipping—"you're quite mad,aren't you."

"Yes—thank blood and sun! Thank(very kindly)the millionary whispers of the anonymous tide—thank(if you please)every leafing leaf of every treeing tree. Thank laughter and true tears(the first curve of a girl)and silence;not to mention that harmonicacoloured fragrance of the tomorrow-behind-yesterday . . . or whatsoever only may completely be afraid to be afraid—"

"da(if I may interrupt)but what has this tirade to do with our present circumstances?"

"dada. Nothing—or the unthing which everyone(except impossibly the artist)must become merely by going to sleep."

"Hm . . . I take it,you consider the artist a peculiar individual?"

"O and how very peculiar! Hark:if peculiar were as peculiar as elephants are elephants,the socalled artist still would be precisely the only(the let us say indivisibly)peculiar thing alive."

"Well" he considers "I know a great many artists,especially

Russians(you're going to meet some of them)but I shouldn't say they were as peculiar as all that!"

"yes,captain;but let me ask you something. Do you know"(I can't help laughing;Virgil's mask looks like a selfportrait of Rockyfeller's Manship)"one rather strictly unrecognizable artist,who comes rather than goes by the terse and reflexive pseudonym of Thih Seauton? Why? Because that there fellow actually(And When I Say Actually)is the artist for me."

"Pff" he pffed "you're joking . . . but seriously,comrade,I'm getting a little worried about your reactions. Do you realise,I wonder—it's more or less my fault,I'm afraid—that your artistship hasn't as yet seen anything which might be considered really important?"

"'really'? —Wait,wait an inch:do you,sir,honestly believe(honestly,I say)that one blind fish,flying feebly along the ceiling of old ocean(at an average height of several nautical miles)might not,if unplausibly,know more about . . . well,let's assume the baldspot of an upsidedown plutocrat(monotonously who is without difficulty clinging to the imported sandalwood poop of his twelve thousand cowpower steamwhatnot)than Karl Groucho Marx or anyone else(including Hop O' My Thumb Carrie Nation and,least but not last,Comrade Anthropomekano Supino)knows—knew—or will know,about humanly inhuman destiny?"

"now please don't let's get all tangled up in abstractions(although,as a matter of fact,Marx isn't as abstruse as you seem to believe)—what I'm claiming is this:one simply has no right to judge one's environment until one has at least attempted to understand it."

"One hasn't? And why? Isn't my environment judging me? Although,as a matter of fact,that there particular comrade(who just moved up behind you with the intention of hearing better)looks as if he were unfortunately doing his level best to understand this here fortunately uphill conversation."

"Where—!" Virgil ½turned ½pale. "—O . . ."(and,almost whispering) "I suppose we might discuss more general topics,mightn't we?"

"Master" I to him said "you unfairly astound my astoundability. One momentless moment it's god save the beatifically benevolent three letter fraternity—"

"sh—you don't understand! Hm. Yes . . . Well,here's our food.

Deliciouslooking,isn't it! Shall I serve you? I see they've generously brought us two plates—"

. . . hadn't that recently upmoving comrade formerly been chattering in some farthest corner with a uniformed friend? Where(I wonder)is now this friend? And as,dissatisfied with the present view,I squirm a little sideways—my elbow touches an elbow. —Of course! Quickly which instructive discovery hands all my proud comrade spine a telegram of anger:then,mercifully,up(out of memory)lifts the immortal dictum of untime's most ignorant how wisest daemon:It's What's Behind Me That I Am. Blessings upon thee,Krazy Kat;may thy poet prosper until eternity!

"why are you laughing?" Virgil looks really alarmed.

"Because again and again an anticommunist teacher of Russianless Russian assured me that,wherever I went in all this vast land,I'd be followed:and again and again I blushingly refused the compliment. Because again and again an anticommunist painter of beneficent devils warned me that to open the prizepackage of Marxism was to find a joyless experiment in force and fear:and again and again I merrily smiled. Now I'm not blushing and I don't smile,comrade. The good New Englanders merely and honestly burned their comrade witches. Now I can laugh. —By the way,what miraculous mushrooms!"

"I'm afraid you're a philosophical anarchist."

"Whatever that may be. However;one good category deserves another" and where—when—did the upmover? . . . and the elbow,too(impossibly have possibly Gay-Pay-Oos an all-their-own method of supernaturally disappearing?)

Thursday 14

Door's(to self's auroral rap)opened by(of all people)dim neatened youthless: who seems 100% better—versus myself's angel;horrific in most wintry underwear,bitterly who wails that last night he died reliving our speakeasy argument("which I insist upon resuming when our bellies are satisfied"). Better 'phones breakfast;grinningly,albeit ⁵/₄starved,refuses to partake. And suddenly—from the squareless square—reverberates Carmen(of all ditties)out whereupon we 3 busily crawl to observationledge and,lo!peerade. It's the wellknown letters,Virgil tells better,manoeuvring in honour of Gorky(whom I'd like to meet;but mentor's darkly doubtful about that President of Writers' Club invitation—Gorky,says benevolence,negatively will be everywhere,not positively somewhere). So "well,are we all set?" . . . and,swopping a capitalistic cheroot for something proletarian(something which comrade better emphatically does not recommend)I just settle down to a long winter's nap—

Q:The whole trouble with you is that,like so many people who were brought up on religion,you can't bear the idea of anything doing away with it.

A:Can't bear the idea of any what doing away with which?

Q:Of science doing away with religion.

A:I see:we're supposed to suppose that the new religion,science,does away with religion,the old religion—tahk.

Q(snorts):How can you be so perverse!

A:I?

Q:As if religion and science weren't direct opposites!

A:Right you are,colonel:every coin has two sides.

Q:Odear. There you go,utterly confusing the issue—

A:Issue? We've all tried paying with one side and keeping the other side for ourselves,haven't we?

Q:But,my dear chap—can't you possibly be serious?

A:I'm afraid I'm being much too serious,comrade.

Q:No you're not—you're being extremely trivial and very childish and rather cheaply amusing.

A:And I'm quoting Emerson.

Q:Emerson?

A "When me you fly,I am the wings".

Q:Who said that?

A:Brahma,the sage of Concord;who(inconsiderately)went to Rome and found—

Q:O,of course . . . but to return to our muttons. What you can't seem to realise is this:religion imprisons the human mind,whereas science makes people free.

A:What I can seem to realise is that I'd just as soon be imprisoned in freedom as free in a jail—if that's any help.

Q:You simply won't be serious,will you.

A:For crying out loud,my dear professor!do you seriously believe that a measurable universe made of electrons and lightyears is one electron more serious or one lightyear less imprisoning than an unmeasurable universe made of cherubim and seraphim? Are you—I am being serious—really sold on the saleability of reality? Do I seriously(very seriously)seem to see your human mind squatting in your magic jockstrap,freely watching Hitchy Goomy Gitchie Koo(the sickest medicine-man of them all)turn your ailments into formulas? Did they ask,seriously,for bread and did you seriously give them Einstein? O Millikan,O Marx! —Page by all means a certain Mr. Cosmic Ray,Mary mother of Joshua ben Lenin ben Joseph ben Franklin ben Stalin ben Roosevelt ben Big Ben ben Big Stick ben Evolent ben Lightningrod—

Q:All right;all right:did you ever stop to think what would happen if everyone were as selfcentred as yourself?

A:Not to completely feel is thinking. May I be allowed to feel,if you please?

Q:Yes? —Well,tell us what you feel.

A:That anyone who pretends to know what's good for somebody else might just as well admit the immaculate atonement's vicarious conception—

Q:Good heavens! If all people "felt" as you do,there wouldn't be any civilization!

A:Is there any?

Q:O don't be completely idiotic!

A:And what(I pray)is idiocy? Falling for this that or the other brand of propaganda. Am I falling?

Q:Propaganda!

A:Propaganda:canned wishes;just add hot conscience and serve.

Q:But is there anything in the whole world which isn't,or which may not become,propaganda? Answer me that!

A:Not in the world. Elsewhere.

Q:"Elsewhere"—?

A:Art.

Q:Art! —Why,my dear fellow:art is derived from religion!

A:And deriving may become almost as much fun as pingpong;unless (like the artist)you happen to be afflicted with seriousness:whereupon all childishly idiotic trivialities like "time" cease to have any particular significance,either as concomitants of a deriving game or otherwise.

Q:Hm . . . I suppose one should rather pity than condemn your illusions of grandeur—which are,after all,neurotic.

A:Strangely enough,I was thinking the very same thing in your case.

Q:—In my case?

A:One should(after all)proceed carefully;as Relling said to—

Q:Who?

A:Doctor Relling.

Q:I don't understand—

A:"Rob the average man of his lifelie and you deprive him of his happiness".

Q:What's that?

A:The Wild Duck.

Q:Wild which?

A:A play by comrade Ibsen.

Q:O—Ibsen's play;yes. The Wild Duck—yes indeed . . . magnificent thing of its kind,but of course I'm interested in the new theatre.

(Proletarian something has long since fizzled). "Life being a mystery at best,let's telephone the perfume girl;shall we?" I enjoin.

"The perfume girl?"

"you said you knew her—the one to whom I'm also bringing a multitude of magazines—"

"O—of course! —Why"(beaming)"that's an excellent idea,really excellent." He turns to better;who nods,locates a number in the encyclopaedia;gorods. "She's out" Virgil translates "but we're to call again between one and two. Odear"—and all at once he looked very very old.

"Kahk?"

"I'm afraid I'm going to lose you."

"'Lose me'?"

"to her." He sighed. "She's such a charming person."

"Indeed?"

"I admire her so much" he mused. "Almost as much as I hate religion" he added dreamily.

"Well:well;well!"

"of course you've heard(everybody has)of her first husband . . . who killed himself—"

"let's not kill ourselves" I admonish.

"That was really a great man" murmurously reminisced my guardian "a leader,a worker,and a fighter—but" giggling "the fair lady married again."

"To whom is the fair lady now married?"

"O,a nice enough fellow—a good communist—but of course he can't compare with his hero predecessor."

"Quite a nice predicament for the nice enough fellow" I sympathize.

"Hm . . . to tell the truth,I never thought of it from that angle before. —Well,so you're going to the great Madame Potiphar. Take care!"

Better coughed,stood. We shook hands;then(angel patting him affectionately;warning him to go straight home,not to catch cold,to guard against overdoing)better slid betterfully forth

"tell me something" sotto voce "don't you think he spends too much on tobacco?"

"He that can live without food can die without tobacco" I solemnize.

"Hm . . . Possibly. Yes. In other words it becomes,like alcohol or drugs,a habit—I don't smoke,myself,you understand . . . But now let's try Volks once more"(he'd 'phoned before breakfast,unsuccessfully)"and see if we can get a Gorky clue. I emphatically believe that your apparently genuine(but,all things considered,somewhat unaccountable)interest in the world's foremost proletarian of letters ought by every reasonable means—"

stairs,stairs,stairs.

"Whither?"

"this man" mentor explains "is the head of all the book publishing(I do hope he's in). Notice these photographs" we've entered a dusty outer office clogged with placid mouldily loungers "of proletarian writers" and the mouldiest placidly lounger,turning himself to Virgil(shyly and entirely and sharingly;or as a child turns to some suddenly trusted stranger)grins—Do you know who they are?

and angel names them:pompously,solemnly.

Good!says the grinner(then,greatly and proudly serious)I—I(pointing right into his own heart with a devout selftrustingness;with an eerie confidence in world in work and above all in Word)I've read them all!

Virgil(nudging)"did you get that?"

"oddly enough,I did."

"Nice,eh?"

"it's something like overwhelming" I must correct him. "Also,something like a universe away from the New York equivalent . . ."

"which would be?"

"sure I know all the speakeasies on this block."

Stunned,staring—"then you don't really hate socialism,do you!"

laughing "so far as I can feel,I don't hate anything except hate." The comrade greatman is unimaginably busy(his comrade associate politely informs us).

"O and by the way—I almost forgot to mention it:we paid,last night,for two orders of mushrooms:did you realise?" "No,I didn't." "And we only had one order." "Correct." "But I don't think they were trying to cheat us,do you?" "Inasmuch as I had no such hunch at the time,my guess is that they weren't"

(and Gorky,not to be located through Volks,is today—quite as benevolence had assumed—not somewhere but everywhere)

obsequiously,ikon joint. 3 or 2 disguised-as-women,Orientally. A reek of junkless baskingly junk and

"how do you do,Doctor!"

deferentially mentor murmurs;while,by junk wonderfully swallowed,marvellously are by junkless regurgitated twain contrasting apparitions—1(individually)huge,Chinesy,dangerous:1 brainless, American,collegiate(type).

"Greetings,professor"

a dull small voice,distinctly from chinful vicinity trickling of much neck, cautiously responds. And his beringed(alive but,or,mysteriously)molluscal hand makes the brittle grabbing of brainless(Gladtuhmeetyuh)seem a handshake's photograph.

"I can't keep away from them,as you see"
twitters angel. The small dull voice glitters
"keep away?"

"you know my ailment,Doctor(you haven't told anyone,I hope!)— well,it's getting worse every moment" then,to gaping collegiate "this is a great secret:I'm interested in ikons—from the business standpoint,you understand" and to huge "I'd only just decided on three simply gorgeous ones,when the comrade in charge produced another(which I have to admit is extraordinary)but I can't afford all four" and with a mocksigh "—isn't that a terrible dilemma?"

The molluscal(upgroping wanderful hoveringly)arrives gently; becoming hand . . . cautiously which papier-maché Virgil by 1 shoulderless shoulder
"listen,professor"
grips;the voice goes wee but its glitter flares
"be careful"
and slowly a far deep mind adds
"of this store."

"O but my selections are perfectly authentic;absolutely genuine: there's no possible question of that—to be sure" almost bitterly "brother Cummings didn't seem overenthusiastic;but then,brother Cummings like" archly "so many of us" and cynically "is labouring under certain capitalistic misapprehensions!"

Left. Left. Left!right!left!tiddledy-AH—Dee:Die-dy;Doe-dy,Dummm . . . Parade,rade,rade;parade,rade,rade. The uniformly moving monotonously uniform comrades imply vision in which dreamless Virgil unwishfully and wishfully my dreaming self swim,through dreamed uniform wishless monotonously walkers &
"here" pointing,giggling "is the terror of Europe. Look at it"
"I am"

"mais quel dommage"(you misunderstood;Gorky won't be visible today—he is everywhere). Genially presidentless president of mightily bustling Writers' Club almost is himself nowhere,but anyhow finds occasion(if not opportunity)to lunch with Look at it & I am. Up,just at most glorious apex of an actual Russian repast—with really for a change beer—floats dingy agreeable diffident somebody whose The History Of One Murder became in god's country Gods Of the Lightning (confidentially,this comrade assures me,he didn't invent second title;did I know,farawayishly he asks,that I'm 1 of 2 poets—the mysterious other being "a monosyllable"—about to be translated except that "something happened" and the translation was put back a year?)

No,I didn't.

Nor did I know that Clairsin Islew,familiarly known to his many friends as "Red" Islew,is the communist idea of a "great artist". . . And anyhow the president 'phones(and what's more gets)the perfume girl;whom perhaps I'm to visit tomorrow(sans—with heaven's help—all agog Virgil "when she calls up,be sure and tell her about . . . not that I wish to intrude,you under . . . I wonder if she'll invite me too:but wouldn't it . . . probably you should go alone?" and,unsmiling "though she did smile upon myself the last time we . . . at least,that was my impression;of course one never knows,does one:Odear,isn't that exciting: is she really going to telephone you tomorrow morning? I believe if I were in your place I couldn't sleep" adinfinitum)

and flutterfully exit.

Hahrahshoh.

—You'd like to see the Something play tonight and present your letter;of course . . . let me—(comrade presidentless produces brisk tall courteous comrade,author of now-in-rehearsal Something play,who takes comrade 'phone;but comrade Something himself is out:will I perhaps be so possibly kind as to return in probably half an hour?)

a poet(but not a monosyllable)wandering wonderlessness,pondering imponderabilities,harshly bump what luscious letters of decipherable (PANORAMA)word recalling childhood(its terrorless pity,pityless terror)—thereupon who,abandoning the parkless park,joins 1 odourous shackful of comrades and(several kopeks the poorer)squirts his lean hungry mind through various peepholes. Punk,alas . . . supposedly representing stages in the torture(sic)of mankind by clergy-and-nobility . . . quite beyond lifelessness dead,excepting this mediaeval séance of drunken old godworshippers(1 showing his bottom);but scarcely less quite lifeless than these all how ominously silent beside me ghosts who,peer,move,peer.

At Something theatre(which,just for a change,looks like a theatre—even a true theatre,possibly a burleskhouse)

self(to him in Administration)"sprechen-Sie français?"

he(smiles)"nein."

I "eng-glish?"

he(grins)"non."

Self "yah cummings." (Producing letter and naming)"comrade—?"

he(serious)"da." (Inspects and carefully puts aside my epistle of introduction)"ein?"(referring to pass,which is good for 2)

I "yes"

(& check coat with undifficulty and with even ease reject proffered multifariously operaglasses)

. . . there is no curtain:sacks clutter the lightless stage;at whose inmostness looms,towers(against not masked theatre building itself)a battleship

. . . but finding my seat were un tour de force,"orchestra" equalling sundayschool chairs(of the more very uncomfortable variety)grouplessly grouped in strictly ambiguous sections. I appeal to a comrade nonman usher. Accurately and with pride who finds me the wrong place;carefully from which voluntarily dislodge in favor of ample anguishing proletarian family—to sink into(by sheer chance)the proper really destination(But hush:sh!dark . . .)

now here's tay-ahter—sense of pretend,promising nonsense of actuality. Dissonant pipings "set the key":stark exposition(Yank-Chink dialogue)sacks are removed by chorus,opening stage which is promptly animated by the crossing of a tiny boat(water,real)and which subsequently is annihilated by the(waterless)movingup of the Chief Object,i.e. battleship,toward audience;abstract use of noisesound to invent space(distance)and place(location);nouns arbitrarily are represented by merely wheres,e.g. sailors face X and look—X being a plane or anything whatever or nothing,being not looked At,being unimportant with respect to looking which itself constitutes its target

and from these promisings am happy. For I taste technique:smell style;touch something(not definably,particularly,logically which seems) thoroughly which Is:understanding the spectator always a never faster than the spectator overstands it.

. . . Then what happens? On the contrary,happens is progressively negated. Smothering happens or occurs—choking accidently or beautiful—behold the(à la Proletcult with a difference)weed of dogma flourishes. Dogma—the destroyer of happens,the killer of occurs,the ugliness of premeditatedly—here stalks And How. Announcement from stage after 1st entr'acte(we have with us tonight certain workers who've completed the 5 year plan in 2 years . . . about 50 shy creatures blushfully arising are vociferously applauded)gives unneeded clue.

Now I'm witnessing a cheap melodrama,so cheap(alas)it isn't cheap enough

the drowned man now in semidarkness gets up to take a bow

now imperceptibly,by dint of Tverskaya,returning—could my lingo be improving?wasn't tonight cheated re 2 cakes(with not ale because cheye and very good cheye)—I(myself:miraculously!)meet horror;symbol . . . via the(suddenly)upper-$\frac{1}{2}$-of-a-man rushing along . . . & I see— feelingly;deep under any dream—that(subtracted from this hope) furiously spectre vanish upon its awful little wheels . . .

Mob

through mob glints—?yes,radiator of what was contentedly Ford sedan till the hind-by vile enchantment?quarters turned into a dumpcart. Now which . . . comprising very pale lad,and girlwoman(?)calmly nervous . . . extraordinary monster's eyes being snapped on,it starts:rightfront-wheelpolygon ally wob b ling;and,stops.

Mob regathers,denser:now very paler lad becomes plural(1 doesn't stir,1 keeps getting in and out and reaching over the girl(?)who modestly cringes toward obscurity).

A whistle! Enter boyscoutcop.

Argument. Now very smaller palest originally singular is being hauled;he manfully resists. Now both lads are dragged forth(downgliding whereupon the woman weaves mobward,unhurriedly around nearest corner disappears). Argument and argument and. Redfaced taller 1,who's hypersoused,tries to extract a badge from his own lapel but can't quite unscrew the emblem—backclimbing angrily into the dumpsedan monster,he slams petulantly its door.

Applause with catcalls.

Now somebody is seizing somebody away;seized somebody struggles; mob(densest,most excited)pursues(I never heard so many "tovarich"s)— tiens!acrobatically the seized-struggler is picked bodily by the seizing up(and run clean off with)for something like if possibly not a parasang

59

. . . upon being grounded,seized violently objects to this flight:seizing immediately pinions seized's wrists:seized whirls free,recoils and(amazingly) leaps skyward—to drop squarely atop formerly seizing . . . down the seized-and-seizing goes(directly before an onrushing mangily Renault which avoids doublemurder by hopjumping this curb)and both seizing-now-seizeds wallow wrigglingly(stopping traffic)and . . . where? . . . aren't.

Not that comrade myself saw them vanish.

Mob,chuckling,unmobs. Traffic resumes. The play is over

i;wondering;visit a certainly spiralling Which

and who appears(with whitely nothing behind)at a vast nearness—implacably,in mist,decorative:very how more than how very relentlessly copious:immutably(prettily)alone. Whereof the wonderful architect therefore did not see our world. (& could this)to(yes that's)my(right),matters unimmortal lay saint Lenin's matterlessly inoffensive claptrap,dimly thosethese mausoleum,something,or cardboard or something,or boxes feel impact(eyes) . . . awaken to glimpse some(thingal)most prettily (indiscreetly who discreetly)retreating giggles. (Omen?) Hark—neuter chuckle of talktoy(a really feminine voice courteously assails me in much-beyond-my-French French,cordially now is inviting me to dine "chez nous" this afternoon,then skillfully skates And How suddenly over the subject of certain gifts . . . "à bientôt,Monsieur!")

Joseph "know thou" announces "that Madame Potiphar has telephoned" . . . unhappy mentor!You have indeed suffered a seachange. Every undeepness was obliterated and each category drowned and all his littlenesses filled with guilt. Comrade(not born,undead)mentor cannot feel;therefore did Resurrection not recreate,it crucified,him—therefore by his own insincerity is comrade mentor overwhelmed—therefore(in a futile attempt to transform even what could have assimilated ignobility into what even ignobility may assimilate)this more or less corpse less or more expires.

Sigh. "I was trying to cash in on you" he confesses. "You should go alone" dismally adding. "O how tired I am!" he groans.

"Pardon me for observing that you look as if you'd met a work of art headon,comrade."

"I have. Extraordinary. From beginning to end—simply extraordinary."

"Da?"

"profound. Absolutely profound,my dear fellow."

"But far,I take it,less profound than if,say,comrade Lenin had been the author."

"Hm . . . As you see,I'm completely exhausted. Sorry:I really can't argue."

"These socalled Russians" truthfully I soothe "are a miraculous people,bolsheh or no bolsheh" while comrade cheerfully better commands capitalist breakfasts.

"So"(over the eggs with toast with jam,over the authentic coffee)"we must plan your campaign. Firstly—a map of the battlefield,"

(adorning with numbers words angles dots and other signs the very envelope containing comrade Kem-min-kz' introduction to the perfume girl)

"—there."

"My general,three salutes and one bravo for this chef-d'oeuvre."

"Don't mention it. Convey my compliments to the fair charmer;tell her(if you see fit)that one of her most ardent,if least aggressive,admirers must admit himself temporarily incapacitated after an evening with the great Tolstoy."

"Sir,it shall by myself be done. And now for the bankless bank—"

"our young Russian friend will guide you safely there and back."

"I do entreat—"

"O,but I insist"

vainly 35 minutes at various guichets . . . then shrug & smile;he smiles and shrugs

"zahvtrah"

and grins . . . Whereas,at that forgotten not to say neglected Mecca of all Meccas,INTOURIST(whither crisp Teuton flipperingly had disappeared 1 fateful morn)a 20 cheque immediately cashes gladly itself in the King's English—delighting almost beyond unbelief our young Russian friend. He dances,winks,gestures,gurgles . . . and solemnly accepts the gaily proffered extra paperohsa(placing,most sacredly,same within how very jacketless a jacket and)humbly,humourously explaining

Tomorrow.

"How are you getting along?" paternally our guardian interrogates 1 disagreeably American thickset undoubtedly not young news-paperman

"okay,professor:I'm using a sleeping-dictionary"

" . . . "

& my trousers fly on. (A great Godlike voice,from somewhere above,continues)

" . . . "

. . . bearded,too,Manshape perches;squeezed against ceiling,tinker-ing . . .

less than perhaps absolutely the original if not only comrade Santa Claus couth do I(desperately putting forward my best foot)comprise

(1)a map,drawn by guardian angel upon letter of introduction—right side pants pocket

(2)a new toothbrush(with an extra brush part)—upper left vest pocket

(3)several neckties—lower right coat pocket

(4)a plethora of perfume—left outer overcoat pocket

(5)a tube of lanoline—right inner ditto

(6)the following extremely soi-disant literary items—stuffed in every helpless nook and cranny of my flowered wall

1 Bravo

1 Motion Picture

1 Ciné Miroir

3 Photoplays

1 La Revue du Cinéma

1 Jazz

1 the Boulevardier

2 Vogues

1 Pour Tous

1 Détective

1 Cri de Paris

1 Vu

Virgil(having staggered in)had opposite a certain photograph collapsed, promptly to regurgitate hopelessness—("it seems to me that I never get anything done,I'm no nearer my objective today than I was yesterday")& sighs;groans . . . totteringly seeks his couch

nab the 16 tram upon conclusion of unusually brief(10 minute)wait. Cross a creek("river" of my map?). Arriving,dreadfully sooner than had expected,at what possibly might be something which map terms "rond- point" I interrogate my nearest neighbour(he nods—"da")also conductor("dadada"). Cautiously descend—into really a maelstrom of trafficless traffic.

Whither now?

ah—Virgil's trusty diagram beckons That Way(whereupon our hero busily hunts the original of a transliterated avenue:he makes a mistake,he retraces my steps;we approach a(mighty young,pour changer)izvostchik and us begs humbly enlightenment. Fluently he directs. Thankfully I spaseebah iz. Pleasefully iz pahzhahloostahs me.

I walk a huge distance.

(Damn this receptacle of giftless gifts,alias my not lightweight overcoat—for am sweating like a fish:besides,the cargo has somewhat shifted;me walks with a starecausing agonybegetting list-to-starboard. Meanwhile everything considerably gets muddier,lonelier,more delapidated. And god help Santa Claus).

Cobblestones—a turn:could such-as-this-a-swamp equal the long sought vista of my mentor's dreams? Yes(and by my capitalist watch just 25 minutes early). O well,nothing whatever like a mild machinemade cigarette(have I?I have)

—of course:no matches.

And no place to sit down,either.

Just a great deal of time,of course,and almost complete(and approximating hysterical annihilation if such things be)weariness . . . I flounder dimly how listingly reeling into a peeling court:sweatingly I for 2 hefty nonmen steer(younger & unyounger,separately who are silently leaning on a flimsy porchrail)

"where this?" in Berlitz remark,lifting with utmost difficulty the blue envelope posterior or mapside downward . . .

nearer,unyounger,does not read:beckons to the younger(who reads,looks,tells me To The Right,points)—Ilessly I list now dimly for a certain houseless house with 2 unportallike impossibly portals.

(The right?)

"da"(both leaners smile,nod). And I point:Up?(they nod,laugh).

Climb 1 tough flight quickly of surprisingly substantial stairs—to face 1 leathertextured door mysteriously flaunting in deep shadow 1 almost polished plaque. And . . . balancing carefully some ½dozen lesser bundles per the bannister . . . prosecute frenzied search for(through a shutness at hall's end I can eye the 2,Elsewhere Looking,leaning; together:silent)matches—find!

da . . .

and it's the long sought name. Hahrahshoh(readjusting my collective self,wondering how not to look exactly like the local equivalent of ye Fuller salesman)I thumb a sunken button:

swish!—angrily frowns nonman with scraggly black hair.

Citizeness(should I have said Comrade?)—?

Come in,please(abruptly & hurriedly).

Swish!—(and am standing nightswallowed:alone. But here's;yes; undark . . . stirring beyond which(O can such things be?)

a woman:tall but not too;not young but not old,and handsome and most womanly moving and instantly I feel—she is honest,she is gay,she is strongwilled.

It's very good of you to come(French).

Please(Russian).

Whereat she laughs—not as the Marxians,not echoing world woes! "Et où" ½seriously,½mischievously "est votre camarade?" Actually as and at every reachable portion of thoroughly amazed me rushes,apparelled in a peculiarly innocuous most sumptuously infantile expression, 1(genus,ugliest)bullpup

"il n'est pas méchant du tout" comrade slightly I said-smiled(while the fiend,after turning 3 somersaults off my left shin,recovered tranquility sneezed and his legs)

"même pas assez."

On the wall,several "artistic" camera "studies" of a very much too fearless,at least 3 fisted,pathetically And How actorish tovarich gogetter;backgrounded by wouldbeforceful caricatures. I.e.,comrade suicide.

You're in the country here(I said,pointing through partly shutness at trees)I like it.

O but we're moving(she smiled)to the centre.

Will that be better?

Mercy yes! The house will be better. And we will have gas . . . Pause.

And how's my sister? So—she must have money if she sends all these things! Yes?

My wife and I spent several delightful evenings in Paris with your sister and her husband.

Perfume!—How is he?

Excellently well,I should say. He's an old acquaintance of mine—

A toothbrush:how nice!—what does he feel about Russia?

To me he was enthusiastic;although I've heard he didn't have an easy time here—

It was in Paris he didn't have an easy time(she corrects). His former associates,those idle aesthetes of the Latin quarter,resented the fact that our friend had turned communist. —Magazines! O that's magnificent!

I'm sorry,I didn't understand.

But is the comrade returning to Russia? He promised us that he would come back.

"Nyez neyeyoo."

Vogue! Vogue!—and may I ask,please,why didn't you bring your wife to Moscow?

I didn't because I thought she'd find Moscow a trifle—well,severe.

Why?(looking straight at me).

My wife and I both . . . ("pourquoi pas?"says myself) . . . You know, there are not many things in Moscow that shine. I'm a child. I like shining things.

Yes?(straight).

Yes.

Would that be a reason for her missing Russia? You think so

Not exactly a reason,but—

Hm. (Pause). Tell me:have you read this book?(pointing to a shelf)

I never read. Why should we read?—that's for the others!

(Laughing)you're right;I see:yes. And you've brought your own books,of course?

My own—?

In this letter,my sister mentions your books with great pleasure;I suppose you've brought all of them with you—

I should say not!

—No?

"Non. Et je vous en prie,Madame,ne me demandez pas pourquoi je suis venu en Russie;parce que je ne le sais pas moi-même." The eyes grew;she laughed,smiled;

she slowly floated about a smallest room,she stepped crisply in and smoothly out of(handling the things,gifts,opening this which skilfully and touching this)sunlight . . .

Are you adjusted to Moscow? May I do anything to help you?

Yes. (And gravely)I'd like to stop living like a millionaire—

(and laughing,she telephones . . . and she gives me an address;and assures me that a certain comrade will arrange everything—will find me some costless or almost costless domicile). Herself,it seems,must the day after tomorrow depart for everywhere.

"Voici" naming husband:undersized,with a shaven(baldspotted) head,blackrimmed spectacles;the walk of a bankclerk and something too serious about(somehow something which he isn't)him . . .

How goes it?(German French).

(I)Confused.

Why?

You behold(I somewhat candidly explain)someone who finds himself inhabiting a workers' republic and a hostelry de luxe—both for the first time in my life.

Where are you living?

Metropole.

Aha! Moscow's most expensive hotel. Ten dollars a day,eh?

Five,with breakfast.

Hm. Well,you have valuta. (That fate worse than death).

Yes,and I used to have an American passport—but,even so,your servant isn't quite John Henry Andrew Ford Carnegie. (He's a writer, she said in the language of unkings). —At one of your proletarian theatres,where those lucky stage-Americans wander about in their dinnercoats and their silkhats,I began murmuring to myself:O to be an American;I,who am only a poor Russian!

All that will change for the better(she comforts,laughing)

Madame is too kind.

But(And How earnestly)you should see the theatres in the factories. They represent our new Russia. They are unique;whereas(contemptu- ously designating the remarkable comrade who didn't meet me;also the charming president of the Writers' Club)are everywhere. Understand? (I nod). You have your books with you?

Alas,not one.

That's a mistake. Next time you'll come and bring your books.

Next time I'll send my books and stay at home(humbly comrade me said,patting the pup)

—enter now a plump gentle dignified(husband,sotto voce:He's a great hero of work!)soldier:modestly whom outflank 3 huge medalbadges plus 1 merely large pin. Who speaks marvellous English.

—Enter collation. Lavish beyond describability

le mari occupies a tiny sofa,not quite en face me,who's next to the hostess,who's opposite the hero,who gently to all distributes edibilities galore and softly to all but host apportions vodka and white wine and red wine from the Caucasus and finally cognac(and entirely whose most mannerless manner I can't help liking;but can't help wondering,too,why Monsieur doesn't do the honours). 3(no more no)lessons in speech had plump from a London woman(result:"allow me to present you with this box of Our Mark cigarettes" previously having dealt me 4 Nords for 1 Lucky "they are made in our factory,you will find them rather superior")but he never hit Paris;therefore when I maintain to Madame that Americans are savages—and seriously she responds O no!the fact that you have Dreiser proves that you are civilized—ensuing argument must item by item be translated for his benefit. And translated it apparently is. Also,Madame insists that I must write an article for the Russian press—

Comrade K:In Paris I was by one American offered the fabulous sum of a hundred nonMexican dollars to scribble about Russia;bravely thereat I sad no.

Madame: Why?

K:Because the offerer happens to be a friend and suppose I wrote something my friend didn't like!

Hero(gently):You might have taken the hundred dollars and returned it.

K:But dollars spend themselves so easily. And doesn't that sound American(I cried)—here's one hundred dollars:now go and write something!—O Merde(I shouted quite forgetting myself)what a wonderful word! How do you translate it?(Madame looked as if she were trying to register shockedness and carefully asked her hero,who said carefully that he didn't know any exact equivalent). Well,suppose I took your advice and wrote something bad?

It would be all right(she laughed).

Really?

O yes(smiling)we have some severe critics.

—Meanwhile speechless mari gulps guiltily dainties;timidly then retires into a back room,with(for consolation)the telephone. I begin to comprehend . . .

"all—you must see all—of Russia"(hero,1 arm tentatively encircling Madame,cognacs). "There are so many ways . . ."

"what a pity we can't all go all over Russia together"(I cognac).

"Oui"(she cognacs sadly)"c'est dommage"

(—but other things are not dommage:for instance,the fact that I'm courteously but firmly restrained from politely bidding these lovebirds adieu) . . . Enter quite ungently 1 exclusively Russianspeaking and leanish Terror(no doubt about him)times a not too unattractive(in her gold teeth)nonman aggressively up-&-coming with scarlet tam. Hero waves

meless me to sofa. Dog scramhopbles beside. Next whom places herself
the hostess(whose chair tam inherits). And looking at leanish I am.

Perhaps you'll be so good as to excuse me for talking only Russian
with these comrades?(Madame asks:comrade myself begs pardon for
not understanding;enter tense intricate debate,punctuated by tam's
mirth:rises then leanish,follows telephonewire to study door,yanks
latter wide,tosses a grim Dahsveedahnyah to invisible mari;and—curtly
bowing—exit with hurry(tam)ingly)

reenter,bedraggled,with his telephone,mari . . . almost who suggests
something which I once never not quite didn't think I felt almost like.

Everybody(almost ½pitying,not less than more than ½mischievous,
Madame unsmiling states)scolds him.

It's not fair(I disapprove as amiably and believingly as possible).

They(to myself himself bedraggled And How solemnly intones)tell
me that just because last night,after a great discussion,I left weeping,I
do not deserve to mention the name of the party . . . simultaneously
hostess & hero,in fact linked,are(have)disappear(ing)ed . . .

action—

—camera!and what a transformation! No more do I perceive a
censured comrade;no more do I behold a hopeless husband. No!
The shorn Samson and the mangled man,rising into(suddenly)what
pathetic ecstasies of annihilation,mutually explode—born of their death,
appears(reeking with itlike vigour)a murdered-murdering impotent
altruist-machine:unhe. Unhe starts. Unhe begins rushing up and down.
Back and forth. Here and there and there and here . . . (Anything which
may have been life and everything which death should have been—and
awful must and aweless anything—echo,horribly to reecho,in singly an
how glib trivially nothing—The Cause!) Words pour out of unhim. The
Cause! Gestures swarm upon unhim. Unhe sweats,stamps,occasionally
slavers. The absencefilled silence whispers,glare of 3fisted brightens,with
unhis brittle cryless most lost cry—all all all for The Cause!

. . . (now ride upon flexible patience of my pity hurriedly 1 by 1 perfect-
imitation-pearls;doctrine by glittering doctrine forms itself this lustrous
circle of a world's unhope,that futile necklace of unhis escape . . .)

unhe:The second(i.e. leanish)soldier is a high official of our Gay-Pay-
Oo. Do you know what the three letters mean?

I:?

unhe:It is a police with noncriminal jurisdiction. Let me give you an illustration—there was a crisis caused by shortage of "petite monnaie";the 3 letter lads were notified;they routed out the hoarders and compelled them to fork over their hoardings to the government. Is that clear?

I:Continue,please.

Unhe:I want you to realise that Russia is in a state of civil war. Let me give you an example:suppose an antibolshevik blows up a factory;the government turns to two poets and says:Write poems,expressing the badness of this deed. Now suppose one poet says:It's not in my heart,I can't do it. Well,he can't;he feels toward the blowerup even a human feeling—HE IS NEUTRAL,THEREFORE HE IS OUR ENEMY. Russia is full of neutrals . . . as if anyone would be neutral in such a struggle! . . . Of course,for someone who believes that art is above everything else,who has oldfashioned ideas like that,who cannot participate in the struggle,who is unable to do anything—it's hard. It's hard for him and it's hard for the "petit bourgeois",who just loves his house and his wife and his children and his land . . . Yes,in Russia everything is "une lutte"—at the factories,groups of workers discuss,argue,battle,over Tolstoy,literature, ideas;as,in America,people do over boxers. You understand?

I:The very feeling of Moscow certainly is different from anything I've—

unhe:Different! Why,when I recently got to Germany I felt as if I'd stepped from a "voiture de luxe" into an ordinary car

(ignoring this to me curious metaphor)I:They do say that Soviet Russian's who visit other countries can't stand it long—

unhe:Most of them can't;and you must comprehend why. You must realise that we,we the Russians,have over us no sovereigns;we are not compelled;we are striving for IDEAS. You must not misunderstand: the fight's goal is REAL,not imaginary—for instance,you can literally see "ça pousse" in the case of the Russian villagers who(only a few years ago)were "comme des fauves". Now what do you think of that!

I(gently):Already I've felt,in the Russian temperament,something or other which makes possible an achieving of such ideas as

unhe:No—it's not at all a question of race! What you've noticed is that each of us has an INNER DISCIPLINE,not a discipline which has been imposed by some outer authority. Let me make this point perfectly plain—people talk of Stalin as if he were a dictator!why,you can't imagine how small he is at a workers' meeting. You can't imagine how small you,an employer,feel when your workmen demand Why did you do that or this?

I:"je comprend".

Unhe:In short,Russia is being turned,from an agrarian country,into an INDUSTRIAL country.—Of course,Russia isn't yet as industrial as America;but observe what progress Russia has made in the comparatively microscopic amount of time which has elapsed since our own revolution!

I(dimly):Yes,I've been told by those who know that the Russia of today resembles the America of a few years ago—

unhe:Not a few years ago—

I:No;a long time ago.

Unhe: Yes,as long ago as the Klondike period.

Are there dancings?(I asked). —I don't mean fashionplate dancings,I mean places where people dance:because the harder one works,the harder one plays.

No(unhe said)people dance in their houses. (Fade-in on Better's "house"). But there is a great deal of sport(proudly).

As in America(I murmur)

. . . Moscow is very bureaucratic(said unhe;and looked scared). Moscow is the administrative seat of the government(unhe rapidly added). He(suddenly referring to 3fisted)was at the end of his strength—it was the system's fault . . .

I hadn't asked. Finally,very finally,comrade Kem-min-kz insists upon taking my leave(having been invited for 4:30,having dined at about 5,and having already been until 8:30 lectured. Unhe calls(using the affectionate diminutive)hostess;who presently enters from a back and beyond dark room,explaining how she had a headache. Headache follows,looking a little if possible plumper and almost as gentle.

When you come to America(quoth K)we'll give you,not so delicious a repast as this,but of our unworthy noblest. (She laughs;almost sadly)

O but(quickly unhe upspeaks)not everybody eats like that and many who do pretend otherwise. Nor do we ourselves,always.

Shall I see you again?(she asks)

But you're going away in two days(mercilessly I remind her).

Telephone me(directs Madame)when you've seen the comrade whose address I gave you;and perhaps we can arrange something for tomorrow evening. Will you?

Yes;I won't,but somebody will for me. (Then,turning to the hero,shake hands)hope to see you again,perhaps in France or England(he seems doubtful. I turn,to dark;find door).

(She somewhat more than avers)my husband is going with you.

Fine(say comrade I;and descend the marvellously substantial stairs: while,ungoing,unhe earnestly chatters with unhis . . . but unhe goes . . . joining me after an ungood minute. (Promptly turn wrong. Unhe corrects me). Together ourselves walk(aria!)toward the "rond point"

unhe(conversationing):Take any hundred individuals. Take them from their houses over there. Ask each one if he or she is contented,well off. Each and every one,without exception,will tell you—NO!the necessities of life,even,are wanting in my case . . . Then put the hundred all TOGETHER:say to the hundred Comrades,we have this end in view,we need soandso;help us. Each will give ten roubles. That's the difference between the action of individuals and the action of a mass!

I:"entendu".

Unhe:It's like poker—a royal flush is not as strong as a common card. One plus one plus one don't make three;they make—

I:Something else.

Unhe:Much more.

Most(I lead)of the autos hereabouts are Fords.

Yes(trumping)Ford sends us the,what is it . . . —parts:and we have plants to assemble them . . .

Do many individuals own Fords?(mildly.)

Nono.

I imagine it would be quite expensive(says comrade capitalist Kemmin-kz). I mean they wanted ten roubles as recompense for taking my poor baggage from the station to the hotel.

Yes?($\frac{1}{2}$amused,$\frac{1}{2}$pleased).

And as for taxis(K continues)I really haven't had enough courage to experiment—

unhe pauses:

opening a taxi,bows me in. Bewildered,very,myself enters

quelle sensation—& it's a real taxi;too(albeit with an odd architectural bump behind the driver . . . reminding of mustachios and the Paris-N coffin)

the difficult thing(tireless unhe thingishly continues)is to understand, first,a mass;and next,a mass's dictatorship—in other words,to realize that Stalin is expressing,not himself,but the mass.

You mean,I presume,that comrade Stalin is not imposing his power on others,but is expressing their power.

(Delighted):Exactly! It is not something personal,it is something IMPERSONAL.

Outside of(taxi bangbumpbangbumps)Russia,one often hears You should have seen it before the revolution!and O,it's all right for businessmen;but for artists—pst!—they're materialists,there in Russia—

unhe:We are materialists,yes;but in our materialism there is much idealism,whereas your American idealism is founded on,and is consequently rotten with,materialism. Now for art:always remember this—if a poet doesn't want to write a poem,that's one thing. But if a worker refuses to do something,his refusal will affect everybody—

(bumpbangbangbump)

—you can't begin to appreciate the simply tremendous ENTHUSIASM which exists everywhere(with,of course,regrettable exceptions;for communism,like every great cause,has innumerable enemies. Example:the rich peasants don't like it,why should they? They have enough). But the peasants who have NOT ENOUGH and those who have NOTHING; they are the ones who WANT it.

(BuMp:ArRiVeD)

Please(I request very slowly)don't misunderstand me. If one doesn't know,I feel that one had better say so frankly,rather than pretend. Frankly,you've been talking to someone who doesn't know.

Immanently unhe:Ah!—but I feel how well you understand!

". . . what a typically bourgeois way of living. And vodka,too? Hm. —I only hope your host didn't think you were going to pay for the taxi" thus,archly,Virgil.

I(consciencestricken):"good god—!"

"yes,it might have been well to offer. However . . . Posleh zahvtrah—of course you know what that means—we're invited to dine with the charming daughter of a very much admired American writer;and(now who was . . . hm . . . funny I can't remember . . . O yes—of course!)the comrade who never turned up at the station to meet you" qui summons? (If Virgil,what recuperation!) Early to bed and. (A telegram?) Anyway,must be out of this room by 12—why,it's the cheerful Deutschspeaking little comrade with my Russian permis de séjour;6½ roubles,and he actually doesn't want tip . . . danke schön,tovarich;now let the 3 letters do their worst

recuperation hell!(whatever's happened?could this comrade's ailment be perhaps myself?)Dirge after strictly unsolicited Dirge

"only two things in life really interest me:the creative instinct and companionship;but I find that they're incompatible,one seems to destroy the other"

then

"if I hadn't been so well educated,I might have known something"

crowned by

"I never can know ALL of anything"

which grief somehow demoralizes the Metropole cuisine(respectful has left us large slices of cheese and no omelets)whereupon comrade better,with a shrugsmile reminding me of yesterday's inefficient voyage,telephones the cheese away and hithers missing eggs

I "wonder" gently "where this address might . . ." Sibyl's frown zooms(so,there we are! He's jealous;still jealous,albeit Joseph did his bitless bit).

"Go toward that red flag" And How worldwearily pointing. "You may have difficulty with the number." Sighs. Smirking "I shouldn't be astonished if Madame's girl friend gave you a room chez elle in"(bitterly)"return for certain favours—"

(very most truthfully,not now are and never have(as I live or breathe)been,or shall be,my favorite studies geography & arithmetic . . . 1st:confoundingly manyapartmented court—brace of politely,if too grammatically,questioned young nonmen(giggling)indicate dark hallway;I pass through which to bump barest big room full of conversing unmale and male:the former glowers;male(miraculously linguistic) suggests "librairie" only a couple of doors away . . . 2nd:irritatingly immaculate "librairie"—where a repulsively distraught neuter comrade idiomatically wigwavewags me next door . . . 3rd:next door—busy-with-some-papers bisexual apparition who says "oben"(and I oben,encouraged by "dadada"

to almost an attic)with twain pseudo-tables,elbowed by twain nonmen. By fleshlessly mournful,by jovially fat. Bowing,offer my credentials to fat;who nods,grins

and(most eagerly)"are you a comrade?" quavers(in sheer Brooklynese) the mournful.

"American" I reply(her comrade face darkens).

Sit,commands jovially fat(even as quick footfalls become Jewish cadaverous much frightened behind slightly askew spectacles he—"vous ne parlez pas français?")

I do,sir.

Good. We've heard all about you from comrade—(i.e. Madame). Now concerning rooms:yourself most unfortunately doesn't belong to any organization.

"Byezpar-teenee" I agree.

"Non"(hastily)"ce n'est pas ça" . . . (coughs)what I'm really worried about,to tell the truth,is your uncertainty.

My—?

Just how long are you remaining in Russia?(he with a certain careful casualness inquires).

Well(casually I and carefully respond)it's thus. I am married. Recently I telegraphed to my wife in Paris,but as yet I haven't had an answer. Now until I hear from her,the duration of my Russian trip must necessarily remain indefinite.

(Pause . . . dogmatic leers are swapped among the comrades. Then)— you mean you might have to leave after a few weeks?

Or possibly before.

Hm. And,as you may have heard,it's unbelievably hard to find rooms—

I've heard,sir.

Whereas in summer there'll be plenty of them.

Really?

Therefore what I suggest is this:prolong your visit. Plan to stay six months at least,preferably a year or two;earn a few roubles by translating,and spend your roubles travelling all over Russia. There is so much,so incredibly much, to see—

I understand

—also,to say(he adds thoughtfully) . . . but suppose you dine with us(indicating jovial)at five o'clock this afternoon. Here's where we live.

Thank you most kindly.

Shall I write it in English also?

Perhaps you'd better.

(He does). When you leave,a comrade will go along and show you the exact spot—

"mille fois merci!"

—otherwise you'll never find it. "A bientôt!"

exit. And foots(feminine)teps. —Enter an almost(by comparison)attracting nonman. To whom promptly by jovial I'm presented,whereupon pull my best Russianless Russian greeting . . . roars of laughter from fat;even mournful cackles faintly . . . pochehmoo?

Pahtahmooshtah—slumpily before me hovers no other than comrade decidedly Radcliffe helpmate:she who,with her pimply American embarrassed-in-a-Russian-blouse stripling plus or minus comrade livid military tactician,bundlefully did depart the Hotel Metropole for a less sumptuous life

then comrade Kem-min-kz also laughs;and Radcliffe(nervously scratching)blushes and . . . feetsteps—"hello!"—enter(with a profound grouch)stripling(the blouse and all)immediately who,unto high heaven,announces that himself and spouse are changing their most recent whereabouts;this time because there's no running water,because the toilet smells terribly,and(in the immortal phrase of Crank Frowninshield) finally because something distinctly flealike picked her up today "in a streetcar" and

(feetfalls)"how"(me suddenly confronts a wee carrotheaded English— man)"would you like half a room with an old lady,eh?"

I feel,look,surprised.

"It's dark" adds Clara "and of course there's no plumbing and you couldn't possibly write there."

"What could I do?"

"sleep."

"How about the old lady?"

"the old lady? Why—are you shy?"

"not pathologically."

"Then there's nothing to worry about,eh?"

"I should very much enjoy glimpsing the layout"(cheerfully,if guardedly).

"Any time at all. By the way:here's a French-English translation for you to look over"(and helpmate—the,it happens,translatrix—winces)"see you later!"

pause.

1 yell—"OH"(explodes)"I WISH i could stop SCRATCHING" (Radcliffe).

"WELL(stripling)"WHY don't you STOP then?"(dittos)&

feetfootstepsfall—agedly full tray appearing gravitates toward fat:now everybody's sampling dangerous cakes,delicious tea(and,if everybody's hungry,something or other like Mr. Khoury's kibbeh krass)very gracefully,and simply,which are administered by comrade jovial. Follows presently much faretheewelling:exeunt finally 3 unleashed roomhounds . . . 1,at door,acquires weatherbeaten nonman with golden molars who("pahzhahloostah")slumbers forth avant—resigned,unearthly—who floats(& we all)left;transcends a fence(past dumpcarts and horses and men)skirting a sandpile braves this lumbercluttered portal and(with me only)climbs;pauses;laying 1 how spectral hand upon thisthat rickety doorknob to now sepulchrally remark

here.

Thank you.

Please

(ghostly;remains)

         —I descend:rejoin the waiting grouch and scratch. We turn(Americans 3)our faces toward luxury

"it's perfectly ridiculous that you should pay so much"(scratching). "I'll speak to the management:they must have a cheaper room. You know,in Russia one simply has to insist—"

"bully,you mean" grouch grunts

coyly(verily)at bar of judgment lurking:cutaway,specs(why not monocle?)& Palm Beach accent. Who myself amazes by giving helpmate a whole single entire full box of reallytruly matches(surreptitiously she slips them to myself,who mucho sorely am in need). Argument And How... No,he hasn't any cheap room. And How argument . . . Yes,he has a cheap room

"—you see?"(she,to me)
which is 4 and isn't 5 dollars per day,with breakfast.

I(to Palm cynically):"is it good?"

He:"very good—I slept in it last night."
Whereupon nab both new room key and old,whereupon 3 comrades mount on foot to the old;whereupon I(comrade)chuck hurl leave and throw all earthly comrade possessions into my valise and into my knapsack and into comradeless comrade myself.

"Let's" grouch growls "make a parade out of this" cheerfully shouldering knapsack

"you've forgotten your soap"(she scratches)
and we all(the Americans Are Coming!)march down hall,in-cantationing Frankie and Johnny Were,to elevator—wherefrom these several poor merely Russians instantly are by another expelled without benefit of riposte

(softly)"I don't like that"(she scratches,rising)

"nor I"(rising)

"these"(snorting)"comrades"(gripes rising grouch)"certainly are goddam fond of their Wall Street . . ."

a grinning thickly antique nonmanbiddy,"klootch pahzhahloostah?" opens—new's gooder than old;cosier,far less complicated,quite a whit smaller . . . view,too. Hahrahshoh. I whereupon pluck yank jerk and twitch possessions here there and nowhere;undo the shutness(it yields only a centimetre);salutingly thank scratch-grouch Inc.;relax—

"come on with us to the Savoy for lunch" he opines "their capitalist food is slightly better than the usual swill."

"Yes,please do"(scratches scratch).

"But I seem to have eaten a flock of lunches today—"

"well,have a drink,then. The beer's almost real."

"Tovarich—your ideology!"

notwithstanding(And How)just as we're sitting(at a real table with a real tablecloth)comrade everybody objects—comrade somebody interprets: This restaurant,comrades,is for valyootah-holders "and I,like a poor fool" blouse proclaims "have worthless roubles,hard won by teaching English to Russian truckdrivers—mphg!"

"isn't the Savoy's rouble restaurant entrance next door?" she patiently (frowning)scratches.

Tahk. Flashy,too. A real coatboy takes my comrade headgear. But(alas for poverty)the rouble restaurant is full. Full(And How)of all sorts conditions andsoforth of comrades—particularly who are grouped grouplessly around apparently something very similar to a(with real goldfish?)capitalist fountain . . . also,when our comrade trio asks to share this table with pair of previously arrived comrades,that("nyet!")wa iter strenuously objects(The Lady Mustn't Sit With People)and grouch grouches . . . and(scratch)patiently argues . . . and(scratchscratch)argues . . . and(scratchscratchscratch)finally

("you see?")

a very most headestwaiterest,truly-untruly resplendent in untovarich boiledshirt(with all the babylonian fixings)pompously unropes large horrifyingly empty space(devoted,as I learn,to lucky valuta-holders)whither 3 humble comrades march;where halting,we collapse in luxe . . .

across,a not so unprepossessing if slightly sticky gent. Am introduced by grouch;but not to gent's(vis-à-vis)sleeping dictionary(she's a little well dressed,very conscious of it. Looks,over & over,at her hands . . .) now gent's newspaper boosts—between her and himself—itself

bien sûr,Moscow isn't a city d'amour.

Shoving protestations aside,scratch&grouch Inc. make me a full plate of lunch from their own dainties. It I partially consume;wholly my beerful dollar beer . . . Grouch:

"yesterday,2 roubles"

—pointing to a quite incomprehensible item;waiter bows;a "3 roubles" diminishes

"parr-dohn . . ."

"The thieves" grouch snarls.

And "shall we walk?" she innuendos. "I love to walk . . . since we left your hotel,I've done a great deal of walking. As a matter of fact,every day I've walked in,from the suburb where we are now;with a wad of trulyreally American toiletpaper(to take advantage of the Metropole's modern plumbing")

. . .
    etc.
    locks
    scissors
    tacks
    nails
    etc.
    screws
    hinges
    combs
    etc.
    garters
    pipes
    etc.
    toothbrushes
(this is a market)

and a refined chap,whittling stickhandles;into which you insert old-Gillette-blades,thus producing the Socialist Soviet equivalent of a regular capitalist razor

and an armyish thug,unsuccessfully performing cardtricks

and a flyspecked booth full of soiledest(how onceuponatime)toys;but now they unprotestingly are Elsewhere—perhaps dead?(& O,the eyes of the silent beautifully bearded toyman)

this sewingmachine,broken

all surrounded by crowd,by mob,by multitude;by peopleless people engrossed by interminably errorless gestures of Buffalo Springfield rollerengine(immortal Marianne! . . . "As for butterflies" . . .)

Free trading. Absolutely against Marxian or whatever principles. Bootleg commerce. Tolerated by comrade régime,for its own comrade reasons

"I once bought a canopener here for a dollar and a half" she whispers shyly

(because a superb burst of wonderfulling rain)we blow ourselves to 8 minutes' tram ride. Impressed by her "see?" I catapult the comrades left and right—even so,scarcely contrive a dismounting via frontend. Brief(less wonderfulling)walk. A slummy doorgate. 3 flights of(Grouch:"there's the elevator. It doesn't work")clambering—to dimly pigeoncote,comprising many audible comrades . . . through hole,into what least nook with bright paperless walls;peopled by worn tomes;wondrously disordered

"it's so messy" she(scratch)apologises

"well" growl grouches "anyhow we have two copies of one book by Jack Reed"

"since you're thinking of taking this room,comrade,you'd better see all the disadvantages right away. Unfortunately,somebody's just dumped water into our nemesis:ordinarily the thing stinks to Heaven . . ."

then I'm manoeuvred to(not so bedless,considering)bed,where carefully protest that can't promise anything—although I'd much(of course)prefer this palace to half a winedark room with an ole davil lady . . . still,something(who knows?I don't)may turn up—

"why not meet the proprietor? You needn't commit" scratching "yourself"

an(ominously afflicted with that quite uncanny mixture of timidity and pomposity which,thanks to Monsieur Potiphar,I now associate with "inner discipline")comrade. A very much comrade of a communist to be sure. E.g.,steadfastly refuses to talk prices—"only as a friend of my friend" naming the blousegrouch "would I think of accepting you here. But his father is such a great writer!" Yet under all—a sturdy,competent(if an American,one could say unimaginative;since a Russian,one cannot)chiefmechanic type(whose flowsy wife hides her redly running nose behind her pallid offspring's dusty curls)endowed with some refreshingly direct aman'samanfora'that spirit. Me:"I wish I could speak Russian as well as you speak English."—"But I ought to speak English much better:it's such an easy language to learn!"

". . . Well my friends"(I subsequently inform scratch-grouch)"thank you both for your courtesy. A victim of the congenital incapacity for immediately deciding anything wishes you well,and begs to take his leave."

"It's really cleaner than it looks" mildly she encouraged(scratching)

"For GOD'S SAKE" he horribly shrieked "STOP THAT!"

now,and while impatiently awaiting tram,I experience my 2nd typically socialist phenomenon,viz.—hosing. (Moscow may lack amusements:

but there's a public water supply. Rain may rain;but streets,of an afternoon,duly are and ceremoniously wetted. Slyly into which collective function creeps how unmistakable the bogy of bogies:individualism)

this,if you please quite expressionless proletarian,aetat 5,starting with that singularly defunct old nonman whose socklets imply babyhood, herds mercilessly a group(including me)of comrade prospective tram clients hither and thither . . . some of whom escape with mud splotches below the knee while others are well goosed or patiently receive the thumbfurthered stream shoulder-high. But entirely nobody protests;not anybody is amused;absolutely everyone Elsewhereishly just simply doesn't somehow care

I move. To find myself stalked by(yet so gently,languidly,that reach nearest stop many seconds in advance of)tram;mistakenly whose backplatform I—for aria's sake—embrace . . . did I say mistakenly?a mightier word is needed here . . .

because,comrade,if you can imagine a cube,black and with silver edges;if you can visualize the gradual prodigious tumescence of this cube,whose substance meanwhile turns through greedy red toward fatal green while its six facets curl with some huge inner strain;if possibly you can picture this warped angry unshape stupendously disembodying,collapsing,homogeneously disintegrating,silently(irrevocably)blossoming into what sheer omnipotence of immeasurability;and if—now focusing on a mere moment of the miracle (glimpsing,without comprehending,some infinitesimally ultra-microscopic slice of never to be fathomed augmentation)—you can conceive dread universe within fearful universe within terrific universe of dissolutely outpouring most murderful corruption,of overwhelmingly ubiquitous putrefaction,of selfconjuring doomfully profound and abominably ejaculated obscenity:only then,O my gentle comrade reader,can(how imperceptibly)yourself begin(and very,very inconsiderably)to visualize 1 universal catastrophe of odour anonymously fathered by 1 fabulous denizen of 1 fabulously overinhabited socalled tram's rear or back platform. . . . In which case,be it courteously said,you're a better comrade than comrade I.

(5 P.M.)

ring,chez fat & cadaverous. Pause

an oldish lively nonman yanks. Slamming!escorts briskly me(through chattering dimness filled with nesting comrades)into tranquility,where

—immediately
am slugged
with(" Ça c'est beau!" I
cry)hue. Recovering,find comrade K muddily standing on 1 of this
bloodredness edge . . . alias blanket,draped over sofa

fat "neechehvoh nyet!" welcoming protests jovially;oldish and
lively(disappearing)gruntchuckles(the;offleaping guiltily:visitor dusts
mefeetprints with my capless cap).

Sit,eat(fat beams). We won't wait for him(incredibly,I'm understanding).
Our(with mutual bowings,wavings,pointings)selves arrange their
distinguishable owners at this most painfully almost table not quite merrily
decked for 3 . . .

1st(the guest's only:a special token of esteem)course=glass,covered
with paper,of yaoort. Jill meanwhile imbibes creamy cheeseyness

2nd=ribs of dense meat;bread;red wine(sweet,natural,also powerful;
the same I'd quaffed chez madame Potiphar)—arrives Jack,panting,sits
(with a brief friendly nod)chews eagerly vast helpings affectionately
lavished by his maternal spouse. Who seems a very human indeed
person. Who frankly(in fluent Russian)volunteers that she doesn't like
and that she can't understand poetry. Who(in French stuttering)likes
only "le cirque,la musique,et les joujoux." And(obviously)the boyfriend.
But obviously not novelist Sir Dry(erstwhile enthusiastically defined by
the bride of Potiphar as "très gentil. Nous avons tous beaucoup bu,et
puis il ne voulait pas aller chez lui. Alors,mon mari lui a fait un lit
ici")whom Jill caustically dismisses

Pff!he writes big books;you could kill a man with them!

 . . . yes,very human;yet(incredibly)who hasn't a particle of
imagination.

I:Do you perhaps know my very good friend John Dos Passos? It was
he who obliged me by sending a telegram of recommendation all the long
way from somewhere in Mexico to the Russian embassy in Paris,and I
happen to think that his telegram really persuaded the authorities that I
was worthy to be admitted.—She:Yes,I know comrade Dos. I like him.
But I think he's strange("strahnyeh").—I:Why?—She:Well,when he
was here,somebody gave him a doll;the doll was wrapped in paper;then
comrade Dos tore out a little piece of paper opposite the doll's face;and
when I asked him why,what do you suppose he said?—I:What?—She:He
said,and seriously "pour qu'elle peut respirer."—I(sub rosa):"Bis!"—She:

And there was a child,who'd seen him tear the paper;and the child asked her mother Why is he doing that?and her mother answered So that the doll can breathe;"alors,l'enfant demandait:est-ce qu'il est fou,maman?"

3rd course=potatoes and beets(?)with heavenly goo

4th=vermicelli soup

5th="volaille"(I stop,reeling,after 5)

6th=cheese(?)

& there's absolutely excellent coffee,plenty of it . . .

this Ritzy banquet—its elements stylefully presented by lively encore chuckgruntling oldish—terminated,fat plumps herself on the colour;begins to embroider intricately a marvellous Ukrainian "robe". The other gorgers,Jack and I,smoke Nords and converse. Jill(apparently far more oblivious to abstract ideas than she is ignorant of the French language)actually,I gradually notice,directs—indirectly for the most part;sometimes directly(What does "usine" mean?Why don't you tell him suchandsuch?)—her Jack's every move;following our rickety train of thought a thought more closely than any ambulance-chasing lawyer pursues his accident . . .

d'abord,regular propaganda carefully intended to convert the Heathen. Having had enough of this crap from Monsieur Potiphar,I politely beg to excuse myself. Jack(Jill inspired)thereupon switches his attack—takes me into an adjoining room—brings forth all sorts of books made in Russia for popular consumption(very handsome they are too,I wish my Persian friend and setterup of poems were here)particularly stressing all the yth and worse rate pro-Soviet "grands écrivains américains"(who look much better And How in Russian)also innumerable mutterings of an orthodox red variety by comrade Gorky,Invisible. Comrade Joyce's Ulysses I presently discover for myself—in the original. I then make bold to ask cadaverous if he knows of comrade Pound,and cadaverous allows as how he's heard of that comrade;so comrade Kemmin-kz faithfully repeats that comrade's message

("tell them to read cantos" soandso at the Régence who,to my "have you any greeting for the Kremlin?" had replied thoughtfully(more than)glancing(very)keenly past himself into a luminous Everywhere of nowhere)

yea,and cadaverous promises to speedily do same. Certainly,1 bookful of paintings by some Ukrainian

("vous êtes peintre aussi?" Yes,comrade Vaillant-Couturier also raved over this peasant genius. He's like Rousseau,isn't he;but he couldn't possibly have known Rousseau. Of course,before the revolution nobody paid him any attention;for the Soviets were the first to begin collecting and preserving the work of our non-bourgeois artists and the Soviets discovered him;it was very hard because his paintings were on walls,on cafés,in bars,and frequently painted over by subsequent decorators. Well well,I'll get you a copy of this book since you like it so much)

leads all the other indigenous brochures by several lengths

(. . . all the factories are feverishly interested in literature,you know;some of our poets,for instance,have a circulation of ten thousand copies).

Again try politely to depart. But no;indirectly directed cadaverous reassumes room 1,pours me a,to put it mildly,beaker of what luscious wine—and—comrade I have fallen,fallen And How;tumbled into exactly 180 minuteless minutes of "materialist dialectic" which(among other miracles)makes sun while the hay shines,opens the key of life with the lock of science,juggles(without dropping)the unworld the unflesh and the undevil,and justifies from soup to nuts the ways of Marx to man.

Feasts from which crumb of reason:

(1)AND MARX SAID

the ideology of any society is that of the dominating class.

(2)Art

reflects the social milieu of the artist. Comrade Kem-min-kz,living under a full-fledged capitalist system and reflecting in his art the ideas ambitions impulses of the system,cannot possibly attain to that state of bliss which is spontaneously enjoyed by a proletarian artist. Item: the peasant art of Russia—a prerevoluntionary specimen whereof was by comrade capitalist Kem-min-kz and comrade socialist Vaillant-Couturier separately admired—is now beginning to reflect collectivist tendencies.

(3)Beauty

(especially intellectual beauty)is indispensable to life. No;comrade Kem-min-kz was not exactly wrong in telling comrade Madame that he liked shining things;he just hasn't been here very long. When he's been here longer—long enough to master the social and economic principles involved— then comrade K will cease to judge Moscow according to those superficial standards by which(most unhappily)his entire life has hitherto been capitalistically conditioned. Then he will joyfully acknowledge the beauty of that supreme ideal whose profound radiance transfigures even the ugliest comrade countenance. That for l'avenir. At present, the sadly blinded comrade K may be interested to learn that the communist party—ever mindful of the worker's inner being—was only prevented from renovating a particular section of Moscow(and making that section quite as "joli" as "joli" could be)by the sacred fact that each and every energy of each and every loyal comrade must, temporarily, be directed toward a sterner goal.

(4)Blunders

have occasionally occurred in the course of applying socialist principles to human beings;but an unintentional error fortunately involves its own remedy. Thus:the socialist state at first tried to force the ignorant peasants into collectivism. Since this only made the stubborn peasants more stubborn, communism abandoned coercive measures;and today the only converting force employed is the all important force of example(e.g., individual farmers of a machineless peasant community notice that their collective farm neighbors not only accomplish more work but enjoy more leisure. Whereupon the wolves penitently beg to be admitted to the fold).

(5)Children

are the future citizens of the world. To their welfare—on which the perpetuation of socialism depends—the socialist state is primarily dedicated. This does not mean that, as capitalist rumour goes, a socialist child is protestingly torn from parental arms;it means that every socialist child is given full opportunity and in every way shape and manner encouraged to express him- or herself, unhampered by narrowing— because essentially selfish—parental influences. Children, as a matter of fact, prefer to leave the ancestral hearth because there are so many more distractions elsewhere. There was at 1 period a perfect epidemic of runaways;not long ago, 1 child left the following message:At home I feel like a bolshevik in a peasant community.

(6)Divorce

having been made easy, an immediate and inevitable result was abuse of the new freedom per socalled husbands who had been led by the nose for years and socalled men who had never been masters of their smallest wishes. All such temporary excesses seem insignificant, however, when compared with certain vast and permanent benefits resulting from easy divorce. Fundamentally, the permanent relations between men and women have been made healthier;and the lives of men and women are consequently happier. From a morbid or fear-relationship,founded on economic fetichism and mentally sponsored by a sense of guilt,marriage is becoming a healthy and spontaneous bisexual manifestation of social integrity.

(7)Home

is where the heart is. P.S.—a socialist heart is in the socialist state.

(8)Kitchen-

slavery is a thing of the past. Any normal woman,given a chance to extend her realm of influence,gladly abandons those monotonous household cares which have been arbitrarily associated with woman-kind for centuries. Unlike her bourgeoise sister,who is continuously threatened by that nonexistence which inevitably results from moral and economic impotence,a Socialist Soviet woman unrestrictedly shares with all her male and female fellows the proud duties and profound advantages of a conscious citizen.

(9)Marriage

though not any longer ecclesiastical,none the less remains a relic of atavism. The mayor(or whatever official performs a civil marriage)is better than a priest,of course;but the mayor must and will go,as priests already have gone,before the socialist state attains normal humanity's sexual goal,viz.—if two people live together,that is a marriage.

(10)Motherhood

is a fundamental instinct. That no fundamental instinct must suffer repression is a scientifically demonstrable axiom. For the socialist state—whose aim is the economic and spiritual liberation of humanity—to attempt to repress a fundamental instinct would be not only ridiculous but criminal. What the socialist state attempts is something entirely different. On the 1 hand,the state educates its male and female citizens frankly and openly in the arts of sexual hygiene,birthcontrol,etc.,thus lifting sex from an abnormal to a normal plane,controlling disease,and combatting involuntary motherhood;on the other hand,the state removes the stigma of bastardy;and extends every protection to the prospective mother,who receives all sorts of special advantages and privileges(including vacation with full pay,etc.).

(11)Religion

has trod the path of all dead things;its disappearance being in no sense a result of any official persecution—for communism's only direct action against religion consisted in revealing to ignorant masses of humanity the predatory nature of the clergy's rôle—but a natural by-product of the instigation of socialist reforms. Religion's imaginary benefits were only a substitute—and a very poor one!—for REAL benefits;when the latter appeared the former disappeared. Take,e.g.,the 5 day week:nobody who hasn't seen them with his or her own eyes can begin to imagine the 5 day week's miraculous effects. Even if you should now ask 1 of the few remaining "petits bourgeois" what day it is,he wouldn't know;he would only be able to tell you which number. And why was the 5 day week such a success? Because it gave MORE leisure to the masses(5 goes into 30 oftener than 7). So with all the other successful reforms: in each case,heaven becomes less necessary.

(12)Transition

is what the presentday visitor to Russia encounters. There could be no darker,no more tragic,mistake than to assume that Russia of 1931 represents the result of socialist endeavors. What Russia of 1931 really represents is an intermediate step—characterized by unimaginable contrasts—between classes and classlessness. If comrade Kem-min-kz returns in 10 years,he'll find no class(I:You mean that I'd find one class only?—Jack:One class is no class,isn't it?)whereas today he may view with his own eyes localities where men and women are passing from feudalism directly into socialism;he may visit certain isolated districts whose denizens are now perfectly familiar with the airplane—which at first caused premature births and droppings dead—but have never yet seen a train or an automobile. Verily,verily,1931 is a crucial year;how lucky is comrade K to have arrived when he did! Imagine being privileged to behold a spectacle unprecedented in all human history:the world's first socialist republic fighting for her very life—at the frontiers,with capitalist neighbors;abroad,with England and the rest;at home,with neutrals! Incidentally,comrade Kem-min-kz had better remember(when comrade Kem-min-kz looks around him)that conditions in the capital of Russia 1931 are comparable only to conditions in a beleaguered city of the middle ages.

(13)Ultimately

the 2 great "petits bourgeois" desires—namely:to possess and to enrich—will completely disappear from the face of the globe. Already they are marching as to doom. Already,in ⅙ of this fair earth,is growing up a healthy and happy younger generation which simply does not understand those needless sufferings—sexual jealousy being one of the commonest—which afflict me and which afflict you and which afflict many, many other comrades of the older,older generation.

(14)Wealth

(in the capitalist sense)is nonexistent;for everything belongs to the socialist state,i.e. to everybody. That at present it's literally impossible to work for one's own profit may be readily seen from this fact:no worker,including comrade Stalin,can gain more than 350(360?)roubles a month;so soon as a worker earns a greater sum,progressive taxes give the surplus to all. But surely(the capitalist exclaims)this must result in a killing of initiative? On the contrary;this results in a birth of initiative. Why? —The answer,everywhere overwhelmingly evident,is:collective enthusiasm. "Quand je suis venu ici de Pologne,j'étais sûr que les ouvriers russes travaillaient par obligation. Maintenant je sais que ce n'est pas vrai;et je vous jure que la seule force qui les fait travailler est celle de la propagande"—and,almost slyly—"Vous écrivez vous-même:alors,vous comprenez la puissance de la parole"

explicit.

Over and over again,during those hours(motifs whereof I hopelessly have hoped to more or less record)find myself standing before A Portrait Of The Artist As A Young Man;watching a certain Jesuit father move heaven and earth to persuade a certain Stephen Dedalus that he,Stephen,is fit for the holy task . . . which Stephen(forever,but only after meditation)knows is not true:only knows because of something around(under throughout behind above)him,or which is always the artist;his destiny. And although,when finally I escape—nearly ecstatic with talk—into the open air,cadaverous's eloquence unaccountably disintegrates,nevertheless my(breathing)self salutes Karl Santa Claus Marx,original if not only concocter of so invincible a thesis:and very thankfully,I marvel that such prophets as KM cannot be poets,that always they must depend upon mere reality,always must attempt a mere realization of themselves by others—

with what fatal consequences!for what could less resemble I wish than It is?less an alive actual tree than the "same" merely not dead tree,"successfully" which has been transplanted?less freedom than unfreedom,less dreaming than doing? . . . yet only the bravest fools have glimpsed that difference;with what eyes!

(now smell earth—no—it's parkless park:here and here shadows embrace;fondle:lovelessly).

For the immeasurable domain of The Verb is actually or imagining, which cannot ever be translated(and least of all resembles its reflection in a measurable system of nouns). For life is mercilessly not what anyone believes,and mercifully is life not what a hundred times a thousand times a million anyones believe they believe.

"May I" ask comrade deskman "be called tomorrow morning,please?"

"Certainly."

"May I order tomorrow's breakfast now?"

"Of course."

"Not merely, as you see,is my Russian feeble;but telephones terrify—"

"You can say French 'bureau'" he suggests mildly "then they give you me and you can say English what you wish eat"

—Virgil,Virgil;why didst thou not tip me off? Here was I,timid,trusting to thy linguistics(whenever we both didn't trust to comrade better's) for eggs and for coffee and for toast;yea,verily,and for marmalade

"I may forget" the deskman comrade grins. "I will try not forget" he smiles

"goodnight"

Elsewhereishly "goodnight."

. . . O but this my roomless(with its speck of small far high view)room is welcome! (Almost I can receive possibly myself,here;almost can feel,invent;dream:possibly almost begin)—

12:30
stroll miles,buying a box of speechkih at 2 kopeks from an old man standing asleep beside a young man lying asleep

Sunday mai 17th

1(jutting through dreams)explosion
Me:"omelet yest?" awakening.

Waiter:"yest". And a finer omelet never swam bellyward. Nor bellyward floated honester hottestly fragrant tea(koffyeh being,like Virgil's matinal nursing,a thing of the past)

and boldly to now consummate my independence by shaving à la russe,in the eau chaude of this diminutive teapot which roosts precariously atop the teapot proper . . . fishing former's cover from peed sloppail,mildly to meditate man's illustrious infallibility,his thrillingly supernatural capacity for spontaneous involition—come;shall we not worship,this bright sunny voskresaynyeh? It's the day I was born;also it's a day which doesn't exist(thanks to the 7thless 6thless weekless socalled 5 day week)

withoutly:sheer barberpolemiracle-pineappleprodigy. Withinly:mere edibility. (You must get used)my Jesuit most expressionlessly said yesterday(to the fact that Russians "mangent beaucoup.") Puzzling tinily overornate corridors—depressed with niches suggesting a certain type of male urinal—chuck clumsily glutting muchnesses of(hurl thickly herethere murderings of)colour(simplicity)everywhere belch nowthens of blunt decoration. Hark . . . noise-silence:a pale,bigeyed consumptive nonman,crisply addressing a huddle of tensely scarfswathed dumpy mothers,of listless dimly runningnose children,of big ponderous timidly earthmen. The earthmen's caps are pulled hard over their eyes. Unearthly they(hearing?unspeaking)stand with what(gruesome)something of the doomed impotence of unwound toys. The dumpies have been particularly told something—probably that they are equal to something—and they neither stand nor writhe,simply they aggress;fearfully,futilely. Pale always is talking by rote,always pale is telling(religion is opium for people)what pale's been told . . . now that conference moves to another corridor:dumpily now listlessly now doomfully now drifting past urinals of ornament . . . I(trying from sly stares at my bare head to disappear) confront,suddenly,head bare;gray—who can this be,possibly? (Am I looking in a mirror? Am I quite so old? No. No . . .) But who,save myself,comrade capitalist Kem-min-kz,dares to unhat in the presence of ye fiend? . . . discover it's patiently wandering penitently American middleaged businessmanness;quickly from whose unsly unstare I(diving past urinals)disappear . . .

look—hush. Of(defeat?triumph?)A sanctuary:on this crude easel,cruder image—a woman with a big baby in her wide hands. (Crudest,scrawled on cruder placard stuck to crude wall of holyroom,7 letters,2 groups of). And which I read

greek X,o,greek D,a—H meaning n,e,t and(hohda nyet)pronounce and finally which(NO)I(ADMITTANCE) understand. So;this little picture is sacred;noone positively must go near it,noone must enter the roomlike negative holiness. . . . Not sacred in the blessed sense;for any more religion isn't;holy in the cursed sense;for the Soviets discover and protect the work of the prerevolutionary nonbourgeois artists(and ikons will go up this winter and . . .) I(miraculously nyet grayheaded prodigiously nyet businessman)actually happening to be myself am therefore he to whom nothing either is(and everything is both)blessed and cursed;gradually toward now the picture,the big baby,the wide hands,who strolling

halts. —Goosefleshed from head to foot

:touched

yes!because(but more lightly than by a whisper;more fatally than by a sword)touched

. . . quivering,scared;I:look—down. 1 hair of string,so thin as to be almost invisible,warned,whispered to,me(touched). Rope nyet and cord nyet but 1 hair(string). Exactly placed at knee-level,accurately stretched(from a wall to a wall)neither waisthigh nor headhigh. Blinding nor eyes which err,neither reminding thighs who sin,but O speaking very strangely to knees which must no longer kneel. —I(& myself)are touched;hitherto,threatened with words,thoughts,carefully who kept,guardedly,our heart. But this—Elsewhereish . . . but of another world;a(beneath idea)universe of thingless alert thing,possibly of string(1 hair)cosmos of ofless not and nowless un-. Conquerable. 1:fragile eternity of the it's-too-late. Supremely,tearlessly of whose inescapable dimension's dumb descending swiftly victims a poet and beautifully

"in which" sings "if they turn and twist,it is neither with volition nor consciousness."

. . . Gently then my(cautioned)self moves;slowly. Moves. Finally:light;space, pompously which fill bad scrawlings of helltorture,cram magnificent photographs of(my totem is the elephant)tractors,clutter snapshots—hangings,lynchings,people sleeping in parks,stuffed(last but)clergymen utterly(not least)berobed. & everywhere captions . . . & the blazingly message everywhere blazed:Down with religion,up with the proletariat!then—aria!

yes

to the true world again:O nowhere ugly,somewhere anywhere splendid world!

Otto,by cadaverous(at the revolutionary literature bureau)introduced, Can't is a Roumanian. Dark. Sentenced to die;he escaped. Untall. Speaks French:keen. Formerly a member of the "très haute bourgeoisie." Can smile. Gratified(immensely)to hear that I'm a friend of Madame Potiphar's sister's husband;ecstatic:even exclaiming "tout va bien!" Halitosis. Much interested in my renttroubles,will certainly telephone me tomorrow;but meantime,comrade,the best way to learn Russian is to(when he was in Hungary himself andsoforthed a Hungarian)marry a comrade and what are you by the by doing this evening?

Dining with the daughter of Lack Dungeon,the great American proletarian writer(myself,cautiously,avows).

Ah(he registers)her husband has(disgust)a bourgeois face.

Yes? "Oui?" Da?

(He smiled sorrowfully)"très."

Dear me,I said without alarm.

Mais c'est une maison

—"why it's a house!"

tartly "what did you expect?" Sibyl.

(Really)"anything except"(comfortablelooking).

"Why anything except?"

"that from you,comrade—after what I've recently heard about that O how invidiously And How insidious institution:home!"

("they live downstairs")whispering("the doctor whom you met rents it to them;he himself owns this house . . . O my yes,very rich indeed. Remind me to tell—but public spirited,very;though he did go out of his way,didn't he,to warn me about those ikons;hm. Whereas her husband—I mean Lack Dungeon's daughter's . . . he . . . well . . . ".)

("I hear he has a proletarian face").

"Proletarian!"—Christ! I almost imagined guardian mentor whoses was about to cast whatses benevolent cats. "—On the contrary! Bourgeois!"

"excuse me—that's what I meant—"

& if looks could kill . . . "Hm. Did you. Well, we're supposed to take off our coats here, I guess" as dumb plump domestic variously indicates somewhat unRussian habits already hanging sundrily in a milewide skyhigh hall. To whom "spaseebah." And sneerfully to myself ("it's pathetic, isn't it").

("What?")and we're climbing a short flight of marble-and-really.

("Why—a maid; for opening the door!")

To begin with:upon entering comfortably(nor bigger nor smaller than should be, if roomy)room, not bothered with(if adorned by)furniture people neither and both, we are cordially, we are also very simply, greeted by 6 feet up and several through and certainly(I feel)much more comprehendingly complex than any Muscovite I've yet encountered—immediately whose exterior implies goodliving and to me suggests a Turk. Who, blessed with deep easygoingness, now easily(or gently)presents acquaints and inflicts ourselves to with and upon

(a) 1 great Russian poet & novelist

(b) 1 great Russian dramatist

(c) 1 small American newspaperman

(d) the best looking female I never quite expected to see in that little bit of Eaven on Hearth, Marxland.

Sightly recovering, observe that(a)=dreamy, almost feminine, slim, ageing, timid; speaks French(b)=active, almost masculine, stocky, unold, friendly; talks Russian(c)=mindless, almost nothing, bignosed, harmless, flat; chatters Winchell.

"My wife has"(announces Turk distinctly, his eyes wonderfully twinkling toward nervous angel's backless back)"the best maid in Moscow and the best cook"(backless cringes)

"both Russian"(smiling she supplements)"but it's all right, because my husband does all the talking—I myself can't speak more than six words"(back curls).

Enter, adorned with hurrying languor

(e) 1 faded chastely angular American matronly spouse of (c). Fearlessly, in addition to her native lingo, spouting to (a) such tourist

French as unpossibly outdesecrates even my very own best Berlitz nonRussian . . .

vodka-&-sandwiches presently are by tumultuous all—save only cringecurl—tossedgulped to Babylonian profusion,whereat I swooningly amaze myself by realizing that the curse of centuries is fit for gods.

Welllighted,wisecracking (c) now dims pinwheelish to vividly sputtering idiocy—(e) scowls,shouts,staggers—(b) romps,snorts, gurgles,gesturefully insists I'm not gulping but sipping,whacks the(fluently Russian murmuring)Turk on a huge shoulder—(d) laughs,toasts cuddling among pillows (b)—(a) delicately expanding, deliberately siftsdrifts in my directionless direction:softly to apologise for never quite discovering comrade I's hitherto whereabouts:"je savais que vous étiez écrivain,mais"(delicately)"tout le monde dans cette gare ressemblait à un écrivain"(smiling).

I:One says that my difficult name succeeded in marvellously mangling itself before the Paris-sent telegram reached you. (Item:pinwheel (c) had just confided that if it hadn't been for the excellent Turk,nobody and more especially my distinguished vis-à-vis (a) would have possibly troubled to guess who comradely comrade Kem-min-kz was will be isn't or is).

(a) softly:O no. Your name arrived in perfect condition.

But that gentleman over there(pointing to pinwheel)said—

(firmly):O no.

(All very Russian,feels myself;speculating as to whether 1 great Russian poet and novelist would be gutted or jugged or mulcted or merely plugged for openly admitting before capitalist cronies that any Socialist Soviet telegraph operator at any given or ungiven time misspelled for any reason or otherwise any wordless word whatever)et

puis;cocktails,white and red wine,cognac;rich abundant spicy food(Turk,twinkling "glad you approve of our American cuisine")really, and not almost,nobly distributed by 1 shunting weazenedly doll with a huge wooden puss and firm gnarled paws.

. . . Cringecurltwitch has rarely,if ever,suffered so. Held by best-looking's frank eyes,It bloats glassily. Stroked by the Turk's implacably smooth deepening politeness,It nastily coils. Desperately It(at myself)flickers a venomous challenge—(You,who pretend to be an artist,sit here debauching yourself with trivial philistine philanderers when your better nature should be flying with mine to the chaste domicile of high

and serious drama!) But it's finally (a),very much and softly the quiet
gentleman,who dares

"Madame—si vous voulez voir la pièce de votre père,il faut partir de
suite . . ."

"Merci Monsieur" bowing the hostessly thanks gaily. "—It's not a very
good short story" she seriously added "and the play's probably worse."

—Crash—

upstarted(vomitgreen)mentor:"excuse me!" trembling,he lays down
cloudwhite napkin. "I—I really must be;er,going"—darting at me what
poisonousness! "Of course,that doesn't mean that the rest of you need
. . . well,you see(scathingly)I take MY theatre very,very SERIOUSLY."

"What a pity" our hostess,gently.

"Hm. Er,yes. I hate to deprive you of—"

"Not at all" lightly.

"Well—er—the rest of the company will be along later,I presume"
Virgil(hatefully shaking hands with the Turk)snapped. "I'll expect to
see YOU"(me)"anyway."

"Dahsveedahnyah" quietly said Beatrice.

but where O where's (a)? At my best- right looking strolls;beyond
her,madly gesturing romps this dramatist dollclown;self(focussing)
collects quick glimpse of—just ahead—cavorting pinwheel most
lopsidedly nailed to arm of what rigid spouse!elsewhere,if near,up
(genially)towering paces the how deepeasilymovingness of Turk
crowned,newly garlanded,with a dis(white-actually-and-which
disappears into blue-really-and-afternoon)tinct:trill;ci,ga ret.t esmoke
Oho—there is noble (a);he's saying goodbye,and we're(all)others
boarding(this)tramthing . . . here(comrades around us all)there
grinning,every(very much enjoying)where somewhat festive,mis-
or behaving,6;certainly:peculiar;these,creatures us—cursed with
of Russia centuries—became . . . 5 of 6 wrigghurlling now are
frontendward-lying;some(how)I(don't)budge,why?(yes)tangled:
must;un-,can't—and it's,the;tramstop:now they(tumbfalling)getting
(wait a)off jiff whoa!and(whoa)am far-far from any-end 4 outside yell
and-tramallthing-starts and here's:a;par(yes)don win(comrade)dow,
Out;We:Fly

—catching,while in air,stares(all)from grinning vanishers—hit,to
bounce;hurtless:bowing,to resume happily distinguished company . . .

why O why should this be all very familiar?—ah. (Proletcult)the same nice managers(brisk but courteous,efficient but cheerful). Politely,if firmly,who put comrade us into a loge or a box or a whatever;not because we're stewed I guess but because we're late;the play's in progress . . . tiens—there's my exmentor—how exly he pulls a dreadful frown—sh! (Pinwheel,pinwheel,thou shouldst go to sleep or thou shouldst be quiet. As for that spouse of yours . . . how disconcerting). Best-,Turk,and my suddenly sobered self are,very fortunately,models of deportment. Romp-clown-romp au contraire expresses none too secret disgust re this how proletarian production. Well,can't blame him. O,what a playless! Not ever,I should dream,thing was worser . . . & nyet,nyet escape?

at the 1st blessed entr'acte:familiar(how excellent)tea and cakes chez DeeDum;but this time served in a larger pigeonhole. Guardian (exly,cool)joins us:emanating familiar Harvard Coop credentials he now begins evolving familiar Socialist Soviet statistics. (I notice—who wouldn't?—that Turkess is deluged with a particular,an almost unearthly,respect as being no more nor less than the daughter of her unmitigated father. I observe that unmitigatedly she(if politely)unlikes these tributes,notorieties,ghostly attentions. I nab the Turk(that bourgeois face!)looking anonymously very much indeed amused). . . . Well,probably lest everything should possibly be lacking,who now tempestuously appears—handing bestlooking's U.S.A. silk stockings 1 peep that would grow waterlilies upon the backside of an airless planet—but The Little Girl With The Big Heart!gotten up right coonily in scarletsailorsuiteffect(and altogether too bolsheh for words)and promptly who pours over everybody in general,and comrade romp,and pinwheel—and even meless—recently series after series of executed And How symbolic(kind of you know sort of)sketches "showing" she modestly announces "the yellows and reds all reaching for one goal."

sh!—back(but now in orchestra)

Turk "sit next to me" murmurs and,to self's complete amazement, punctually translates(in 1 velvet whisper)literally,wordless for word,yes for da,quite such an unforgivably dramaless preposterosity as improbably would have been assembled by the Lindbergh baby.

But there is a god . . .

all of our partyless party,save Big Hearted exmentor,tea-out next-to-the-last act in directors' pigeonhole(and for this truly supernatural reason:a miserably diffident sadly gangling youth,who has the additional misfortune to be the play's father,guiltily mumbles something anent Dum & Dee,something which—by twinkling Turk translated—means "the next part is really very dull;may I advise our distinguished friends to skip it?" bravo,comrade!one should never judge by appearances)and 2 of us might also have escaped act last,if Dum hadn't seen pinwheel sneaking 1 cigarette

(previously I'd abstained from ditto vice at the behest of a perfectly unidentified tovarich whose tone nobody would forget soon . . . give something ever so small(e.g. "the mind")something ever so little(e.g. "authority")and what huge so to say enormities result . . . not that this behester was healthily rude—"inner discipline" eliminates the very possibility. He was putrescently sanctimonious)

however,the worst we get is back row orchestra

"bring in any roubles?"

"No" I whisper.

"Why not?"

"Why should I?"

"Good god—don't you know the rate in Paris?"

"Thirteen to one dollar,is it?"

"Thirty,you mean!" a pause

"did you?"

"Plenty" he boasts.

"Get caught?"

"Nn-nn. Correspondent"(in other words,superman). A pause. "No good,though" dreamily.

"What do you mean?"

"Roubles."

"Roubles?"

"What the hell" he sighed "you can't get rid of 'em! All the big hotels insist on valyootah"(that foul capitalist malady).

"Glad I didn't bring roubles,then."

"O you can travel on roubles,all right."

"Yes?"

"Not that anybody'd want to" he groaned. "Except to leave this"(censored) "place" he added;almost weeping.

Yet(out of the mouths of sucklings)do I learn that for exiting you positively must allow at least 3 days and all of 25 roubles. My blood shudders. I imagine mislaying said time or squandering said sum(or preferably both)and—not getting out,getting not out,not getting even nyet . . . "What's that?"

"that?"

I point to a mysterious flourish on his open passport. He smiles cynically "heaven."

"Exit visa?"

"Yep. Leaving in two days,and the"(censored)"can kiss my" (censored).

"Been here long?"

My confidant stares roundly,thundersmitten "what the"(very much censored)"do you think I am!—I just got here!"

Interim.

"That playright's not so lousy" grudgingly admits our socalled gentleman of our socalled press.

"I thought his suggestion most gallant;wish his drama hadn't—"

"Nn-nn. You don't mean what I mean."

"What do you mean?"

"The one we got" meaning,presumably,romp.

"O—seems lively."

"Know where he's gone?"

"Gone?"

"Sure. He's gone home—to give us a party."

I confess to astonishment,not unmixed with awe "but isn't he one of Soviet Russia's hundred best communist writers?"

Pityingly "sure. That's how the"(censored)"gets away with it. If you're okay with the comrades around here you can do anything." He yawned. Then,simply and profoundly,"same as anywhere else." —And out of the sides-of-the-mouths of journalists!— "That"(censored)"told me:I like you,we drink" adds contemptuously this moronic epitome of commonsense

beautiful pages,pages of Proust which are a paragraph(whose end occurs rather because than when his readerless reader has completely forgotten its beginning)brutally are by 6 comrades' search for comrade romp's "home" suggested;or as a person's idea of the person is suggested by that person's distortion in a trick mirror,and La belle au bois dormant by Glossina palpalis. Caplessly ExVirgil & spouse,pinwheel

& Turkess,Turk & self wander(to rewander)wonderingly(during 20 minuteless minutes)Moscow,U.S.S.R.   Now and again,genially Turk converses Russianly with that startled(with this total)stranger;always I see a shrug:then it's either the truth("nyez neyeyoo")or a sheerly fanciful stage direction,involving 6 comrades in revolvement ad absurdum

gradually whose ranks falter.   Even ex- totters.   Spouse reels(but no Cambridge arm is there to save;"inner discipline" has no arms). Tranquilly Beatrice desperately takes fair advantage of this doorstep and(removing with a sigh 2 Frenchheeled toys)asks

"is this Kiev?"

"Nn-nn" pinwheel gasps,sudflopdenpingly in nearest gutter "Naples."

"Breathes there a man"(gently Turk most unruffledly continues)"who cannot utterly despair when he beholds a supreme idea juggled by vaudevillian bureaucrats?"   And as for comrade Kem-min-kz(now who's many billions of millions of miles from translating that by the Potiphar's sister's husband "poem" which Otto Can't so generously did impart)marvellously he feels—as he has felt throughout this extraordinary evening—Release.   "Yes,they're certainly far from their"

(grunts. Groans. 6 comrades movelessly move)"ideal of classlessness. I should like you to meet a very good friend of ours,a professor in the fourth."   I ask "what is the fourth?" and learn,from no journalist,from a human being,something distinctly significant concerning that unreality which M. Potiphar and comrade Jack term idealistically,And How,"transition"

(1)heavy workers
(2)light ditto
(3)families of (1)&(2)
(4)intellectuals
(5)S.O.L.s

might or might not have been the layout.   At any rate:

our friend,comrade professor,a scientist,found himself in class next-to-bottom;he 1 day refused to "volunteer"

"as they call it;such a charming word"

for woodcutting:this audacity cost him all but 1 microscope and all his specimens and his laboratory(not to mention almost his residence)and his past present future

"but not his,shall we say,life?"
murmurs my(far more gently than even gently)informant.

Door:velvet-leather effect(cf.Madame Potiphar's). Suite of "nice"(très bourgeoises)rooms. Admire blue wallpaper—romp poohpoohs same and introduces,to all 6 exhausted comrades,a bashful(hair kittenish over unface)nonman who serves bashfully compôte and cheese and who bashfully retires

item:6 bottles of(Russian)"champagne"(bootleg).

Ex- drums me up to romp(and vice versa:"look around;see how many special privileges he enjoys? That's because the comrade is one of their hundred picked authors" etc.). Romp,abandoning pinwheel,warms up to me

"voo,pas payer,moi,ensemble,toujours,montagnes,très bons,splendides, magnifiques,suprêmes—oui?"

the which altogether too generous invitation our heroless would have accepted had

(1)I been so anatomically disposed by versatile mother nature

(2)I believed anything said by any member of the ruling or unruling class of any country

(3)I not discovered that the dites très bons were 4 days away by slow freight(Russia's "rapide")

(4)I come into Moscow without any idea of going out,e.g.

"take these only" her stone face cleaving. "There is not too much. Nobody can prevent you"

take(partially wrapped in wilted pages of Le Temps)1 small can of George Washington coffee,2 small bars of Swiss chocolate. The dreamish slenderest sahbahkah arches,bows;fluently:himself into that tiniest room

—back!(stamping,she in)will you get(Russian cries)back?what? (snatching a whip)yes?(glares)you,I mean!

slenderest fawns,simpers;lazily:retires dreamish to its nest beside stove.

"I do not ask you to bring them" cleaving,but proudly "to my mother. I only ask you to mail them from Moscow. See;here is the address in Odessa. Do I ask too much?"

"no." Am looking into room's corner;at wondering moistly eyes,slim heads,curled marvelously animal marveling bodies. "But of course you would prefer—if I decided for any reason to visit Odessa—that your gifts were personally delivered?"

"'prefer'! That would be better!a million times more sure! I should be so happy;for she was sick;very sick:and because I am afraid . . . However,if you do not go,you will mail them."

"Odessa is a seaport,isn't it? I might leave Russia by Odessa—"

"listen:Odessa was once a most beautiful city. Very beautiful like this,even like Paris. (What beautiful streets,how gay;life:people—O everything. Yes.) But all these are I think no more,no longer . . . I do not think" she smiles "I feel. It is no longer."

"If I don't leave by Odessa I will mail your gifts from Moscow. If I do leave by Odessa I will personally deliver them."

My Russian teacher's face,caving "take for me a little earth—so much"(a hands' prayer)"from my home" slid,collapsingly "thank you"—quickly she became a column(made of something much prouder than steel) . . . you are terrible!(her own death shouted at uplooking 3 mildly slimness heads)you villains!(sobbing)I love you! . . . And,slowly returning a quite tearless self "till tomorrow" graciously;with a graciousness beyond possibly iron. Then(something)distance,something(unbelievably vaster,always,than from a moon we call this earth to our earth's own moon)gradually entered(everything)her now(nowhere looking steadily)eyes:eyes very gracefully which have disappeared in(silently) Elsewhere. "Dahsvee-dahnyah."

The Savoy. Actually,same room where myself once lunched with blouse & scratch;changed And How! (When did we now 7 find all this?why 7 are we are here?—)because the "champagne" eventually wasn't and eventually we were drunk and all and said 6 goodbye,but romp 7th came with us all eventually "pour" drunkenly "manger quelque chose" . . . but look:2 comrades and 2 nonmen,1 of latter actually attractive! In red. Music(not bad)I dance with spouse—actually she can dance! And with actually Turkess. —What's? "Fowl?" Moorhen? All right. A feastless feast! The Turk whispers "don't worry:I'm Rockyfeller." Arguments. Am arguing. Fiercely with stewed romp:furiously amid vodka,also peach wine &

"voo,moi,ensemble"

—not a chance. Why won't I go to Magneto something? Well,what's there? An "usine?" But in America we have those,comrade. O we have millions of thousands of hundreds of tens of those things,comrade. But I am a poet? Am I? Who told romp that? (The Turk,smiling,denies it). Well if only I felt free to speak,I'd tell you,comrade dramatist romp,at least what I'm possibly anyhow not—

("go ahead" gently,Turk).

("And the three letters?" I whisper)

he laughs. "I am god. Give him" indicating romp "the works." Pause.

You seem to me(myself Frenchwardly addresses romp over worst music and through worse noise)to be filled with zeal.

I am. Why shouldn't I be? —To Russia!(he gulps).

Who filled you?

myself.

How recently?

not long ago. (Then,with the hysterical expandingness of a mythical I Confess contributor)listen:not long ago I did not believe. They told me—I said no. They argued—I said impossible. Then they took me: I saw—not possible,real—my own eyes believed;and my own voice said yes!

where did all this occur?

here!(bangslaps his bosom).

"Ask" earnestly I request twinkling Turk "ask our dramatic friend,in authentic Russian,precisely what corner of this fair world is most associated with his recent conversion." (Pause).

"He says" Turk twinkling announces "that it's the very place he cordially invites you to visit with him"

"voo,moi,ensemble,toujours,usines,grandes,montagnes,magnifiques, très bons,splendides" raves romp vodkaing "buvez! —A vous!"

"tell him I drink . . . to the individual."

A pause "he says that's nonsense."

"Tell him I love nonsense and I drink to nonsense." Pause

"he's very angry. He says you are afraid"

"tell him I am afraid to be afraid"

noisemusic,a waiter's glaring. "He believes you are mad."

"Tell him:a madman named noone says,that someone is and anyone isn't;and all the believing universe cannot transform anyone who isn't into someone who is"

item

3 A.M. l'addition(150 roubles exactly).

It came(by request)to romp,who thereupon sagely decides that each of us 7 comrades owed exactly,¹⁄₇th. (According to spouse,who prefers Hemingway to Joyce but had moments of surprising lucidity re people around her,140 roubles go romping rompward—I knew that I apologise to the company for a certain financial aloofness and I knew that ex- coldly regrets his inability to pay my share while Turk gently insisted upon so doing). Wonderingly now,behold 1 proud 100th of all Russia's foremost living literature pompously And How extending what vast sum to glaring . . . and

("he—he gave THREE roubles tip!")Mrs. Pinwheel,gasping,slides into her capitalist Mr.'s laplessness

—is glaring angry? Da. (Will he,perchance,bring an humble cheye in behalf of Turkess? Nyet). Possibly we'd all better be disappearing

a toy,alive on top of a ladder. The toy looks down;seriously it asks

"isn't Moscow Boston?"

laughter. Toy,descending(becoming gradually me)waves:goodbye!to Turk-and-Beatrice away galumping in battered droshky . . .

you,I,together,my house(romp grabs. Toy pulls aside).

Listen,comrade,I have a wife and seven children at the Metropole.

"Alors?"

"alors . . . il faut avoir sept enfants"

and(in the morning)Moscow somewhat resembles Wien,and guttering pinwheel and spouse dropping and declaiming ex-(and toy toppling) wend wend wend wendfully toward marble-or-something-or

"if" right cheerfully "as rumour hath it,every Savoy waiter is a member in good standing of the Gay-Pay-Oo—" thus chirps ex-.

"Prud." Muttered pinwheel "prud-didge. Puff-ikly prud-didge. Usheeveningk—r-a-a-a-a-y!"

"you have dropped your hat" ex- postulates.

Looking(a thousand hundred million miles)note 1 now little Else- wherecoloured Savoy doorman-comrade dollishly grinning;almost heartily:looking,looking

Mon. 18 mai

That even a 1strate capitalist breakfast cannot quell devastations of nthrate soviet "champagne" troubles me(American)not at all;that whoso leapeth through a moving tram's window waketh zahftrah with 1 sore foot I(fatalist)deem irremediable

distantly ex-,mightily hungover,intones

"I've been watching all Moscow go by on the ceiling." Nor was anyone ever more horizontal. (But he's naughtily pleased with himself,too). "There's a little hole in that curtain,which acts as a cāmera obscura— you've no idea how really magnificent one feels,lying here in a kind of daze with a procession going by continuously over one's head."

"Comrade,comrade,I fear you're a dreamer."

Sighing "perhaps I am."

"In that case,may one make hay with your English-Russian speakeasy?"

"I don't know what you mean,but for god's sake don't start an argument." (And while cautiously I'm finding Switzerland for the benefit of a cautiously worded postcard)"wonderful,wasn't it,the devotion with which" naming romp "defended his socialist principles against the combined onslaughts of you five rabid bourgeois individualists—"

"how much for l'étranger,by any chance?" waving my missive before his unopen eyes.

"Ten kopeks . . . and I felt positively nauseated at times by the unbelievably vulgar journalist—remember what I told you about correspondents when you arrived? A creature of" sitting pyjamadpink up "that totally degenerate variety should be automatically disbarred from:O!" falls back . . .wilted. "—Hm. Well,it's my own fault. Wasting an evening with drunkards when the whole world cries out for revolution . . . "

always glad to see me,President of Writers',very kind as usual,telephones Bolshoy;alas,the somethingorother organization has engaged every living seat. So comrade K won't witness that great socialist soviet opera "Red Poppy"(and he hears it's unco droll)—never mind;President gets me located for this evening at an art theatre . . . not The art theatre,you understand . . . and here's its name which I can't read or even its address to boot but that's

"bonjour"

sleepily my nonmeeter. Not quite Latin Quarterishly apparelled (suddenly am sick for unimaginable Paris!)

I see you aren't dead(he whispers most pleasantly). Then we lunched: I very heartily dined,rather;he languidly translated the scrapofpaper menu,he ordered gradually for me deep food and thick cigarettes and large beer,he dreamily conversed re his old friend the Russian-living-in-Paris novelist,re novels and novelists,re Paris,re—looking carefully everywhere into the crowded Club diningroom—re. And,Elsewhereishly smiling,he invited me to telephone him day after tomorrow morning. Perhaps,possibly,it could be contrived that I should meet on Thursday another. Indeed,seriously,however,he is delighted to have encountered a "sympatique" person—

&,willowing the uptorn yard outside,we abut romp. Nods. Stares

I quite(LQ murmurs)understand your admiration for what you have called the Arabian Nights cathedral. Doubtless its extraordinary story is familiar?

story?

Ivan the Terrible,Emperor of Russia,commissioned a particularly famous Italian architect to build the most beautiful church in the world(LQ resumes)which when the architect had done,the emperor extinguished the architect's eyes,saying Lest you should create something yet more beautiful. (A beggar lurched at us:LQ sidestepped him gingerly;frowned:spat. In a not more than whisper)and those were the days when art was highly valued . . .

"yah pahnyee-meyeyoo."

"Tahk." This is my street—how much?(to a forlorn slenderful unyouth clumsily whose both wings hug white frail trafficshaken flowerings. And stooping,LQ inhales)"incroyable. Ça sent la vie." (He chose,dropped slowly coinless coins into the un-'s outstuck handless hand)smell. (And we pass on). Isn't it Spring? Is there anything more beautiful—even a woman—than a flower? And women are so rarely beautiful;that's perhaps why we worship them if they are. Whereas flowers almost never succeed in being ugly,therefore we are inclined scarcely to notice them.

(K)there is an I Feel;an actual universe or alive of which our merely real world or thinking existence is at best a bad,at worst a murderous, mistranslation;flowers give me this actual universe.

Give(he said)yes(he stopped. Eyes:looking dreamily toward me with something beneath shyness;through me with dreamingly something beyond agony or all pain). Thank you;poets don't speak often

it's about 5:30 when explore the Revolutionary Literature Bureau. Can Otto Can't possibly have kept his fantastic promise of yesterday? Can Otto have 'phoned the Metropole management and ordered them to reduce my rent? This being Russia—nyet:nevertheless,might as well . . .

—with you in a moment!(cheerily. He's 'phoning now,all right;but to no hostelry . . . quite a call. 15 minutes elapse,and heaven knows how long the comrade was at it before I came)—well(thoroughly gripping my palm)how are you?

I'm about to say "pauvre" when

(clumpcrash!&)

in stagger 2 extraordinary caricatures(1 grim little ratfaced chap swamped beneath somebody's much too big overcoat,somebody else's differently much too big shirt,Charlot's pants,and a hatlessly dripping hat remarkably similar to some recently tossed custard pieless pie:1 big, ungainly,gruesome,horribly everywhere who from a far too tight boyscout uniform protrudes—and more especially aloft,via lump of totally hairless skull). Simultaneously which(sinking upon hard chairs)bozos bombard Otto in vernacular German . . . Painfully myself gathers that there was trouble,that trouble went with them night and day,that trouble followed the 2 of them for unimaginable hours all over Russianless Russia,that trouble got into uncounted trains,that it finally arrived in Moscow,that(doggedly dogging their faltering footsteps)it moved heaven and earth to eliminate any resting place,to make the inscrutable housing problem more inscrutable,and that's what you call trouble and here it is now and here they are now and what the etc. etc. etc. is Russianless Russia alias comrade Otto Can't going to do about these here now 2 good comrades and this bad now here 3rd unshakeable comrade trouble?

What is Otto going to do? Well,Otto's 1st going to soothe them. That's,so to speak,Otto's business:he's in the Soviet soothing racket. He's going to sympathize and soothe and tell them everything will be all right.

But sympathize skilfully:he's going to bandage their battered spirits and mend their fractured loyalties and flatter their flabbergasted vanities just as much as possibly is possible. And(hope springs eternal)he's going to promise them fantastic things;for that's part of the soothing. No more trouble,for instance. Trouble kapoot . . . I know.

Know,did I say?

scarcely do I guess the ⅓ of it . . . Yet,after a ½hour's intensive bandage-mend-flatter-ing of the most magical socialist variety,our Germanic communist comrades are still faintly rumblethundergrumbling— particularly Herr skull;who turns out to be a "Shockbrigader"(i.e. a high pressure idealist,a professional whooperup of the Cause of Causes: a 2fisted redblooded gogetting supersalesman of Marxian axioms). Well,comrade K has heard enough. Despite his woefully unlarge acquaintrance with Deutsch,this comrade has learned more than enough to make him thankful that he's got a roof over his head in the cityless city of Moscow,U.S.S.R. Good god!what if he'd accepted comrade romp's hysterical invitation to abandon the Metropole for distant climes!(though of course it's just possible that the 100 best Russian writerless writers only have a 100th of the trouble so copiously enjoyed by comrade piehat and comrade boyscout. —Adios,comrade Otto!

but nyet.

—Exeunt also boyhat and piescout;in a jiffy,am joined by comrade Can't himself. (Apparently the Can't's conscience pricks him with my unmentioned not to say unsolved financial problems;anyhow he pats my shoulder affectionately and confidentially coos)

I'm going to walk with you a few blocks:I'm going to show you a special store where you can buy Nords cheaper.

Nords?

that's what you're smoking,isn't it?

O yes(I say hurriedly,offering him 1).

Opposite the Lenin institute(opposite the aggressively unreal boxlike structure pompously,with a toy's pomposity,flying a red flag)there's a pseudo-square;in this squareless square people scurry,nonmen and men;through all these people circling vertiginously a rickety automobile street-sprinkler—with the sprinkle going full tilt—ploughs. Men-and-nonmen stumbling rush thither and hither;some get drenched,some merely spattered;all are threatened,several escape. Not 1 scurrier,however, registers anything approximating indignation (and—from safety of sidewalk—Can't pointed,chortling)it can't be turned off. That's Russia!

the actuality of which metaphor gives me pause. I actually feel(at that moment)how perfectly the far famed revolution of revolutions resembles a running amok streetsprinkler,a normally benevolent mechanism which attains—thanks(possibly)to some defect in its construction or(possibly)to the ignorance or(probably)playfulness of its operator—distinct if spurious loss of unimportance;certain transient capacity for clumsily mischievous behavior . . . very naturally whereupon occur trivial and harmless catastrophes

the store was shut.

Too bad(he observed,shrugging).

Well,guess I'll be returning to my gilded cage,comrade.

I'll go along too.

Don't let me take up your valuable time—

not at all. Not at all(another Nord goes the way of all flesh). What have you seen today?(he asks briskly).

A man buy flowers.

(The hard eyes quickly which looked at,stopped some distance from,myself. Dismayed—flowers,certainly,are not his dimension). There is so much to see(an emptied voice,almost ex-'s,commented with polite almost contempt).

Quite so . . . do you know him?

—who's that?

(I named the flower buyer).

(Shrug)O yes(and with the finest,most deadly evenness)a companion of the way.

A which?

that's what we call them(almost jocularly).

Why?

to contrast those people with the proletarian writers.

What's the difference?(I ask innocently)

enormous. The proletarian writers(he lectured)work,and describe their own work. The companions of the way don't work,and describe the work of others. Can you imagine a greater difference? The former are active,positive,original. The latter are passive,negative,parasitic. The former are building socialism,are creating the new Russia. The latter are playing an ignoble role,are remaining cowardly spectators of the greatest struggle in all human history. —Take,for instance,the man you mentioned:I know him well. "Il veut la révolution"—and when we encounter an obstacle,his eyes turn back to the good old days;but when we surmount the obstacle,he cries "'vive la révolution mondiale!' Tout de même"(pityingly)"c'est un type pas méchant—"

(the filthy under feet sidewalk arose:reelingly sank;then,in a city named Moscow,briskly walk beside walking briskly fellow-human-creature)

"—même pas mauvais."

Do you know the(presently I ask)church which makes perpetual revolution?

(a positively dirty look)"comment?"

I don't know any other way to describe . . . the whole thing marvelously whirls and this total supreme whirl is made of subsidiary,differently timed yet perfectly intermeshing,whirlings—it suggests to me and probably for no reason the Arabian Nights.

"Je la connais"(he said briefly). It's an antireligious museum now.

So I saw. (Pause)

there's an interesting story(he stated).

Yes?(pause)

during the struggle between reds and whites,the whites planted machineguns in that structure. Lenin promptly ordered his red gunners to clean out the enemy. Lunatcharsky thereupon resigned. Lenin sent for Lunatcharsky. Why have you resigned?Lenin asked. Because I cannot bear to fire on one of the greatest works of art in the world,Lunatcharsky answered. If,said Lenin,the revolution demands it,we will knock down a thousand cathedrals. Lenin was right,of course;Lunatcharsky,realizing that,withdrew his resignation immediately.

"Vraiment?"(I say,watched by hard $^1\!/_2$s of eye).

"Oui." And then the reds fired,and cleaned out the whites. "Comprenez?"

"comprend."

Later,when the struggle was over,the victorious proletariat appropriated a sum for repairing the injured edifice—did you notice any mutilations?

no.

There are none(said,eyeing,Otto Can't). In the first place,the damage was negligible. In the second,the restoration was scientific. And a great principle had triumphed . . .

the supremacy of life over art?(I hazard).

The supremacy(he said,carefully and almost gently)of humanity over everything(2 comrades are moving)

except(I,eyed,murmur)principles.

The principles which protect humanity are an integral part of humanity "n'est-ce pas?"(away looking,coldly affirmed Otto).

"High" croaks thickly at my stepping from elevator at pyaht self.

Surprised "hello" greet the sleeping dictionary correspondent.

"How's everything?" who grunts amiably.

"Fine and dandy. And you?"

"in a hurry?"

"sure. I was on the way to my humble hovel to shave before a show."

"Live up here now?"

"right."

"Come and give a look at my dump."

It's a roomlessness really larger than mine and actually 100,000,000 times smaller—crammed(as hope I'll never and have never seen and see anything crammed)with comfort modern(e). Why,he even has an imitation stove to cook over. Not to mention imitation sherry glasses,willfully arranged in an imitation cupboard . . . and almost if not quite knives and forks and really a spoon. Also a flockless flock of notably useless objets impossibly unnecessary d' utterly junkish art.

"Homey,eh" the proud possessor of these ad infin. horrid trifles barked solemnly,ponderously reaching into almost curtains.

"I'll say so." A bottle.

"Fixed it all up myself" he growled happily(cautiously selecting 2 almosts). "But the gal" ceremoniously pouring something which might be port "(here's luck!)keeps it neat."

"Looks like a million dollars"—and which tastes like awfully watered vino rosso à l'américain,N.Y.Eyetalian style,aetat nil.

He put down a glassless accurately:something nearly like fear(exactly travelling into the once corners of something facelike,of someone possibly who had been young?)sharpens this timeless(and how incredibly lonely!)dense unwhisper "the woman's touch."

"Tovarich Pavlov?"

nods.

"Yah Kem-min-kz."

Well,what of it?(doggedly this facial bigness inquires). Have I picked the wrong window?—no:it's comrade Pavlov,certainly minus familiar Xmas whiskers;but whiskers were not specified by comrade Writers' President when he certainly told me to visit a certain comrade Pavlov at the "Vtoroi Mchat"(as comrade flowerbuyer so kindly wrote it all out and as comrade deskman how kindly looked it all up and as comrade I so kindly tracked it all down And How)

"beelyet?"

Silence

(then)"bfghjklmpqrstvwxyz"(or something,whimpers dogged;cocking 1 shaggy ear and very almost suspiciously viewing my—produced desperately as a last resource—Russian passport) . . . American writer(his dumb grey faithful eyes read darkly). "Da." Pawing,upstaring,scratches in my direction 2 frontrow seats!

. . . out of this crowdless crowd sticks ex(upstanding to be observed under pretence of observing)Virgil:next whom cowers his not lame "secretary",she of Gahlstook. And immediately we 3 collide;and immediately he's persuaded("well of course if you don't like to sit so far front I'll be glad")to exchange his modest for my immodest places:and scarcely have some fleeting thankyous disappeared than

"pahzhahloostah"

halt.—No earthly use embellishing a comrade unknown oxeyed nonman's lapless lap,even though she(and her bepigjowled boyfriend) happen to coincide more or less exactly with exmentor's exterritory . . . a courteous comrade-usher kindly disappears with my mutely proffered formerly angelic twice told tales . . . "nyet!"(find myself repulsing sternly several gesturing frenziedly comrades;variously who would hand their sundry tickets to him whose expressionless savoir aplomb indicates that he is somebody else,e.g. the usher—eventually they understand— foreigner,1 says to 1—and all thereupon RedRidingHoodishly survey grandma . . . and now semidark. Shs everywhere. Glimpse ex-,safely ensconced in row A,lawandorderfully scowling around himself;while myself,also 10 or 12 other comrades,miserably await their sundry locations . . . wellwell . . . lights:'twas a false alarm. And mildewingly enter the(judging by his lofty gait)manager;salaaming prettily who personally escorts—would there were a band!—Americanitz peesahtel to far better than ex-'s exvantagepoint;pahzhahloostahs;vanishes

SH:

dark

incidentally,this translated from the Ukrainian and featuring Soviet education might well be called A Wolfboy's Domestication,or Hooray For Lenin. 1 little happy originally wolfboy(living in a nice hole in sweet mother earth)meets the new religion and brushes his teeth and proudly arises to humbly become just another honest citizen of good Master Stalin's(fooled you)great USSR. Heroine isn't so bad;but much too immensely tall and(like 4 out of 5 native nonmen)boastfully pianolegged. Moral:children can teach their teachers something about revolution. Villain=a bourgeois professor,crazily who roars his wrongful ideology:hero(the good Marxian)winces;listens—tightly selfcontrolled— and,when roar subsides,patronizing smiles to you and me and meyou and youme and comrade us

which,then,is the new formula. Different from Christ's "hit me again",different from Mammon's "yesun ifyuh wannuh make sumpn outuvit stepout soyd";telescoping tolerance and implacability,altruism and egoism.

There's 1 peculiarly excellent set:a colossal picture which rhythmically has been torn.

"What did you buy?" ex- motheringly demands(entr'acte).

"One piece bread and one piece ham,sixty kopeks. One glass tea,ten kopeks."

"That's five kopeks too much for tea" he remarked very severely,giving me a purchased beforehand cracker. And politely she of Necktie insists that I accept 1 also beforehand purchased sweet wrapped in muchly gooey paper. And at the endless end of the showlessness am caught in sinful act of departing—"I've had no lunch" ex- pleads;until(with a brief farewell at she)we're offlessly off to the underground beerjoint

peevoh,alas,has risen;1 rouble 50 after 6 P.M.,it seems. And 1 rouble apiece for these("you must eat something too")cakes which,praise heaven,have no cream and taste somewhat,or almost somewhat,like cold minceless hot mincepie("delicious,eh?" smacking lipless deadman lips)and there's a much more than far less concealed orchestra of partless parts which most wickedly,all furtively,renders 2 very very very Very hoary jazz(2 youthless youths guiltily stand,wiggle briefly against each other,sit wickedly)tunes in devilishly rapid succession.

"Do you know" he confides "I feel very queer."

Amazed "you feel?"

"almost as if . . . as if I'd been poisoned"(hastily)"mentally,I mean.—Physically" belch "I never felt better in my life."

"Perhaps the music" myself sympathizes.

"O no. As a matter of fact I like jazz;now and then. Hm . . . interesting,isn't it,how unutterably prejudice can distort facts. Here we are in lively Moscow which" lifelessly he unsmiles "is controlled,says the capitalist press,by an unscrupulous group of fanatics,operating a vast insidious political machine for grinding millions upon millions of helpless human beings into abject slavery;yet" sighing "we've just heard two jazz tunes,played spontaneously and with(you must admit)great spirit by supposedly cowed and miserable workers,for the entertainment of their fortunate fellows."

I stare

"put that down in your diary" he said "just as it happened:a group of Russian workers supposedly isolated from the rest of the universe; supposedly denied all the fruits of their labours;supposedly scourged with poverty and famine,supposedly tortured and terrorized by inhuman Marxian oppressors—but really(put it down!)taking their ease at their inn,drinking beer,and listening to American jazz."

Recovering gradually "I'll try."

"In describing an unfamiliar environment,it is always best to let facts speak for themselves. Truth is after all stranger than fiction" ex-stated,peevohing. Pause.

"You feel better now?"

"Much. I really think the only trouble with me was that I'd been feeling guilty about something or other—I can't imagine what."

"God knows it's in the air—"

"come:none of your Freudian nonsense! There are enough real problems,heaven knows,without imagining any" scowling.

"Do you imagine Freud makes people imagine?"

"I imagine he makes them mad. That's his business,isn't it? Then he can treat them."

"Possibly. But I should rather guess that the gentleman from Vienna spent most of his time reconciling individuals to a system—"

"well,I think that's very bad!"

"as I sit here,thoroughly not reconciled to this earthly paradise enow or socialist system,I'm inclined to agree with you,comrade. In fact,there isn't anything that gives me the jitters quite so rapidly as imagining myself,after ten or twelve years of heaven-on-earth,waving a red flag to beat hell."

Ex-(with dignity)"to my mind,a person is more loyal to a court if he criticises a bad judge." (Burp)"I trust you would retain your critical sense—now,WHY"(suddenly glaring over my shoulder with horrifyingly more than ferocity)"does he go on swilling beer when he's already positively sodden?"

squirming,glimpse(3 tables away)precariously by him(seated)self swollenness;all drunkenly now which mutters,all(pointing)who gestures . . .

(annihilatingly)"I can't understand such people!"

"perhaps the comrade's unhappy—"

"'unhappy'!"(tonelessly voracious tone of scorn)

"—look:he's talking to you"(he is). "What is he saying?"

"don't be silly!" ex- snarled "such a creature is absolutely incapable of saying anything."

"If I could only understand—"

"pay no attention. It's disgraceful;positively—"

"come come,comrade humanitarian. Besides,I'm curious:against what or whom is that tower of peevoh leaning?"

"himself,probably."

"No. It's something about"

(was pronouncing "rabohtah")when—goes miraculously over slowly over backwards drunk chair mutter all-in-1;former,landing on his (graspingly at same momentless upsetting other 2 chairs)very hairless

thud:

head,

"there! —Now are you satisfied?" while a pair of(of whom hurrying 1 upsets angrily 3rd chairless)waiterlesses grab(pluck dazed him)drag muttering that drunk-gesturing(the a)this which:off;up,out . . . And "how can you sympathize with such depravity!"

"O,he's got his world."

"—world?"

"a world in the head is worth two unworlds in the hand—"

"comrade" icily "one should restrict one's pity to worthy objects; otherwise one is one's self pitiable."

"May I ask why you despise our vanished fellowman?"

"I don't. I despise what he represents. I despise idleness. I despise self indulgence. I wonder that you can ask such a question."

"And you probably despise comrade Kem-min-kz for wondering what mysteriously underlies all this concentrated hatred of fleshpots which seems to have permeated every molecule of Moscow's atmosphere;you despise him for wondering what,fundamentally,all this hyperZiegfeldian glorification of Rabohtah presupposes."

"Presupposes!"—he glared helplessly. "Why do you pretend to be so stupid? Haven't you your work? Haven't I mine? Isn't work one of our greatest blessings? Well?"

"but actually" comrade K marvels "what does the thing mean? Everywhere you hear it,'rabohtah'. Is it god? What is it?"

he glared.

"See" pulling out faithful(and opening)pocket dictionary and finding "that sacred symbol of symbols!"

"well?"

"see an unsacred threeletter word just above it?"

"Rab,meaning slave:well?"

"well?"

he eyed,frigidly. "If" cunningly his unvoice,neuter,said "you intend to entangle us in a discussion of original sin—"

"—which reminds me:Mr. X of America" K said "is an editor. Don't go to Russia,said the American editor:in the first place,it's too big for any one person to understand;in the second place,you are singularly not equipped by sociological or economic training to understand it."

"Excellent advice. Considering the bourgeois source."

"Then we had a few drinks(on Mr. X)and Mr. Bourgeois American X observed that mankind had eaten of the tree of knowledge and that mankind was being punished thereof. He alluded to the sufferings of a socalled world—"

"imagine any seriousminded person deriving our present economic situation from some antiquated theological doctrine!"

"—meaning labour pains,Mr. X's ignorant interlocutor mildly observed. Let's hope the child is not born blind. At any rate,I shall take along some argyrol and a brace of open eyes."

Something—mirrored in his eyeglasses—

"sh"(who whispers)"there's a Phi Beta Kappa."

"Where?"

"exactly where that drunk was. Hm . . . We'd better pay our check and go."

"If this happens—"

"no,really"

"—again,I shall begin to suspect we're both slightly paranoid. But speaking of guilt,comrade:the Russians have certainly developed a 6th sense in that direction."

"You mean" whispering "toward their government?"

"government? Government's merely an exteriorization,isn't it?an outward symbol?a projection? Or did the conditional reflex discover comrade Pavlov?"

he seems almost to think. Then he whispers "why did Lack Dungeon's daughter's husband emphasize to me last night the fact that these companions of the way are better writers than these proletarians?"

"so?"

"in America" ex- almost angrily stated "we don't expect senators to be writers."

"Bravo! In other words,an artist's mind differs per se from a politician's—vahshezdarohvyeh!"

going(up,out;)

"I wish some kind soul would invent"(ex- groaned)"a satisfactory solution to the apparently insoluble problem which confronts one really to be pitied creature:I mean the sincere socialist who,through no fault of his own,has a little money . . . by the by:that's what I've been feeling guilty about!" he added,brightly.

Behind 2 moving comrades moves a 3rd

"let's slow down" I suggest. The 3rd passes.

stoops,picking from the floor a little Polish coin. Which gave itself to me only yesterday. Neatly,even youngly,arrayed. When I showed it to ex- he didn't believe. A towelled head;short skirts. "You"(said he)"probably brought that masterpiece into Russia with you." Her white coarse stockings show off almost unheavy legs. "There's no reason,comrade,to suppose people are dishonest." But when I discover her face,it's 46

(which all somehow reminds of the Paris-dwelling American communist's remark by ladybug echoed:everybody in Russia is so very young!

if comrade foreigner dodges a native comrade hose,or if he glimpses that multitude of native comrades dodging this gaga streetsprinkler,then cowed and mossy Moscow seems to be overrun of and by and for oversize children . . . but if foreigner I haven't forgotten—shall we say x,tacitly therewith including comrade censor's face?—then,beyond the(feelfully impulsive trusting friendly)children are unchildren(astute,premeditating,diplomatic)—under the seem,then,of everything lurks an(as adult only is cruel)adult compulsion. Behind spontaneous yes,implacably And How because)

"let's play a game called YOU" said the unchild to the child . . . poor child! Poor everywhere child(in wasman's shrug,in dim of youthless; even in non- of spattered nonmen and who look down(twistingly)at (everyone's)muddied(not my)unnew(not your)stockings,to expressionlessly uplooking resume Elsewhere)

something—uncertainly meanwhile trying to locate the moving Art Museum,whose present whereabouts comrade flowerbuyer had(speaking sacredly;or perhaps not quite as a man condemned by death to life might impossibly speak)indicated rather than defined—is sure,I feel; something's certain:Eros wins. Eros wins;always:through a million or a trillion million selves,musically which are 1 who always cannot perish— plural:the nonworld of denial;spectres of defeat,repression;shadows of agony—singular:form of all names;ecstacy,triumph,immeasurable yes and beautiful explosion . . .

therefore;he(whatever his creed)who would subvert Eros,the form, shall become shadow. Who would contain form in formula only shall be contained in spectre. Who would any when or where limit(however hugely)miserably must undie the least undeath of measures;always cannot always live;believingly may therefore trivially multiply or worship the mere nonexistence of himself.

A strange,a very muchly labelled,structure. Art? (Why not? And why?) —I choose that strangestness of this most strange label over its grim doorful front;opening dictionary,search. No;that unparticular word isn't:wait,wait a minute;here is a word,to which that word might well be cousin and which means

"insane"

Moscow hears laughing! 1 starved(suddenly eating green sunlight)tree chucks a(to me from where?)shy(when?hurtling)leaf into my eyes;hears distance,this Ving filth of avenue which and momentarily how expands with silence;O but these comrade ghosts leftward or rightward stare,amazed;2 stop(whisper . . .)

curiously very much more than enough,the next-most-promising comrade edifice turned out to be a planetarium. Shut

return in time to meet my ex-(at 2 P.M.,my ex- has said,we're together leaving the Metropole for Volks;you ought to visit Volks,everyone at Volks is so very nice and sweet and kind and good—"although I really must admit they've proved singularly inefficient whenever I've wanted most to see a particular show;not that I think it's intentional,you understand"). No my ex-. No,at least,answer to crisp thrice repeated knock . . . upon a bench at the end of ex-'s couloir sit 6 whitecoated surgeonlylooking persons,chatting almost cheerfully: comrade bellboys. Well,I might almost sit(and cheerfully)awhile in the nearby reception almost room(or what haven't we)conveniently adjoining the Metropole's almost farfamed barbershop. I might sit and unread Russian magazines,fortunately which are filled with(marvelously bad) photographs of tractors and travailleurs . . . then I might float upstairs to my own hot couloir and unlock my roomless and write a letter and hunt a map(it's lost)and lock my roomless and wander slowly down and reapproach my ex-'s door(to be crisply told,by a surgeonly,Nobody home)and down,and post my(noticing that ex-'s key is in the rack)letter;and to hell with sweet kind good nice Volks—am off,now,to our next appointment;am off to the palatial residence of the Chinesey doctor who(ex- said)asked us to dine with himself or with the Lack Dungeons alias Turks or with both or neither or who only heaven Russianly knows:

if this doesn't especially resemble anybody's door, that clumsily authentic maid I recognise

"dohmah"

disappearing. And also these very various coats. Go upstairs, toward voices.

In a little plushy room sits(feeble?or merely not as I'd remembered?) Chinesey(sandwiched between 2 typical American business gents of the Quiet,and how,variety)towering who politely inquires(dangerously)whether I'm looking for(naming)the Turk or for himself? —Reply that I just want to know when(naming)Virgil's expected. —"Very soon"(he mysteriously reassures)and,allrevolveslowlying,presents lazily to both Quiets myself . . . sighs . . . retires(eyefully)behind thick glass;becoming swollenly a submarine mind. Pause

"have you been here long?"(self,selfconscious)

"no" the nearer of the Quiets answers me quietly "about a year." Pause. From Baltimore. Pause. Yes,has a match but no,doesn't smoke. Pause. Mild snowy head. Interested in railroads.

By(guardedly)Chinesey escorted,conversation(remarks in hand-cuffs)begins;re an automobile excursion to "the country" and a lake. Briskly—but respectfully or as a supersecretary to his infraboss—enter empty American whom I met 1 dayless at ex-(then Virgil's)ikonjoint. Jumps into the conversation almost happily,with youngmiddleaged swagger . . . —what kind of a car?desperately demand.

8 stares:the most recently arrived coldly replies "only a Ford."

"O,only a Ford" I repeat.

"But they're pretty good,the new Fords"(aggressive,bristling pompadour).

"I think so" agree "I have one in the country—" oddly,if not quite queerly, the more imposing(hitherto unsampled)of the Quiets contemplates father of this assertion. Apparently I should be quiet, too . . .

. . . "spasEEbah" ex-'s

voice—and,for once,welcome to my ears! Now enter same,enter the selfunpossessed personage,the really genial scholar,the actually frigid New Englander of Russia

"so"(marching at our heroless and gripping my fin not more as if we hadn't seen each other for a millenium than less as if we'd married the same woman by mistake)"you found it yourself!" Airily "that's very clever of you!" And with a look I'll perhaps remember if somebody wants to eat me "you don't need my guidance any more!"

"but I knocked at two o'clock. I waited for you. You weren't in" vainly plead. For he(somewhat too glibly)protests that it was all a mistake;that I was surely wrong,that we weren't at all to meet at 2 or ever visit Volks this day. Turns—

enter Turkess and the Turk(she smiles,he winks)social,subdued:

Quiet the more imposing accepts cigarette:politely preferring humanity's Nords to my Camels . . . would that un(I think to myself)smoking ex-,then And How mentor,had only a little fiercelier refused that fond arrival gift;a whole a single entire a homogeneous complete intact package of Luckies—however,perhaps dim got them;and here's hoping! So stroll helplessly around;infinitely lonely:smashing (carefully)a burnt match in my hand,

pair of nondescriptly overdressed Russian nonmen guiltily appear. Bow,glowering at Turkess;guiltily disappear

("have you seen the beautiful—?")unvoice whispers. Beneath railroads

"if she's one of those—"

"O no. Sh . . . Come!" bringleading me to inner("sh") doorway. Very painstakingly seated,at a pathetically real piano,now is by us beheld("sh!")1 rather reddish distinctly homely maybe Celtic vision;bountifully endowed with handless(premeditatedly pale)hands "artistically" guttering

"who's that?"

Ex- crowned me with a stupendous "SH!"(and to this day,comrades,I know no more)

next:in the very diningroom where vodkaful romp romped while the alarmed flowerbuyer fluttered and ex- sulked vodkaless,a pompously incoherent conversation fetters 9 tensely untogether—e.g. to my right,a "Russian actor" who doesn't speak anything else—nonindividuals. Luckily for beckoned me,not luckily for not beckoned ex- who vividly tried to get there first,Beatrice adorns my left. So runs the world away. With luscious viands and intriguing wines. With jokeless New England jokes and scholarly quipless quips. With catastrophically irregular silences. Recall only 1 remark

"would you like to go to the Arbat with us and dance?" Beatrice said.

"—Dance!?!"(my totally being registers everything celestially beyond astonishment:why,if casually The comrade Virgin Mary had appeared from comrade frigid's full wineglass armed with a special delivery letter from comrade God summoning to the vacant chair of Slavic languages in Paradise University comrade K,I couldn't have been ¹/₁₁ as quite permanently surprised)

"we're going to the opera. Why not meet us afterwards,if you care—" and stops,frightened by my faceless

nn-nn,can't be true;impossible:nyet. "Please" I murmur "don't joke about sacred things—"

. . . "well,are you going?" ex- has risen. Had said something about getting me a seat at the show which he's attending this evening,hadn't he? Glance at Quiets,at pompadour,at the(whom haven't met yet)nondescript nonmen(who are they,anyway?)at "actor",at Chinesey

"yes" drivelled from my capitalistic shoes.

"Please call"(Chinesey,courteously looming)"again." I bowed,the nonmen flicker,the Quiets grunted,the "actor" jerks,the pompadour coughed brittly. The Turk and Turkess and ex- and self,descending,seek hastily apparel and

(bluntly)"can you find a place for him with you?" ex- asked Turk . . . I squirm. . . . Turk,not dropping dead(not perturbed even,not annoyed)smiling "I think so" answered;and with a wink which more than expressed many things "come along with us" says,gently . . .

everybody crazily shoving,hurrying . . . copious tongues of humanity protrude from all ticket windowmouths. And very("we have a minute and a half")placidly Turk joins a queue. It balks;he placidly changes to another:at window arriving,placidly produces presscard and Russianly converses re American poet. Is refused. Cheerfully("nothing left")he beams

"please—"

but is gone. Around us lunge,bumping,squirm,jostling,wrestle,milling fiercely and literally tearing themselves apart,frenzied comrades of innumerable sexes and denominations and dispositions;Turkess smiles: O;there he is(at still another window)placidly how Russianly conversing: now a frantic nonman covered with children and desperately waving a very soiled piece of possibly paper yells,screams up into the window, shrieks over his shoulder—quietly(very)turning but suddenly(not quite

122

quickly,much more than easily or fluently;fatally perhaps)he perfectly
with implacable placidity calms instantaneously her . . . (And,fatally
gently miraculously out)

"we"

(of such unvictory as never New York subways even at rush hour could
imitate now floating peacefully)

"win!"

(vastness redplushful goldish)10 times 10 times 10 times etc.(=humanity)
every- no- some- anywhereing:

hyper incredible:top—swimming directly against the gilty ceiling—
box even which is crammed with(to chins foreheads eyes diminished)
faces

"bolshoy." Splendor ad infinitum;imperial magnificence Plus;Big
lifted to the Bigger power of Biggest & all these comrade spectators
impossibly aren't dressed alike(all don't seem quite as if they hadn't
been recruited from sewers ashbarrels swillheaps and coalmines not to
mention probably factories)—but not,you understand,that the least
well dressed member of this huge audience isn't very much more well
dressed than whatever Russianless Russian have previously seen. . . . Item:
within comrade Stalin's otherwise glaringly empty lower left proscenium
box de(unutterably regal!)luxest,occurs("that's Gorky" Turk whispers)
shadow;itself cringefully hiding behind a firmly placid nonman:the
shadow's face is timid and old and tired . . .

Prince . . . superbly processioned,costumed;thoroughly danced(O
ballets russes!)amply,loftily,thickly sung . . . Igor. I sit during the 1st
act with extasiée Turkess;alternately plumbing a monumental cavity of
stage and noting the Assyrian backless of Turk's,in row B,dome,which

"have some kwass?"

placidly during 1st entr'acte suggests. (Meaning a softly not untasting
beverage

"made from fermented bread"

says Turkess,refusing

"but this kwass is watered" mildly adds he). And then we exchange
places:solitary myself inspects 2ndrate opera sometimes and sometimes
1 swooning-with-pretend,utterly-satisfied-with-it-all,row A comrade
(perhaps 56?who wears obliviously an,if you please or if you don't,highly
becoming blue working blouse). And solitary myself ponders a recent

incident:just as I sit down,some softly appearing young comrade in shirtsleeves whis-pers something or other(verily would have fled—thinking,nyeh pahnyeemeyeyoo,"that's how the Turk got me my place;the management gave away somebody else's:how Russian!"—but soothingly now he pats my shoulder,quietingly murmurs Don't disturb yourself,that's all right . . . and vanishes). O my country 'tis of! O "fur Cry sake git duh Hel owt,dis iz muhih seat,sea?" Verily does comrade foreigner deem Moscow an extraordinary cityless.

The 2nd intermission produces("they have so many roubles they don't know what to do with them"—roubles,not dollars)1 suppressed almost sallow Jewish "doctor",1 smallish emptyfaced(his wife)blonde,and 1 timidly too eager charmingly childish daughter. Americans who claim to be;but O they're far too courteous. And when Igor is over 6 will walk to 3's present residence,alias Grand Hotel,and there will 1,alias daughter,be deposited;whereupon 5 will visit celebrated dancehall district,alias Arbat

place:Big. Time:almost act last. Characters,ghosts,and Americans. A very charming lady(to proudest comrade Kem-min-kz,respectfully who am again beside her seated)

"Charlie asked me to ask" lights dim "you if you'd"(silence)whispering "do us the very great" Big dwindles "honour to be our guest while you're here—"

boo—&—BOO

(so comrade I'm goldilocks,but where's the 3RD bear?)

follow Turk to a balcony(pleasanter than anything at Metropole because openly overlookingish:under,street-darkness;undistantly,lights suggesting,for what unearthly reason,Venezia!near,in 1 corner a soldier mildly jumbling a woman)

"it's too bad" he gently wondered. "Putting her to bed like that as if she were a baby—and her first time in Moscow,too"

referring to daughter;minus whom,presently emerge parents and Turkess. Now for the nitlif! Rarely(if ever)did this comrade feel so irremediably wicked . . .

great bargainings. Bargainings and bargainings. They all concern a Ford taxi. They all occur in Russian. The protagonists are driver and Turk,duly abetted contradicted encouraged and hindered by motheaten Grand doorman himself:finally—just as we 5 capitalists miraculously have into closedness squeezed—driver explodes verbally,igniting doorman(who splutterfully corroborates

Five is too many!)

Tell him(protrudingly Turk directs doorman,re driver)

"Nyetnyetnyet!"(doorman twitters)

—Tell him(almost on his head now crouching the Turk whispers)I'll give him a tip.

Tips not allowed! Tips not allowed!(shouts doorman)

warily opening nearer door,untangling,Turkess starts forth—also the M.D.—but suddenly Turk gently speaks;immediately Grand salutes: slams 2 outgoers back-on-top-of-us-3 . . . —an illegally 5laden cab lurches awayly

"what" inquire,when everyone's righted "were the magic symbols?"

"I merely" gasps curving Turk(whose chin and knees unpractically blend)"told him that then we'd all five of us get out." Grunt. "Rather than permit which catastrophe he's very sensibly breaking the law."

"O you should have seen Gene" upfolded Harem murmurs. "It was a huge Packard;with the Tunneys and two other comrades and myself. —Only four allowed(somebody cried)and poor Gene almost went mad"

arriving,

. . . "my treat" the doctor said. "Three roubles we owe." (And,to driver;handing him 5)—here. For you!

(enter a flock of spaseebahs)

is five too many?(the giver grimly asks)

(silence;a square hesitates,a puzzled scowls,a dirty face thinks:then)five is not too many(gradually the taker and very sullenly answers).

Now,O now,here's a dump

abandon our protective colouring in chill small nasty(emptily containing 2 hideous whisper-sitting weirds)roomless

—& march down steep stairs into a large stohlohveyeah,jammed with du monde of the almost too apparently demi- or less brand:patron

("doesn't he look like Balieff?" asks Turkess;he does)almost too enthusiastically welcomes us slummers . . . yes,yes with pleasure,just a moment,O plenty of room,excuse me please . . . and balloons his avoirdupois hitherthither;beseeching,imploring,entreating this those these that comrade comrades to move along and to make room and to yield ground and to give way and to get out:1 and all gloweringly And How refuse

("he's in a hard position" she calmly pities "they're citizens of this republic,and they're staying")

whereupon balloon vanishes.

"Don't worry" Turk softly admonishes.

"But—but all the tables are full!" Mrs. M.D. protests nervously

"if there aren't any places he'll make us a few. I know."

"How do you know?" M.D. challenges. "These people look to me like pretty tough customers."

"These people are not really tough" Turk murmurs "these people are really hungry—for amusement. But if these people were really tough it wouldn't matter;because the patron's really crazy to go to America and really open a real restaurant and"

. . . balloon(serenely,from rear)beckons . . .

"you see" Turk tranquilly added "we're Americans."

. . . Sit right down,sorry to have kept you waiting,so glad to see you,etc. etc.(balloon). 1,2,3,4,5 hard chairlesses gradually come and eventually all 5 hardly unsit weless

—nonmusic strikes up itself—promptly outstrides from audience a lanky(in wornheeled slippers faded brown stockings tattered once grey frock and wilted tam)ghostmannonman,simperingly followed by a hebooted maletrousered shebeshawled pugnosed fuzzyhaired spectral it. They clutch;bob,dreamily Bostoning—

("it's a she" I maintain)

("it's too tall" Mrs. M.D. objected)

("I should dislike to investigate" Turk avers) ·

("it has no breasts" the Turkess remarked)

("O that's a man all right" M.D. states)

("but it dances on its toes" I insist)

take your choice.

And what is this nectar? A pitcher of cherryish liquid which— absolutely unbelievably(and I remember the roar unlike dynamite and romp pouring chez lui "champagne" into glasses marvelously unlike champagne-glasses while to everybody commenting shrugfully

"il n'y-a pas de ice") . . .

Looks rather dangerous

"is that a gift from the management?" innocently M.D. asks.

126

"Nooo!" says Turk

"is it alchoholic?" demands M.D. suspiciously.

"Nooo!" says Turk

"then I'll have a beer" M.D. announced.

And so will I—not that what we get isn't warm soapy peevoh. Nobody seems to need food except self;the Turk,however,relents(enter 2 extraordinarily tough versions of shishkabob with wine sauce).

Twice comrade I,with Lady and M.D.'s . . . quelle lopsided comrade musique! . . . dance(?)

overhear a(between Mrs. M.D. and Turk)tremendous argument—"the state is queen" he tells her "and you'd be the first to hate that,despite your pretended procommunism." Carefully meanwhile M.D. sips,alert; silent(Turkess,inspecting queenfully a subterranean world,sighs).

"Why?"

"suppose you were here" supposes Turk "and your husband had a private practice;he'd be unable to make large amounts of money—"

"I wouldn't" M.D.'s haughtily asserts "let him practice privately." (M.D. sips).

"All right. That's out. Now suppose he's attached to a hospital. May we suppose such a thing?"

"of course" blonde magnanimously permits.

"And" mercilessly Turk supposes "suppose a little stranger arrives. The government,suppose,orders your husband elsewhere. You can't go with him. He must go alone. Does he go? He does. Alone? Alone. Why? Because he simply can't do otherwise."

Her empty face darkened. Her darkening face stared. At the,at this,blunt pair of much too manicured 5s

"then,to make everything perfect,it's discovered that you have more room than you need. Comes a knock at your door:you open:there's somebody standing on your threshold—a total stranger—all ready to live with you."

Blonde squirms.

"Perhaps a man" queen adds vaguely . . .

straightening:outraged "I—" and stared(bigeyed,helpless)at the at slowly sipping at her husband;almost who smiled . . . Turk:

"would you let that total stranger in?"

Handing him contemptuously the bad essence of Grand Rapids morality in 3 monosyllabic installments "I—would—not!"

and M.D. looked down;down into peevoh,down among bubbleless bubbles. The Harem smiles frankly

"my dear lady" Turk pities "you would not only let that stranger in but you would make her him or it welcome"(vainly her hating eyes beat on)"unless,of course,you preferred not to eat for a few years"(tranquility)

pause. Upflaring "it's a lie!"

"as incredibly true" smiling said he "as that this meat is meat"

pause. Her stare smallening "tell me . . . something else" 1 hard new little voice commands

"I'll tell you. But do you know why I'll tell you? Please don't imagine I'll tell you because I happen to know things which hundreds of other people don't know. As a matter of fact(my dear lady)not hundreds,but thousands;but tens and hundreds of thousands:but literally millions of human beings know infinitely more than I—or any foreigner—can so much as begin to know or ever begin to begin to guess. But here's the point:not all these knowing millions can tell you a single god damned thing,because they're Russians. Do you understand? Russians. All of them are inside communism;not outside it,as you are. All of them are actually living(or rather dying)an unprecedented experiment,not merely observing it with an analytic eye;far less dreaming about it with a sentimental brain." (Eyes shining)he into all of her emptiness put(very quietly;peacefully almost)"what I tell you,I tell you because I can do what all those millions of human beings can't—speak."

The M.D. straightened. "Bravo" he whispered

the Turkess smiles

"you . . . you mean—?" blonde

"Russians in Russia must suffer and shut up" Turk said softly. "But correspondents in Russia have special privileges. They can't get a really good story past the Russian censor,of course:but they don't have to swallow their tongues while they're here and they're not obliged to be here forever"

once upon a time there's a fond old revolutionist. The fond old revolutionist has a son. And the fond old revolutionist joins the unfond new communist party,for his son's sake,so that his son will be in good odour. And 1 day son discovers that father is backward and 1 day son denounces father to father's own friends . . . "I was talking recently with a man who took me aside and confidentially explained that his own daughter was a communist;and that he didn't dare say anything before her because he was afraid that she would impeach him,even as other children impeach their parents—then he grinned and remarked,with a shrug 'the child's duty is not to the family but to the party,you know.'"

"Demolish the family" M.D. muttered "and automatically you make everyone suspicious of everyone."

"I" wonders Lady "wonder why the glorious future of mankind should consist in everyone ecstatically minding everyone else's business . . ."

this(oddly enough)cheque isn't huge—proudly self contributes 2 chernovitz(20 roubleless roubles)but only after much protesting by Turk,who has to be reminded that someone didn't pay someone's share at romp's little early morning Hotel Grand breakfast. Then,O then,farewell to the sausaging sphere of patron . . . so glad you,come again
up
and(plucking hats coats,while still sitwhispering 2 hideously glare) out. Aria—
bargaining:no(says the M.D. in Russian)that's too much. A flyspecked izvostchik pleads—for himself,for himself's children,for himself's asleep horse,for himself and children and horse's Russianless Russia—"we're walking home" says the doctor. "Will you"(to me)"come with us?"

Turk "an excellent" murmurs "idea,let's all walk."

"Never" the Turkess said.

And so farewells occur and Turk and I and Turkess dangerously now sail into dark(she,by very skilfully shifting from lap to lap,balancing— often scarcely—this continually seasicking vehicle,that treacherous highbackseated jauntingless 1 car hoss)

dawn marvelous. Squalor killed;every(loom)where silhouettes extraordinary the of domes,complete(silent)ly with their feathery crosses:
life. Day
. . . "and what did the driver ask?"—"Why don't you go back to Sweden?"—"And you said?"—"Why should I go to Sweden? Then he looked at me,amazed:why what are you,he said,German? I told him we all were Americans;but he shrugged and wouldn't believe"

(in a very little downstairs room just off the coathattery)triumph cries out
and she's just found America,laid on a desk. And the cable's from her 10 year old son. Who's healthy and happy and who

(marvelling)meanwhile the(quietly)Turk stands(sharing)agreeing
(wondering)quietly with her enthusiasm.

Exists a smallish comfortable—which will be mine?—

("if you think you can possibly live in such a tiny spot. Of course
we'll have all these papers and things cleared up tomorrow;then it will
look bigger,anyway!")

em eye em ee. A deepest warmly thankfulness upclimbs through
myself . . . &

the Turkess makes its bed,despite myself's protestations—and
"behold"(elevating brilliantly striped pyjamas of immense amplitude)
Turk.

"But I'm a wolfboy—"

"what?" they both ask

"everybody in Moscow" I explain "everybody(including my former
mentor of sacred memory)doesn't know what everyone in capitalist
America has known for years:the definition of a Soviet Russian
wolfboy."

"Does a wolfboy bite?" said the Turk.

"Does he cry 'wolf wolf'?" said the Turkess.

"You're both wrong. A wolfboy" I assure them,accepting the more
and more unimaginable pyjamas with a philosophical anarchist bow "is
somebody who never wears pyjamas"

& so at twilight we 3 enter this forest;him(now and now I see the great
shoulders peacefully among leaves floating)self then her(leaping)lithe
then my(this by twigs whipped wincing)spectre. Now they're
climbing—(look)trees!are,stand;rise:now dreaming the wincing feels a
how mysterious theness of air . . . of twilight . . . of all(smells-and-selves-
and-silences)till his unself—shadow,almost which once my life lives;ghost
almost who now I merely am—pauses(with its real companions)beside
an actual tumbling nonsense of water . . .

(and 1,he,cuts living fir boughs. Which(carefully she,1,lays(all
together pointing. Shingling chosen earth)))

. . . How,after they'd gone,frightened I was:lying on a springy roof
of fragrance;how(more and more swirling)darkness with its thousand
deaths marvelously around unme(covering more and mercilessly more
my)closed(ghost with magic,very drowning skilfully my lost image
stretched on boughs . . . beautifully)alone

who this night dies.

Beautifully and who awakens(that day)to find itself,always living
beside a tiny noise of water;who—stands—is:moves. Breathing(silently
marvelling)an opened newness;called "light"

. . . ?

(Alive)

. . . Room?

but that's this tumbling

(where am I?

hark)

handorgan,unearthly ghostgod . . . into thisthat littlest yard
has(old)wandered man?capped(and bearded)overa:ndover-who,
turns;andover this-overo:vernessly & while warpedly bare(shaven)headed
look(stares)ing unboy droopstands;and. Starelook. And,see:a—
perched(over the but?differently)alive;Bird! Green,proud:

upon—sulkily by clumsy wooden authentic best maid in Moscow
served—fresh Russian eggs(3),good(and tough blackish Russian)
bread(Russian)smoothly better cheese,the(Russian)very best butter,and

United States of America coffee(2 glasses of,presented simultaneously)I very royally breakfast with very cheerful Turkess . . . breakfasting,regally inquire for mine unseen host,Turk

Turk,it seems,has been up for hours. Not only has Turk been up;he's been doing. Reading his newspapers,in fact—but not as you read(or I don't)our newspapers:for the Turk's are Russian newspapers and the Turk's reading is a duty . . . very grave duty—he,oddly enough,is the only 2legged Englishspeaking correspondent who can read a Russian newspaper in the original . . . not,of course,that doing his duty gets the Turk any particular where. Even should "news" leak into(by science knows what dreadful mistake)a Russian newspaper,the resulting "story" would surely unfail to dissatisfy al- big chief hole-in-the-forehead's mightily meticulous sense of censorship. However,comrade unseen Turk is now(in that tiny roomlet where a Transatlantic cable has found itself)reading his newsless newspapers;under the watchful(to err is human) eye of 1 ½Russian comrade secretary . . . "but" smiling "I'm not jealous"

—enter,radiating those rarest rays:good & nature,he.

"But I don't want one" she protests.

"You must take it."

"There isn't time—"

"I know. But there's one there."

"Why don't You take it?"

"I've taken mine" he protests "while you were snoozing;I'll be lynched if I take yours" he adds genially.

"But you know that it's not my fault if—"

"Woman" he cries,smiting his chest "—would you break our bourgeois household into Marxian fragments? Take it . . . and hurry."

She sighs. "The eternal problem."

"What?" I uncautiously demand

he whispers("—solved!")giving her a twinkle . . . "solved—!" she nods,happily smiling. Both rescuedfully observe me. "That is—if he'll accept our solution" Turk adds. "Why don't you ask him?" she asks.

I stare.

"Will you perhaps" to comrade myself "do us a supreme,a really prodigious,favour?"

With scaffoldsmirk "please" I reply.

("Ask him" blushingly she encourages)

blushing "you must know" Turk confesses "that this apparently spontaneous lovenest is actually dominated by an ogress—"

"absolutely" she corroborates

"—which monster,being of Czarist Russian peasant extraction—"

"and unutterably devoted to her employers"

"—brutally insists that,come what may,willynilly,at least twice—"

"not counting her own" Turkess

"—a certain ceremony should be consummated" blushful the Turk continues

"every day" she

"right. Now since(one)I have long ago taken mine and(two)my spouse refuses to take hers(three)will you take it?"

"If you don't take it,she'll go cuckoo" the Turkess said,seriously.

". . ."(Meaning hot). Drops blunt paw on a starry faucet.

"Da" I nod.

". . ."(Meaning cold)dropping another blunter on another starrier.

"Dada" nodnod.

Bluntest points:to the very longest artificial womb in the world or unworld

I "dadada" nodnodnod

—abruptly clumsiness chucks sickly wood into sulkily grumbling furnace of primitive heating machine:shuts off Meaning cold(which I'd turned on)horribly scowls;growls:—& in a cloud of steam vanishes

. . . please leaving as clean as didn't expect to find the imperial tub of Chinesey's palatial mansion,but only after much vivid of it scrubbing(this is my 1st regular ablution since socialism,for a bath at the Hotel Metropole easily transcends our heroless means)I,considerably weakened,pass faintly Elsewhereish nonman;staggering,graze dimly crouching millenial crone—housekeeper?—who burgeons rubbery disgustful mistrusting frown. But

"your latchkey" presents hurrying Turkess and "—please have dinner with us here if you're not already dated up" . . . she disappears with adieuwaving Turk

(latchkey?not,perchance,really and truly a latchkey? Noyes? Well,I'll try it;to make sure—)

"wawz eet nawt shutt,thee dough are?"

(—spin:confronting pallid funnily attired wouldbeladyish à l'américaine but somebody else's . . . probably it's unRussian ½ of 1 ½Russian secretary)mumble something. Flee

Club of Writers:nobody
   et comment

INTOURIST(nothing for either Kem-min-kz or Cummings,as usual). And,as usual,naturally:considering that all letters and cables etc. are slapped into wideopen pigeonholes where a little child could reach them and moreover anyone in Moscowless Moscow momentarily who is wasting his or her 5 day week stands dismally around busily shuffling somebody else's foreign correspondence.

   Now I'll move

at capitalist keydesk suddenly(appearing out of the usual nowhere)accosts me livid tactician;militarily(and sombrero and raincoat)with myselfless now who mounts,luxuriously inbreathing a priceless camel . . . but(as unusual)there's a reason:I remembered flowerbuyer;livid finally got him for me,now I'm supposed in the French language to come right over.

   "We" grunts still(livid)breathing "shall also look Under everything" and "these in Russia you must not leave" sombrely affirms;producing goofey Parisian boteenkee which somehow escaped our comrade notice

   "thanks"(reopening valise,incramming shoes,jumping on sum total).

   Peacefully—nay;comfortably almost—the tactician "and so,involuntarily,I participate in your leaving" muses . . .

   "What" proudly sitting on shut total "is new?" I ask.

   "Not anything" livid said darkly. ". . . Your comrade" naming exmentor "will miss you" slyly.

   "Not anything at all?"

   "And I—I too—shall miss you" cannily livid pursues,staring cockeyedly at the camel's rear end. "Fortunately,though,I have your new address." He sighs "and,believe me,I shall call very soon,to take you to the country."

   "That's most kind" rising.

"—The communists" rising he said "have imposed a government on the Russian people. We are sterile,at the bottom"(snapping into humanity's sloppail a merely exmy butt)"but" distantly "time will cure this"

down "goodbye"

.

. . . "I'm leaving in an hour" tell the ghost-in-charge;it,boosting 1 weary eye,replies:Good

comrade flowerbuyer's personal portal is,like Madame Potiphar's,ornately leatherish. Hesitatingly am admitted to a branching of overfurnished (semivisible)roomlets;my admitress retires fearingly. Nonmen suspiciously peep at heroless. Fearlessly returning,admitress now graciously ushers guest up a brandnew flight of shiny stairs to—

the master himself . . . & bows me in

lighttoned "studio" room;acreep with sunight. Everywhere quaintly cluttering knicknacks. Silence. The sense,smell almost,of something frail and disappointed.

"Ça sent l'espace"(I say;standing on a tiny porch and looking down over gardens,earth,wheres,children peacefully sitting under trees)it's space we need

(and he hasn't opened the box of chocolates;the gift of his Russian-living-in-Paris friend,which I've somehow remembered to bring. He has daintily,almost sacredly,thanked me;put it aside).

Our verily conversation bore an imperfectly negative relation to a perfectly positive fact—each of us understands the other without conversing . . . Each of us holds socalled "art"(or whatever actually is)beyond "humanity",or whatever really means. Yet each of us(according to his skill)faithfully for almost an hour played the gameless game of ideas:played the gameless sociological-political game which I've already— given how different circumstances!—played very badly And How with Messers unhe and Jack . . . I begin seriously to wonder if noone in Russia must actually be near anyone,if everyone must from everyone else keep that meaningly infinite distance known as Altruism

—&(for instance)

he says that the soviets take good care of Russian writers(i.e.prominent writers,i.e.himself)who automatically are either paid a lump sum upon delivery of a manuscript or receive an advance by installments;and he says(for instance)that Russian writers may travel(let's hope it's not via roubles!)"comme ils veulent" in foreign lands(provided,of course,they receive their passports). Also,re his living-in-Paris friend-writer,he dismally avers it's too late.—What's too late?I inquire.—He(says flowerbuyer)never can use a Russian theme again;for whoso absents himself from home during Russia's true crisis may not thereafter return:which makes the comrade in question doomed.—Doomed? "Pourquoi?"— "Parce qu'il a l'âme russe";he has what you(meaning me)couldn't possibly understand unless you stayed here a long time;and even then,you,having a European "âme",couldn't possibly write more than a very few books about Russia. (A miracle! "Soul" is spoken with incredible naturalness;quite as if our little friend Behaviourism didn't exist)

(for instance)when I inquire about a city called Kiev—"O,que c'est belle!"(involuntarily. Then)but it's only the old Russia. (Calmly) interesting? O yes. There are catacombs;wherein,against windows,you perceive extraordinary mummies,of sundry colours. (Timidly)I'll give you a letter to a "très belle femme" who lives there,only I don't know whether she's there now,nor do I know whether she speaks anything but Russian. (Grimly)travelling alone will be hard for you if you don't speak Russian . . . of course the Russians used to speak French,but now—(and suddenly wrenching once more out of himself)please don't forget,when you tell of your experiences here,to mention that we Russian writers are regularly addressed by experts,each expert being the most prominent member of his profession;and don't forget to mention that we Russian writers are given free seats in aeroplanes,and that we Russian writers fly for nothing all over Russia,wherever there are aviation routes . . . (I promise). . . . Come again,come tomorrow evening;tell your host(i.e. Turk)"et sa femme" to also do me the honour to come,if they will . . . "à demain"

"May I have my bill,please?"

Foxy(in the usual spectacles)Grandpa regards benevolently my pomum Adami. "Now?"

"an hour ago I told you I was leaving in an hour."

Nods,sagely—then(scratching an earless)contemplates the billdesk. "Shchot!" Foxy cries. 2 soggy comrades at the billdesk pay no attention:1 continues to thumb hundreds of filthy roublerugs,1 continues to watch 1 thumbing.

"SHCHOT!" cries Grandpa in a terrible voice.

No response.

"Hm" he remarked. Strolling vaguely to billdesk, languidly between the comrades' legs groped. Returning with an almost large bit of whiteness "hm." 8½ days. 4 at $5 = $20. 4½ at $4 = $18. "Hm."

I produce my Pay To The Order Ofs; follow vaguely toward comrades wandering Foxy. "Please, a fifty"(I give). He gives to comrades. Also bill. And vaguely toward the keydesk isn't . . .

. . . the(having, perhaps, counted to 10,000)roublethumber soggily stuffs his rugs away. Sighing, begins worrying over my bill. Sighing, abacusses my bill. Sighing, cries out faintly for Foxy Grandpa—who is . . . Yes the bill's too little "you can count it if you like"(not that comrade I could ever count anything!) Pause. "Sohrok syem" announce, at random

billdesker smiles tiredly. Now he begins busily to worry about the exact change which is due me, the somehow certain amount of roubleless roubles. Pause. And worries. I helplessly drift to Foxy's desk; I helplessly yield my new location, I helplessly inquire about conveyances "what's cheapest?"

"well" F. Grandpa hms "the taxi cheapest, impossible to get. Next" he adds semimysteriously frowning "our taxi."

"How much your taxi?"

scowling, F. profoundly surveys(through-under-over his usuals)me. Then(and then only)awfully, unluminously "you are one?"

bravely "one" I admit.

"Two" said Foxy "dollar."

"Hm" I hm

"izvostchik" lightly he murmurs "charge you six, eight, rouble." Pause.

"I'll take your taxi" I hazard.

—Put two roubles on his shchot!(F.G. shouts in Russian). The billdesk comrade groans. Groaning, he indites a new receipt; he soggily shoves it at me; wearily he garners newly roubles. Sighing, he rebegins abacussing . . . after perhaps 10 minutes he abacusses 20 and 20 and says Ten . . . finally, sighing he countes out an unco few coinless sickle-and-hammer contentedlys. I(amazed)recoil upon Grandpa—who's now all warm and troubled persuading this total knockkneed stranger that "here, foreigner hotel; you, pay valyootah" (that unambiguous catastrophe!)

"I'll go up and get my bags now" shout

but(up through over under staring)he protests "taxi not here yet!"

"make it come here,will you please" I groan.

"I telephone you when it come" he wailed.

Pause.

. . . Up

out

—sit. Rather winsomely pondering l'âme russe. Rather winsomely
¹/₅smoking perhaps the vilest cigarette on ¹/₆ of the earth;purchased
last night at Arbat . . . "No,sir,taxi not yet"(telephone replies).—"I'm
in a terrible hurry" self truthfully telephones,gently.—"What,sir?"—
"I'm;in;a;great;hurry" très pleadingly.—Pause "all right,sir,I go out and
see;and if taxi not here I get carriage,yes?"

knock

waiter & ("klootch,pahzhahloostah")maid. He grabs valise plucks
typewriter nabs knapsack. I open her with a look,I close her with a

Please(meaning thanks)

rouble

Thanks(meaning don't mention it)

& somehow turning now just happen miraculously to glimpse my
only soi-disant overcoat—almost which is trying so hard to look like
me that it's gone and hung itself on a hookless. Seize. Descend . . .
prophetically fishing out $2 receipt . . . into

Foxy—beside whom slouches a sensitive(perhaps mechanic?)looking
comrade

"no,sir" very distantly spectacles respond "taxi did not come. I have
get carriage"

"yes,but you see" winsome "I've already paid two" sighing "dollars
for your taxi" softly I remind him.

"Now?" incredulous.

"Well,perhaps all of twenty minutes ago."

"Hm." (He nods painfully;groans,and at comrade oblivious billdesk
yells)give him!—but I . . . am looking,looking at sensitivelooking . . .
Grandpa fol,follo,following my looking encounters and meets and
sees(through Grandpa's comrade usuals)1 comrade head,1 comrade
neck,1 comrade torso . . . "AHHHH"—with a kind of ecstacy;perhaps
the ecstacy of Columbus discovering mutiny—"he come!"

thereupon exeunt. Promptly sensitive skips to wheel of a spic

Metropole Model A. Unpromptly Columbus respectfully whispers my new address . . . hovers . . . hopeless,recedes. And now occurs prodigy unsurpassed:now I hand the waiterless 1 roubleless;and behold the waiterless(I shall not forget)actually is pleased

& up now pullulating Petrovsky(screaeaeaming)flagship swirls up (screaeaeaeaming)up
   this time others are jumping,I'm riding.
   Yes,and although it's really my 2nd socialist taxi it's truly my 1st soviet joyride;for,quite unlike unhe's chauffeur,sensitive has 1strate machinery at sensitive's playful beck
   —and leap un- shrink thighs dart feet jump legs hop arms dash(out of)Else(shaken)whereish corpses & for very nonlifelessness frenziedly (undivelessing)dive . . .
   ah,if I could have pronounced There or said Stop or even remembered the Russianless for Number 8 . . . nevertheless,and aided by lazily sidewalkdusting comrade,we("dadada")arrive . . . Ah,what transformation of comrade sensitive! Speed,the by all morons worshipped(each according to his skill)undaemon,almost him has metamorphosed into an if not quite American!which glares,when bestirring itself to extent of pushing my lightest piece of baggage meward. Which glowers,when pocketing far from tipless tip. Which(lunging down among cushioned)jams,fiercely into;low—spurts:wreNChing vio(screa)lent(ming)ly

yes. Yes,that's a latchkey
   wooden,via pulpy lingo,tells(unassisting sulkily)that neither hostess nor host are "dohmah."
   When dinner?(I sweating,lugging,venture).
   "Shest"(offlumbering the ogress growls).
   —A cry. Cries . . . the ecstatic Turkess caracoles inward;seconded by drifting unhurryingly beaming Turk(weirdly whose life is framed by threatening shapes,who wonderfully sprouts purchases,objects, treasures,items). Foremost whereof,and never to be forgotten:this most deliberate collection of intensities,organically these unmeanings carved into warm ivory and which most suddenly turn time trivial and machinery idiotic and communes common—this most leastful chessset;how which fills an immediately peculiar room with deep blossoming aesthesia . . . Now,O now,almost I begin to live that differing $\frac{1}{6}$ of world for whose new

mysteries myselfless quit mysteries experienced,myself fled the smellsounds of mai;that ⅙ who until now hid from me herself under what imitated samenesses of echoful industrialism(a rose by any other name)under what ponderous wheelwhir of the most ignoble ravenous "equality"

. . . while,in bourgeois tranquility of a(darkened,not to make it smaller but to make us nearer)room,comfortably 3 comrades sit at their meat and at their drink—while 3(sternly by ogress guarded lest any fail to annihilate her or his capitalist viands)children of luxury and despair enjoy leisure—can't help wondering how much longer the more chessconscious parts of this worldless world will play,for some reasonless reason or(such as fear)unreason,checkers with themselves;can't help wondering how much longer intuition will submit to ideas,human beings will bow before humanity

the Turkess & the Turk are departing for a theatre.

Now I am(whose implacably negative definition of poetry equals: whatever cannot be translated!)trying less to "translate" an occasionally not poemless "poem"(mostly a hyper2fisted supergogetting ultrared-blooded certificate of Mme. P.'s soeur's mari's conversion And How)than to possibly salve my New England conscience,re Revolutionary Literature Bureau alias Jill Jack and Otto,Inc.

"cheye hahteetyeh?"

ogress.

"Nyet—"

who whereupon looks so especially destructive that I instinctively understand her query.

"—Da"

renig. Appear twain(simultaneously)glasses of steaming tea

(knock)

as begin the delicious number dvah:

"might I" a bourgeois head beams "suggest some more possibly alcoholic beverage?"

"you might,tovarich."

"With comrade Kem-min-kz's permission we'll step around the" Turk suggests "corner to a socalled stohlohveyeah of note"

and "but the real reason for this régime's" smiling "existence is that everybody" 2 comrades are moving "here has had enough of war. Not

140

long ago I was strolling" moving "this very street with a fine woman;and a hooligan passed. And she jumped:so I asked her why she was frightened? I said 'I'm here,and if I couldn't handle him we'd call a militiaman.' And the woman told me 'yes;I know it's senseless—but I was thinking of the time they put a revolver to us and made us lie down for them'"

sits(bored)in that shoddy dump(frankly)hard by this dead evergreen tree,Turkess. Opposite,1 semimiddleaged demifairy with a pleasant(almost infantile)smile and an absolutely unmistakable Southern accent and pink flesh and strong eyes.

"I gen'r'lly"(he compliments me on my 1st)"f'rget books" . . .

genially dogmatic "why,th' m'jor'ty hates th' present gov'rnment like poison—why,th' workers are throwin' monkeywrenches into th' machines—why,th' biggest Russian tractor plant only makes two tractors a day but does that affect th' propaganda?—not a mite:th' party-members go right on congratulatin' each other in flowery terms and talkin' about Immense Industrial Gains and readin' off a million statistics t' prove that two hundred tractors will be manufactured ev'ry hour only three thousand hours from now!" He grinlaughed bitterly

seriously "Russians" and slowly remarks Turk "often confuse desire with achievement. Besides,they're not used to machines . . . it took even us quite a time,you know—"

Dogmatic barks. "Looka that feller over there with a head without a back,that's who's supposed t' govern this country an'"(Turk's Assyrian dome crisps)"how can he,I'd like t' know?"

"Isn't there any single redeeming feature?" I timorously inquire.

"No" snaps genial.

"Yes there is" Assyrian quietly contradicts "the idea's right;the means of carrying out the idea are wrong—"

"Pfg!" semidemi,indignantly.

"What" I ask "idea?"

"The idea" Turk explains "of greater individuality."

"Greater Garbo" snorts omnipotent.

"The idea" explains Turk "that if everybody has to work only twenty minutes a day there'll be more leisure,which will enable more people to experience the socalled finer things of life,which will result in more individuals—"

"yeeeruh" sneers almighty. "And what's been the effect o' that idea? Huh? How's it worked out? Eh?" leaning forward

"the effect of its application has been" Turk almost silently stated "more disastrous to Russia than was the tyranny of Peter the Great."

Satisfied,backleaning "you said it!"

"I say it" Turk confirms "but I don't say it gladly."

The other shrugs. "Le's all have another beer" grinning "not that it's beer."

"You mean" I venture "that socalled progress has not occurred, after all?"

almost blushing "a prodigious regression" Assyrian answers.

Peevohs

smacking pale lips "lis'n t' this one:there's a wom'n hodcarrier(I m'self pers'n'lly investigated her)with a drunk'n husband an' chil'ren. He keeps gettin' DTs so he's sick all th' time. She keeps s'pportin' him 'cause she can't d'vorce him 'cause he's sick all th' time. Some system,eh?"

"she can't divorce him?"

"a Russian woman" Turk placidly explains "can't divorce a Russian man if he's sick—"

"—an' if she can d'vorce him she's gotta pay al'mony t' help s'pport th' chil'ren" genial chuckles. (Nudging Turkess)"you wouldn' like that,huh?"

"No" calmly Turkess states "I wouldn't like that."

"Lis'n—I wanta tell y' 'bout my cat" suddenly pleads this peevoh-enlivened fountain of disillusionment. "Can I?"

Assyrian laughed. "If the party says it's a cat in good stand-"

"to hell with th' party!" he shouts. Staring around him,fiercely he fixed with glittering orbs an innocent comrade sitting with a sunken nonman(both cringe. Waiters pale,shift,wilt). Satisfied,grins;sprawling, lordly "—lis'n. This one's good:I gotta mighty temp'rment'l cat. Been gettin' milk an' I gave her meat an' she wouldn' eat th' meat so I gave her a kick in th' backside. Some cat. Well one day she had a kitt'n—just one kitt'n(that's how temp'rment'l She is)—an' that ole dev'l wanted t' come into th' parlour with that kitt'n;so I chased her th' hell out an' threw ev'rything 'cept th' typewriter at 'er. Well—lis'n— nex' mornin,I was sittin' in my study with my translat'r"

"who,by the way,is an Indian" Turk twinkles

"—yes an' a dam good Indian,too:god knows what I'd do without him!" glaring "this dam lingo sure is too much for any white man" god avows "— well,I was sittin' there workin' and mindin' the world's business when . . . what d' y' s'ppose?"

aimiably "what" Turk queries.

"Th' door op'ns" said almighty "an' in stalks my dam cat with that dam kitt'n clasped in her mouth."

"Nooo!" cries Turk,alarmed.

"Honest t' god. An'—lis'n—she goes straight over t' my chair,an' she jumps right up in my chair an' lays down th' kitt'n right in th' dam middle o' that dam chair o' mine."

"Impossible" Turkess cries.

"Swear t' god it's true. An' d' y' know why that old dev'l did it?" we all shake comrade heads

"that" he(twisting impotently)whines "was her dam Russian way o' showin' ev'ryone c'ncerned who was respons'ble!"

"responsible?" Turkess

"for th' kitt'n" god. Swinging—"PEE-VOH!" bellows:

—scared,the(here there ½drowsing)waiters up-in-out-down jumpleapflick into various directions;almost colliding,hither whither who(darting)everywhere sprint like minnows . . . & balefully,& bigfish ishly,he(squinting through this little room's dead submarine undepth)

"yeeruh" sneers:grins "niggers!" And amiably,if contemptously,addressing the nervous left-and-right-lurking comrades "you-all got th' slave in you. —Niggers. I know." (3 boys of perhaps 18,haggard and slipshod,creep Russianly across the seafloor . . . gradually arrive behind bigfish—)

"yeeruh" casually ½turning to confront with cool insolence trio "slaves. Niggers" . . . scared,hating,they cringe;trembling,recede. Over-each-other-tripping disappear. "You-all get on my nerves" he snarled.

"Why" Turk,gently.

"I know why. Durin' th' civ'l war my gran'fath'r bought himself a subst'tute"(the weakly face soured)"that"(it squirmed)"I always r'garded as a spot upon our wellknown escutcheon." Pause

Turkess to Turk smiles

"that ole dev'l lived t' be a hundred" god dreamily murmurs . . .

("by the way;give me your American passport and your Russian birth-certificate" the Turk directs "and I'll have comrade Kem-min-kz properly registered at his new address . . . it's the better part of valour." I give) "shall we—" Turkess nods toward doorless

"—MY check" quickly god snatched. "Here"—shoving rugroubles to nearest cringing. Then "lis'n:the oth'r day I said to a Russian,I said Why is it that nobody ever laughs around here?"

struggling from a dead evergreen "well?" Turkess encourages.

"Really" rising god affirms "I did."

"What did the Russian answer?"

"Yes,but don' f'get that th' Russians have nev'r had anything t' laugh about." He laughed,tottering

goodnight gentlemen,goodnight lady,goodnight,call again— obsequious bows,insidious smirks:4 capitalist(3 unbeerfully)comrades move

"and that reminds me of" remembering flowerbuyer myself says "what a Russian remarked the other day:The eyes(he said)of the Russians are sad,but they're eyes which think"

"—Pff!—" god scoffs "G' night. —Come 'roun' an' see me soon, writ'r!"

sick?
    change of address?
        Russian censor . . . ?
This is getting troppo paranoid for words.
    (Hope to god I find a letter soon)

after de luxe breakfast,the Turkess begins frankly discussing "my dad". . . a name with which,owing to 1 seayarn greatly consumed during childhood,have associated free-and-easy hale-and-hearty rough-and-tumble devilmaycareness. He seems,alas,to have been somebody very much afraid of himself(whom he therefore made the mistake of taking seriously). I am even led to believe that nothing in this celebrity's life became him like a meticulous exposé of sadistic vices enjoyed by animal trainers;also that his later years were swathed in obstreperously negative luxuries of most sheer frustration . . . Hastily when she adds "I'm going to write a book some day with" Turk,unhastily I excuse myself;now is perhaps the timeless time to tackle Otto Can't's giftless gift

HE PUT ON A STARCHED COLLAR

    "there are cigaretteholders between cigarette and man"—. Correct. Machinemade "civilization" isolates every human being from experience(that is,from himself)by teaching mankind to mistake a mere gadgety interpretation(e.g. the weatherman's prediction)of experience for experience itself(e.g. weather)
    "worldliness . . . delicacy"—. He doesn't like them;probably because they're as overrated in Europe as are pigheadedness and insolence in America(by the way,he's never visited America)
    everything's "advertising"—. Right. The "modern man" equals a defenceless literate bombarded with slogans mottoes pictures and whatever else will tend to unmake him;i.e. make him need something unnecessary
    "how sweet is the groan which comes from ruins"—. Bullshit
    "the bursting of gunfire adds a hitherto unknown gaiety to the landscape"—. If you're not within range. If you are,you'll be apt to accept even communism rather than endure that same gaiety

"hail to materialist dialectic and its incarnation,the red army"—. Anciently,de gustibus;or as(anent "modern art")Professor Bliss Perry of Harvard used to chuckle "it's all right if you like it"

"spare nothing"—. Nyet. Hardboiledness is dull
dressez-vous contre vos mères—. See complex,Oedipus

"the most beautiful structure isn't worth the splendid and chaotic heap which is easily produced by a church and some dynamite"— Untrue. Dynamite,however,is an easier vocation than poetry

"abandon night pestilence and the family . . . you are holding in your hands a laughing child . . . a child such as has never been seen . . . he knows beforehand how to speak,all the songs of the new life"—. And let's hope he also knows that all the microtelescopically rhetorical optipessimism of any premeditatedly Un(or possible)world may not catalyze 1 spontaneously singular impossibility or(shall we say)workofart

"a star is born on earth"—. Very neat;the "star" being Russia's cross

"dawn rises over the salles de bains"—. Fact. And over a great many other things,cher maître;for wonderfully dawn,unlike the propagandist, and like the poet,is no snob

"history led on leash by the third international"—. Also,muzzled

(and now,comrades,we come to this paean's infantile climax:now the language,fairly wetting its drawers,begins achugging and apuffing—"all aboard!" the paeaner now ecstatically cries—"everybody jump on the red train!"(alias,N.B.,the bandwagon)—"nobody will be left behind!"(and of course Prosperity is just around the Corner)—U-S-S-R,choo-choo-choo-choo(your name's in the paper)wake up and dream(let's all get arrested)Pippa passes the buck

P.S.—HE GOT THE JOB

interrupting above translatory labours,Turk
"this is my secretary"
(but not the ½Russian à l'américaine;far from it. A RussianPlus nongal, somewhat undersized,almost intelligent,very much on guard;speaks immaculate English. And horribly whom twitchjerk-yankplucks compulsive nodding).

"There occurred,not long ago,a really touching scene" leads Assyrian "when a Russian battleship,having saluted an English battleship,was in turn saluted." And gently through paneless panes at rain staring "the communists wept and kissed"

Silence.

Pause. Then

"will you(tic)please(tic)give me five or(tic)even six roubles(tic) for(tic)your pass(tic)port?" tic tocs.

"Please" I do so . . .

"you know" Turk amiably releads "there's a fascinating old folk tale about the origin of the word 'cuckoo' . . . " and that fascinating old folk tale fascinatingly retells itself—

"are(tic)you not in(tic)terested,please(tic),in Russia's(tic toc)industry?" toc asks me suddenly.

"But as an American,I've seen industry before" confess.

"Yes(tic)?"

"never shall I forget watching the first automobile try—over and over and over again—to climb the steepest hill."

"(Tictoctic)yes?"

"a onelung Cadillac,nothing less."

"Did it succeed?" Turk asks,twinkling

"no"

"—you(toctic)felt yourself ex(tic)cited?"

"very much excited. Perhaps even as excited as a Russian peasant of today confronted by his first Ford tractor."

Pause. Silence. Tic.

"I(tic)was walk(tic)ing in the park(tic)here(tic)and I heard a speech(tictic)—before,said(tic)a worker to another(tictictic)worker,these parks were(tic)for(toc)indi(tictoc)vidualist couples(toctic);now(toc)they are for only(toctocticketytoc)collectivist couples—"

marvelously,his soul opening,laughing "hahrahshoh!" cries Assyrian.

"Yes(tic)" toc confused said "re(tic)ally!"

& tim(at Turk,at me)idly al(not quite)most smi(tic)les

et il pleut.

Ogress frowning demands her technical lord's whereabouts,yah

"nyet" pointing(through paneless)to rain;busily making the walksign. She scowls,hesitating

—"may I come in?" incoming Englishly blueshirted cleancut youthful completely enclosed by(1)Oxford accent and(2)friendofthefamily manner

"they're both out. He said he'd be back at five" I very cautiously explain.

Dripping "five,eh:thanks old man:cheerio!"

exit. Who? But this is Russia . . .

lock my suitcase. Don overcoatless and my cap and(verifying nonabsence of latchkey)fare forth,into

il pleut. (Walk). Air very hot. People a little smaller than usual perhaps. The doorless doors of INTOURIST are shut and locked;foiled I note comrades sitting(chatting)just inside:tantalized I observe ecstatic nonman actually gripping a big letter. Neechehvoh nyet . . . invade Metropole

keydesk comrade nyeh gahvahreet,waves me to maindesk comrade who's(luckily)comrade DAwailer . . . not at all disagreeably who stops DAwailing,just long enough to very personally superintend a desperate inspection of capitalist hostelry's daily correspondence. It all seems to be for the Bs—all,that is,until(And How firmly)I absolutely insist on seeing the Cs . . . that mighty deluge of Cohns and Cohens

(damnation)

whereupon,for innumerable unreasons,or because my name begins with what in Russia is an S or because my name is spelled by Russians with a K or nobody loves me or my hands are etc.,comradeless Cummings cordially hates the Soviet postal systemless

frankly it's a wonder he didn't imagine me a victim of the Gay-Pay-Oo. Lo—at precise moment of my dripping arrival chez(wipe your)Turk—up 1 gagging droshky reels and out 2 Englishspeaking spew unknowns(just behind myself who enter,staringly also who mount marble somethings . . . very mysteriously who salute a suddenly appearing negress. She joins the pair. All 3(still staring)threaten Chinesey's lofty quarters. (Upon downstairs breakfasttable are accusingly Turkess's gloves)

et j'ai faim!

voices aloft,chez Chinesey. A dishrattling. Foodfragrance drifts. And should I go up? And no. And why not? And because I wasn't invited. (Yes,but my not being invited may be a specimen of Russian confusion—or possibly of American indifference—or maybe something to do with the factless that those gloves' owner was depressed this morning;or that,after she had mysteriously outgone with tictoc,the twinkling

"it's his vacation" Turk whispers.

"Your secretary's?"

nod,not tic. "And how do you suppose he's going to spend it?"

"God knows."

"As a shockbrigader." Seriously "that poor little overworked devil is leaving Moscow for points uncouth,and(believe it or not)he'll spend his playtime putting the Marxian urge into motheaten kulaks"

"Jesus Christ" I marvel

"you often hear" organizes leisurely he "that in Russia nobody is without work. Often you don't hear that,in Russia,everybody's leisure is organized")

Writers'. Downstairs:president,emulsed with 4 comrades. Lonesomely I buy 25 Nords for 3 roubles. Timidly I touch president on shoulderless—guiltily who starts up,guiltily grins;guiltily chatters:they'll make an exception,they'll have me in at a conference on the 24th,would I like to participate in the Gorky evening tomorrow,if so will I please be here at 5 P.M. to meet the great tovarich Gorky himself(etc. but enter several obviously hungry comrade clubmembers;hugely which cheers me,who'd previously asked the president's comrade permission to join a group of guzzling busily comrade obviously waiters . . . did he look dubious! Now,by Pavlov,I'll eat! By peevoh,I'll drink!

"c'est—"(naming hushfully Something,of Something Theatre)coos Writers' President(indicating prayerfully 1 of foodbents)"vous voulez faire sa connaisance?" But,And How dubious "je ne sais pas s'il parle français . . ."

My friend the sculptor,the man who gave me a letter which I left for — ,assured me many times that both — and Madame — speak French(wearily now I counter)

Hm. We'll see . . . (and aflutter returning)"il voudrait vous voir demain soir à six heures!" handing me utterly most terrifying address never had seen in a comrade life. Times,with an almost tender solicitude "mangez maintenant" . . . yea;and himself cordially now orders me ham mit beer for 8 roubles(and "non non—seulement trente kopeks pourboire,ça suffit"). Every cloud has a silver lining. A man is known by the company he keeps. Triumphantly then arises comrade erstwhile Nemo;shakes a swift dayday at highly respectable comrade president; slowly wanders toward comrade "petit bourgeois" companion of the way flower(tell it not)buyer

the admitress recognises. But I must wait until she properly warns the master. Down properly who comes
"où sont nos amis?"
(flurried):I gave them your message,I ate dinner alone—
& we climb to knicknack lodge:where "répond pass"(hanging up receiver of telephoneless:where he drags 2 chairs,a huge and a tiny,out upon porch. Waves me into huge,droops into tiny:looks;at the whitely raining buds of a tree. And he now smiles,whispering
"peuplier")
and I sit,breathing Spring twi(after rain)light:
"ils viennent!"(phoneless worked,that time)—they left their house only 15 minutes ago,comrade.
—"Didn't you get my note? In red pencil? I put it on the desk" Turkess
—"our ogress faithfully hunted all over for you" Turk. "A great American industrial was upstairs. You'd really have been amused by him,I think:ten times as enthusiastic as the most ardent shockbrigader of them all;has thirty times as much pep and he'll never see fifty again."
"Look" I(prestidigitator)—emanating frayed visitingcard
"why,it's his son!" Turk-Turkess cries. "How did you—?"
"once upon a time I was honeymooning. The boat was Dutch and no bigger than a pickle. We found a baby with a woman and the baby told the woman about life and death and also Russia—"
"his son's wife!" they amaze.
"And the woman confided in us. The pickle,I'm sorry to say,ended when it got to where it was going—"
"encore une chaise!" ⅞ of sofa hides twittering ⅓ frenziedly flowerbuyer
. . . yes how glad is(to see a very charming lady)Soviet Russia's gallant poet-novelist! Split,skies;rain down your stars—drop,moon,into her beauteous lap—sing,you birds of the night,for Life is born again! For hope is born,wish is born,and laughing,and poetry;and this(eyes which

think)master-of-masterlessness feels,almost(and his castle's formerly something-disappointed almost-fragrance vanishes before what entering everywhere invisibly flowers—

yes & now for its lifeless leaps the fearing ghost of disillusion!)

even these knicknacks move;are magic—now I'm even told to pick up the receiver of a hitherto unnoticed extra telephone(and suddenly little doors fly open and begins frondish dim tinkling song!) Look:even a clock,performing tricks solemnly!solemnly this lion's mouth spouting. Try,please,that snuffbox(there will out come,into how more than nothing there will disappear,exquisitely excellent Dreambird!)

yes & eat & drink & be merry!for even Friendship's here—for suspicion has fled,fled with theories:nobody's even dreading anybody now,everybody understands everybody now and everybody is alive! Yes;vodka,more vodka,most vodka;white and red wine and saki and a specially prepared burntsugar punch of the master's own . . . Eat,drink! And eggs and fish and salad with truffles and most more much more mostness until especially these(sacredly,proudly)emanated teacups cautiously shall fill,carefully to all the reeling guests transport,1 trembling(this most adoring)nonman-comrade-bigeyed-maid. "Vous voulez du tabac?"—(look)from silver box with(see)two openings:a small which shows itself to you;a big which keeps itself for me! And O that's the way people really are;that's just why people actually aren't for us,who really aren't people ever any more—we,possibly until who die(probably until tomorrow?)entirely—and even perhaps beautifully(laughing wishing hoping living)—who now are Friends!

Friends!—

. . . Turk and Turkess sprawl-droop,exallhausted

friends!

then the flowerbuyer winks,smiles,points . . . "WE ANSWER EVERY LETTER" hugely boomjets unvoice from wall . . . O,just another trick!—just "science" this last time! Just dear fine old Santa Claus science,quickly stepping from the sweet old unchimney of nice old human credulity to fill all the good old little believing nonchildren's shoes and stockings and even heads with(now it's Russian . . . now it's the International)—now he sits—back toward us—with earpieces at his ears—trying to connect with a conference(which isn't somewhere taking probably placeless)

now,toward morning,I find myself seated opposite(look)1

opendoor-framed warmful slenderlyness. Flowerlike who(without
saying)speaks,Is
   "est-ce-qu'elle est vraie?" whisper
   he,turning "qui?" rises
   —"la lune" I point—
   . . . & wonderingly l'âme russe,smiling
   "oui"

"If they should allow us(because we've been good children)to play tourist today,would you care to grace the company with your distinguished presence?"

"I should more than care,comrade."

"Volks" the Turk said "is earth's most inefficient disorganization. For weeks and weeks my semiRussian secretary has been trying to establish something like human relations with Volks. Over and over she's told them that we'd humbly accept any one of several tours—the Kremlin (where the government's kept)or divorcecourts(where marriages are made in heaven)or even a jail. But whenever open covenants were openly arrived at,the whole damned thing secretly fell through. Nevertheless she claims that today we've a fairly good chance of making it—"

"the Kremlin?" Turkess asked,excitedly.

"Nooo."

"Divorcecourt?"

"nooo."

"In other words" Lack Dungeon's charming(if disappointed)daughter said "a jail."

"Did I say a jail,my dear?" Turk beams "—a thousand pardons. What we're going to see is a blossoming branch of the socialist soviet society for prevention of cruelty to criminals"

neither at INTOURIST nor at Metropole exist letters—is,precisely,the letter. I've(even in French)asked,chez former,if there's possibly any hidden endroit where mailless mail might conceive itself:nyet. Even in Russian(?)I've superintended,chez latter,the searchful(dismally groping through always more Cohens and Cohns not to mention Kohns)searchless

Moscow today is very hot . . . & returning,via worn earth feebly unfunctioning as park,perceive white here and there flowers . . .

4 comrades move:Turk and Turkess;½(cautiously not,today,à l'américaine)Russian whose name appears to be "Nat",and nonself. Long

stinking tramride. Short burning walk. We corner a corner:we behold an ordinary house—no sign of bars or cops or black marias:we unmolestedly enter a peaceful(almost)kind of anteroomparlour

—where prowls,by heaven,Grouch;still à la russe,but wearing capitalist overcoat on 1 socialist arm:beside him,but not today scratching,Scratch meanders

"good for you!" she said sincerely,when I told her my new address. "That's the stuff!" he admires(also graciously;if somewhat grimly).

"Are we anywhere near Volks?" whisper,avoiding an armless mantlepieced ⅓ of John Dewey,Esq.

the Inc chortles—"and where do you think you are now?"

"in a socialist jail. No?"

"No,comrade. At least,not exactly. This is Volks"

staggering "and this is" I gasp "my benefactress" presenting Turkess;who bows and "look" points. Poster:2 + 2 = 5 . . . (meaning? Meaning impossibly). Possibly meaning that the 5 year plan will achieve itself in—

Assyrian escorts me,through doorless,to cruelly sunsmitten unspace. To(something)tired,a pallid wisp of(not;not butterfly?)what? droopstumbling-which(yes!)alights—folds;hang(itself)ing from some lilacunlikeish but nonfragrance

"he will not come I think" said Nat.

"Who?" said Turk.

She named the chicly littlish man-with-the-goodlooking-European-girlfriend:the manless-on-the-balcony of my first Moscow morning.

"So you're coming too?" I ask Grouch-Scratch.

"Sure" grin "we've been taking this tour for months—"

(after tramming down-and-out to the "market",and descending legally,and suddenly being hit with a cloudbursting climax of hailstones—how they crash and hiss!—how our group disintegrates as comrade I jump for this tree and as 4 comrades scatter 4 ways and as ½Russian,calmly amid tornado pausing,signs-yells-points and as all 6 are now rivering together squeezed under the how brief eavelets of bearded toyman's boothless . . . and shivering and soaked and stared at by flyspecked Elsewhereish unghosts)why,there heaves a tramless into view and out into hisscrashing go 6 and shovebumpelbowhuddl-ing(all sopping all melted all awash)roar away off to a nowhereish world'sendful vacant lot;away and away off to a judgmenttrumping misery of tin cans and ruined fields and(there:here)a shack,a hut,a something:

pleasantly greenswarded yard;mouldy house. 5 comrades hug this decayed hallway(Nat having mysteriously disappeared). Gradually around 5 comrades gathers a collection of slouching,dimly wondering, mildly curious,staring vaguely,beings

now—

brisk handsomely youngish masculine appears:firm curling hair: firmly unofficial if modestly authoritative manner. Who,seconded by ½, leads Coxey's army to a big steel shut—immediately which and which unostentatiously opens per 2 mouldily soldierish dolls;now we all enter(lasciate ogni)something remarkably resembling the below-waterline portions of a formerly transatlantic liner . . . around,tier on tier,steel catwalks:on which poised(in semidarkness)stand(staring) what might be(silent)members of an engine crew . . . almost,or quite, everywhere are metal shuts . . . and not 1 sound . . . only the soundless of feet(our?)climbing this how particularly laddery steepness into

(now)

thunder! . . . Long thundering corridor,crammed with thunderful (from each,a pluckingly wandering rod jumps)together-all-shimmying looms. Boyghosts,childghosts,slouch;pallid:start,sprout(as we enter)— . . . stare. Every(outleaning)spirit(peering from enormous depths of thunder)stares,silent,at comrade guide and at comrade ½ and at 5 American deafened comrades . . .

(any questions?

By grouch—how old are most of the prisoners at these looms? Fifteen?

By guide(via Nat)—O no. The very youngest is eighteen)

& into an(only which is only full of merely racket)room. Spools. And extraordinary rays which,infinitely,are being focussed,by this stolid deadeyed expeasant lumpful(whose deads lift,find,drift,blur)&

(any questions?

By Scratch—what is that comrade doing?

Answer—he is selecting threads)

into room 3—not-quite-filled by stuffs(and quiet as only wovenness can be quiet!) . . . there and here lurking(are handling)are(budging are)shifting rolls bolts cylinders these timid unspeaking gnomes . . .

any questions?

K—does the room in which you can't hear yourself shout harbour archcriminals;and the less murderfully noisy,those less arch;and the quiet,those least?

O no. The noise has not any connection with the gravity of the crime

& up(now)ladder(and now down)and we all suddenly have entered hell's mouldering pitlike dank well;guarded by(nudging "trustees" says Turk)uniform spectres-in-uniform;staring silences labelled,at the necks,B.O. Around,shuts. And shuts. And. Creagnk!—

1 is un-

(squeakfg)

locked by guide:voilà—

a winsomely microscopic and under untable crouching oldness(its babyback toward us)scratching,clutching,at dirt,dust . . . scooping, brushing

—Bong. shut

&

(kngaercgfkaeuqs)

erect—oblivious—upon its unbed,a distinguished old man sitting strictly . . . the long gray fine beard . . . lost eyes. Beside whom twitterish leers a notold;in whose ungrin something has been broken

shut. Bong!

(and no "any questions?") Yet I dare to ask:who is the comrade that cleans his room? —Handsome's eyes freeze. Angry . . . sputters at Nat. Grunts—shrugging. (And she translates "he says:probably you are meaning Russian captain of the old régime")&

distantly a crowd,seated,in sun. (Feeling,remembering La Ferté,now comrade myself descends these steps—treads this unfree earthless. Whom all around all now floods now all gushes genial flocks rumbling jocular chatteringly mob:this,younger than others,pulling at my jacket,jerking,wriggling

"izveneetyeh,yah nyeh pahnyeemeyeyoo"

earnest,wants something,all,now

("comrade!" I call to Turk,but he's not)

must,wants,now,all,gush,floods,

—then comes Nat

"O!" who sees(with disdainful almost terror)the comrade American (surrounded by bubbling greedily splutterfuls)writer. "—Please! We . . . we are going—"

"ask them,please,what they want"(must-want-now-all wheels spins floods toward her,toward ½. Rumbling)pause

"they . . . they wish to know" she above hubbub explains "who we are."

"Who are we?" I cry.

"So I tell them of Mr."(naming Grouch)"and Mrs."(the Turkess)½ stutters,blushing with something like hidden fear(—when they made us lie down—)Nat,aged perhaps 17 "and" cringing "I ask him"(younger) "please,show us the prison newspaper;and he tells me:show us,please, some of your newspaper first." —Then,her English mother squirming through a shrill nearly scream "now,come—please?"

("papeerohsa,tovarich?")

—flockgush rumblechatters—

("ahdeen. Izveneetyeh"

which was true).

. . . the younger grabbed it

&

now

"here,you see hospital." (I shouldn't have guessed it was a hospital)where,lo and behold—very properly indeed horizontal—the younger!the grabber! Comrade handsome guide is very much astonished,if only because younger isn't sick. Handsome comrade guide lectures younger(gently but grimly,softly but firmly). Younger shrugs: grunts,twists and—uppeeping—winks. And there's also a middleaged person with hungering holes which always stare. Dimly who smiles. Unspeaks,even. & "now"(Turk,skilfully lingering,tosses to 1st un- then to sick a cigarette;smiling to both)"the

dentist" (A nonman. Victim's closecropped skull unmoves)

"and the doctor"(empty)

"and the library"(solabelled).

Enter dispute.

By Grouch begun,re fact that every socialist cell boasts—high above its shut—a radio;and that there are plenty of wires visible but nary a switch;and therefore Grouch inquires whether the prisoners can curb their entertainment;and if yes,how? Guide(crisp):"Da." But Grouch presses him. Flinching,he hovers;consults this straightstaring comrade perfect stranger who says(crisply)"nyet." At which both Russians fall to Russianing Russianly and ½English also Russians,and Turk(twinkling) Russians. And after 5 nonminutes generally and irrevocably and solemnly it is and mutually decided(1)that a prisoner can turn off his radio but(2)that a prisoner cannot turn his radio on

"here" quoth Nat "the club. Formerly this is church"

yes. Long ago. Altar has become stage. I glimpse(in a kind of otherwise uninhabited balcony,near the stage)1 familiar(if this time in plaster)comrade,blindly from scarletdraped pedestal glaring. White letters upon bloody ground scream,shriek,yawp over proscenium: REVOLUTION HAS CONQUERED CAPITALISM AND WILL CONQUER CRIME

. . . ah. & here,forsooth,is a tobelivedinness. No cellless cell,this. Cosy little apartment with open windows—are these fragments of tree?(yes). "Please—sit down." All of us do:then guide. Follow 45 notable minutes of Any Questions;Turk,meanwhile,having numerous Russian conversations of his own and taking notes continuously . . . Questions. Answers.

By Grouch—what about punishment?

Nat—O no.

Grouch—no punishment?

Nat—he says,never is a prisoner beaten.

"That's odd" the Turk gently remarks "because our comrade friend just told me something distinctly different—"

½(flaring,Russian):"What?"

"he said that if two prisoners fight,the authorities beat them both up—"

pale,she Russianizes to handsome. Who smirks pityingly. "He says: O no;he meant,what is it?mental beating."

"That is" explodes the daughter of a merciful him who exposed animal torturers "the most naif thing I ever heard in my life!"

"what does he" Grouch snarled "mean by mental beating?"

long(by wily handsome;interrupted by twinkling Turk,interpreted by blushing Nat)explanations

"—but" Grouch objects angrily "there are some guys you just simply can't discipline mentally—you've just simply got to use physical force—"

O no. O no no. No no no no. Nyet. Absolutely NO corporal punishment is tolerated in a Soviet Russian jail("three times" $\frac{1}{2}$ blushes, $\frac{1}{2}$weeping "I have been to this prison,and O I am sure!")

"what no straightjackets?" Grouch sneers.

Mercy no. The idea! Although it does seem that there's solitary confinement. But what takes the place of force is a grand mutual collective Bronx cheer,issued spontaneously by all wellbehaved members or member. And that,it seems,fixes the culprit—be he to Hercules as Hercules to a Singer Midget

"my god" Grouch moaned "it wouldn't fix an American sodajerker!"

"how about repeaters?" Scratch faintly inquires(and is abundantly reassured and is copiously fed statistics which ultimately are all proving that crime everywhere is miraculously disappearing). And

"ask him,please,how he came to have his job—"

—I probably said this distinctly(Nat being only $\frac{1}{2}$ Nat's mother)but I certainly spoke less forcefully than,e.g. comrade Grouch . . . whereupon that hitherto solely Russianing and accessible only through bilingual intermediaries tovarich blushes much redder than the reddest rear of a zoobred monkey,not to mention a red poppy. And(blacker than a capitalist heart scowling)deluges with my untransmitted question's answer Natless Nat

"he says" summoning supreme "in Russia it is not customary to ask such a question" courage

and 8 eyes stare,2 twinkle

"for in Russia the" bravely struggling "personal issue does not exist"

1 comrade smiles,4 wonder . . . And it also seems that handsome, having been well educated,was appointed to a job(i.e. this job)in which he "later" became "greatly interested."

Turkess "have they sterilization?"(this time he really doesn't understand) . . . and Nat translates,with even greater difficulty

—O no!(immeasurably shocked)

"three cheers" the daughter of kindness-to-animals cries "for the red white and blue" adding almost gaily "we've had it in California for years—"

"I don't" Grouch grouches "know . . . sterilization might be abused."

"Not at all" with complete conviction. "It's only for the feeble-minded."

"But how can you" cynical Grouch growls "be sure they're feeble-minded."

"That's easy. Most of them have inherited syphilis."

"Is it painful?" asks Scratch. "—I mean, sterilization."

"Not" the devoted mother of a devoted son assures "with a new electric process for sterilizing women, which makes operating unnecessary."

Pause

(no more questions?)

"I'm supposed to be at the Writers' Club at five" guiltily inform Turkess, who soothes and assures that Turk will telephone President immediately &

. . . down—over catwalks, past starers, past was, past past— . . .

"say" calmly Turk directs Nat "the American writer is unable to meet the President at five; then ask the President to kindly save three seats for the Gorky production and to please telephone me tomorrow morning" gently then (while obedient ½ wrestles with Santa Claus science) "this, comrades, is the fatal book in which visiting spirits record their reactions" he turns large pages; slowly reads immense unsentences, rhetorical balderdash . . . himself, coming to blankness

"very interesting"

writes, and signs.

"But I don't—" Turkess objects.

"O go on" he twinkles, giving her the pen.

"What shall I write?"

"what you feel" he replied with a pleasant smile (and, Russianing to negatively all observing handsome: allow me to present the distinguished daughter of —. And beaming handsome, to her positively bowing, radiates respect admiration pride: many of your distinguished father's books are in our library) and she writes . . . at great, great length . . . and signs. And

"now you have to" (meaning me)

"is it obligatory?" I ask Turk.

Twinkling "no."

"All right." Hand (without signing) pen to Inc.

now

O

now, gently and swiftly is by dolls unlocked the big shut. And a hallway(in which happens what extraordinary poster;depicting 1 huge striding ultraman,fettered by many unexpected infrathings such as a person in bed)

air—

Sweet!world

. . . turning,see a(staring at poster,at us,at poster)doll all grinning merrily all chuckling all muttering

"—please! It is not that way!" Nat calls to the Turkess;who had mistaken merely greensward for freedom

obviously,comrade,the very next hour will demand of you an utmost concentration. Luckily provided(by sympathetic $\frac{1}{2}$)with a pencilled map,I must not only find Something's residence;I must,after visiting Something,find god almighty's. For god almighty,it seems,is having a partyless this evening,and the Turk said he'd bring me. But 1st and foremost,comrade myself must return to Chinesey's palace and shave . . . that will be easy,anyhow;since both Turkess and Turk are 1stly homeward bound ere 2ndly going god's way

"I'd be more than happy to send Nat with you" he offers,corkscrewing from among tramcrammed comrades

(but even comrade myself cannot quite impose upon human nature to such a degree)

"then" reeling;collecting himself "we'll all" gasps " three take a droshky to" naming Something "there's plenty of" grunt "time,really"—.

Self(shaved)and Turk-Turkess forthstart. Pause;

"as a matter of fact" Turk recalls "I haven't myself the remotest idea where you ought to be going. That map of Nat's is wrong. We'll ask"

but various passersby don't know.

"Why not a droshky?" opines Turkess.

2 sleep across this street;dreaming brown horse of nearer turns to us a beautiful forehead . . .

"he knows" Turk smiles "but—to drive three comrades thither and two from thither to whoses party—the bastard wants eight roubles."

"No walking both ways" Turkess.

"Come come" heroically upspeaks comrade Kem-min-kz "a miss is as good as a mile—see you later!"

ecco!ecco the arriving(but nobody,least of all self,knows how)K stands
before a leatherish shut;behind me,pausing,a nonman . . . or might it?a
. . . woman—
knock
again
who's not bad looking;in fact(where have I seen?)attractive. Dressed
in red poppyness. (& a flustered jowl opens;and behind which squirts
the apparition of Something;and a gnarled—pointing across the
landing—finger. Shut)
"c'est par ici?" I tried poppy
"oui" the red answers
& by flustered now(by jowl)the opposite shut's opened,by a
nonman,respectfully who greets calmly entering red;nervously who
regards comrade nameless-murmuring K insidling.
Luxe?
not quite. Luxuriously a sunlit but cool,a comfortingly colour-filled
but quiet,room where(miraculously)do you smoke(appearing)asks
Germanly Something himself—"oui,mais"(produce American . . . he
skips:dartingly returns with dull large box of long Turkish keennesses).
And gestures;Smoke!(very genial spidery oldish. Almost gay. Cyrano
nez). And also here's—O,elegance!—"tabac du Caucase"(making me a
sign:to roll my own,by means of nothing less than irregularly torn pieces
of papernapkin)
"vous êtes russe?" she said
"je suis américain." Rolling my.
Indescribably a sigh of ultimate relief—"then let's speak English!"
1 fanée at which moment enters,shakes my hand,vanishes. (& now
occurs what ungentlemen of the pressless do not call An Interview . . .
now Something—darting,smiling,peering—Germans to poppy;now
poppy translates)
Q:Are you staying in Russia long?—A:No,I must go back to plant
a garden in New Hampshire,otherwise we won't have fresh radishes
this summer.—Q:Where do you live in America?—A:Country three
months,city nine.—Q:Would you care to come to a dress rehearsal on
the 24th at 11?—A:I should more than care.—Q:Have you seen my latest
show?—A:No,the only show of yours which I've seen is Roar China(he
made a face which said "it's N.G.")

162

"Piscator" she said,during a lull "is almost crazy."

I smile appreciatively.

"He is used" she said "to being treated as somebody. And here he is not."

I smile.

"He wanted to do" she said "something about revolutionary Germany. At first they encouraged him,the Russians."

"Are you from New York?" I ask(amazed by her accent)

"Vienna" she said. "He worked and he worked. Finally he had the idea. Everything was finished. He was so happy. He came to Moscow,all ready to . . . to put it over(is that right?)"

"right." Pause. "What happened?" I ask.

"But the Soviets,having recently received money from Germany, turned upon Piscator." Her face burned "it's not a good idea any more,they said"(& I now realize that this girl stood upon a porchless porch of hotelless Metropole 1 fine sunny morning)

"so—?"

"that was all" turning childfully toward Something,she pours around over through and under him German . . . instrolls a biglegged boychild,cutely willful(its ears jutting from neck at a mischievously rakish angle)and flees . . . I know,I understand(Something soothes red)"TairREEBLE" and bangs his head cheerfully against wall— Come!springily he escorts her,beckons me,to a tiny table;gestures,Sit. And immediately reappears fanée,smiles;reclining on divan behind me . . . Potipharish fullblownly

exclaim "dam good tea!" He smiles. Glance wonderingly at(here,here)bright flowers in slender vases. He smiles . . . Speak(he signs)to her(red). And obeying

"my eyes have been very hungry lately."

She looked.

"What a change is Russia" I cried(laughing)"after Paris!"

"which" she said almost coolly "do you prefer?Paris or Moscow?"

carefully "Paris."

"O" she said "of course Paris is statically pleasanter"(& Something encourages me:Moscow is very dirty;why even this room—this place here—is entered by dirt)and red,sighing "I like Paris" whispers. Smiles.

Now socialism—it seems—is a good form of government;but when "dummkopfs" try to dictate in the theatre,getting between a director and his audience,then(suddenly his eyes spidercrouch:are)Don't misunderstand

ah,but I don't. And fanée,forsooth,is the leading lady of Something's next production;whose dress rehearsal am to see. Fanée,who speaks French as well as Russian and who understands German. Fanée eyes me interestedly;more especially when(wondering)I stoop,to inhale the beautiful strangeness of actual flowers . . . including always to be remembered forget-me-nots . . . and Something(from his crouch) carefully,gravely;watches:&

the room's quiet(says quietly)isn't it?

"Wunderschön" myself hazards.

I waited a long time(he whispers)to get it. (And had been living in a "furchtbar" place. Here 2 years. Wants to retire and be only a playwright. His present theatre isn't big enough. Needs "grosse Bühne";and machinery to match;you know—cranes,derricks,engines)everything—

a very lovely little girl,quite as dreamlike as boy wasn't,peeps at(through a curtainless)us. "Vous êtes sa mere?" the red asks the fanée. "Oui" simply

O these Russians!not once did Something mention our mutual friend,the man of the strayed face,the mind with the bravely cringing eyes,the noble and droll little sculptor who gave me my letter of introduction . . . "Bitte—ich muss ausgehen" plead,putting down cheye number drei. And to red "please tell him."

"What."

"Tell him that my next jump is dinner with the official Moscow representative of the most influential extant branch of capitalist journalism. To miss farce perhaps is tragic"

"he says he understands." Something understands. If only he could speak!—not English or French(or whatever language is not by me not spoken)but that marvelously only language which may or may not speak itself according as the soul is free or is afraid. If—comrade Something aside—the(somewhere invisible)millions upon literally millions of somebodies who all breathe and move and who like light and who all love Pretend only could freely speak! If at least this(perhaps this most magical)$\frac{1}{6}$ of a worldless world somehow were not afraid;only did not remember wars;impossibly could forget everything and opening its spirit pour a true structure into space and into time! Something understands that I understand—that I feel(if only because knowing is impossible to anyone who feels)how finitely Herr tovarich director Something must merely know,when the human Is within him would how infinitely prefer(if only once!)to feel . . . this human Is,still wondering who I am,wondering for whom he shall reserve a seat at Something's theatre;coming now at my(with a huge blunt carpenter's pencil)self

"schreiben Sie"

and this fragment of paper . . . but spiderless,uncrouched;almost alive. Almost no longer,in a kingdomless of spectres,clownking(ghostdirector,unmaster of shadows)almost someone utterly how lonely in a nonland of un-.

"Yes"

= 1 word. Yes cannot possibly imitate(whose original may never be translated)a poem,or steep alert prodigy. Cannot imitate the(indescribably everything and suddenly which is ourselves,which self is and whatever only creatively annihilates hatred with laughing)spontaneous immeasurably true swoop of Actual. In proximity to which all systems assume their negative unnecessity—appear quite as valuable(for living)or invaluable as a book of etiquette for dying.

Stood—

utterly pulling Yes from a new dimension;emptying(with a syllable) uncouth dustily fixed dead solemnly tumbling clumsiest idiocies;easily (with a word)opening the swift inexhaustibly generous total everywheres of serene instinct

—1 perfectly beaming negress. "He's home. Come right in"(nor vestige of distrust,nor trace of suspicion,of doubt. Welcoming direct authentic heartiness)

"who's that,mammy?"(petulant wail)

"gen'lm'n t' see y'" she placidly,cheerfully replies.

"F'r god's sake" said god "we all thought y' weren't comin'. Y'r frien's been here f'r hours"(I gravely bow to dormant Turk and drowsy Turkess)"how 'bout some reel 'merican food,eh? No trouble,y'll have t' eat it re-warmed,tha's all. Here,boy,have a drink. —Mammy!"

"Yes sah."

"C'n you give this feller some'n t' eat? Or don't he rate food? Huh?"

akimbo,flushing pale black "c'n Mammy give a reel 'merican boy sumpn t' eat in this house?" indignantly "she cer'nly can!yes sah!all th' time!"

"siddown." I sit "'nother vodka." I drink "there's m' cat;lookin' f'r h'r fool kitt'n" stooping,he dug a squawking inky tumbling smallness from its nest . . . the staring silently mother(gathering)hopped into his lap "—y' ole dev'l,I'm not goin' t' hurt y'r chile! —Feel 'im. He's soft,eh? Now look—" the cat seized-up the inky;leaped(with inky)to the floor: strolled smoothly(staring)to the nest,dropped child. "Did y' notice th' li'l feller's tail?" god asked me.

"Yes."

Cunningly "w'at's it like?"

"a starfish's arm."

He thought. "That's right. —Mammy!"

"I'm comin' sah,comin' right away. Give him 'nother drink—"

—to Mammy's(literally American)cuisine the spice of imagination adds itself And How. Thanks to god . . .

"tell this feller 'bout y'rself,Mammy" god now orders.

"Yes sah." (Worldfully orbs roll). "I was a dancer. O yes. Yes indeed. I've danced f'r all th' crown heads."

"All? " gently(dormouse)Turk queries.

"Yes sah:George of Englan';queen Marie(there's a dear!)Albert o' Belgium,what's his name that Danish feller,not t' mention Mussolini o' course—O yes,ah know 'em all;an' mighty p'lite they was t' Mammy. Yes indeed. Liked m' art an' said so."

"Mammy's an artist" god solemnly corroborates.

"Yes sah. But f'rs an' foremost,an 'merican citizen" deeply and with colossal dignity asserts Mammy.

Turkess registers surprise.

"O yes,dear" Mammy soothes. "No doubt 'bout that. Th' bolshyvicky tried t' prove diff'rent;but Mammy fooled 'em . . . "

"how did you do that?" I inquire.

"Buried m' passport" she said simply. "That fooled 'em. An' don't you let nobody tell you there ain't some bright boys in them bolshyvickys,'cause they is!"

"I believe it."

"O yes,they's bright all right" Mammy mused. "But they jus' couldn't prove I wasn' 'merican."

"Didn't you have any trouble proving you were American,without a passport?" the Turkess.

"Yes dear,I did. In fact,I fin'lly had t' dig it up again,jus' t' reassure 'em. Yes;but in th' meantime did I have fun with all them boys! O they liked me,they did! All of 'em called me Mammy. —Everybody calls me Mammy" she added,radiating stupendous pride

"Mammy" god said solemnly.

"Yes sah. That's m' name. That an' Sunshine. In jail they called me Sunshine. Thirty days I spent in jail an' they treated me just fine! —Course I was married then,an' my husban' pretty near went crazy 'cause he didn' know where I was. But they treated me just fine,they did. An' I sang for 'em an' I danced for 'em an' I bought 'em something good t' eat an t' drink(poor things,they was almos' starved" she said pityingly)"an' one day th' minister of th' interior,I think it was,he saw me p'form an' asked me if I wanted anything an' I tol' him,No,everything was fine 'cept m' poor husband';so right away he sent for m' husban',an' ev'rybody was happy."

"Wond'f'l disp'sition Mammy has" god said.

"Are you married now?" I ask.

"Mercy no chile:we lived t'gether sixteen years. That's too long" she sighed."—O yes;I had three chil'ren but they's dead." Her worlds upspun. "Mother's a beautiful word"(the Turk opened 1 eye;sank into slumber)"the mos' beautiful word" said Sunshine Mammy "in th' world."

"Charlie!" harem shook the sleeping.

("Put a piller under him" Mammy Sunshine murmurs "he looks so nice,he ought t' be more comfortable . . .). That lovely 'merican head" she(reverently touching Turkess' crinkly hair;smiling)whispers

& into god's study a street seems to run point blank. Into which street as you do not step I'm standing on a tiny porch(even tinier,if possible,than comrade flower-)with

sunset &

whispering,angels(hirondelles;quickening space which over is through under the wonderfully and around this)everywhere possessed cityless floats in a genitive now of silence

. . . "I like t' sit in m' study with m'" slightly-staggering-god joins me "fiel'glasses an' watch th' soldiers marchin' down this street t' get their baths in that buildin' over there. Marchin'" dreamily "an' singin' an' makin' all sorts o' horseplay"

& sunset

Greyly—"don't y' let anyone tell y' these people like their government." Silence

And dark

"today I enjoyed my first Volks tour—"

chuckles "I never go near 'em. That ole reporter instinct o' mine keeps me from believin' a lot o'—"

Turk(tot)appears(ter)smothered by(ing)hiccups . . .

"push 'im in th' nose!" god cries to Turkess "that'll cure him!"(and bumrushes Turk sofaward;and pinioned by Turkess and fed much waterless water prot(fee)est(bly)ingly he sub(gasp)sides:and this immaculately who has("my")meanwhile entered("secretary")Hindu observes,through dense lips

"it is a pleasant evening"

item:the choice of soviet socialist movies—at least in this district—painfully limits itself unto

(1)Harold Lloyd(ages old)

(2)a serial:featuring,per creaky stills,minuets and bustles;entitled Princess somebody

(3)—& apparently best bet—"Don"

being ½hour early for Don,3 comrades visit a redhot(sic)"café" where—after prayers etc. re the eczemaish tovarich who isn't,or is,a waiter in his non- or existent spare time—I dare beer(combining the best elements of floorsoap and roadapples)while Assyrian adventures,infinitely to his woe,"icecream".

"Only"(thought tovarich Kem-min-kz as he followed his more or most dissolving 2 friends into odouriferous cinematographic redplush)"unfavorably can hell compare with" . . . so He stole another man's wife and She was left chewing the ground and That was how,according to occasionally moving Don,things used to happen in yee goode olde dayse(why?because Free Love didn't exist. And the moral is,be natural comrades)

naturally "you mustn't spoil these bastards" Turk murmurs.

K,however,purchases for a really and truly uncouth sum 1 sprig of actually lilacs;hands ditto to Harem;hurls his cap in the air,and—hugely to amazement of 3 comrades move—elicits from never-before-seen-or-after comrade 1 ineffectually muffled cry registering appreciative encouragement plus awe

. . . (ferocious)ogress chattertotters

it's my passport.

The militia wouldn't sanction our Americanitz peesahtel's change of address.

Because his Russian passport hasn't a red seal.

For instance,comrade Turk's has(or had)a red seal.

And a red seal is was always will be a red seal.

And you simply must have a red seal

("but mine hasn't" Turkess correctly observes)

"Nat" wearily "will take care of all this tomorrow" soothes Turk.

"How?" I ask timidly.

"She'll tell them your passport is foreign and they mustn't meddle with it. Don't worry. The meticulous comrade is probably somewhat afraid of being shot for underzealousness or something—"

"but if the Metropole is"—I marvel—"made for foreigners(as a communist told me)how come no red seal?"

carefully "careful" said the Turk. "We'll all begin feeling persecuted if we don't watch out"

"—now that I think of it:how come the Soviet Embassy in Paris delivered my visa just too late for May Day doings? And how come the socialist soviet republic granted a single month's séjour instead of the promised double? And how come—"

"may I read" placidly "your thoughts?"

"please!"

"you're wondering whether you'll ever leave Russia. —Right?"

"right."

"A foreigner"(Assyrian comforts)"may be kept out of this earthly paradise but he can't possibly be kept in:sleep well" through unshutness;2 cry-men—"oh:boy"(a beardless)& "sope"(a bearded)—with limp(wandering)sacs over(stare)gnarled

"this tovarich is off on a joyride that's going to jolt my guts out and"
"—where?" darkly
"chez a great American Russian electric light and icechest man-among-men."
"Why?"
"to get packingcases" her frown dissolves. "Lest" he added "your ten thousand souvenirs and my twelve million tomes should never see the statue of liberty—comrade Kem-min-kz:forward."

Modesty perhaps dictates splinterful naked tailend of springless and seatless plank(not quite balanced over warped differently wheels)but a most tremendously excited,a reverently solicitous,a mudcovered dungcoloured(patting grunting winking bowing)tovarich beckons his distinguished guests toward supreme luxe,viz. this mouldy fragment of once cloth. Outfacing now,who(now feet dangling)sumptuously now enthroned move—a big blue horse dreamishly strolling—for 20 some minutes;at the unrate perhaps of 1 mile a yearless . . . passing(passed by)streets,by people,noises . . .

(that man-among-men emerges from brandnew stucco officebuilding. He looks blackish,energetically little. Because that man-among is "businesslike",has everything to do,because that man- cannot "waste time"—lest a single hint of himself seize that and he perish—Mr. Electriclight and icechest radiates aggressive timidity,reeks with defensive initiative. 83(count them)oblongs garnish that great American Russian's backyard. And that leads hither and thither Assyrian;that kicks which box and shakes what;that vanishes)

"yes—?" producing the honeymoon visitingcard
in shirtsleeves Turk(sweating,wrestling an oblong)nods.
"Here's what we need!" cries reappearing that;blackishly brandishing the glitterful epitome of Yankee ingenuity,a nailpuller
&

(wastelessly)"Yes? Really? What boat? How long ago? Indeed? Oh,if you're only staying a week I'll surely see you"(soothes me)

&

(busily)"try this"(to the blue horse;uplifting a wisp snatched from nearest packingcase). Blue's eyes bulge:blue outfeels a lip,grabs;blue smiles. "Good,eh?" and

American—(tiny severe round Russian cries,appearing)—hay?
yes(that,proudly)and see him eat it.

See him eat it!(the blue's exultant driver ½wails ½moans)
give him some more(says blackish to blue's;indicating nearest).

Yesyesyes—(spluttering,stumbling,quivering,chuckling,tovarich-the-driver totters to box,gathers how sacredly least wisp;smells, Ahs!nods;grinning uplifts toward blue)

wonderful(the round tiny,himself gathering a less than least,sacredly it sniffing,whispers) . . . Hay . . . American . . .

"now why don't you give these boys a"(out of corners,angles,rush claimants)"few" blackish tells Turk "roubles? They'll pull all the nails you want in no time at all." And Assyrian elevates host,presents the nailpuller;and 4,5,6 comrades handle,caress,touch it;murmuring . . . American . . . good . . . see?

"it must have been one nice job getting all your stuff unpacked" rejacketingly elevator

"job? You said it! Why,I had all the customs men down here working all day. I fed 'em and I wined 'em and they opened every dam box and they carried up every last bit of furniture on their dam backs—this being Moscow,the lift isn't in—every single dam thing they toted. Eighty-three packingcases-full. Yes sir. At the end of the day those poor chaps all of 'em fell sound asleep in this very yard. —And I don't blame 'em!"

. . . good . . . see? . . . American . . . (chortles the nailpulling cult)

"come on up" invites blackish(patting asmile blue)amiably us "and see the sights."

New.

Everything new(and sharp).

Sharp à l'américain;crisply carpentered—fresh

a series of sharp crisp fresh identical rooms filled with fresh crisp sharp identical objects,each and every proudly wearing its crispsharpfresh American brandnew label "we're completely" proudly blackish announces "standardised. I mean absolutely. Even down to the dishpans and the dishmops. Yes sir. With one exception,there's not a thing in this building that isn't American. And what's more,every office in this building has absolutely the same equipment:all of it brandnew and all of it Americanmade." He,punching a Beautyrest mattress,leers "but you haven't seen my room."

"Have you" gently "your own frigidaire?" Turk asks

blackish "you mean General Electric" corrects quickly

"yes—of course."

"O yes. I and one other fellow have our own." Bloatedly "here's mine—" and how solemnly pointing,through this just-painted doorway,at 1 peculiarly ghostful superrefrigerator. "Pretty swell,eh? Yes sir. Imported 'specially for me" great pompoused

"what's the exception?" I beg.

Angrily "this" tapping a chauffebain. "It's German." (& in apologetic confidentially whisperless "we couldn't help it")

. . . nails & nails . . . pulled & pulled . . . pullers & pullers . . . tips & tips . . . and several packingboxes sacredly have by boys been boosted aboard springless . . . now exultant tovarich the smileful blue's driver looks,lookstoward,looks toward 80-something ob-

take a little hay for your fine horse(the Turk suggests mildly)

Will I take!(replies among other things tovarich,ecstatic,taking & taking and)

"possibly are you aware what that Russian soul probably is going to do with it?"

I ain't. Unless he has an elephant chez lui?

"make himself a bed;and his wife,and even his children. They're all embarking tonight for reverie upon American hay,even like kings and like queens."

. . . Careful the driver stuffs carefully hugest wads under that behind this;carefullyer(with our very thronecloth)covers,hides some few, carefullyest conceals certain protruding wisps . . .

"what does he say now?"

"he said:America HAS everything" Turk translates "—we Russians can only TALK . . . ah well;suppose ourselves march decently on before . . . that Russian soul desires most mightily to disappear;believe me,that good tovarich has no idea of delivering packingcases. Whether or no my boxes arrive will depend on nothing less than fate;and so be it"

172

park. Unearth

sunstruck(in dream?wandering)comrades. "I should like" wearily said Assyrian "kvass. And you? —Dvah . . . we'll probably get hoof and mouth disease" cheerfully elevating(and this furtive softdrinkful comrade hungrily watches our chipped glasses,seizes them away hungrily,quickly them rinses in untrue American sodafountainstyle,them quickly shoves at sunstruck thirsting other comrade-wandering-dreams?)"the Russian substitute for lipstick being,as it were,made of horsefat . . . look,there he goes"(pointing,very placidly,to blue-and-soul who're guiltily turning a cornerless)"so we don't any more need to worry about our earthly possessions. It's up to him and to his conscience . . . see" nodding at white-once-flowers wilting on ageless(an asleep)stationary comrade's armless. "We'll buy." (And softly to ageless)"Skoylkah,tovarich?"

(and ageless,not awakening,mutters):Not much

they're tired(quietly the Turk said)these flowers

so are these(unawakeningly now a little once basket of possibly less white even or probably more tired flowers opening mutters ageless)

"I've" triumph "got it!—I'll say" triumph "tomorrow is my maid's day off. I'll ask if we may all dine with them." Triumph. "Then I'll leave the food"

"splendid" her lord compliments Harem. "And perhaps this comrade will accompany you,while I answer telegrams?"

"will you?" she

"Gladly. Who's to be fooled?"

"you may not or you may remember the scientist I spoke about—the unfortunate professor who didn't 'volunteer'?" he

"I remember."

"Well,this unfortunate and his faithful wife are quite as proud as they are poor—I don't mean proud-narrow" smiling "I mean proud-erect. So it's a problem to prevent them,once in a great while,from not eating nothing. My young confrère,however,is good at solving problems"

am standing glued to confrère. A tramless moves. Confrère's passport inhabits my least pickable pocket. Most of me hugs a huge package. Some of me holds 1 rouble

so am beside confrère staggering through heat,dirt,a suburb. 2

comrades enter this buildingless. Are challenged by glaring nonman;whereupon confrère calmly pronounces 1 scientist's name and unmolestedly we climb worn stairs

a flowery,frail door

"O—!please come in"(ironhaired,not old,gentle,not young,and very perfectly erect person)"it's good to see you!" By his alert slenderly patient face also is confrère told(quietly by intense lonely eyes)that to see her is Good. And here,taking my hand in his,exists miracle—ecco the phenomenon of phenomena:a man,a human being,natural and unafraid. That prodigy of prodigies;no ghost;someone certainly who creates always a universal dignity by always the very modesty of his aliveness. "My wife"(a little blonde eager starved courteous woman—no nonman—and who surrounds prodigy-phenomenon's each utterance with the unutterance of her love)touches from time to(and touches)time the confrère sacredly("yes,she is real");smiles. That premeditated smallness,that unroom,logically clutter books,papers;and it contains chiefly(and it celebrates proudly,how proudly!)this beauteously glistening serene microscope whose very sacred self inhabits 1 huge bubble of clean glass

. . . whereupon we almost politely discuss,softly,jails. Our hostess,also,has experienced them;she timidly,eagerly is explaining how—

knock!

(words cease)come in(host bows,courteously opening)

middleaged brisk(gently the host presents him to us)tovarich. Curtly to company nods:ahems—plunges into questioning . . . simply and unhurriedly the priest of the microscope visits the shelf,removes carefully the tome,turns almost prayerfully to the engraving of a flower;briefly speaks,kindly . . . another tome:again the same flower's picture . . . until Is your question answered?

Yes(angrily almost. Brisk turns,nods)thanks. (Stumbling—eating confrère with a ferocious admiration—hurries to the flowery & frail)

"and he wished to know something" phenomenon told,smiling "and" proud-erectly "I was able to help him." Quietly "we may relax again."

". . . What lovely buttercups!" the Turkess said.

"Please" said the hostess;lifting(carefully 5 or 6 taking)from a tiny vase near unshutness:and

"OooO" the Harem shivers,while cold stems dive between breasts.

capitalist pensivities while donning a nexttolast shirt

how(rather surrounded by than surrounding)distinct an aura of something slightly more ultimate than generosity appeared,in that steep moment when he—having escorted us to the street—½turned;waved

did the faretakeress of homecoming tram merely forget to give me change?

what about continued absence of mail,both at INTOURIST and Metropole

da,these Russians are extraordinary . . . for instance,the poor creature who disappeared only a moment since. Possibly 46. Haggard. Best friend of Turk's exgirlfriend. Am told she amazed the Turkess by welcoming her with("is that Russian?")open arms. And can certify that Turkess did nobly;even kissing affectionately that sagged withering welcomer;accepting even graciously the pathetically earnest offer of theatre tickets;perfectly submerging even whatever most natural suspicions may have darkened her own spirit . . .

He gradually(very)awoke. After dinner gradually he(verying)stirred: groaning—observed

"circus"

(I cheer)

"—you'd rather see a circus than a play?" Harem demands,surprised

"ten million times;any day,any where"

"why?"

"probably I don't know . . . but for one thing,the smell—" she's laughing "will there be elephants?"

"I gravely doubt it" Assyrian answers gravely

said she "I should think" gravely "that about the last thing this country could manage would be elephants"

"and" rubbing eyes "imagine" himself wonderingly murmurs "a socialist clown!"

15 minute voyage,through darkening air. Tired structure . . . ungay, colourless,not from whose noiseless portal seeps any least thrill of magic . . . he purchases tickets . . . Turkess studies grayness . . . & I'm elsewhere(a blessedly steep reek

—no cowardly manstink—no sickly of human pores whimper or

dismal cringe from comrade bowels. Reek:thunderous unmitigated reek,authentic ripe reek smiting and entire;

the hulking truth of smell. (Drenched in whose dimension fatally occur forms hurl curve angles glide lights crash shrill spiralling mesh poems and immense squirmfully occult float alive now suddenly
dreams))

and gradually and who darkestly from elsewhere now returning,marvel there should nonexist uncertainly certain gameless games . . .

each a because or system merely;when fears,wishes(placed at certain angles to each other)become facts,boxes. If the game or system is unkind,these boxes are cages;through which even may communicate(peering sometimes)the defined inhabitants. And if the system or because is kind,these boxes have no perforations and these(ignorant of ignorance)prisoners do not suspect that they are these prisoners. And each measurably system(and miserably)must remain negative,merely must remain real;must dreamless mean,untruth

e.g. an altruistic game of human prisoners,uncircus of noncreatures,calling itself "Russia". Almost—now I apprehend—are within whose realness decently embedded hints(directions,pressures)of actuality

. . . & entering now which almost-play-within-a-playless,only and swiftly I feel:

the machinemade tool of the selfmade man stutters on the impression of a pterodactyl

item:scattering of sullenly("the Russians have never had anything to laugh about")unresponsive timidities=audience. Lethargically before whom caper 2 thoroughly dejected how cautiously(general order number P.S.:all fun must be clean,i.e. political,fun)clumsying scarecrow ghosts-without-makeup . . . who? "Socialist clowns"

strongman trio,in dirty buff jerseys,murders several handstands and applauselessly departs

pepless banjo & piano act,undone by a rather frightened Fairy and a quite frightening Lesbian,drivels

juggler juggles wobbling fire

next:series of very intricate manoeuvres,executed with the greatest spirit and dexterity—a precise high deep instinctive and altogether miraculous demonstration . . . (per horses)

1 terrific dose of propaganda. Vehicle=argument between Comrade Right-O,alias ye bold Soviet Sailorman,and Mademoiselle Pasbon,alias

ye wicked émigrée trollop. Argument,capitalistically enough,couches self in rhymed(much against its will)prose blatantly reminiscent of ye French academy. The very vile bitch makes every conceivable objection to noble comrade Stalin's 5 year plan. Right-O,in his very rough-and-ready way,does not bother to answer any of her points;contenting himself with very personal insults,plus several hale-and-hearty generalities. Climax . . . whore(cynically shrugging):You haven't any pants!—hero(ferociously swaggering):No,but we will have;and when we do have,all the world will be afraid! (Enter most mild,perfunctory applause)

"at" quietly "least" Turk during entr'acte murmurs "the Russians are frank."

"Why did you leave?" innocently I ask the(who'd with a passionate cry disappeared mid equine actualities)Turkess.

"Read Michael" almost angrily "and you'll know" she said.

"A book" softly he interprets. "By her dad. About animal training—" the 2nd act begins well:twain comrade-ushers lug in a big perforated silvery ball and deposit same at base of a 6 tier spiral. Silence. Ball,of itself,rolls(very slowly;gropingly)to summit of spiral—pauses:from 1 of innumerable perforations outjuts tiny red flag,which . . . falling . . . is caught by an usher-comrade. Now(slowly,very;gropingly)the;ball,rollstops. Down. Down-down. Down—arriving at base of spiral,it pops!into $\frac{1}{2}$s . . . from lower now unfolds a little nonman wearing the world's oldest faded bluegreenish tights

and worthily continuing part 2nd,this pig gleefully unrolls with quick nose that longish palered carpet,lettered DUROV CIRCUS. Flourish: now enter Durov(an extraordinary 5th musketeer who's much above 70;vastly who enjoys threadbare silken doublet literally shingled with medals,and pantaloons to match). Looking like a depraved Buffalo Bill,who addresses his populace(how glad I am to see the people in the saddle,etc.)bows;and is heavily encouraged,by several tovarich-retainers in once-scarlet jerkins . . .

whereupon follows the nonplay-within-the-almost-play-within-the-playless:Durov's circus proper. I have not read Michael;but Durov's circus undoubtedly constitutes everything which comrade Lack Dungeon how ruthlessly exposed. Very drugged,very starved(some of the canine protagonists have apparently met comrade Pavlov)and very non compos members in bad standing of the animal kingdom,less or least(with noteworthy exceptions)lifelessly now cringe now stutter through more and most infantile and generally excruciating—but Harem does not disappear—tricklesses

("Durov was a celebrity" Turk whispers "he used to carry his own show all over Europe. Even the ogress proudly claims she knew him as a young man")

such as:

a terrified collie making patriotic sentences with wooden words

a motheaten fox and ditto rooster eating out of the same plate

a mildewed cat,with a rusty rat on her back,willowing among obstacles innumerable

a drowsy cheetah(having raised a red flag by pawing a revolving drum)firing a toy cannon

2 bloated-bondholder badgers—they also resemble very amiable bedbugs—pulling up this diminutive bucket from that miniature well,playing a specially constructed organ,riding down a chute in a car,and finally(heads tucked between legs)somersaulting

—Grand Finale;animal orchestra,viz.

(a)white donkey . . . White Russia

(b)black donkey . . . fascist Italy

(c)momentous dotardly walrus(minus teeth but capped and earmuffed and mitted for the occasion)who sucks his thumb and beats a drum labelled Alarm . . . Pilsudski

(d)a big black seal . . . Lithuania(?)

AND

(e)grey O how mysteriously glad elephant;carelessly who leads the band with a baton while representing(via bannerblanket which immediately he begins tweaking off—and is by innumerable agonized tovariches most forcefully restrained)ALL EUROPEAN CAPITALISM

—and even as this irrevocably playful personage is with huge difficulty compelled to walk on 3 legs,K hears the just behind me comrade's unvoice trumpeting to comrade some unworld:Capitalism limps!understand?good!

Superfinale(the equivalent of a Ringling chariotrace)equals 1 troika;drawn by peculiarly delapidated dogs and in which Durov totteringly circles the ring;feebly fluxing backstreamingly scarletness while painfully through wobbly mustachios at possibly you and probably me grinning;and undeniably comrade Death

street. Night

far,up(whirling—wonderfully how—through,such;keen:agonies)
climb(tense)sprouting explodes wholly a:now;bright,thickening—
scream

("my god" he & she whisper. 3 run toward)

people,arms heads feet backs hands,surround It. It,dwindling . . .
gushbubbling undrooping,which stiffens;bursts:

& a glimpse—from black(skirts?)something—of chewedness thrice
lifesize. Of chunk of mashed bloody steak

. . . dizzily Turkess,fingers in ears,slops against nearest wall.
("They've called the" Turk soothes between geysers of scream
"ambulance. He" pointing to a trembling militiaman,helplessly
who bends over black (woman?)something,repeating monotonously
Tovarich "just said so")

I hear myself saying "let's wait,and see how soon the ambulance
arrives"

"right?" he turning to her. She,nodding,"I'm all right"

8 minutes

during which the screamIt rhythming has wilted. Enter now
ambulance:very very large and very very very efficient. 4 figures
descend;calmly. & sudden puddles-of-Itscream evaporate . . .

"they gave her a shot then"(he whispers,staring over heads)"I could
see the syringe"

China is wonderfully filthy.

Japan appallingly is clean and comfortable
(the Turk tells meanderingly;stories of Elsewhere,rapidly:blossoming
trees,fertile flatnesses,mountains nonsense and kimonos)

"good evening" Nat

(start guiltily)4 comrades from leftover(cold but somehow mightily
comforting)bleenihs

"your passport" almost severely,if not quite proudly,she addressed me
"it is good. I took it there of myself;they shall now submit it to their
housecommittee."

"How many thousand thanks" I don't pretend to say.

"Then we'll have it back tomorrow?" Turk mildestly inquires

"yeehas . . ." And(wisely)How 1 semiEnglish semiRussian eyebrowless
"pair-haps" boosts

ogress's day off.

My host and hostess depart early to buy a present for the scientist's child;soon they'll return and escort me chez god almighty for "real American breakfast"

(grabbing original hymn of hate,also my "translation",I tack for Revolutionary Literature Bureau)

beside whose shutness 2 unknown nonmen & 1 carrotheaded known).

"We're locked out" explains,with a brief shrug,Clara Bow

"please" pleasefully "take this . . . it's only a literal rendering. There are gaps where the French text was mangled. You'll probably have to change this and that"

"then the person to change it is you" he said brightly,trying to regive

grimly "I've done my best" K states,hands in pockets

"but wait a while" the Bow soothingly invited. "Someone's coming with a key directly;and I want very much to read your translation. Besides" slyly "we owe you a few roubles."

"Sorry,but I—"

"come come—"

"but you have my present address—"

"the comrade's due any moment—"

"yes,but I've got a breakfast date with the Ay Pee man" desperately announce. Carrot suddenly recoils

"with—?"(faintly)

"so long!" Our heroless smiles,waves. Scandalized 6 eyes stare . . . 3(muttering to each other)shocked comrades look . . .

Mammy,née Sunshine,seems 15 years older;the nonexistence of Sunday has also afflicted god. Yet(after 1 singularly unsolid hour)when "real American breakfast" makes its immense appearance,everybody—Mammy even—forgets everybody else's troubles . . . crisp the sausages . . . juicy the griddlecakes . . . fresh the butter . . . steaming the coffee. Furtive the(unvisibly entering)Hindu "where y' goin'?" almighty grunts,at myself

"hate to admit it,but I have a little dress rehearsal on my hands, comrade—"

"why not meet us at the Art Theatre later?" suggests Turk. "We've got three perfectly good Gorky-festival seats:the Writers' president sent them to me this morning;and,according to Nat,comrade G himself will be there."

"Which theatre did you say?"

"walk down Tverskaya to the telephone building" Turk directs. "Turn kittycorner,left;the Art Theatre's on your left again. Here's a ticket. We'll see you later—"

("not me" god mutters,drowsily sucking god's teeth)

Something's(I walk in unchallenged)showhouse—feeling of emptiedness; of inefficiency,looseendsness. At 2nd floor a genial ugly nonman inquires my whither;hearing Something's name,grins,nods,leads("dritte étage")me to next landing;and(remarking that rehearsal lasts from 11 to 3)vanishes—I perceive(in a tiny open room)several tipsy reeling soberly youths,painfully who are balancing paper cornucopias on their noses . . . I shyly peek at stage:the battleship is coming down . . . no anywhere comrade Something. Occasionally,from far nearness,a band snorts

mother earth's foremost living proletarian writer. Himself,not a picture. Not a shadow—not that shadow which,very scarcely,I glimpsed in $\frac{1}{2}$darkness of an opera loge

but am lost. Or yes? (Woodenly this droshky-comrade views my ticket;he nods solemnly;gradually evolves circular distant gestures: I comprehend. I must go along that street. I must go and go. I must go until I see a rapidly revolving theatre,preferably upsidedown. Spaseebah)

a not closed shut with certain dreamish comrades negligibly idling beside. 1 sign—which compares favorably with the inscription on my beelyet. Enter. A comrade who takes away my cap and gives me stare in exchange. Another comrade,who doesn't want my ticket;who gestures heavenward. A gentle personage pointing behind himself. I push through shuts. & approaching 1 possibly comrade-usher

Is this here?

my gifted self queries:he doesn't look surprised or unsurprised:taking,lazily scrutinizes ticket:mumbles:gives,lazily. Perhaps because he's standing with his firmly back to still another shut,something tells me that Art Theatre is now enjoying blessings of drama—accordingly,wander that almost vacuous corridor(filled with educational photos:boasting a 1st-of-May section which somewhat resembles Arabian Nights' antireligious museum). Unpresently turning,see comrade possibly-usher peering timidly through the final shut—timidly which the possibly comrade presently now opens. And duckscoot through opening

into arms . . . President of Writers';whom I've scarcely(you only just got here? "Quel dommage!" But there's still much to come)greeted when up glideth exVirgil

"your" caustically unsmiling "whereabouts are unknown."

"I left my address with the Metropole—"

whispering("come:I must present you immediately to the author of Roar China")

I "hello!" wildly shout,spying the Turkess

ex- stares:ex- also spies;ex-'s nonface bounds—"aha! the beautiful daughter of" . . . and for herself unhe dashes—"how do you do." (Bowing)"I suppose you just got up"

wearily she demurs "not just"

"of course not. I'm joking. As a matter of fact,I just got up!"

and the(kicking out comrades who've occupied seats whereto they belong even less than the same don't belong to ourselves because everything really belongs to everybody)Turk

"welcome."

Darkness

(1st a dramatization,on dit,of the short story which made comrade Gorky famous)2 men. 1 idiotic,with haycoloured hair. 1 not;older. Eventually,latter throws some money to former:babbling who embraces latter. Latter then hurls former more money. Former thereupon waxes ecstatic. Latter then takes all the money away from former. Former begins to cry;changes his mind,and chucks a large cloth rock at his disappeared friend . . . the rock disappears hitlessly,the friend (considerately)returns to drop dead. Remorse(etc.)by former:whose passionate tears bring latter to life. Joy(etc.)by former—neechehvohs by latter;who(still rubbing his head)departs;leaving dumb kneeling dumbly with untouched wealth before dumb intermission

(2nd)2 nonmen and a(superb;almost immobile)man. 1 of nonmem,the Turk fortunately explains,is a boy;son to the other nonman;who's a whore(dragged in by the man and laid on a couch). While drunken whore(boy's mother)sleeps,boy and man converse. Exit man. Darkness. Light:enter same man bringing toys. And he has brought the(now awake)whore food,but won't have his reward,despite her "go ahead and sleep with me:you can ask any of the boys;they'll tell you I didn't give them anything." Finis as whore embraces her sleeping child in an ecstasy of motherhood

intermission

(3rd)beginning of The Lower Depths("the tovarich who plays the baron is a great actor"). Set—levels,heights,distances—excellent. As in 2 preceding plays,an almost infallible homogeneity transcends the merely unsentimental;easily averts the merely real. When,at last,clamour indicates that the hard lodginghouse unlady-in-red beats her in-pink-daughter for loving a blond blueshirted thief,this(at least)comrade has experienced actuality(O categories!O "proletarian" O "art"!)or if possible what more surely despises propaganda than dream always is under deed—nay,suspect it's only propaganda which this rather whitish little character brooms busily while the tovarich curtain descends

& straight to Chinesey's proceeds Harem,Assyrian and myself pause at ye Lenin institute("one of the few places where you mustn't tip" he whispers. Tiptoeishly we abandon headgear in a downstairs chapel-coatroom. Tiptoefully—propitiating all undaemons—purchase,upstairs,devout souvenir postcards from a devotee who's nigh hysterical at thought of changing 1 rouble). Promptly we're sacredly asked,by another devotee,who we are? And:Americans(Turk replies)but my friend here understands Russian . . .

2 steeped in the odourless odour of sanctity floors,of about 6 tiptoeingly rooms

fondly now this(among other things)ex-wouldbecommunist,my friend Assyrian,crisply discusses that revolutionary document or that revolutionary photograph;fondly now explains,concisely,many unthings . . . e.g. why comrade revolutionary Trotsky very incidentally occurs only 3 times("which is worse than leaving him out entirely"). —Everywhere we're haunted by propaganda-in-the-fleshless. By 1 rigmaroling tovarichpriestofhumanity who Russianizes to groupless pallid group of dirty clumsy probably schoolchildren

. . . bust. A statue. Photos galore. Flags. Gifts to L from workers' association. The automatic which did not kill(beside which occurs an official document testifying that this is The automatic). Clothes. Wig(exile). Occasional glimpses of L's W. On the 2nd floorless,phonograph(softly "a speech of Lenin's" Turk marvels;and,carefully replacing record,winds up slowly the machine)&

("that's the man who's introducing him"). Cracked voiceless ("Lenin")

   brisk short barking skilfully perioded harangue

—I turn—

behind are,greeting that magic horn with precisely an His Master's Voice expression,tensely standing rigid youthless in uniform,lostfaced civilian,nonman usher

all:spellbound

I retreat slightly—am sternly eyed by uniform—

(Assyrian would have reversed the disk;but the nonman crisply states)No more(and 2 atiptoe comrades pass onward)

why then should there be no(between arrival of 2 chez Chinesey and departure of 3 for professor scientist's)time to try Disappointment Square? Not that a letter's waiting for 1 comrade

this unbelievably enormous jar,violently labelled COLD CREAM and cadeau from Turkess to Mme. Professor,isn't exactly the oriflamme K would have chosen. But it's much too heavy for comrade Turkess;Turk already totters under vodka and light wines . . . miraculously the uncrowded tram stares merely,shrugs,neechehvohs.

Why should our party be met at the scientist's portal by a beautifully dressed little boy with warm serious eyes,who rushes at hastily unbundling Turk and embraces him? 4 comrades climb worn stairs—pausing at this landing,inspect a large unshut cubicle of patriotism(an official roomless or "red corner";furnished à la modeless with tawdry banners dirt and a pair of oldish men,vehemently seated in obstreperous silence). & climb. Until the flowery door. Until erect welcoming dignity,and erect's wife;and her stocky greyhaired sister(as I learn after several vodkas)completely who,deftly,seems by delicate mannerisms enclosed.

Why then should easily dignity locate an extra group of perfectly different sitting-contri-vances(choosing a stool for himself)? And now our wellwarmed company essays good soup;melting sweetish chicken with fluffy rice;a tasty homemade dessert;featherlike cakes;cheese;and more and more coffee and more . . . Who peers through sexless nervous wellbred atmosphere-of-kindliness may discover that all cooking was accomplished via single round gas burner almost big enough to unchill 1 thimbleful of milk. (& throughout this miraculous repast,Assyrian and serious-eyes are playing;when More finally ceases,eyes leads his playmate to a tiny couch where playmate falls asleep embracing the Arabian Nights in Russian)meanwhile my righthand neighbour,hostess's sister,once or twice shyly has emerged from her(showing me a bravery and a gentleness of spirit)selfless

"you like?"
wife,delighted,cries.

Yes,I even more than like. In fact,have just(rudely through wellbred pointing to diminutive mantlepiece)asked whence comes this woman-and-child miracle?this Giottomodelling of doubledoll?effigy almost not made with hands,almost beyond mind unreal.

"A child has made it" proudly. And rushes for tome of all coloured photographs all portraying child statue-dolls—"this is good"(she says)"I mean,that the child shall make. It is a good school,we have many,many good school"

"you have also a most wonderful museum which I never can seem to find;you have Cézanne,Picasso,Matisse—"

"il faut absolument visiter!" exclaims her sister "c'est le meilleur du monde!"

thereat host,beckoning,smiling corroboration,maps me very patiently whereabouts of socalled Western Art . . .

—(rising,finger on lips)pilfers the sleeping Turk's kodak. And(perching cautiously it atop most fragile assemblage of mutually incongruous objects known to nonscience)4 times mortalises that oblivious guest. Alone;wearing flowers and a female hat;with an empty vodka bottle beside him;threatened by Turkess posing Salomeishly). While serious-eyes dances for joy silently

—and,the comedy concluded,(pointing briefly through unshutness) "no bells. They don't ring" at a distant spire smiles hurtly.

"Doubtless" not to erect himself I suggest,not to any human being;but

to that excessively that mythically unhuman Mankind whose nonexistence seals each slaughter "no doubt socialism is here exercising the
benevolent prerogative of psychological protection" dare to continue(for
he's now smiling not hurtly)"the silencing of all churchbells is of course
directed against that psychic demoralization,that derangement of the
spiritual machine,which must inevitably occur when a tension is not
followed by a release or(which may heaven forbid)an expectation remains
ungratified." He's almost laughing "thus:ringing infers,comrade;ringing
is a comparatively worthless prelude to something very definite and
positive and valuable,some particular sort of manifestation—god,for
instance,should appear,or a bellboy;otherwise the anticipations aroused
by ringing are disappointed,otherwise the confidence of humanity is
violated. But,comrade—by the sacred tenets of socialism,god and a
bellboy are strictly forbidden" he laughs,almost gaily "therefore" the
Turk stirs "humanity's strictly benevolent vicar,the holy apostolic socialist
state,formally forbids anybody ever to ring for either—while graciously
permitting unpoliticallyminded comrade Pavlov to stimulate the salivary
glands of his young dogfriends"

quickly erect—pulling out a few coinless coins—"this is the reason"
with deathly contempt "that is the only reason"(and what eyes!)

. . . & finally,long after Assyrian's awakening,a hint of tragedy:
when(Turk "read this" whispers)I peruse document inviting the
distinguished to a distinguished conference of his distinguished peers in
the land,O comrades,of the statue of liberty. How distinguished would
give all except his very all to attend!yes,but something named "Russia"
demands that his very all remain as hostages. Therefore distinguished
will not attend

(fervently)K:An "idea" was never "put in practice"—never is,or will be.

T(leaning across how solidly between us situated daylabouring
tovarich):Never?

K:Suppose it were even "scientifically" established that the best
"idea",when "put in practice",produced the worst results;that would be
1 face of the cube.

T:Right. But disagreeable . . . probably because I sincerely tried to
believe in this religion of humanity.

K:What a murderfully vast difference exists between "standing
up for an idea"(between combatting unvalues;for instance,American

unvalues)and inhabiting the "practice" "of" an "idea",inhabiting socalled socialist Russia!

T:Machinery came to exalt mankind. It remained to degrade human nature. I cry shame on capitalism,for making a fetich of machinery in behalf of personal profit. I cry doubly shame on the 5 year plan for glorifying gogetting,in behalf—if you please—of impersonal profit!

K:This comrade feels very humble;this comrade begins to realize that soandso enters the pigeonhole for the same "reason" that suchandsuch doesn't. Take,for illustration,my good friend—who will soon be my good enemy—the talented author of that hymn of hate which I've been unbusy "translating":well,whatever "reason" for this conversion to communism is probably a fair lady,which is probably whatever unreason for my own nonconversion. Amen

and we pass(or this time I notice)brutally disembowelled corpse ecclesiastical,its frescoes unpityingly here and here exposed

& now(now alone,infinitely alone among all unalone lonelinesses(I'm through this very small parkless strolling;in the hot darkness . . . 3 gypsy children together,3 little girls in bright rags,earning kopeks:1 claps while 2 wobble—a comrade-man gives a comrade-almost-pretty-nonman gives;an earnest scrawny comrade-unman questions abruptly the wobbleclap trio and clapper immediately sidles off(immediately follow the little chubbier dirtier and littlest chubbiest dirtiest wobblers)and the how littlest utters 1—not to be measured—gesture of scorn,and the onlookers(except scrawny)laugh;nudge . . . & I pass the Metropole Hotel,I round the forepart of that large parkless and I emerge;to climb a steepish street,into an oval,past L's M and the "internationale"-striking tower(to my right:incredibly a near sector of moon!)and the Arabian Nights cathedral;on whose steps 2 coiffed crones dream . . . & past joking astroll man-and-nonman almost-lovers & down to the left through emptily dark soiled streets & back through very small(same almost-pretty-comrade-nonman;she's talking now with the comrade-man-giver)park & past this dolled up Oreye-entully scornful miss all swathed in blue veils & up Petrovka to a corner. Where

something(lightdrenched)is being uptorn . . . backs these hurl pavingstones . . . hark:unequally now intermingling rhythms of the shovellers(perhaps as if molecules of surf perform,always,some to ourselves invisibly usefulness?)

& Tverskaya—almost but not quite deserted—& into and out of
sandy treelined lane,where am grazed by gouging furiously tram(its very
din neither saw nor noticed;far less heard!)&,miraculously not turned
into steak,now down now left and past & back
. . . faintest star points in hot dull sky

that unpreening "publicity!" Turk to preening this Turkess raves. "It's the
only thing! —Jesus:what I want is a good loud publicityman!someone
to get up publicity for comrade Kem-min-kz. Not to mention comrade
Lack Dungeon's distinguished daughter's unknown" they've returned
from a functionless function "husband;né professor-in-extremis of
advanced Russian at god knows which 4thrate American university
but my class had only one student,a hunchback,and how I hated him!
Help—help—for the little fatboy—who's down in a corner of beautiful
somebody's nuptial photograph:au secours!" He chuckled,beaming

"when we get to New York,I'm going to steal away to a quiet speakeasy
and give you all the publicity" she mutters,preening

"'I see you' she said to me 'with two children—there is a little girl,I see her in your arms'" sighing "—I'd love to have a child . . . another child." Pause "that was just a regular medium. But somehow I believed her." And almost desperately "because there really are some things we don't quite know about!"

"I should hope!"

"O . . . I'm so depressed"(she cries)"and it's silly too. I know it's silly. This wasn't anybody's fault—"

"this?"

"you see,Charlie just got a cable saying that too much news had been sent. Well,Nat was off sending still more and nobody could get in touch with Nat to tell her to stop . . . things happen queerly,don't they"

"but they still happen:then let's be amazed"

"all right" the Turkess agreed,laughing "let's"

and what a mood poor Nat inhabits! more accurately,what a pair of ½moods;for Nat's Russian and English differently suffered when the Turk lost his temper(who's now sorry;being a happening by god's grace or sensitive person incapable of hatred)and Nat's English is all pulled back up far into itself,making pain;but her Russian is all spread thin over everything which itself isn't,making grief

and as for me,I've merely walked with each portion to its(and deposited both at their)dentist's,all of a griefless painless angerless today-morning

. . . in Disappointment Square,comradeless Americanitz peesahtel consults caringly a scared diagram(gift of a caring comradeless professor scientist). Caringly the former now fights into this earth's feeblest tram. Caringly(as per latter's directions)unfights at 1 now golddomed cathedral. He walks too far. Halting,inquires his caring way of nyezneyeyooing boyless;of silently tall ghost who points

. . . oasis

enfin!

1st:anteroom(containing much giltedged bourgeoise merde plus several early Cézannes). Follows a roomlet;together jumbling certainties

& incertainties . . . next propaganda stalks:ponderous(wouldbe proletarian)unvisions of amorphous "workers"—and may Marx help the cause of labour if ever these should come to life

4th:

incredible—Picasso!

1 entire room. 1 hollow cube;solid with only(upon all its walls) beautiful,beyond wonder,murderings of reality. Fatal strict rocketings (deep most fluent)swoops floatingly seethe and(cool huge)absolute volutions,are Mind—utterly are alert(wholly which inimitably provoke now the serene velocities;the now how furious tranquilities,of Form)Spirit

. . . I feel—"suddenly"=a word—why comradeless Kem-min-kz made pilgrimage to socialist soviet Russia

5th,unbelievably Matisse!

—above this doorway,5 gradually distorted heres(flat upon a flatgreen aslope insolently that;or against crudely blue skyflattest this;or andishly among both's neither)splurge;opposite,swiftly reproportioned,if of no world,creatures lymphatically pauseflowing(what neverdancers alwaysd ancing!)reel,droopingly are precise of rhythm perpetually selfinventing the constituents. & from ceiling unto floor:and from floor unto ceiling,Colour(blossomingly moored with hue alive Shape;swaying— steep orchestration of ripe optical Emptiness—wandering melodic to harmonically return visual Vitality)tugthrusts at its at such at anchoring what mercilessly Contour. Mercifully,from up to down,from far to near,unimaginably luscious navigations of Silence

I("feel"=a word)suddenly why socialist soviet Russia made pilgrimage to Is

my silently not big with smallness of all humanity(& as mind makes: silently)self small with bigness moves of every universe.

. . . Aussi il-y a des excellents Van Goghs,especially the billiardtable. Also an entirely luxuriant and where you sweat with the tropics Gauguin bower. Also old man Renoir. The boys and Derain and Vlaminck et al. Also 4 Maillols;no Lachaise(and a wretched Rodin) . . . I touch(for luck)lightly 1 idol,this by Something's friend:bonjour,

&

out

(now

. . . into merely)human(not . . . which? . . . a)street?(does it perhaps
or do these people think they exist or it exists?)
  neechehvoh,tovarich!

exceedingly chez Chinesey lurking,my friend the Turk seems not
quite exhausted. His unmiraculous today had brought—in addition
to news-woe—2 separate visits from illstarred compatriots. (Seem
to understand that the adoption,by any socialist soviet wife,of any
capitalist husband's nationality marche pas. Also,that Russian divorces
aren't any too good in the land of the free. Then alas that American
citizen who,tumbling for a nonman,tries to export her as his bride!
And,just for good measure,no official spokesman of god's country graces
Moscow;therefore an American wouldbe exporter of wouldbe American
womanhood weeps on an unofficial shoulder. "It's" Assyrian,pointing
upstairs,murmurs "tough")
  & through the ceaseless miracle(my own today)enters(quietly)agony
of a man crying;despair of a woman sobbing

3 comrades this evening adventure Stanislavsky's for magnificent
Boris.
  When the 2nd(the inside church)scene tremendously's applauded—
not so much for its mountaining caesuras,for its most sunny and colossal
music,as for god's comfort in ungod's comfortlessness—1 comrade
understands . . . yea;these miscellaneous(sensibly celebrating a singularly
stifling occasion with their suspenders and even bathingsuits)children
of nondeity are glad of bells!

". . . something about dogs?"
  "she said the dog is loose" Turk translates ogress
  "well?" Turkess
  "loose in the kitchen" he amplifies sadly
  "dog?" K vaguely interpolates
  "a mighty mastiff cur. Whom the good doctor"(Chinesey)"personally
releases late each night . . . "
  "why a dog?"
  "to keep the comrades out" twinkling. "Poor soviet Cerberus!all day
long who must remain enchained."

And she groans "then we can't have anything to eat?"

"suppose" he suggests "our servitor should open that can of sardines which dwells in the bathroom?"

but Harem shook her head.

"Nyet?"

sighing "there's no fork"

"—my god" he cried;terrorstruck "do Russians use forks?"

"This Russian does;at least,to remove the skeleton—"

"come"(solemnly taking my arm)"comrade. Let us from this most bourgeois boîte remove our own tovarich skeletons"

& out of inn of ye dead Xmas tree sprouts a young(whom accompanies a very tiniest orchestra)violinist until the airless now tinily quivers with forsythialike gypsytunes

. . . ½ while am remembering the very back of Mr. Moscovitz himself,not a picture,seated before his cimbalom,not a harpsichord—un(smoothly wholly per peevoh & Assyrian)rolls the paradox of paradoxes;till &

"our little universe is headed that way."

"Toward socialism?"

"Yes;but I think it will come to America as a series of more or less gradual modifications."

"That would please Ezra,the son of Homer. Or any man with roots. And that would displease all uprooted and rootless unmen and 'radicals'"

"revolution" the Assyrian said "cannot be ordered like a plate of beans. Somebody most truly has remarked" softly "you gotta have a lotta people poor first"(revolution?

We of whom Is partakes,only to whom our deaths are births—savagely makers beneath docile time(and beyond conquerable space travellers)who are not contained or comprised,who cannot fail in wonder—possibly we conceive dreaming and impossibly freedom:opening and mind's agony of first joy—stern we,the hugely forever-pitying genitals of spirit

continue not to be,arithmetic of unwish!die on,measure with your nonexistence our existings! Unplay,very O most trivial marionettes,unplay—so solemnly—that gameless game whose ignorant beginning neatly predetermines its knowledgeable end,or which can merely be to living as an equation to a smile . . . continue not to be,die on,unplay:how you shall always everywhere perish! Not here and not there shall,nor then nor now,perish;not "religion" and not "science" shall perish,but what undreams would deny feeling shall attain the end of their beginning(always they shall know the everywhere knowledge,which death is) . . . whatever knows must die.

& live—lovers of To Be!eyes of the world,relax;open and feel,give yourselves only to the giving walls of this single house—only whose ceilings and whose floors frame the Self's full perfect doom of imperfection:doom untranslatable,doom of which all exhortations constitute unplastic parodies—breathe in this house,makers of Is,not hope and not despair,but timeless deep unspace,the single poem,which builds unconsciousness:immeasurably this house only shall live! Only these walls may not wilt;only cannot drown with any earthquake,any wave. "Revolutions" everywhere must perish,but not these walls:only these walls are Revolution) outside my(barred)unshutness,in sunlight,7 things entered descendingly 3 times—& I looked out—a bronze face,boy,vizor up-and-back,black hair,his arms hanging limp,wandered in;approached;looked:turning looked:looking;turning,went(".o.o.o..o..o.o..o")—the 7 things I do not know,therefore they were dressed for me as dreams . . . the dreamer might have been offering me all wealth of another planet,or merely love hope dream birth fear death always:nyez neyeyoo.

(Distantly breakfast tinge upstairs-and-down consolations(again the sobbing Russian nonman and her crying American wouldbe exporter: Chinesey consoles former;Turk latter) . . .)

now,this little engineer came to the earthly paradise on a low salary;came earning $150 a month—which sum remained in America for the uses of his family—plus maybe it was 80 roubles or maybe not,which here he spent himself(and all because this little engineer was "interested in building socialism") . . . now,the socialist republic kept this little engineer idle . . . and this little engineer objected("I came here to build socialism") . . . whereupon,the socialist republic framed this little engineer And How by immediately assigning him to a job about which he knew less than nothing . . . now,this little engineer(who came to Russia to build socialism) knew nothing for 2 long days and then resigned . . . aha,then quoth the socialist republic;we thought so:you are not an expert,you are therefore a spy("I don't care,I have my visa,I can leave;it's" choke "her!") . . . not so much being unhappy because she can't leave(with this little engineer)as because certainly she'll be called to "the big house" and examined re him and probably won't be jailed and will only be kept under surveillance and already has lost her job,which was writing,and she's utterly helpless,and can't move anywhere,or do anything(or love anyone else but this little engineer)and all because "I was serious,I came to Russia seriously,I came here to build socialism"

at the Turk's "we're off to the Kremlin" cry,all our hearts hop
   . . . the Kremlin!

& away darts Turkess(to don her best)&
—the Kremlin!
off Nat scoots—I rush to(the Kremlin!)my razor
and:
and;
&,
1 Hour's Wait.
. . . Finally
—ah—
rings telephone the
(quick)
and "sorry" and "very"
(sorry?)
"we aren't"
—aren't? Aren't! what do you mean Aren't?
"taking any more for the Kremlin today;good-bye"

(INTOURIST)helplessly angrily ploughing Ks now,now lost:desper-
ate;gloomily,now sullenly harrowing the Cs—. Find
    O did ever shutting perpetuate
    did opening invent
    ,or surface(touch!)feel,Alive(with an how deep-full an eagerly what
dream-near)ness . . .
                        So let's have the merry World!—feel . . . a(most
forgotten glad immensely what universes aeons having travelled)Now
firstfully(peering through space newly through created time rising a
mysteriously)Here;
    (pity only those who cannot love
    do not pity lovers)even if lovers may not(only with those silences
which are most certainly love's Together,certainly each under where alive
Voice or beyond when)murder death;suddenly(themSelves)touching;
with every(and with always)where becoming a single(darker,a greater
perhaps stranger;large more impossibly than what quite is never to be
imagined)Self

. . . then an—in dream moving—madman wanders:toward something
called Turkish something called consulate

he rings at a house.

Out of which drips a small dark comrade saying "yes"

—make as if to enter—

seizing my arm,mutters dark Russianly;points:to a shedlike outhouseness . . . powerfully growls

Thanks(nod)and investigate:entering shed's unofficial dirty roomlets where dazed sit 3 tovarichs

"c'est ici le consulat turque?"

"non" 1 responds(gradually pointing to mansion from which had been bounced)"c'est par là"(and turning away)

can you tell me(ask 2nd)something about leaving Russia?

you can ask here(2nd points to 3rd)

what do you want?(number 3 asks)

I want to know—

know?

—whether I should get my exitvisa in Moscow or in Odessa.

In Odessa.

How long does that take?I mean,to get a visa in Odessa?

one day.

And do ships go from Odessa to Athens?

the soviet ship goes only to Constantinople(grumpily)

I presume there are other ships?

"je crois."

And the soviet ship goes often?

often.

How often?

often enough.

Are you sure?

"je crois."

There's perhaps a boat from Constantinople to Marseilles—what do you think?

"je crois."

And I suppose Greece and Turkey and the other capitalist nations require visas?

all visas may be got in Odessa.

Then I may take a train from Moscow to Odessa;I may get all the necessary visas in Odessa;and I may take one of several ships,from Odessa to—(I almost said The world!)—elsewhere?is that correct?

"je"(off myself sliding his to a lapless lap eyes tumbling)"crois"

&(Presidentless nowhere at Writers')proceed dreamingly(buying in dream speechkih of silent ½armless)to Torgsin;& buying 6 Troikas and 3 Yahvas there in dream for almost 3 dollars(after waiting exactly 10 minutes while 3 Germans—of whom 2 unmale—buy 3 lemons and some candy and 6 boxes of cigarettes) . . . am staring at
  would these perhaps like to travel?
machinemade dolls,when hear behind
  "thinking of all the girls he'll give presents to!"
(unvoice). Ex-:
  "hello" I dream
  "—pathetic,isn't it,this display! Just look at all these foods and clothes and trinkets"(and why forget the ikons upstairs?)"obviously intended to convey an impression of native luxury and abundance;when of course they're really here for the sole purpose of catching your and my valuta" (that fish which sings!)—then,at a tovarich who's now solemnly stuffing with many small parcels the vast babydress of this peculiarly enormous effigy "see!" pointing,uneyes aglitter lewdly "nice,eh? Hm . . . Pleasant occupation,I should think—and so safe,too!" obscenely he whispers, nudging
  (care)"did you know"(fully and calmly I observe)"the military tactician's a wellknown Phi Beta Kappa?"
  recoil!
  "or so they tell me" K vaguely pursues
  "now You're getting them!"(unhe trembled,pallid)
  "'getting them'?"
  "getting the Moscow heebee-jeebees" ex-(pallid)trembled
  "no no:I merely thought you might have seen our friend,and"
  "I've"(explodes)"seen nobody else!"
  we look. At we.
  "—He'll be here in a minute" adds this sweating cocktail of hatred and pathos
  "indeed"
  "hm . . . —Well" violently collecting himself "if that's" confidentially "really so,I'm glad to hear it"(sneer)"My trouble is finding a bolshevik in Moscow" with how not describable what dense bitterness "one meets more bolsheviks per day in New York!"

"I shouldn't be surprised."

"Hm:yes;but—speaking of fraternities—he says,I mean our military friend,that we completely misunderstand a certain remark of his . . ." pause. "About the Russian soul . . ."

"in the days of the Czar,a Russian's soul was his passport?" I quote

"yes. He says he really meant that the Czar owned a Russian's soul and his body too;while now they only have your body—or something like that" ex- almost "you'll say it's crawling,I suppose" smiles

the K comrade began laughing—

"—well if you" up-and-out-flaring(And How!)"Will live with millionaire Jews!"

"what's that?" I said.

(Snicker "I didn't mean anything derog- . . . as a matter of fact"(amiable)"I myself sponged off the doctor more than you;I didn't even pay for my room,and"(sly)"I assume you are . . ."

"I'm not paying" I said "one kopek"

"—no? Hm . . . Well,nobody could accuse me of antiSemitism—don't" suddenly pleadful "let them poison you" ex- begs. Tearful,almost "I'm really So disappointed;you . . . you came here with SUCH a nice open mind!"

"pahzhahloostah"

"—you ought,really you ought,to meet the other kind. You are meeting some of them,I suppose . . . no,but someone like what is his name now;of the Harvard Crimson,Barnes—no no,that's a different Barnes,Harvard M.A. I think,but he said he came from another college—or did he? O:I know what he said;he said I wouldn't know his name;and I said Tell me,I'll know;and then he told me,and . . . I had to crumple up!—they live together!"

"so long"(waves comrade fleeing capitalist Kem-min-kz so shortly)

still stupefied(by a cannonshotlike Good from ogress,apropos of inadvertently taking 2nd soup at dinner)who meets much more than extraordinary windowdisplay—something like a pawnshop and a picture gallery rolled into 1. The pawnshop motif existing chiefly via defunct totally clocks,the gallery per merely unborn natures mortes infinitely overframed,but heaven only knows how many quarreling objects here coexist. Homogeneity,nevertheless,results. Actually here jets into the street a profound spasm of uselessness—

&,spattered by uselessness,possibly the most motley hypnosis of tovariches(immobile,clumsily)occurs

. . . who marvellingly continues. At Something's theatre,I soften the Administration with a glimpse of American passport plus tidy little formula of Turk's;promptly receiving ticket,I enter The Last Decisive.

Peculiar audience. Audience neither childishly here-I-amish—e.g. Gahlstook—nor(with due allowances for political climate)effete —e.g. Prince Igor. An audience painfully,not to mention strainfully,Try-ing:¹/₃ whereof=soldiers;99% of whom=Phi Betas. Find for a change my own seat. Near(incredibly)a girl(unbelievably)handsome;squired by a flaxhaired certainly not comrade and whose capitalist face belongs on the end of a horse's neck. Both beauty and the beast,meseems,are under escort—per this almost animated wondrously dumpy nonman

(scene 1 does not belong to the play at all:dumpy—to beast "ex-cuse,please I will get pro-gram for you"—vanishes. Comrade-usher orders a seatless tovarich to dumpy's vacant chair. Immediately mine ears,and everyone else's for 13 rows,wince with that strictly most appalling of sonal atrocities The Great American Voice —"This!Seat!Is!Taken!" beauty twangs . . . Christ,how the usher cringes,how the seatless scuttles,how 13 rows of("slaves—I know")Russians bend upon America their hating-silently but mutely-worshipful attention)!

as for merely the play itself:words do not fail.

Title,broadcasts dumpy returning,is("some-thing right from our nash-un-al an-them which" genially "is the in-ter-nash-un-al") short for the last decisive Struggle "be-tween the cap-i-tal-ist world and us"("how interesting" beauty suavely smiles. "Hm" politely horseface muses)

given such a title,nothing less than Ragnarok can legitimately be expected of comrade director Something;who,nothing loth,fills the bill in a big And How way—I don't mean maybe, comrade.

Boogeyman blood and infantile thunder . . .

—utterly to me extraordinary=1 fact:a brutally(almost but not quite beyond recognition)caricatured American Sailor wins,not murderous rage,not patronizing mirth,not disdainful silence,but tremendous applause—the 1st(incidentally)and last strictly spontaneous ovation of an entirely incredible soirée. He moreover deserves it;with a mucho original hornpipeful of mingling softshoe-&-Diaghilev tricks well buried in semiobscene gesturings

. . . thunder and blood. Our Side Wins;this time,by losing(if only to make things slightly more heroic) . . .

"for forty hours" severely if politely expostulates twang,whom the earliest entr'acte's pitiless glare reveals as a middleaged midwestern matron "for forty hours,mind you,on the Riga-Leningrad train we had No Diner. Absolutely" Voice complains,turning on poor dumpy a wellbred complaining stare "NONE!"—"I know,but" dumpy writhes.— "But how can Russia" beauty with dignity continues "expect Americans to come here,when the most elementary facilities are lacking? You claim you want us to see your country" she protests with gentle irony "and yet you do everything to antagonize us while we're in it!"—"I am so sor-ry."—"Yes but" calmly "that doesn't help matters. O;and then our trunks!do you remember?" leering at beast,briefly who and wearily nods "why,that was simply outrageous!just preposterous!why,we were actually INSULTED!" she flared.—"I know,but" dumpy fidgets.—"Now listen: what it comes right down to is this:before your country does anything else,she'd better reorganize her whole tourist system from top to bottom;if she doesn't,do you know what will happen? Civilized people,who are used to living in a civilized way,will refuse to visit Soviet Russia. And you can't blame them,can you? I'm speaking as a friend of Russia,you understand"

: . . blunder and thud. During which our American matron unshakenly maintains a mild,an almost peaceful,demeanour of superior illumination: now and now ½turning,smiles:benevolently—then,as she notices this or that wideeyed comrade placidly sopping up the slop,pityingly . . . & now,now comes climax

a balcony voice denounces The Great Experiment of experiments, alias 1 stage-trenchful of Our Boys . . . who thereupon squirt not only said balcony but entire audience with machinegunfire . . . nevertheless(ars longa,vita brevis)Our stage-trenchful Boys dwindle . . . in fact,capitalism,or the enemy,operates with such efficiency that 1 lone loyal soul remains.

Now(please don't believe me)the sole survivor begins to die;thinks better of it;squirms upright;emanates something remarkably like a piece of chalk;yearns anguishedly toward,finally touching,something comparable to a conveniently appearing blackboard and(all things considered)heroically writes,most very And How legibly,a long long long long string of figures (162,000,000). Do not believe me.

Further dying:then he chalks a pathetically brief number(27)under the string and groaningly endows the former with a crisp minus sign. Eventually,after multiple incredible sufferings of most approved ham species(gutgrabbing, staggerstuttering,plucking of adam's apple,etc.)he performs a subtraction of the small number from the huge. (He subtracts absolutely correctly,I may add). And only now—kerplunk!—drops dead. Or is he dead? Yes;he's dead this time,all right(and apparently the string of figures expresses mother Russian's present population and apparently the tiny sum states the strength of Our trenchful and apparently the subtraction means "you capitalists can do-in that or this handful of comrades,but notice the thousands and hundreds of thousands not to mention millions who're alive and aching to in-do you")

at which pugilistic point Something's play(so to speak)throws away its truss—the final defunction of the interminably hero suffers a most startling resurrection—out(And How)strides real 'live socialist soviet tovarich matelot:How Many Men In This Audience Are Fit To Go To War?(rogat)

—trying to(any port in a storm)identify with serene beauty and her unruffled beast(leaning toward tranquility and toward compatriots)I hear

:ALL THOSE WHO ARE READY TO FIGHT FOR RUSSIA AGAINST THE WORLD STAND UP!

—beast(to dumpy):Do we stand up? Dumpy(rising):Yes—

(the shall we say audience rose to an apparently comrade).

Comrade I(rosing)couldn't resist a cheerful memory . . . scene,some or other New York theatre;time,Yee Olde Ware Toe Ende Ware;action,the band plays O say can you and(capitalist)comrade I and a(comrade) capitalist friend capitalistically-or-comradely(or otherwise)just simply don't budge:patriotically over ourselves And How lowers a comitalist caprade—"WUHSUHMATTUH"(shrieks he,baleful)"YUH FEET HOITUH SUMPN?" . . . now,even as comrade I arise,feeling just simply ashamed,not feeling quite like a poodle begging for a biscuit,suddenly comrade I catch the wonderfully laughing comrade eye of a stage,a not real 'live,comrade-sailor("isn't it a good joke on you bourgeois?" this genial member of the cast seems to be decisising "you must admit it is!")whereupon I grin. Whereupon he grins

&

homeward wandering(by his grin dazed and mine and by serene and beast and by machinegun-chatter and by pistolshots and last O not least by the click of unloaded rifles)

rapidly we are passed by a Gay-Pay whom had especially noticed in the upper foyer of Something's theatre this very evening

(an aggressively ugly sawedoff kike type,striding hohenzollernly along as if he owned the word that made the world).

Female yells
   du monde
   middleaged nonman(sporting the usual extreme babyclothes)bawls heaven out of a lean angular toughlooking guy. Who,tossing purgatory over 1 tattered shoulder,slants off.
   Laughter

—on our left,a brilliantly lighted houseless:from whose topmost unshutness an almost girlish head protrudes,the head looks down(at me?)
   is singing!

Turk's 1st remark—(primevally as heroless frames unambiguous annihilation of The Last Decisive)
   "would you like to go on a party with some Russians?"
   K(reeling)
   "chez a pathetic old lady,who used to have a salon"
   sank—
   "and talks too much,and is a grandmother"
   —on 1 of several(originally 83)count 'ems(so blue and blue's obeyed their conscience!)
   "well,it's just as you like:nothing exciting;thought it might amuse you to watch the remnants of the olden days" Assyrian soothes.
   "There won't be elephants" entering states Turkess.
   "Provided" I mutter "there won't be castrated machineguns,provided we won't have to stand for the Interspangled Bannational,provided nobody isn't doing everything except trying . . . that's" comrade Kem-min-kz exploded "what's lousy here!Trying!everybody's never feeling;never for a moment relaxing,laughing,wondering—everybody's solemnly forever focussing upon some laughless idiotic unwonderful materially nonexistent impermanence,which everybody apparently has

been rabotatically instructed tovarich to welcome. God damn undream!
May the handshaking hell of the Elks and morons bugger to a bloody
frazzle everybody who spends his nonlife trying to isn't"

"my" A quoth to K "friend,not only shall now we sample this socalled
Slavic orgy but you will then get as stinko as I can—'

"Charlie!" the Harem said "your ideology confounds me!"

"a pox on ideology" cheerfully he replied

ring. & through most desolate very smelly anteroomlet("ugh!" confrère
scowls)a how(exsaloniste)tiny lurching shabbily atremble mound of
wrinkles spiritedly spirits—with exclamations(in French English and
neither)of delight and not infrequent duckings—us;and into larger
roomless,containing 1 groaning board,1 askew piano,infinite(especially
candlesticks)knicknacks,1 highboy,7 chairs,and

(a)gruesomely foreshortened cuss,whose allheadness completely has
been shaved

(b)not pleasantly elongated unyouth with something very unimportant
on his possibly mind

(c)much too neither Young Woman

(d)gent with a goatee and a mysterious smile

(e)chipper little plump hoppety robinman

(f)the sweetest sight that any 6th sense could clutch in any 5
day week. She's blonde & she's beautifully(simply)dressed(un-)in
darksmoothlyestishful &

(g)1 cat,grey

Hors d'oeuvres obstreperously à la Russe,pompously vodka,grandly
wines . . . small(and hungry)grey perches itself next Assyrian. "Funny"
who marvels "the only thing which is really repulsive to me is a—"

("nice garçon,vous" wrinkles atremble next myself seated strokes
lurching mes cheveux)

"—a cat,and I always have a fatal attraction for them."

("Artiste?" atremble uplooking spiritedly "oui?—Bon! . . .
hahrahshoh")

"is there a reason?" I inquire

"well" sighs the Turk "my mother collected stray cats for a considerable
number of" blonde,draped over arm of opposite the robin armchair,cups
dreamily "years" her left "she even used to give them milk" he
murmurs.

(Brightly)Stravinsky's(chants robin)"weak";Scriabine,a "great" man(translation by much too:retranslation by blonde)—after which robin honours us with a touch of something remarkably like The Old Apple Tree and(when applause has died)spins sputtering at K . . . "you" saloniste caressing translates "play-please?America-something,yes?" . . . I whereupon,possibly inspired by blonde vodka or whathavewe,render Old Man River crossed by Everybody Loves My Baby(with a mere dash of Nearer My God)

"hahrahshoh!" lustily robin cries,clapping me on gluteus maximus dexter and cutting a clown's caper

"why—nospeak—you—rooskih?" lusciously blonde ventures

I wish(I reply)

"HAHrahSHOH" robin,rocking with mirth,chortles

"woon dare fool" the mysteriously smiling goatee approves

Is the comrade a Norwegian?(from something not unlike stupor momentarily emerging hints foreshortened)

"guess my wife'd like to teach you,all right" proclaims a lank unvoice;almost if not grimly—turning,I confront elongated—"she's tryin' t' learn English herself" darksmoothlyestishful's unhe continues,faintly jocular "we're both goin' to America in a few weeks"

"Mair-kuh,yihz" ecstatically blonde nonlooks

"I tell her" the elongated said darkly "she'll marry a rich man." & in that word "rich" occurred something unmistakably genuine;something which might make a stone feel suddenly very sorry indeed for elongated "I tell her" confidentially "she won't stay with me long there"

"what is your profession?"

"engineer"(proudly. He coughed:bowed,strode elsewhere)

. . . what the? . . .

("heez wife,she-belle;no?" caressingly slyly the mound grins)

"encore!" chirps,merrily pointing at askew,robin

("do you perceive any glass of water?")whisper to Turkess,under hubbub

("don't think water exists") Turkess dittoes "but we'll try"(and weaving her wayless to antique wrinkling)"He"(pointing at myself)"Wants —a Glass of—Water" (shouts fiercely into earwrinkles)

"DANCE?" antique instantly exclaims "—dadada!" and(atremble) seizes among herselfless me . . .

"here!" the Harem cries

. . . and giving tiny lurching shabbily 1 last decisive whirl,I bow,trip suddenly over goatee,pardoning wade around elon($\frac{1}{2}$hating $\frac{1}{2}$fearing) gated,gain highboy

"but I wouldn't drink it if I were you"

but I'm I. And let's hope immortal. (For never was water like this!)

"good?" atremble,miraculously recovered,inquires

"DeLicious" shout

"funny boy" she atrembles

"Americans Are Funny Boys" loudly I inform her and seriously

(me almost lightly touching)"I want you"(whispers)"to love" tremulously upherselflessdrawing "this com-pany,this coun-try,and this gov-ern-ment"

—K salutes—

"listen"(touching)"we Russians are sim-ple . . . here"(points. To heart)"but not sim-ple"(to head. Points)"here"

"pahnyeemeyeyoo,tovarich"

the atremble wrinkling stood:stares;now for the 1st time I realise(that mound has eyes,that long long ago these eyes marvellingly were unafraid)some—perhaps fragment of an aspect,of a shadow,of that unexplorable negative thrown by the infinite mystery of old age. And quietly "I" said behind all wrinkles exquisite Theness "think you are like us"

Now it might have been Theness which begat Aness

now it came to pass that I saw some thinga live Mov ing(which in my now hand is:hugest 1 amazingly;black,omen!)

"OH"

why gasp,Turkess?(& tick-ling-ran-up-o-ver-me-all-my-neck-fore-head-down-runs

mr)cricket

. . .

without the hearth. (It tickling ran up ran over my ear forehead and down and yes disappears . . .)

at askew bangs robin

,now the gallant,Turk foots featly,blonde upyearning,in his arms,now the Harem,scowls ungently,featlying,in bootless mine,

now "you can en-gage to dance" antique encourages—heartily whom therefore I(until she squeals with joyful terror)twirl and myself mightily dizzying but not mightily enough to miss those(now here now there)anguished . . . less hating,more fearing . . . glances,with which elongated surrounds she-belle,now who seems to hurrying be into her

"isnit funny" Assyrian's whisper booms "whnevr yfinda goodlookng Rushn grlshis Poelish"

coat(are we all going?hahrahshoh)and

"you—didn—hava—cap" Turk totters,tells;me:wonderfully,laughing(quite right,too. Didn't. Why?)

feel pluckings

("come" suddenly Harem whispers)

"But—?"

"yes,I know" she sympathized "but come." . . . And,as past shoulder-patting robin past salaaming goatee past offish much too and foreshortened and(where's elongated?and where O where is blonde?)farewelling gradually and(through the wrinkling slyly finally bursting gradually with many caresses thanks promises congratulations)us greets Aria "I've been" Lack Dungeon's proles vandinefully observes "doing a little detective work tonight"

silence. 3(2 at random)comrades move

("the")at("engi-neers have shaggy")random("ears")misquote,upholding the who's me upholding 1

("and p-")1 starewiselying meward essays("pi-")his big eyes laugh helplessly("pis-")

"Charlie!" she admonished

("stolsintheirbreeches")he succeeded.

(O what a comrade stomachache)

the was of canned fish which vaguely recall sampling,among other à la russe hors d'oeuvres?

or that glass of waterless?or

(heat—

"well it's hot in this room" towerful Chinesey(the gradual knock proved his)opines gradually,gradually disappearing)

—or 1 bath . . . heavenpointing(language having failed)ogress recently compelled this O how helplessness to agonies of steam . . . scarcely could who locate tubplug . . . scarcely could,fainting,yank same from its suctionloved socket

(hey nonny no;& today absolutely must follow up twain long since mailed without result letters of introduction from Americans-living-in-Paris to a brace of socialist families)

—probably "just nervousness". Cause:not being seduced by 1 very husbandful gentlemenprefer at 1 very polyglot soirée intimest—"a submarine?" respond I dimly,re Harem's O distant cry

"lost in the gulf of Finland. Cable just arrived."

"Tell me" severely asks K "have you—"

"almost dead" cheerfully she agrees. "But I shall eat breakfast if it's the last thing—"

"comrade" assailing lathered Turk "as one tovarich hangover to another,what should not be undone about this comrade's exit visa and god knows how many—"

"there's" lathered faintly recommends "no sense in worrying,especially in Russia. Just you make a little list for Nat—write down quite illegibly everything which you don't want not to know—and then very carefully put that list where the ogress will be perfectly sure to throw it away. The rest" he added,sopping blood "is silence,unless—but please don't let me go against your better nature—unless you should presently feel like perhaps dropping any soiled object into yonder socalled laundrybag"

"I cannot" almost tearfully "impose . . ."

"you" busily "New Englanders are a very curious" sopping "folk. Folk you" he,beaming,said.

Irremediably bent upon delivering gifts,young Joseph left the Hotel Metropole;more or less mistaking himself for comrade Santa Claus. Now,for a change,I bear no burden beyond knapsack containing 1 immense coffeecan(its lid,battered by customs-comrades at N,is secured with a precious substance called "string" which I've permittedly stolen from 1 of the lathered's "ten thousand souvenirs")plus 2 books

goal,those socialist families,fortunately lies in general direction of Western Art

mail nyet—what care I?

battle into number 34 tram.

Un(having allowed others to cut the forward swath)torn,descend (smothered in dismay—for we found no kopeks;then the outraged tickettakeress bawled Comrades,pass your change:a Rouble has arrived!)near oasis,trudge dimly to Kropotkin perioolok;dimly left,along shady little streetless,past 3 smirking striplings;and without care enter a positively black courtyard.

Now of these portals which might harbour a certain socialist family?— Not here!(this unold nonman washing these Nfaded thinglesses recoils: terrified,when I pronounce dimly the name)—Not here!(that's all she can say)

& carelessly beat retreat;overturning almost that "cultivated"looking (that not young)nonman—who points,wordless,across the yard to a cleaner than others(newer)portal

knock.

A child opens

"yah americanitz"

—he semisomersaults with joy!rushes(ecstatically crying Come in!)down a short(The American is here!)hall. Returns,joyous;beckons

2 nonmen adorn a sunful porchless. 1(Hausfrauish,ample)=larger version of Jill—1(tranquil,grandmothery)=something from my past? White ample sit-bulges in a spicandspan frock. Neatandclean grandmother smile-rocks in a black shawl. Both greet myself cordially

I'm sorry not(white sputters French)to have answered the kind note which you wrote us but you know we really couldn't tell where you were because three times a comrade friend came to your hotel with his new film which he greatly wished you to see and three times your hotel didn't know your address or who you were or anything about you . . .

How interesting(marvel)—I certainly remember giving the Metropole my address,although you probably don't believe that

O(she assured)yes I do indeed. It's not your fault;not anybody's fault: just a Russian habit. Well,you came here anyway! Sadly enough—(cheerfully naming her husband)isn't returning until tomorrow or the day after. He's been for several weeks away on business. It's the cultural park,you know. That's one reason I couldn't come out myself to your hotel:now let me(exiting)produce another reason

And how do you find yourself liking our country?(genially asks in French French grandmother)

I am(K,dimly)confused

(smiling) Very natural!

(enter white;by child pridefully escorted and proudly bearing reason number 2—a babyboy bouncing beyond description . . . whom catching)"citoyen russe"(proud grandmother announces)

"il est fier"(and he is)dit K

"oui,il est fier!"(black agrees;then,proudestly from fier to me smiling)"le citoyen russe vous salut!"

The American citizen salutes the Russian citizen(to fier I bow. He burps)and proudly delivers to the Russian citizen a slight but sincere token of esteem from certain of his American friends

—O!(everybody,including the baby,shouts. And gloating,and sniffing)"café!" (And white and black and child and citizen exclaim transportedly)"merveilleux!"

My husband can speak(white,coming to her senses sighs)only Russian,with German—see;here's a translation on which we're working together(K's foot in time spears flying page)thanks . . . but I'd like you to meet my husband. Well,how about dinner tomorrow,provided he's here? So:you're stopping with friends—well,give me your present telephone number and I'll call up later and we'll arrange things:O,and will you please take the telephone number of our friend whose wonderful film you(carefully white does not mention said friend's address:uncarefully I wonder if said friend ever came to the Metropole)absolutely must see. You yourself are living where? "Merci. C'est entendu"

What!(black grandmother)you haven't yet visited the cultural park? (I promise to see it,provided there's time between now and my next socialist family)—why,that's a very important thing(she solemnly said).

There's one mighty handsome church not far—(before I thought)
what's its name,please? (Look of pitying scorn from black to ample. Of
altruegoism . . . then,calmly,black names the golddomed;adding calmly
    You've witnessed Bread?)
    What bread?
    Bread the play(severely)
    O;yes(dimly)indeed
    Such a crisis exists in America(white announces,quite as though myself
were 1 Tibetan)
    (ignorantly)"oui?"
    (black,rock-)O yes!(ing grandmother,serenely,nods)all our friends are
coming back to Russia. Of course it's expensive—
    He(meaning bouncingest)eats two potatoes(white cries joyfully)he's
a three rouble boy!
    —I say it's very expensive(grandmother resumes)here in Russia.
But(grimly:And How)here only there is HOPE
    Yes?(gentlyest;K)
    (heartily at whom)"BZFGL"(leering the citizen observes)

no more 4 P.M. . . . no cultural park today. Find the named domes;at
carrefour turn left. Enter,through a sticky gate,grey courtyard:grown
little nonmen sit in pale sunlight(& in a sort of garden wanders a little
ungrown nonman)—bow;present my 2nd envelope of introduction;the
grown chatter,point:left,straight ahead—bowing,K enters a portal.
Climbs,dark:darker . . . in darkest of halls looms another,a huge,nonman
further who directs me
    Come in!(perfectly as my Russian teacher had pronounced it;almost
that might be her voice
    but a depthful darkness dogless)spy(at lower end of highceilinged
which)3 mediumsize(1 seemingly young,outslouching lazily and whose
undress reminds of uncouth rougeetnoir backlesses sported at The Last
Decisive)non-s. A tall a forbidding a nonfemale nonfigure advancing
toward myself
    I,American(state;hastily adding the living-in-Paris names which mean
apparently nothing to advancing. Who courteously invites me to sit
down)
    "do you speak English"(timidly inquire)
    "ay-yuh leet-el"

210

"books—cadeau:please!"

"she-yuh ah-oot,wark"(feel from depth negatively hostile stares)

"I"(sitting)"write:name—mine,address—mine"

& the room entirely bulges . . . tall pulls curtain

"telephone"(writing;noting that outslouching is not so old)"—mine"

"gallantly I give you" Turk uplifts gallantly his tiny brimming "the Soviet flies!"

"where?" confrère

"in my vodka,not to mention yours. —Drink them lady. They are socialist."

"They taste socialist" she scowled

"impossible" Assyrian contradicts "all -ists are tasteless."

"Do you know Bread?" I beg,toasting

"Bread the play?—da"

"having said I did,I feel I ought to"

"briefly" he proclaims "Bread is this. The man loses the girl and wins the day."

"No more flies"(she refuses). "Which day?"

"my dear—you ask that?why,the socialist day,of course."

"And who wins the girl" K queries

"O,the lover wins the girl;but the lover loses the peasants. Therefore the husband,who's also the man,bawls the lover who wins the girl out. So the girl,who's also the husband's wife,accuses the husband who loses the girl of personal antagonism;whereat the husband is" Assyrian said "aghast."

(Capitalistically)"there seems"(comrade K mutters)"to be a good deal of aghastness kicking around here"

"but,comrade,what can you expect" he asks "when everybody mistrusts everybody because every- . . . —have a bite to eat with us,Nat?"

"no"(entering ½)"thank you"(English haughtily)"very much." But,relenting,does not refuse 1 coffee,1 cakelet. And she's on her way to her family. Mellowing,presents Assyrian with a "story,I got it all by myself" about particularly cheap store recently opened for noble comrades who've done their 5 years in a year(whereupon he "good girl" congratulates and Turkess "what would you do without Nat?")then, admitting hunger,rises:bows,goes . . .

"voilà" he said gently. "The very thing we were discussing. Nat's just as nice as she can be(whenever I lose my temper with Nat I'm genuinely ashamed of myself—though she can be enormously stupid!)and my confrère gives Nat clothes and I try and everyone tries to help the poor girl . . . but—do you know something?I can't trust her."

Face of comrade peesahtel expresses wonder

"not that she's dishonest" Turkess said.

"Quite the contrary" agrees Turk "Nat's as honest as the day. Which makes everything much,much worse for everybody,especially for Nat" pause. "I simply can't trust her with messages to embassies,for instance— it's not that she wants to spy;she's compelled to answer the comrades' questions. So I have to go myself,or send my socalled literary secretary who's an American girl." Pause. "Never" spilling wearily himself over couch "trust a Russian . . . "

and enters dreamland.

Dreamily "I hate war" the Turkess said

"as a woman,you should" peesahtel affirms

"you mean,war destroys what women create?"

"war is your only rival,I mean. Or isn't it?—both woman and war being essentially . . . shall we say Sexual Phenomena?"

she thought. And asked "what's sexual about war?"

"everything is. Not that I've gone over the top with a dreamgirl clenched in a heart of gold and a kind of a knife on the end of a gun,or anything like that . . . little me has only fallen into the merciful mud by day. And by night I've only seen such flowers cruelly opening . . . if there's anything more sexual,probably it's—"

"you mean something by Sexual that I don't" she said.

"I mean intense. Magic,I mean. Among those flowers,nothing is real merely. Everything strictly which they touch or which I feel somehow is transformed;is dreamlike,amazing,actual. Every actually amazing universe—really which has been asleep in(say)a piece of steel or a mountain or an eyelid or particular kind of darkness or hunger or the rain or this or that word or any silence or some gesture—wakes:lives"

"I know a" she muses "girl whose son had to have his toe amputated. And she was ecstatic—No army for him!she cried"

"I want" comrade poietes said "all my toes and I'm sorry for the son;but let him join an ambulance corps when the time—"

" . . . well,I'll finish typing Charlie's stuff . . . "

that(awakening who observes)man with the goatee and the mysterious smile equals "a glimpse of old Russia." Had the misfortune,the tragedy,to be born "a gentleman"—son and grandson of landowners;fled from the bolsheviki:returned during nep. "The type of fellow they don't want" in communist Moscow;but goatee "has languages;so he probably earns two hundred and fifty roubles monthly . . . it occurs to me,by the way,that you might get a thousand roubles if you wanted to sell your typewriter"

"how much?" I gasp

"a thousand roubles. Don't stare. In purchasing power,a thousand roubles is not five hundred dollars. It's about one hundred"

"my portable cost only forty dollars new;maybe it was thirty-five"

"yes. But do you remember those Russian boys with that American nailpuller?—let's try it,anyway:I'll have-in a buyingandselling tovarich to look at your wondrous wordmaker,and then we'll see." (P.S. he didn't get the job.) "O—here's" departing "an article which might possibly"

(called Pioneer Americans in Russia. "The American engineer is the 20th century's man in the covered wagon" and "master of the machine,Soviet Russia's god." "Feed an American and you have a civilized being. Half starve him or ration him and you have a savage"—luxury and efficiency being(Marx save the mark!)inextricably intertwined. Capitalist U.S.A. is the model of Soviet Russia's 5 year plan,but "the Russian's idea of the shortest distance between two points is a circle"(. . . isn't it?)) . . . Voiceless of a nonman whom I've somewhere met. Probably in this very house. She's by French-English bargaining with Turkess in the hall,re trinkets. Enter(yes;I saw her upstairs,with Chinesey:& she might have been handsome once?)training a powerful pair of eyes upon meless . . . enter now a plumper harder nonman . . . Now 4 comrades stroll to Turk's "office" where the Turk's tovariching with 2 tovariches—the cheery youth of the rainy day,he with the Oxford accent,and another . . . 7 comrades now are mounting this by heat murdered perioolok

"excuse me"(Oxford quoth)"but—are you a . . . what is that—. Poyayta?"

(accept the compliment)

"I've heard of you"(he said cheerfully. Pause). "That" whispering,pointing to Harem "is the first time I've seen a woman wearing eveningdress in Moscow"(and right merrily chuckles)

at Tverskaya cheerioing,with his Englishless friend.

"Her husband" to me confrère whispers,indicating bargaining

eyes "who's now in exile for ten years—perhaps his sentence will be commuted—has translated some of your poems"

Kem-min-kz stared.

"That's a fact" the Turk whispering nods

"and she speaks French" the confrère said

halt 5 comrades;gallantly while Assyrian coaxes wilted muguet from that shrugging curbstoneghost:beflowered,we wiltingly proceed

(O Paris!I dream)—noone speaks freely here(I try eyes)

"personne!" eyes replies:and burst into Russian

"but certain" to Turk "artists have their own revolution" K insists "compared with which,the socalled social revolution isn't worth . . . I won't say"

"yes" shyly "don't tell her"(winking toward eyes)"that"

& at god's—it seems we've been on our way to god—door,Assyrian holds me;whispering "the flesh is weak. The comrades ask questions. Careful"

god introduces nobody(everyone—including Chinesey,more than ever submarine,and the gentlemanly more than ever censor of censors and not exmentor and not comrade Gorky—seems to be chez god ce soir). God says that if his guests can't get acquainted without being introduced they're a lot of somethings(& quite tight he is;& very genial). I'm through a welter of 30 or perhaps it was 40 very singularly untovarich really males and females espying somebody . . . who's all dressed up fit to kill,why it's Nat!when

"how long have you been here?" asks casually briskly total(short of stature and mighty of eyeglasses)stranger

"not long"

"how long are you staying?"

"not long"

"did you come with anybody?"

name names

"I'm from the embassy" he said jauntily,looking a little like a goldfish(and,drawing me cornerward,fully describes during several brief businesslike minutes each and every person of personality chez god)"how do you like it here?"

"I feel" truthfully I assert "as if I were standing on my own head."

The total hms,smiles. "Well" he cried crisply "it's like this"—then(slowly and very(very very)softly)"people here are DOING something . . . but whether it succeeds or not is quite UNimportant . . . and nobody GIVES a damn!"

vanishes

Are you married?(eyes)

"oui"(K)

Do you love your wife?(Chinesey is watching;submarine)

"oui"

(sighing)I was with my husband and now I am alone

—whereupon(Marx bless her!)Nat suggests dancing . . . Nat dances as Nat exists,in ½s(eyes watches)

"maintenant!"(eyes shining)

&,all her selves skilfully to mine gluing,copiously eyes-&-K Inc. meander among watching abundantly And How watchers . . . "vous êtes un merveilleux dancer" . . . "et vous,madame" . . . until

"AGH—mon coeur!"(it clutching;which was knocking to be let out? She sat down

)look around meless

everywhere a terrific(modelled and remodelled and unmodelled by always drinkbringing Mammy Sunshine)putty of nonproletarian of badly thirsting of nobodies—deeplycynically on whom beams the more and more distingué censor of censors;communists don't drink. Whereas the a little drinking Doctor Chinesey more avoids and more these brightly dressed these screaming flatly these lurching dolls("and nobody GIVES a damn")

Are you acquainted with Dos Passos?

"oui"

A very great friend. Every evening in Moscow we went to low dumps. I can see him now,dancing,with his—

"first" Nat's ½and½ voice shrills above tumult "we shall have"(god pounds for hush)"gypsy songs. Then"(her shrill drowns—"SHUT UP" god yells:unnoise)"we shall have the gypsy dances. I take very greatest pleasure to introduce the very greatest singer in the world"(Turk,almost hidden behind 1 female back of beef,grins)"which will sing now for us the first song." Murmurs . . . as putty pushed by amok god and frantic Mammy forms horseshoelike hole—

occurs,mothered and smothered by hairy vagabondloverish impressario(almost who might be a burlesk edition of comrade

215

Something)unremarkable singing. Then,dancing dishonours having been equally shared by a fatarmed partially dusky hoor and a tiny earnest negroid tart(both immeasurably under wraps)emerges now 1 song,beginning and rebeginning with a moist dark tone;cringily climbing (tumbling;crazily,upyearning)collapsing:smoothly,and languidly, building . . .

"d'amour?" consult now the now ringside Assyrian

"redhot" who nods

—suddenly enter 1 lusciously young female. Timidly who embarks upon the very most completely censored shimmy imaginable . . . uproar: the(hole-in-head having tactfully departed)male population squirms with untrammelled ecstasy. And squirms. But sans remuneration:even god can only make a tree,shyly female(and hurriedly)disappears. . . . A motley flock of dittyless ditties "in the"(comrade Natannouncing)"gypsy language" tramples hopeless hope beyond repair.

Hopeless hope threat invades boisterous banquethall(or god's study,to whose minor side is tacked a porchless)and promptly is greeted with caviarful closeup of our genial host in the actless of presenting the if possible more genial guest-of-honour:Wood was unfortunately that man's name. "Unfortunately" because Wood scarcely is known unto all men when 1 of these twain Quiets(whom our heroless had erstwhile encountered chez Chinesey)uprears his much applauded head and— "spEEsh!" wails god:Dum bows. An hush is with difficulty propagated. Mammy instantly falls through the doorway;while a dinnercoat from which most carelessly she'd not detached herself curls most carefully over backwards even without spilling his Tom Collins. Reigns havoc. And unreigns. Eventually Dum speaks

—in numbers!(for the numbers came. Sometimes with difficulty, sometimes perhaps a thoughtless thought too easily;but by and large and considering Dum's an engineer—or perhaps that's why—uniformly). On,on,on they march,Dum's uniformly verses properly preceded by the cross of capitalism,during all of 3 whole agonizing minutes and once only are(per somebody's godgiven how prodigious hiccough)punctuated . . . each and every(need we say it?)verse comprises,willy-nilly,nolens volens,a freakish,an even treacherous,ambiguity(or socalled wordplay)re Mr. guestless-of-dishonour i.e. Wood's helpless nomenclature.

& I here solemnly pray,devoutly I here beseech,that— whatsoever may or may not happen—this here comrade will neither do a Daphne nor be a Dum(which of which horrifying alternatives were the more perfectly degrading,your correspondent knows not. He knows only that Wood endured to the endless end;arose—by any other name—ducked twice Wood's head toward everybody:grinned,and said

"thangs"

. . .

shortly after,this here contrives the pretty acquaintance of a Miss Spenceish(previously cornered by Turk)young lady whose papa follows Dum's calling. Lady whose whole family—including grandma—inhabits Russia(it we're more than less successfully attempting to cause to disappear when porchfinding Queen Mab,née eyes,appears:vigilantly to demand

you have eaten?)

"oui"

"which" the also appearing Turkess unvigilantly asks "of that" pointing "pink lady's legs do you think's the cork one?"

"the left" I guess. "Which?"

"I don't know" she admitted. "Have you met Duranty?"

"where is he?"

"sh. Right opposite us"(an earnest if a jovial poise between tovarich and human being. Seatedly who argues,cheerfully,with a standing heatedly how protesting tuxedo)—"good law!Here's a 'meric'n chile who aint got no gin fizz!" cries Sunshine,handing me same—"do you want to meet him?" the Harem asked

"nn-nn. He's busy. —Any more one-legged people at this party?"

"at this party" she mused "there are many,many threelegged people—O:see that gal? Look out" wandering "she's a reporter"

. . . too late. "Are you Mr—"

"he is my halfbrother—"

"well,I'm connected with" and a very huge connection indeed;my halfbrother's favorite yellow journal,in fact. "Would you mind saying something—"

"never speak"

"—anything you like."

"Merde" I said

"I mean,about Russia."

"Russia?is that a disease?"

"is it?"

"I wouldn't know. I haven't got it"

"don't be silly:you're in it."

"I may be in it" grimly K states "but it isn't in me."

Wearily she smiled;sighing "then you won't tell me what you think of—"

K(staring)"for god's sake:do I look like that?"

pause. "No" she said "you don't. All right . . . sorry"

"EYE play TENNIS" cried suddenly entering god's study American "do YOU play TENNIS?"

probably my face expressed doubt;at any rate,

"—DO you?" he cried

and vanished.

"You are from New England,aren't you?"(hysterical,whisperless)

"I was born in Cambridge Massachusetts" our heroless admits

"tell me" this not-quite-woman with dishevelled locks not quite gasps "isn't it wonderful"

"isn't what wonderful" heroless counters cautiously,cautiously edging over into a porchcorner

"everything" ecstatically. And How

"that it isn't" I cheerfully contradict(and wondering if porchless will endure her enthusiasm)

"you're joking!"

"look" said K "there's a street. With houses on both sides of it. And look—there are windows in the houses. —Miraculous!"

a blank stare of complete incredulity "but Don't you See?"

"were you also born in Cambridge Massachusetts?" comrade K suggests

"yes" dishevelled nods "I was."

"Listen" I said. And she listened. For 5 or 6 or even 7 minutes. But no puns. And her faceless turned the hue of drunkard's puke;her arms tried to make gestures:and(desperate,quivering,amazed)she

"b-b-b-b-B-BU-BUT!"

"take off those machineguns" we command "I know you"

"—but . . . you—" upwrithingly "you're just like A Little Boy!" sheless sobbed.

"Not just like" K begged.

"Yes!" sheless howled. "Just like!"

"no. Not just like. I Am a little boy" pause

"are you?"(wonderingly)

"and I like little boys. I like children. Perhaps—" turning through doorway suddenly perceive titanic squabble between god and Wood "—it's just possible"

—"you got My rushn Hat" god shrieked "haven't Either" Wood yelled "You got Mine"—

"that,being a child(and not ashamed)I actually feel these people(actually who are children)directly,entirely;and not as per theories"

her face stopped. Vaguely "you . . . you're not horrible,are you . . ."

"horrible?" politely we recoil

herselfless recoiling—"don't!don't,please don't! —You mustn't!" screams she faintly "you have No Right to put such ideas into my head!"

"if there's any right,you mustn't,you have no right to have been born in Cambridge"

"no but don't you really think—"

"down with thinking. Vive feeling!"

bitterly "the world needs thinking!" her unself insists

"are you the world?"

defiantly "I'm a part of it!" and contemptuous "—but you're really not!"

"quite so. Actually,the world is a part of me. And—I'll egocentrically tell the world—a very small part" ("comrade Kem-min-kz—

    upstairs" confrère)

    & leaping heavenward meet Chinesey;graciously who,if solemnly, indicates a remarkably reallooking telephone

    which answers nyet. "Probably they will ring again"(smiling who comforts and soothingly)"if you hang up." Sil

    did he like the gypsies?I ask.

    "before you came" vaguely(through glass)elsewhere staring "I had one here,in this house." Ence

    "indeed?"

    "she was much" staring(avers)softly "better" silen

    . . . al-lo!monsieur Kem-min-kz?ah—bonjour!dites:voulez-vous venir demain soir chez nous,pour diner? Oui. Justement,mon mari est revenu. Comment? Vers sept heures. Oui. Entendu—à demain . . .

    ce

    "younger" he said simply

(eheu fu(labuntur anni(rugis et instanti sen(adferet indomitaeque mor

    "Sam!")said)Mr.)Pickwick)

    & bolshoy means

    "Sir," said Mr. Weller

Big(chockful of pipples who've with pains attired and almost taste themselves;I'd scarcely know we were in Moscow this afternoon!) everyone glances elegantly at everyone . . . plump,eyes' friend,3 in;Turk 2;Turkess 1;myself on the aisle(positively effete,this grimly chic in clothes of years gone mostly by assemblage . . . and,now tense expectation warbles to unearthly(now;the maestro will appear)heights(& a nervous now:orchestra awaits)sh . . . quel)moment

    PRK!

    off flew entire back of

    —I grab Harem)—

    . . . & don't by some . . . miracle;

    "aha" genially;rising,the Turk. "A counterrevolutionist!"

    (whereat this proximate tovarich immaculate in black smock

threateningly scowls)And. How very cautiously comrades K & T kneeling reassemble 1. Partially dissolved(comrade. Stool;cautiously And How very(partially K thereon deposits his comrade)posterior; very)cautiously Assyrian . . . re . . . sumes Assyrian's

ONGK

—it's off again;it disappeared when a comrade waded into the row behind

"hold on to it" his whisper advises "and throw it when you're bored"

(which never more I was by "music" more less,more simply darling,than "Pickwick". "Conducted" with eheu vastest ceremony by a(portly Englishman;né a Russian but born,A's murmur whispers "a footballplayer"). Harem—and throughout the Big scattered "musiclovers"—applauds fiercely;venomously)

"isn't" chairbackless I during a lull groan feebly "it amazing how people applaud;amazing that probably they'd much rather applaud than be applauded!"

"comrade" the Assyrian whispers "it is—"

"more blessed to give than to receive" whose confrère quelled us.

Now they're rushing a stageentrance. She knew Football then,she wishes to now congratulate(why is my life heavy,so improbably dark? Certainly not all the darling music of any worldless—)

INTOURIST

there'll be a letter?

da

. . .

(so

& he did it at last . . . with a)pistol,of all things remember:us;all jammed in his Voisin coming at 73 miles an hour up from the midi(and remember killing a sheep?)en route to Wien but he never got beyond Paris,he liked Paris;Paris made him feel all right again;no more worries now. Everything fine now and no more need for any great doctor of the mind everything now wonderful(remember,

a thwock:and something;flew—which doesn't fly,but this—didn't fall which;this should and now . . . that . . . now,That:began very how horribly dancing?)

President of isn't at Writers'—I'd daydreamed of asking him for 3 seats
. . . I'd daydreamed of taking my friends . . . I'd daydreamed of playing
the host(just for a change!)at Red Poppy

ecco

—1 splendid landscape!much the best comrade landscape have
beheld!more than best!bestest!very unreally on a nonpiece of uncloth
painted,it deathfully hangs in landscapeless parklessness. Itless hangs
heavy and limp in the airless. Micro(before itless)scopic crouches a
tovarich notquiteasleep. Memo:get snapshotted;now if only my pocket's
fortune did not comprise only 4 roubles(item:in this socalled civilization
travellers must prove they exist

&)what,what do you suppose would happen if every camera on
earth stopped functioning at ½ past ½ tomorrow? I don't suppose;the
seaelephant said—futurefully noting nonunless's terrestrial location

"have you seen?"

I hadn't. I thank Harem

(and what don't you suppose would not happen if all—absolutely
all—the newspapers on earth killed themselves tonight?probably there'd
be less suicides?) As I peruse this Bit of News,as I unglory in this
Bedtimeless Story,am almost and hopefully but humbly certain. Not
that himself once—our heroless—didn't stand on a little hill at nothing
past nothing blowing my brains out:but that mercifully something
occurred(a feeling)You possibly might not be at our funeral! Orete

sh

—in the very next to "my" room lies a man. Motionless. Something
familiar . . . assez!halt;comrade:we are not in 2 places at once just now(just
for a change)no. No. And besides—look:that breathes,see?that's bigger
than this was . . . poor this(so K marvelled;observing the noble Pickwick
perfectly weary of conducting,lifelessly draped over Assyrian's bed)silently
by nonsilent whom sits boltupright 1

private secretary. Now whom brings into "my" room the(plus a huge
bebeaded cocktailshaker)Turk and jumbling now her strange big necklace
Turkess

p.s. nasally,from K taking Troika "pretty boxes. I like the boxes better
than the cigarettes—"

"here's"(and Assyrian's eyes salute another world)"luck" and

"luck" and she hopes.

This afternoonish(this was it eveningless)plump,eyes,Pickwick,p.s.,my hosts,self,all together did chez solemnifgracious Chinesey dine. Nobody saying almost(nobody except the Pick and the priv,explosion and echo)anything. Explosion re glories of Russia—P's brisk(he too had a cocktail)portliness twitters with Russia—P & Russia,Inc.—I dare say P remembers being born in Russia

"whaduhyuh thinkuv Mawskuh?" cordially portliness flung at myself while we descend

"well,it looks rather delapidated—"

"and always did!" P flopstruts "just the same in the days of the Tsars!just as dilapidated!just as ramshackle!just as feelthy dirty!"(he unsuccessfully attempted to throw away his arms)"—I love it!"

(unlike other playlesses)play of this unevening happens to be a musical burlesk show.

Often this—when somebody hangs somebody's coat upon a convenient cloud—when someone else jumps into painted water—unevening am in the National Winter Garden in the City of New York in the Country Of America in the universe of the world. Mostly,I'm wandering from the unworld or Moscow into the world and back again;sometimes very occasionally,I enter some 3rd(and miraculously therefrom depart!)realm or Afterwards . . . into which has permanently escaped a dollsmall body and a huge head(and that volcanic face,something believed,seen through a telescope at night.) Dollsmall and believed once upon a time made large,made weakly(if little and shrewd)caricatures—always such people are Of themselves!—made something not so unlike the stage-pictures at—in this "Moscow" or unworld—which I'm looking . . . "well. That's the end" said Harem. "Of that act"

. . . someone has placed,among other unthings,upon this stageless,for my amazement,a pretend audience watching a pretend stage.

("I thot she was geeving me the ayer")confides p("naow I daon't theenk so!")—

da:

in honour of Pickwick,twice,during entr'actes,the entire cast honoured our boxless

("deedn't you heayer me ayering my French?")this private asks injuredly

—O but she wasn't so much,my good man!you shouldn't worry about that parlayvooing nonman-chorine. Life is a bestery at myst,comrades,or the man who killed the sheep killed the man who killed the

   . . . it is over.

Now comrade who,not I(my life?)quite alone;sit:watching the now much even more than ever theatrical stage—workmen(now)silently are taking apart a platform used in scene the last—the open pit between no audience and nyet footlights elicits a now all-by-itself tovarich (grinning)creature who's fiddling—now a(smiling)comrade teases the piano. Meanwhile appears obermensch,carrying a metal tower topped with an electriclightbulb;who opens a hole near the footlights,the bulb glows:and who disappears. A plainly,a becomingly,dressed nonman(with a how small contented simply face)begins(placidly)outspreading—forever and forever and forever—hugely long strips of amen

   & Assyrian & probably then the burlesk's young producer are by my solitude accreted;quietly who together go aRussianing,3(now)smokes of cigarettes upwobbling:peace;ful,ly

   . . . below us . . . before us(on the more than stage)lights . . . blossom-wilt

for health's sake;that's why absolutely needs must walk our Pickwick. "Certainly sir," said Mr. Weller.

   "I"(1 yellow-journal gal seems to have joined our party centuries ago)"feel submerged in Russia"(and seems now to be unjoining)"I like that."

   "Here" K hears K hereing "I feel sometimes infinitely more than physical—a perhaps mythical—pressure"

   "I know" enthusiastic "I know what you mean!"

   "—as if I were strolling the bottom of the sea."

And salaams "with the compliments" Turk "of a rival" gallantly. Presenting to yellow oncelilacs. "So"(and nervous yellow grins farewell) "for the censor" sadly he breathes "come on tovarich and listen in"

   wearily "I'll wait" confrère. With P and p pausing

   (nonmen occupy both booths. In the right booth,2,in the left booth,1. Cheerfully "for crying out loud,hurry!" he raves "don't you realize you're holding up tomorrow's news?")and for some reasonless 1 does. "It works comme ça" baring not so secret secrets of an automatic socialist soviet telephone which for some timeless doesn't "hello! Mr. —? This is —. Anything new? No? Thank you. Good bye . . . nothing has happened" twinkling " . . . poor world! My confrère wants to tram it;well do I know that look. Will you,perchance,sacrifice your normal love of exercise? As for abnormal me,I'll walk those bozos foolish,curse them."

"Une dame russe" speaker "voudrait connaître" equals "vous. Et monsieur"
eyes
(whom Harem tells Bring on voudrait).
Voudrait,brought on,being subdued New Englandish tovarich
the ogress produces koffyeh
Tell me(K begs voudrait)frankly:what do Russians think of Americans?
In general,they don't have a high opinion of Americans(voudrait replied immediately)
So I imagined.
They consider Americans parvenus. They think that a rich American buys a picture by its size.
I understand.
(Encouraged)that Americans are childish,obstreperous. That they(she hesitates)live . . . exteriorly
Correct.
For instance,the American idea of what's comic differs from the Russian. If a man falls down,an American laughs—a Russian doesn't laugh.
Are there("they've never had anything to laugh about")many soviet painters?
O yes. Moscow swarms with painters and with sculptors.
Good painters and good sculptors?
There are no firstrate ones yet. Our actresses,on the other hand,are great—it's in the Russian temperament.
So I feel. And is there a new Eisenstein film?
No. You've heard,of course,how he was forbidden Hollywood—
Forbidden?
As a communist.
Yes,that's so(eyes)
Excuse me:I think you're both mistaken—
(shrugging)It's(New Englandish admits)possible(calmly). Have you met any of our writers?

I've already had the pleasure of meeting(name flowerbuyer)and I anticipate making the acquaintance of(a poet;"très grand" according to the flowerbuyer's Russian-living-in-Paris-writer-friend;"authentic" the Turk says)

Neither(coldly voudrait)are writers

That's(eyes cries)not true!the poet is a writer,a fine writer!

(frigidly)Why do you say that?

(eyes)I say that because he's a stylist

(shrugging)I cannot accept your point of view

But—

Yes,but—

K:Probably Russians think of Americans somewhat as Americans think of bolsheviks

Monsters,eh?(cheerfully eyes' friend)

In the(ventures this here comrade)Russian temperament socalled,I seem to have felt something eager and naive?

"et comme les américains." And she not unsmiles

but Mr. Assyrian Turk wonders . . . because the world is a strange, strangely enough,place. And you can't get along when you're with it or . . . twinkling,who chuckles to confrère

"did you hear that secretary-bird twittering about the bolshoy concert to all those little actors and all those little actresses?did you hear him announcing that Moscow went wild over Pickwick?"

boldly Harem said she considered Pickwick's conductor a very fine fellow

"O what's his name's all right enough" Assyrian chuckled "it's his yesman who gives me the pip—not that you'd really expect anything different"

"—just an art-racketeer" comrade K observes

"sure. Nothing more nor less. The woods(to use an engineering term) are full of rackets great and small,musical and unmusical . . . but forgive me,friends;I deviate" then(and noting my ignorant mien)"—remember a naughty sailor in The Last Decisive who goes to a whore's? Well,he didn't go to a whore's;he deviated. By gratifying an individualistically carnal whim,he betrayed the collectively spiritual obsession. Dadada. Not so,as you probably recall,the mass-hero"

"meaning that comrade who takes so long to die?"

"precisely. He wasn't a person. He was an idea. I mean,the tovarich who plays that part isn't trying to become an individual,he's trying to symbolise a mass—and there's the rub. There,my countrymen,is where certain grand old inexorable laws of aesthetics come strolling quietly in to spoil the best laid mice. A play's a play. A play must pack a punch;which means concentration on our hero. But the more concentration on our hero,the less our hero symbolises a mass;and the more he becomes an individual—right,sir poet?"

"page" peesahtel "a comrade named Darwin. Or do I err in assuming that the very deus ex machina of evolution is deviation?"

"in that case,we must liquidate evolution"

(beautifully now someone inhabits "my" room,not someone,someones. Flowers;have miraculously arrived now 2:most extraordinary, someones—

deux roses roses).

"Madame,I accuse you of a most serious thing:kindness"

"but not quite so serious" she laughs "as if you had given them to me" on bended genou "please"

"and why—"

"more blessed to give than to receive,I am informed"

"bourgeois" that bourgeois face benevolently frowned "proclivities . . . good night,peesahtel"

"good night,deviator" she said "and thank you for my own roses"

"amoeba is" K modestly insists "my name. Good night"

& now I(only now!)discover that,where they meet the ceiling,all "my" walls are peopled by(so little as to be almost undiscoverable)kittens; echoes,possibly?of(over "my" bed)that big little kitten with its very pink bow after breakfast,Assyrian and myself climbed to Chinesey's;patiently there for 5 or 15 or 50 minutes the Turk sat,Russianly wrestling with time's own space—crisply then doffing talktoy,stood;spoke

"they tell me the poet left yesterday for Magnetogorsky."

"Why that's" I remember "where a certain recently converted tovarich-dramatist begged my humble self to go,expenses paid."

"Luckily,you could decline"

"whereas Soandso who left yesterday could not decline?"

twinkling "I should say he couldn't! Soandso,who left yesterday,is first and foremost a poet. That means something to you and me;but that means something else to a good tovarich. It means to a good tovarich that Soandso,the poet,isn't a good tovarch—because a good tovarich is a good tovarich first and foremost. Tingalingaling . . . and make it snappy . . . the poet drops whatever he's making and the poet goes arolling down to Magic City with hurrahboys to right of him and hurrahgirls to left of him"

INTOURIST emanates nyet

"I'm leaving Moscow"(Foxy Grandpa,unasleep at desk of Metropole, nonrouses)"and I'd like to see comrade Lenin before I leave"(blinks)"—could you please tell me when he's open to the public?"(and stares:dustily retiring,consults now 2 doingnothing tovariches)

"from sefen to neye nafter noons" advancing 1 states

& the other cries Nonono!

"twice week frum noon" Foxy decides

Nonono!cry both

Why doesn't the(pleasantly asks a languid spectator of this frayless)comrade go there and find out for himself?

we all register That's an idea

There isn't far(gently our spectator hints)

. . . please(I beg 1st copscout I see)mausoleum Lenin

(copscout)!!!

(K)What?

he reiterate,even more vehemently. I(hearing a "tahm" in the !!!)go
There. I find There. Sure enough,There is Lenin's mausoleum. Outside
whose gateless airily lounges another copscout

When is this open,please?

Seven evening

Tomorrow?

Every day

(so that's done. . . . And now to acquire information regarding
Moscow-Odessa transit—Nat,suddenly I recall,advised INTOURIST
. . . back,patiently,to Soviet Russia's official travel bureau K wanders . . .)lo
and behold,comrade

grouch.

"How's things?"

"hellish" grouch groans quite not uncheerfully

"toilettrouble?"

"nn-nn." His most solemnly uprearing pimpledness "BEDBUGS"
answered.

"I used to stand each morning before a furnishedroom mirror"
reminisce "prior to greeting P.F.Collier & Son Publishers Of Good
Books;and ambidextrously I would pick them off my necktie"

"and do they stink" he pondered

"once,my very considerate roommate saved a rather splendid specimen
to show to our aged African housekeeper—there was a moment! She
jes-shrugged and she jes-grinned. He coughed a couple of times. She
laughed. He blushed. Finally,most politely,he asked Where,er,do they
come from? And—very majestically leaning upon her broom—she
replied most mysteriously Some Folks Sweats Em."

"No doubt as true as many another theory propounded by the
socalled human race" grouch scowled. "Crabs"(scratching)"are a
localized nuisance . . . I prefer crabs" he assured himself. "A little service
here!"(hammering on counter)

"is it your opinion,comrade,that yonder oblivious comrade-lassie will
ever be waiting on either of us?"

"she may be waiting on me,but she won't be waiting on you. Because"
grouch shouted "I'm god damn tired of all this Russian vagueness
and,believe me,comrade,I'm going to stand right here in my tracks and
ask and ask and ask and ask until I find out something—even if it takes
until the day after tomorrow"

"what would you recommend in my case,comrade?"

"if I were you I'd go to the Sovtorg Flot. It's quicker. And I really think they know more . . . not that they could possibly know less,of course"

ah,but they could—

—Bang!this door slams which a redcoiffed nonman opened(only to pour Russian all over myself:who obviously shouldn't be here now. Because probably humanity's lunchhour or something)—hahrahshoh. I wait until the deluge ceases;then(mildly)

Shut?

I suggest(glimpsing 1 bushyeyebrowed unyouth leaning through 1 inner not-shutness

"DA"

. . . at the foot of these stairs,unusually pallid bust of Lenin(pedestalled in red)usually does not see . . .

it didn't take until day after tomorrow

grouch is nyet

a lank measly coldeyed American occupies the unattention of comrade-lassie. In coldeyed's angry forehead lives a dollarsign.

45 minutes pass

now coldeyed triumphantly attains the apparently summit of his investigation:what are not,and what are,the trains between Kharkov and Vienna? Oblivious(sometimes aided by a possibly comrade manager)is reading a German timetable wrong way up. 3 separate times oblivious miraculously presents her client with a train which does not exist. Seeing whom(the dollar deepening)coldly businessfully heartlessly refuse—for perhaps 20 comrade minutes—those 3 nonexistent trains,I begin to begin to almost if not quite understand why god made Adam before he made Eve . . . at last a train exists:coldeyed inspects it thoroughly and with the utmost suspicion:takes it. And(dollar shallowing)isn't

. . . my turnless.

Immediately purchase 1 "soft" on the either 8(nobody knows):30 or :35 P.M. to Kiev,due next day at 6:35 P.M. Fare,51 roubles 70 kopeks. Hotel in Kiev,Continental. Same train continues to Odessa,arriving the following morning. I positively can get my exit visa in Odessa. Armed with my visa,I may select 1 of 2 kinds of boats—Russian,direct to Constantinople,June 8 & 22—Italian,stopping a dozen times(but never at a town called Athens)June

14 & 28. The Constantinople transit à la russe consumes 22 days. There exists no French timetable "heyayr orruh ay-nee whayayr",hence there exists no way of telling how many days separate Constantinople from Paris. At("ol spihk ingleesh hotel con-tea-nayn-tol")Kiev("hooweye doo-yoo goe-too Kyif?" & what a frownscowl!)comrade K positively may again obtain the inestimable,not to say immeasurable,assistance of INTOURIST(happily situated in the "street of Karl Marx"). And . . . no indeed!he most certainly canNot have his ticket now! He can only pay for it now. The comrade must return to this very spot posleh zahfvtrah,at 3 "and hwun haff" P.M. And "goood-beyeeyeeye"

but I don't believe a thing

well,let's believe a thing! Why not? I might almost,just by way of believing,buy some gifts of departure—which would prove(if,O if out of this Un- myself ever should awake)that a human being named Kem-min-kz did not for 1 month live and neither did he die! A case for the medical profession;a condition to be analyzed,a sickness to be explained . . . probably due to some worm or germ
    and we shall come home with toys

at toy-and-knickknack counter of exmentor's ikon joint(otherwise known as Torgsin)a blond comrade's clumsily(I couldn't do it worse)immersing in 46 varieties of paper(none of which remotely resembles wrappingpaper)this singularly(by contrast)homogeneous teakettle. All for the benefit of that tallest tellurian(maybe English maybe Scotch)elsewhereish dame with the frozen nose. —Come layer 31,blond reels;and is promptly replaced by a brun tovarich. Brun(who's big and strong)goes right after the teakettle:in a trice,he's unwrapped all the wrappings:in another,he's placed the(confused by its sudden nakedness)object in a modest crib of once-upon-a-time cardboard. In a 3rd,he's tied everything with more knots than Houdini himself required(the substance employed as string may formerly have served as a gahlstook,it may be something extracted from old shoes by a new process,perhaps it's just a lot of tied together donkey's tails)
    "yesssmadmmm!"
    —frozen came out of her elsewhere with a silent crash:glimpsed the finished product,gasped . . . clutched. And ran!

(ingratiating)"sirrr?"

"I see you have toys" K

"we have"(this dark bozo pigeons with pride)"every-thing!—all-most"
he sadly added

chose dolls,bowls,an ashtray,a necklace,a sort of cupboard
(diminutive)&

"here is some-thing verry nice,sirrr" which it is. A box

"how much?"

"thir-ty-sef-en roubles"

"I can't afford it" I said "I'm only a painter and writer"

"what?"

"I paint paintings and I write writings"

"you?"

"here"(pointing to me)

"so!" he murmurs,astounded. Adding proudly that there was another
American writer at this very counter not long since. "Blond—you
doughknough?"

"you doughknough his name?"(I suggest)

"knough"

(I shook my head)"knough"

we contemplated each other. "You must have it"(he said softly)
"because it is be-you-tifool!"

"it is" I agree

"you are judge of be-you-tifool,you must have. —How much you
give?"

"well . . . with all the other things I've bought,I can afford just thirty
roubles;no more"

(suddenly he whispers)"wait." Disappears. Reappears,mysteriously
bearing 1 large most potent magnifyingglass. And applying same to
cover of be-you-tifool("see!")whispers

. . . & appear letters,words;skilfully which to the human eye had
masqueraded as design—as something ornamentally more or less emanated
by the driver of a troika;but a regular troika;a troika whose steeds(unlike
Durov's)are not canine . . . & now(whisper)"you read Russ-ian?"

"I can read the Russian letters" I also whisper "but I doughknough
what the Russian words mean"

he gave me a German verb

("to drive out?" I guess)

"da!" upglancing keenly;with much the same(I feel)unmalicious mischief which had greeted our heroless from a stage-tovarich-sailor's eye at The Last Decisive. "Yes" he purred happily

"is that capitalism which the driver is Driving Out?" I ask

"da. Yah:yes!"

"very neat" I comment,remembering trick-gadgets chez comrade flowerbuyer and wondering if comrade Thurston had Russian blood.

"Here—a-nother. Good. . . . Fight"(it was a smaller box adorned with battlescene)"more cheap" slyly bozo observes

"no" boldly K states "I like your first box better. The painting is more Russian"

"why"(sharply)

"the painting of the man driving the horses" sternly I protest "is more here"(pointing to my bosom)"and I feel that in his heart is where a Russian lives;and that's why I like the first box better"

"but you do not like the writing" he said as quickly as a mouse does not move

"O yes"

(startled)"you—are not . . . a cap-italist?"

I hear myself now,laughing now gaily for perhaps the now 1st time since a town called Paris—"no artist ever is a capitalist!"

whereupon he went away. Group gathered. Bozo's excitedly declaiming. Group eyes myself. Miraculously(almost)the dark bozo has now drifted and mousefully to me,is whispering("I give you. For twenty-sef-en roubles")

"thank you" I said.

I saw(why?)the "Russian citizen"(I saw myself saluting)

. . . and dark will fix me a bill-of-lading for all my various purchases and this and this and everything will be quite all right at the border . . .

and I tell him I'm late for an appointment . . . and he tells me "you leave some-thing—you need not leave some-thing—come to-morrow—I have every-thing read-y then" . . . and he runs after me "your name, please!" . . . and I write my name,leaning the bit of paper against a convenient wall . . . and we shake hands(I stepping on the toe of an enthralled bystander)and we grin . . . and we part

. . . Aria!

I'm going,going out of the unworld;now I feel it:now I feel that it's true

true. & instead of turning cartwheels—which might be misunderstood
—let's get ourselves snapshotted now(let's see for ourselves what the
world's absolutely most delapidated camera thinks ourselves look like

& sometime perhaps we'll say to somebody:This is what I wasn't;this
is how,without ever dying,I didn't ever live)

microscopic landscape-tovarich speaks German
dirty as only dreamers are dirty he dreamingly proclaims
"vier Stück. Drei roubles"
But how many do I actually need?
"vier" dreamingly announces;if the comrade would "fortfahren"
so dreamingly "vier" it seems to be . . . I sit,looking into the un,looking
into the -world;looking into the unworld's:looking into the unworld's
absolutely most delapidated camera and marvel-,always marveling-,
marvellingly altogether contemplated by 2 always boys sitting on 1 always
bench
"vier" micro- mutters "Minuten,oder fünf"
—I shall spaziergehen(gesturefully,upstarting as if resurrected)and
hierkommen
"bitte" he mutters
I'm

. . . going
,going out
going out of
going out of the
going out of the un-

world

a new victim's seated(look-,looking,looking in-)when comrade gradually
I reappear. The dreamingly(all-now-crouch-together,squinting now
through an eyepiece down into the camera's posterior)grunts;tilts his
head;recog-nizing gradually me,smiles—"fertig!"
(and tosses something into an open pail at the foot of a treeless
tree)
. . . that pail attracts fatally myself. Fatally moving,my(feeling
that am doing a deed more than dangerous,am committing a perhaps

crime)self approaches the fatally attracting pail:now,over fatally it(dangerously)stooping,peers . . . &,breathless,sees(recoiling!) . . . horrific afloat images of meless,images in a dim liquid,images dreadfully themselves warping . . .

now the latest victim arises. Whom-negative now gently micro- pastes upon a board. Me(positive)micro- fishes gently from pail's witchy broth. &,studying carefully atrocity,asks solemnly

what are you?are you Swedish?

American(I claim;tottering)

businessman?(ruthlessly he pursues)

"NYET!"

engineer?

(calm,now)"peesahtel ee hoodozhnik"

I learned German on a steamboat(he whispers)

"oo mehnyah mahla d'yehnyek" I whisper

(micro- smiles sadly, studying carefully atrocity)"gut für Passeport. Nicht gut für Fräulein"

"da."

Magically 2 always boys arise from 1 always bench—altogether both magically advance—magically pausing,each regards atrocity . . . cries out . . . flees

quite "I want you to meet"(unmistakably for summer unapparelled)"a nice American" and mistakably Jewish "girl"(loftily who's vanishing as I'm entering unloftily coolish palace of)Chinesey who's

"having one hell of a time getting stuff shipped to America" laments cheerfully the Assyrian "—god only can tell" at confrère "how our poor treasures will fare"

she,bridling "the proletarian class is inferior—"

"but" mildly Turk

"it only deserves" scathingly the Turkess "to be governed!"

"a what might be termed" that bourgeois face reproves "sweeping statement"

"I rather guess I'm just a good old proletarian" sweepingly capitalist comrade K tells both comrades "I'd rather be governed than govern"

German baldness. Vivacious. Little. Is the great electric light and refrigerator's dad. Is the greater,greatest. "The really electric personified,

the truly refrigerator incarnate." He hops about;frowning;grinning;
twitching;always lustily(lustfully almost)chattering. A quite unpitiful
optimist. Thinking much than his son faster about more things. And
if this chattering paused,this optimist might explode. Unpitifully
who kids the veriest pants off poor(in the opposite corner miserably
squirming)god. Stabbing each Bad which feebly god wafts against
U.S.S.R.,wafts against the choochootrain,feebly against socialism,this
wild old sudden man reverses it and it brutally back hurls;brutally with
Good pinning his opponent. Such a marksman!how robust an insanity!
. . . Russia's miraculous . . . nothing like Russia . . . never anything
approached it . . . painter(to me)are you?well,there's more here to paint
than you'll find in the rest of the universe . . . writer?well,Russia's the
only topic which really exists today . . .

the unrecognizably subdued son(I didn't see him enter)says "where
are you going from Moscow?"

"to Kiev,then to Odessa."

"Got your exit visa?"

"they tell me I can get it in Odessa"

"get it here"

"I doubt if" doubtfully "I have time—"

"get it here. With a letter of recommendation you can get it right
away. Don't you know somebody?" he asked

K names Something

"anybody else? —Well,here are 2 addresses. They may help you and
they may not . . . Where's your certificate?"

"my which?"

"that piece of paper they gave you at the border,saying you came in
with so much money"

I search. Nyet.

"Don't worry"(he said severely)"you'll probably go through all right.
But be sure to get your exit visa here in Moscow. It's much safer"

1st beyond miracle 34 full. 2nd,miraculously,empty.

bouncing's brother greets me with a great "O"

—& up bobs a hairless compressed somehow not aged doll
("pahzhahloostah")& beckons(brusquely)K into tidy studioish. 2
colossal "mod-ernistic" photos:woman,man. Circular,"cubistic" à la

Picabia,oil painting. "African" idol,female to a fault. 1 small table more than neatly set for 4.

Germanly doll are contriving and myself constipated politely conversation when enters(welldressed,smiling)doll's Frau,alias communication,alias the(more or less)French language:whereupon politeness withers beneath statistics—why am I here?what do I do?who are my friends?where have I been?how do I react to what I've seen? Swiftly the somehow sickly(ah!but now I remember—and guiltily extinguish my cheroot—those Paris-living American communists expressly warned me against smoking in this particular socialist homeless because doll's a consumptive)the tense the not intense doll-host feverishly sifts,analyses, tests,examines,proves,this very suspiciously human guest. No Jack,by Jill directed indirectly! No hysterically ranting unhe! . . . Now,having gratified but not satisfied his communist conscience,doll permits me to relax. Now,secure in 2 respectful silences,he discusses Asia with himself a 3rd(almost grandmother's age and plumper)silence,equally respectful,conveys "le citoyen russe" to his proud doll-father's arms and tiptoeingly serves a Spartan meal. (Odd hors d'oeuvre. Cold good herblike soup. Cutlets. Jellylike desert with milk. No water and no wine. Propaganda ad lib). And presently,to my huge regret,the immaculately cheerful citizen's bedtime arrives. I like the cheerful citizen. I cheerfully feel that the citizen likes me . . . Now and solemnly And How am given 2 real communist schoolbooks thrillingly illustrated with gory(upon land and sea)annihilations of capitalism . . . These are for children?(ask,just to make sure)—Yes,for children(and beatifically)Children adore them! Courteously now,but firmly,I am asked to carry into the other world certain gifts for certain comrades. Doll was a painter,"la peinture est morte":hence 3 big excellent photographs of the socialist family(starring "le citoyen"). Also,1 charmingly naïf little pottery horse.

Clutching cautiously all which,muster respectfulest salutations
—till we meet,
doll and Frau!

And in all of that unworld 1 cigarette never quite tasted so delicious

&(everywhere-looking)that redcoiffed collectress of kopeks not(at now illegally descending this myself)quite grins a stranger.

. . . She had been sick(she was tall)

physically,mentally tall. A simplicity;a dignity of honesty,and a quietude. Nothing did not matter;everything differently mattered. Values were herself,were not Of herself—not something taken or grasped,but something giving

lived within her eyes a person who had tried to give to someone who could not receive;perhaps it had almost killed her. It had certainly not killed the someone;who merely had killed himself,as someones do—whereupon nothing remained for her but to grow. This(a sometimes marvelling of her eyes,occasional inflection of voice,told)is much harder than even being born

to grow is a fate.

People may dare to live,people may be taught or may teach themselves death;noone can learn growing. Noone can dare to grow. Growing equals that any reason or motive or unreason becomes every other unreason or reason or motive. Here exists no sign,no path,no distance, and no time. The grower has not any aim,not any illusion or disillusion, no audience. Not even a doubt:for he is doubt;perfectly all outward or inward points of reference are erased. Drunk and becauseless(talking about a cyclone,telling how at last with the disappearance even of impossibility himself found actually himself and suddenly becoming the cyclone;not perishing in and not surviving;Being)the poet Hart Crane was able to invent growth's likeness

Assyrian,almost casually,asks his fatal guest whether she enjoys humanity's régime

"no" a startling(how beyond fearlessness!)frankness "I do not like it all. Of this system many things must change themselves. But—?" a directly smiling mind. "—That is not important" simply the tall said with(possibly thanks to her voice)mediaeval innocence. "You can" wearily whispers a granddaughter of Tolstoy "not turn the wheels of history backward"

nods approvingly her companion,the spouse of Soviet Russia's foremost prosewriter(and he's that tovarich whose intricately cinematographic portrait of socialism the Turk from day to day miraculously is translating)

"What are you going to do?"

"why,I was going to write"

"go with Mr. Cummings and help him out—he might not be" suggests that bourgeois mercifully "able to read the blanks"

"so" Queen Maryish. ". . . I don't mind"

("I think she does")I said at Nat,to Turk

"no-uh—" supershrug. Languidly embracing a large cylindrical limpness "well?"

"allow me"(K)"if you please"

Nat allowed. "I shall come-back" grimly

"there's a good comrade" twinkles the Assyrian

"may I ask"(shifting limp cylinder to his other armpit)my "where we're going?" self begs

airily whereupon she "to the dry cleaners" answered,every inch a queen.

2:

   comrades;

       move,

a shop.

Yes;a real shop,tended by a really shopfaced(respectfully delighted) nonman,who welcomes Nat;burden:me. Various in all stages of disintegration stuffs lie,lean,lurch,where,there,everywhere . . . Begins Russianing. 15(with devious,with intimate,protests—with rages, explanations crammed)minutes. Meanwhile the cylinder becomes a quilt. Stolidly meanwhile standing—listlessly watching the now cordial the now furious protagonists—1 tiny tovarich. Whose dead right hand milks a dirty sofapillow. . . . Solemnly

"come"

& burdenless 2 comrades reenter sunlight

"this way" ½ directs dreamily

"when will it be ready" inquire

"which?"

"the quilt." Pause

("queel-tuh")she murmurs "that is the name in English?yes?"

and on and

"will you be able to get it soon?" I ask

"O yes"

. . . sunlight(over decaying streets,lazily over decaying comrades,over deadnoise)drooled

"how" K "soon?" ventures

(& regal she ½turned to his a perfectly expressionless mask)"in August"

. . . threatens us 1 immense ochrepillared mansion. Us swallowing, becomes many and littered—now echoing to clumpthumping smileless tovariches—corridors now into wearily which breathe unrooms nasty with fearhush. Queenly(1 particular fh finding)she enters;knavely I follow. Demandings. Officially gruesome slips of paper . . . Now(seated at chewed table,comrade K beside her)Nat toils. Nat's among nastiness pale voice lifts

"it says:when do you come here?"

& K consults this by-upsidedownoutinside-jottings-en(crazily)crusted notebookless. And facts disen(from smell feel taste look sound)tangle how painingly

"come."

At the not-shut portal of a roomless-within-unroom now 2(bearing more even than before gruesomely official)comrades(slips of)wait

—now we enter. Approach sitting twain:a man,tarnished;a nonman,worn. Nat,proud-erect,Russianizes quietly . . . To tiredly worn upglancing at me;to nervously tarnished downscowling on slips of

why did you come here alone(rasps tarnished. Nat translates)

for no good reason that I know of(and he gave me 1 mighty dirty glare. Then)why are you not with tourist-bureau?

because with tourist-bureau one generally finds the most objectionable type of being—

what do you mean,objectionable?

a great many things;such as something which the comrade would probably call bourgeois(Nat,translating:he says he means bourgeois)

but you would be with Americans

please:I'd rather be with Russians

(dirty glare number dvah)you do not like Americans?(almost can feel
myself eyed by La Ferté's commission)
I like people(here the worn really smiles)
but not bourgeois people.
How(angry)on earth could I possibly like bourgeois people?
(surprised)why not?
I'm a painter and a writer(softly enter dark bozo)
are you a member of the communist party?
"byezpar-teenee"(and smashed and dogs and a stove)
"pocheh-moo?"
"ask him" I tell Nat,laughing "why he isn't a painter and a writer?"
(she,blushing):he says he is an artist
(frown)have you seen anything while you've been here?
yes
how were you impressed?
I was confused
what did you like(frowning)most
probably the theatre
ah—so you came to Moscow to study our theatre?
("must I" helplessly ask Nat "have a purpose?"
"pair-haps" she unanswers coldly).
"Da" I say
. . heroless can stop at Kiev if and(why are you going to Kiev?)only if
he's out before the 10th. From us thanks and bows . . . At another not-
shut portal of another roomless-within-unroom,23(count 'em)roubles
depart. Bows and thanks from us

& when I hit aria,when I(not fearhush but merely deadnoise)again feel
and am,find myself grazing a peculiarly emptied parkless,peculiarly little
kino-theatre,peculiarly less little nonkino—burgeoning,both,fresh new
much harsh paint. & among green trees bulge redcloth slabs:having or
not some connection with
"here they give Rose Marie"
(that universal language!)"not really!" K exclaims(really seeming to
recall how Paris was reeking with Rose Marie when he)
chin soaring "I am tired of it" Nat spake.
The sun dissolves. (Grey came over unworld.
But not cool)

"so:it's going to rain." The palely heavengazing Queen intones

"yes" peesahtel avers "mother nature is sorry to see me desert mother Russia—"

Nat flashed 2 ½s—"O!Americans are So egoTistical!"

"correct" agree cheerfully

"I"(stiffly)"have worked for Ameri-cans for years. But I nev-air fall in love with one" her royal boasts

"pocheh-moo?"

pause.

"I used" vaguely "to know"—exmentor of all things! "He was very kind to me"

pause

"but then"(almost)"he must have for-gotten me"(softly.

pause).

"Are you happy here,Nat?"

looking "hap-py?" and(greyly)away "well . . . I'm spoiled" ½smile "I live at home,with my pa-rents." Solemnly "Too Much Love"

"that's the whole trouble with America" brightly said the perspiring K comrade

"what"

"Too. Much" brightly "Love. That's what makes all the damned difficulties"

staring,dubious

"much better" brightly "to be hated"

—starting:nodding "Yes!" &(to herselfless)"that's right."

The brightly comrade sweating hoodozhnik and the regal palely comrade translatrix not quite reach a certain doctor Chinesey comrade's when

"Who married YOU?" she smacked(YOU as in ape;possibly as in idiot)

"see?"

pointing. To a photograph—not a likeness,not an unlikeness. Nor abstract nor anecdotal. Not that Woman(not that Man)chez doll;chez unhe,that Tovarich suicide. (Remember(crunched into alert)breathless a . . . troll:snarls "wunMo-Ment"—who labours underground;but whom occasionally I drag into le soleil,but who verysmilingly returns).

"Ohhh" Nat breathes

"feel" and "suddenly" are words. "Epic" is word. This on "my" table image—the buoyant,the firm—renders,impossibly and only gives: Word(in beginning was;shall be in ending). . . . Human,the Word.

A face.

Head . . .

Rising—not(the invisible skull afloat upon the invisible column)from shoulders but from itself. A-3rd dark. Eyes. Capable perhaps of wonder?merely of bravery?

("what does she")Nat whispers("do?")looking("is she . . . an— actress?")

before our arrival,the ladyreporter of K's very favorite yellow journal telephones;the Nat queen(still awestruck,living in the dimension of Malkine's camera)ascends with me dreamily;dreamily essays in my behalf talktoy:succeeding,writes dreamily directions,streets,trams . . . all needless—for it so fell out that Assyrian's trustworthy American "social secretary" plans to drop in later this very afternoon;and she full well knows the yellow lady(in fact,tovarich,they're hand in glove)

"I" Turk now suggests "suggest that you permit my naturally honest pal to guide the unnaturally erring footsteps of peesahtel and of hoodozhnik"

which suggestion both accept. With pleasure. Hastening now forth in search of

mail(nyet)

toys—and we shall come—

yest. Spacelessly friend bozo has boxed them—a very fortunate procedure;considering that suitcase and knapsack together boast more unspace than even a 2nd class Paris-N coffin. Verily "mysterious" doesn't describe bozo's look,"occult" doesn't;neither does "arcane" when(climbing into my ear)he whispers

"I-want-you do-me a lit-tle fa-vor"

then—all around ourselves with horrifying care looking—

"look"

surreptitiously(guiltily)darkly sliding(toward comrade me)a billet doux. (Darkly)guiltily(surreptitiously)I turn billet over on billet's front(behold! tidy succession of English nouns,each accompanied by a number,e.g.

butter—2
sugar—4
cocoa—½
tea—1

wickedly I upraise inquiring eyes).

"Here"

villainously(passing from his right fist to my nerveless left hand a clump of roublerugs)he gasped. Nodded twice(gruesomely)

"twen-ty rou-ble"

"yes?"(I say)

"buy eight-een rou-ble some ko-pek"(hissing,at billet)"pay two bill to-gether.

Ah. . . . Now I understand! —I must visit the next alcove. For there's a counter at which(but only for valuta,that indispensable atrocity!)may be purchased reallyandtruly food. I must order so much,so many rouble's "worth" of,truly butter really sugar trulyandreally cocoa reallyandtruly tea;I must pay—with my truly own and really valuta—for same and simultaneously for my sundry gifts;then I must surreptitiously reestablish contact with bozo,guiltily confer upon bozo the valuta-bought groceries,darkly treasure 18 roubles plus some kopeks of the 20 roubles which bozo has villainously just given me . . . All because only by such accumulation of infantile deceptions bozo will and bozo's family and perhaps bozo's friends really have something truly to eat—just for a change—in socialist soviet Russia. The worthless roubles,with which he's paying me for what he can't buy himself,our heroless may get rid of as best our heroless may:18 roubles and some kopeks will(as I reckon)stake me to a few Marxian peevohs in soviet socialist Moscow or possibly even elsewhere

so,for the 1st time in my life,I dabbled in high finance

(and bozo's lighting face!his almost tears;more than prayers;of gratitude . . . these no coin of any realm creates ever,ever destroys)

street:a young nonman is selling forgetmenots.

Trustworthy was a "nice girl"(of 36 perhaps)with something static in her manner,in her eyes with something stopped;accuses promptly myself of not having made her acquaintance chez god(where trustworthy must have been a prettyish fluffily dressed ashblonde;now she's only herself And How). Trustworthy insists on paying her own way in the tramless.

We got off at Gogol's statue
walk(turn)turn(walk)turn

most should certainly never alone discovered have yellow's
whereabouts—then 2 comrades climbed 3 flights of stairlesses:are then
admitted by a genial oldful nonman to an,if you'll believe,actually
colourful roomlet

yellow knows what yellow's wearing:this time it's chiefly 1 unsleeved
blouse.

Announces that she's "adjusted"(methinks the lady doth).   Follow
anecdotes . . . our friend Sir Pickwick got in bad:suddenly told a large
political gathering all about "me old friend Nic",who used to slap
him(Pickwick)on the back and was "just like anybodyelse";whereupon all
the good tovariches "looked down their noses" and "there was an hush"
. . . Exmentor,that "old woman",squealed on trustworthy to trustworthy's
boss(the editor of a Moscow newspaper)—ex- repeating,verbatim And
How,a justified wisecrack uttered to him(or her)by trustworthy in strict
confidence . . . Etc.

toast has meanwhile appeared;also dates(which "came in the
Zeppelin")also teacups and tea;also "cookies".

"It's mighty good to see colour" the mightily dateeating K
exclaims,anent vivid here-and-here-placed landscapes

"why,Russians" said yellow "love colour! The only reason they wear
dull dresses is that the dyes won't stay"

I said "I believe.   And Russians also love textures.   One evening my
hostess and my host and myself were walking to a theatre;she wore a
velvet eveningdress—"

("she certainly dresses,doesn't she" trustworthy muses)

"—and a tattered woman put out a long sharp hand:and,very wor-
shipingly,touched;felt of,my hostess's robe . . . I haven't forgotten that
toucher's smile"

"my father's arriving" yellow said,after a short pause "I'm worried"

"there are four censors" muses trustworthy "connected with my
newspaper;and it's humanly impossible to please all of them"

"I'm afraid he won't understand the way I live" said yellow "you can't
teach an old dog new tricks"

"once" trustworthy muses "something which I wrote was finally
published. But nobody,including the censors,had the least idea what it was
all about;because each of them had chopped it up to please himself."

"May I" I ask "ask you why you came here?"

"this is her second visit" yellow said

"yes" muses trustworthy "I came here originally because I believed in socialism." She added "then the system began to not matter;because I began to feel horribly homesick—never,never shall I forget the first time I crossed the border,going out of Russia! But everything in America seemed terrible;so I came back to . . . well,to recapture my lost illusions."

"Did you succeed?"

She smiled and shook her head "no. The other day I saw the American flag in a movie and I almost cried"

"they held an exhibition of paintings here not long ago"(yellow has suddenly relaxed)"and one of the pictures was a stilllife,representing a branch of an appletree—but what do you think the title was? 'Apples in a Kolkhoz.' That's propaganda for you!"

("everything's a question of politics here" trustworthy muses)

"somebody else"(yellow's now quite at ease)"painted a picture of pigs. Well,that picture was barred from the exhibition. Guess why"

("not because it was badly painted" muses trustworthy)

"I should say not!" says yellow gaily. "That picture of pigs couldn't be shown because the pigs were dirty;and a picture of dirty pigs is demoralizing,because Mother Russia wants clean pigs"

("bigger better and" muses trustworthy "cleaner pigs")

"fortunately,however,a high official sustained the artist's plea"

"what" trustworthy inquires "was that?"

"the artist said that it was all a dreadful mistake" yellow said laughing. "He said that what he was trying to do was to prove how shameful and disgusting and vile and low and inefficient dirty pigs were. —No,really: and,believe it or not,the dirty pigs were accepted;along with his apology. I even saw them myself."

"How dirty were they?" K asks

"I'd give them E minus on dirt" she said. "Why,they weren't dirty. They simply hadn't washed behind their ears"

"were they" asks K "pigs?"

"nn-nn" she said "just trying to be"

("and probably not trying very hard,at that" trustworthy muses)

"are they very different" I wonder "—Russian and American pigs?"

"very"(end of yellow's 2nd phase)"here's an American pig" angrily pushing at me large clipping from favorite. A—smeared in clipping's midst—bumptiously tailoured physiognomy . . . cruel as only she who has exchanged being for having can be cruel;hard without firmness;unhonest;older than old . . . "read that." All about(not Russia)a mirror. In which cruel,in which hating,saw her own death reflected livingly. All about a surface impenetrable,or on which always occurred her own projected Without and Un- and Than. . . . The shocking immorality . . . I saved my husband's life,I got him something to eat . . . —"That's" sullenly yellow "My censor trouble. Imagine trying to write for a sheet which prints Her stuff."

"you're no worse off than I am" quietly remarks trustworthy. "My censors even cut part of my translation of a Litvinov speech"

"but at least" desperate "you have the satisfaction of dealing with intelligence,whereas I'm up against stupidity!"

trustworthy shrugged "intolerance isn't intelligence. To be intolerant is stupid. I'm up against stupidity as much as you are—just a different sort of stupidity;that's all."

"A better sort than mine!" yellow flared sourly

"a far less excusable sort than yours" trustworthy rather gently said.

"How do you"(yellow whirls on)"feel"(K)"about this?"

"as I feel about thinking" who answers

"about thinking?—how do you feel about thinking?"

"it's a" peesahtel hoodozhnikally feels "little like swimming in a straightjacket and a lot like making love through a telescope"

. . . on the tram back,trustworthy allows me to pay her fare.

Whom should for dinner magnanimous Harem have invited but Darksmoothlyestishful(and Her husband

"more detective-work?" suspicioning I suggest

"we'll see . . ."

& what a dinner)

—they arrive late.

She looked like the tovarich devil:perhaps he even beat her up after that party?anyhow she is scared beyond belief of every one or -thing,she's most commonly and much too- clothed;she suffers(And How she

suffers)from that ultimate despair of the spirit which even an impurely
an unsimply prodigious headcold cannot quite symbolize

nor all Assyrian's gentleness nor Harem's gloating tact nor comrade
Kem-min-kz's comraderie could rout that 1 time sprightly eyeful from its
nowish agonies of behavedness. That formerly eyeful but who(emptily
eyelessly)cringes at each glance(at the glance marital,who imitates 1 now
undead fly subsubsiding inininto glue)O marriage!

(. . . her father was killed by the bolsheviks . . .)

facefacefaceface
    hand-
            fin-
                    claw
    foot-
        hoof
    (tovarich)
                    es to number of numberlessness(un
    -smiling)
with dirt's dirt dirty dirtier with others' dirt with dirt of themselves
dirtiest waitstand dirtily never smile shufflebudge dirty pausehalt
    Smilingless.
                    Some from nowhere(faces of nothing)others out of
somewhere(somethingshaped hands)these knew ignorance(hugest feet
and believing)those were friendless(stooping in their deathskins)all—
    numberlessly
    —eachotherish
    facefacefaceface
    facefaceface
    faceface
    Face
        :all(of whom-which move-do-not-move numberlessly)Toward
    the
        Tomb
                Crypt
                        Shrine
    Grave.
    The grave.

                            248

Toward the(grave.

All toward the grave)of himself of herself(all toward the grave of themselves)all toward the grave of Self.

Move(with dirt's dirt dirty)unmoving move un(some from nowhere) moving move unmoving(eachotherish)
:face
Our-not-their
faceface;
Our-not-her
,facefaceface
Our-not-his
                —toward
Vladimir our life!Ulianov our sweetness!Lenin our hope!
all—
(hand-
        fin-
            claw
foot-
        hoof
tovarich)
                es:to number of numberlessness;un
-smiling

all toward Un- moveunmove,all toward Our haltpause;all toward All budgeshuffle:all toward Toward standwait. Isn'tish.

The dark human All warped(the Un-)toward and—facefacefaceface— past Arabian Nights and disappearing . . . numberlessness;or may possibly there exist an invisible,a final,face;moveunmovingly which after several forevers will arrive to(hushed)look upon its maker Lenin?

"pahzhahloostah"—voice?belonging to comrade K. Said to a most tough cop. Beside shufflebudging end of beginninglessness,before the Tomb Of Tombs,standunstanding.

(Voice?continues)I,American correspondent . . .

(the toughest cop spun:upon all of and over smallest me staring all 1 awful moment—salutes! And very gently shoves)let the skies snow dolphins—nothing shall confound us now!(into smilelessly the entering beginning of endlessness:

—between these 2 exhausted its:a

bearded,and a merely

unshaven)now who emotionlessly displace themselves. Obediently
and now we form a dumb me-sandwich. & now which,moves

3 comrades move;comrade before me(comrade I)comrade behind
me . . . un- . . . and move . . . and un- . . . and always(behind comrade
behind me)numb-erl-ess-ness

(at either side of the Portal:rigidity. Armed soldier attentioning)

—stink;warm poresbowels,millionary of man-the-unanimal
putrescence. Floods up from dark. Suffocatingly envelopes 3
now(unmovemoving past that attentioning twain each(& whose eyelids
moveunmove)other facing rigidities)comrades

as when a man inhabits,for stars and moons,freely himself(breathing
always round air;living deeply the colour of darkness and utterly
enjoying the sound of the great sun;tasting very slowly a proud silence
of mountains;touched by,touching,what never to be comprehended
miracles;conversing with trees fearlessly and fire and rain and all creatures
and each strong faithful thing)as when the man comes to a where
tremulous with despair and a when luminous with dissolution—into
all fearfulness comes,out of omnipotence—as when he enters a city(and
solemnly his soul descends:every wish covers its beauty in tomorrow)so
I descended and so I disguised myself;so(toward death's deification
moving)I did not move

bearded's cap slumps off. Mine. Beardless's

. . . now,Stone;polished(Now)darklyness . . .

—leftturning:

Down

(the old skull floating(the old ghost shuffling)just-in-front-of-me
in-stink-and-glimmer &

from)whom,now:forth creeps,som(ething,timi)dly . . . a Feeling
tenta-

cle cau,tiously &,which,softly touchtry-ing fear,ful,ly how the
polished the slippery black,the—is it real?—(da)amazedly & withdraws;
diminishes;wilt

-ing(rightturn)

as we enter The Place,I look up:over(all)us a polished
slab reflecting upside(com(moveunmoving)rades)down. Now;a. Pit:
here . . . yes—sh!

under a prismshaped transparency

lying(tovarich-to-the-waist

forcelessly shut rightclaw

leftfin unshut limply

& a small-not-intense head & a face-without-wrinkles & a reddish beard).

(1 appearing quickly uniform shoves our singleness into 2s)yanks bearded to the inside pushes to the outside me . . . & as un(around the(the prism)pit)movingly comrades the move

(within a neckhigh wall

in a groove which surrounds the prism)

stands,at the prism's neuter pole a human being(alive,silent)with a real rifle:

—comrades revolve. Wheel we. Now I am somehow(for a moment) on the inside;alone—

growls. Another soldier. Rightturning us. Who leave The Place(whose walls irregularly are splotched with red frieze)leave the dumb saccharine porebowel ripeness of stink . . . we climb & climbing we

're out.

Certainly it was not made of flesh. And I have seen so many waxworks which were actual(some ludicrous more horrible most both)so many images whose very unaliveness could liberate Is,invent Being(or what equally disdains life and unlife)—I have seen so very many better gods or stranger,many mightier deeper puppets;everywhere and elsewhere and perhaps in America and(for instance)in Coney Island . . .

now(breathing air,Air,AIR)decide that this how silly unking of Un-,this how trivial idol throned in stink,equals just another little moral lesson. Probably this trivial does not liberate,does not invent,because this silly teaches;because probably this little must not thrill and must not lull and merely must say—

I Am Mortal. So Are You. Hello

. . . another futile aspect of "materialistic dialectic" . . . merely again(again false noun,another fake "reality")the strict immeasurable Verb neglected,the illimitable keen Dream denied

what crispedged flatness does a dexter comrade-hand meet in a sinister comrade-trouserpocket's darkness? 1 ticket(given by Turk as I fled toward another darkness,a different tomb). Blonde and mari,Turkess and Assyrian,are visiting a "musichall" near Something's theatre. I'm due to join them there(comrade Lenin permitting

and comrade Lenin—hearing the wholly miraculous words "American correspondent"—permits)

the lush with lounging comrades foyer recalls Shaving Hour in a pullman. Somewhere confrère and wholly that bourgeois emerge from a corner near a telephonebooth and

blandly "our poor sick" Harem said without batting an eyelash "guest came here with us;but when we found that the show began at eight-thirty(instead of at seven-thirty as we'd all thought)she went home with her nice husband"

"who'll return. And what" Assyrian "to do with one extra seat? . . . I'll try"(flowerbuyer

10 minutelesses)

"he answers nyet." —Comrade(addressing a shrivelled stranger with a huge gorillaface)here

it's too expensive(snortgrunts the gorillaface. Mucho cautiously,nay suspiciously,having surveyed 1 extra ticket)

where do you work?(Turk asks)

(shrugging)I don't

well(that bourgeois more than shrugs)here's the seat—(& 3 comrades invade the pleasantest theatre have yet beheld;leaving 1 comrade dazedly studying a crispedged flatness. Almost immediately enter mari:sits next myself;agreeable and halitosis. So has the(infinitely wretched and absolutely dragging)show . . . weary "gypsy" dancers,through split skirts waving most unlike legs legs,spiritless "gypsy" songsters and -stresses bellowing semioperatic atrocities—I recognize,with unglee,a pair of god's entertainers . . . next,an educational program of(apparently not for me alone)unmitigated dullness(even the whole audience protests rather feebly after 2nd entr'acte)during which Assyrian disappears to 'phone hole-in-the-forehead and Turkess draws out hal

he's a busy man,hal is. Installing a new(to Russia)automatic railroad signal system. Which is much needed,it seems. For the cheerful Russians decided to replace wornout materials such as cables with other such as cables made by themselves. Result:an intricate ruination of the whole shebang. What do you know—out of every 50 chances to make a mistake,those greedy tovariches took advantage of 4(versus 1 mistake out of 10,000 chances in America). Hal stresses the point that foreigners who are called in to take charge of enterprises find themselves sooner or later helpless before communist doctrine:and they can't ask why such and such workers aren't paid more;and over all "experts" are "bee-essers" who hand out "bee-ess" ad lib,no matter what happens;and statistics,in this extraordinary country,have become a fetish

"you know how it is here" he sighs "they believe that if a four-cylinder automobile is running on two,it's fifty percent efficient."

"I actually" Turkess "had a communist say to me:we're turning out so many(I can't remember the number)tractors;what if they don't run?we're turning them out!"

"slightly to change the subject,why" K asks "did we have the leg stuff first tonight and then the enlightenment business? Was the latter supposed to make us forget the former?"

"my no" cried hal "a few legs don't mean anything to this bunch. Have you seen naked bathing?"

"no"

"you ought to look around" said hal

(who himself has not;I discover that he's merely heard—from certain of his Russian associates—about places where men and women disport in the alto-,separated only by 2 yards of sand "and a rope";and a woman will take off everything and will cover her face with a piece of paper and will enjoy a nice quiet sunbath). We glide to marriage

"they've got that all sewed up" blonde's mari affirms "of course,it's not perfect—(nothing is)" he added darkly "but most of the husbands who find themselves divorced feel,well,relieved . . . I know" dreamily "of a girl who divorced a man and married again;the second man moved right in—as her husband—and shared her room with the first"

"no news" appearing Turk murmurs. "Poor,poor world"

. . . "why,do you realize"(I'm dangerously leaning on the pedestal of Lenin's huge black bust,which looks dangerously like Lenin's little pale doll . . . across this corridor dangerously looms comrade Stalin's effigy,the first I've seen—Assyrian and Harem are ½listening to allhetup hal,½watching 3 uniformed ghosts who simply can't seem to leave our entrancing vicinity)"do you realize"(hal raves)"that there isn't one Russian engineer with more than what you and I would call a highschool education?look:suppose I,an expert,tell them This is the way this has gotta be done . . . know what they do?they go into a conference. Well

now,why shouldn't we do it another way;that's how they talk. It does
no good to tell 'em Say listen,I'm not just trying to gratify a personal
whim,I'm talking from the experience of alotta wise people who taught
me—d'y'suppose they'd believe that?huh?HUH?"

the haunting trio approached gradually. Less gradually the Turk
soothed hal into silence . . .

now we're all going

"I've seen nothing native" says K "to compare with your charming
lady"

"no" agrees halitosis gloomily

"who is Polish?"

he nods

"where are all these raving Russian beauties one hears about?I don't
believe they exist"

"sure they do. But they're Asiatic." He shrugged "the Poles are more
refined . . . you know,more European"

"do you think she'll like America?"

"first she's going to Cambridge Ohio to meet" his voice squirmed "my
folks. I tell her" he scowled "in America everyone will be flirting with
her on the street. And" darkly gloomily shrugging squirming tragically
scowling "she'll marry a millionaire!"

& momentously

"I've come to a truly"

pouring

truly Scotch "momentous conclusion—this land is run by two
classes:

by exjailbirds and by

shyster

politicians" Assyrian affirms.

("Strange")he said suddenly("I'm only happy in three ways:when I'm
drunk,when I'm efing,when I'm working")

Sun. May 31

(. . . day I was . . . which doesn't . . .)today;&

the ogress's birthday

—by way of celebrating which occasion,Turk(a)begs respectfully the ogress to go ashopping(b)courteously requests the hallowing presence of that most distinguished visiting celebrity,myself. And blow,trumpets!—andfloorshaveanall-their-ownwayoflookingunnecessary-if-not-dangerous and never have I seen anything quite so both as she: not who,forsooth,as the scribes moveth;but as 1 whose wooden soul did scrub and did wax and did rub and did polish itself to such a purely surreptitious frazzle as might tempt only the footfall of a Jehovah(and even that's more than doubtful). Gazing upon superslippery which-whom—from a far beyond respectful distance—I feel that whatever's been hitherto told or sung in song or story concerning Russia's revolution equals bunk. I feel that Russia was not once upon a time,and what a time!any number of cringing peasants ruled by an autocratic puppet—Russia was any number of kings,so perfectly so immanently and so naturally royal that(with a single negligible exception or "Czar")they did royally disguise themselves as humblest slaves,lest the light of their royalty dazzle a foolish world. But a foolish world is more foolish than royalty can suppose. And what has been miscalled the Russian revolution surely is a more foolish than supposable world's attempt upon natural and upon immanent and upon perfect and upon kinghood;an attempt motivated by baseness and by jealousy and by hate and a slave's wish to substitute for the royal incognito of humility the ignoble affectation of equality . . . so muses our(happily ignorant of "history" and "economics")K comrade,alias peesahtel,alias tovarich hoodozhnik,alias Poietes

the ashopping over(Turk's presscard gave us immediate access to 1 most dismal roomlet where dull stuffs guiltily are bought,whisperfully are sold. Had we been merely Russian,like the interminable queue next door . . . !)bowing grandiloquently royalty departs;humbly the scribes turn their faces toward Torgsin

my salesman,dark bozo,greets us heartily

I purchase cigarettes for me,a necklace for Harem. And for royalty—?

"let's ask him." To bozo "what should we buy for a servant?"
Assyrian

"for a?"

"servant." (He doesn't know the word. Turk translates)

"—ahhH!" the salesman,grinning amply,produces a 10 rouble box
with a plump young woman on its cover;winking,shows us the pricetag:
whispers "for you—six roubles"

"is that good enough?" I query

"plen-ty" says salesman,frowning "too-good"

"do you really think it would please her?" I ask that bourgeois face

"I think it would positively delight her" who assures myself

("come back be-fore you go")bozo commands,looking at me with
mysterious sternness("because you kind,I have special sou-venir")

& 2 comrades visit another counter,where comrade I buy some
large pretty bad photographs(1 of Arabian Nights)and 12 faintly
sentimental postcards and a very terrifying indeed map of the world
in Russian

(& was that good enough?did it please her?

nyez neyeyoo. She certainly gave me a dreadful look and she certainly
said something almost softly)

Assyrian "when you deal with any of the lower officials,the trick is to
knock 'em over. —Remember how that 'American correspondent'
worked at Lenin's tomb?I knew it would. I knew they'd never dream
of asking for your credentials . . . Always let 'em know who you
are,make 'em feel your position:what harm can it possibly do?none:
you're right,anyway"

a tiniest wooden shutness

(Turk raps loudly)

magically it flies open—appears faceless

"visa" that bourgeois said briefly

Good(faceless very respectingly answers,very respectingly taking my
receipt)

. . . 1 nearby wearying nonman grins 1 sickly grin & "how are you?"
accosts bourgeois . . .

"her trouble is this" he confided,when 1 trilingual rapidfire
conversation had enjoyed several not natural deaths "she was born here

but she's an American citizen and she wants to stay another month. The poor thing's hung around this miserable dump for weeks,waiting for some idiotic tovarich to make up his assinine mind—but she's lucky" he added "if she only knew it."

"Lucky?"

"sure:they haven't killed her yet. Why,there was a nicely broughtup girl who came over recently to build socialism—a girl,mind you,who'd been vaguely associated with the labour movement in America for years. Well,that girl made the big mistake of thinking she'd automatically get a job teaching ignorant peasants how to think or heaven knows what—something interesting and stimulating and something she could write home about . . . little did the poor creature realise that a person of her type is as welcome here as a shortcircuit in a powerhouse. That's a fact—if you're a bloody bourgeois,they'll clasp you to their bosom and either take away your valyootah or convert you to communism or both. But if you claim to know something about the way this country ought to be run à la Marx,good night!"

I asked "what sort of a job did the radical lady get?"

"scrubbing floors" he replied "and she died a raving maniac. There's a Fontainebleau for every Katherine Mansfield"

(with born-here waits a timid little fellow;timidly who now questions,in timid English,the very nonman whom Nat successfully and I encountered—he takes a prompt "NO!" and slinks behind a post)

"well,voilà your serene and lofty permission to quit unholy Russia. Pray for me,comrade:pray upon both your knees,each night before retiring,that little comrade I will be getting mine soon!now let's see . . . yes. A Turkish visa. You could really grab that just as well in Odessa;but since we have plenty of time and space,why not mount yon stinking trolley and ramble up to the charming consulate?"

(shrug)we're closed(shrug).—Closed?why?—Sunday.—But this(Assyrian marvels)is Soviet Russia.—That's all right,comrade(the consulate comrade-caretaker genially assures him)we're closed on Soviet Russian holidays,too.—Are you also closed on Turkish holidays?—Of course,comrade.—Listen,comrade:I know the comrade consul personally;I've had the enormous honour of playing bridge with him at comrade doctor(naming Chinesey)'s. Will you be so very kind as to send in my card?—Certainly comrade,if you like.—It would be a great favour.

—Don't mention it.—Thanks.—But I must warn you of something, comrade.—What.—It won't do you any good if I send in your card.—Why not,comrade?—For a serious reason.—Reason?—Because the comrade consul is out for a walk.—Are you sure,comrade?—Absolutely. —Which way did the comrade go?—I'm sorry to say I don't know, comrade.—Did the comrade say how long he'd be gone,comrade?—Un fortunately,comrade,the comrade didn't say anything:he just went

"consulate" Turk grumbles "—an atom of crap completely surrounded by holiday . . . aha;Christo et ecclesia:hair of the dog!let's go in"

"that—" a not delapidated unnecessarily ornamental cottage wrapped in grim wall

"no,comrade. That used to be Volks;and very convenient for all of us. But the comrade state decreed that comrade Gorky needed a nice comrade home in Moscow;so Volks was shoved off to its present site in the distant outskirts,where no non-Russian-speaking cultural-relations-seeking foreigner could ever possibly begin to find it. —My church"(pointing)"is there"

("hohda nyet" K whispers.

We enter a squashed toad)

between 2 lines of buzzing entrails. Of stopped semihuman. Of asquirm muttercringing. Of busily begging shapelesses

we(enter

comrades)move:

a coo(lish-& a smallful-ness;sweet,how Sweet—with flowery!)breath(with flowersilence). Unold an unyoung blondbearded a rustystoled leanness is reading is from a dark book:behind him guttering low candlelike pillars;around whom cling people,eagerly,beings,women . . . this lifts a baby . . . 1 deaconcreature;limply completely bowed. Kissing of the dark book:then the priest turns—. Singing(simple sweet). He holds a little cross. Kissing of the little cross . . . the baby won't kiss it!he smiles. Almost everyone's hands have flowers. Hands. Flowers. Hands. Have(further in,old relicy woman rubbing softly the glass over a madonna;now which she stretch:uping;kis,ses.) Ceremony performed,leanness disappears with creature(who's by many not excluding Assyrian's kopeks richer)to the left. Now 2 comrades move toward sunlight:beholding here a group of saints' heads,here a Christ—under occurs complexity;inscription("that's church Slavic" A murmurs. "My old professorial instincts rouse")eagerly which l tiny female and how proudly Russians for,reads to,him. "What are the three symbols" ask "set in that jagged halo?"(a crowd. He asks various women;they don't know,they shrug). "Nor I . . . but the inscription says:a napkin-image,not made with hands,the one and only napkin and miracle which is the true image of Christ." K smiles—

NO!NO!NO!(shrill! Pair of flameeyes! Of savagely flames hurtling;yell insane scream angriest reaching for me,shriek,leaping upon myself,against my)it's TRUE!(smile)TRUE!!(at peesahtel comrade hoodozhnik frenzied daughter of Russia wails,this quivering horribly ghost)TRUE!!!

that bourgeois face:Everything is loosening. Since you've been here,you've seen with your own eyes a naughty market;you've seen a wicked nightclub—or the equivalent—you've seen an ecclesiastical function. I tell you(he smiles)or rather,you tell me,that ideas cannot succeed at the expense of instincts. What is an idea? Idayn,a pattern. Superficial because incited. Instinct:the fundamental,the what you call Is;the inciting power,the instigating force. Not in their own right do ideas exist,but by virtue of instincts—the greater an idea,the more expressive of true force and power,the more liberating and the more redeeming. I believe that the Russian revolution was founded,not upon any mere idea,but upon an instinctive need. I believe that in that revolution a fundamental human wish expressed itself. I believe that the wish was the wish to be free. So far,so good:and what resulted from that revolution? Tyranny. Boss government. Boss Mussolini,boss Stalin—do slogans matter?they do not. Freedom is what matters,because the only freedom is happiness. All of which,you—being a poet—feel directly,instinctively,fundamentally;whereas I,who am not a poet,must come to it(as I have come)painfully,crooked-ly,gradually. . . . How does that fellow Emerson put it:I went all the way to Moscow and I found a goddamfool named Charlie"

sun hammers us our bench humanity's parkless

"the tragedy of life always hasn't been and"(he added quietly)"isn't that some people are poor and others rich,some hungry and others not hungry,some weak and others strong. The tragedy is and always will be that most people are unable to express themselves"

reels with Kohen,with Cohn staggers,INTOURIST mail department . . . but less than staggers(less than reels)Cummings with Kem-min-kz.

"Come" reelstaggering Cummings begs "let's collect our ticket!"—
"Wuhtiggid" Kem-min-kz wonders.—"Our ticket for the world."
—"Wurl?"(comrade Kem-min-kz doesn't seem to understand;it's all
his sober friend can do to keep himself out of a tailspin as "wurl?" the
drunken staggerreeler repeats incredulously).—"Surely:we're going
out."—"Wear?"—"Out" patiently "of hell. Into the world."—"Awreye"
abnormally straightening "buddeye doughn bulleevid"

however,I finally succeeded in bringing him to the travel counter.
We leaned on it together for some time;perhaps 10 minutes:
imperceptibly a sourish little tovarich became not unconscious of
our presence:eventually I caught the word "receipt". ("He wants the
receipt he gave you when you paid for your ticket")I whisper,nudging
K. "Awreye"(and K fumbling spills from my pocketbook a veritable
flock of receipts;all the sundry all the various receipts of all 1 monthless
in U.S.R.R. And . . . frowning . . . sourish hunts through receipts
and receipts and receipts for the receipt and frowning finds and takes
frowning and

"do you remember—"(I'm about to ask sourish something,when)

"I can-not re-member every-thing!" he snapped.

And went away . . . Returned . . . And I saw . . .

en route to goodbyeing Arabian Nights(comrade peesahtel hoodozhnik's
come out of his stupor;the actual sight of the ticket convinced him—I,on
the other hand,am beginning to feel strangely inebriated)we run plump
into

"well well!—this Is a coincidence:as a matter of fact,I was just
wondering whether you were still in the land of the living. I want
you"(ex- turns to a pair of shoddy unyouths;dimly suggestive of,but
more gangling than,dim youthless)"the American poet Mr. E.E.—"

we bow. They smirk

and he onrattles "hm,yes;you're looking very well indeed:prosperous,in
fact . . . I suppose you've been dining and wining with the American
colony to your heart's content(and probably a little of something
else,eh?)why,my dear fellow,I do believe you're blushing—and very
becoming it is,too. Hm. Yes yes;there are compensations for the
hardships of a Moscow existence,after all. Even stodgy professorial
I go swimming every day—what? No! You don't mean it! Leaving
Moscow?tonight?alone?you really mean to say you're going all by yourself!

Well well well:that shows very great courage . . . hm. I tried to do that once. But do you know what happened?"(we shook our head)"just as the train was pulling out,I had the most extraordinary sensation—no really,I never felt anything like it before or since—a kind of overpowering desolation;a profound unreasoning inner conviction that what I was doing would end in some horrible disaster,some unspeakable cataclysm. Mercy,that was a dreadful moment!—whew! . . . And do you know what I did? You won't believe it;but I suddenly remembered a lecture engagement and jumped right off the train,leaving every bit of my baggage on board! Absolutely! Why,it took me months to get those things back—you know the present standard of efficiency?well,it was very much lower then. . . . Not that they haven't done wonders . . . But of course you're coming back to Moscow? O,please don't do that! Why,you haven't yet scratched the surface,my dear fellow! But it's positively criminal to leave Russia after such a short visit! Really—I mean it!"

"I must go" I said

"dear me. What a pity. —Well,we'll meet in New York and you can see what's left of me! Bon voyage"

the ganglings smirked

& just beyond Grand,bang into

?

not—

da. Swiss. Toolbringer lui-même

but . . . in the name of prodigy and miracle,quel changement!

(shrunken,wistful. Almost voiceless. Ghost. Gives me a ghost's unhandshakeless. Nonsmiles feebly. Around with scared eyes furtively itself glancing,this ghost whispers weakly:I want to buy dollars! Yes. Nods faintly:I want to buy dollars!do you know where I can buy dollars? We cannot think of anything to say,we sadly wave our head,we do not know,we are sorry. It;stares;at;and;at;and;at;ourselves—then:"vous avez cigarette?" Immediately we produce Troika—"ah" the ghost marvels . . . Also speechkih—"ah." (We're going away. It cannot go away)it smokes; stands:stares. S-t-a-r-e-s . . . &(suddenly)winces)

"bonjour,camarade"

(we-turn:and;wincing,it. Mumbling who me includes)

—Glad to meet the comrade. What does he do? (I answer:write).

Indeed. Very interesting. (Pause). This is a writers' paradise,comrade. So cheap for a writer. You just write and take roubles and living costs you practically nothing and you spend your roubles travelling all over this vast country. Of course the comrade has met our writers? If not,I should be only too glad to recommend him to the Revolutionary Literature Bureau and to the Writers' club and to—

thus spake an entirely out of nowhere appearing tovarich,whose French was faultless and his small tight face a mask. Now who takes(firmly And How)in tow the lost(feebly-the-weakly-farewelling—and those eyes!)ghostless . . .

"au re-"

gone.

my luckiest(returning from Arabian)self
passes a hunchback.

Softly unintrudes eyes-nonman:They tell me you're going

I must go

have you any magazines or newspapers in English,which you don't want?

I haven't any;I am very sorry. (Eyes sighs . . . wistfully eyes eyes this tin of 50 formerly,now of 3,American cigarettes)allow(offering contents)me

"merci"(but continues to eye. Presently)could you—perhaps—I mean(timidly) . . . the box?

box?

(eyes touches tin)This(and rapidly eyes,removing American 1 by American 1 American 3 cigarettes)—like this:may I?

(now we understand)Please.

A gift(steadily eyeing)from you?

pardon(while taking the 50 tin gently from her)I must autograph it

yes?(amazed)how?(stares. & my right hippocket yields a very old jack-knife:I thumb forth its little blade;now slowly steel coasts over the inside of tin's cover;making rollercoastering from C an arching skid into gs).

What is(alarmed)that?

that,my friend,is(protest,laughing)my signature

your—?

my signature;the way I write my name. "Vraiment." Sh—once it was worth five dollars

(eyes' eyes open,understanding;she laughs softly)"drôle homme!"(then with a,to myself,completely new part of herself;a secret a luminous—and scarcely which might dare to recognize its own existence—tenderness unadventured,lonely;not with ideas not through ideals nor by comrades by a million or a billion or innumerable or humanity explored)"comme mon mari"

dinner quietly:Assyrian,and Beatrice,and departing,and tall("you cannot turn the wheels"). Tall said

"Russians have never been owners."

"Artists are never owners" I.

"And" she "Russians are artists" said. ". . . But this is a tragic time. What you" a mind smiling "may say with truth is:better—much better—this,worse even,than war would be." (When they made us lie down). ". . . I like Volga country best . . . since I was a little girl . . . eight thirty-five?no;I think your" reading punchedin merely puzzling numbers on my arcane ticketless "train will go eleven something . . . please,I give you an address;my brother—you can read?explorer club:he is a nice man,even if he is my brother" directly smiling. "I can say it" and. "No"(to Turk and his camera)"excuse me,I must hurry-to-go: dahsveedahnyah"

& she hurried-to-go:

she went,after shaking hands.

Outside Chinesey's portal,within sunsmotheredness,Assyrian shoots Harem and departing. There she shoots that bourgeois and departing. Departing shoots Turk and Harem. A couple of perfectly unstrange total strangers refuse(scared)to(frightened)be included(terrified).

3 comrades tram

unstructure with eagles. Despair. A on filthy floorless sitting perhaps drunken nonman. Confusion,timidly. ("See the")whispers("nomads") Turkess . . . (stolid hugely faces poke from rags & bags:sullen squat drearily scratching lost ghosts. Men. Grunt nonmen. Their pyramid—of fear,surfaced with asquirm naked babies—does not move. None have any shoes but some are wearing instead baskets. 1 is smoking).

Turk drops coinlesses,a machine spews quai-tickets. Now(baggageladen 2)3 comrades,through despair timidly through confusion through perhaps wearily and through(you cannot turn the wheels of)irrevocable un–,move . . . beneath curving steel-and-glass nonroof now finding (asleep,foreverfully)tattered train.

Boldly(skilfully)Turk-and-knap(linge et Corona)sack boards this crammed all with staring all with human with condesfusionpair with all with beinglesses slightly-more-than-others-mildewed segment of asleepness,rotting particle of putrescent foreverfully—I-and-valise following;me she(with a gasp at omnipotent immense incense of primordial toejam. With almost a cry)&,backed against that shutness,totters,handkerchief-at-nose("let's get OUT!")—while sternly he politely digs vacancy from a jamcrammed 4 bunk hutch;depositing sack,upheaving valise,turning . . . grins(

3 comrades flee

toward)aria! "You can imagine" A remarks "what Hard is"(and I reply

"I can imagine"

and)"really I prefer not to imagine"(she prefers,really breathing . . .)

"by the way:did you perhaps telegraph the hotel in Kiev and reserve a room?"

"I never thought of. Should have,probably"

"I'll get Nat to do it when we get back—come come,tovarich;no mammonism. Besides,it'll only cost a song. And you'll need all those dismal little things called roubles before you see the lights of mighty Istanbul"

". . . it's been marvelous to—" she began,giving me her

"—jump!" he whispered

                     . . . away silently went with waving me a train

someone
asks something.
—Please I don't
understand.—"You speak English?"
—"Yes,do you?"—"Yes."—"I
didn't know."—"Now you know."—"Yes"

(a writer. Ecstatic re Russia(and having learned a thing or 3,we'll wait)who arrived by special invitation from New York and was promptly in Moscow paid 1 "lump" of 2,000 roubles as royalties for a wellknown opus entitled The Other Side Of The River or,via the language of unkings,I Am A Jew)

he is;& a very gentle Jew

(finds out for me that this particular car is the only car without linen. That this particular car is just a Moscow car. That this particular car's conductor volunteered although this particular day was his day off)

a very gentle

. . . meanwhile space:and through a ½shut– ½unshut-ness air;night, we meanwhile pass woods,a fire—smell of!

Why is(angrily)nothing ready?(appearing demands industrial hero whose badge is almost as big as himself).—Because this particular . . . (the conductor begins)

we pass this particular village,these particular dark crowds—a thumping screaming band!

What's going on?(gentle shouts down at 2 boys at 4 eating the oncreeping softliest untrain eyes)

Soldier(barks bigger briefly)

Our men are going for 3 months(smaller cries)

Want to come to Odessa with me(gentle yells gaily)

"DA"(both)

Why?

"zdyes plokoh"(barks bigger. Smaller nods)

Why?(no answer)why?(shrugging;wry faces:then)

Nothing to eat(smaller disappearing bawls)

we pass darkness

night

(gentle persuades the particular conductor to look in Hard and see if he can find an extra blanket . . . particular's Russian answer is to shut the shutunshutness)

Why is there no light in our compartment?(angrily demands badger reappearing).—Because this particular car is just . . . (conductor be-)

&

"bread?" gentle is offering me something,some bread,some of his tough dark good . . . "chocolate?" am offering gentle something,some chocolate,some of my for export only . . . "together"(he beams:pointing,to bread;to chocolate)"hahrahshoh!" Good together. Sharing is good. Is better than alone than bread than alone than chocolate than good than alone than than.

He never ate in New York—in Moscow his appetite was simply prodigious

the Writers' Club in Moscow is just as good as Paris(he thinks)or better

have I noticed the "free Russian woman"?no?why she's everywhere! probably she escaped my notice because I was looking for something physically different;which of course is preposterous:"Nature,always, same"

Leningrad . . . a wonderful place . . . the October hotel with a special for foreigners oldstyle headwaiter a 20 year old with a red scarf girl in charge of the whole Tsar's palace imagine!

"now I go"(sleepsign)

. . . But I must have a light!(badger).—Here is a light(conductor,warily emanating earth's oldest candle,grins).—Thanks!(badger,outreaching greedily).—For all,comrade(the candleman snickers;mildly grinning, chuckling;shoving mildly hero aside and sticking;carefully;candle into this;single;and;world's;ancientest;lantern of just-a-Moscow-particular-car . . .)

BUT—(exploding,hero)

Neecheh-voh(to myself winking,the all-server)

. . . space:&

wigglewoggl

ingl

y the nontrain the untrain the trainless,

—wogglewiggl

ingl

y the lightless the uncandle the nonlantern

under which sitting;

under which

under.

I

I;write

I write wogglewiggl,ingl y

from that lower shelf:ears and wrists—a mother and her children—
protrude. They are eating(for all,comrade)quietly . . . perhaps not only
quietly;perhaps(we don't know)obliviously?I feel charming and little
eating-to-be-eaten(but everyone must eat)animals:neither do which
question my presence nor do they accept,they are eating;even(we may
imagine)pinkeyed rabbits cannot be quite so hatelessly aloof,even they
cannot exist as if both privacy and its cancellation did not exist;or so I feel.
This temporary this how arbitrary juxtaposition of myself and themselves
completely(I am aware)is negligible—by comparison with some infinitely
greater,some togetherness allcomprising indomitably,allpenetrating some
indissoluble promiscuity

called "socialism". These(thoroughly accustomed And How to a
mercilessly enforced psychic promiscuity)human rabbits are not any
longer conscious of themselves . . . (who must not despair,meanwhile
they unlive,cannot laugh)meanwhile their deaths eat. (Flat I to
nibbled)planks I shunting(now and I now shifting with the of trainless)
train's(moveunmove)this is morning—where's

gentle?

(upboosting cautiously,ach)ing:hop

—down

. . . he's occupying 1 apology for a strapontin,in 1 apology for
an aisle. He's gently glad to see me "you sleep long!"(enthusiastically).
Accepts after great persuading chocolate. Halts trainless but door of
next up car(a wagon lit)'s locked and our car's ends both,and next car
down,and everything;locked:locked—LOCKED seems to be The
Verb

"here Ukraine begins:richest soil in Russia;see,how it is black"

windmills drunkening. A tree bowing to a tree. Lush dank vast
s-p-a-c-e. Shiftshunts budgeshufflingly un(non)train(less) . . . through
land,through a sea of land

now & here,creatures of the sea of the land,seacreatures of land,and
there silence,& then of the land things of the sea,of land seathings,

but every(soil earth dirt)where lush dank vast land silence

but;

:Smell

—yes,alert through even ½unshut shutness always dark sonorous the always the vastly alert the enormous fertile reek of soil and of silence.

(Now I understand that once upon a time there was a village—like even this village,this(½ through unshut shutness glimpsed,with a man with a horse with a wagon,and they're turning a corner,and the wagon's lurching the horse is galloping the man is shouting and he waves and as down goes and man the and the but horse lumpstumbles and off away offoffoff rolls andAnDaNd wonderfully 1 wibbleAwabbling circle a wheel A—now I understand that even to this village,which once upon a time was,to this village in which gentle lived when gentle was a child,came 3 armies:a white and a Polish army and a red . . . that the Jews hid in the earth . . . and finally the red army triumphed "and I wondered what was with them" because "them" did not have guns and "them" fought with whatever "them" found or with even their hands,even with their bare hands;like this:their hands;only their hands)now we stop at a station called "Settlement". We I & gentle descend through mysteriously unlocked doors;move we,stamp,gentle,walk,I,stretching mysteriously ourselves:purchase,across the track,salty- soggy potatochips—drink then hot milk & there's a cake in the bottom of my glass now. Ascend(and from these wars he escaped and also his family escaped but "accidentally not." Once gentle was caught,once a guard took gentle into a café,whereupon gentle quoted the bible and the peasant soul of the guard became soft and the guard said "what can I do?" and gentle said to the guard You can lower your rifle and I will take your arm as if you are my friend,because why?because otherwise the peasants who had guns would have shot the guard before he could bring gentle to a superior officer,and the guard did as gentle bid and they 2 strolled along unmolested by anyone peacefully until they heard(clear and near)firing!and the guard cried "what's that?" then gentle answered Perhaps it's the bolsheviks?and "goodbye" said the guard,then gentle was alone;and for clothes only uniforms were sold:and the women made dresses out of uniforms. Yes indeed. O yes. And the peasant soul is mystic—a man from this village would kill another man,then he would see something else and start to shoot at it and it would be a cat,down would go his gun(he would remember kindness to animals). And there was a woman with nothing to eat,a man brought her bread because he was sorry for her,when she went into the kitchen to put the bread on the shelf he stole from her. Yes,O yes,the Jews always lived under ground during pogroms,nothing was always sure,and there were tricks always,everywhere tricks,nobody knew anything,messengers arrive covered with dust as if from a long journey and ring the bells of this village and the people of this village(who are peasants and who are ignorant and who always do something because their fathers and their mothers did always something)they all come hurrying in from the fields when they hear the bells(the custom is that because that was the custom)then—"communists in cities are Jews" the messengers tell the peasants—"communists are Jews,Jews are killing peasants,will you stand for it?" and)gentle grins(the peasants cry No!because they are children are the peasants)& it seems that he looked into our hutch on this trainless,early this morning while I was still asleep;he saw me,and I looked like a child;he saw the woman asleep under me,she looked like a mother—like my mother—the mother of the child who was I who was asleep)

. . . gradually,but perceptibly,gentle's(he'd been paid big royalties—edition of 10,000 copies—to write on salary—everyone kindly—in Moscow what should immediately happen but a total stranger politely asks "are you a foreigner?" and when gentle says Yes the stranger without a word helps gentle carry his trunk up 4 flights of steep stairs just because gentle is a foreigner)enthusiasm becomes transmuted into(doesn't feel happy anymore—must be something the matter with him—had success in America—beautiful girls there—coming here he left the very most beautiful girl—a Garbo type she was)anxiety and from anxiety quickly drops crudely drops into(this train is taking him to his old home—mother deathly sick—he must go to her of course—everything will be changed)despair via nothing less than contact with grim reality;viz.

2 phibetas appear on a platform. Train,travelling at about 6 miles an hour,stops bumpily. Phis board train,1 at each end. Bumpily train resumes. Presently the rounder cop appears in our car. Entering compartment after compartment,searches tovarich after tovarich,opens bundle after bundle box after box bag after bag;attains—I'm(with my back to the unshut)lounging in 1 apology for a corridor,lounging at a point most very directly opposite the apology for a doorway to gentle's and to my apology for a compartment—now our very unown hutchless and my nonmother and the human rabbits and innocent gentle himself and all unour whatnots . . .

possibly this comrade may have supposed that he knew something about fear. He possibly may have for weeks inhabited Moscow(that citadel of guilt). And yet my every memory of those most merciless vibrations bows to when tovarich Gay-Pay entered comrade rabbithutch. . . . Cringe—but not a quick with-bright-edges good lively cringe—did hutch have for hutchless. Not even a slow edgeless bad deathful cringe: rather,a negative subsiding;an unmoving-out-of-focus(blurring of something so intrinsically flaccid,so hugely wonderless) . . . never,no never a syllable of introduction uttered Gay- —nor was any syllable needed(with his entrance,our stinking chattering gesturing car assumed a perfectly collective numbness)—no permission did Pay- ask,no credentials did Oo show. A not human voiceless and greylyness orders

open this

this opened

give me your papers

papers appeared(but gentle's American passport provokes,loungingly I am pleased to observe,something almost like brief apology)and now

why(almost savagely)are you carrying man's clothes?

(savagely if a machine can be savage)darts,at the poor rabbit-mother

(because my husband—

from an immeasurable distance her answer begins)

why?why?

persists,repeats,machine,thing

—I am taking them to my husband I am taking them to the father of my children I am taking them to him.

But you are not a man(thing snapped;spurning her luggage:and,out stepping from hutchless,looking all-around-(why-not-at?)me vanished. Into the next compartment

. . .

long long long long afterwards,after long the train bumpily had now paused to discharge our visiting thing with his fellow-machine and retchingly now had resumed unspeed,comrade capitalist K turns to the still pale comrade a Jew gentle and inquires

"what did they want?"

gentle,gripping my arm,a Jew,glancing everywhere apprehensively,still pale,replies "SH"

"no,but—"

"please!" he entreats;solemnly;with great eyes.

& . . . and(gradually)unlife resumes;chatter . . . chatters,gesture . . . gestures,stink . . . stinks(all in a how different,a nervous how and timid,keyless)

. . . the land has an itself-taking-care-of-itself mien
at stations tower barefoot beggarnonmen . . .
&—ecco—heaves into view a(clumsy with sun)city
Kiev!

    —farewell,gentle.
Trainless,farewell

no,O no visible porter. Begin therefore,with the pride of a child who's learned his alphabet,reading signs;finally I decide on Out To Town. Ecco— 2 tovariches,1 a soldier—Town?I cry—both nod sleepily. Wander,now,with knapsack and valise,down a long rickety lane. To the left espy row of sickliest hacks. Then a delapidatedest extouringcar for which(it's nearer)steer. Now a part of most delapidation sprouts;becoming comrade—who glowers hungrily at me—now bounding from autoless grabs that my this. "Hotel Continental?"—"Dadadadada."—How much?—Twelve(that's what he wants,he doesn't and can't want anything else). Whereupon wavers my better nature. My worse accepts

bom bim bum bam bem boom(hobbles now humpily weird contrivance now taking on solitary a now single cylinder if not less what must be steep hills now don't know the battered top eliminates vision)BUM—jerk-hideous.

Haul . . . aching . . . my(lost)self to-gether;crouching,now un,climb; forth:A,Street.

Really a(little)street. (Driver,the elsewhere staring,makes no slightest least move re baggage;now I gr-ad-u-al-ly subtract which from delapidation all-by-my(lost)self. Paid,never smiles,doesn't scowl,seems not to exist). I—boost—belongings through a smallish dark brownish portal . . . into what might have once been a little hotel . . . into cool. To what might once have been the desk of. Where birdlike is something(someone?)are grey eyebrows & wispy moustache,is the uprising essence of politeness and he's(apparently)been hatching this surprised to find himself alive boy? Now birdlike and(having thrown me for a loss in Russian)boy announce to each other raptly A Foreigner. "Da" feebly I agree. Presto!appears the Turk's telegram—behold!our Foreigner is an American Writer . . . everyone at which is vastly amazed not to mention gratified(and,since "yah nyeh mahgoo" fill out these blanks,up now yah and now baggage and the boy stutter via once-elevator).

Ecco undersized lowhung highstrung tovarich-director,seems to be somehow a younger(a much less authentic)edition of birdlike. Speaks German,so don't I. Immediately takes away my passport. (On being pressed,promises it grudgingly for what in certain languages would mean Tomorrow;in the Russian,Any Time At All)

(boy now the bags and quailing with "zahvtrah" I resume stutterupwarding . . . horribly lurch-wilt,

cease). A 12-foot-ceiling-exlovenest. With a 2 foot mirror. And a 7 foot fake-mahogany-screen panelled in blue cloth:behind. Cautiously. Which;peering,K seems . . . almost . . . to glimpse tiny—in complete darkness—bedless. . . . Boy Tipped Scuttles.

& wearily how my(lost)self slump(And How)lurches upon this strangely loneliest big chair MightilyPromptlyAccurately which hurls(into fortunately broken-already of the ornate bookcase glass)me . . . lie,laughing . . . squirming to all 4s,grope toward microscopic porchless . . . cautiously essay its sizzling surface:seizing baked rail now,yank slow;ly self?e-rect:& breathe;bReAtHe,BREATHE

sweet

air:sweetest. Acacialaden

almost like Fayal,

O how can flatness possibly contain mountains?how?O but the flatness which am holding in my hand contains the mountains which am climbing with my thighs;the merdecoloured piece of paper's silence contains depth and height,I(following the torn map)mount and(tumble along streets leading out of the circumference of a sky into the centre of an earth)I am not afraid(BrEaThInG

sweet

air:sweetest)

of anything-of-anyone-of-me-of-myself-of-zahvtrah,or Of

tiens—an amazing grove;lushly greenness inexcusable,here & here lazily tovariches(wanderingly among shadows within cOOlness)happen: dream . . . now among cOOlness newly now within shadows and luckily I moving relax:am. Happeningly who pursue dreaming a path;gradually ribboning trail quietly which me leads my(finding)self to(suddenly opening immense)SPACE—the

ocean?

—nyet;this most miraculous distance yields no ocean!I am standing on the brink of the terraced hill

far beneath,

a manybodied paleblue river coiling through prodigious air extends foreverish and on it vast rafts of logs each raft with a toy house creep tinily and rush sharpprowed launches tinily while updrifts music of existing invisibly musicians

. . . (here pause;coolness. The midges don't eat me. And I gradually behold now a sort of forum a kind of dreampergola and—with nothing prodigiously behind them but distance—peacefully old men quietly are,on the world's edge,talking). . . . Always view opens beyond view newly as again I move . . . striking how gently 1 narrow street which is full of a blackbearded solitary man-comrade playing an accordéon—and past motionless him-whom past silent 1 emptiest whose tin his cup past now caracoling wonderingly lucky tune my(more than by any vision wish dream alive)self burst

into a realm of churches.

The churches are drowning with stars,everywhere stars blossom,frank and gold and keen. Among these starry miracles time stops,lives a silence which thought cannot capture. Now(touched by a resonance of sexually celestial forms)the little murdered adventure called Humanity becomes a selfless symbol(the doomed assertion of impermanence recoils;falters the loud insignificant intrusion)whereas these stars eternally and all their cathedrals march to some harmony beyond themselves(here the lone star of socialism dies;defeated by all stars)

within the largest-form-the starriest,voices are singing

K enters:a dark of frenzy tattered lump locks this 1 high man in gold and 3 these lower in green. Of trees—everywhere who at this moment which now are blossoming(whose wishlike fragrance drifts through every instant)whitening all twilight—the flowers,clutched by that slim hand desperately or by that huge hand,live;tremble

. . . outside,all all around,dirty are people are lying in dirty was grass . . .

now possibly I encounter a new a than others fatter cathedral;I begin climbing many steps;passed am by a now descending handsomeness dreamily twirling a padlock,and who,moves,as if who had shut,not this,form,alone but a hundredhundred formforms. Toward a sunset I turn my face. Below me,a street(yes)drops dizzily—above: incredible tranquilities of ripe beckoning flame surge;not(and building mingling)believably who greaten(unimaginable)now to outtowering crash . . . all through most sweet air heaving a thousand(thundering with alive mind)smooth million lost explosions until that now around myself town of these domes with their new stars and until streets trees even I(we all)writhe,boastfully seethe—strict possibly and eternal in this shuddering agony of colour.

Re(past music cup accordéon tovarich-chehlohvek(through darkening grove,comrades & shadows)

enter)intrusion,en

ter doomed

selfless . . . Kiev is full of sodafountains

—you pay with checks received at a kassa

am tired of standing in line and go buy myself under the sky a nahzahn cash down

next to comrade-"my" hotel there's a bright door. There's a comrade-passage. There's 1 summergardenless with few uneasily sitting impersons with 1 central(notfountaining)fountain with a lot of big papery flowers with embarrassment.

I have eaten,however,of sunset

—where?

   possibly can't imagine

   . . . &—what might not have been the last

thing you didn't?

   (the last thing I did—might

have been . . . was to . . . do something 3 times;some . . . number;to write some number over,and over,yes:to write 8;and then 30,and again and then again. On a slip of . . . what looks enough like paper to have been—)

   & then somehow to impersonate to imitate . . . someone knocking— whereupon!that hitherto merely interested creature with somehow this poise of a bird—the

   deskman?(no other!)of the

   Ho-tel-some-thing-of

   what. The. Devil. Of

   whyareyougoingto

   . . . KIEV

which O-so-near-yet-so-far seems from somewhere called Odessa which Is-so-far-yet-so-near to a(whisper it)city sometime which somebody has called "istanbul"

   (alias The World

)

  knock

   it worked.

Arise in sweet air

. . . summergardenless much empty. More,when occasionally(on his way to disappear)appears a this a sleepwalker

   (given perhaps a good and perhaps-not ½hour,decide I'll investigate: easily dig(from the usual nowhere)fadedblackblouse fellow,very kindly,likes talking pidginGerman. Occurs next snappy,but patable,little blackandtan bitchless. Then most drowsy that maybeish waiter?

And—before quite all of an hour's up—1 omelet,1 piece buttered bread,1 ditto cheese,1 cup tea). 5 roubles 25 kopeks. Myself anchors an extra rouble(with K's plate)& faded embraces maybeish & smiling beatifically bitch keels over-on-her-back & all the paperish flowers applaud

so now to locate INTOURIST
    please,where Karl Marx?(accost birdlike)
    you did eat?
    I did eat,where Karl Marx?
    great man.
    Street—
    ???
    street Karl Marx;where that street,please?
    (with a horrible grin)—here!
    (also pointing to the here floor)here?
    (grinning horribly)yesyesyesyes!!
    (mopping heroless brow,pronounce desperately)in-tour-ist?
    here!!!
    "dear god" we murmur "is thy servant gaga?"
    —he flutterreeled out of his cubbyhole;grinning(but not horribly) clawed my shoulders;turning,a little edgewise,my;self:pushed— me,through-a-sideways-corridor toward-a-darkish-roomlet(probably thinking I want a shave?yes?or
    no. Nor could this even be a toilet)—where in-tour-ist?(now I salute this grimly round rubberfaced stranger)
    "hier"(placid).
    "Hier?"
    (placid)"wirklich."

Ah yes. I remember:coming home,very drunk with sunset,beheld a very large sign INTOURIST next door to "my" hotel. But didn't at all believe and not at all believing saw Karl Marx street. And was drunk with height and had eaten colours with flowers & forms
    . . . everything's very simple. Leave Kiev today. I have paid the round comrade 45 roubles for a Soft ticket to Odessa. At 8 P.M. myself must be waiting in a certain railroad station;near the 1st class newspaperstand,which isn't hard to find,in fact anybody will tell me.

There and only there shall I meet an INTOURIST man,who will give me my ticket("etcetera")and this remarkable man will know me(although I don't quite understand how;but I quite do understand how I shall know him,which is by the word INTOURIST,which word is written all over that wonderful man in letters of light a square mile high or roughly thereabouts). We having known each other,all will be well or something like that. —Incidentally the train for Odessa leaves at 8:35 and is due at 12:05 tomorrow. (Round comrade politely accepted a Troika. Graciously laid it aside . . . for some worthy occasion?he'll probably smoke that same cigarette at the next meeting of the local Soviet or possibly when comrade Stalin's assassinated or perhaps on learning from a newslesspaper called Truth how capitalism hovers on the brink of Highme Wokker or what not)

stutter to director's. Of course,he's nyet.
    "Später" assures a nonmansecretaryorsomething.
    "Passport" I insist.
    "Später" she assures.
    I go away—today—Odessa(insist).
    I understand—good—later(assures).
    NOT "zahvtrah"?(very most suspiciously)
    (comfortingly,And How!)nonononono:this afternoon;one hour . . .
he will return—you will have passport. YES!

& so during 1 hour I pack everything except myself. Return
    not yet,soon(assures).
    When(insist).
    One hour. "Geld zahlen"
    I go away—
    yesyesyesyes
and so dive into roasting sun. By the,where's my receipt from—hunt everywhere not forgetting lining of capless;but nyet. Odd. (For round gave me 100 roubles when I gave him a $50 Pay To The Order Of and . . . did K get a receipt for?no . . . and)then we paid 45 roubles for 1 Soft ticket which somehow won't exist until . . . and he didn't give K any for that . . . (moreover we don't really know when we'll get my passport;just because nobody really knows. And if K doesn't get my passport I cannot go to the station;and if I do get K's passport,and

can go to the station,we may not meet the comrade and if I do meet the comrade he may not . . . but that way lies . . . have our(mad-)ticket . . . and incidentally how long by accidentally what means is it from "my" hotel to which if any station?merde—yes)Merde!

no wonder that poor exVirgil,after paying for a ticket to Kiev,and after receiving a ticket to Kiev,and after finding the right station,and after catching the right train,suddenly for his her or its(remembered a lecture engagement!)unlife jumped.

But,come to think of it,unlife's not worth much

I,very seriously . . . breathing . . . doubt if unlife's . . . sweet . . . worth anything . . . air:feel that unlife's certainly worth nothing. & comrade(I feel)Kem-min-kz(really nobody knows how)is actually leaving Kiev today;& from Kiev he's going actually to Odessa,& from Odessa actually to

& the if nothing else very idiocy of the abovementioned capitalist comrade Kem-min-kz will somehow actually bring(I feel)him out of hell.

INTOURIST shut

—to hell,then,with INTOURIST!let same remain shut as long as ditto wants to . . . what care I?(and by what caring we'll open magically somehow it when the time of times comes). That,

only,is the thing in Russia:to whatcare—

yes

see?whatcaring already bears fruit!2 comrades now are conversing outside the director's office and if 1 comrade isn't the not a picture director who himself courteously produces comrade whatcaring Kem-min-kz's pass(and affably nonmansecretary makes out whatcaring comrade Kem-min-kz's bill and comrade Kem-min-kz whatcaring pays 10 roubles 90 for less than 1 day)port and pocketing pricelessness-i.e.-passport airily murmurs peesahtel hoodozhnik

I suppose there'll be no trouble in getting to the station with my baggage?

just ask intourist about that(easily)

(languidly)I happened to notice that intourist is shut

shut?(gentle surprise)

not(sleepily)open

(shrug)
(shrug)

& at such moments cherchez la femme. Sometimes who arrives à la special firechariot with thunderbolt on the side—more often than not,not . . . Generally she isn't where you almost always expect. (My humble own receipt,based upon years of if nothing else very idiocy,equals:when in doubt,buy a postcard)

. . . and there she was.

Didn't speak German;like me

so we just have 1 long intricate calm-and-pleasant marvelling warm conversation in the if you please English language,which this fine little lady speaks effortlessly and gratefully and unselfconsciously and altogether not as all the tovariches(and she says:

that she quite understands my inability to quite understand the Russians' inability to quite understand the Americans' idea of time— which she however quite understands,

that comrade-director really is now out there in the street conversing with really some comrades and probably they'll all come to some strange really conclusion about me and about time and about baggage and about America—if they don't all of them get sunstruck first;

that if she herself were I myself,she herself would soothe my nerves "it will not do harm" by entering the Torgsin or "giftstore" which is "in this house" and there inquiring ad lib;asking there anything which comes into my head:slipping,in Tad's immortal words,the rubber off the roll and shooting the whole works:

. . . eskmih. Deed eye beye puzcardz)

apparently K's aren't the only nerves which need soothing. As our heroless enters giftstore oasis mecca or Torgsin—which is most by the by agreeably cool and which very peacefully indeed stinks of cheap And How Ohreye-entul incense—heroless quite accidentally trips over . . . what do you yourself guess?tovarich-director. Who's chattering now wildly re life in general with a presumably tovarich-headfloorwalker

—whereupon our h(now unutterably restored)feigns mildly astonish-ment,shifts dimly our postcards to the other hip,lights("always make 'em feel your position")lazily 1 for-export-only-no-mere-Russian-could-afford-even-if-he-were-allowed-to-buy-it cigarette,dreamfully lolls upon a capitalist leg,and(only now!)begins elsewhereishly unstudying embroidered skullcaps.

(Whereupon forth float houris,exquisitely garbed in provocatively diaphanous robes;& who do minister unto his needlesses,e.g. chocolate & crackers,with that forsooth almost unhealthily celestial eagerness too rarely seen by mortal eye upon this socalled earth. & of their generous joy do freely give our h glad information,to the effect that INTOURIST will reopen in 1 hour).

Somehow I tend to believe. (Probably because we're parlaying?)

. . . extra—whatcaring bears more fruit—extra . . .

but where is round?

nyet.

Maybe this also waiting,maternally And How structured,Jewess can tell . . . who

you want a light?(Germans suddenly)

"yes"—K,surprised into our native tongue,drops my cigarette.

Very severely "you will find at every streetcorner matches."

"Zoh?"

"And at the desk of this hotel you will find"

—returning(stuttercomrade gave fire,I gave stuttercomrade export) "will you smoke?"

"naugh" she snarls. Pause.

(BRGONXFH!)

　　　　　　　　　—& in And How rolls roundish,just as if not more than sore as 7 deadly boils. Barks to her. Growls re me

"you first"(maternal shrugs,at Kem-min-kz)

pleadingly "listen:I'm just an ignorant American who's trying to get from Kiev to Odessa. I want to know"(such and such). "Will you do me a very great favor?"

guardedly "what" maternal

"will you ask this comrade"(so and so)"for me;in Russian?"

& 2 big tired shallow kindly eyes wonbulgederingly—"off-Course!" gnädige cried,widegrinning . . . and(whirling slowly,bangs with questions round slaps round with contradictions round wallops with affirmations:& round sputters & round pounds & round outscreams)

eventually:I must be downstairs with baggage at 6 sharp. Because the train leaves at 7(not at 8:30,which is tomorrow's train but not today's). A reallytruly INTOURIST driver will take me in a reallytruly INTOURIST car to the station and will buy my ticket for me with the money I've already paid. Here's a certificate of that transaction,why didn't I ask for said certificate at the time of said transaction? Marx knows this office has other things to do beside reminding comrades of things which comrades ought to remind themselves of,etc. Incidentally:there never was an 8:35 train;where in capitalism did the comrade ever get that idea,the train was 8:30 but that's tomorrow and this is today and today's train leaves at 7 and the comrade-writerpainter had better be downstairs in his hotel with his baggage packed at 6 sharp if he wants to leave for Odessa today. And anyhow this office isn't responsible for trains understand we do the best we can somebody can't be blamed for everything get me see all right goodbye get out scram!

"thank you kindly" I say and I bow to maternal.

(Shrugging,grinning)"it is nothing."

"Spaseebah" elegantly self observes to puffgruntsweatpanting round;then(very loftily twirling our imaginary mustache)faultlessly we disappear

. . . restored?

rather!

even(risking both time and space)who grope my lordly way by map to a certain monastery of note,a very famous And How sight or more than justly celebrated spectacle,situated upon the very fringe or even outskirts . . . Arriving quite in time to depart,now deeply who breathe sky height very space,luxuriously now who breathe farewell to most sweet air . . . Grabbing this tramless now we screetch down hill—

a little blunt wearing o'er his rump my knapsack hechambermaid betwixt nonknees hugs a suitcase. Presses the stutterbutton. (Pause). Pressespresses. (Pause). Shrugging,he p-r-e-s-s-e-s. (Pause). Then he bawls out—then,turning,shrugging;wearily,remarks "nyet"(&,of course!up comes stutter)

dadadada,my magic is working. Why,even now—behold!a onceupon-atime Renault lounges foolishly before Continental's portal . . . my private comrade-car,ready to take me to my private comrade-station . . . with a private most remarkably reckless looking,if not perfectly idiotic, chauffeur:spewing cigarettesmoke like nobody's business and meanwhile reaming his(if not ominously)noticeably vast right ear. Tip hastily hechamber,seize belongings,dash through portal,nod to reamer,boost belongings—

"nn-nn"(the spewing reckless asserts:forcibly)

—halting,spy another machine;make for it:

Later(gaily whose whitebloused chic nonchalantly occupant grins)

"Intourist?"

(nodding)"dadadada"

I?station?Odessa?

Yes(chic assures)not now. Later

whereupon the with a yell exRenault disappears. & whereupon soldiers now begin heaving boxes into chic's machine. And whereupon comrade Iless return through portalless to the cool foyerless of K's hotelless and park our maybe brains . . . Off larrups chic

5.

10.

15.

Minutes

. . . enter(through portalless portal)a sort of a kind of a bum

circuitously,and diffidently;approaching myself:it mumbles something;about trains,I nod:it shrugs:I shrug—we grin—it sits down very disconsolately and seems to sort of fall kind of asleep. . . . Is it really asleep? Silently,I proffer 1 export . . . mercy no!no I should say it wasn't asleep!far very far from asleep very far in-

actually & it says Thank you. Disconsolately . . .

actually we now smoke(disconsolate & the American)

5.

5.

—Leaping:starting!jumping;collaring both my burdens crying COME ON whisks mightily through portal bum followed by me and by myself and K and Cummings by all of us now rushtearing behind it out through and up to chic boosting hurlheaving bags us into bangslam hophurdling selves . . . Grrrrrk:off—

Ta

  -De

    -dE

      -aHhH!

bring on your foghorns baby. Cheest I scarcely never drove widuh reglur Cheehoo like dis. Out of the way,scum of the earth! And watch them scuttle And(just missed)How(that telegraphpole)look at them go-white and skip(up right on the sidewalk by Christ:and Lord I thought that old woman would sure drop dead . . . Chic,backtwisting for our approval,winks;resumes unsidewalk) . . . Honk!give 'em hohlee-hel—here:take a cigarette for yourself,pal—howl brakes:chic skids him-us-all into immobility(all-traffic stopping on this particularly-busy-corner while,yknow,taking his royal goddam time about getting a regal light from capitalist comrade imperialist memyselffless's)G . . . rrrr—K,we're: off. . . . Go it babe. Sic 'em,Mussolini. Tease 'em and threaten 'em and scare the living mud out of 'em:that's socialism;make 'em eat their own livers and like it,talk to 'em with sudden death,atta Stalin!

 . . . chust youmun beeinz maydin gawdz(HAWHAW)imidge.

Just the spawning dumb lost ignorant hopeless count 'em masses;yknow,that's all

huge huts. Crowd(ing wil)ted clamor(ous ir)regularly(always throbb)ing un(things,people,despairs

station?)yes

apparently—for we swirl up in high style;among all these tumbling to right(terrified retreating)goddam left(recoiling horrified)comrades . . . & now very gradually as bum(baggage bearing)and(empty)I outclimb,1—1(one)only out of awed myriads—mutterwhimpers some (semi-sarcastically,semiplayfully)thing yknow about the well spirit of the hawhaw revolution . . . & busily the into unmangling manunkind beginsbum burrowing. Questioningly & I point at bum:Jehu nods,lackadaisical, nods,listlessly n-

(I)Ticket?

(J)Go with him

How much for you?

(he hesitates,he scowls)Four

Four roubles?

(curt nod)

pay. And a long long dirty dirty look for no tip. —My(desperate) plunges into self the how maggoty how seething the

 & glimpse(passing through a sort of open kind of)bum. (Whom pursue. To so to speak restaurant:cheye and peevoh:tables:waiters,even)

Sit
the bum said. (Upending valise)K sits:my back against low fence;we
watching innumerable humanity squirming,in line,toward beer toward
tea;tottering,out through an open kind of,presumably trainward . . . ?
  —time moans in time's
  6:30(a big clock)
  bells ring—
  (the restaurant deflates,bulges,redeflates)
once,through dimness of legarms welter of finhooves,behold we the
bum talking about humble myself to a sort of youngish waiterless
  6:45:
  6:50
    1
    2
    3
(hell,what do I care?)
  7?
  7:05
        . . . well,gentlemen of the INTOURIST jury,that settles that.
  Sweat,comrade Kem-min-kz(it will not do harm)sweat;but keep your
comrade-shirt on;for the honour of comrade-honour;we're comrade here
because we're here because(a ragged Micawberish waiter approaches
comrade patience-on-a-suitcase—softly(stooping)tells said comrade
something which that comrade doesn't a bit understand—journeying
gently to nearest table,slowly rotates(for that said ununderstanding
comrade's a bit benefit)1 vertically existing card upon which is
emblazoned in letters of something)
  But he can't understand!
the(with semipitying semicontemptuous gesture)youngish waiterless to
the ragged:who shrugs. Whereat good comrade-notunderstanding(unless
it means No Loitering?)patience,alias K myself,rises abruptly from our
suitcase . . . (and(And How)realize we haven't eaten since perhaps breakfast)now,leans;against:low;1,foot;on:monument . . . we very much should
like to buy ourselves tea . . . damn that Kassa—(waiters confer,waitering
shrug,waitering point at)
  . . . 7:40(in agony self espy no not really yes the bum him)It's All
Right!(self)

these words IweK comprehend. Pidginly who ask when my new train leaves?

"sept" comrade the bum begins "—vous ne comprenez pas français?"

O—!I don't,eh? . . . After which,the sweet blood returns to my soul. Is bum delighted to speak this language?did he work at the Grand Hotel? And so it seems that everything just was somehow a you know great mistake. Because my train will really go at 8:35. So we travel,bumI,arminarm,to so-to-speak-shall-we-say bar and drink a hideously warmish beer on me and—O incredible occurrence!—another,yes,peevoh on(actually) him.

But—but what's(but this?this weazellike tovarich full of stealth & briefness who)to,me,nods,briefly(who consults and stealthily combum)now the both,shrugging now face rademyself.

(B)"mon camarade—il dit:pas de beelyet"

I say exactly nothing

pause.

"Kommen Sie." The weazel said

"wo?" inquire faint-

"gay-pay-oo" . . .

(Sie could have felled ich. With a moonbeam)time,8:45—abandoning baggage to bumrade,comweazel and the I fight through a station,mauling through unthings through men through things battling through nonmen through childrenless now at last winning a brief suffocated bad glimpse of track and trains

—to be shoved endwise by this soggily hysterical guard.

("Wo?" comrade inquires faintly

weazel the beckons:I follow . . . side by side through unthings)childrenless men things nonmen savagely he and the length of the station I battle we brutally now burst(floundering)into—a YMCAish roomlet;amazing 2(at that neat desk seated)soldiers-of-Marx,1 extraslow awaylooking and 1 medium sallow scowlish . . . to and whom and now and immediately and the weazel(erect how desperate)speaks . . . (desperately)and while (wiltingly)I(outing passport)say

American correspondent—

whereupon sallow explodes.

American correspondent

—again whereupon sallow explodes.

American—

hurriedly enter a youthful gay-pay;brushing past meless and bending over desk who in low tones reasons with the twice exploder—straightening,nods;grimly:exits . . . immediately(erect)and now (desperate)weazel speaks . . . immediately(and wilting)I

American corres-

now older officer almost quietly appears;entering,leaning almost calmly on neatness,remonstrates(al-most-mild-ly)with exploder who

. . . (There is only third class)weazel Germans to wilting

That makes(myself hears crisply meless stating)nothing. I MUST Go

pause

(He's writing you a third class ticket)the weazel

He'd BETTER(hear I myselfless) . . .

Take!(shouting)exploder flips his scrawl at the weazel—me who now very madly embracing—we might perhaps have kissed properly if there'd been any time—lugdrags(and I him)now(pellmell arsy versy husteron prot)at things-life-death-people-objects. . . . Hurling we now our combined(tripstumbling)selves bru(tally a)gainst wild(ly in)to (savagely)through thatthis-wail(scrambling)UN-

. . . to a windowless . . . to all around which a swarming all yelling mob a battles with 1 commonordinary all soldier who's acharging and plunging and atossing insanely himself through into and against myriads. Now the weazel the tries to crash waitingline—the soldier the bangs now him in pit of stomach—& I & wave frenziedly & passport—soldier grabs me now snatches to himself now plugs me against wall beside windowless,now rOArs . . . Weazel the now beckons. I(ducking)follow the;a

backdoor:he knocks;pause . . .

Out pops benevolent grandma

"shtoh?"

and weazel the chatter,the flourishing a scrawl,& I wave & passport . . . ("nyet" she refuses) . . . relenting takes now scrawl disappears shutting isn't door pause—door RoaRS open:emitting most midgetyish Jew-in-twisted-spectacles &(scrEEtchscrEAming)and he slams scrawl and into weazel's and face,fistshaking all he all bellows all fadedly . . .

"pahzhahloostah" very coolly indeed comrade weazel replies . . .

dashes(and also comitalist caprade I)back(to windowless)weaving (duckbobbing)among fins hooves(we)appear(in very midst of the line waiting)—horribly astonishing And How commonordinary(not-to-mention these all serenely bovine tovarich-sailors). Here common comes:I block thundering common's bulldive just as nim(now)bly weazel slips,scrawl-in,to-windowless clutches;out-coming-something &

we're(—but no. Ono. A waiting comrade protests,wants to fight us,must be served first;who are you,this is Russia;shut up comrade,go to hell comrade;there isn't any,comrade . . . all right. Go ahead. He's served. And now)

"SCHNELL!" weazel twitters exultant tumbling over a toandfro rocking moaning beshawled mountain of maternalish miseryful makes for restaurperhapsant(behind him I,fully I recovered,I completely restored,boosting him by the scruff of his weazelneck over lesser objects smaller unthings)frantic wavings the bum sees us & now(fallreeling)gallops with baggage—"beelyet?"—"da" I cry,squeezing into his handclawfin all my change sicklemyhammers my all contentedly—"au revoir,monsieur" salutes(beaming)almost(tearful)"bon voyage!"(I seize valise,weazel knapsack)rush at into through against &

". . . nyet!" a guard snarls;blocking the gate to the trains . . .

& and immediately weazel chatters and the & expostulates denies yes affirms no the argues

"NYET!!"

—then,with upon my wet faceless that expression which Supplicating no more describes than Lovely conveys a sunset or Awful defines dying—out of what actual profound inestimable fathomless and unpredictably solitary depths of exactly 1 human spirit I,kapoot,remark

"pahzhahloostah,ameriCanitz corresponDyent"

nothing else.

& a gate opens

(a little boy told comrade the weazel it was probably further of 2 trains,a 1armed conductor with metalrim spectacles said:Yes,this was the very train;but weazel must get right off)& right off got the weazel without saying 1 syllable to me . . . who vaguely now am through a shutness looking(watching a locomotive plough screaming into through recoiling hordes cringing myriads) . . . Furtively my saviour reappears: he's whispering that 1armed will find me a seat later,that I should write Kiev's intourist about where in Odessa to send what they owe because

I paid for Soft but this is Hard . . . tell them to send it "schnell" to the Hotel London(whisper;and weazel;tipped;& promi-sing;vanishes)

(long wait. Longer.

Also unplaced seems to be an almost handsome astonishingly not unwelldressed nonman)

about 9 the perhaps train shudders;sighs;not unmoves:

the,entering amiably,conductor amiably escorts elsewhere the also unplaced—returning now,now beaming,beckons to comrade K

Nononocomradenonono!—that dripping(beside all of whom amiable was suggesting that I sit)nonman indignantly howls through sad fat

—Nocomradenocomradenocomradenocomradenocomradeno-comrade!her(insulted to the proletarian core)skinny vis-à-vis cackles stubbornly. & amiable justshrugs:You must excuse my selfish compatriots:I'm thoroughly ashamed of them myself:but what's to be done?—& K(wearily)nodgrins—&(winking)amiable redisappears . . . to instantly return;to(leading K now deeper into crammed carless) produce(see?)almost invisible hole between these violently objecting comrades;& now(gesturing)explain—something may be pulled down— may transform said hole into heaven knows—perhaps a seatless?

& I grin & I grin

&,gradually,the objectors subside . . . now,unmolestedly,K upheaves baggage—to a shelf above 2 merely somewhat disgruntlednesses . . . now(of their own accord)these twain invent sitability;nay—they even request the honourless of ourmy presence. Thankingly comrade peesahtel hoodozhnik collapses(and O most cautiously)—and wearily now who is staring at,just across unaisle of carless,hutchful of eagerly And at Ime staring How tovariches . . . see? . . . a dumb type with a pipe a shaggy elf a curly blacksmith a bold brakemanish fellow a ghost with a pulleddown cap a big animated with pointed raven-beard creature a shavenheaded dreamy youthlessness in much soiled not much blouse.

Animated(from the inside corner of the hutch's left lower sleepshelf authoritatively booms):"Sprechen Sie Deutsch?"

Yah:"Wenig,sehr wenig." Pause. "Sprechen Sie vielleicht Französisch oder Englisch?"

Animated:"Nein"

—& a truly Russian really evening opens

what do I do?—I write and paint

with what organization am I affiliated?—none(consternation)I work for myself(!)

where do I live?—New York and New Hampshire

whence did I come?—Paris

why?—curiosity

how long ago?—O about a month

what have I seen?—the Moscow theatre,a jail,Lenin's tomb,all sorts of similar things

how did I happen to go from Moscow to Kiev?—well now,I thought I ought to see something of the country

yes,but why Kiev?—but Kiev is,after all,on the way to Odessa

why Odessa?—that's the way I'm leaving Russia you see

leaving Russia after only a month?—I really can't afford to stay any longer;besides,I must be getting back to my little farm in New Hampshire

but why leave Russia by Odessa?—just because the only other financially plausible way of leaving . . . unless I went out as I came in,through Poland . . . would be via Leningrad;in which case I wouldn't see so much of the country would I?

how much do I earn?—sometimes almost as little as a thousand dollars a year,sometimes almost as much as nothing

how big is my farm?—perhaps several hundred acres(amazement)

its chief crop?—rocks(this was good for $\frac{1}{2}$hour)

what do I spend per day in Russia?—I guess something like ten dollars(?!)

in America?—much less(!)

why am I not with tourists?—they bore me(15 minutes)

why didn't I earn roubles in Moscow by writing?—I kind of needed well a little vacation

how long do I work a day,on the average?—from none to twenty-four hours(horror)

what am I taking with me out of Russia?—"Puppschen"(this puzzled everybody)

no valuables?—none whatever

none at all?—none at all

nothing?—nothing

. . . which preliminary interrogation(to whose thoroughness the memory of a Muriel Draper could not possibly do justice)over,I'm very formally now presented to youthless-in-blouse—Meet An Ukrainian Artist—we riselurch,and(bowing like seals to each other)cordially shake hands—Whose Specialty Is Paysages. (I bow). Have You A Piece Of Paper?

How about my notebook?

A pencil?

Here

(pipe-elf-blacksmith-brakemanish-ghost-and(my principal interrogator the)beard lean-bend-yearn-stretch-twist-writhe all toward youthless)train unreels and(now,to breathless everyone's joy,youthless . . . cautiously upon 1 knee centering this opened-to-a-blank-page diary . . . it,very . . . And,How skil . . . fully rotates,beneath poised karandash begetting—a somewhat-more-than-miraculously-circular Circle. . . . Skilfully within which,now,live a cottage and,trees and now,a,stream and sky and a bridge and now birds,and)

darkness

! . . . I hadn't—so vivid was my examination—noticed the flick-er-ing of e-lec-tric bulbs.

Groping;locate speechkih

—1 striking,

proffer(respectfully)its frail illumination:but(gently smi-ling)eyes-of(declining)youthless say patience. &

dark.

est(comes:now blundering;comes some(with,something)one-becomes(and who bearing a very littlest candle)amiable. And)which(with quite prehistoric care)light-ing(now)he sticks,in;bashed:this;nearby, unlanternness . . .

—appearS-thE-hutcH-yearnwrithE-staregriN

. . . &,waiting,youthless . . .

&

Flicker Resumes:

the picture also.

. . . Courteously which its maker to myself presents;after entitling,and dating(he'd have signed it but 6 hands cried Don't 6 voices whispered No . . .).

Hahrahshoh! "Spaseebah,tovarich"(grinnings)

—Is he hungry?(re me the blacksmith asked the brakemanish)

—Are you hungry?(the brakemanish asked myself)

Mildly.

—Are you really?(the elf asked me)

Yes.

—Hungry? (the ghost)

A little.

—He's a little really hungry(said the type with the pipe)

—When did you really eat last(the loudly munching beard inquires)

Let me see . . . "Frühstück"

(surprise)No!yes!no!

—Give this man(pointing to brakemanish)money and he'll buy you something(the munchbearding directs). "Da" assures nodbrakemanishding. "Da" they nodding all assure me,solemnly danodding;and . . . wearily . . . we discover 5 roubles . . . wearily I hand 5 roubles . . . to brakemanish. Who,takes,inspects,says,Five,Roubles(& in-an-all-his-own way quite dis-ap-pears . . .)

not really since breakfast(the elf murmurs). As trainless bumphalt (gradually)ing itself. Stops:

. . . quite—train(starts)less—reappears that bold brakemanish fellow. To myself(solemnly)presenting 2 shellless eggs;a pinch of garlic;2 little soft loaves;3 roubles and 10 kopeks exactly.—"Spaseebah"(K faintly).—(Shrugging)"pazhahloostah" he(& resumes his place . . . Now pipe ghost blacksmith elf and bold emanate little trunkfulls of food;all eat)everybody's eating now;as for comrades Kem-min-kz and Cummings,together with comrades peesahtel and hoodozhnik and also comrade memyself,that oaf,why we're all 5 aplunging and awhirling into our ambrosia like nothing even a Russian ever saw and ever heard. (My silent neighbors to left and right stare amazed). The hutchers register approval:good,eh?(ghost winks). (Loudly)—you couldn't have bought those things yourself because nobody would have sold them to you,and even if you could have(beard munches)you would have paid three times as much

. . . & O for if only a touch a whisper of nectar!(but Patience).

I pass my pretty of Troikas all around all

oos & ahs(Export!everyone laughs;greedily all seize)all but beard;
who—Say:aren't Russian men good?(suddenly after very much indeed
mysterious whispering with elf and with curly,shoots)

"da"(puzzled)

—And Russian women?

"da"(cautious)"ich glaube"

. . . oos & ahs . . . much licking of many comrade-chops

"aber ich bin amerikanisch" I pidgin genially.

—Say—why are you travelling Hard?(shoots beard straight at my)&
therefore we explain that there positively was no room at any inn . . .
(reelstrainreelstrainreelstrainreelstrainreelsun)

—Sleepy?(pipe type said softly)

we,shrug

—What's(a stokehole character appearing points briefly to)this?(me).
—From America,for Odessa(shrugs,beard).—I'll give him my bed.—
But(all of us 5 Americans protest).—O,that's all right(the hutchers
chorus nodding assure solemnly).—But a man can't take another man's
bed away from(we all seriously protest).—Don't worry about(they
nodding they all assure).—But the comrade—.—The comrade
says(beard translates,yawning)he's overslept;so move your baggage a little
further down the car on the same side,where the comrade's bed is,and
go right straight to bed

K accompanied by a multitude of assuring Troikaites obeys dazedly
instructions

—See?(the stokehole proudly points to,neatly adorning his
sleepshelf,twain glowing linen sheets! Linen!) More-than-dazed,
seeing,thanking,attempt to shove-our-valise under this palatial lower. &
—Nononono!(everybody-including-stokehole vividly corrects us)that's
your pillow,that bag,tilt it up like this. —And make yourself at(brake
manish)home(grins)get undressed

. . . (now)—May I?(offering sheets' owner a fragment of completely
forgotten chocolate)

—No thank you(slowly,very calmly)I'm not hungry. But;you might
give some to these(pointing at many startled animaleyes. Almost among
a snoring motheranimal buried,beneath sacks)

—nono(whisper the eyes fearfully the refuse)

—Take it(stokehole,very gently,suggests) . . . & scared the small the
pawhands clutch;

& now:that(minus
  its shoes)oaf me-
myself slides inbetween coolAndHownesses!& care-ful-ly its
Troika(upon filthy tremulous planks)ex-ter-mi-nates. ½ . . . dozes

he said he was a writer and a painter,but he's a worker. Good. And that's
his typewriter. Ahha. I tell you what I'll do I'll telegraph. Good
  (½ . . . hears;somehow,through much-more-than-dazedness,feels:
strangely,½ becomes aware of,uneasily . . . something—.   Because of
something I said?or didn't?my cigarettes?that stranger—he who laughed
loudest he who cried And here's what Russians smoke!Have one!and
because I accepted(not a cigarette,perhaps a wisp of very-old-indeed
manure)well;O well . . . too late now . . . haven't got any what on
whatcaring me—O what the hell anyhow)
  . . .

over & over
  voices
  of comrades(voices
  of several comrades especially
  that beard)are telling saying Do something?ordering Something?with my Baggage commanding
someThing?but
  what?but
              (Wake!but
                      wake)Comrade(wake)
&(I)open my . . .
yes(there's the beard:why does he look)scared?saying
—Valise! Valise! Valise!
—Open?(I request;vaguely)
—No!(then something I can't understand)shtoh?qu'est-ce que?—"Was?"
—"Schnell!"
  this wakes me quite—I'm sitting. Looking into . . . and against . . .
1 young immaculate gay-pay-ooer who is with a shootingiron on his
hip placidly standing very most immovably over myself. Slide-from.
Sheets;stoopgro. Ping,find and be. Gin donning our left unshoe—
  "nein" 1 says,expressionlessly

. . . I nonmove:upstare . . .

"bleiben Sie ruhig" expressionlessly says 1,and not moving

. . . I stare . . .

"bleiben Sie ruhig"(not moving 1 and expressionlessly repeats)

. . . smiling gradually "spaseebah"(the K myself we Cummings I comrades hazard)

"NYET spaseebah!" 1 snarled. "—Bleiben Sie ruhig!" . . . &—isn't . . .

every(eyeseyeseyes)where . . . watching

but not of Artist,not of Beard;who aren't

(is the not so bold brakemanish is the blacksmith not so curly is the elf)

but no Ghost

(and the dumb type with a pipe)also I locate stokehole now who's playing with the little animals

. . . and these all other watching strangely are—seem to be how old—new. But . . . —Has this carless,for all these new-old eyes,wonderfully shrunk?feel as if myself were much smaller;not merely very different:another person? Morning. Trainreels through. No;I'm I(or whoever's passport safely this may be,may safely be these Pay To The Order Ofs,this discwhispering now safely toy). Day. How extraordinary:how wholly unlike anything . . . last night for instance:or anywhere . . . here,for example:or anytime . . . or now. Yes,it's actually day;day through those shut those unshut shutnesses,day reeling flimsily(not like itself,more—impossibly most—like a memory of quite what hasn't yet happened)day palely silently creeprushing.

& where's my gay-pay?my ruhig?my Sie?my bleiben and my NYET spaseebah?tell

me not that while you slept he snitched our—no:here's 1. And . . . the other. Hahrahshoh! Thank god. 2 shoes. Not identical,either; fortunately if symmetrically dissimilar,even as these(luckily)my feet She Had Her

shoes on when she fell(so what the hell bill what the)& I breakfast with oaf memyself esq. passing up the 1st 5 or 6 courses and taking the conundrum's dilemma with all things considered for dessert(hello there,you!comrade K?comrade C?)you're going to Odessa yes you are(and no nobody not all the eyeseyeseyes can stop you not all the counterexamcrossinterrogations and shootingirons plus hokum plus or minus inhunonmanity times bunk divided by the square root of Jesus subtract heaven what's the answer?)

never having found the answer,we invite stokehole to share our partially remaining chocolate with suddenly remembered crackers

stokehole(whom we seem to remember glimpsing through our

dreams,once or twice crawling on all 4s hither and thither)courteously each declines;but willingly administers both to 5 count 'em kids(the animals)toward whom he seems to feel a distinctly agreeable responsibility—maybe he's been put in charge of them,or is he their mother?(the snoring motheranimal has utterly disappeared)or perhaps,who knows,he likes children . . .

pipetype feels very jolly today. Slaps heartily the wood of his shelf;I sit beside. Curly and brakemanish farewell shake hands and hop off at a stationless in a forestless. Elf presently vanishes. Pipe and myself and a sleepy whoish tovarich(just arrived out of nowhere)nod at each other solemnly and do not understand a word each other say and smoke each other's cigarettes incessantly until each other become so mightily athirst that pipe purchases for K 2 nahzahns and nobody has a bottleconquerer so comrade I gradually ruin the cap of 1 with a dull penknife but 1 taking whoish thereupon mysteriously opens it all now completely over entirely comrade poor pipe

—who grins,marvellingly:"NYET"(winking)"spaseebah."

Which accident invigorates whoish to such lengthless lengths that presently he begborrows my next-to-the-last cracker &(solemnly upholding the same beside his own metallic nonloaf of tarlike unbread)exclaims

Import . . . Export

& returns the cracker,with polite merriment. Also he proffers(shrugging "plokoh")canned fish,& to pipe's horror C samples plokoh via tar. & this nowhereish creature keeps getting off at nonstations & hurrying nowhere & returning out of nowhere emptyhanded(cheerfully "neechehvoh nyet" shrugging)

. . . well . . . well . . . the country's getting flat. Seaishland.

Why,here's the elf:he produces an incredible species of map-timetable;he wants to show us where we all are now,but all he can manage to show us is something quite otherwise,i.e. where we all are when. — However,something has not or has been definitely proved and irrevocably established:we are really going to Odessa:that's a great relief to everyone. Probably this now entering piglike pair(middleagedly lecherous)prove something too they sit opposite they gleam at they(whenever not vividly pumping whoish about peesahtel)if pigman wore gahlstook hoodozhnik would think him a bourgeois her nobody shouldn't think anything god in his infinite grant

that of such is the kingdom of Odessa not made.
Shtoh?
but. Unbudge:halt;jerK,
impossible!
. . . but
            —but comrade I am goodbyeing with stokehole with children
& elf's downclambering already from trainless(& now pipe lights,K;then
him:1 merdeish final import)we . . . shake
    hANDs
    —dahsveedahnyah
    HandS

(not far.near.5 minutes
    starved)
just down there:at the end of that street
    (smoldering stringlike
right around;the,next corner)
    shruqful sinewy stutterish(Germaning always assurances mentioning
this occasionally that naming)strolled(on top of his narrow head
balancing my swollen valise wearing my bloated knapsack between
hollow twitching shoulders)
    for 20 no-more-
    no through a once(imagined nobly,breathingly with wide treeflanked
avenues planned)city;now dream aswim in vision tottering now with
memory now clenched by madly silent enormous heat
    -less minutes
    until i glimpse It and i cry(and he squirms—"yah"—grinning)Ocean;
never to be
    imagined,or planned
    all His planes;every Her magical
    colour
    the substance of tomorrow:lying among yesterday,a bluegreening Is
    bright with(whitely)Nows
    "und" amazed C pidgins to strolling stringlike "es ist Blau!"

the down come stringarms with valise(shoulders slough knapsack)freed
the head turtles(smoldering leanness the now snakes escaped)
    "shoylkah?" K

. . . What you like . . .

(& off "danke schön mein Herr" proudly deepening a drowning in-with-by sweat strolls nimbly apparition.

Ritzy,this hostelry!situated upon a great esplanade overlooking formerly (paralysed)mighty harbour;

foyer coolly,spacious.

Structure aware(despite revolutions levellings reversals—but Ocean has all these:are these not all integral portions of a very life called Ocean?)of itself,I feel. Wonder

what the Hotel London used to be?wonder where I'm standing?how many skulls leaked,how many slowly brains drooled,over

this immaculate coolswift floor?)O progress!

courteously Germaning deskman efficiently leads around that wall,through carpeted corridor,K into INTOURIST;where am served welcomingly in(of all things)the French language by agreeably worried young gentleman who suggests almost softly that K should return to Kiev should procure a Polish visa should leave for Paris via Poland.—Ah,but my present visa specifies Odessa.—Ah,but all that may be changed.— Why should all that be changed?—Well,you will save both your time and your money.—By returning(I suppress a shudder)to Kiev?—Exactly,sir . . . at least,that's the way things look to me now;I shall be able to inform you further about four o'clock,when our manager arrives.—O and by the way monsieur:will you kindly get me certain moneys which your Kiev office owes me . . . the time which it owes me you never can get.—Pardon?(innocently uplifting servile eyes,eyes perfectly untrust-worthy,polite) . . . O what a shame:you were indeed unfortunate;we are of course not responsible for the train service you understand . . . Well,sir,I suggest that you come back at four and we'll try to settle everything to your satisfaction . . . "entendu?" Good day.—

the sonofabitch(me thought to Kself)

the bastard!

(lazily reclining amid regal splendour,an unkind kind of superwhore-houseness;draperies galore,galore redplushery:dooble-vay-say magnifique and salle de bains suprême—aussi a bidet. Quel sentiment:a bidet in hell).

And rapidly having bathed,having made several rapidly sketches,sally

I forth in my last not-clean-but-unfilthy shirt(we dreamily inhabit ye esplanade . . . sit,hypnotized,in the real shade of the real trees,beside a distinguished really generalissimo of a sortless;I breathe we ocean tense air sunsunsun . . . while almost-naked children(by their teacher eyedeyed-eyed)play near(directedly)and al(prettily)ways behave

4 P.M.)
    a rather deaf
    & quite offish lump of tovarich(my timid young gentleman murmurs "malade")grumpishly scolds that it will take all of several,probably 5,days to change my visa and doesn't advise anything whatever and be sure to
    come around tomorrow morning early and goodbye

—given "civilization",a man(an indivisible or individual,roundedly not flatly(naturally not obediently)alive:spontaneous,firm,sensitive and very humbly of his own impulse proud-erect)is amazing;in hell is overwhelming. (Overwhelming,my 1st glimpse of hole-in-the-forehead . . . here,against how trying fanaticism,occurs(looms)certainly the candour of a truly human spirit. Overwhelming more(deeply)gradually,Assyrian's continuous curiosity;his merciful humour:his fearless gentleness). Moves now toward my(faintweary)self now a perhaps 3rd integer:
    "c'est par ici le jardin?" whom ask
    "oui monsieur par ici" quietly(seriously)proud-erectly headwaiter replies. With a dignity quite at right angles to both that dumb lusting after selfhumiliation and that assertive dread of selfabasement which respectively afflict unmen in general and headwaiters in particular. —With a roundedlyness perfectly unlike this behind me how flat suddenly American Voice
    "puddun mih—"
    (ilah preserve our spirit!whither may we fly?nowhere!too late . . .)
    "—Mistur Cummins;eye wusn here wen yoo come in,but they tole me ubboutun Umerican arreyevin this mormin;eyem un Umerican too: pleasetuh meetyuh Mistur—"
    & cleverly low desperate sticky vitality(ensconced in a small oldmiddleaged imperson of defunct eyes a twisting lip toadstool feet pudgy claws)hales me to a not outdoor(a merely diningroom a not "jardin")table;summons with And How fabulous authority plus loftily And patronizing How friendliness the(who immediately impersonates

a summoned)headwaiter;snappily now relays my hesitant order of soup & turkey & beer & compôte.

Caught:that's what I am—

stuck. Well . . . let this devil's minion strut his. Ecco food,anyway(and damned good it turns out to be;actual it is and not imitated) . . . as for ecco peevoh,it's(shtoh?)beer!—The defunct watchwatchwatchings go almost undead

"good,huh?"

the twisting quiverquiverquivering now itself almost straightens . . .

"eye node yoo wus"(whisper)"uh Noo Inglundur by yur axen. Lissun. Eyem uh Noo Inglundur too"

—whereupon my burleskloving spirit lifts a shout of joy:all's well! 2 Noo Inglundurs. Hahrahshoh! Beacon Hill and Veritas. You simply cannot complexly beat it,short of perhaps Minsky's(and doubt if even—"funny" grimly K whispers "I recognized your accent too!")

"aintid odd" he said "—no,eye meanid:aintid mysteerious."

"You and I" we contribute,munching.

"Meetin like this" he contributes,nodding oddly

(& was born in New Haven. But inhabited Russia for past 22 years. The local only official representative of a tourist service recently organized by outraged foreigners to protect themselves and dear ones from INTOURIST. Why,my own little agony in the Kiev station "aintuh thing". It seems this diabolic INTOURIST is so unhealthily and absolutely bad that the Russian government has gratefully endorsed and joyously acclaimed INTOURIST'S sworn most deadly rival. Why,everything you can't begin to so much as imagine has happened to the illstarred clients of this diabolic contraption how loosely entitled INTOURIST;not merely have people been raped and robbed,they have also "been disuppeered" now and then:whereas courtesy and efficiency,combining with knowledge which is power,do reign benevolently over these or them or those who park their lives their fortunes and their sacred honour with)"uh reely seerious kunsoyn. Now look. Here yoo are,payin too much fur uh grade big room yuh doaneed—cuz yur un Umericum. Thad ain fair isid? Well,eyel shoot yuh right intoo uh room thad's chust us good fur half thih price—how ubbout thad? But lissun:thad aint all . . . anythin eye kun doo fur yoo eyel gladly dooid,un wen yoo come tuh leave yuh kun chus gimmih wut yoo thing is right;I ain gonnuh charge yoo nuthn. How's thad? Thad's fair uhnuf,aintid? Wumun ur shows ur liqur ur anythin yoo wan—chust ask mee . . . How long yoo gonnuh stay?"

we thereupon outline our latest encounter with the daemon INTOURIST. Defunct turns 7 shades greyer

"lissun. Here's thih card uh thih kunsoyn eye have thih honur tuh woyk fur. Un here's testuh- . . . puddun mih uh momun"(ambles wildly away:fiercely immediately returning with letters,papers)"testuh moniuls"—several of which am forced to read;1's a long intricate wail about being gruesomely overcharged by INTOURIST's benevolent rival("nuttuh woyd uv truth inid" defunct states proudly)the others are of an almost painfully laudatory nature. "Now take yur choice"(fixing me with a glassy And How stare)"cuz meye feelins ain gonnuh get hoyt eethur way. But lissun—"(crouching twistedly toward)"—US WUN YANG TOO UNUDUH take meye advize un leave Russhuh like yoo wuz suppose tuh,by Udessuh. See? In this country it ain woyt taykin chances,get mih?"

"and from Odessa?"

"ware yuh goin?"

"Paris"

"chus like rollin offuh log. Yoo take uh boat tuh Kunstantunople—thad's uh swell city!thih goils is thih best in thih woyld;buleev mee. Ut Kunstantunople yoo gut thih Orien Express—thad's thih crack train uh Europe—straight tuh Paris;un no monkey business,get mih? . . . Well?"

well(us wun Noo Inglundur too unuduh)I think there's a lot in what he says. And I wonder if

"lissun"(reading my hope!)"here's sumpn els:suppose yoo gut sumpn" e.g. a diary "yoo'd chust us soon thih kustums didn see—well,eyel fix all thad,free uh charge. Thad ain nuthn tuh mee. Weye,thih boys down there,they nose mee like eye wus their granfathur. They'd doo anythin fur mee,they would;anythin!"

"it sounds almost too good to be true" we guardedly comment

—starting up "kummon!"(he snapped)"seein's buleevin!"

1st we tiptoeingly view(he having snappily asked for and promptly received from salaaming deskman its key)a summum bonum or inside room on the ground floor with a toilet and bath attached—all for $2.50 per diem then,snappily crashing the gate of a plump gestureful tovarich-manager,comrade defunct demands said bonum in my behalf;only to find—via multiple apologies—that it's already taken(I later learn the real cause of gestureful's refusal,viz. that the bonum had to be "fixed all ovur cuz sumwun wus sick:no wut eye mean?"). Whereupon,powwow;result,am to be very shortly(NYET "zahvtrah")changed from my present how more than luxurious to a smaller but more than sufficient chamber,which latter plus or including 3 square meals a day will cost our heroless only the very trifling(the almost negligible)catastrophe $6.50. At this distinctly And How minimum rate our heroless will quite easily be able to survive the Hotel London for some timeless,or(joking aside)until next Monday;when a Russian boat absolutely departs willy-nilly for Istanbul. P.S. initiation into the Society For The Prevention of INTOURIST To Foreigners doesn't,it seems,depend upon transference to less gaudy quarters—here and now,with the approval (nay enthusiasm)of comrade gestureful,I am handed a neat little booklet of mealtickets;now and here do I sign away forevermore ticket number 1 . . . representing my recent contact with the Hotel London's cuisine . . . drinks,by the by,are extra.

And so we pass to higher things:what should I like to do—take a little personally conducted tour of the town,perhaps? No?not today?just wander about alone;well,that's all right,of course. But lissun:an educated man like I ought to carry a good book with him:now here's a perfect corkerino,a knockout,a gem,a jewel,more than as good as they come,something you'll never regret having read(just lending it,you understand;wouldn't part with it for a million dollars)nonono,please take it,bring it back when you've finished,I'm only too glad,I've got a lot,piles and piles,heaps and heaps of them;when you're through with this remember there's another waiting and

"yoo woan"(reluctantly me releasing at the curb outside our portal) "run away withid,will yoo?" defunct wistfully inquires "—but eye gut thih drop" & mentor-the-2nd's unface brightens;remembering cheerfully "eye gut yur passport!"

—and so into sunsunsun strolls comrade Kem-min-kz,helplessly clutching The Ringer by Edgar Wallace.

Our heroless walked . . . keeping as near to the shore as architecture permits(which it doesn't) . . . all of several miles;encountering everywhere bathhouses:and once,through a ragged hole in a stoney wall,Ocean returning,he parked a masterpiece and changed his fast disintegrating booteenkee. He also wrote 1 letter. Descending—armed with antiINTOURIST bible—to the Hotel London diningroom or salle à manger,was quietly greeted by dignity;together dignity and heroless ordered dinner,comprising 2 huge redhot schnitzels lurking among many fresh tasty vegetables(& it took ½ an hour to cook & 3 waiters to serve)and very floweringly as that svelte baronial candelabrum of this vast indoor diningroom glowed in presumably our hero's honourless,we gradually noticed that I did not dine alone. Opposite was sitting,probably had been sitting for some time,a too blonde nonman amid bad makeup smothered but betraying something like not ungoodly figure—K recognizes artful directress of the hotel's Torgsin,she to whose over(And How)stocked precincts comrade-mentor-defunct had previously me escorted lest me lack for dainties(& I also recall there was then a little boy tumbling around the central showcase:defunct snapped,at tooblonde "doan ledim play with thih knife!" . . . which set us awondering

in our quiet way). And now as,glutted with nutriment,we quit now blondeful baronial,after K pants agalloping a waiter awaving our forgotten holy booklet

. . .

dark(unmoving,perhaps 10 yards from "my" hotel,
Bleiben)ness
night. (Night)a crowd a swarm of young young of faces comrades boys and girls of boys not men of girls not nonmen and not women girls who are pretty who are gaily dressed and young with bright eyes with golden skins girls with small high bosoms and young with slim legs with French heels and not men boys young boys tall with broad shoulders wandering awkwardly moving shyly embracing the young graceful with French heels the girls laughing the girls not women kissing in shadows the boys the young girls dancing in shadows with the awkward tall young boys with the young boys not men and young a swarm young a crowd a wandering young embracing moving kissing dancing dancing in shadows bright eyes dancing with awkwardly shyly dancing with golden skins laughing dancing with broad shoulders gaily dancing with tall and pretty with young and graceful with young and slim with young and young with young and high young bosoms dancing and French heels dancing dancing not nonmen girls not women girls young girls crowding

303

swarming wandering laughing young embracing kissing moving young
moving

cringing amid magnificence 1(in its left claw a box in its right fin a
rag)$\frac{1}{2}$implores my all $\frac{1}{2}$threatens all my proud-erect most dreamfully
reentering new selves
    ("shine?")

Thurs. June 4

pronounced absence of bugs despite prodigious antibug-stink

pack,ready to transfer

I breakfast with comrade defunct,now who(magnificently bowing)hands me an(offering me in the next breath from his own private collection a Red Book)all the way from Paris telegram . . .
    after which the comrade dons his 1911 boater and with K awanders through sunsunsun up mysteriously empty by huge trees full of memories shaded streets into

1 dirty small office. Here at timid clerk-comrades defunct chucks slapstick greetings. To a cheerful most homely here nonman very now courteously ducks,tipping the straw à l'amérique. And now commences(And How respectfully)Russianing.
    " . . . Meye purticlur frien wus out but eye ingaged yur passige chus thih same:evurybudy knows mih uhroun here;yool get thih bes there is,buleev mee."
    (. . . And judging by cheerful's grin,I shall)

a visa is an unnecessary evil completely surrounded by "toykish kunsulit"(disguised in tumbledown whereabouts). 3 dank unflights of darkish filthy stairlesses.
    & past swash(a frightened mother a terrified father several merely scared children who are and piously which have been waiting)buckling gaily defunct plunks me right spang into the innermost sanctum of glad-to-see-you-ish comrade-consul and gtsy welcomes copiously myself who(blushing)produce 1 horrorimage and . . . clic-clac . . . all's
    ("—wudduhyuhmean Pay fur id?")indignantly("He ain gottuh pay fur Nuthn! EYEM gunnuh pay fur this un Eyem gunnuh pay turMorruh,see?nut now!un Hee's gunnuh pay MEE wen Hee leaves thih ho-tel tuh take thih boat—get id?"
    10,000 apologies from consul

"woulduh beer go good?"(particularly after battling with Odessa's telegraph system)

"would it?"

"if yoo ask mee,kumrad,it would."

"I ask yoo,kumrad."

"Okay . . . there's uh reel beerjoint eye know,thih beer's suhwell . . . nize un sudzy un beeg un cool . . . yunno—nut like this fuggin peevoh!(thad ain no goodun nevur wuz)but" apologetic whisper "thih dump ain vury highclass"

"thank god for that,kumrad!"   .

he stared at me in unsheer wonder "eye like yoo" he said "yoo ain fulluh shid"

a faded open to the sidewalk in almost every direction roomlet unswallowing many faded tables. Unto its faded counter stroll we regally. Where comrade faded bartender greets defunct,where defunct greets comrade presents myself("eye tole him yur uh reel Yang un tuh to be good tuh yuh")where from

no-

where float

foaming glasses("les siddown")

. . . I could have siddown until doom's-(it's actually,icily,Beer)day . . .

"shooer" mentor encourages "leave him sumpn. They all want id,pooer devuls;but thih kummunists keep afturum woysun fleas. Lissun:bihfore thih revulution,thih Rushuns wus kinely un husputuble but . . . yunno." Darkly "things get toyned upside-

dyuh mine if eye ask thad" nodding violently to a now scarcely now a silently "felluh tuh" entering the salle à manger dwarflike individual(whose And How more than big head wears perhaps the most perfectly discon- solate face I ever saw)"eat with us?"

"why,no" I say;uneasily

"HAY Kummon ovur!" rotating . . . smil(through pain)ing slowly . . . the more than head,ghostfully;the much more than head(upon its tight very little)"he's turruble unhappy . . . wans sumun tuh talk tuh . . . talk twimun trytuh cheerimup!" mentor hastily admonishes(stunned body approaches

"monsieur:bonjour" this)tiny he,arriving stood;rigid. & through-pain-smiling.

(We meet)"merci" sits. "Comme vous voulez"—politebrokenly,to
very that with now large eyes quietly him searching maître d'hotel—
"n'importe" briefly

. . . an Italian. Ravenna and Palermo. An electrical engineer. Says
ghastly he's "perdu". Says faintly he needs something "pour me donner
du courage,monsieur". Says that what's killing him is the neither-yes-
nor-no indefiniteness. Fortunately however "le consul italien,un brave
homme" has stood is standing and will stand behind him. Stunned
expects to hear the final result "ce soir". He closed up his business in
Italy and left his wife and his children to come to Odessa to work for
the soviets at their request. Great by them things had he been promised:
immediate work;a big salary to start with,rapid advancement. Stunned
was most particularly instructed not to take any money with him and
most particularly informed that,just as soon as his boat docked,he
would meet(at the Odessa customs)a mysterious and omnipotent
man who would immediately take complete charge of him and would
instantaneously do everything for him. . . . Arriving,as per schedule,he
met no mysterious,no omnipotent,man. Met nobody and nobody ever
heard of him. All day in agony he waited and nobody came near him
nor did he receive any message from anyone. There must have been
some terrible mistake. Finally,desperate,he decided to look around. The
Odessa customs-comrades affectionately advised comrade stunned to
leave all his baggage in their loving care,and almost cast kittens when he
picked up his suitcase and walked away. He walked until he found a taxi.
He said hotel to the driver. The driver drove him here. Here he explained
in French that he had no money and told why and asked for assistance.
Whereupon nobody believed him. Whereupon comrade defunct
miraculously appeared,heard his story,believed him,paid the taxi,and
actually bullied the management into loaning stunned room-and-board
until stunned's incredible arrival could be unbelievably investigated.
Comrade defunct also lent comrade stunned money to immediately
cable Moscow for instructions. Whereupon no answer. Whereupon
they visited the Italian consul,who(being "un brave homme")cabled
Moscow again. Whereupon,despair . . . stunned can never thank
defunct for what defunct has done for stunned in stunned's despair. If
it weren't for defunct and the Italian consul,stunned would have gone
mad. Whenever stunned thinks of his wife and of his children and of

his home and Italy and of his friends,stunned believes he's going mad. His wife and his children!he has no money to send them,no assurances to give them,nothing—nothing. He says he feels somewhat as if his honour had been taken away from him but more as if he had been castrated. What can be done? Nothing. With the exception of comrade defunct and of "le brave homme",nobody,absolutely nobody,believes stunned's tale of woe:why should they? Stunned himself openly and frankly and in anguish admits that the whole thing from start to finish sounds highly improbable and completely fantastic. "J'étais fou:c'est tout" he was idiotic enough to sincerely and really believe all those rumours which he'd heard . . . that socialist soviet Russia was a vast country with unlimited resources devoted to the welfare of mankind;an earthly paradise,nothing less,where all those human beings who really and sincerely wanted to work could find the kind of work they wanted and work to their hearts' and souls' content("et c'est seulement Ça que je demande—Travailler!")that's,above all,what's killing him,what's breaking him,driving him mad—not being able to Work;to express himself:to do something "et je Sais travailler,moi!" very desperately eager is stunned to prove that he really knows how to work and that he sincerely wants to work. So eager,that he's willing to go to work for nothing,just to show what he can do;and if his bosses aren't satisfied,why they have a perfect right to ship stunned home. But what no human being on this earth has any right to do is,to keep another human being in limbo,without any assurance,any definite no or yes;without any chance to vindicate himself,to fulfil his responsibilities toward those he loves.

"Il Me FAUT Travailler!"(desperately—out of the big head perched on the very much more than little body a lost)voice(leaps)

&("excusez")small fists dash from eyes tears . . . now,

(upstarting)"those sonsuvbitches uv shoemakurclerks wouldn buleevim" defunct snarls "—hee may be uh fake:O ids all right,he doan unnurstan Inglish:but thih lidl cuss looks like hee wus onnes tuh Mee. Weye see here:hee mightuv run up uh big bill,un didih?hee did nut. Weye" scowling "ids all yuh kun doo tuh getim tuh eat" the Noo Inglundur Frum Noo Havun marvels

now

"écoutez,monsieur"(& disconsolately to myself now stunned silently

turning
. . . "s'il vous plait?")
I believe you.

"shine?"
          in its left claw a box in its right fin a rag
"zahvtrah" mentor said irritably. And 2 through portal comrades
pass into sunsunsun:descending;slowly;via the immortal Potemkin
stairs;wander a stopped desolate mess of wharflanes. ("Id ain fur me so
much,ids fur thih ole wumun" he guiltily insists
     & us smites finally Cool).
Than previous Torgsins less preposterously artificial. Bossed by
a positively hearty deepbrown comrade-in-shirtsleeves. To right of
doorway blares the far and away most audaciously mendacious specimen
of internal superpropaganda which I've as yet(dazedly)experienced:1
poster,gaudily depicting 1 tiptop rollicking jolly monarch-of-all-I-survey
Rooshun seated at his lordly ease and gladfully inhaling,to its And How
delicious depths,1 export(sic)cigarette . . . to darkness . . . to the Kiev-
Odessa trainless,darts And How memory!
     —transaction:we're here because we're here because we're here because
we're buying(ostensibly I'm buying;with mentor's kind assistance)uhlotuh
canned stuff and 2(guiltily "eye doan drink usuh rule,thih ole wumun
woan let mih,but . . . yunno how id is;uh felluh needsuh drop now un
then. Eye tell yuh wut:yoo buy wun un eyel buy thih othur un weel share
um—eh?")bottles,1st containing something "strong",2nd containing
something "weak". —High finance:hearty takes all my receipts(looks over
carefully all my receipts and receipts and receipts)selects 1 which had been
already drawn on via the Kiev Torgsin,and now—carrying same himself to
a supplyroom—arranges with this dumb bedizened nonman that comrade
I should run amok to the extent of 20 roubles. Dumb can't believe;dumb
takes it back to hearty;dumb is reassured;dumb returns,dumb fills "my"
order—"Tayuk theeiz pleeas!" And comrade I("yoo bettur take id,id
looks bettur")receive 1 huge package. Then,with defunct,revisit comrade
hearty . . . mysteriously whereupon evolves a mighty discussion re that
supernatural substance,valyootah . . . and apparently(Homer having
nodded)defunct got a receipt endorsed(so that he could draw on it)when
and whereas defunct shouldn't and "if he gave it to us" hearty Englishes

for my spellbound benefit "we wouldn't let him buy at our store."
Whereupon hearty's genial if albeit hitherto speechless associate begs
hearty to inquire of myself

"how much do you spend in a day?"

"between" cautiously aver(for most of my innumerable receipts
represent Pay to the Order Ofs)"five and ten dollars"

whereupon(2 comrades well-nigh-swooning)2 far from swooning
comrades unmolestedly carry a quite unpaidfor package into
sunsunsun—& if 1 comrade,alias defunct,hadn't surreptitiously all the
time meant to get rid of a certain oldissue-10-roubles,that very same
unmolested package might be unpaidfor still . . .

"lemmih take id now!"

. . . quel transformation:quivering(shimmying)a ½crazed dotard
clutches(pallid)at me(with splayed paws)greedily(at my bundle at his at
)I give

"—gud-bless-yuh Mistur" babbling now hysterically loonily hugging
now package "Cummins" chortling "I'll pay yuh" now whispering "back
Mistur Cummins us soon us we get tuh thih ho-tel un"(guiltily)"wait
Mistur Cummins wait till thih ole lady knows she'll bless yuh too she'll
say gud" piously "bless Mistur Cummins chus like eye doo—"

thus,comrades,was the Hotel London Torgsin doublecrossed.

"Wanuh see" radiant "how yur goin out?wanuh see" grinning(clutching)kookooishly "thih vury place?huh?yuh?"

(K's heart hopped)"sure!" I said faintly

"thing eyem kiddin,eh?—but eye know all them gud dam kustums-
bastuds back un forwuds. Weye,eye gutuh nuf un thad lousy stinkin
bunch tuh sen thih hole kuhboodle uvum tuh kingdom come:un doan
they know id! Here;take this—waituh minute."

He packageless reeled off. Toward a rambling shed. . . .
Upon a capstanlike iron(mercifully situated in a merciful pool of
darkness)something I now deposit—very,very,and very cautiously—
this how sacred brownpaper burden:I stand(marveling,at life,at
unlife,and at lifelessness . . .)

"—HAY!"

there he is,beckoning like a windmill. . . . Resume the load;aiming
for through sunsunsun said shed.

Defunct chuckled,contemptuously thumbjerking "wannuh look inside?hee" nodding curtly to this—lounging before unshut shutnesses— brighteyed tovarich " 's gut sum tartus in there" and spat.

"All right"(dizzily K

glimpses who,entering,1 lengthwise dirtily disordered silence:and at whose endless mutely now are squatting ragswaddled-nonhuman-shapes framed in a chaos of thingless soft-filthy-things)

"well,id" defunct nudges me "ain so turruble,is id,huh?"

"—this is where I come when I take the boat for Constantinople?"

"shooer. Right here un no were els. This is thih kustums,kumrad. Lovuly,ain id?" he sneers with a scornful shrug. "Les ride back in thih rubberneck waggun"(meaning INTOURIST's officially parked outside chariot)"with them buggurs"(the tartars) . . . "ids too fuggin hot tuh walk" he snorted

"will there be enough room?" I wonder "those comrades seem to have lots and lots of baggage—"

"and lots of money"(a voiceless at my elbow said. Turning,confront 1 steadily elsewhere-gazing tovarich-total-stranger. And who)"lots of money" repeats now dreamily

"yes?" comrade peesahtel-hoodozhnik politely Poietes

"uh-huh" the total(vaguely and almost but not quite greedily) murmurs.

Well,I got him up that hill. —Poor defunct! This sunsunsun is much too much for him but anything,worse even,were better than waiting any longer for those "dam tartus" when he can almost if not quite taste something which we're going to sample the very moment we reach the London . . . & luckily for my mentor's by no means robust constitution there proved to be a winding wayless,a crooked pathless,up(but gradually,crookedly,painfully,up)Heartbreak Heights,via innumerable terraces adorned by here-and-here sleepily lolling comrades:this route 2 comrades did pursue;resting(he cursing)occasionally,occasionally (he groaning)sitting . . . and after a goodbad ½hourless 2(I bearing burden)comrades attained the will-o'-the-wisp summit

pausing near where those great stairs begin their steep music,we look(breathing)down—down . . . to the fatal shed-of-sheds

&(breathing)comrade(looking)I remember dimly how,as we left it,there came against us highleaping horses over which yelled a

blondmustached salmonshirted backleaning charioteer and:we,dodged
the horses;leaping which came to a black chain,and the chain:gave;as
ponderously an(at 1 end)drum humming began spinning whirling
fiercely to this outrushing now nonman's wildly cries—

now probably(I wonder?)being the psychological—"remember that
woman I told you about" looking ask looking "the mother of my Russian
teacher?"

"thih wun yuh wanuh take sum presuns too?" he gasped,fanning
"right."

"Yesn rumembur" gasping "wut eye said?eye said ids dayngurous!"

"I remember—"

"buleev mee"(solemnly gasps defunct solemnly fans)"yur leyebul tuh
get yurself intoouh lotuh trouble if yuh doan watch out." . . . Quickly a
fat whisper("I ain kidn yuh. Look:here's uh wumun whose dottur made
uh getuhway durin thih revulution by bribury un kurruption;thads wut
yoo said,ain id? —Well,thih muthur uvuh goyl who done uh thing like
thad is uh suspicious charactur. Un suspicious characturs is watched,see?
. . . Now lissun. Us wun Yang too unuduh")stealthily("keep outuh hur
way!")

"but" stealthily very stealthily I remind him "you said that,if I took
YOU along,everything would be all right—"

"'all RIGHT?'" nondefuncting:unstooping:upheaving And How a
chestless "weye,if yuh take MEE uhlong,yuh kun Piss in thih Eye uv
thih Gay-Pay-Oo!"

"fine!but how about her . . . I won't get her framed up,will I?"

"Yoo might;but"(assures my mentor,sumptuously strutting into the
superluxurious foyer of the hyperserene("shine?")Hotel London)"WEE
won't"

& who(duly having mingled "strong" and "weak")even votes that I
embellish my Russian teacher's modest gifts with a bit of Which and of
What . . . from the copious larder of too-blonde. &

suddenly "now eyem gunnuh make yoo ucquainted"—after 20 minutes
of sunsunsun based on K's scorn of mythical taxis "with un inturnationul
young lady—born in Umuricuh un doan speak Inglish."

Alias 1 plump bronzed missie. Who's placidly sitting beside an unshut

shut,through which catch almost Parisian glimpse-of-courtyard. "You siddown there next hur un eyel be right back"

. . . somehow his daughter has the air of a Booth Tarkington heroine

is absorbing 1 small book very very diligently . . .

Electricity?(asks,peeping at its nearer page,Kem-min-kz)

smiles she and she nods. And she resumes her busy memorizing

. . . along this streetless slouches past us a bigeyed youngold nonman and from youngold's right finclaw droops a warping babe:missie starts—smiling,she hellos. Resumes memorizing

whoretype upsidles . . . the neat,head memorizing sinks,deeper, in memorizing the,small

"kumon"(mentor's all excitement)"in!thih muthurd like tuh meet yuh—" & dragleads me through court into long and large and tidy and darkish room which,with 2 smaller others,he boasts of sharing 12 short years with a cordial gentle housely wifelet. German Jewish. Takes my hand in both thick moist paws:thanks(almost weeping)me for "your kindness". And(and trembling with terror of the Demon Rum)watches:while pompously sir mentor mixes me sir and sir himself just another chus wun more weakstrong . . . who wouldn't trust those sacred bottles out of his sight 1 moment;not he! —And presently wifelet brings("take sugar,please")tea,cakes,jam;and seated in state,teaing,statefully now 3 comrades converse. . . . Do I notice those photographs? They represent the benefactress of mentor and of mentor's Frau and of mentor's(at present perched near the window,reading always reading electricity)"propurly raised" Tochter("none uh this free stuff fur hur" he whispers fierceproudly "she doan love nuthn but hur lessuns—un us!")not to mention Tochter's elsewhere unfortunately Bruder,a gentleman and eke a scholar,an earnest tall honest strapping credit to his parents("yunno" nudging "they wanted him tuh join thih kummunist putty . . . but he thought too much uv us!")cheerfully who took a poke in the nose from a certain angry kulak only the other day("meye boy wus up North investigatin kunditions fur his papur—sum uh them peasunts hates joynulists woysun poisun un they ain vury fond uh kullective farmin neethur"—"sh!" wifelet admonishes) . . . well,this benefactress of the whole family,she for whom naught is too good,this very angel,inhabits(I'll be agreeably surprised to learn) Constantinople. And when I go to Constantinople,buleev me I'll go with a letter of recommendation such as never ain't or was;a letter And

How to angel from mentor,stating via the King's and Queen's English in no uncertain terms that comrade K is the pot of gold at the end of every rainbow(if yuh know wut eye mean) . . . the which will do everybody chus woyls uv good and very considerably foster the spirit of international amity. Also,be I informed that angel's husband is the greatest American engineer in soviet Russia today—witness his chef-d'-oeuvre of chef d'oeuvres,the universally renowned Stalingrad tractor plant,which does-or-does-not turn out tens-or-thousands of tractors which do-not-or-do work. Also,that a charming daughter graces angel's Constantinople villa;likewise a clean upstanding son,the apple of his mother's eye. And that these worthy scions of an illustrious house attend Roberts College. . . . Imagine wut fun yool have wen yuh get tuh Kunstantunople!chust imagine!

"these rooms are delightful"(and oddly—for I'm certainly now in a stronghold of bourgeoisieness—not cluttered)I comment

"wee used tuh have wun more wee did;but" mentor scowls "they took id uhway frum us,thih"

("sh!")she said. (Smiling)

soon rain.

Everything says. Rain

& these starved untrees this parched nonair

—standing;clutching a giftpackage somewhat augmented per the Hotel London's giftshop oasis or Torgsin;I hear untrees speak and nonair(speak of only and wonderfully Rain) . . . & verily I ask myself where am I not in the world(where in the unworld-nonworld am I?)—pausing on an edge of such a hollowsquare of buildinglesses?

while not quite clutching "yool luv um" detective stories pumps 1 shrugging much more than middleaged ghost in babyclothes(and who What who What Name who O who wickedly sneerfrowning "nyez neyeyoo")?—again while something while someone with skin like a drowned angleworm bats now madly with an old straw hatless that hanged(rustily)high unbell which clongclingclungs . . . and out of the nether dark sprouts 1 nonface(who What who What Name who O who You Mean The Cripple who frownsneering wickedly Down and To Your Right now disappears?)

—now do we the further angleworm groping and the I halt before unshut shutness before this comprising 1 bespectacled oldyoung hideous

314

nonman(who What who What Name who sneerfrowning wickedly "nyez neyeyoo")?

—possibly does myself behind himselfless(quitting the speaking of Rain only nonair)enter now blindly unportal(now are we do we climbing climb through blind unlight stairless unstair nonstair & into and within silent perhaps & now)corridor appears(or seems)1 silentness(who What)now,points . . .

—now—

(or am I dead)

the worm knocks loud.

                    Come:In;

. . . or am I dead?was;that is,this(a voice?

—he-or-it opening now-somethingless which might-once-unhave been a-perhaps nondoor)

                    & we come in.

                              Cluttering beyond belief images cluttered beneath disbelief with portraits photographs pictures clutter. Warmdim. Trinkets everywhere a littleness this obsessed littlish by trinkets. Roomlet. Everything to kill but which cannot(pictures clutter photographs cluttered portraits cluttering)loneliness. . . . Lonely. Alone

& up

rising out of what unimaginable loneliness(rising without moving: being;as only Beauty shall,is always)this . . . head:not a face;not,merely,a look—

elsewhere created,nowhere perhaps invented—and proudly never for any nonworld,for some unworld,made . . . the once how(a now dwindling)tall how erectly(a crookedly now)body marvellously whom this Head magically once upon a time inhabited(broken a now almost nakedness sits,feet hidden by pails and pans,on couchfilth)pulls hastily(with latharms)over its(deadlap now)self quickly that faded this:

What

(& by Voice withered,withering at a Syllable,wilts,as by a lightningbolt, mentor . . . hinging,droops and stuttering . . .)

My Daughter?—

                    (2 eyes leap like shot deer;crumble)

. . . gave mister cummings . . . some presents . . . all the way from paris

Paris?—

hearing Paris . . . an entire a neverishly Self relaxing a swiftly opening an almost-smiles . . . ("est-ce que Monsieur parle français?")

Yes

You are from Paris?

Yes

You are French?

American. But I studied Russian,in Paris,with your(the wince;crumpling) daughter. Who asked me to take you these—may I put them here?

(latharms 2 outspurt)"non:s'il vous plait;ici"

(so then I put,carefully,between latharms,this. Magically and they became,not starved,became slender)and this marvellously something else . . .

"should uh brought uh" grumbles(staring through roomlet's unshut shutness)mentor "raincoat"

"why don't you run along?looks to me as if we'd have a cloudburst—"

"yes uh guess uh will:here;take"(unclutching murder and sudden death) "see yuh latur." . . . Timidly "ohree vawmuh dum" (bowing)scoots now

I go to the unshutness—I sit opposite a Head;silent;we. Light suddenly blossoms,the topsyturvying roomlet bulges &(with now all smell of deep-of-opening-of-swiftly-all relaxing)comes wonderfully wonderingly perfect everywhere immense Rain descends

through It girls & on little porches now of opposite buildingless with flowers are smiling & nonmen laugh are & talk & looking

alive(Rain making alive)ness uttered comes(all marvellous transforming magical all being Rain)newly,arrives hugely(& swooping the)merciful;now(amazingly)with how alive gifts laden:beautifully the sharp the great wish;the,Now(falling from when immeasurable where with a forever cry)!

watches Head me. & Rain. Gradually(among upsoaring instreaming cool)herself begins. Begins. . . . To suffer(I believe)is what Head can only and must do:her poem:by suffering now she must,and only can,express her being,fate. Now isn't,now cringing itself everything(just for a change)reverses,disappear(into themselves stealing)all timidly values,leaving this alone Head,who therefore suffers,therefore who does not yield. & therefore in noone who will confide,has confided. Only who confides because or when that real that unexisting now—singly

against which battles the crippled then of her aliveness and will battle—
falters,during these few moments,under my coming,gifts,memory,
world;under the Rain's actual wish or Now.

She somewhere does-not-have 2 daughters(my Russian teacher,whose
merciful somewhere equals Paris,and my teacher's younger sister,whose
cruel somewhere equals Moscow). A suffering motherless of 2
undaughters broke her foot:a doctor said it was nothing,prescribed
massage;and twice a week a masseur visits her. Once a week a nonman
arranges her room.

I try gently to not quite suggest that here are other sufferers,sufferers in
the world(New York,even,has its breadlines)to punctuate,quite without
puncturing,her isolation . . . Boldly she agrees that Moscow is ugly;she
never thought Moscow beautiful—but have I seen "Petairsboorg"? No.
Boldly I admit that Paris changes;however,I love Paris and so I love
changes. And it rains,I say,in Paris all the time. But Odessa,I say,has
wide streets;you feel space here—"c'est ça qu'il faut"(she:"Mais c'est tout
détruit!détruit!")—and Now I'm slowing my Frenchless French as Head
strains Now to apprehend this unexpected,this unpredictable contact.
. . . Occasionally she groaned nervously.

These walls—except directly behind her,where live(O exmentor!)3
vertically placed greenish ikons—literally are embroidered with
images;mostly(there must be literally hundreds)photographs of
Head's family and coloured drawings,portraits. Especially a dashing
generalissimo—NYET tovarich(Head's father?)with the very head of
Head(or perhaps merely some ancestor?) But here drowse and here
very colourless paysages in very guilty gilt frames. . . . Never possibly
have eyes beheld,never shall behold,such clutterclutteredclutteringness.
Finally Now turns into again now,the Rain becomes merely rain . . .

—Would you(touching)go out when,by waiting,you could come to
your house dry?brokenly me
     who(clutching sudden death
     smile)—I like everything

even I like being which am now lost. (—If courage only could give,com-
municate,courage!or possibly I slightly how slightly gave?)
     wet . . . ask a wet comrade with bright neckerchief("syoodah")
     wetter,passing a wettest unfamiliar homeliest church,approach 1 quite
unwet cocher(2nd)pointing(left)

& arrive at Flower Alley—yes;

flowers!particularly amazing blues & daisies & O roses . . . pelted gently(smiling)with r-a-i-n and nobody is buying nobody is selling but these comrade flowerpeople don't care it doesn't matter because flowers are always flowers are

and

now,distance;Moryeh

a steamer farts:going right,foreshortens, turning goes left and farts again. I(alone,lonely)stand at top of Potemkin stairs,beside barefoot among women talking saying things about the ship laughing(yes)& behind myself now myself quite can feel girls(giggling)and boys(touching). . . . So I come to a new room,a small but neat,uncluttered,a facing on a courtless:I open these closed shutnesses;and at the unshut across from mine but higher is a face,a boy's sometimes,sometimes a girl's.

Doves sexually(creating elsewhere)coo and(somewhere inventing)strut . . . An atom of sky builds pinkish

extraordinary today

learns. Learned. Learning. Not merely by encountering a specimen of the "4th(is it?)class" alias a human being in agony(alias Beauty,or a Head). But also,via that obscenely unhead;via that with-or-without very old strawhatless nonagony(alias my present guide philosopher and friend)who,during our plentiful rambles,has confidentially emitted

"eyel show yuh thih tram,all yuh have tuh doo is take id tuh thih end uv thih line,un there'll be wumun lyin uhroun naked . . . sure eye hoyd Lenin speak. How wus he?well now eye tell yuh:Lenin wus uh good Bryun but thih trouble with him wus he died too soon . . . weye let um call their noo ruhligion kummunism ur socialism ur any gud dam ism they please—it doan fool mee! . . . lissun:thih pass few years has taught thum buggurs uh lessun:they uctually foun out sumpn,they gut id intoo their dumb heads thad they kunt doo without this thing called capitulism . . . eye buleev money rules thih woyl"—and(glittering)"—wen uh man's gut thad bright gole thing in his fist,he's strong

"lissun:meye fathur wus uh doctur. Meye fathur lived in Noo Havun un meye fathur used tuh make hundruds uv dollus uh day. Yessur. Well,wun day meye fathur stopped. Un meye fathur called mee un meye brothur bihfore him un meye fathur said:Boys,eye wan yuh tuh unnurstan sumpn—eye wouldn doo nothn fur yoo boys wile eyem uhlive. Eye

318

made meye own money meyeself,he said,beye thih sweat uv meye brow un eyel spen evury stinkin cen uv it meyeself,says he,un if there's any left wen eyem dead idl be duhveyeded uv course but lemmih warn yoo too boys here un now eyem gunnuh live furevur if eye can. Now,meye fathur says tuh me un meye brothur,eyem gunnuh ask yoo both uv yuh uh question:ansuh me this,he says:should millionaires be kuntrole by thih state? Well,meye brothur un eye we chus didn know wut tuh say tuh meye fathur. So he ansuhs fur us;he says:Yes,they should:thih rich man,he says,ain gut no right tuh do us he gud dam likes with his money irruspective uv thih rest uv thih gud dam hyoomun race;un doan yoo boys furget id!" Pa,eye says,yoor uh sociulist. Eye am thad,says he "wannuh see uh propheyelactic station?"

I "is it interesting?" ask

(he shrugs)"naw. Chus wun uh thih sights. But they're dooin good woyk thad way:they gut uh lot uvum sprinkled all ovur thih place. —Gud knows they needum!"(he added grimly)

cheerfully "I hear prostitution's been practically eliminated"

"uhliminate prostitooshun?" mentor cries "Nevur!weye,yuh kunt uhliminate wut's nachurul;un thad's thih mohs nachurulist gud dam thing there is:yessur. Always has been,always will be. —Weye look here: uh goyl has uh frien,un wun fine day she sees hur frien walkin uhroun with silk stockins,un all thih boys lookin at hur—well,nachurully she's gunnuh get hurself sum silk stockins;ain she?un if she kunt oyn um with hur hans weye she's gunnuh oyn um with hur budy. . . . Uhliminate prostitooshun? Weye yuh might chust us well uhliminate eatin!"

"so there hasn't been much of a change—"

"there's been uh change" he said slowly "fur thih woys. Weye?bihcuz, ware in thih ole days uh wumun could be un onnes whore,now she's guttuh doo id in seecrut. Uh-huh. Thads thih only change there's been;un uh lousy change id is,too.

"Eyel han um wun thing" he said "they gut good docturs here . . . excellun . . . there's uh suh-wel doctur here that give me thih best upuration eye ever had . . . took uh piece uh skin frum here un sewed id in here;un yoo kunt tell thih fuggin diffurunce;can yuh—wunnurful!

("wut yuh thing uh thih ole wumun?)yuh? Well,she's been through uh lot,now eye tell yuh! Vury rich payruns she had but she nevur gave uh dam ubbout no chewls un things—chust inturusted in hur famuly un chilrun,thads all. Thih goyls chus like hur muthur thad way too:no monkiy businiss,always lovin un obediun too hur payruns. —Weye eye know kids,they tell their muthurs un fathurs tuh go tuh(ex-cuse meye Frensh)Huleenuh Muntanuh. Weye only thih othur day uh wumun says tuh meye wife:How dyuh doo id?she says. Yoo say kumeer un she comes. Un meye wife says:bihcuz if she didn eyed wring hur neck,weye eyed break evury bone in hur budy!"

"there must be something good about the present system—"

"uh hole lot" he mused. "In thih foys place,people feel freer. In thih sekun place,bihfore thih revulution,dyuh know sumpn?meye chilrun couldn have gone too uh good school!"

"a remark" I said "you made about all the waiters and chambermaids of all the grand hotels reporting regularly to the secret police about all the foreigners they serve—"

"eye didn say any such" quickly "thing!" (He had. And more.)"Nn-nn—there's uh lottuh talk ubbout thad,but yoo kunt be shooer . . . uv course" easily;shrugging "there May be sumpn uhroun mee un there May be sumpn uhroun yoo,but Eye doan know uhbout id." Pause("look—") nudges;pointing to a statueless pedestal("—Karl Marx himself!")

"where?"

"they had tuh take him down" mentor(chuckling)confides. "Know weye?bihcuz his wiskus wus so ridiklus!"

"really?" comrade K

"woysun Santuh Claus" said,tilting itself,the old strawhat "evur hear thad wun ubbout thih kullection?"

"nn-nn"

"yuh know in Paris they guttuh White Army un they support id?yuh know thad,doan yuh?"

"you mean an antibolshevik army?"

"shooer. Supported beye thih anteye-bulsheviks. —Well,thih story goes thad thih Whites in Paris duhceyeded tuh give uh putty un raise some money. So uh lovuly young goyl's uhsittin un thih steps;un wen un Inglishmun comes up,thih lovuly young goyl she pulls up hur skoyts tuh here un shows thih Inglishmun uh gartur with uh pixur uh Kink George,un thih Inglishmun he gives uh good look un he sulutes un hans hur ten shillins. Then uhlong comes un Eyetaliun un she pulls up hur skoyts clear tuh here un shows thih Eyetalian unuduh gartur with Moosuleenee's pixur,un thih Eyetaliun he gives uh good look un sulutes un hans hur uh hundrud liruh. Well,pretty soon uhlong comes thih genurul uv thih Red Army—up he stams with his spurs un evurything clingkity clank clong clunk right tuh thih vury place ware thih lovuly young goyl's uhsittin—un wen she sees him,weye she" mentor spreadeagled "un thih genurul uh thih Red Army,he gives uh good look un he sulutes un he hans hur wun rouble. . . . So afturwuds thih Inglishmun un thih Eyetaliun they get tuhgethur un kumpare notes,un thih Inglishmun he says:She showed me hur leg up tuh here,wut did she show yoo?un thih Eyetaliun he says:She showed me hur leg up tuh Here. Un thih Inglishmun says:Eye give hur ten shillins,wut did yoo give hur? Un thih Eyetaliun says:Eye give hur uh hundrud liruh he says. Then thih Inglishmun he says:Hm;I wondur wut she showed thih genurul uv thih Red Army?un thih Eyetaliun he says:So doo eye;les ask him! So they both uv um ups tuh thih genurul uv thih Red Army un they say:Genurul,we unnurstan thad thad lovuly young goyl showed you sumpn. Un thih genurul he says:Shooer she did,un eye paid hur uh rouble. —Uh rouble?they says—is thad all? Wudduhyuhmean is thad all he says,id wus too dam much. Weye says thih Inglishmun she showed me hur leg uhbove thih knee un eye give hur ten shillins,un she showed meye Eyetaliun frien here hur leg half way tuh thih thigh un he give hur uh hundrud liruh;but yoo only give hur uh rouble:well,wut did she show yoo?Mee?says thih genurul uv thih Red Army—pff!all she showed me wus Karl Marx's wiskus"

verily 1 tiniest fable may illuminate huge problems . . . When 3 (including comrade "he chus gutuh good ansuh" stunned,who's possibly some worlds less("merci!" ecstatically wringing my congratulating hand)despairful than at déjeuner)comrades can momentarily hear themselves unthink(a 2piece pomposity having thoroughly polluted this soi-disant jardin with semieverything and demilightsomeness)comrade our heroless illuminated K demands of illuminating comrade Noo Inglundur

Suppose America went officially bolshevik . . . do you believe that our funloving countrymen would stand the gaff?

"ob,so,loo,mon,NAW" mentor replies

Did you hear that sombre bandmusic after dark on the esplanade?(I ask comrade not yet quite unstunned) "musique? . . . triste!"

There's certainly something profoundly sad in the Russian soul(K platitudinizes)

"eel nuh foe paw shooshay lam roos paw settuh moo-seek settuh moo-seek say lays or-kest milly-tare shooay paw sample soul dah son ree-an son edoo kassy on" mentor objects "prenny luh moo-seek easy don luh shawdan say baw paw treest gay"

But the music here isn't Russian(I protest)it's—

Yes:what is it?(stunned wonders)

Something calculated to make bourgeois foreigners feel at home,perhaps?

(shrugging)"sais pas. Comprend pas le système ici. Triste!"

"poor quaw voo deet treest toot ay treest wee may say paw luh foet duh lam roos lam roos nay paw treest"

How about Russian literature?(dare inquire)

(stunned almost-smiles,nods fiercely)"oui!voilà!triste comme tout!"

"poo-tet" jauntily mentor admits "ay on too car eel ay un graw playsear duh ron kon tray duz om untelly-shon"

. . . the shawdan,incidentally,possesses 1 most nontruly extraordinary ("baw nes paw")fountainless;all made of metal in the undolce styl nuovo,and obviously(like 2piece)a truc bourgeois,a capitalist heart-gladdener. Of course it doesn't work:but what of that?there it is. . . . "La luxe"(murmurs—re nuovo—distinguished headwaitering dignity & with 1 such miraculously prodigious wink as,for 1 magical now marvellously moment,sent comrade peesahtel hoodozhnik's heart into New Hampshire)

—O yes,in Italy there are crises. But the Italian people would never stand for bolshevism. Never. (Twilight:young begins;girls and boys, moving "excusez-moi,mon ami. Il faut que je rétourne à notre hotel;j'ai une réponse très important à faire . . . bonne nuit. A demain!" & comrade myself

alone

wanders this twi(young)light

what

what edgelessness

what does a rookah meet in a darkness of myself's of my jacket's of my pocket?something crumpled. This little piece of boomahgah:on which is something written(and here's a circle of youngs here's a fireauto with pompiers with actually Parishelmets who are busily all screwing something now into the ground and they all cry Stand Away There and here's look a gush a gushing of silvery and ooz and ahz it's beautiful isn't it O and look and now there's another cry a cry Return and see the gush dwindles stops and look they all dash at the fireauto now all the Parishelmets all now firelessly all together roll away forever?disappearing)written by someone by whom by me . . .

(a sketch for a telegram—sent?today,sent;this
:mourning
Don't

     Operate e for someone's name t for two and two for tea a for a name r for reality I suppose e for someone's other name p for probably

preposterous perhaps perfection possibly pain O for O civilization Unless

that next god damned word?

                  Reason)

et quantumst hominum Venustiorum.

Fri. June 5

almost unfairly reeking with almost serenity(cause:the successful—not
that all of them are clean,most of them aren't;but that most of them
almost dried during the night—scrubbing of sundry shirts socks
kerchiefs and almost whatever your well behaved foreigner sends to his
hotel's comrade laundry)this little pig(almost sans Pay To The Order
Ofs)languidly floresces amid the arboreal shawdan

into which now is by hulloing mentor coasted 1 avec inferiority
complex neatly apparelled and otherwise americanitz customer who,left
to ourselves,begins patting right feverishly a cat and grumbling and

"you have to wait for everything" complains "and when it comes it's
wrong!"

"true" I unguardedly agree.

Whereupon it seems that he went through the whole revolution. That
originally the revolution was made by students. That he the grumbler
thought he could never forget it the revolution. That now,however,the
whole revolution is "all like a dream"

"I know. The socalled world war became a dream for me"

"why not?everything's a dream" he said simply.

Forever will remember his all too recent experience of returning to
Russia from America as a tourist. Thought he'd save himself a lot of
trouble by so doing. Good sweet darling kind INTOURIST had said
he'd get off easier with the customs that way. Found himself stuck with
a "simply disgusting bunch" of quotes-Americans—almost all of them
Russian Jews. 1(life of the party)Jewess particularly got grumbling's
goat;never saw anyone quite so "shamelessly vulgar":wouldn't have
believed that any such a person could have existed. My god. Is only
somewhat now and partially beginning to recover his mutilated senses

"that must have been lousy" K sympathizes

arriving at the customs,my illstarred vis-à-vis encountered trouble to
the n plus 1th. And all . . . all . . . because of those "accursed" quotes-
Americans! Why,each of those damned tourists had brought(can you
believe it?)ten,no less,pieces of luggage—not for each's self,O no:for
each's quotes-Russian relatives. Naturally,the customs became "peeved".
Whereupon those horrible Jews began all squabbling and dickering and
raising cain generally. Nothing doing. Thereupon those hideous "kikes"

began weeping and wailing and gnashing their false teeth ... Finally,the customs just confiscated whatever they "jolly well" didn't approve of and let the whole dam thing go at that. But can you imagine? Can you conceive of such a mess?

K "it must have been simply" sympathizes

as for my vis-à-vis himself,he'd only brought in a great many pairs of silk stockings. And(discretion being the better)he told a customs tovarich all about silk stockings. And tovarich was much pleased. And tovarich said:Never mind,comrade,I won't take all of them,I'll just take all but two of them,and here's a receipt for all but two and if all but two aren't claimed after a certain number of months they'll be officially auctioned off by the socialist soviet government—or(if you prefer)you may send those silk stockings to someone outside Russia. Not inside Russia,comrade:outside. O my god. O . . . those accursed quotes-Americans-close-quotes with their ten separate items of luggage apiece! —My god!

"simply lousy" sympathizes

as for the revolution:well now,look at the revolutionary leaders. Look at them. I ask you:what did they have in common? What? Prison. Yessir:all of them spent years in jails. And naturally all of them were,well;hardened. —Not that all of them didn't have hearts;all of them did:but the jails,well;hardened those hearts of theirs. That's how it is: prisons harden people;and the revolutionary leaders were no exception. No,indeed . . . why,look at comrade Lenin:never had a luxury in his life!

(suddenly I remember 1 doubtless faithful reproduction of Lenin's own unroom;we bumped into it,Assyrian and I,at the Lenin Institute—or rather we were bumped into by a NO SMOKING sign,whereupon L's un- followed . . . very,I remember,discomfortable . . . très early Christian,remember feeling

& now for the

shift?yes)

now listen,listen while I tell you a story—

(K's listening)

—I was at the Swiss border. I was standing just outside the douane. My friend had gone into the douane to register the Citroën. Suddenly something happens. Up from behind comes a huge car. A vast American gets out:stretches him-self—yawns . . . and cries(clapping a little French gendarme on the back)"Hel-Lo Buddy!" The gendarme looks annoyed but he doesn't say anything. Meanwhile the American stares. The American stares at the French gendarme pityingly;then,very earnestly(and in a flat injured almost pleading tone)inquires—"why the hell don't you learn English?"

"we" immediately K agrees "Americans are egoists"

And How. Why,you simply can't imagine the difference between . . . well,a Russian student for instance and an American collegeboy. O no. It just can't be conceived. Absolutely impossible. Why,tell me:what does the American collegeboy know?huh? Baseball!

"thanks"(this comrade murmurs)"to some unimaginable,some inconceivable,intourist stupidity,I had the very great luck to travel Hard from Kiev without a berth"(vis-à-vis registers "!!"). "I say luck,because one of my fellowtravellers came forward and gave me his berth"("??")"sheets and all,in a way which actually taught me something about Russians. I even learned that what a distinguished young woman had assured me in Moscow about Russians is true:they're artists." ("!?!") . . . "They're artists because giving is their nature,their self,what they wish to do and what they can be. Take this fellow;the Russian who gave me his bed—he wasn't being magnanimous or selfsacrificing;not at all . . . it was as if he,quite simply,felt:I have something,a bed,therefore I give it. If he'd had three beds or five beds he'd have given three beds or five beds but since he had one bed he gave only one bed. —The American attitude under such painful" K marvels "circumstances would certainly have been:This is MY bed,You get the hell OUT"

"dirty" quoted quickly vis-à-vis "foreigners"

"meaning which?" as Joe Gould says. "Meaning that everybody else and the artist,meaning that the keeping psychology and the giving,are incommensurable"

pom("comparisons")pous("are")ly("odious")

"not merely odious,by god. Futile"

he muses(shift?)"Odessa was a great port . . . but"(yes)"when they lost Bessarabia,the emphasis changed." Pause. "These waiters" he solemnly frowned "have been waiters before and always will be waiters,you can't change 'em . . . That's what's true about the common people" sic "you can't change 'em" he said solemnly "—take my father. There,god knows,was a perfectly unchangeable person. Me?(my father would

shrug)Why should I live in the future?the present is all I have!" . . .
Pause. "Whereas" shift?yes "my nephew—who's only so high—knows
his" won-der-ing-ly "Karl Marx like the bible:why he can put up an
argument against anybody!"

K ventures hereupon that some of the Karl Marxian theorists remind
me only a luscious trifle of certain most saintly gents who'd argue until
the comrade cows came home such burning questions as how many
angels can comfortably camp on a needle's point. . . . And now we
discuss the English;who have such nice manners(although grumbling
cannot say for sure,not having lived among them)who are crazy over
Russian soap and raise hell anent 1 shipload of "good Russian(can you
imagine?)butter" until

"She is living for the future" sighing

"when She'll have the world by the balls" cheerfully

"well,She"(eyes)"has that"(aglitter smallening)"already." Pause. Softly
"I wonder how the Russians who live in hotels like ours can afford it"

"so do I" the(feeling his almost dry shirt)K tovarich mildly wonders

". . . nice girls here." Elsewherelooking my vis-à-vis

"young" ditto

"the" ditto "younger generation . . ." Caesura and. "D'y' know
what"(here)"they've been"(it comes)"brought up to believe?"

"what"

"that people"(leaning across tableless)"like you and me are"(sub-
whispers)"monsters."

"Noo!" I,seated in a shawdan of Hotel London,marvel

"sure!—Do you realize something? Listen:Russia's entire younger
generation hasn't the faintest,not the smallest,conception of what the rest
of the world is like." (He grimmestly nods)"talk about education!"

K is listening

"the moment a baby pops" my shifter less than whispers "out of its
mother's womb,what do you think happens?"

"what"

"the state begins pumping propaganda into that baby like mad and
the pumping never for one instant ceases,not for one single instant—
see?understand?"

"pahnyeemeyeyoo"

"ever read the headlines of a Moscow newspaper?"

"you bet"

"well . . . there you are." Relaxing. ". . . That's the sort of nonsense all those boys and girls are fed right from the cradle. —Imagine!"

"which probably" K "accounts for the fact that,after my first most drunken amazement at suddenly encountering a flock of actually young and goodlooking Russian girls,I somehow couldn't help feeling a most unbelievable sameness—"

"SAMEness!—that's it" himself quicknods. "They're all of 'em dumb little chippies,no mental development,dead from the neck up,believe everything they hear,just" contemptuously And How "factoryfodder"

(now

while 2 comrades stroll from shawdan through salle à manger toward foyer,realise I have been entertaining a chipmunk. Whom— seated—we took to be at least a(shall we say)lion?

"eye doan see any"—nor ever heard K sadder than mentor's voiceless. Woefully who's on our wayless to a very particular tramstop & there,under his august tutelage,I'm due to catch a particular tram which will rattle myveryself all the particular way to a very target particular goal particularvery bullseye or . . . why not allow such eloquent nomenclature to speak for itself?"Arcadia")but mentor's feet hurt him dreadfully and in particular 1 of them,the right,adorned by a comrade bunion of no uncertain size,and he wishes to god or something he had some shoestrings for these his only his extraordinarily infra(cross between sneaker and sabot)shoes,and maybe . . . if we're both very very particularly good and if we all hold our comrade-breaths and don't see speak hear think no evil . . . there will be peutêtre a shoestring in Odessa today!—so 2(he woefully groaning)comrades make a slight détour and find ourselves now hopelessly investigating fabulous windows of particular shops(of only,you understand,the very largest the snootiest flossiest the ritziest supershops: for they,they alone,might . . . sh . . . be not—hush—unlikely to(don't breathe!)boast that most impossible really you simply can't have any idea of how(in this choochoo union of kookoo socialist poopoo soviet googoo republics)perfectly unimaginable luxury,A Shoestring.

"Nut wun"

so cela being cela,on we—he limping,steadfasting refusing K's offer of 1 of my own—dawdle . . . & presently the martyr is hailed by a roundshouldered young comrade and Russianing occurs and the rsy says "very glad to",whereupon exit martyr and now am standing,alone,in a huge waitingline waiting for comrade-tram number what? "You!"(rsy's waving at me:so's a nonman with him;K,beckoned again fiercely,breaks from line and makes for wavers;now 3 com(pushfightsquirm)rades wickedly brutally madly into this presumably Arcadian

. . . "my wife" rsy. Tramshimmyjerkhunches;reeling,I bow

"you're going to the beach,too?"

"bee-utsh,yis"

"nice day,isn't it."

"Nay-us,yis"

"how far from here to the beach?"

"no-uh far." —Whereupon it seems that he works 8 days;and then 2 days "no-uh". We meanwhile skirt peagreen imposingly flimsy gates . . . within are parklesses;bits of greenswardless sprinkled with unhumans in all stages of semidecompostion . . . "wear-kears" enjoying themselves,happy laborers taking their vacations. Not as in the very bad not so old days. Then no for poor man vacation,none. Only for rich enjoyment,then. Now all,everyone now,labourers,now even youme

"is that it?"(we ask,pointing to the finally appearing Ocean)

nonono. That's just a beach,we're going to better. To much very better,Arcadia,fine!a wondrous place. Arcadia. Reminds me somehow of comrade Julia Sanderson twittering "eightyintheshade-they say-Just FAN-cy" my sundayschool teacher,having a lech on someone I had a lech on harkthe pipesof Panare calling,he took us both to a Short-life and a G-A-Y;one. Here we are

ecco:

this is

it.

Tiny plage. All very fenced in. (Men,trunks. Nonmen;trunks and brassières. Only the children sport nothing). Atmosphere tout-à-fait bourgeois. Formal to a degree,familystuff. Et l'on paie—

"yoo go-uh inn?swhim?yoo-uh can!"

"are you going in?" I ask them,ask him and ask his thickishly shy nonman

"oooooooooooooo—noh!"(screwingup an eye)"deartea"(they say)good-bye and they stroll away toward flimsy gates of a softdrink parkless with tired tovarichy lawns adorning this nearby singularly uninviting nonsummit cragless or disprecipice

. . . well. So what? Hot as

but beach NG;what there is of

—why,then,shouldn't our heroless wander a bit?not rightward,for mucho worldwarwire blocks the way,but leftward via this proletarian much too trod dustful unpath? . . . On-and-on(along low semicliffs)for possibly miles comrade optico-erotico journeys;and journeys:and journeys. Noting

(a)soldiers-with-fixed-bayonets,apparently guarding starknaked phi-betas;1 of whom's as-you-like-it fully warrants telegram to exVirgil come-at-once(and he,that melancholy Dane,wasting his timeless on the nonbanks of the Moscow unriver!fie). A family,of Russians but a family,a bourgeois picnicing honesttogod family,who immediately do precede my ever erring feetfalls along the cliffs,pause oohahingly before that manly vista—the comrade pater proudly points;the comrade mater sighs with pleasure,all the comrade infantes collectively nod . . . traffic resumes

(b)unguarded-by-bayonets ancient impersons,of various species,laving their strictly not to be described hideousness. With exception(possible)of a single jejune couple—completely bathingsuited—no faintest trace of sexual or otherwise or in fact any whatever emotion

(c)now and then—mercilessly silhouetted against the wave—gangling nude hes;absorbed by their failure to catch imaginary fish with several thousand substitutes for A Shoestring

(d)a nook alias cranny. 2 alias flowers-in-the-crannied lassies. 1,young,in only her trunks:with pouting bubbies,of which she's actually conscious . . . presently ties something red around her head and coquettishly advances,giggling,toward what we should prefer to call 1 mere spectator,alias comrade optico. Who now perceives hard by the twain(and them completely ignoring)a mouldy comrade-father plus innocent kiddies. . . . This couple of boys of about 16 go scampering down from my cliff to the shore of cranny;squirm(from shirts and pants)naked,plunge,and swim far out away from cranny's flowers. Halt,on my cliff,a pair of youths:stare;giggle,vanish. Beside me now stand a much dressed brun swain and his much dressed blonde heart . . . looking,amused mildly,mildly admirative . . . Meanwhile advancing actually conscious coyly essays now wavelets—stooping,splashes poutings dunks—retiring to safe sand,sprawls(pinks up)with a little black rag over her eyes "got a match?" K asks the in state at Hotel London's desk seated mentor

"—Streichholz!yah!"—& comes Shine & fumbling &

"danke"

"he wansuh cigurette" mentor suggests,rising "givimwun"

I do

"kumon les eat." . . . And dignity greets 2 comrades . . . "Well"(genial)"howdyuh like id?hot stuff,nes-suh paw?"

"not" I "so" zephyr that "hot" steamingly now soup

"HUH?" amazed

"rather disappointing,to tell the truth."

And he stares And. —The swirling into wisdomknot his pallid foreheadless;ponderously grad(ually nodding:leering "tuh)Morruh"

"know what I'd like?a good swim at a good beach"

—"tuhMORruh!" mentor grimlyandhow promises

with back to luxury,facing the paralysed(dangling our)harbour(heels)perch upon esplanade's most ample parapet,almost where begin mightily what stairs;dangling in a quivering our eyes in a parkless in far below the (diminished a multitude a foreshortened)myriad of children of all who are these who playing and this are others who playing another playing those throwing some running but while—and up wanders stunned,shakes my hand,jumppivoting seats be(himdwarfself)side—hundreds:of;and now of hundreds children(distance—mov,ing look)& here they're;rock:ing in painted gaily huge toys

futures tomorrows destinies

(fore)futures(shortened)tomorrows(dim)destinies

(inished

multi

myri)

    & & &

        Down. dowN. mightily stairs stair by stair men(a babycarriage reel-stum(bump)bling—

foot:feet. foot

die:dead. death

        . . . and seconds and minutes hours and days weeks years and time the merciful time who does not live who cannot die time

change & up from paralysed floats from parkless & dreams a rocking
& throwing running mulmyritude change myrmultiad NowmultitudemyriadNow

playing).

. . . Whereupon it seems that the fundamental idea of fascism equals
no "lutte de classes":cooperation of "ouvrier" and "capitaliste";"Mussolini
certainement un grand homme politique",yes was formerly a socialist and

"nous" the Italians "avions besoin d'un homme fort parce qu'" whisper
"il y avaient des désordres"

How is fascism sustained?(K asks)

dwarfish "comme"(points to myriadplaymultitude)"ça":by organizing
the children. By taking them when they're young and moulding their
youngness

"je comprend"

They say that down there(stunned whispers)there was a great
park;once upon a time

(pause)

I was at a beach today

So was I

Arcadia?

Arcadia. (Danglesit lazily near us whistling trio of sabotsneakers . . .
just and beyond whom,this boyfather derricks his over chasm baby that
girlmother mildly protests the atom squeaks boygrinning thisfather it
now restores to a most ample parapet)"rien,eh?"

Nothing

"oui" he shrugs "ils sont habitués"

& in far distance tiny individuals collecting make circle now which
entirely mimics the centre,each little child taking pose of,little heads
following,teacher:now the finally all now the entire circle together the
children littlenesses all are . . . see? . . . Fly-ing

at whom look mothers look nonmen expressionless look at Fly(play)-
ingThrow & running. Look. At something(at not-themSelves)which
all they have lost?cannot be?

painted down-

up gaily up-

down

huge

downupdown
         Toys

alone am,several aeons later,entering luxury—ecco:dwarfish(but how changed!a certainement corpse)supported by

"lissum yoo speak bettur Frensh thun mee,yoo" mentor

"explain tuh this felluh we guttuh bad ansuh from thih am-Bassy tuhday un thih kunsul he woan be ruspunsuble he's forwudid thih fax tuh Moscow un if they sen money okay un if they doan weye he says it ain his uhfair see?"

K translates

stunned's chopped face goes dark—I understand:my consul is naturally afraid,since he hasn't documentary proof:but why hasn't he?because at Constantinople the official Soviet representative who gave me a Russian visa said that it was unnecessary to consult my consul—I understand: arriving here I went directly to the Italian consulate where I was asked for my passport and was told that it was not "en règle",now it is being "réglé";I understand . . . (so a voiceless continues while a heart discontinues, manyness of words framing nothingness of hope,talk gilding despair)

K is very sorry for dwarflike—the(K understands)hardest thing,it's to wait

gazing heavenward;stiffening "mais . . ." & splutters hangedbird gestures

I ascending(not mighty,stairless)of luxury stairs 'm salaamed by crumblefumble saluted by Shine mumbling who Germanly inquires concerning the health of my very distinguished shoes?of my godsent miraculous shoes?of those fabulous tokens of mythical power my wonderful shoes?

we throw him a zahvtrah

gulps Shine(wibblewobbling)seallike our(down)zahvtrah;flopflipyearns toward us for more for(anyeverythingthingless)sillywhiskering "sprechen Sie Deutsch?"

A little

I shine them I bring them I shine shoes I bring shoes to you bring to your room bring them your shoes back your shoes home to your room to you

All(weary & curious)right

ecstatically hunchhoppingnudgegallumping me pursues—I learn German I at Antwerp I from where everyone speak anyone German not good German nono not good

"besser als ich"(we guess)

"DA!YAHYAH!"—much better(Shine twitterchuckles lunging me after. To "Zimmer". Cringesquirms through door,standing;rapt:begs)for both pair,of my wonderfuls

How(sternly)long?

"zehn Minuten!"

"NYET zahftrah?"

—O god O my O my god not not tomorrow nono now right now directly immediate sooner than instantly without a minute delay within a few seconds before you can bat one eyelash absolutely certainly no doubt about

(hand him both. Standing in socklesses)"nicht vergessen?"

I know(proudly,taking)a "Herr" when I see one;understand?

5

10

15

    knockknock enterenter ShineShine withwith bothboth gleam-gleaminging . . . takes thanks takethanking a 1 rouble . . . salutesalaams . . . salsal uteaams . . . suluums . . . & as K moves toward a cigarette Shine automatically asks for a cigarette(then,shrugging;laughing gaily at his own request)cries—thankyouplease! . . . we give . . . Shine takes laamlutes salsal his Shine's eyes droop see 4 toes 4 naked from 2 socklesses protruding my-not-his K's-not-Shine's 4—give old socks!(Shine begwhines)I "nyet" I no have I "nicht" I . . . so we promise & he fumblebows &

"pagohdah hahrosheyeah" K genteelly observes

"da!pagohdah hahrosheyeah—kooshaht nyet!"

& vanishes.

Yes

    fine weather fine and nothing nothing to eat fine and eat weather and to nothing fine to weather and nothing eat nothing. Dadada! Ahgoo

. . . at dinner,strolling through salle à manger toward shawdan,unhappen most gruesome couple,a dumpy toobespectacled pugnosed unhe,an unhe

thinbeaked pincenezed weaklychinned with heavy head upon light body
with undeveloped trunk and limbs and both unhes unexisting not-dying-
via-the-brain(focussed incompletely above the neckless)arbitrarily now
& unspontaneously regarding me anyone with a tensely a not intense
a superficial or missing-nothing lookless did you ever keep caterpillars
did you ever have them make cocoons did you ever wait did you ever
hear a rustling a dim thudding a desperate thin knocking it was a moth
trying to escape from the cocoon but something is wrong it can't it will
die in there you must help it you really can't help helping it you can't
stand the tinying noise you slit the cocoon Out Flops A Monstrous
Unthing which Dies dies because it did Not escape Itself because it was
Helped because it canNot Grow you let it out but It Cannot Grow it
had better have died inside the cocoon at least that would have been a
natural death a doom caused by itself's weakness by itself's inabilty to
burst forth and to live!living to grow!growing to be!

politely(rather to shawdan's fountainless)"good morning"(than to K)grumbling smiles

"we wus chus" gaily "talkin ubbout" quoth "yoo" mentor;thereupon who now proceeds to talk And How about himself:

meet the good old days. Meet a city called Odessa,recently invaded by Germans. Meet comrade mentor,proud proprietor of "uh suh-well lidl" Odessa hotel. Meet—last but not least—an unidentified man. Man walks into hotel and says in broken Russian to proprietor,alias mentor, Can I Pay My Bill?"maykin uh sign". Mentor,alias proprietor,alias "thih seecrit soyvis",alias a sworn performer of all patriotic duties,understood. And mentor took the visitor upstairs. They went into a room and they locked the door and mentor tore up sheets,knotted the sheets together,let the visitor carefully down to a taxi in which "too uh meye men" were waiting. But "clevur us eye wus eye madeuh mistake"—the secret service allowed himself to be hypnotized by 2 American newspapers which Mr. visitor left behind. Well,as hypnotized secret service is peacefully sitting at the desk of mentor's hotel,busily reading 1 of those fatal American newspapers,who should come awandering in but the Germans and the Germans they say Come Along. Why?says mentor("un huly Cheest wus eye scaret!")—We'd Never Have Thought You Were A Spy,Come Along is their answer;whereupon terrified secret service came along. At German headquarters he submitted to crossquestioning during 4 hours,which somewhat fatigued him. They then shut him up tight in an office;which greatly encouraged him,because at least it wasn't jail("so eye says tuh meyeself maybe they ain gunnuh shoot mih"). And it so had happed that "chust us they wus draggin mih outuh thih ho-tel,meye wife seen mih;un she says tuh mih,Wut's Thih Mattur?un eye says,Eyem Urrestid"—moreover the soldiers who did the dragging were hard beset by "meye lidl boy" who kept on following the soldiers;who kept on telling "meye lidl boy" to go away,but he wouldn't:and they threatened him—and he said You Leave Pop Alone. Well . . . even as "meye lidl boy"'s parent,alias mentor,alias pop,was wondering busily whether he mightn't be shot after all,out go the Germans from Odessa and in the Poles come strolling. Whereupon(meet "thih muthur")his gentle housely wifelet got by hook or by crook to the Polish general's headquarters "in this vury ho-tel"(alias the Hotel London,whose arboreal shawdan 3 And How florescently breakfasting comrades adorn). "Un shee broke through thih solejus;un fell un hur knees bihfore thih genurul,un spoke pewer Polish un broke his heart." The wifelet,or a neighbour of hers,had decided mentor was a Polish citizen;the distinguished son of an originally genuine Pole who subsequently changed his name. And it worked with the Polish general. And they let out mentor("un wus eye glat!"). But then,O then,the fun began—there were exit visas for himself and his wife and his son;but there was no exit visa for his baby daughter,just because she'd been born in Odessa:so of course nobody could leave. And nobody did. And everybody prospered. And eventually the government paid mentor a simply colossal sum,something like 300 roubles,for every day he'd been in jeopardy "absulootly"!

(pause. Grumbling "sounds like a detective story" murmurs)

so after that mentor—now a rich man—is peacefully sitting at the desk of his greatly improved hotel,sucking a very big cigar and dreaming of America;when up comes a little bellhop looking "scaret tuh death" and the bellhop whispers to the manager that a Polish officer has secretly occupied the room of a Greek who skipped without saying dahsveedahnyah or leaving any forwarding address. This,it seems,is really bad news;for the very same Polish general who'd erstwhile spared our mentor's life not unrecently issued an ultimatum,in which he expressly forbade his officers great and small to stop at mentor's hotel without official permission. Furthermore the officer in question was drunk,moreover he was with a woman,incidentally he couldn't be budged. . . . Well,3 days passed. Then down the stairs comes Mr. officer tottering;and calls for mentor,and so mentor appears;whereupon Mr. officer begins to bawl hell out of mentor,and mentor protests;whereupon Mr. officer hauls right off and draws his sword and hits mentor in the eye with it. (Mentor,it seems,"wus reachin fur meye gun;but thih blood spoytid.") —So across the street "with meye eye hangin out" runs mentor to a little pharmacy,in which was a kindly doctor who "pushed id back in." So then Mr. highly insulted officer complained bitterly to his general,whereupon mentor was promptly arrested. But everything(you'll be glad to hear)came out "okay";for Mr. insulted officer got 2 rebuffs:1st,the general refused to see Mr. officer at a grand banquet when Mr. officer sent in his card:2nd,Mr. officer was stripped of his uniform in the presence of mentor("eye run out")and "meye lidl boy";who(unbeknownst to anyone)was "undur thih table,dangim!" Well,that very night—just as Mr. rebuffed officer was leaving mentor's hotel—"meye lidl boy"(who was watching and waiting)up and just at the right moment "hee dumped sum—ex-cuse mee—shid" from away up above on the luckless guest's departing head. Whereupon Mr. officer "hee swore like hell hee'd cut out . . . no,nut mih eye . . . mih heart!"

(pause. "That reminds me" murmurs grumbling

"wut"

"the way that story ends"

"wut does id rumine yoo uv?"

"a Jewish story. Maybe you know the story?"

squinting warily under pallid foreheadless "m-m-m:y-e-Z?" mentor muses)

"buzzjoo mushyoo" are the mystic words which Virgil's comrade successor hurls at a dwarflike foyer-haunting stunned ghostless. And forth into sunsunsun voyage now K mentor and grumbling. After perhaps 1 quarter of an hour who all safely reach the(I learn)ex-best bank in Odessa(which looks even more,if possible,barndancey than even the customsshack at N:being all adrip with banners agog with slogans askew with mottoes). Happens here a huge todo re grumbling's letter of credit—3 comrades float from guichet to guichet ad infinitum,if not worse;finally I locate a bench:Munchausen joins me

"no wut all those flags say?"

I certainly don't

"he" nodding toward grumbling,who is just now raising particular hell with a very pahzhahloostah comrade-gent in droopy mustachios "can't read id eethur"(chuckle)"ids Ukraniun"

I ask for a translation from the Ukrainian

"wee guttuh doo thih five year plan in too years" mentor renders

—"outrage!that's what it is:a damned outrage!" grumbling fumes,gesturing frenziedly

"wutdid that kumrad with thih wiskus tell yuh?"

"tell me?he told me he knew nothing about American letters of credit and so it would be necessary for him to write for instructions to Moscow!can you imagine?the idiot's actually going to write to the soviet government in Moscow and ask them whether or not this thing"(waving loc)"is worthless!—my god!and he told me he hopes to have an answer . . . when do you suppose? . . . in Six or Seven Days!"

"well,it used to be woys—"

"WORSE!?" the loc's possessor explodes "my god!why,years ago I came to this very bank;and was served in five minutes!"

"eye mean" placidly "since thih revulution."

"O. Hm—perhaps . . . but" objects this leonine chipmunk "it's the assininity which gets my goat!the stupidity!—why do all government officials have to be morons?"(shifting)he pleaded. "You know,a fresh young fellow in the American consulate actually had the nerve to ask me why I was going to Russia!can you imagine?well,I told him a thing or two. D'y'know what I said to him?—I said:listen:I didn't come here to give you a political argument,if I'm good enough to play for your president I'm good enough to go where I please . . . that's what I told him! Just Like That!"

(nor would I ever,ever in all this un- or world,have guessed that comrade shifting grumbling chipmunk lion was a musician).

Next stop:comrade deepbrown hearty shirtsleeves. And comrade mentor,in the usual manner,obtains fish jam and butter,crackers,and a bottle each of weak and of strong . . . the magnitude of my purchases amazes grumbling;who(after parlaying to soul's content with dumb bedizened)feels quite certain that comrade K should buy me a $1.50 shirt and "why do you take so much for your voyage?" keeps asking: then "why don't you buy at the Hotel London Torgsin?" & K shrugs & K points helplessly at mentor as if to say,my life is in his hands.

Which it more or less is

which isn't always not exactly unpleasant(e.g. when into the nonprivacy of this kohmnahtah hurries(with pudgy claws;on toadstool feet;a twisting lip;defunct eyes—all quite as we'd first glimpsed them;quite as before peesahtel hoodozhnik went anti-INTOURIST,partially thereby from death diverting him who is now to death rededicated—now who is deresurrected)comrade Noo Inglundur

. . . "bad noos!")

"shtoh?"

it seems the manager just informed mentor that he,the manager,won't have stunned in this hotel any longer without Geld. And it's up to

mentor to pass this pretty greeting along to stunned. He,mentor,hates
to do it,of course. But he's after all just a hotel employee. Therefore it's
his duty. But what will "thad eyetaliun doo"? . . . quivering,comrade
pallid wad of low desperate sticky vitality plucks(twittering)from
beneath a faded jacket 3 bottles:1 empty:1 full of weak:1 full of strong
. . . greedily,shimmying,uncorks fulls,pours strong and weak into
empty,plugs result with shakily improvised paper cork,hands comrade
me the strong bottle(in which remain 2 noble drinks apiece)and whispers
gruesomely

    "wee needid!"

we less or more do,I feel.

Waited. In corridor. Wondering

    "—kumon in!"

enter "thad eyetaliun"'s kohmnahtah:slightly than "mine" less
unspaceful,not nakeder. A pénible scene. Mentor(very drunk,mostly
with vicarious pain)slapping stunned on various backs arms and should
ers,blubbering,gulping "voo zate moan amee";himself strumming with
pudgy fists,snivelling,choking "shaw fay too poor voo";stunned silently
is sitting on a tiny tableless:he looks,I feel,only like someone who wanted
very much to be born and couldn't somehow ever be born

sunsunsun

    & unshut-shutness framing some(face?)to whom waves Noo
Inglundur

    open-shut. Noo leads stunned(dreaming?)and K into 1 crammed cubic
untidyness—he-and-we spurn queue of densely waitwaitwaitings

    a deadish office:2 little labourers,1 in blue. Immediately Noo spouts . . .
They listen . . . (stare carefully;at Noo,at me,at stunned;at 2 little in blue
labourers;at At)—stooping now,reeling,Noo whispers . . . Stare,listen.

    "Kumon." Too-straightening;

    K Noo dream(stunned)ing march,spurn queue of densely(of Wait-)&
out:

        Sun

    "they prumise mee they'll write thih manidgur tuh wait three days
un-til he"(wagging toward stunned)"gets his ansuh frum Moscow"

    "—god damn it,comrade,I beg to congratulate you!" K cries;clapping the mentor on the Noo's back with such force that they nearly both nosedived.

"Un they kun doo id,too"(re-Noo-cov-men-er-tor-ing chuckles)"thad's thih yoonyun,see?they guttuh thorrity roun here!well,mushyoo—kom on saw vaw?"

shrug:& dreaming "mercimonsieur" and does not smile

"maymush yoo!eelnuh foepaw ayter kum saw;too vaw byan,kum prenny?"

"vous" gently "pensez?"

"Maw shuh Say!!" Noomentor And How proudly proclaims,angrily wiping a tear "—kuh pon say voo dun shongemon duh sane?"

which I feel is 1 god damned good idea

8's our tram.

Hour of it.

. . . Dismal flats(from time)filthy(to)shacks(time stunned)loom (winces)

(exhaustedly Noo dozes) . . .

—now a hyperDilsuperApiultraDatedness=parkless?   Nowmen tor-rou-ses(now)"day"(yaw)"son"(ning)"day"(&,stunned;up:starting)we 3 un-

climb;

follow(in Sun)worn un(Sun)path winding through(Sun)low ground . . . to right are high hills . . . to left

shtoh?

      a barbedwire fence

?O

Dante,O comrade poet;aid me now,

beyond that wire(moveunmoving)seem not beings but items,unearthly integers,shapeless corruptions,baleful unobjects;not creatures not things but grotesquely how hideous entities(or such foul monstrosities as might arrive only with the disintegration of a universe;only behind life's final sunset,awfully vomited out of depthless nightmare . . .)

&,as we approached,awfully(there dreadfully & fearfully here)appear omens,signs,tokens,disastrous hints;resemblances and presently the very(but everywhere immeasurably deformed)lineaments of mankind: now I am beholding,faintly and sick at heart,some unimaginable parody of human flesh-and-blood;am viewing a demented most preposterous distortion—now itself cruelly this catastrophe reveals:now my eyes celebrate the transposing of man and of woman(and of their natures flesh spirit or proportions)into such fathomless vocabularies of unrecognition as must dwell beyond any dream or every darkness.

Beyond the wire passes,only to repass,a gruesome masquerade: unmoves-and-moves a doomed assemblage of folk most horribly who are themselves painting & have painted with a blackbluish slime;smearing—some only their noses and legs—others their genitals and upper arms—still others their shoulders and their rumps—while the rest go embossed with mud from feet to head

"baw poor luh sontay" cheerfully declaims,nodding approvingly at the slime-folk,my mentor. "Thih gate's up here" indicating a distance in which the wire seems to end;and("gimmih sumpn fur him")whispers,referring to stunneddreaming("thih poor cuss ain gut no money") . . . I offer 5 roubles;mentor will take only 3(himself has paid out 1.50 tramfare). —Proceeding,3 comrades eventually reach the endless wire's end:also a miserable hovel,from which leers a witchlike redkerchiefed nonman who mutters ShutShutShut

"what is shut?" K timidly inquires ·

"thih bathhouse uv thih mudbaths. Doo yoo know sumpn?"

"nyet"

"this mud" solemnly(not to say pompously)our guide intones "is thih vury bes mud there is. Absulootly! Heals anythin that ails yoo,frum roomuhtism tuh syphulis:uh posutively shooer kewer fur kunsumtion lumbago headcoles puralusis livurtrouble indeyegestion flatfeet un evurythin. No kiddin. Eye mean id. —Weye in thih ole days people come frum all ovur thih woyl chus tuh get uh crack ut this mud(idsimplywunnerful). . . . Well,yoo ain gut no ubjection tuh undressin un thih beach?"

"not a bit"

we're rounding the wire's

                    —Christ!(?

???

        :yes,yes)comrade Kem-min-kz,

a drooling female vast naked unfirm continent,a flabbily mountaining irregularly progression of every-which-way swooning balloons;a 250 pound bellyup—almost I stepped on it—nonman:sprawled utterly

over(and ⅔ ensconced in the)sand;with . . . neatly,even coyly,between
colossal unlegs laid . . . possibly 1 square inch of rag

And How cautiously turning now the uncorner of that hugely slopped
bosom,next K avoids this(placidly slumbering bellydown)poodful Juno:
whose very listless rumplet rises somewhat higher than my quaking
knees

and close beside which basks on elbows a(through slime dimly
peering)merely fat mancomrade,wearing complete mudeveningclothes
. . . "mushyoo!voo voolay nawjay?baw!baw poor luh sontay!tray baw
poor voo!" mentor encourages stunned. "Naw?say dummawj mushyoo.
Ulor,voo garday nose ubbee,nessuh paw?wee?—mussee!mussee bohkoo"
& strips with a will,to a pair of blue bathingtrunks,now proudly showing
me his "upuraytion" scar;proudly "eye ain gut skinny legs. Nut bad fur
fifty-six,huh?" now "—Cheesus doan go in like thad,yoo guttuh wait
uh minute;wait un-til yur dry undur thih arms:then id's all right,nut
bihfore,weye we'd catch ur death uv cole in thad watur!"(& stunned
sits,surrounded by our wardrobes,holding in his hand mentor's to-
mentor-priceless watch,gazing vaguely through big sunglasses at the
tiny stretch of greyish liquid now which 2 not quite nudists threaten to
invade and at the miserable hovel alias mud-bathhouse and at all around
us oddly lounging strutting uncouthly specimens of chaos and at At)

then comes the moment:
. . . "hay!" mentor splutters(emerging from a duckplunge)"yoor
tallurn mee—reach mee sumuh thad mud! Naw" disgustedly "thad's
chus clay."

And now from cureall exiting most reluctantly
"opun um up"—handing me his box of priceless crackers—"thih poor
cuss ain had nuthn tuhday but coffee. Mushyoo—!MONJAY!"

retraverse 3 comrades a parkless en route to funiculaire whose price turns
out to have quintupled . . . encountering merely a couple of not unlovers;the
masculine ½ of which pair is—to my surprise—calmly carrying upon
his backless just such a ponderous weighingmachine as graces New York
Elevated Station platforms.

Repass 3 the unshut-shutness
    now which frames 2 comradefaces
    wherewith Russians at great length mentor-Noo-Inglund

announcing triumphantly that the "manidgur"'s got his ultimatum.
"Say baw,mushyoo!"

(but comrade stunned always does not smile)

. . . & enter we("shine?")the Hotel London:whereupon stunned
gently but firmly informs comrade Noo that Noo must immediately
consult the comrade manager,for stunned absolutely refuses to enter
the comrade diningroom unless officially invited by the manager to do
so—If I am a thief(quietly)at least I am proud . . . & Noo vanishes. &
returns:looking as if Noo had been hit with a batch of 5 year plans and
several collective farms to boot

"well?" says the by this time distinctly angry comrade K

"he gut thih lettur all right" Noo whispers "un he says thih mushyoo
kun stay three days more but he says he woan give thih mushyoo nuthn
tuh eat"

. . . whereupon the mushyoo,understanding,perfectly collapsed in an
enormous sob(and under Noo's my and Shine's guidance something-not-
unlike-a-corpse drifts up certain stairlesses into K's kohmnahtah,folding
up silently on what-might-have-been-a-bed while twittering shimmying
quivering Noo suddenly pours a big drink of strong and shoves quickly
it—tears bubbled over his cheeks—at)rising suddenly

"salute!"

(suddenly behind despair disappearing down hinging) stunned . . .
"MonJay!" Noo implores "MonJay!—seel voo Play MonJay!"

Let me lend you a little money to buy a meal(K prays)

"merci"

But if I were in Italy and had nothing to eat(this comrade insists)you
would do the same,wouldn't you?wouldn't you ask me to share your
food?

"ma maison serait la votre" he said simply,at a pillow

"eh bien:permettez-moi—"

"écoutez,monsieur"(faintly)I'm proud. I ask and I receive no presents.
There is one source and one source only from which I will accept
money;that source is the soviet government,the soviet government owes
me money and I shall get it. Please do not be offended. Explain my
attitude to your comrade and beg him not to be offended. You are both
unbelievably kind:I shall remember always . . . Till tomorrow(spurting
slowly erect bows gravely then totters through my open door feebly into
the hall and toward his)

. . . eye'll.stick.with.thad.buggur" Noo Inglund murmurs "if.thih. hole.gud.dam.kumunist.putty.plugs.mih.in.thih.gut.fur.id

how'sthihfugginduck?" he asked wearily.

"high"—which it was And How—I answer

"yunno"(flopping beside me,Noo stares dumbly at fountainless)"there's sumpn bihine all this. Eye tole thih manidgur yoo said yoo'd back thad poor cuss un he said,Weye eyed doo thih same,he said,excep eyed be ruspunsuble fur his hole bill,he said. Yunno he ain uh bad sort. . . . But wut kun Eye doo with Them gud dam bastuds?" Noo wailed greyly "—they gutuh eyedear evury furinur has uh bag uh gole!"

so that was lunch.

Shortly thereafter,through Sun stroll 2(passing subdued Tochter minus arithmetic plus a giggling girlfriend)comrades laden with all "my" purchases(1 whereof he mysteriously deposits with a mysteriously unprotesting comrade kiosk-keeper)to an almost-Parisian glimpse of courtyard,to a long and large and tidy and darkish room—where gentle cordial housely wifelet's thick moist paws prayerfully me welcome;and she cried a little over the fish,

and she said god bless you Mister Cummings

thereafter unshortly,a(gentlest)knock. Not(quite)loud enough to be earthly. (Ghost?) "Entrez"(orders K)

& it's stunned.

Almost calm. He has seen his consul.

"Un brave homme." Understands. Inquiries are being made.

I offer him the strong. Which he accepts. Subsequent to persuadings infinite.

"Salute!" Almost smiles.

Talks very softly of that and of this . . . "maintenant je vais à ma chambre,entendre la musique"(refusing my offer of dinner politely and kindly for biscuits nothanking)

(medium shot

comrade peesahtel,1 invisible boil adorning his hoodozhnik tail,½not-sitting on parapet)

(multi

myri)
NowmultitudemyriadNow
(and a palpable comrade blister upon his Achilles heel)
    playing.
(And behind me silently nears a—and nearer—and—touch-ing
stands,absolutely against myself—
    you're wasting your comrade-time,Patroclus)

(day which doesn't exist)
   not because of the 7thless 6thless
(longest day of my comrade-life)
   but because of tomorrow which is when C and(Tomorrow)myself
and I together with comrades hoodozhnik peesahtel(tOmOrrOw)and
Kem-min-kz
   (NYET zahvtrah—TOMORROW)

but nothing could possibly happen syehvohdnyah. . . . Then it is no
doubt impossibly that comrades Noo and stunned accompanied me
throughout meandering this comrade tramride? Impossibly it only was
that we descend at almost the ending of the unworld?shove 3 selves now
through 1 solemn little turnstile,3(our)souls finding now on a skynear
beach lashed with Black(nicht Blau)est(chorneeyeh)thunderingly &
ocean . . .
   this little comrade capitalist laundry improperly entitled or properly K
strips to my drawers(most of the—buried with deafening surfyell—he-
or-she to-right-and-left socialist comrade laundries retain lengthful
underwear or else nightgowns)whereupon all we run 6 of now to &
plunge:hitting warm fatal entirely kind darkness:morhyeh.
   Later sometime C is for child is strolling(with whom moveun
(dreaming?)moves our this dwarfish shadow)hunting . . . further,
farther,from to what eagerest homely("used tuh woyk with mih")nonman
gesturing mentor busily . . . treasures:after perhaps decades perhaps
centuries impossibly arriving the silent captor of these few magic stones
magic these few shells
   & we shall come home
   with
   toys("vashezdarohvyeh"—I positively hereby insist I am inexorable
no absolutely refusal both of you immediately at ecco boothless sample
must a softdrink than which unlife holds nothing worser a concoction
$\frac{1}{2}$pretending to be made of lemons something which tastes vaguely as if
honey not unmixed itself with floorsoap note that dash of whatyouthink
the shall we say resultant stupefying potion is to me a sumptuous symbol

of reform reformers and reforming is to mentor "turrible ainid")is to
stunned "Dio!"(he horrified thereupon siezes a large cake made all of
sawdust)

curiously,certain of the child's comrade hitherto not quite unfaithful
trouserpockets this(how unexisting)day disintegrate,my watch departs
twice;and twice it—by K and C—from sundry trams is variously rescued:
the 2nd("nevur mine we'll get yuh unuduh tuhmorruh")sundrily various
time time stops.

Et "je suis au"(a
      strong with Noo chez K)
      "bout de mes"
      stunned . . . exploding . . .
      weeps.
                  AK-shun—KAMera! the moment's here. It's here because &
      Up comes dignity
yours to command,yours for life unto death,yours against lifelessness
against undeath stupidity against fanaticism cruelty fear against hate
or(utters the proud-erect silence:say the great sensitive eyes)every
meanness and
      who taking a trio of(quietly accepting 1 strong glass but gently
depositing which ½emptied)good,of solid,of selfish,commandes
hereupon now bows. Marvellously s-m-i-l-e-s
      —up comes merely a waiter(but looking as real as an American dentist)
who clutters(with 17 times more joy than Nero fiddled)the whole vicinity
alias very meager environs alias Kem-min-kz's comrade komnahtah with
goulash and with turkey and with items of ambrosia too numerous to name.
Then who receives wonderingly a cigarette;wonderingly quaffs(exactly ½)a
glass of strong:smilebows
      et puis "MONJAY!"
                  (O how 3 mushyoos go at it!
      a bite for intelligence a bite for tolerance and a bite for pity a bite for
courage and a big bite for love and a bite for generosity)how they bite
those trois mushyoos!
      "BOOVAY!"
                  and a doublecup to living-and-dying "BOOVAY!" a self-
ish,a solid,a good twiceswig to the abolition of altruism("ONGKORE!")give
me a triple toast to Everything Which Is!everything which somehow cannot

be compelled warped terrified or perverted!everything whatever,under the sun or the moon,which does not seek in others a parasitical negation of its own unfulfillment

Salute!

laugh—REEAY—comrade mushyoo stunned!

REEAY—laugh—drunken mushyoo comrade mentor!

(only yourself—you,the 3rd shoorade or mushcom at this feast revelry banquet—smile only;do not quite laugh,keep(by an atom)sacred your laughing;now gather it into deep you and now preserve how very skilfully itself until tomorrow;until a ship—with you . . . your laughter . . . all your spirit—shall foreverishly out of hell go

25 Karl Marx street

well that movie's to die,it's so funny. Why that "filum"'s the funniest filum anybody ever saw anywhere. "Wee wee wee" the word funny doesn't even begin to describe that indescribably ridiculous,that absolutely ludicrous not to say unbelievably sidesplitting,masterpiece. It's called Morale. And just the very thing friend comrade(fell among thieves)stunned should visit "sur swar" with comrade(good Samaritan)K acting as chaperone? Karl Marx knows,if you'll pardon me,that stunned deserves a change of scene: well,that filum fills the bill. As for K he'll never regret having seen Morale: the most intelligent of us enjoy some relaxation now and then "yunno." And is Morale relaxation!—funny?why it's so funny(is that dam)you don't even need to understand it!

I,therefore pondering psychological axiom to the effectless that sad people should be shown funerals,approach 25 comradeKarlticket-Marxoffice murmuring Two

Two What?

Good.

In the comrade foyer,by a lazily comrade amiable comrade tick(hair like 1 feather-sticking-to-an egg)ettaker,we're quite slowly made to feel(that all late comers await Morale's 3rd séance;which doesn't begin until)via this most imposing placard also devious fingercountings(9). Or in other words:comrade-time to burn. Time to burn and to play the comrade-hose on. Quoi faire,donc? Perhaps a wasteland toast and a tea?or "Café?"(timidly stunned dreamundreaming suggests)

ah—

but where? Why,just around the comrade-corner! Dadada. "Café restaurant" le voilà. Certainly isn't prosperity but has a troolyreely terrace:including 1 completely elsewhereish not much more unrousable than good comrade-Sphinx I do believe(we might try anyway)waiter. Da-da-da. It's a waiter. It admits that it's a waiter—not openly,of course;for that would be très bourgeoise or something:but tacitly,by seeming(ever so slightly)disturbed by our unique proximity. Eventually it budges,sighs,and shtohs. Eventually we make it understand 1 thé and 1 café crême—not,of course,via French;for that(in a restaurant labelled Café)would be having your cake and eating it too:but à propos of universal signs and a few merely local nouns like "koffyeh" and "cheye". The prompt shchot threatens us 25 and 85 kopeks. Promptly I seem to perform a necessary transaction,unpromptly Sphinx appears to mutter unnecessary nothanks(or whatever's the au fait socialist mot when pocketing a tip) . . . whereupon stunned suddenly desires to see a menu. 15(pocketdictionary)minutes later comrade stunned sees a menu. And by god's grace it's français as well as russe and we learn that a cup of consommé costs 2.20 and a chateaubriand 5.50 and to put it a little differently almost any hotel is cheaper. That's what we learn. Stunned and Kem-min-kz,Inc.

mais('gardez-moi ça)from neighbouring sidewalk into Morale people are disappearing like bedbugs(allons vite)we might be impossibly missing something but I don't think so neither do you however—much to nobody's considerable astonishment un brave homme,alias the heroic Italian consul,graces foyerless. Whom And How masking,snootily attendant brace of demoiselles both apparently shall we say capitalistes: ready for anything not excluding a quiet game of croquet. I therefore, marvelling that moi j'ai no mallet,slip the electrified stunned Two Good(& off sparks he)and Kem-min-kz peacefully observes dopey comrades ½playing is-it-checkers(& back stunned radiates full of all sorts of god knows what news,e.g. precisely where our seats are and the factless that comrade masked bravo just promised to 'phone stunned in the middle of the night should any réponse de Moscou which of course will occur but paraît qu'aujourd'hui's a national holiday meaning("an island of")everything's shut well not that is everything only the consulate all whereof good comrade chaperone doesn't quite under-)

Two Good equals not so far front on the aisle within a huge a comparatively stinklessness. House ¾filled(the usual brand of thoroughly

housebroken tovariches but O how not so dismaller than equivalent
Moscow audience!how very much having a somehow more time for
themunselves!and(for ghosts)how alive!)

then . . .

(how is Fate changed and merciful!nyet from un- rudely into life
Who would hurl me—as me how mercilessly from life She into un-
hurled!Fate,mercifully to this worldless myself who now presents a
spectral premonition of that myselfless world—reveals,to a stranger
inhabiting a shadow,a shadow-image of what strangeness!)

very as via probably earth's oldest film rickety Berlin un(church we
knew?park I)folds,throughout K's blood flesh muscles nerves certainly
a returning unsuspected hugeness or existing begins;now millions
trillions now swarming more than ever even the stars are in summer
even the stars even in New Hampshire quintillions of always memories
are approach impeach always threatening—O,with what curves!smells!
cries!tastes!colours!—now and rush maddening storm suddenly the
forever lost portals of almost-forgetfulness!now—now—in every corner
of my open being(stands a man,whom once I and I only knew;again
whom—soon!soon!—I shall know only,shall even and shall always alive
wonderingly how erect proudestly be!)

nyet gesture not a sound comes,from this around us breathless
ghostliness. No minds,thoughts;(but 1 single immense simple wish them
breathless all glues to any rickety to each moment of earth's probably . . .
children living a fairytale)

& which is all about how An Old Professor Suddenly Finds Himself
Locked Out In The Snow Even Without His Pants By A Girl With Lots
And Lots And How Of IT.

Selah

(. . . here's a negro
alive—

(a very black nigger a real coon not stuffed not a ghost he might have
stepped out of Small's Paradise)but O O how on-your-guard-baby O
how watching-my-step-baby never did we quite see anything like it quite
so cautiously illatease impossibly quite leery . . .

"américain,eh?"(stunned nudges. We're)moving(toward homeless;I)
and(stunned,stunned and)myself,

inc.

"heeyoor eez owoor beeug struheeut" explicating 1 shrimp of a tovarich upon the American alias African's left

"beeyooteefool;yooer theenkuh?" 1 tovarich-lobster rhapsodizing upon AfricanAmerican's left

"so! . . . uhHuh . . . yeas?" Americ(murmurs,apprehensively)An(d, How)Afric

—sudde(nly for whom lunges toothless—this—drunk stunted-a filthily non("—HUH??"—(he terrified cries)back)man(stepping:a-l-l-q-u-i-v-e-r-i-n-g— . . .)))

now

comrade-something's happened,around these comrade-partless-parts;what:which?who

somenotsocialist somenonsoviet someunRussian thinglessome-

"Ecoutez!"

                child seizes shadow:we're passing through the London's

"quoi?"

I heard laughter(stunned,whisper;to stunned)

Really?(won.der-ing)

. . . Will you sitwith me in the garden?(to a shadow says a child)

(won:der:ing-l;i;s;t-e,n,i,n,g)"avec plaisir monsieur"

—aha! . . . so That's the accident!well well well Well. As for this shawdan 'tis all quite jammed with That why That's everywhere plastered against aboreal That smackup against fountainless and shouting quaffing That grinning chuckling LAUGHING!

"étrangers"

you And bet How. My Karl good Marx god. Yah da furinurs. Doyty furinurs. Kepitulist doytiest furinurs phooey. Dutch?Germans?Swedes?4 who?or what?6 odd which?languages?al(together)ragingly?hubbubery

(&—so That's why,disappearing into the night like bedbugs,inc. met far beyond usual dressedup comehitherings—)

item:What Price Silk Stockings?

—so very utterly,so unbelievacredibly shameless and indeed depraved are truly all these(& of all drunkest this hogbellied really Deutscher) capvanitdaltalist whowhichwhats,trooly and reelly and onnesly . . . nay,I exaggerate nyet;absolutely it happened,upon my sacred positively honour as a peesahthoodozhn . . . 1 fiend(you may not or you may believe)raps, actually raps;raps almost heartily:upon a comrade glass with a comrade spoon! . . . PHOOEY what deathwishing glares those—not really waiters,of course;all that's just bourgeois alias bushwah:what I mean is certain truly highminded tovariches,most of whom ought to be if they're not Phi Beta Kappas and they are,certain quite-as-good-as-in-fact-rather-better-than-you-and-me-and-don't-they-know-it soldiers of Jesus né Lenin alias comrades who well just are sort of temporarily(for the immortal benefit of mortality,you know,for the eventual kind of goodofhumanity orsomething)PreTending to be brutally enslaved victims of a hopelessly idiotic system or what have you(we haven't)those loosely entitled for public convenience and otherwise very vulgarly nicknamed—"waiters". But they don't call themselves waiters and you don't call themselves waiters. They're "comrades". Better remember that,too;or somebody might think we were blowing up the Kremlin with my safetyrazor: then—byebye!

well;so utterly etcetera are all these drunk etceteras,that(literally etcetera)they call highminded etcetera comrades etcetera "Herr ober"(sic). And they bang for service(sic). And this very-much the much-very—who doesn't seem to know that the sovietsocialist reason service really isn't is that service really is bushwawbourgeois . . . that is,all service isn't of course;only the service that doyty furinurs mistakenly expect from Gay-Pay-Oos(I confess I really quite don't or metaphysically speaking)but anyway . . . well:

so drunkest wants to know.

So the almost-headwaiter(dignity having wisely vamoosed)wrestles, mentally of course,with drunkest;but that's sort of just the trouble,it seems that drunkest kind of isn't mentally wrestlable,drunkest apparently if you'll pardon me fools people that way—even gay Phi pay Beta oo Kappas(perish the pensée!)at any rate K never saw a quite so futile treatment of a so quite trivial situation. . . . All that happened was,drunkest took it all not as a little bit of clean fun but as a direct and highly personal insult affront and somethingorother not merely to drunkest but to all his fellowshawdaneers each and every . . . not omitting a rambling shambling blondish gangling who keeps visiting drunkest with dire results and then wan-mean-dering back to bevy-of-angry-cronies at distantly-situated-tableless . . . also(and very much)not omitting this dark slick tart now jabbering FrenchPolish-Somethingelse right exactly behind me & meanwhile

almost-head- strokes:whispers;soothes,blushes

and drunkest raves

&(as if to cap the sortofkindof soi-disant climax)Inc.'s pinklampshaded light goesoff and comes-on & comes-off and goeson until really Ragnarok was by comparison just a pardon me ½arsed Episcopalian praymeeting.

where . . .

the Last?

(nyetimposscan't

But)

da . . .

K:well,don't think about it or perhaps it won't be

C:"think"!it's nothing to do with thinking or not thinking!it's I—it's to feel—I am—already who am feel begin who

K:sh

C:"sh"?to think with "sh" who the thinking cares about "sh"! We're leaving this thin thing think "sh"(don't you feel?)we'll be all miles away,beautiful new all green away miles,tonight—

K:the boat might not sail . . .

C:(censored)

K:you have a lot to do today,remember

C:I have to keep from laughing my fool head off today and slapping dignity on the back and throwing mentor up in the air and handing stunned my final few Pay To The Order Ofs & taking a thick big swift poke at that pussyfooting son of a manid-

K:pour l'amour de Lénine,behave!

C:for the love of love,wonder at ourselves:who are in the greatest luck of all time,having visited places under existence(or such as with a certain Florentine's enormous dream impossibly compare)only we;only who were defeated upon the hemisphere of this world,who through Un mightily must descending penetrate cordially hell;after,shall welcome stars.

"Weye,hee" meaning out of Noo's angelbenefactress by Stalingrad's tractorplantmogul Robertsycollegeyprodigy "'s gunnuh show yoo uhlotuh things yoo nevur seen bihfore"

Noo halts

"here's thih pawnshup." Whispers "doan yoo say nuthn. Eye'll do thih talkin"

well,it seems that in the cityless of Odessa—A.D.MCMXXXI—a good

2ndhand timepiece costs 110 roubles;i.e.(2 roubles equals 1 dollar)$55.
Artfully but we have with us today just a few—going going—specimens
of the art of crafty tovarich Ingersoll who made the soi-disant watch
which made the socalled dollar as it were famous;and these,O gentle
comrade,will naturally cost you considerably less. Dadada. 2ndhand,O
comrade,these originally $1 timepieces are really a tremendous bargain.
A bagatelle. Practically rien de tout. A just without the reachless of
every honest working unman nonman and manless trifle,get me? $40

"what about repairing this one?" timidly K(2 comrade-merely-
capitalists having regained 1 comrade-socialist-sidewalk)hints

Noo "pretty late" frowned "they oughttuh have ut leas too weeks. But
we'll try" he added;courageously "—now gimmih thad un yoo chus walk
uhroun fur uh wile un eyel cross thih street here un doo sum dickurin
with uh felluh eye know"

. . . 15

      no more no
           unminnonutelesses
a horrifying and horrified ghost spurted from a tiny shut:wildly
then hurtle(crazed?)lim-pin-gly on-toadstool-feet through-traffic-
less and(spitting sputtering redfaced redjowled speechless)shakes
now,mad?pudgily ferocious unhands before amazed-verily-mytheself—
recoiling who("what happened?")whisper

"w . . . wuhWut—WUT HAPpuned?!" ghost(quiv)ering(shimmy)
ing(the ar)tic(ulates cra)zed

"yes"

"l-Lis-LISsun"(almost with wrath bburbursting)—"dyuh Know wut
thad Sonuvuh" etc.etc.etc.etc. "thad Bastudly" etc.etc.etc. "thad" Etc.
etc. "had thih Gud dam bastudly Noyve" etcetera "tuh ask fur ruPairin
yur Watch?"

we-shake our-headless

"—Dyuh kNOw?" ghost

"WhaT?" K

"Uh POUND Uv BUTTUR" . . . he suddenly screamed . . . "In Thih
OPEN MARket!"

breaksansfastly puffing amid foyer("shine?")a bentvery cignonalessretteun
stunned has already this nonday seen brave homme;stunned mutters
feebly that brave has renewed brave's demand for immediate decision by

Moscow,weakly that brave has offically lenthened by deux days of grace stunned's limbo,faintly that brave has most forcefully directed stunned to go without fail to go subito go tout de suite go right-away-quick to somethingorother it's called the what the the commissariat of of of labour(which appears thereupon is where Noo took stunned also me. Thereupon is where 2 comrades,1 in blue,finally agreed to write a letter to a manager. Is where a lot of unmen and nonmen and menlesses and even babies were waitwaitwaitWaiting.

Hah,rah,shoh

& bring ye your buzzbabberooz).

Haps(of course)that nobody's home at said commissariat of labour: therefore we all of us need a coffee to put it mildly;and yet(or of course)the Casino just over the redhot way is shut. And How

"—you go back to our hotel" K offers "I'll take charge of him for a little while"

thereupon 2 most comrades dismally are strol . . . ling,such beneath sunsunsun as anyhow nobody somewhere heard(why of stunned course doesn't collapse god knows I don't)let alone probably felt ever tasted,when bejeesus!behold . . . the . . . . Franco-Italian . . . Restaurant . . . & which(of course)doesn't speak a single wordless either of Italian or French but quotes desperation brooks no barrier;also we're wise to cheye and not incredibly koffyeh—also,enough is as good as a feast(which even K impersonally inclines to disbelieve while personally C verily doubts it. And somethingorother like "peeroshkee" turns out to be in to be cakes—both my shy "gateau" and stunned's humble "biscuits" having failed,and peesahtel's dictionary being for no reason nyet. Now I lay me 2 roubles down on a 1.65 conto . . . now his nibs alias the highly enlightened walks off sullen with to not return.

Hah;rah;shoh

. . . it won't be long now. "Well yoo guttuh shake meye han" upsprouting from non("shine?")bench mentor ecstatically hailfellows clapping stunned's unback gaily & cutting a sort of a kind of a caper a.

"Why,what" genially we ask "have you done now,kid?"

"siddown!"

wilting 1 comrades 1 flank trium3rdphant

"shoot" the comrade K encourages.

("Shine?")"shine?" begs

bumbletythumbletukScrunch!(at a fleeing-instantly-"shine?" Then ruddy then jovial tummied then bowlfishofgoldfullish SantaClaus minus-the-whiskers slaps!my knee . . . leers:awhi-sp-eri-ng "Eye Fixed His Uffair Fur Him!")

" . . . no . . ." gasp I

"Hees Gunnuh Woyk Here,But"

"—Noo!!—" gasp

"DOAN tell him nuthn NOW" mysteriously Noo commands

"réponse?"—stunned's faceun o("non" I shrug)pens & closes blacken("mais je crois que tout va bien enfin")unblackening.

&.

Through

through ing Waiting waitWaiting waitwaitWaiting waitwaitwait Waiting through were through babies through even through and through menlesses through and through nonmen through and through unmen through of through lot through a.

The comrade in blue

very serious,nods(we nod)seriously;

briefly,brings out 3(and we sit)chairs:& seriously now accepts K's temporarily last export.

1 tall agilefaced pincenezed immediately tackles our stunned. Immediately in excellent French. Tackler speaking quite crisply very seriously really efficiently. (But not coldly)about voltage and wiring and amperes and. To whom—inwardly straightening slow-ly,slowly uptakingslackof(for the 1st absolutely time since I have known positively him)self—stunned;out of dream rising:sLowly;replies un(rapidly answers,quietly)stunning

& quietly & watched And How & by the in blue

And rapidly How by e.g. to blue's right comrade-not-blue by i.e. this plumcoloured aleaning along desk upon silent hands blouse

also & by speechless blond a pale curly- viz. a to blue's left seated headed husky

sun

  Sun

    SUN

       (des larmes

a new with-tears on-

its-cheeks creature)un peu less dwarfish a little

taller(moves not-quite not-very-not really-as-yet-be
liev
. . . ing "je
Vais
—TRAVAILLER!"

mentor,as comrade(not K)C gives him 1 package of imitationGillette
safetyrazorblades,now almost drops dead. But "shine?" as comrade
C(not K)gives him 3 pairs of unheeled toeless socks almost now floats
alive(& what eyes!)

flutters the fattily a nonthing called "manidgur" all this over
tumblefumbling over that K's all reckoning takes now these trembles
those Pay Tos addssubtracts fumblesunhands & finally & bows handing
bowfinallying 28 and-tumbling-swirls and roubles and & thanking(it
won't be long now!)to my
self.

Hah:rah:shoh

mentor and K,Inc.(triumphers extraordinary overnonright)down
vodka under amazing chandeliers

& "monjay" with much-taller-now who has just reseen rebrave
rehomme so everything's now different people believe people are like
"c'est bien étrange" that but much-taller will really never quite ever forget
2 very Comrades viz. mentor and K who were not like that e.g. who
were not merely people,2 who believed him when nobody believed when
believing wasn't the thing 2 Comrades who were Comrades and who
believed because they believed when there wasn't any reason whatever
any at all not even the really very quite least reason:and that's what
Comrades are Comrades aren't afraid Comrades don't hesitate Comrades
aren't ashamed Comrades dare:not because Comrades know they don't
they never know nobody ever knows but Comrades don't have to know
because Comrades can feel because Comrades are not like people because
Comrades are Comrades

"—how much may I give" dignity alias "him?" whisper . . . "O give him
three" allvanquishing mentor shrugs . . . whereupon dignity becoming
head(is very graciously grateful)waiter suddenly now into himself turning
seizes(heartily)my right hand with his right hand:"Bon Voyage!"

and this highminded(alias tovarich merely politely waiter)gets exactly 1
and that desk-tovarich(courteously who greeted me upon my arrival

once when everything upon a time was bien étrange and the black sea
once upon a time was blue)gets precisely 2

and the(already And How at shut of komnahtah number 29 alias
"K's" roomless)tovarich(supercourteoushyperpolite)porter gets 2 too

and(one)1 remains on "C's" tableless for invisible chamberish and

. . . Trumpets!
Within-
&
-Without!!

Ordnance!!!
Everywhere Fireworks!!!!
—Cannon every(Bells Guns)where Rifles
Pistols(everywhere Rockets Romansplendcandoursles Torpedoes
Mines)Cheering Searchlights Pinwheels!!!!!(mentor & very-much-
now-taller and I now jump in a not a picture a Henry Ford sedan with
peesahtel's valise with hoodozhnik's knapsack with 2 unidentified blokes
positively both of absolutely whom look like posolutely the manidgur
alias manager & why the absitively hell not—

why the doesn't everyone here look like everyone

why isn't only 1 face worn in all hell

?

(Yoo

Kun

Beye

Um

All

Fur

Uh

Cigurette)
shed. Lengthwise dirtily disordered. (Where are the
Tartars?elsewhere. They have been taken away

somehow)chaos but somehow different probably because am here(not
K)myself I(not a picture,not a tovarich

but a beginning;

but:a)

dream. This as it were undream:this picture;this socalled tovarich,this
customs-

soi-disant he proceeds O how and very languidly . . .

—("doan leye" beside me standing whismurpermurs mentor)—

&

. . . (a)how much Pay To The Order Of did you have?(but,so soon as we produce the And How considerably smaller of our twain lumpoftravellerschequesstubs this short white(big)bloused dumb grey(youngish)capped examiner pushes it away almost if not quite wearily)

(b) . . . give me now all your receipts(casually now he looks at 3 of them,listlessly he hands them all wearily quite now back)

(c)"shtoh?"(Typewriter,quoth mentor. Examiner kind of lazily makes sort of a note of a yunno a typewriter)

(d) . . . (peering into knapsack,feels,it shoves sleepily it away)

(e) . . . (carelessly inspects my various toys. 1=a doll outside a doll outside a doll outside a doll outside a doll outside a doll outside a doll outside an almost-not-believably-quite-small-Doll. The: shrugging;young-ish scoops,8;dolls:to-gether—he)

(f)Any Roubles?(asks almost briskly awakening almost perhaps quite not possibly unfiercely)

. . . but roaring down to the shed in Henry's "lissun:there's" whismuring "chus wun thing;yuh kunt take any uh this money out with yuh,get mee?nut uh kopek!see?eye wouldn wan yuh tuh get intuh no trouble?See?GET MEE?"—O yes,I get him;I give him my change:all of it. Every kopek:14 perhaps or 15 roubles;not one,1,atom of hellmoney have I now . . .

Languidly very and how O by he disant-soi now

my baggage is weighed(g)

(h) . . . my passport's handed by me to mentor who hands it to some tovarich who hands it back to mentor who does not hand it to me(but as soon as the good boat starts I'm to have it back from all sorts of and from every kind of people including,of course of course,the marine police and—eventually I hope not—the captain himself

&

HAH.RAH.SHOH

. . . just outside shed,both my are seized hands by seize both hands of now an how-very-much-now-taller . . .

then & A Dream alias ex-comrade ex-peesahtel ex-hoodozhnik alias Poietes follows dreamFulLy 1 low desperate sticky vitality(ensconced in a small oldmiddleaged imperson of defunct eyes & twisting lip toadstool feet pudgy claws)upandupand rick-etyhang-ing stairs &

what?

(tovarichporters tovarichsteward tovarichofficer canNot possibly unshut this

possibly canNot unlock this

locked)

—but mentor Can. . . . Absolutely empty cabinless. —Baggage dumped. Relocking . . .

& "yoo doan have tuh tip nobudy"

. . . O,

there's my Italian comrade,standing in sunsunsun down away down miles years away and he waves and he smiles and I smile and I wave . . . (where is he?nowhere,certainly,that I've ever been!O no. Nyet. You can't persuade me I ever stood down where a black haired a very short-and-tightly-knit an individual whose big head wears perhaps the most—no,not the most perfectly disconsolate face—no,not now,now that face extraordinarily has changed,it is now beginning even to be alive,something amazing has somehow happened. To me,also. I am not comrade K,who descended from the Paris-N train 1 day into a world of Was—O no;nyetimposscan't:who passed from mentor-the-1st through Assyrian and Beatrice into starry churches and thence through Bleiben Sie Ruhig and—but,da—into sunsunsun

into down away down years away miles . . .)

—"LISSUN".

(we recovering turn. It's the 2nd mentor,now about to become ex-

"yes?")—

& now his both claws somehow have tangled in my left arm. & he stared up-at-myself. & away,below us;stood a person:who had been dead . . . as the imperson(whom I shall not see again,the now lifting its not quite defunct eyes up-toward-mine its almost dead really its doomed)suddenly shoving in a kind of a sort of pushing anguish boosting all-against-my-own-self desperately its unself—now—spoke—said—whispers

"Eyem. Gunnuh. Haveuh. Good. Scroo. Tuhnight. Uneyem. Gunnuh. Thinguh. Yoo."

amen

(8). Via recently not unglimpsed $250 probably(of once- possibly
even the captain white nowhere vacantly beside myself staring once-
uniform)timetoy

   hah

      rah

         shoh.

(Dirty little)was of a boat's(there)labelled every(here)where
French Marine(pocheh-moo?). . . . Chugging:she?nyetimposs—
2 hideously prote(filled with Gay-Pays)sting antique launches
are(off which dive he-heroes)play(idly)ing at running-down-their
-fellow-antique-French-Marine-alias-

   me.

Mixture of(très très très proletarian)3rd(Hard if you prefer)class
passengers-and-friendsrelatives—men kiss farewell;a girl bursts,dropping
her head,& is led grimly away by gigantic grinning nonman

   on this(years miles)wharf—whores,side by each in a puddle of shade
seated,2,munching—up strideth encorewhite gallant encoreuniform,tips
his cap,converses. (Locked in the same dimension of non(down
miles;years)existence)is 1(angular squats)motherlump(droops hugging
a)gently a babyunshape(a)

   it

   would

   take

burglars,and pretty good burglars,to solve "my" cabin's combination. So
what? So no overcoat(now the sunsunsun's gone,now a dampreekcoolness).
So I overcoatless move among these those all betattered patchmendeds,
feeling conspicuous;nay,even bourg- if not bush-

   8

   ,05

   ;10

   :15

      —moving,I gratefully spy now somebody else who's(nonchalantly
conversing with a patchful a betattered)conspicuous;but not like me
merely nyet-miserably-dressed;O no:a dark really & truly groomed truly
& immaculately really attired milordship. . . . Excuse me(I of dude
inquire)know you when we leave?

   Not before eleven(the elegantly dude responds,also in Bastille)

   Thank you very much

Please
move I now
". . . ou peutêtre demain!" he calls,cheerfully.
(Time moans in
time's)time
moans
in(time moans)time
dang
        doong
                deeng
                        dung
. . . so mouldy tovarich so feebly appearing so steward so rings colossal
this handbell.

Rush the patchmendeds. Squirmsprawl(I too)into . . . Deer in
Snow?nyetim. But ultradilapidated really a quite superior brand of very
wasness with 2 tablelesses diningunroom. Opposite I too are 7(count
'em)kids. Seem to hear "monsieur" from other tableless?dude's beckoning.
Resit,beside dude and opposite a superSemitic nonmale next which horror
lolls shaggy hyperditto unfemale e.g. husband with perfectly false teeth(too
late,yah pahnyeemeyeyoo. Dude can't speak English. Dude guessed I
can. Dude therefore summoned me to entertain these undoubted and
nondoubtable Palestinebound Americanos). Presently un- wishes they were
getting off at Constantinople. Whereupon And How states non-

"but we've SEEN Russia!"
back and forth and insideout and all the sights and always travelling and
always INTOURIST and always excitement three coats one very valuable
stolen while my husband merely turned his head for just a second to
look out the window for just a moment always excitement guide almost
killed trying to keep me from falling off our deelux train with three
dozen eggs which I'd really insisted on buying at a station somewhere
always excitement and when there weren't any trains why what would
INTOURIST do but charter a special with private rooms and even
private baths yes really can you imagine baths on a train I wouldn't
believe it Russia is simply wonderful so immense so throbbing earnest
vital people so happy everywhere thrilled with communism building
socialism everywhere a feeling of freedom everybody everywhere on
their toes exhilarated you know just aching to work full of the shwoddy
veev bursting with energy all free all liberated all madly wildly almost

364

insanely enthusiastic everywhere the train was met by delegations by wildly enthusiastic delegations of madly enthusiastic workers by almost insanely beautiful hundreds of splendid upstanding youths and noble loftybrowed maidens and always always everyone seemed just crazy to show the tourists everything everyone always really seemed only too glad to do whatever they could and were O so sympathetic O so kindly O so appreciative especially of the splendid work of American engineers who made such really great sacrifices to help rebuild this really vast country and everywhere everywhere everybody felt so wonderfully you know conscious and aware of all the incredible really quite unbelievable if you hadn't seen them with your own eyes advantages of communism you know socialism why you simply can't picture it just a different life altogether something absolutely new positively undreamed of really stupendous and opportunities for educating themselves and reading and writing and taking baths every day and leading their own lives for the first time in human history imagine just miraculous that's what it is isn't it just can't be described O if only people could know what's really going on in that really colossal land how human beings are being benefited everywhere how poverty and sickness and disease are things of the past if only every American could somehow be made could be just compelled by force to take that tour to be courteously guided willy-nilly all over that really prodigious nation by INTOURIST my my my I ask you wouldn't their eyes be opened can you imagine can you conceive what a difference it would make can you?

"D'y' remember that Cossack?" he grins

that cossack of course will I ever forget I wanted to take his picture and this was away way off in an outlandish part where the train stopped for just a few moments and all the natives instantly came flocking around us in their O so picturesque costumes I really never saw anything like it and were they men those native men my I should say they were my goodness the fiercest looking fellows you ever ever saw in all your life I really was almost afraid of them but of course I simply had to have a picture to show to the folks back home I knew they wouldn't believe because nobody would unless they saw it with their own eyes so I just said paw jawlus taw and snapped the fiercest biggest brutalest man of all those men who were really men and I thought he was going to murder me why he came right after me why the guide had to interfere and all those outlandish people carry huge great knives they're only sem eye civilised of course the soviets are doing all they can working night and day the five year plan and the collective farms and everything it's all so perfectly miraculous everyone working all together without distinction of any kind for the good of all you know the future of humanity lovingly cheerfully each one gladly doing his or her bit everybody never expecting the slightest reward O no all just working for you know the common good of all you know for the sheer joy of just working brothers and sisters fathers and mothers side by side just one big family and aren't the children perfectly wonderful just so happy and so contented it's simply marvelous unbelievable yes I really never imagined children could be so healthy looking!

(. . . meanwhile feeble-tovarich-mouldy-steward serves rather indeed amazing parodies of food. At which the young milord occasionally pales:but superSemitic goes marching right And How on until unfull of food-parodies passenger-parodies creep from full of luxury-parodies diningroom-parody. When dude,esquire spills me latest parody-dope i.e. l' on part at parody-2 A.M. 8,11,2—always not forgetting "peutêtre demain"—hahrahshoh. & parody-I stumble to the French Marine's topdeckless. Where

O have you seen a prophylactic station?never?no?not ever?not one!impossible!not really!why it really doesn't seem as if you'd seen anything!why but don't you realise it's the greatest achievement of the revolution I mean the way they've dealt with prostitution which of course was perfectly terrible under the Tsar simply widespread positively prolific and well you know what they did the communists you know the way they dealt with prostitution don't you well I'll tell you perhaps you may have heard of a splendid organization it's sometimes referred to as the gee pee you well of course most foreigners don't understand they think it's like our police but it isn't at all O my no the members of the gee pee you are persons of the highest moral calibre especially chosen for their lofty ideals and devoted to the cause of humanity and they never call themselves police O no they always call themselves guardians of the proletariat because you see that's just what they are they're really just protecting the proletariat from bad influences you know external and internal both well so prostitution had to be liquidated that's their word because it corrupted everybody and was bad for the state so a few fine young men of the gee pee you volunteered to cure prostitution and they dressed themselves up as ordinary civilians and they allowed loose women to take them to hotels and when they got to the hotels they just paid for the rooms and immediately I mean just as soon as the rooms were paid for instead of doing anything immoral with these women as the women had expected they just explained who they really were and then took the poor diseased creatures right straight to fine homes which the communists had provided in advance especially for that purpose and O my you know these homes are really the most amazing of all I want to tell you I've never been so moved in my hole life nothing I ever saw in awl Russia and believe me my husband and I we've seen everything but nothing absolutely nothing was quite so perfectly wonderful as what I'm going to speak of now of course you've really got to see it with your own eyes otherwise you simply wouldn't believe it nobody would absolutely nobody it's just simply positively incredible quite unbelievable you know what I think I think everybody ought to be made ought to be really compelled by force to see with their own eyes one of these extraordinary homes where women who used to be socially ostracized and avoided by all nice people as a social menace and looked down upon by everyone who had any selfrespect and treated as vile degenerate utterly depraved outcasts are now really accepted for the first time as human beings just like you and me only of course they never had our cultural advantages but now they're given everything which will help them to better themselves morally and physically of course including free examinations and treatment by the very best doctors and for the first time they all have really good books to read and their minds are kept interested from morning till night isn't that wonderful in all sorts of healthy and profitable and really important things and of course they appreciate it indeed they do why shouldn't they why it's like a rebirth for them why nobody despises them everybody understands them and wants to help them why they begin to feel important they begin to take an interest in what's going on in the world and they all of them begin to want to be good citizens mercy no they're not compelled to stay in these homes I should say not nobody uses force not for a moment the point is this they'd much rather stay because it makes them feel they're really somebody after all not just parasites and menaces to the community of course once in a while they do run away but only very seldom it really doesn't count and then you know when the poor creatures have been cured of all their horrible diseases they teach them an honest trade so they won't have to sell their bodies and then they all go out and they all become hardworking selfsupporting selfrespecting citizens and if they meet prostitutes anywhere they tell them all about these fine homes and the prostitutes go to the homes voluntarily to be cured of prostitution and so now there isn't any such thing any more as prostitution can you imagine isn't it miraculous you know I think just that one great single unbelievable incredible achievement I mean eliminating prostitution makes up for any mistakes the communists have ever made or ever will make I mean nothing like it ever happened in the world before I mean you've got to see it with your own eyes to believe it but it's true really true seeing is believing I mean I've seen it and I know

. . . meanwhile comes,through almost-night bumping,an antedeluvian (a crammed with tovariches)camion and(ree-ling)lurch-es,along quailess, and(arriving finally beside Frenchless Marine)halts—outspilling every which(tovariches)way tumbling who all sprawl(revealing 1 tranquil large iron disk). A cry:for a man's man to man our good ship's shoreside crane;lazily someone appears,someone wearily wrestles with rusty mechanism(pistons jar and stick;yield—steam:jets—& up slow;ly from:truck up;to lo,wer deck:tranquil;the:disk;now is,pumpatumping-ly-es-cort-ed). . . . Instantly 3 blond boys wearing overalls pounce feverishly begin plucking at are dissecting all-to-pieces-taking are for the once homogeneous tranquility substituting a chaos of mostly arcs . . . which chaos 3 unitedly attack feverishly grabbing at seizing trying to reassemble the now picturepuzzle now fumbling blundering and juxtaposing segments mutually(to my humble own ignorant eye)hostile. An officer. He tells them to stop. They stop . . . & now the seg-ments,fragments,elements,pieces,guiltily are most slowly lifted(1 by 1)are carefully leaned against this bulwark,in something very like painfully immaculate disarray. Calm whereupon resumes . . .

exit nonmale.

Enter unfemale. Lectures me(through)for(popping)an(teeth)hour. Russia,that dark continent,is really it seems just perfectly marvellous "now take me:I'm worried;just heard stocks hit new lows" perfectly wonderful "I'm in the drugstore business,see?and now I gut two competitors" perfectly elegant "but here a man don't have to worry,everything's done for him" in fact he really thinks I really ought to really go there some time

1

  0

    :5

     9

—just to make everything perfectly perfect;upwanders esquire,dude with a perfectly portable phonograph trickling dizzily jazz. Paraît,says smiling perfectly he,that this good shipless will leave "peut-être" at 2. Questioned most roundly by Kem-min-kz,the perfect smiler flatly affirms that a wouldbe circular portion of our noble engine's vitals was only yesterday discovered to be imperfect. That at the factory or the foundry or wherever this portion contrived to conceive itself apparently somebody worked too hard or may have enthusiastically hit the portion in question with a hammer when somebody shouldn't at any rate the portion in question isn't perfectly round. That well you know the crew consulted the captain and the captain consulted the crew and they all of them notified the police who thereupon notified the foundry or the factory or the wherever(and incidentally began a secret investigation of this indubitably Counterrevolutionary Atrocity not to mention Right Deviation). That naturally the wherever boys with the fear of Marx in them immediately voted to work overtime and whoop it up for the honour of Odessa and produce with recordbreaking speed one perfectly circular contribution to our engine's noble vitals. That which they did. That perfection having just arrived and having been taken completely apart by people who couldn't put it together if their lives depended thereon,absolutely nobody now knows what to do next. That all of which stems from the gruesome fact that this good boatless is very ancient and quite unsuitable for travel and was actually condemned some 10 or 15 years ago.—Then why are we on it?(the(pop)Jew(ping)asks(teeth) nervously).—Well,it seems that a boat named Tchicherin which is twice as big and thrice as fast and four times as new and five times as good as this one . . . a boat by the way whose name occurs on your so to speak ticket and on mine and on the tickets of all the other soi-disant passengers . . . decided to lie down and take a little nap only day before yesterday. So what?so nothing. So rather than disappoint all the other passengers and you and even me this very benevolent government of peasants and of workers just simply shoved me and shoved you and shoved even everybody into this leaky old tiny and very by socialist soviet workers frequently repaired in all the wrong places probably more for the fun of it than anything else ark.

"I wonder why it's called that" I wonder

"what" says pop

"French Marine" I said,pointing

"what's called French Marine?"

I point

"frANZ" he cried with dis(pop)dain "MERing!"

"so it is" wonderingly we admit. "But what does Franz Mering mean?"

his jumping teeth stare aghast. His to portable's meanwhile trickle wriggling meanwhile obscenely wife moos pityingly

"is it" I generously hazard "somebody?"

"one"(pop)"of the great"(ping)"est socialists who ever"(poppop) "lived!"

. . . "voulez-vous danser madame?" dude elegantly of wrigglepityingly inquires

So there we are. So,marooned upon a desert island=the harbourless of Odessa,that feeble old buccaneer Franz Mering dreams of Ye Happy Hunting Grounds. So meanwhile from his topdeck jazz leaks:unto the which somewhat anachronistic(given our locale)cacophany whirleth now this perfectly embarrassed dude;now whom clutcheth And How huggeth 1 quivering stamping eyerolling dugwagging gutthrusting upper-middleaged specimen of Hebraica American(—and,for no reasonless,I begin to begin to remember to remember a certainly uncertain musician who once went all through the revolution and he was good enough to play for . . . yes). So there we are! We're there because we're there because we're there because we're ex-

hausted(but perfectly having bowed to specimen . . . who,meward glinting,continues her unconscious imitation of a typical proletarian theatre's idea of a typical capitalist female)esdudequire blushfully now gropes portable;on slips now another record,now winds the infernal(. . . as for I,busily am And How elsewherelooking)&

up:

    from;the,tiny-black-box sprouts(mir-ac-u-lous-ly ten-dril-ing,cLiMbS rapidly-into-dumb-unsky)a finenes(s a f)rail shrIEking(dis:lodged, very a cruel;ly tumbling)sobbing(a,spilled,a,prodigious)new squirmsnow akeenverilypillarofmostswiftly

Alive

    —wonder

                ing faces peer out of a nether darkness and the once chattering beneath us ceases—

Voice!

of The World of where we out of hell shall go if only something happens if
   only this
               agony will not become eternal if our unlives only do not linger forever under this(mir-ac-u-lous-ly ten-dril-ing into which now Is climbing bravely Newly reaching is while all Our unlives listen breathless itself-frail ly-sure ly-feel ingliv ingfeel ingbe ingfeel ingmoving a.l.i.v.e a Song!
   Alive is singing of love(what else is there to sing of?)Voice is climbing toward love(what else is there to climb toward?)& a Song is feels (inventing)being(feels is imagines)mov ingcrea ting(Only is For and always Is and was And only shall be for always Love!
   without whom nothing is everything does not exist;or shadows. Kingdom of hell,Un)
   —the frozen Jewess flopped:scowling slunk—
   pop,spellbound,whispers "Turkish?"
   dude. Nods
   "gut any more?"
   dudenods
   . . . "why does he like jazz?that other stuff's much" to my(amazed) my(almost weeping)self mutters false-perfectly "better" . . .
   and,ecco!a littlish Turk—sucked from below up by a Song—flutters at upon toward our dude wildly gesturing begins with whom achomping (under nonsky)a vivid acrobatically an uncouthness they standless bathed in somersaults of dislanguage

2:15. Franz unmoves. Heroless might as well retire. I descend. Sudden a manreeking a & pitchdark:where?but . . . no;within this(thunderously snoreful)corridorless(gutters 1 big candle)shadows writhe here(and)here around sprawl(corpses?asleep?)manthings carefully over(and)between blun(strik)der(ing)matches a the "my" cabin(which of course is unlocked of course:which has 4 shelves,2 upper 2 lower,all minus any slightest bedding;under left lower repose safely,of course,knapsack & valise) . . . re-tur-ning care-ful-ly bet-w-een(asleep?)ov-er(corpses?)c-arefull-y locate T-h-e,of all soidisant conveniences ever which have the pleasure of encountering me had,much And How filthiest;can you believe it? Da I can:dada I can indeed,dadada . . . God almighty I'm not going to bedless. —Maybe there existless unstars in the nonsky outside?let's. Ascend—

371

near Mering's bow a group of shadows murmur,I recognise our dude

Can you tell me what to do about getting a blanket?(ask him politely)

Have you no blanket?

None

There should be blankets(he murmurs). Have you looked?

My cabin isn't made up;I just went down to see

How many of you are there in your cabin?

Myself

(I thought he would have fallen overboard. Recov(infinitesimally)e ring "OH-HO-UH!" dude mar-vel-ing-ly exclaims)

"pourquoi?" je demande

"oHH-hoHHH-uHHHH!" noddingly he smiles "c'est comme ça,eh?" And—bending upon me a grim but perfectly courteous stare—"nous sommes cinq."

In that case,why don't you share my cabin?

Look—I'll show you(he insists). And we descend. And,sure enough,in a cabin only slightly less full of unspace than "mine" very violently are playing uncards 4 shadows,all of whom greet dude most merrily with vast inquiries for his supreme health his total happiness & of whom all register now falling-overboard re our heroless re his wonderful 1man coffin and of whom all perform now gladly And How immediate transfer of dude's innumerable belongings from pyaht to ahdeen. Which thereupon becomes dvah. Whereupon immediately dude shakes,out of innumerable elsewheres,that feeble shadow;who seems to be the diningroom steward alias the waiter but who unpresently awakens as the bedroom steward and may(for all I know)be innumerable other people including the captain(I rather hope not)and this remarkably very mythical person digs from the usual if unusually nowhereish nowhere not only merely blankets but even sheets which pahzhjahloostahing dude directs him to lay on opposite lowers and that he pahzhahloostahing does and vanishes

empty Troikabox

wedges un

shut open

(more tired ever in life?yes.

in unlife?

Non)

372

and,so i wonder(what
  colour's the
  ocean?we probably aren't
  very far out Franz doesn't seem to be rolling,even to be pitching;she's
only very busily throbbing)&
  from
  "my" sleepshelf wriggles drowsy 1
  inhabitant-of
  -hell with(not
  open)with(shut)careful
  ly eyes &,very now erect stand
  ing
        to smiling to himselfless;whispers
:Wait. Don't look. Feel. All you have to do now is to open these
comrade eyes—whereupon you'll be another person. Wonderfully
whereupon yourselfless will become(how silently)myself. Not among
doomed and transparently millions a shadowcasting shadow spelled
with a K. Not you,peesahtel-traveller in shadowland. Not you,tovarich
hoodozhnik. Not you yourselfless;you a solid shade,a loneliest
uninhabitant of unloneliness. For unloneliness or shadowland is no
more. For all you have to do now is to open these closed(these carefully
shut)carefully these not open eyes. And yourselfless will be myself. You
do not believe? Because you cannot see. Then open wide these eyes and
become silently myself seeing who will believe
  (whispers hoodozhnik;and having whispered opens peesahtel's eyes
&—tovarich unsmiling suddenly Kemminkz saw,framed in the futile
porthole,
  Odessa)

while anything that's left of whom dazedly adjusts K's gahlstook,feebly afar
off Jack-of-all-trades ringrangs his superschoolbell . . . pochehmoo?probably
breakfastless. Thereupon leaving our dude fast asleep with his neatliest hair
ensconced in a net,we stagger grimly parody-forward. Sit. Lonely gulping
in wasness parody-koffyeh crunching parody-hlyeb. Totter lonelier to the
top deck . . .

dadada.

Not 1 one inch has Mering budged.

Not 1 one centimeter has Russia receded.

("peut-être demain"?)

"gumornig"—it's of

course Jerusalem pop—"I gut some news"(just to make parody-
everything parody-perfect)"we're leaving"(who sputters beaming)"in
Haffan Hour"

"do" loneliest "you really think so?"

"think?"(his eyebrows independently begin orchestrating a hurt
glance of mild surprise)"I KNOW it!" Which isn't all he KNOWs.
Nyetnyetnyet. E.g. i.e. viz. and for instance

everything here in Russia(Q:what would become of pop-and-spouse
if,by some some curious—some quite unexampled if not positively
unique—collaboration of paralyzed time and hypnotized space we should
ever leave Russia? A:probably nothing)well everything here in Russia
isn't politics and that's where you're wrong in saying it is because what
you say isn't right you just haven't travelled so naturally you wouldn't
be able to understand you wouldn't say that if you'd been anywhere and
had things explained to you see because what you say is just superficial
but underneath everything everything's different I mean the hole point
in this everything here in Russia is economics. Politics doesn't exist.
Politics is the mouthpiece of economics it's like the violin(sic)which is
the expression of the inner man(sic)playing

"but everybody here" wearily And How objects our parody-heroless
"seems to play the violin"

tut. That's just your ignorance you see the way it is you just can't grasp
the fundamental issues everything here in Russia is economics now take
the fight between Stalin you've heard of Stalin and Trotsky you know
Trotsky well take the fight they had it was all economics it wasn't politics
at all politics don't exist the hole thing was like this Trotsky he said to
hell with the peasants see that's what Trotsky said just keep that in mind
and what did Stalin say when Trotsky said that well here's what he said
when Trotsky said to hell with the peasants Stalin he said no that's what
he said see Stalin he said no see so there you are Trotsky saying to hell
with the peasants and Stalin saying no well now listen here's the hole
point see the hole point is this why did Stalin say what Stalin said when
Trotsky said to hell with the peasants huh when Trotsky said what he

said why did Stalin say no huh because that's what Stalin said see Stalin he said no and that's the hole point see that's what I'm asking you see I'm asking you why did Stalin say what Stalin said when Trotsky said what he said?

"I give it up" faintly admits heroless

well now the answer to that question is very interesting because it proves what I said and maybe you don't remember what I said I said here in Russia everything is politics I mean economics not politics no that's what you said politics see remember that remember you said everything was politics here and I said no I said politics is just a mouthpiece of economics remember my saying that and then remember what I said I said Stalin and Trotsky remember and Trotsky he said to hell with the peasants and Stalin he said no remember that and remember I said keep that in mind and then remember what I said I said why did he say no that's what I said when Trotsky said what he said why did Stalin say no and you don't know why you don't know do you you don't know why Stalin said no do you no I thought so well now listen I'm going to tell you something very interesting I'm going to tell you what else Stalin said see this is what he said he didn't just say no just like that O no he said no because see and that's the hole point if he just said no that would be different see but he didn't he said no because not just no see that's the hole point and now I know what you want to know you want to know what else he said don't you when Trotsky he said to hell with the peasants Stalin he said no because and you want to know because what don't you I thought so well I don't blame you because it's really very interesting in fact it proves what I said see now listen here's what Stalin said Stalin said this he said no because Russia is seventy-five percent peasants

"where's your wife?" I ask desperately

O she's terrible she's bad today my wife she's had cramps for three days now just simply awful listen you know something I had terrible cramps yesterday myself for three hours solid no really but I feel better now it must have been the food terrible isn't it and what service just simply awful pretty soon I'm going right to the captain of this boat and ask him right out because of course I speak Russian like I speak English and you know he's nice the captain of this boat very nice and young quite a young fellow I'm going to ask him for some paregoric for my wife say listen you know something you know it's a funny thing when my wife and I first came here I couldn't speak at all not a word no really

isn't that funny but then well I just don't know I guess something must
have happened I just seemed to you know suddenly remember it all

"just like riding a bicycle" I said. He(frowned)nodded. "Or skating"
I said. He(nodded)frowned. "Or dying—"

whistles

—11:53—

. . . she moves,does Franz . . .

behold,

the quailess(miles aeons)shifting now droops gradually(away)
& on it almost noone only perhaps a few and it who unhe waves sheless
wave . . . drooping to(shifting)gether now with 1 blackish that with a
reddish bow a losing much paint freighter labelled KING EDWARD!
we—(not French)Franz we Mering(not Marine)departing are from
this breakwater the paralysed harbour spins gradually the defunct town
the mouldy cityless of Odessa it's(a soundless eternal)raining(sound)
quietly(foreverish)very raining really q-u-i-t-e(raining raining)aeons(raining)miles Raining(away)grey rain cold rain dahsvee al(ways rain)ing
dahnyah &

"now I'm a type" Jerusalem proclaims "who's constipated. I can't"
ponderously "move my bowels without an oil or sumpen;but" radiant
"here—you know that bread?well. In Russia" he cried "I never missed
once"

parody-our-middaymeal passed like unto a dream(& we're moving . . . !)
and occasionally pop,pop of whom all his travels haven't yet made a
sailor,stutters:mutters thicktimidly—"she's goin round!"—grips des.per.ate.
ly his;paro;dy,knife(! . . . vingmov 're we)a smallish alertful passenger with a
fine little boy in tow Russians now glibly to dude who painfully translates
that paraît the captain is merely trying out the compass—whatever that
may not and may mean,or whatever may mean the factless that ever since
breakfastless all our electric lights have been going full tilt;or

soon I know.

We're back,in Odessa of
course(abeam's the parody-breakwater with its un(tiny)lit
lightnonhouse)MERDE

—but

soft:

376

softer;
     softest,O

SomeThing's actually happening. Not merely really. Now you can feel
actually somEthinG in the airless . . . & ecco!—alongside,yesterday:
yesterday itself,in person;via those 2 these And How antique Gay-Pay-
Oo launches—well . . . that is encouraging;maybe we're kind of moving
backward since we you know can't move sort of forward. Maybe there'll
be Kiev and Moscow and N and the very Paris I left at the very moment
I left(that's something!)—1,wallowing expectantly at the very foot of a
mysteriously by our good shipless emanated ropeladder,oncelaunch is
held off-and-on(by that youthless-with-a-rope perched upon its stern by
this dotard-with-a-boathook crouched upon its bow)something looks
like somehow business! . . . & now verily appear 3 ecco mysterious
strangers
    (a)cadaverous officer with obese portfolio(b)soldier in green
cap(c)foxfaced civilian carrying(pochehmoonyezneyeoo)large kettle
    & all dropping by the ladder win now launchonce safely—Bill the
Boathook,instanter,grunts!into nearby speakingtube—an invisibly
industrious engineer cranks andcranks andcranksand cranksandcranksand
cranksandcranksandcranks and—choo-choo goes-byebye-goes launch-
away(Bill and Ralph the Rope dropping inward)goes-choo-& all
choo-3-strangers-mysterious-simultaneously lift their mysterious trio
of various sundry headgears to 1 to that most battered this old socialist
Mering(not Tchicherin)O so farewell solong so be it and so's your old
    ,by;god:we're;actually,Off
    —yes.
    Actually. Now,at 1 exactly:30 P.M. on. Tuesday,June precisely
9,begins. The very same in fact identical voyage which merely. And
really or so to speak began to begin at 4 P.(miles)M.(years)on uncertainly
Monday June certainly 8
    MCMorwhathaveyou?I have
    Hallelujah
    (amen)

. . . and(O no they're not like you hear the gee pee you they do good all
the time for instance just listen to this there was an American woman
who came all the way from American to visit her sister in Russia well

it seems the sister had really been secretly speculating in American
dollars and one fine day she made the mistake of advertising a sale of
her furniture in a newspaper called Izvestia but they knew all about her
the gee pee you because that's their business)I fell(they have to know all
about everything all the time because they have to otherwise you know
the proletariat would be victimised well so the gee pee you just answered
the advertisement and some of their men'in disguise they came to see
her and they were very nice and they agreed to buy all the furniture
and they left a deposit and said goodbye and then of course they turned
right around and arrested her for speculation see well the woman was
kept in jail for two months see and then she was tried and then she was
given two years and they sent her off somewhere away from Moscow
for two)into a deep(years just as a punishment for speculating well do
you know when that woman's sister came on all the way from America
just to see her do you know what happened do you know the gee pee
you those fine people they released the criminal in the custody of her
sister for two hole days no really can you imagine why in America she'd
have been kept locked up why the police would have treated her like
a criminal why nobody would have been allowed to go anywhere near
her not even her own family but the gee pee you is different the gee pee
you isn't really police at all they're fine unselfish human beings the gee
pee you is doing good all the)slumber . . .
    transposing
    into colour and
    quickness diving into laughter a
    youngest now ocean plucked by white breeze
    we're lazying and dawdling toward the Azores creeping in immense
sunlight dreamingfully suddenly cries everyone rushing up out almost
tipping-clear-over this world's by-far-the-feeblest oldest than-it-none-
slower freighter:Mormugão,20 from New Bedford -something days to
Lisboa;O then everyone danced wonderfully laughed everyone sang
everyone cried Look!& it was dolphins
    more
    . . . (it's simply wonderful the factories they have their own theatres
and wallnewspapers and everything we)than ⁹/₈(saw two lists the workers
had posted them themselves and one was called heroes and it was all of
the workers who'd done the five year plan in three years and the other
was)expecting to—dare you now open your(called slackers and it was a

very small list O just a few names written on a camel I mean a picture
of a camel and those workers were all of them pleading to have their
names taken off the camel you know when everybody's doing their best
it somehow don't feel good to be different)eyes? . . . At
   no-sun-no-laughter-no-dancing-but
   . . . At
Last
   !No
       Shore.

Esquire,alias heaven knows who—he's meanwhile been faithfully trying
to fill unfillable wasness(alias our parody-diningroom)with sundry
brands of(canned or phonographic)culture—suggests "thé";the man
with the boy—who has also(no thanks to feeble)discovered a samovar's
whereabouts;who moreover doesn't need to be told that Marx helps those
that help themselves—joins us. How(offering exports,he inquires)are
Afghanistan's diplomatic relations with soviet Russia?—Thus(rhythmically
twitching his particoloured suspenders,my immaculate cabincompanion
blushfully replies)and so.—You wouldn't(expressionlessly to myself
remarks boyman)think he was an Afghanistanian,would you.—
"Nyet"(agree I very wouldn'tthinkishly. Myself's fuzzy(à la Kipling)wuzzy
idea of an Afghanistanian being somebody more or less 7 feet tall with hair
all over him her or it and a poisonous spear in 1 hand;less or more yelling its
his or her bushy head off)"du tout."—O but there are many "gens sauvages
chez nous"(blushful,reading my thought,asserts)"il-y a même des gens très
difficiles!"—Civilization's a(with an almost-wink the boyman solemnly
proclaims)wonderful thing,simply(scowling at almost-entering pop . . .
who promptly changes his Palestine mind and retires in vile order)wonder-
ful. I wonder(this philosophical personage murmurs meward)if you
happen to know a former "concessionaire de crayons" whom his admiring
friends call the doctor? Or perhaps you have met a former professor of
Slavic languages who's temporarily occupying the post of a temporarily
absent newspaper correspondent?or possibly his charming wife,the
celebrated daughter of a worldfamed American proletarian writer?—
(Cautiously)I shouldn't wonder($\frac{1}{2}$ I reply)if I'd had the very great honour
of knowing all three.—At first I took you for a certain(he murmurs)
American who came to the Turkish consulate in Moscow some few weeks
ago and gave us a long tale of woe ending with the pathetic statement

that people were pursuing him and he didn't know anybody. That was a mistake(he said gently)on my part. (Pause).—Are you by any chance acquainted with a socalled companion-of-the-way named(the flowerbuyer)?—Acquainted with him I am(he answers)indeed.—Who seemed to be worrying(I venture)about getting a passport from his native land?—It's not easy(Mr. boyman grimly said).—What seems to be the trouble?(I ask).—Nothing(shrugging)except that two million Russians would leave Russia tomorrow if they possibly could. (Pause). But in the case of a Russian writer like your friend(he continues)the passport problem is less annoying than the valuta problem;valuta being a quite indispensable adjunct to foreign travel. . . . Why(severely)didn't you leave Russia by Berlin or Poland?—Because I(rain:rain reminding me of Rain reminding me of Head;Head reminding me of dogs-and-stove and . . . suddenly,realize I forgot to;didn't:bring a little . . . earth)because somehow Odessa sounded more(guiltily)interesting.—What are you going to do when you reach Constantinople?—Well,I've been told there are boats direct to America.—There may be;but I doubt it.—At least there's a fast train to Paris.—Which is both expensive and hot(he sniffed. Pause).—Anyway(I brazenly said)it'll be better than Russia.—"Oui"(solemnly And How the boyman nodded)"c'est la misère là-bas."—"Parfaitement"(nods the dude solemnly).—Tell me(emboldened I)can a foreigner,who is so unfortunate as to marry a Russian,get his wife out?—He(grimly boyman)can if he persists. But it's very difficult;especially for Americans. And if the man should succeed,the woman is given an exit visa forever. (Smiling)It's not logical(he daintily said). . . . But what(simply)is? . . . ("Everything's a dream" the musician said simply) . . . now take those two accursed Jews:they're just dumb tourist-sheep,they've gone wherever they were told to go and they've seen whatever they were supposed to see;well,as a result they know absolutely everything. You can't argue with cattle like that. Why those creatures are a thousand times as blatantly enthusiastic as the very most enthusiastic professional communist who ever lived!—"Bête" the dude grins "tout-à-fait bête! C'est drôle;pas?"—Unbelievable(I sympathize)and it's much worse for me,because I speak English,because I'm an American.—"C'est vrai"(grinning).—Do you know(I add)what the husband told me?he was boasting as usual about how he'd seen really everything,how he'd been really everywhere,how he'd done really and truly everything,and finally I couldn't stand any more and I asked him pointblank Did you ever try a Russian meal?—"Et qu'est-ce qu'il a répondu?"(dude,grinning,asks).—He answered that once,once mind you,he did try a Russian meal;but he found to his very great surprise that he couldn't eat the meat.—EAT the MEAT!(boyman explodes)good GOD! why,there ISN'T any meat for the Russians!

(thereafter descending,fuzzywuzzy our dude dons wondrously ornate pyjamas—the gift,paraît,of a most adoring Russian-born . . . but luckily for her not inhabiting Russia . . . spouse. Who also,paraît,showers her lord and master with multifarious blankets quilts etc. if not(I strongly suspect)1,2,3,neatly And count 'em How pressed complets vestons.

And now ornately fuzzy strolls with wuzzy me Franz Mering's loftiest deckless. Ornately strolling loftily fuzzy now explains that things are so perfectly bad là-bas that he,himself,in person,slept with a Russian girl,not a picture,in the Hotel London in Odessa for 1,not 2,not 3,pair of silk stockings and she was only 18 and she gave him her photo and he said Suppose my Russian wife should see it and she shrugged Tell her it's your "amie" and he replied "Aaah-hoh!NON!" And paraît que the dirty people are now on top down-there;but will the dirty people remain on top?"Aaah-hoh!NON!"

—"I gut it!" pop suddenly rushing at us stutters me grabbing "here it is!listen!"

pyjamas elegantly And How pauses

"what" I say;freezingly.

"No but here's the" wildly pop pops "difference—in America a man don't work too hard because he might be out of a job;but in Russia that aint so:see?get it?huh?"

"wonderful!" I commend icily

"sure it's wonderful!" pop stutters "in Russia you don't have to worry!everything's taken care of!everything's done for you!get it?you're free!Free!FREE—"

"SAM!" a voiceless rang

". . . yes mother" wilting,he("I'll be right back!")hurries

next we have:Forsooth.

A seaman bold was he,actuated by(aren't we all?)mixed motives. Such as the highly laudable desire to further his negligible—about on a par with my Russian—English. Also a not to be underestimated evangelical impulse to do a seaman's bit or trick in the come-to-Lenin-all-ye-capitalists moveunmovement. Plus,last but not least,plain downright honest curiosity:that very greatest of all the virtues.

A gentle being with a horse's face

childlike

very proud is Forsooth of the crew's "clubhouse";particularly he stresses the fact that tovarich captain eats with tovarich crew(whereas "my-very good-friend" the second mate—who acts as if he were being punished for something—"he-eat with-you pas-sen ger" than which I incidentally can conceive no more awful punishment). Very excited is bold Forsooth by something which once occurred in Italy:there it seems the crew of a Russian ship exchanged visits with the crew of an American "export line" boat("on-the chim-ney is-an E")and there it seems was clean fun with real things to eat and delicious speeches ad infin. and even . . . he smiles shyestly . . . dancing and then(O joy!)it turned out that the E's 3rd mate had once upon a time been a member of the I.W.W.! Very very definite is that bold seaman Forsooth all about the world. After France—alias Marseilles,alias la Canabière,alias a bar which I can't quite identify—Germany is apparently gayest;Italy—alias apparently Genoa—sad;England—alias,if you please,London—"big historical building";Norway and Sweden "no gay". Very much indeed Forsooth became delighted when once upon a time an English captain at Marseilles borrowed money from his crew,once upon a time who were also very much delighted. All in all and altogether seaman Forsooth approves of Marseilles which tovarich Forsooth solemnly describes as an "in-ter na-tion al-port".

Item:he REFUSES a not-for-mere-Russians papierohsa &

GIVES me 1 of his own private personal strictly-for-home-consumption cheeroots.

O yes,Forsooth enjoys now and then American cigarettes:especially the camel. Assures me(simplemindedly allgrinning)that Russian boats are models of sanity of probity of goodwill of all the(except 1)virtues—e.g. engine workers,says F,have "of-ten er-hol id-ay be-cause work-har der." Was really himself on a "three mast barque" with a cargo of wood during very terrible storm off the Orkney(?perhaps)Islands. Did not die. Was himself really on another boat with a bad cargo,a very bad cargo:stone;which shifted;and so one sailor who was an Italian really got "fright-en"—jumped right in—whereupon apparently all the other sailors never have really stopped their laughing

. . . while this bold seaman Forsooth and I are conversing,sundry and various unmistakably members of Franz's soi-disant crew survey(from the most divers points of vantage)us. More and more acute the chaperoning becomes. And I'm not unsorry when

"ex-cuse me-I go-now for-lit tle-sleep be-cause mid-night I-go on-the watch"

(&

salutes)childlike. Grins.

"—Comment dites-vous 'je ne sais pas parler anglais'?"(desperately esquire whispers)"'I Do Not speak English'?"

"'I don't speak English'" whisper I sympathetically

"'I DO NOT'would be more"(Sam's partially from cramps recovered helpmate helpfully corrects)"correct,wouldn't it?"

"O take uh pill!" her husband said wearily

. . . & amidships there's a ragged stripling;kne-eling,before rusted vise . . . in the rusted,gnarled chunk of wood;on which I presently descry nothing less than or more than pencilled outline of 1 shoesole . . . patiently the(with a broken roped handled saw)kn-eel-er:saws sawssaws s-a-w-s a-long the-outline . . .

meanwhile!over us!over all life!over sea sky & air!

(Magnificent

—in whom here and here(see)are blossoming—

Forms of Destiny)

—few,early,stars—

. . . lift & the following hills-of-wake;sink & cry the of mown waters . . .

Space

        ("you know" pop said "I gut a drugstore in Buffalo—"

"so you told me"

"yeh,but I didn tell you this:I gut seven clerks;four at the fountain")

(from behind us)"yes and when we have guests for bridge you know I always serve ore-dove they're well you know so tasty everybody likes—"

"Take uh Pill" wheeling he groaned "TAKE uh PILL!"

silence.

Then

". . . I always travel with my own toiletpaper" omnithepotent globetrotter most sepulfalsecralteethly remarked "it's the best brand"

—pause—

"See Pee Doubleyou."

Splendours:Forms;fates,over us!

("but I made a mistake" he "one day" whispers "I put my hand in the wrong pocket and" sheepishly "used a rouble")

air Sun:

cry(ing thick)ish(troll grun)ting(is ho)sing(decks oaf)ma(king ev)er
(yone)jump(grunt cry)ing(gnome)

ecco professorial & with a goatee spectre approaches;studies the whirl-
unwhirling disk of
    Walker's
    patent
    CHERUP
    Mark 11
    SHIP LOG
and,unto myself bowing,politely observes "kraseevayah pagohda"
    . . . which it is.

Good morning(said the man with the boy).— Good morning.— I saw you
talking to an officer of this boat yesterday;what(the boyman asks)did he
report?—O,he told me(which he did)how everybody was so happy and the
captain eats with the crew and the clubroom is being repainted and under
the five year plan Russia's fleet will be seventy percent larger . . . —Hm(the
boyman smiled)hm. Well,here's something he apparently forgot to tell you:
every Russian ship has(lowering his voice)in her crew a communist—who
may be a mate and who may be an oiler,but whatever he does or pretends to
do he's the real boss. Comrade socalled captain's job is merely to navigate this
comrade socalled ship;comrade communist whatnot's far more important
function is to note every word,every action,every tendency,of her socalled
personnel. You can easily imagine what it means . . . "tiens!" here comes Mr.
supercommunist himself;looking a trifle pale to be sure,but that is perhaps
only natural—he vomited all last night

omni(immediately buttonmeholing)potent says boy(disapnowpearing)
man is a most remarkably intelligent fellow it seems last night they
enjoyed heart-to-heart talk and m.r.i. confided to omnipotent listen in
Turkey everything's terrible bad just simply awful and then he stated in
his opinion bolshevism was the only salvation of a dying

"why do you suppose worlds die?" we wonder

worry,that's it;worry about tomorrow. Everything that's wrong with everything is wrong because of worry about tomorrow. "I like a country where you don't have to worry about" pop sighs thickly "tomorrow. I came here;but my heart is dare"—my heart is in America,worrying about tomorrow,worrying about possible new competitors,worrying about whether the chainstores will undersell me,worrying because I once refused sixty thousand for my store and I don't suppose I could get fifty thousand now and I dropped fifty thousand in the market and the very day I left a loan was called in so I had to fall back on my wife's savings and her brother's a bank executive . . . worrying always worrying,worrying about the fact that I had twenty-five hundred when I got to Russia and right this minute I only got a thousand making fifteen hundred I spent for two but anyhow everything's paid as far as Palestine—

"you're coming back to Russia,I presume?"

(shrug and clinching of eyes)"naw. How could I?" but listen just the same I had the idea to sell my store for fifty thousand and then deposit my fifty thousand with the soviet government and then take my eight percent interest in roubles and "live like a king"(SIC)in Russia:of course with the understanding I'd get my principal back in dollars whenever I wanted;O that could be arranged with Amtorg all right;well,believe me,if it couldn't they'd never see a red cent of Sammy's fifty thousand!listen,tell me something,why didn't you visit a single factory in Moscow?now I went to a rubber factory myself,it goes in one end and comes out finished,there's two girls and two doctors and every ten minutes the doctors examine the girls' eyes isn't that wonderful?listen,tell me,what's all this talk about capitalism encourages Initiative?Initiative for what?Initiative to undersell people?Initiative in cheating people?huh?that's the thing I'm asking you!I'm asking you is it right that thirty-five rich guys control the whole population?is it?and yet you're complaining to me(nb.I wasn't)about the dictatorship of the proletariat!dictatorship?why what else have we got in America but dictatorship?huh?look at how you and I are!look at America!look at thirty-five rich guys. Day dictate to us,don't Day?don't Day dictate what you and I do and how you and I live and what clothes you and I wear?huh?of course Day do!so what happens?why you and I we worry you and I we worry about tomorrow!but does a Russian worry?he does not!why should he?just as soon as a Russian gets a Russian's money a Russian spends it all because a Russian's sure of a Russian's job because

Russia's a country where everybody don't have to worry about anything!
... how's that?huh?say listen what do you mean this boat ought to be
one class?—"Day don't claim Day GUT socialism—Dare BUILDING
socialism!"—and just you wait and see what's going to happen!just you
stop worrying about(I wasn't)today and look into the future!well what
do you see?rosy is no name for it!why in the rosier than rosy socialist
future everybody will work two or three hours a day then everybody
will do what everybody wants all the rest of the time there won't be no
worrying done by nobody see because everybody won't have nothing
to worry about understand? ... etcetera. Whereupon these possibly
immortal words

"earning a living will be like going to the toilet"

sun;air

"I aint no fanatic!" he screamed at lunchless.

"I should hope not" quoth nonsoup-swallowing our unhero

"But let me" crazily "tell you one thing:they gut the best sanitayriums
in the hole world right here in Russia!"

"That's good" we said. "A friend of mine was telling me all about
a socialist lady who came here to build socialism. By way of doing
which,she went"(up he-eat with- quickly looks)"crazy"

"wudduhyuhmean crazy?"

"I mean bughouse."

"But . . ." staring "but . . .—but what should make her crazy?"

"what makes anyone crazy?"

pause. "Maybe" solemnly he suggests "she was crazy with
enthusiasm?"

"maybe" we shrug.

"You couldn't have seen nothen of Russia" suddenly omnipotent
challenges.

"O yes" we trust we are laughing lightly "I could,and a helluva lot
more than you—"

"but . . . but you don't speak the language!"

"I have eyes though" we trust

"—well,you see in the" Sam's(crampfully heading tableless pea)And
interposes How(green spouse)"old"(soo)"days"(thingly)"there were a
great many places where Jews" sic "were not allowed to go."

Actually!

I dropped my lozhka.

The boyman totters. Amazed fuzzy wuzzy gaped. And believe it or "my-very good-friend" who eats with passengers ½smiles

then

"NOW it's DIFferent!"(pop gloated fiercely)"—remember the time there wasn't no train?"

Eyerolling "that private car!" peagreen

"and so our guide"(gloats pop)"telegraphed ahead and I never see such a thing . . . all the furniture reel mahogany not a scratch on it. Was there"

"just" corrobo(peagreen)rates "imagine"

"there was twelveofus and we" poppopping "took the Hole thing:Six Compartments"

"and a bathtub" coyly she murmurs

"and you gut your own toilet!" he triumphs "how convenient that is!" Pause. "But my wife and I"(pop(gloat)ping)"we gut the best compartment!"

. . . do I believe which?

da da da . . .

Hav(ing bel)"we serve lunch" ched he(said)

"you serve lunch" I echo

"fifty cents"(he)said and(belched)

pause. The,blushing,dude wrassles;vainly;an inedibility. Boyman: un-eating:gazed nowhereward

"what sort of" politely "lunch?" I inquire

"—well" pea "really we" green "have access to all the" gushes "best" bestly "clubs and we never once found anything like it at six times the price. Why really some friends of ours came back from Europe just before we left and do you know they told us we certainly are glad to get food again and do you know a group of young people from the art school who take our lunch every day said when they heard we were going to Russia you'd better take along some of your own stuff you won't get anything over there like this—"

pause.

Gutturally("if our boy was here!")mutter perfectly false. "He"(prideful) "says Some people eat to live but I live to eat"

"we have a" bestly cultureful "little daughter" informs "too" voiceless
guttural "he's only thirteen but" outchesting "—big?why he's as big
as Seventeen!" Proud(pop)ly "I Want him to be Big"

"well I" cul-ture-ful "think it's natural for" voiceless "boys to eat,don't
you?"

(time
     or un
     existing(or
     because,game-
     less of ghosts &
     fools;invisibly
     believed disease of measurable nonthings)
     was.
Was(everyone
             except myself
             -less seemed to consult whispering
             toys:except my un-
             self,everyone seemed
             measuring how many whispers of
             seeming exactly of whispering
             what Time it)when
hell
     did not disappear.
     And
     did
     not
     disappear
     ;when hell
     was)
but hell and must ought fear disappeared. But finally even a ridiculous
ship departs almost bravely. Steering out into what becauselessness.
And,silently my unself becomes I. Gazing I;I(from ridiculous)silent(from
almost brave)ly(I staring into oceanic afternoon)perceive

—the World's
   coast

　　　　—grim & conventional;spattered with grey ruins,dilapida-
tions(whenlessly which opens like a
　　dream.

)...(we,
　　un,big en,ter
　　a trif,ling har,bour)...
　　　　　　　　　　　　crisp!2
　　　　　　　　　　　　launches make for
　　　　　　　　　　　　dow-dy-Franz

& over & whom strolls & horseface. Gently clumsily & who summons
all each & everyone
　　(venite,adoremus)
into a & pahzhahloostah will you come into my & said the to the stifling
parlour situated & how at lousy Mering's so to speak nose
　　everyone each all surrounding stand
　　stand all surrounded wait are each by
　　w-a-i-t-i-n-g
　　(fragrant
　　ghosts in
　　tatters;stinking spooks
　　in rags;odoriferous And
　　How denizens of can you
　　believe it bags sacks
　　or whathaveyou)I
　　　　　　　　　　have curiosity.
Not the unmerely ferocious,unmerely contemptuous, the perhaps
unmerelyboth,stance of twain erect with("shine?")moonbright weapons
　　hyper(Turkish)cops
not the demisuspicious glance of;sitting immaculately;twain
semidespising
　　super-customsbrutes-ofthecrescent
(let 'em twirl their dread mustachios!)can move your perhaps
correspondent quite as much as this e.g. how pallid viz. maculate i.e.
slenderly & unweaponed threadbare envelope or socalled nottomention
captain:patiently who
　　—a spectre—

and even very humbly;beckons . . . & reallytruly caviar(upon preposterously thick hunks of almostwhite almostbread)plus 2(count 'em)bottles Nahzahn appear before capitalism's emissaries. Rudely-very who,shoving-aside-untasted these-not-imaginable-luxuries,begin now their most dreadful

  and

  how

preparations

  (possibly whereby moreorless a cargo of lessormore unbeings shall attain a perhaps and World?

  but)

most me moves this—clutching for undear nonlife rotting 2 $1 bills—sh-ing feeblestly nonmangoblin. Ever whose idiot . . . drooling always often moaning sometimes clucking . . . unson threatens to attract the notice of dread twirling dreadfuls. (& I supposed that I had known agony!—O mothergoblin of a than any universe older faceless;and such eyes,flowers of complete pain:what can you do? You sh must not hide your monster you cannot sh calm it). Quietly now approaches 1 little item of the unimperial Russian navy;smiling now to citizeness goblin,stoops(gently)beside loathsome droolmoancluck: points. To a lowhung unbig wallmirror . . . and in which suddenly viewing itself,loathsome allfreezes:looks . . . Looks . . . and LOOKS. Silently not-clucking not-moaning-scarcely silently-drool-ing. (Then . . . out of enchantment entering unenchantment,laughs(softly: sputtering;googoo,bubbles!)& . . . reenters magically a the soothing mirrormystery)

  (I have

  curiosity).

Horseface comrade Forsooth,my life is in your hands. A little passport is my life. A little passport has disappeared in a heap stack pile of passports clumsily shoved and gently by Horseforsoothface at twirlings

  (1 by 1)passports are from pile stack heap(cautiously or almost as if they contained dynamite)by twirling A removed. & opened. Name is called(by twirling A). Denizen spook ghost answers(cautiously whose features are with a little photograph—what magic!—by twirlings A and B compared). Question(where are you stopping in Constantinople?) Answer. Something is written in several places(including a passport)by

both twirlings. A little passport is by twirling B presented cautiously to the

— . . . sud(be)den(side)ly(me)fuzzydudewuzzy ob(sotto)serves(voce) probably at least K of Franz Mering The Ghostship's pour ainsi dire passengers won't get their visas ce soir & won't go ashore tonight . . .

yes. But I don't happen to believe in probably

no. I happen to believe in happen,in impossibly to believe;I in I believe but not in probably ever reality:never;nyetimpossi,Nyet

but(look)now(at myself winking gently)horsecom clumsy facerad slyly stacks this pack(inserting slyly toward its top my little;now:But . . . twirling A shuffles

)& little capcom Kem-min-kz disa . . .

ppears

    —to?

        Re

!YES

I am

Kahmin Koomeegs Kommosh

Anything you like never

mind trying to pronounce it

you twirler Yes I'm American am

only passing through Istanbul en route to

stopping at("quel hotel?" demand of

fuzz. Wuzz repeats. I repeat

1 blooded hostelry 1

veritable Ritz-de

-la-Ritz)

      THANKS.

(Never before glimpsed)Do You Like(via the very purest Parisian)Paris? (phantom this accosts shoddy tiniest but a somehow)So Do I(styleful fe-notnonman-male me now & smiling who & adds wonderingly) Especially The Trees The Avenues And Gardens And Trees The Beautiful Trees

unbig departs from:trifling

   . . . O,now everything begins

everything expands increasing now even the air celebrates(the sky's
building within the sky a steep incredible pleasure out of what far Forms
unbelievable;springs a sun,but no mere world:1 atom—of blood of life of
all)every-and-thing & opens lifting quietly rising growing-and-upward
infinitely opening & throughout coolness alive always deepening growing
beside wonder and height rising among promise and dream lifting upon
immeasurable
whereless
silence
whom float the unimagined swim the not guessed or at whose eternal
brainlike deepness drift the shy immortal
wanderers invisibly(and visible pilgrims fearless
of no thing conscious except themselves moving within themselves
drifting by their own light swimming a selfcreating everywhere now
which is against our life possibly more close than dying)now impossibly
beyond our mind less than death near floating futures easily how past
how indolently present voyaging toward endlessness brave(travellers
wandering always always not despairing unresting visible now and now
invisible & always pilgrims never tiring fearing
swift dolls of unutterable wish dressed with mystery and hope)
poems.

& ghost-cries . . . ghost-gestures
                    look—
(new Stars!Stars not-of-heaven awfully
begin;here
multiplying suddenly become the
very arising magically
is:looms!a
. . . now . . .
allblossoming finite Firmament of throbbing frenzied Ifs of leaping
fiercely Whys. Now insane structure of To Be;finally sprouting terror
ecstacy and semblance—now a profound a trivial an architecture of
mortality—moves at us like a
Yes)unfaltering
& toward our ghostship comes,inhabited by thousands upon millions
of manlights,the World

with its smell hints its follies hatreds laughter mistakes whispers its sins(a murdering and mimicking)rhythmic devoutly through incessant birth a perishing World(fatally Whose womb hugs the sparkling seed of timelessness)fearful unfearing(greedy a most and hungry)dream(World) supreme unmeaning doomless alive spiral(never to be imagined or subdued)World of disillusion and of illusion,always forgetting no complexity of imperfection always through doubtful certainties remembering each contradiction surely and beyond hideous victory all beautiful disasters . . .

Langu
      while
            packing
    idly "vous savez il" casually remarks fuzzy "y a des types très méchantes là-bas qui" much enjoy murdering strangers;you'd better stick with me,I know the ropes:surtout,don't give your baggage to anyone—
    (& his advice disappeared. As tumult swarmed through our porthole)
    tumult,the child of . . . as,gripping baggage,American & Afghanistanian emerge grimly . . . pandemonium:milling wildly And How all around the solemnly itself trying to anchor Franz Mering are(and hither sprinting rush thither madly colliding disentangling crazily and darting)boatlets glitter areel with unhumanly gesticulating screaming shrilly threatening dully bellowing cursing and thislike imploring thatish(here faces hands backs here)begins skilfully made of nightmare
    nightmarish & enclosing vividly(vividly nightmarishly everywhere laid over the)skilfully with lights athrob waveless(everywhere upon the chewed with wakes waveless wave)an unfathomable the tone of wailing
    not,sorrow. A spherically mysterious,than sorrow deeper impossibly larger richer(something only and dreamingly true. Impossibly which may or actually wear sorrow only as a dream may wear a universe)some without past or future immeasurable and always itself predicting intensity complete resonance directionless
    . . . which only to feel,have I abandoned hell . . . Aliveness,never by whatever theorem contained;not unpain not nonjoy:Being. Not speech—Breathing

&(

   . . . s-Pl-UtT-eRiSh,chain-quake;grateofboatlets

)

   aboard now leap myriads:

—"le" in such uproar as makes(gripping fiercely baggage)me dizzy "consul soviétique" wuzz very calmly mutters;bowing,to that every(bowing)where(nodding)hatless grimly cheerful noodle which has just swirled up a gangplank . . . "mon"—and my 3rd mentor presents this remarkably Eddie(bouncing eyefully)Cantorish(surging with dilating with hysterical with excitement)individual—who shakes my hand fiercely,gives me 1 quick huge stare;then—turning to dude,pommels weird night with gladly uncouth syllables

   and hands grab tug our bags voices implore hint command and

   . . . wheeling frère speaks "vous êtes seul?"

"oui"

From Paris?

Yes

Know this town?

Not at all

Where you staying?

"Ce monsieur"(alias fuzzy)gave me the name of a—

What was your Paris hotel?

In Paris I had a studio

Where

Near the Gare Montparnasse

Moderate rent,eh?

Very

Want a moderate price hotel here?

Surely

(with a You see?gesture to dude,frère resumes violently uncouthing) and tug hands grab hint command wail voices implore and

   Frxchtg!(or something quoth Eddie)whereupon 1 fiendfaced crouching wailer gloatfully pounces

—shall I(over-1-shoulder yell,pointing to down-the-gangplank-rushing valise-&-knapsack)follow?

—yes!(dude yells)in our boat!

—what?

—together!"nous trois!"

(how the)stumbling(devil)seaward now(shall I)and(know)grab(which)
hands hint voices(boat?

seem billions everybody's plucking at American wail pouncer's
vanished

"par ici,Ici,ICI!"—ecco)several wrestling scratching cursing biting
somebodies just have dumped some(mine)things into tipsy tiniest
craft(manned;And How:by 2 of)the entirely quite piratically ferocious
most hogsticking-bloodlapping-sons-of- who

Where are my friends?(sternly of pointing pleading plucking we
demand)

Coming(in especially French a hundred voices)get in,yourself(cry)
quick!(—& if all-at-once 3 big lusty murderous huskies haven't boosted
poietes-kerplunk in-to tipsy tiniest,which . . . skwEEge . . . LiLtS:i-n-t-o
space;wail(into,dark)ing—far(from gangplank Franz and

"MONSIEUR!"

from gangplank.madly beckoning.dude the

"ViEnS!i-c-i—")

"Arrêtez!" poietes addresses briefly 2 And How busily

labouring which thereupon

And How more busily!labour:night's rap(wail)id(ing)LY swallowing;
tiny(d-u-d-e,still beckoning,smallens)

. . . sToP(said poietes

Mering dwindles).

I WILL(I,very sincerely indeed en francais,said;advancing)KILL
you—

—the:2 cringe—leer—

YOU GET BACK THERE IN THE NAME OF GOD AND BE
QUICK

. . . wilt the;twain . . . speechless. Swerves,sicklying-tipsy—toward
expANDing now Franz Mering we. Move—out,of slow(wailing)ly dark.
Ness—slow-ly. Toward. Yzzuf . . . beside whom flutters(with perhaps
the whitest face in the world)frère

That(who screams)Isn't Our Boat!

I Followed My Baggage(I approaching slowly roar)

Kqlzb(or something he snaps at the leer-cringe wilters. Then to)Pick
up those bags and jump in here with—(me)

"il faut" dude peacefully murmurs "faire" while PullPull pulLpulL

pullpull this much larger much & much tipsier(& in which we-3-much-by-all-belongings buried lurk)craft s,1;e:w.s into(Franz leaks-out-of sight)dark "attention". Adding,serenely,that my recent companions would certainly have robbed me of everything I—

Robbed!(splutters the frère)why,they'd have murdered you!

Really?(poietes doubts)

Listen(the amid be(whiteface)longings angrily chatters)you're in Turkey now,understand?people steal and kill!you're not in Europe,understand?anything goes here!

"Il a" offering "parfaitement" cigarettes "raison" murmurs gravely fuzzy-wuzzy

. . . a match's yelp.

pullpull(silence)pUllpUll

What O what in god's name my newborn self expected going-ashore would be like,god knows:a golden carpet laid from dazzlingly bejeweled seastairs to mysteriously beperfumed silence becluttered with moving of discreetly-butnottoo lascivious houris wouldn't have startled our almost our not quite bekidnapped hero in the least

(pity poor realists!

all whose minds cannot wish;

those who do not dare,

have lost their wonder)

. . . but:night's;colour troubling are outlines,but the huge tranquil(w-a-i-l)ity of space murder acute temporal whispers . . . and;I feel a beginning of:dimension . . . hereless and unhere jagged somethings stand up into what stars! & now our hitherto(puLl)silent(pulL)oarsmen,groan &;both(lean:ing)swoon-us-all suddenly throughagulping greatly-white cuRve—(what's?f-l-i-c-k-e-r . . . stOne,embankment;st(oo)ped a figure,the who reaches) . . . now;cautiously bala;ncing,the dude-out steps. Now,care(full,y frère) . . . NOW

(terra

how oddly,how unreally

firma)

I. I am. I am standing

breathing lost dark(w . . . a . . . i . . . l)ness,and smelling the a smallness of land

1 bare damp scarcely lit shed.

Already Franz Mering's ghosts are here:I recognize the(seated on a nearby bench)mother-goblin and her loath-droolmoancluck-some;she's weeping. Beside loathsome squirms a fragment of old burlap,merrily wherein is fishing for inexhaustible toes a cherub;beside the cherub sits an expressionlessly staring rigid boy,whose longest hands frame a mightily sobbing little girl:lurches beside rigid this once-tall now bowed once-very-handsome(face tight with)woman(anguish,tears tumbling from her shut eyes)—that wearing chiefly a hat father of which family squats before mightily and shoves at sobbing a large dark thing of bread. . . . Which loath. Some sees. For. For which. For which loath. For which loath somereach es and . . . reaches:cap-turing(as the shover;shrugging; rises)takes. Lifts . . . Putting toward. Its

now cherub's asleep,handlets together

(the woman's eyes are open;she has taken the sobbing from the rigid and the sobbing's sobless. Now the once handsome holds the once sobbing away from her . . . she pulls slow(ly at wet)ness(at-her-once)dress once(self. And as her now her slowly her pale lips move upon each other nothing fails to happen in a kind of smile))

. . . with a very remarkable exception of a perfectly occult tin trunk,all Afghanistanian and American belongings have drowsily by 1 demiofficial been semiopened. And by Eddie Cantor have been immediately rushed to a neighbouring corner("vous savez,on VOLE ici!" . . . customs officers volent worst of all,I take it). And somehow or other I guess that all isn't going well with the dude—not that the dude turns an immaculate hair;no indeed:even while Eddie feverishly seems to be waiting for somebody else to examine somethingor(that trunk?)other,his dudeship languidly informs myself that once-very- is the Russian wife of a Turk,alias the chiefly hatwearer,who went to Russia "en cachet" and who was located and who was brought back . . . and just now(the dude explains)once-very-handsome said I'm Not Crying For Myself But For My Children . . . & "oui,ils sont des sales types ici" sympathetically he adds,unhatting and becombing his raven mane.—Well,what or whom do we await?that's a question for men and mice. Eddie's so horribly nervous(not to mention ruffled)I don't dare ask him;dude nerve-lessly doesn't quite seem to understand how anything could ruffle anybody. Perhaps I seem to remember that somebody,during out voy(wail)age from Franz Mering,mentioned something about slipping something to someone:perhaps the proper personage to tip somehow or other hasn't appeared?—but how's this?comment?shall we leave our luggage here and call for it in the morning?—I answer emphatically "NYET!"(and jump at that hellword

O well . . .

                    anyway,we aren't any longer in hell!)
we aren't any longer in
we aren't any longer
we aren't any
we aren't
we . . .
12:
     4
      5,by unruffled's whispering toy
—arrives a supercivilian(just as I'd on behalf of the U.S.S.R. etc. managed to slip chocolate to shrug-the-ging chiefly hatwearer & now who offgoes with all his especially once-very shouldering prodigious-miraculous bundle family)arrives the no doubt and of course the long awaited somebody else. Who briefly inspects and with lightning speed okays Americana. . . . Beckons,with grue-some-ly narrowing eyes,at perfectly at perfectly occult at perfectly occult tin

    Nononononono
(Turkishes or whatever Eddie Cantor)
    Yes
    Nonononono
(cries Eddie)
    Yesyes,
(narrowing insists)
    Nononono
    Yesyesyes;
    Nonono
    Yesyesyesyes:
    Nono
    Yesyesyesyesyes.
    No
    YesyesyesyesyesYES!
whereupon(wuzzfuzz's peacefully meanwhile "c'est défendu" smoking)E most very grudgingly produces trunk . . . with hyperproviso that super

shan't on any account open it. Whereupon super commands Cantor to open it. Whereupon Cantor refuses. Super insists. EC agrees . . . with ultraproviso that super shan't on any account look in it. Super insists. "Frère" condescends . . . with infraproviso that super shall only glance at the contents;shall on no account touch anything—

&,trunk unpromptly being opened,super promptly does touch NononononononoNO!(attempting to shut the trunk without taking the trouble to remove super's hand) . . . whereupon out comes super's(the worse for wear)hand,& in that hand a letter

—which is snatched by Brother

resnatched by super—

& Eddie locks the trunk,demands the letter;super refuses:& Cantor opens the trunk;directs super to insert letter,super refuses:whereupon EC commands and super refuses and frère relocks the trunk and brother reopens the trunk and both protagonists threaten(peacefully fuzzwuzz's smoking)menace each other grab wrestle(plunk at the letter)scream pound pointing at their bosoms jump-up-and-down snarl

. . . finally,however,the letter's reinserted—whereupon Eddie Cantor immediately seizes the trunk in his arms and hurries it to a corner. There(he says)that for you you lousy soandso son of a suchandsuch. You show me your credentials(super shouts)you give me your name immediately! Here(says Eddie,holding a visitingcard before super's crimson puss). Give—(super snatches card). You(Cantor leaps at him)why you vile degenerate unmitigated—. Keep away you foul you impossible(super yells)child of andsoforth! Return that card(frère trembling from head to foot shrieks)return it instantly if you care to live. It's none of your thisandthat business what I may please to do with your efing card(super howls) . . .

finally,however,the card's returned—whereupon brother,tapping himself hideously And How cries Frenchfully to me:You will write about this wrong,understand?because you are a wrong-about-writer!yes!you will take down the customless pants of Constantinople's ignoble customs!you will take up the customary offense of your profession in defense of lib liferty and the perhap of suitiness yes!you will positively turn no absolutely leaf unstoned!—

&(wf exhaling tranquilly languidly flips his butt)now super and dilated are squabbling murderously over a mere Afghanistanian suitcase containing a quite unbelievable amount of Because You Like Nice Things:which(it seems)are all for the dude's wife—but suppose they weren't,whose business is it?nobody's;would you like to see his diplomatic passport?no:apparently nobody wants to see anybody's diplomatic passport—well!what's this?this is an inventory:explain it if you can;explain it yourself,why should I?I didn't ask you to explain it,I asked him;you have no right to ask him to explain the contents of this valise!understand?O go to—

so now the ark of the covenant's back again. So now it's hopping from inside the examination-enclosure to faroff portions of the customs-shed. It's skipping hither it's darting thither. Eddie hugs it and runs. Super chases him and tackling they both fall down super regains the Cantor tries to shove super into a bench,down and both they fall all and the falls trunk down rising 2 protagonists call now each stands perfectly motionless other everything impossible

. . . I seem to be guarding the dude's hatde and overcoatluxe

where has everyone gone?

is everyone except me arrested?is everyone settling everything out of court?or is merely everyone murdering every—

Get away(I vainly tell a perhaps porter . . . now all the American all the Afghanistanian luggage has is will been be irrevocably escorted toward a fatal . . . but(tout va bien qui finit bien)and here now comes peacefully my deluxeful beckoning mentor;I thereupon pick up whose overcoat and whose hat and I follow whose beckoning around this

—through that—

into.night;light(dark(unwailing)ness)Aria,

. . . a narrow:asleep street. A small open taxi,already full of Afghanistanian baggage plus Eddie Cantor. FW begins gently climbing over whom

Where are my(myself begs)things?

"Bon!"(a banditish very enthusiastic charioteer assures. Stabbing forefingers at his craft's bow . . . and behold!from the radiatorcap dangles per a strap my knapsack—my valise being tied with string to 1 mudguard)

What do you mean Good?(I ask,amazed)

Firm secure safe Good!(very very very banditish very very enthusi-astically very maintains)

All abroad!(frère commands)

But;my luggage—

It's perfectly safe utterly secure completely firm(the very very very very pushing fiercely me into what's left of a front seat asserts)

"Il a" the dude remarks "parfaitement raison"

Ilah!of all the(wildr eelingj agge)d rides I(either dre)amin(gly or drun)kenl(y ever or otherwise for instance on rollercoasters or)shall(for that matter and even of all the which anyone would for example)en(joy if he straddled a rocket and rode up to the moon have en)joyed,that very thisful omniverous(thisslamthatbang strictly AndHow delirious)voyage from heaven can tell where all through devil knows(which twisting)what lanes right over the top almost of 1 almost per(pendicular al)most mountain mostwasal willisbe & i(mpossibly must re)main perhaps peculiar(ly the fatally even perhaps magnificently the)most(by quite all means meaninglessly)unique(bad and perfectly mad). As 1 probably of those unpoets whom a selfhating or nonfeeling world pompously has entitled scientists would feel,were he compelled—instead of really or merely believing or assuming—actually to live,Isfully to experience,his inexperienceable unlivably universe,even so felt myself. Should unpoets live their unlives,people would live lives,people would eat when hungry;people would unlearn how not to hunger without eating(that most redoubtable goal of progress life civilization whathaveyou etcetera)

etcetera curiosity

how(as we swirl)long(as we whirl)will my ba(as we all on 2 wheels now take hairpin turns)ggage alias knapsack & valise endure?—answer: as long as long can be. Banditish was right. Dude was right about banditish. Good safe secure and firm were all correct adjectives. . . . When,tottering,I descend from a(stopped so suddenly all our heads flew almost off)taxi . . . behold!2 utterly covered with dust of ages but otherwise entirely unharmed items.

Which enthusiastic(dismounting)detaches and verily toward a smallish

"voici l'hotel" Eddie-outtumbling-Cantor nods

door(as I glimpse a sign Roma)lugs. Apparently the American and the(sprawled his dudeship's feebly lighting cigarette)Afghanistanians are inhabitingseparate domiciles?I shake my 3rd mentor's nerveless hand:

follow items,brother. Who begins angrily ringing conciergeish bells. A
door opens . . . peacefully itself shuts . . . anoth

er emanates interrogative gentwithsuspenders(of whom

asks en francais EC)Have you a chambre?

For(gent en francais asks)how many?

One(I Frenchly said)

Yes

(I said)How much?

One pound and a half

(pound?ah yes. Am in Turkey:Turkish pounds;now I remember,defunct
promised he'd put me in touch with a Turk on the Franz Mering who'd
change me a few American dollars—O well,anyhow he wrote me out
1 hyperultrainfra laudatory supergreeting to angel-guardian's-Roberts-
College-model-son)

You can(frère states)look at it(frowning)

(I)Can I(at suspenders looking)look at it?

Yes

Well I'll say goodbye(to starting forward me announces Cantor)

Thanks(bowing my,self salutes)infinitely

"S'il vous plaît"

he and the dude and enthusiastic and taxi and street
and night are & nowhere:gone

come;3 narrow flights of mouldy stairs

atop hides tinily door labelled,8

—suspenders pushes which . . .

mouldy. Clean

-ness the gentleman doesn't need to descend . . . Up presently
up suspenders climbs,upbearing(valise in hand,sack on shoulders)
dustitems;shows me a mightily spacious W.C.:demands politely my
passport until demain matin—promising to wake me sans faute at dix
heures absolutely "bonne

nuit mon

sieur"

. . . and this little room reeks with all strangeness with alive(with
follies hatreds laughter mistakes whispers)ness sins

(yes & here is a window and are night & nowhere

—good;how good,to lean:into Nowhere!

to be in beautiful hideous imperfection(mimicking murdering)to be in spiral doomless unfearing fearful(birthfully perishing)to be in(rhythmic and disastrous)lewd(victorious)fatally how chaste complexity

& breathe

b for beautiful r says remember e begins eagerly a that's always t spells true h makes how e begins eagerly.

Now(not any more threatened by ought:not by must any more wounded:not by un deceived any more)

. . . to lean into)Nowhere

Thursday, June 11

new

glad(new
glad Newwhere

cries)
criesstrange
glad(Where)alive

newcries Glad
(any- Every
-some-)

Strange Where cries
(gladnew

Here)

(cries)strange(cries)alive

some-(new gladnew
hereglad!Cries:any

there;a)live(every
new,Strange -where)
Glad(aliveglad crie:sgladA;live)

O & wonderfully are moving(look)hurrying are hither people thither
look(look)skilfully wearing on their invisible heads huge glittering
look trays of candies and yoked with bunches of(look)eagerly green
grapes and shouldering look mountains of bread sprouting coronas of
artichoke(look)there & meandering are goats(here float flowers)daintily
atiptoe donkeys(O &
    smell breathe feel
    . . . glad

alive . . .
the people)are everywhere moving(the flowers)the colours
move(cry)ing any(every)where the
—& a thousand noises & million smells
billion & gestures—
the little animals even are alive they are not ghosts either nobody here
is a ghost(each wonderfully has his and her shadow)wonderingly here is
sunlight(look)anyone and everything here and everyone and anything
is breathes feels moves,
    breathes(moves;
feels:
Breathes)
alive.

Down
        the very street of my window(a street called Payrah)in newness in
morning in billions of cries smells thousands I millions wander with a
marvelling little(the Roma's probably garçon)boy(genially by the Roma's
presumably patron selected to show me a socalled Wagons-Lits where it
seems that miraculous tickets—tickets to any-,to every-,to even somewhere—are bought openly;openly are sold). Not French not English
German not Spanish and Italian and never American does(luckily smiling
moving luckily)this little marvelling know. But even luckier my(luckiest
impossibly)self:who knows nothing,O absolutely nothing!—not even
that his stomach recently breadfasted via exhell's last export chocolate
and crackers,that his passport safely inhabits once more my pocket,that
a perfect gent would certainly have insisted on contributing toward last
Walpurgisnacht's taxi,and that a human being(or even an American)
might by his hotel's proprietor be supposed to recognise the name of—a
street called Payrah—where he lives) . . . I only feel:here isn't hell:hell
isn't any more;ought isn't,and should and hideous must aren't(I feel only
that here everybody isn't supposed to,isn't expected to,know;recognize:
for each is what only himself is(does what himself only does)loves
unrecognizably suffers murders ignorantly weeps laughs hates(building
not known immeasurably how doomlessness—building the fate
of,weaker than every stronger than any,Someone Who becauselessly
toward light's darkness tends:Whose will is dream:Whose lives we only
die:only Whose language is silence

à gauche,French

(I'll reward your kindness later)communicate to little. He(that's quite all right sir-stranger don't you worry)communicates luckily disappears

the jeune homme très gentil of Wagons-Lits says beaucoup. Says,in any case you'll gain much time by taking Orient express to Paris and catching next transAtlantic steamer. Says give me your passport,I'll get you the necessary visas and a ticket for tomorrow afternoon;you'll arrive Monday morning. Right?

(. . . just like that!)right(exhellion murmurs quite unbelievingly . . .)

money changed?certainly. A receipt for your passport?with pleasure. Roberts College?allow me to call them for you(. . . —an Oxford accent summons another,which describes the apple of my defunct ex-guardian angel's eye as inhabiting "Beh-bek"—)it's 15 minutes by taxi;you'll find taxis everywhere. So:then I'll see you tomorrow morning—good day!

. . . incroyable . . .

O sir this is a Watch;not just a watch:why,this Watch is "incroyable" and "suisse" and "guarantie" and it costs—not a mere $50—only 32 Turkish lire. & what should the face of Watch of supremely of perfect of wondrous of just-like-that be labelled but

"TOSCA"

—Farewell sir(the aged and elegant the vandyked,cleanshaven the and the obsequious adolescent,chorus)return again!O come to us,whenever you are in need of jewels;come,whenever precious things and things beautiful occur unto your spirit:or if a fluttering heart remind you of some beauteous lady—come if you should wish a ring

(encore

       Pera.

Opposite 1 totally most(&
supremely)vile world-war monument wakes
husky-taxi-ruffian).

Hurtle we mindless if mildly compared with Walpurgis up dale fatally wildly down hill arriving now finally beside this how very splendourously blue ocean &

—scRCrunCHcH—

at imp(challenged)osing gate I dis(mutely)play defunct's apple-letter to antique sagely to caretakerish worthy nods who & opening

—climb(windingly)taxi(and)we 1 sheer(neatlykept)young-mountain.
Halt,radiator aboil,atop:

a plain. Mucho educational pomposities. I breathing distance height
ocean sun dismount

challenged:show my wares to 1 guideful biped;thereupon which(beckoning sagely)escorts into that most & supremely uptodate(and
totally)publiclibrarylike-elegance(whose immaculate And How office
elegantly seems to be full of strictly . . .)me. Biped shrugs . . . nobody.
—Outflummoxes briskly-educational dameandhow("good
  morning"
her gadgetvoice gadgets
  to guideful;which Turks)"is
  there anything I can do for you?" gadgets to
  my(who ex
-plain)self:thereupon gadgetvoice gadgets from round the gadgety
corner a prettily-primly her suitcase-bearing schoolgirl-damsel. A
healthy-minded well-fed apotheosis of shy American maidenhood—
minus halitosis,without B.O.,and possessing The Skin You Love To
Touch—promptly who(just like that)offers to personally conduct the
apple-letter-stranger to her brother-the-apple who's out on the sea for a
sail in the sun for a while with a friend in a boat on the Bosphorus

will you then come into my taxi said the writer? "Sure" the handing
him shy said suitcase and,coyly adieuing the gadget,inclambers
  . . . ec- . . . !—
ruffian- lets
          (meanwhile-shy's-cheerily-chatting-these-are-the-
college)all(buildings-lovely-view-so-high-up-isn't)
  fall
  down;young(kept
  nea-tly)sheer:1
  moun
      t
        a
          i
            n
          . . . to blue,Splen-dor-ouslY! &
where chat(flat)ter swOOns into an affectionate nay an incestuous
suddenly s-c-r-e-a-m hAIl(name)ing 2 they're-trying vainly-to-hide

behind-the-sail-of a-near-shore-becalmed-yacht improvised-from-
something-suggesting-a-Rangely laddies

"stop!"(s tax-ruff. She

now-flut-ters-forth,waaaaving;lyr-i-cal-ly:lustily;wa-ving-at-the-
2,meanwhile I'm cautiously descending her valise placing it I'm
cautiously beside the cab well out of ruffi's

reach

"s-o-m-ebody for y-o-u!"(lyrics lusty)"S-O-M-EbodyforY-O-U!"

. . . twain be-lyric-ed,grumscowlbling,now out-oars,sulkily rowpull
shoreward . . .

and I'm pointed at. And defunct is mentioned. & with an illconcealed
sigh thinner clam(now shakes feebly my hand)ber

forth "there it goes"

-ing,said,cynically.

Damsel-&-me;turn;following,his illboding—behold taxi backing
right-completely-squarely-carefully-over her suitcase

"don'tDon'tDON'T!" she wailed,running at the ruffi

"arrêtez!" helpless thunders C,also at the ruf runningly

(bong:

     off suitcase slips a rearwheel;

g-r-r(& up & on esactius climbs a & front))—"you

stop that!" damsel orders.

The an glared sheepishly:&;stopped,with his leftfrontwheel upon the
saitcuse . . . Then why did you tell me to stop?(shrugs. And would have
carefully run all over it again if both we hadn't all snatched aw(it)ay at
the quite moment)

"You ought to be ashAmed!" shy scolds husky;and,cheerily to me
"there's no harm done—it's just a little split:I can get that mended at a
store in the village;but of course mother Had to tell me to take especially
good care because it was the best valise she—. Well,I'll walk right over
now. O no,it's only a step . . . no,no:please. You're going sailing with
the boys. We'll see you afterwards,I hope?"

Take This You Es Of A Be(C shoves at taxi-ruffian ruffian-taxi's fare
plus monstrous tip)

Hey,What-the,Listen-here-now,That's-nowhere-near-enough,You-
can't-get-away-with,etc.,etc.,etc.(automatically that Turk protests
implores rapidly;nor("Turks are like that" thinner calmly shrugs)ceases
when our skiff weighs anchor). But,au contraire,emanates imitation of

Harry Greb,plus couple of luscious Bronx cheers,times 1 triplebarrelled fullyfledged omnidextrous That For You,Count Tolstoy!which I've never seen everywhere equalled

3,

took;

turns:

rowing.

defunct's angel's eyeapple's freckled pal:son unto the chemistry professor at Roberts;rows,best rows;long:est

. . . heading(a(dodging crisp dar)cross(ting stea)blue(mers)splendourous for "sweet waters of Asia" which be-

"look at those darn towers back there:that's where the Turks asked permission to build a huntinglodge and made forts instead and used 'em to clean out the Christians"

gradually)comes 1 drowsy creek(flanked by uptotheirknees all inwaterhouses vividly allbeggingrepairs all cravingallpaintdesperately

"there's a tax on painting your house so,hek,nobody does").

"How do you like Roberts College?" I ask

"Gosh!it's one hek of a place" said freckles

"run by old maids" thinner "and,gosh darn it,we never have any fun!"

"do they let you play around in Constantinople?"

"O sure" freckles shrugs

"but Constantinople's not so hot" thinner scowls

"no?I'd always imagined—"

"you're thinking of the Arabian Nights or"(. . . barberpole?miracle! pineapple?prodigy . . .)"something" said thinner. "I know. Before I got here I imagined a gosh darn swell place;with,you know,the sultans and harems and the veiled women and everything. But,hek,all that's shot to hell!"

"Mustapha Kemal" nods solemnly freckles "he fixed all that stuff for keeps—gee!"

"isn't there something left in the old city?"

"the bazaar" both

"and Saint Sophia's worth seeing" thinner

"how about that Blue Mosque" freckles

"you'll come to lunch of course" thinner said "O hek:mom will be simply delighted . . . and then we'll all ride in together(you can get off" to freckles "can't you?)and we'll show you what we know of this town;which" a sad shrug "isn't darn much. —Gosh,let's try the sail,what do you say?"

& the darn sail promptly ripped

(and presently 1 goshdarn oarpin sunders—

&,hek,shore;where happens ad infinitum hek-and-gosh-palavering with a darn mummified creature the good raft's no doubt owner; doubtfully twisting who wilted forehead accepts a very indeed copious reimbursement for damages rather remarkably insignificant

"so that" thinner,sighing " 's that.")

. . . Angel-the-guardian's

viz. mom's

apartment reached via this prettily picturesque courtyard and per this unpretty staircase even more picturesque,spells COMFY. To find a gosh darn comfier—outside the(always to be excepted)gosh darn U.S.A.—were gosh darn difficult,hek;if not impossible:sofas and pillows I chiefly seem to remember . . . and a lot of bric-of-course-à-brac of souvenirs of distant-you-know climes . . .

"I didn't think Russian was" flourishing image of 13-year-old-insouciance "hard I just picked it up playing with Russian kids" i.e. other sister of

thinner "here's something about dad" handing me the Paris Herald. Where read & read. About tractors about the readily learning about machinery Russians about how quite unexpectedly successful what perfectly incredible really results are obtained and a little patience building momentous achievement the startling transformation of

enter mom a most

large sensibly welcomish smiling

corseted very

genial being.

Graciously & we all now sit down to a comfy table to all do full justice to a believe me comfy luncheon with(in my special honour;at mom's particular bidding)a comfy And How bottle of "but not too"(smiling coyly at apple)"much" Bulgarian wine & we all now discuss from various comfy angles comfily to our hearts' content a singularly uncomfiness called Russia

"but of course that's" meaning Paris Herald "for foreign consumption" she sensibly smiling pleasantly said. "I haven't heard from my husband" cheerfully "in weeks—but anyone who knows Russia isn't surprised by little things like no" Disappointment Square "Mail!it's a miracle if you ever hear from anybody!"

"gee. I thought Russia" quoth quaffing surreptitiously thinner "was the berries!everywhere I went I just pretended I was an engineer and,hek,everybody turned the gosh darn place inside out for me and of course—dad being a big tractorman(you know how cuckoo the Russians are about everything mechanical)—why:we had all the gosh darn roubles we wanted all the time;and we just all of us lived like kings"

"a slight" cheerfully "exaggeration" his mother smiled

"no;we did mom! . . . at least,I did"

"well it's an extraordinary place,Russia" she muses "but of course I'm very glad to be here,in a pleasant house of my own with my children around me"

"O gee,mom! . . . don't talk like that" he pleaded

"we want to get back to the U.S.A." softly spoke shy

"AND HOW!" thinner loudly corroborates

"my children" corsetted beams largely "are inclined to criticize the educational institutions of—"

"you Know it's Awful!" The Skin You accused

"I don't know anything of the sort" affirms mom "Roberts College is a very fine institution"

"shucks"(thinner shrugs)

"you know it's run by a lot of old hens,mother" B.(poutingly)O.less

"you mustn't talk that way my dear"

"—but it's true!" the apple exploded

"I only know" genial quietly observes "that Roberts is managed by a group of grownups who are sincerely interested in all young people and the social life is—"

("oouh" he groans)

"why Jack dear"

. . . "may I ask" I ask "how you happened to get acquainted with" naming defunct.

Pause. "My son made his acquaintance first" mom said calmly
pause. "I felt sorry for him" her son said simply
(and the accident to the suitcase having been dismissed with a
cheery smile,permission cheerily is granted thinner to enter town as my
cicerone

"I only wish there was something else we could do for you" said la
matriarch

"spaseeba" C bows low

"—I can tell you one" upflaring "thing:the Russians are going to get
away with their five year plan!" at guestcomrade me glares eyeapple.

"Why,darling" mom gently & very indeed softly reproves "he didn't
say they weren't")

&

   on "we"
   reel(here's)monument
   Pera "always take" doW(nD)OwN
   "him when we"(look!)awriggling
   quais(—now—)o penin gcriessu nhar
   bour "go" wHirl "to Stamboul(he"(&)
   swiRl(then)up.sharp "knows all the roberts
   boys")curve,keen;sweep:this;hill,this
   up(hark)u(hark)p
   Hark(now)wail(Now)WailIng
   w-a-i-l
   -i-n-g-
   L-y
and.

&

hugE
    ness(in am tinil)yin vast
Ness(move am wander)ing and
   & over not-floors-but-heavens
creep
    in(gwithi)nmovin(gnot-immensities
    -but-u-n-i-v-e

                rse)sO than
high
        less pe(rhaps credible
        slowlier than hig)her(much
        than highest easily more floating)
        more skilfully s(ilen)tthan(the
wonde
            rfully highest fragrant more)&
            beyond joy(be
            -yond skill Or and even
            si-lence)even(And or total(how
            Complex-ly)serene most now of Dreams(i)wan
der(than my tinily self smaller wondering than the world smaller even
than a very insect move(dizzily who i am)cre-eping move through this
how all gigantic and with what colossal petals harbouring immeasurable
steep each amazement)Flower(beyond skill dream silence)only myself,i
only tinily now discover universe not(not height)immensity;and:am;now
wonder(joy)& wander-ing not,floors,but,heavens)
    —always(lurking . . . hysterically at our arrival they out)swarmed
chattering they wildly gesturing fought struggling shoved curse wrestling
to escort us;then,recognizing my companions,nodded crestfallen all
grin sheepishly all shrugging cynically away floating relax everyallwhere
and(resume quarrelsome and indolence hugging carefully & shadows)are
before Saint Sophia lice called "guides";of all colours. At the most very
portal of hugeness our liceproof trio waited . . . while 1 most scurrying
wizened haggard very being brings out old slippers;the being daintily
has knelt,has daintily pulled slippers over our shoes . . . when we shall
all depart from this vastness the old slippers daintily will from our shoes
be pulled the being very kneeler will receive coins—
    "what"
    (through infinity i timidy staring i at Circles enormous of writhe-
gallop of-lilt of-squirm mysteriously-&-cUrLiNgS)
    "are those"(I whisper)"are they
words?"
freckles and apple explain. That those Turks put these darn circles
up wherever there used to be pictures in this darn Christian church
because hek the Turks don't allow any pictures in their religion. And

414

sure all those funnylooking wigglewoggles painted on those circles mean
something I don't know probably verses from the Koran I suppose

. . . & else
                (with its
                minarets,
                the white shapel
                y against(how-
                blue,SpirEingA
                mong sky(keen:ly;ness the,
                a(mong greenleaves lif-ting(from
                winecoolish;a,frompaved(court
                yard.of.alive(memories
                Splendourful)Visitation)deft)
                magnificent)Sublimely)
                Voluptuous)
                procession eyes,death;Love)
. . . where &

we pass to a. Gate. Here are trees. Shadowmade,under the trees,incredible
fruits and sitting. People. Over whom here are hanging from limbs of
that tree gay cages. Moving,moving,in those cages are moving birds

Enter
        (city:a. Dollcity. With its own sky;with not`our. With its. A sky
painted. Blueembroidered. Streets,under a ceiling. Dollstreets. With
people;dolls:with unimaginable hues innumerable noises not believable
odours. Throb. City a,alive within arcades;from athrob arch to arch
throbbing:and whose dollhorizons are a painted distance. Alive. Not
real;doll. Actual. Here are dollstreets and dollstreets and each street
giving its particular alive kind of smell its very sound own colour dollish
& alive & throbbing. All over most paintedly around the always all
the streets dollsky made of embroidered walls made of arches made
of silence and distance. Into this distance rush dollstreets,out of that
silence dollstreets creep:move streets with wandering chattering with
echo are and teeming with alive dolls;everywhere incredibly drifting
who swim a distance of silence shy chattering alive wandering teem are

415

and who become nearness. This,a;city:with a painted sky,with its not
our. Doll)

timelessly I'm drifting(myself)herein through impossibly;
mauvechrome and scarletlemon:down(myself)drifting am I a street
of silks possibly and beyond swiftly into a street of jewels. Gradually
& now I am approaching new silence;entering alive am a darkness(of
dusty air clogged)skyhigh with everything dead everything which ever
was alive is no impotently more

(Clocks furniture
mirrors
and especially)
Weapons
        (—axes swords daggers pikes halberds poignards and
scimitars once sharp and every glittering fatally all tools for hewing
pierce to cleave for stabbing wound to wickedly to hurt mercifully
and murder & now helpless how dead now useless all imperfect
now superceded)hundreds of forgotten thousands(arquebus musket
matchlock flintlock and pistol every dreadful once now foolish machine
and every once terrific extension of man's insufficiency projection of his
hatred smallness all now not alive silly now useless not amazing now
without magic all defeated now all timeful things—)

negative monuments to love.

High on(among dead)padded shelves loll fat not-quite-asleepily-
dingy mencreatures;each,as we approach,up-most-lazily-reaching lights
a little electric . . . out hop-jump helmets!glittering-strut,leap;suits-of-
armor(flash)goblets candlesticks glint(thrones)and

everything must be bargained for

"they get sore if you don't try to beat 'em down:hek,it's all a game;if
you don't play they think you're insulting"

. . . & freckles,who's been negotiating during weeks with a particularly
quite dingy not asleepily re 1 useless and antiquated and magicless and
unamazing perfectly pistol,today buys. Buys for $^1/_{50}$of original price and
$^1/_2$again what he finally offered and easily 3 times as much—our apple
claims—as the gosh darn thing is worth but hek you get tired and they
know it they take advantage they

(while myself confines me to a probably the fair lady Scheherazade's
necklace to improbably something which certainly was Harun-al-
Rashid's mouchoir)

in
   -to af-

        ternoon we're

   floating our sky real

afternoon the realness of a hill but hill of always dollstreets teem
echoing are dollfolk and chattering gesture now it's here a rushcreeping
dollstreet of(—O how not like the flyspecked toys of hell!—)Toys:
only and immensely,flutter;stand bulge,lie whirl stare;and:s-m-i-l-e . . .
millions of SmilinG!

   at this hill's base

                 we're,su

                 dde

nly tur,ning a corner(hit)with silversaying-fish-keen trillions!of!glIstenIng;
by all the musical shapes fragrant the colours tactile rhythm the of ocean's
rarest people;with bright centripetal shouting architecture;by polyps and
anemones and dreams and miracles. . . . Beyond which exists,facing the
harbour in a great gentleness of shadow,crowded garden of sitting men
young & old dark & gay(skippety-1-song phonoed,from;be:hind)lis-
ten-ing . . . driNKing . . . grinning

   —over "the Golden Horn" we stroll,treading a bridge of boats;pass
(ing,re)pass(ing are)hurrying swarthy statues wearing upon their small
heads pedestals—the(each atop other all rising perilously swaying
fatally)pedestals are boxes:everything itself seems to balance,nothing
falls. Nothing falls and we(& 2 Greek?priests with blackblack spools
balanced on yellowwhite foreheads 2 with curling immense blueblack
beardmanes pass)enter a tunnel;board a little metroish train;ride through
dark;stop;descend;emerge. A street called Payrah

   "hek,let's have a beer;it's gosh darn hot!"

   not a,but 3(apiece)beers. —O

how not like hell's peevoh!how not untasting how not lukewarm
how excellently actual! 3(apiece)in this Italian . . . if you please . . .
restaurant-café:where everyone speaks everything noone is supposed to
know everything somebody only is what himself

   is

      e.g.

        Drunk . . .

(clg)(clgclg)(clgclgclg)

—I

o

-pen:why—

it's;the,dude!

come out with me and see the town(smiling says the entering dude softly)

fine(blink tight I)but first let me pay you my share

You pay Me?

of the taxi we took from the customs to this hotel

O(fingering his immaculate chapeau)no(glancing genteelly through window)it's(smilingly)nothing. I didn't pay for it

then your friend did

"peut-être"(softshrug)"allons"

. . .

where(inquire)do we go?

"taxim"

"taxim?"

(childwisdomishly uppursing 1 eye)"poules—chic."

A cool vast garden-café,built upon the edge of rather Rubensy distance or wherein gradually create themselves hills farness. Stuffed with(would-be)European-to-a-degree peoplesit tingdrinpeopleking chatpeopleting every(a-r-o-u-n-d)where us &

"qu'est-ce que ça veut dire?" point;to. This flaring curtain,dropped behind those. Unlighted footlights of that tiny stage;to surface squirmwrithing with language:what does it—

"où?"

"là-bas"

it says(genteelly And translates,to poule de How luxe nodding gildedly,his nibs)always Ford cars are the best.

& hereupon page we Mustapha Kemal . . . And that's what became of Constantinople. I now learn that veils are violently forbidden,that there positively is no Arabic anywhere permitted on the streets in the trams on the menus in the mouths of Better People(to be sure,you still encounter it ad lib across the harbour:they are still very ignorant over there,they are dirty and very uncivilized over there and still live very primitively a most miserable dirty horribly ignorant life of thieving and prayer and lice—good old religion!listen sometime;you'll hear a kind of Wail . . . that's the socalled muezzin calling his microscopic faithful,he's allowed to do

418

it everywhere;but only there-and-here a few a very few respond . . . now
all now look around here all all around all you;and say,tell me:if possibly
you wouldn't think you were sitting in some big terrace-café of perhaps
Germany or even France? Are not all of these all chatteringdrinking
sittingish all people quite as(if not rather more)uptodate as(perhaps
than)you'll probably find among Europe's even great capitals? —Poor old
religion:foutu;not yet everywhere dead but now everywhere dying—now
enters everywhere a new age,an epoch of scientific achievement,an era
of progress! Look around all around around all here and you're sitting
in progress you're really chattering in achievement you're drinking truly
in new O all the people are emancipated why they even serve excellent
whisky-and-soda will you have one on me? Well,isn't it excellent? Best
always Ford. . . . Mustapha Kemal

    (genteelly)they call him the lion

    . . . so always waiting I but no & not for some reason today:& curtain
didn't stirmove;& nothing will for me,now or ever,happen upon this
tiny stage.

"Jolie,n'est-ce pas?"

    as you like,my friend;have seen prettier:who even knew how to use
makeup

    —meanwhile she's hunting downstairs for a record which dude insists
I should take as a souvenir home to my country and Ford's. Meanwhile
the phonograph spouts creepseetheishly darkdeepl

    "chanson d'amour. Toujours" waving elegantly forefinger
"d'amour"

    ydeepseethedarkcreep-l-yish

    dar-kishdeep-ly spouts love Love LOVE—

    there was in his attention,as he watched me,watched me always(and
he meanwhile always always listening to chanson)a beginning of almost-
curiosity quite beneath pathos. What(seemed to ponder watcher to wonder
listener)may this person be,anyhow?who,American,naturally prefers a cake
of soap to a country of soviets:well,he's right,I understand;yet when I
show him Constantinople's capitalist splendors he actually appears bored:
ah well,that city which is called New York probably eclipses my wildest
dreams

    I hope you're staying a few(dude murmurs,turning-over elegantly
LOVE)

days I know a fine girl who'll be
(l
 -o
    vE)here a personal friend of mine(he shouted through upspiral
OUtblossoMing Derk-dape)

& did insist we dine at "American" restaurant. With a reassuring
sawdusty floor but very nearGreek food and no drinks & himself doesn't
eat for some reason presently himself excusing traverses the dingy room
him(sits)self converses with 5dark lean5 over5dressed fellows about all
heaven knows perhaps what . . . including life?

how are the(having parked my 2 LOVEs safely at hostel experiment
now with elegantly beside me now Pera strolling-always-Pera)
whorehouses
    (starting)O—very bad. Dirty:dangerous;very.
"Are there no other streets?"
    (stared,amazed;opening both eyes wide:responds)yes;streets,yes;well?
I mean,why don't we try—
    (shocked)because this is The street.

(Education:from the Latin ex=out + ducere=to lead. 11th June
synonyms—cries tasted in a bed;sights smelled and colours touched from
a window;lucky my(through itself,morning)self moving;sea glimpsed and
young mountain;magical wandering afternoon,Sophia & Blue Mosque
& 1 gate & the bazaar & hill of wonders & a bridge. —Explicit)enter
dude:Payrah became something else
    at whose almost end,paraît,is The Best Dancing In Town,alias
a roofgardenlike whereless of people overdressed not(people)many
darkish selfconscious acclaiming people elegantly genteel And they
are bejewelled boiledshirtful How ditties culturously propagated by
pomaded by nymphs by perfumed by gigolos—are especially now are
politely encouraging 2 Real Russian(—believe it or:sic;not a,picture—
)Dancers
    now
    (a dark overconscious selfdressed)
    now I
    now I'm

(youth joins us immediately who &)

now I am whiskying

now whiskyanding

now(actually positivelyandnegatively goodbad and I whiskysodaing about everything about argue anything with dark about nothing youth about some(about)thing a(finally)bout about)

stewed. Round swings the rooflike the gardenful boiledjewels darkish revolves whereless around elegant(not)ly best stutter people better stagger people whirl bestest spin talk I Talk I'm TALKING saying whatever telling what arguing Declaiming SHOOTING my face!for the 1st time in heaven knows!killing nears in droves slaying almosts massacring myriads of notquites banging into darkness all into eternal night all false timid all -Less all Un- & O how darkconscious stares O how he frowns I don't care & now O how youth laughs Laughs and I also am LAUGHING!actually can you imagine at ideas at ideals at ideology at anything which would corrupt the natural pervert the distinct poison the eternal warp the incorruptible & O now how falsesmilingly dude his timidtwittering esquire nibs finally now fuzzy nodding almost-heartily me wuzzy now clapping upon the-my-back("c'est juste!")why!even thisthat-alias-waitheader lookseems amused,peepsleers;intrigued grinscowls:& the musique dindledondles twittertwattle the danseurses whirlspins pomadeperfume &—& I!LAUGH

. . . under me a month of hell!

over me are stars

(ecco). Round swings a star swoops Talking LAUGHING drip-faintdivinglyanddis-appears

forever?

—O all unyous,all whoever seem around me who me despise pity cannot comprehend or who give to myself nothing,all you all fallacious you futile all un,nothing-wishing anything-accepting something-missing everything-rejecting,how the hell should I(not in hell any more)care what you thinkless who you areless why you dreamless when-where-wherefore-whenever you do not live(destructibly you nonexist;corruptibly you,very And most unnaturally How,foreverneveringly strut)cringe . . .

—can't(you Cannot)that's your trouble(that's your evil)that's your hate(your woe)your shame(that's what gripes you)that's what turns your wouldbe into a hasbeen(and puts O just the least(a teentsyweentsy)bit of merde on it)makes you eat it right all up with a nice and pretty(sweet

swallow it all down now smile)Cannot(that's nonyou)that's your
stuffless(your unfate)you impotents(all you pasteboard haters)O paper
lovers . . .

—what is alive,say:what are skies are trees to you?and moons worlds
smells stars suns flowers?they are nothing(and Love,what is Love to
you?nothing!you create nothing;therefore you cannot Love,and because
you cannot Love you create nothing)—

O you all unyous around me now seeming,and elsewhere,and nowhere
somewhere anywhere—O all youless nonalive ungivers—wherever in
hell,whenever not in hell,arelessly who Cannot;dreamlessly who Can't
  :I
   (about
  to
    be)
      alive
  —salute

you'd-taxi bucks-surely-have says-been-robbed-when totters-skids-you-got-
off the-volvereing-Franz-Mering-I-know I-outstraightening-was-the-
first-time-I arrived-rapidly-alleyes-said-Eddie-now-side-be beside-me
-mightily-down-now-up-now-bouncing-Cantor

Friday, June 12

Simplon Orient Express: Stamboul à Pythian Transit et l'Enclave de Karaghadge ou vice et versa, Pythian à Svilengrade Transit sans l'Enclave de Karaghadge ou vice et versa; Svilengrade Dragoman Granitza ili Dragoman Granitza Svilengrade; Putnik Beograd, Rakek Caribrod, Caribrod Rakek—Ferrovie Italiani dello Stato, da Iselle Transit a Postumia Transit o da Postumia Transit a Iselle Transit; Vallorbe Gare Iselle Transit ou-oder Iselle Transit Vallorbe Gare via Lausanne; Vallorbe Gare à (paused suddenly my) Paris (heart) via Labergemet Sainte Marie, Dijon (very politely he murmurs)

    it's(whisper to Mr. Wagons-Lits)magic

Parcours: TURQUIE

    BON pour: GOOD for

        UN

                DINER

      ONE

Parcours: YOUGOSLAVIE

    BON pour: GOOD for

        UN PREMIER DEJEUNER

      ONE MEAT BREAKFAST

Parcours: YOUGOSLAVIE

    BON pour: GOOD for

        UN

                DEJEUNER

      ONE

Parcours: YOUGOSLAVIE

    BON pour: GOOD for

        UN

                DINER

      ONE

Parcours: SUISSE ou ITALIE

    BON pour: GOOD for

        UN PREMIER DEJEUNER

        ONE MEAT BREAKFAST

Parcours: ITALIE

              BON pour:GOOD for
                    UN
                              DEJEUNER
                    ONE
        Parcours:ITALIE
              BON pour:GOOD for
                    UN
                              DINER
                    ONE
        Parcours:(heart my suddenly)FRANCE(paused)
              BON pour:GOOD for
                    UN PREMIER DEJEUNER
                    ONE MEAT BREAKFAST(politely he murmurs)and here's
your passport with all the necessary visas
        (handing whom dollars)I can(7)scarce(90)ly believe it
        ninety-(gentil Mr. Wagons)seven(-Lits taking my)dollars(dollars
politely murmurs)

 . . . incr
          (oya
              bl
)e . . .
O
re
mus

just inside hugENess,a poet is praying.
    I feel that he is blind
    (by dreamlike what serene totally adventuring ecstacy surrounded is
this(beyond now all imagining)small—dark,tinier even than my(than
even a timidly very wandering insect who may name itself impossibly
my)self—dark poet;blindman:a beautifully communing he.
    Everything,for this(I feel)he,exists;everything lives only for this
very(perfectly communing)dark man
    his always the alive whom I now feel;joyously are his the always not
substance merely(the not merely spirit)secret of how more than life
or death;joyously always the and under(and throughout all perfectly)
surrounding poem,

                              424

therefore who may not know merely or unlive,worship by denying,
measure:only who(than all more;than dream becoming)feels,poet:darkly
communing with impossible light;

perfectly whose amazement is beyond every aspect any(comprising
what begets tomorrow's yesterday)dimension;sizeless,entirely creating;
impossibly alive:his

voice is made of silence and when his voice pauses the silence is made
of voice.

(Silently

          as now to

               whom my,pray-

                       ing my

-self;bows)

       . . .

            Look—
!children(suddenl
y:invade
(not-immensities
-but-u-niv-e
rs)es
all are gaily these playing heads bright these flicker bodies(and all
gush gaily how like petals over
not,floors,but,heavens
&)Float-inG(past that row of—seatedsolemnlybeforetheirshoes—
women)& flutte-ring lAuGhInG to(a(much
than highest easily more floating)
mong)joyOUsly
vanish
)
& . . .
      now)
          . . . far
away a. (Reading with magn)old an. Older(ify)all. Byhim(oldest)self
singsonging(book,The;which)leans(be;fore,whom). A(which & now
toward,reverently now;and;now hum,bly leaning now who)reads. Who:
sings
   . . . &.
      i

am-floppingly(and my tinily in-too-big-slip-pers)&(
self wondering,dizzily-than-the-world-smaller-i'm and
)wander. No- &(among The every-Flower a)deeplyening within
And;where,total or(how
Complex-ly)serene most now of Dreams(i)wan
a
n
d
  here
a flapping dove
                    A
-light
    ing
        (low.
              That
(like me wanwond ering)figure hurlshis capupat
itanditfla
            P
          Pi
        Ngl
            yRis
                  esint o
more skilfully s(ilen).

In such very littleness of cooldark someone is sitting at a piano
  I feel that we've met
  remember something about
  . . . re(spurning these)vis(lice)ited today Sophia? Dizzily out-
wan-der-ing was curse led gesturing fight to called guides struggling
buy 20 pic"wheer?"ture"airyooer?"post"fraynz?"cards? & who(alone
dreamfully following silverish ribbon of sunlight)enters(with its minarets,
SpiReingA)nd?again:worshipping . . . Wandering now wondering
remem(You're not in Europe)bering seeks and(You're in Turkey now)
seeking cages-of-birds hanging from a tree-of-people. See,king
seek,ing(With its own sky;with not our.) . . . Loses he finally among
w-a-ILI-n-g & 1 hill myself and him(upon a bridge)self found,standing
before this very-(this most respectfully viewing And per How
drunkenly wuzzy scribbled words)-not-ruffian(driver this tim)idly

wagging a long(this climbing from his)ish head(disappearing)&
rea(with shortish drowsy)ppearing & sleepily that adjusting spectacles
gen(tly taking studying busily puzthic-kis-hlyzling)now,that;man:
readingaloud. —Presto(camera)longish-&-self & the taxi all-
are-together rushdownupinglying-S(kyfall?)-tOp.— Ecco . . .
1sortofkind?ofshallwesortof?maisonde?luxe? Self,my,pays the,lon(unthe
protesttheing)gish. &. Rings:lingadinga. Wait. &. Rings:dingling-
adinglingding—. Pause. A,girlface;peeps:¹/₂opens;discompre-hends,very
suspic(quite à la can you imagine speakeasy)iously receives fuzz-
scribbling(quickshuts-vanishes). A:u:s:é:p:a:u.s. (Dude's guttural
accents. Lyplacidingpeer)o-pens . . . in a can you Russian imagine blouse
over silk("bonjour")pyjamas sle-e-pily & waaaves me into so much such
a little darkishcool;opens a window:stands;filletted vacant motionless;
forthgazing(& now silently disappears)

Some—
and I feel he is I
—One
        begins:with piano this;piano and,begin understanding impos-
sibly someone's
Joy
(O but the probably house forever would collapsed O have entirely
collapsing would all diplomats embassies consulates(perfectly even O
holidays))
    —comes-how!subito!es(minushairnet)quire nowbeck oning Some(&
Joy)One up-a-great-a-many toosilent stairs-to-great-to-many toosilent
rooms . . . bowree ling,fuzz enters somewhat unfeelably comfortandhowable
chambre fa intly wuzz takes comfortmoderneish AndestHowest throne
deeplyestthroated. Je m'asseois
"c'est" f eebl y "pas mal ici,n'est-ce pas?"
Very(I retort)
pause
"excusez-moi" langui(placi)dly "je me rase maintenant. Il-y" bur "a"
ping "des livres"
"merci"
    —exit via gor("voyez:c'est presque américain,pas?")geously betiled
bain de grande luxe(de quel chic de tout ce qu'il faut)de what hast
thou?
de la curiosité.

Readread. For 45. Minatory minutes. Terse history of Turkey
. . . why

       the devil did Cantor's crony insist last night I absolutely
positively must be here tomorrow midisansfaute?(marvel.

&:probably;so does)

bathed,shaved perfumed,smoothed curled anointed,lux(un)urious
(steadi)ly who dis(nattily his semiapparelled presence)posing vagu
(now)ely di(observes)mly

"café?" —Knock.— Entereth both upon pins walking and upon
needles girl("jolie n'est-" nudge "ce pas?" As you like,my friend. I have
. . .)face plus very elegant tray frasmograkinntgllyy

SIPpauseSipPausesipPAUSE

                       (&

                             paraît there's pas d'argent for lunch.

I offer to treat)

             dude answers "bon".

So perhaps(after several parts of

                   an hour)

                         of un&dress(with-the-cri-
tic-al-aid-of-count

less-mir-rors)ing the young mi

                 lord Seems to be al?

most
All

   set—whenallat

once:hush. & sh!—paraît that Another Embassy Arrives . . .
courteously I(if)am(quickly)ensconced in much much more than
de(quite sequestered am in a positively very negatively palatial
drawingroomish)grande luxe far from not suggesting just a trifle the
Mille Et Un?). . . . Cru-cial-l-y,fuzz;wuzz:tip-toes-out . . . i-nto a
hall(now . . . returning very solemnly whispers that self shall depart he
murmurs he'll meet me later . . .)

I say "bon".

My(clutching its ticket)self(passport)deciding meanwhile to(whatever
we do or don't)avoid diplomacy . . . N-ow

(stea-l-thi-ly)stairs . . .

-down-

. . . cree-ping-we2
gain
por . . . tal;SH:a,-n-d—

                       leaPforWardIng suddenlyundersized guy
(with blue glasses)starts em(innumerably)bracing fuzzdudenibs
   the
may we add last time I ever beheld his imperial majesty Tintrunk 1st.

Payrah. Italian really truly French anyway not de luxe anyhow nectar
   culled from of paradise
   flowers the of once-upon-a-
Now
am
F-e-e-L
-ing
as . . . who?
            "Captain Bonavita and his matchless group of twenty-
seven forest-bred African lions"
   . . . except that he had 1 arm. The lion chewed off the other. That
was chez Bostock:Frank,"The Animal
   King"
         who modestly called himself. . . . My miracleprodigy father toted
me there & we spent a stupendous day(tiny I rode an elephant)when
we came home the family smelled us and wept . . . Then during years I
was—not The Animal King,O no;that didn't satisfy me:
   The Animal Emperor
                 & I drew and drew pictures(& hundreds of
pic-tures)and thousands & millions(of me)pictures,of myself(of 1 tall
big high strong man with a mighty cap which always said(that. Which
never said anything during years but that,just(during years)that only)
   . . . pity poor realists)!
   yes:Bonavita was a dashing man. —But speaking of dashing how
about what was his
   "Danger Deriding Death Defying Desperate Dare Devil Diavolo
Loops The Loop On A Bicycle" very much more than suspected of also
being "Porthos Leaps The Gap Over Nine Elephants"
   —?

except that loopleaping signor DiavoloPorthos was killed in
Havana;he suddenly came down the slender track(with a black stripe in
it)just as I(breathless)'ve him seen come & . . . someThingHappened—or
let's
      not
         . . . probably the little white bicycle collapsed under him
—or Let Us Pray:
Forepaugh & Sells World's Greatest Shows The Only Living.
BON pour:GOOD for
-sitan et haec
olim
      (ninety-
               seven,
                     doll;ars
)a
:men
& then came Buffalo Bill.

And after Buffalo Bill(a graveyard "New York" &)what fireflies among
such gravestones(afterwards mai and les chevaux de bois & death)we
have arisen,who were dead;having died we are as only Animal Emperors
of the imagination shall be(and as only poets arise:again possibly to
die,impossibly again & even out of hell ascending who shall keep our
circus hearts against all fear).

You es es are are es vee pee pee dee kyou kyou ee dee ay men
   it's passing very skilfully along an edge of a sea. It's wonderfully hot.
The way he said Are you going to Paris,monsieur?I shall always remember.
(Such a jolly little if how respectful man)! Tranquil,that shore of that
ocean:filthy,those un-"there's a tax"-painted alldecaying rapidlyhousesand.
We are steel. Bright,we;indestructible. (Such trusting gayness if a French
commerçant;going to Dijon coming from Syria—The only people
worse,he says,than the Syrians because a little more if it's possible mongrel
are Greeks,he says). Meanwhile but this is Turkey . . . serene,slopes;
now:we're. Climb. Ing. A,train;Is:We. We are a train are the express
we are that Simplon Orient train from Stamboul to Pythian Transit and
the enclosedness of Karaghadge from clavis meaning all the windows are
open. (The,he says,all the Syrians have not changed simply will not and

cannot change,why,they make all their rugs by hand—these changeless Syrians—quite as if a machine age never had occurred)a which,we;now: are. Moving a,machine;the:Orient machine moving now through fields loosely to which are glued little staring almost angrily soldiers. & it's here in this deuxième terribly hot but everywhere even here must be cooler soon because the night will come:we are all going toward night moving all toward darkness. Meanwhile space;country—pushing,angrily almost: against the gradual dully reddening sky . . . now skilfully,all,we moving-are-among poppies . . . (& they lie the Syrians and all,he says,the Syrians steal; but they none of them attack you.—Why not?—I don't know,he cried merrily;they seem to do everything else.—Is the pays jolie?I ask.—Great place for ruins,he grins;for ruins and)moving we n,o,w among flowers we(for tourists:and not really)we all an epoch all we a machine(expensive. O,you can live for seventy francs a day everything included,he smiled)an era now wandering skil-ful-ly through a sunset

seething an era with its now here and there everynowwhere now all its how innumerable lights

. . . impossibly

j'y suis. Door of little(named Roma)hotel in a street entitled Pera in a mythical city called Constantinople. (Knock). "Quatre heures!" the probably patron enters. Now he descends my belongings now I pay for merely 2 days now he wigwags an(out of ruffian by longish)taxi(downupish whirling we)and a. Station. Is this—hell?nyet,without confusion. No waitinglines. Merely the few neatly takingthingseasy officials who inspect my visas my ticket my passport and last but not;presently who—alone—wander a lonely platform;staring alone at those lonely groups of And How Americans lonelier English. . . . Pause. —Enter(slipping dreamfully us silently toward)il treno der Zug la machine,magnificently concentrated(gliding a)sublimely It.— Noone seems particularly excited:perhaps nothing would excite those(now they heavily hoist themselves into spicandspan rooms now they emptily talk to friends via opened without difficulty windows)ah . . . here's an exception;this ferociously-old with a black kerchief lady shoutsqueaking vividly-almost to large crowd of very docile indeed boys;she just won't let them simply all leave her window,they really can't get away all those wellbehaved lads or ever say goodbye . . . ecco!boisterous bevy of bouncing beauties,1's truly not hard to look at and now she's(also her aged Aunt Matilda)gracing the recently furnace I temporarily vacated(maybe Miss Turkey?bound for the land of the midnight movie bound for the shores

of the bathing beauty bound for the realm of the baby parade). Chatter
sHrIlLs . . . A. Lurch
   —&
      (yel
   ling)&
   we're
   m o v Ing(
            &
            f,are;wel,l
   -ing)

pavots(through;we're,
   c-o-m-e-s:twilight)
ah!but not hell's Red(but alive nyet proletarian but universal not idea
but esti—fear never:always Is). And so we went to Russia and so we were
found by some Picassos. And so we came to Moscow and so we found
some Matisses. And so he ordered bleiben Sie ruhig and so I murmured
spaseeba and so he snarled nyet spaseeba. But there were stars in Kiev and
there were Assyrian and Harem and the flowerbuyer at Moscow and
   USSR a USSR a night- USSR a nightmare USSR home of the
panacea Negation haven of all(in life's name)Deathworshippers hopper
of hate's Becausemachine(U for un- & S for self S for science and R for
-reality)how it shrivels:how it dwindles withers;how it wilts diminishes
wanes,how it crumbles evaporates collapses disappears—the verily
consubstantial cauchemar of premeditated NYET
   . . . BON pour:GOOD for(The Greater Hotel St. Regis New York
Where Fifth Avenue Is)sic(Smrtest)

c'est la vie,et non point la mort,qui divise l'âme du corps(MCMXXVIII Paul Valéry)

and it came to pass(in the year of grace '31)that certain inmates or occupants,viz. Miss Turkey & Aunt Matilda,of a phenomenon portent or hereinbefore mentioned Simplon Orient Express did most maliciously monopolize and most premeditatedly appropriate 1 without exaggeration indispensable contrivance and did wantonly,by a foul abuse of godgiven freewill,deprive other inmates or occupants,viz. jolly if respectful & myself,of the benefits naturally accruing to all 4 parties through a discreetly alternate use of said indispensability,as originally intended and providentially provided for by the architect or architects of said Simplon phenomenon Orient portent or hereinbefore mentioned Express. And as frivolously inferred via the following by me faithfully imitated yestreen inscription,viz.

PASSENGERS ARE PARTICULARLY REQUESTED TO NOT EMPLOY THE WASH BASINS DURING THE STOPPAGE sic OF THE TRAIN IN STATIONS. THE USE OF THE W.C. IS ONLY ALLOWED WHILST sic THE TRAIN IS ACTUALLY MOVING

consequently memor(of a sunset tangled with heatlightning)ies begin dissolving memories of a starry night but black and holding(just outside the rush of steel)a chatt(through are which ingrush we allourlights)erish scream of frogs dis(begin)solving into respect with sweat standing on jol's brow is ecco if jolly's if respectful if pyjamas who

It's A Crime!

"oui"(& to whom the very benevolent mogul potentate very sovereign conductor nods verily)

an outrageous offense against civilization!

I know

a simply abominable blot on the lilywhite escutcheon of progress!

true. But(YouKnowWhatIMeanfully smiling)they are women—

but we are men!(ScotsWhaHaeishing jol affirms)we have our rights!

(nod)life(with the compassion of omniscience)is difficult(our deus
ex irrevocably mused)

pause

Can't you open it?(respectful whereupon challenged

1 allcomprehending of angelic sleuthfulness wink partially warms
his interlocutor's near eye)let us(and)see(re(spect,ing)ly)knocks. (The
And How locked gateway to paradise budgeth not)"tiens"(graciously
producing illimitable clefs,selects mercifully the very largest;it
benignantly inserting,t.u:r;nS)

—O my(jol recoi)lord!(ling from by no means numerable garments
of a distinctly intimate not to say quite undeniably female nature)

there(the conductor said)you are

I(quaking)'m . . . afraid . . .

of what?

. . . I . . . might abyss them(quoth he)

"bien"(closing re(spect,ing)ly portal)come with(&;bec-kons:sol-emn-
ly)me

like(pyj)this?

I pray you,my good friend,distress not yourself unduly;noone,my
dear sir,adorns the immediate vicinity at this moment

&

—excuse!(spinning in great alarm respect catching sight of)I I I you
you you havewakedupn'est-cepas?!?

& & &

we are(are we Express is)pursuing(Simplon is Orient The)a swollen
bluebrowngrey verblike silently thunderous life swirling animal among
wheres now dizzily a to or itself droopingful in plains expand and an in
narrows newly fiend bristling

(past now float he-shes chiselled from darkness,slicesofnight with
greyrockfaces—also)once,a spoolhat priest with a bellhat(all got up fit
to,why it's . . . with redder than orange than redorange petticoats)bride.
Savage gradually country;and

(Once a)portion(oF)the(skY be)comes

mou(NtaiNs are S)now

. . . flowers:mauve;&,chrome &,cobalt;& scarletnyetproletarian:pavots.
fields . . .

whose(wilfully fragrance translates wilfully our voyage(into a dream
into)nyet cauchemar into(vision or memories perhaps into)Being. fra . . .
gRa . . . nce
   and
Amazing(over their whom to(from-far)near rhythmically swOOps
wind)ly illimitable(fields-from which protrude(ouTleap)little!shepherds.
abrupt.staunch.jagged)
   nowhere
         &
               herethen,fragments;of(merely language of unkings echo-
ing the not merely of kings language of poets)hell's
   alphabet but:this
   machine-der-Zug-our-
   It does not flinch;Gathering
   fluently·Its(scythe)self,mows them all down . . .

Bulgaria?
         means pink(cochons!scared by tiny dream-(allstrangealldif-
ferentallqueeralldeceptiveallbyitself blunderfuling)locomotive within
whose very much warped cab live(are smile)dark(sharp)blue(flowers.;
   &)look—out,the()window of our reeking this with heat with
us—lo:ok!fe,;el!air . . . A-r-i-a(&:far be(turningnowthatthen)yond,the
dangerous;superb the:hungry head-of-folding OrientSimplon segmented-
un-folding-nobly Worm))
   —hark
         :again & sky Be(the)comes;once,s
                              N
                                o
                                  w

(10:30). spelled à la russe Sophia:1—gorgeously sprouting upon,sucking
greedily the,what mean midst of rustyredd ishtile ddesolatio nness(of-
suburby-misery-of)And how Hopelesslyness—(one)hot gold authentic
mushroom
   alias
   Religion
   . . . a piece of string Hohda Nyet

11
   (o Tosca My tosca)
             40
                    hellspelled Dragoman,alias possibly Serbian?
frontier.

   Behind:dry sandy peaks.

   Near:gruesome relics,of agriculture sheep(etc. perhaps folk,nailed to
notmerelydead,to neveraliveever)grass

& are-cautiously we en-ter-ing a sullen crazy arid-drenched occasionally
in paleblue. Flowers land. Care-ful-ly we are scaling & now stratified
slopes(we flow-ing are precariously past black-&-white wavingglaring
humanthings now-&)observe dreamfully these creepdreaming al,ways
these,oxen someBody's ploughing in Somebody's world!

. . . Niche
             engines.
                  That:larger,proud-narrow. Those:silent,not
   corpses:they are
   machines,perfectly all awake(utterly untired,who inhabit whenwhere;only
their semblances
   obtain)—1 wearing a red cap
   sic
   &-cattle are-up-to-their-bellies-in-a muddyness(somehow
   remember A with a,and they're turning,and the wagon's lurching the
horse is galloping the man . . . andAndaNd wonderfully 1 wibbleAwabbling
circle a wheel A)item;2 porkers are sitting in the
   shade,nyet
   whores(weye yuh might chust us well uhliminate eatin)or whom an
encorewhite gallant encore
   uniform will salute(but
   up hob)bleth somebody is examining po(ki)ng is who now grey
(dis)turb(ing)the which who now up-stAring all;smiles,dolefully:the
blue is asleep.

und Zeit moans
            in Zeit-
                flaunt

                                        nudegals all over the plat(And How)
form
(less)of
  1 dullbrown sickness called beograd.
  "—Où allez-vous?" jol,vested & almostifnotquite melting,respectfully
fearfully queries
  of forthstrollingmygaily shirtsleeves
  To visit our oracle
  Give it my(respect said,earful grinning)regards—

. . .
  . .
   .

     then thennow thennowthen thennowthennow noW no N
NOWT NOWTH NOWTHE nowTHENthenNOWing it
  there therehere thereherethere thereheretherehere herE her he H
HERET HERETH HERETHE HERETHER hereTHERE-there
HEREing it wel
  comes
  my(
     marvelling wholly
)self
& "metal steed,very treacherously wherefrom descending the
promiscuous urbans plundered rus!through you I greet all itgods. And
I tell them of a singular He,indivisable or individual,one Being natural
or unafraid,for whom exists no sign no path no distance and no time.
Strutcringing inexistence!through you I greet all cruelly enslaving
deities of perfection. And I tell them of a totally adventuring Is Who
breathes,not hope and not despair,but timeless deep unspace—I prophesy
to handless them that they shall fall by His hand,even by the hand of
Poietes;for guilt may not cancel instinct and logic defeat wish,nor shall
tasteless hate obtain against the fragrance of amazement. Unspontaneous
sterility!through docile you I greet all deathless,all the not alive,wheelgods
of real. And I tell them of a million or a trillion selves,musically which
are one always who cannot perish;I prophesy to faultless them a moving
within feelfully Himself Artist,Whose will is dream,only Whose language
is silence—heartily to most heartless them I say that their immaculate
circles are mere warped reflections of one selfinventingly unmitigated

Spiral(of selfdestroyingly how strict untranslatable swooping doomlessly selfcontradicting imperfection or To Be). Hungrily premeditated angel of because!through youless you I greet all ravenous ignobly equalizing symbols:I pityingly cry to pitiless them that pitiful children have become the untoys of toys;I cry that when the toys have unplayed with the untoys,the toys throw the unchildren away. Cordially myself,a lover who completely feels—savagely a maker and to whom his deaths are births—joyously one citizen of the miraculous Verb,challenges(with only whatever beautifully shall not mean:strong fire and faithful rain;sunset and moonrise and impossibly all shining things who may not be comprised or known)equally every purveyor of impotence and alikeness to mankind. Hear me,O go-toy!and escort very fearingly among your how vicarious beatitudes the sinful giver of love's homogeneously chaste complexity;own child of luminous forever-pitying sternly immeasurable Yes"

    who prays.

    To the orient almighty,now in elephantine whom glidebulges then,dwells in hereful which exact how murderfully there. Uttered:cries said. Speaks

    "he who knoweth the eternal is comprehensive;"
& the station rose

    "comprehensive,therefore just;"
exploding all naked flaunt the becoming

    "just,therefore a king;"
as flags flutter are spilling all nipples tossing and thighs eyes all

    "a king,therefore celestial;"
opening shouted and ecco:all the air is filled with millions full of little filled is full with only

    "celestial,therefore in Tao;"
girls(drifting suddenly and like lice)

    "in Tao,therefore enduring;"
girls with teeth gestures perched smiling prone weeping(young)with lips hands laughing dreaming clenching young pul(ling into young wonderful deep them wis)tfully keen adream wonderingly millions of alive(lice)men

    —χαίρετε—
    "without
    hurt

he
suffereth
the
loss
of
the
body"

     .
       . .
        . . .

could possibly that(could a(possibly this the)impossibly not)very bluebeautiful
   Danube?

to-work:men—hoes(risef rfall rifa risfal risingfalling inging)
   to;keep(woman—&)her(white nice)ly geese wob(ble) . . .

Copyrightissimo Portraitissimo of an Americanissimo,
   (a)forciblissimo
      anent Ispeaknolanguagebutmineown customsofficial
         "THAT. IZ. AY. TYPEWRYTER"
   (b)protestingissimo
      re nokomprennytablemate
         "mYPLESHEr"
   (c)implacablissimo(And How)
      telling ye world
         "OW rfathuz nmothus dIDnh AV them UNeewEEh AV"
   (d)loudly
      to sovereign potentate mogul benevolent very,peacefully who
surveys 1 nudegal flaunting Young at beo
   "why"(injured)"don't you let us know when the train's leaving?"
   "I do" smiling our genial upglancing conductor protested mildly
(incredulous)"yas?"
   "I" very indeed gently our "say,four minutes before:En voiture
messieurs s'il vous plaît!"
   (scowandhowling)"what does that mean?"

"that means" cheerfulest "All Aboard"

(snarl) "doesn't mean anything to me" (shrug) "y' might as well say" (sneer) "tuhtuhtuh tuhtuhtuh" (sic)

"everybody" omniscience almost "can't speak English" invisibly reminded him

(!with a hideous starestart and a low kindof sortof lush groan) "A-hh-hhH . . . I never thought of that . . ."

"You should" very, returning, to, verily "have a dictionary"

pause. Then:horribly

"you should have a" the son of mammon yelled "sign saying—GET ON THE TRAIN"

night

(through cricketsobs & birdcries the train ploughs;the train with its own shadows,its own lights)

unI am sitting(the nexttothelast timeless)in shawdan. To unmy right,unsheltered by a not quite ridiculous unhedge,the nonwoman shaped like a bear is wooing the nonman shaped like a seal. Some (ponderously)where behind unme,lolls apelike redsoldiershape; unhis footlike hand framing a cigaretteless. To the left unis an unembarrassed disyouth,possibly European probably not—he almost might be not quite anything. & the fountain before unme brings not quite tears to unmy almost throat:such complicatedly And How simplification;4 timid jets emphasize a semihearty 5th—and snug under this 5th(in a sortofa kindofa rack-or-cradle)sleeps a huge ball,drenched by real descending water;a painted sphere . . . doing nothing. The foolish fallen water rattles softly;the curves and angles of the metal pipes shimmer with a tranquil and credible silliness. But through the pretty idiocy of metal and foolish samely plash—directly across from herenow myselfless appears:structure,5 human heads 5 mortal faces. They unexist differently each from another. They not quite might be alive. (What are they doing? 1 seems speaking,gently;seem 4 listening,earnestly. The youngest talks now,the others hear;the fellow with the cap says,his friends wait). Do I understand those 5 heads? No. (Would they cheerily wring this neck? Pair-haps). Might all be gangsters or merely politicians? Possibly both:but all seem filled with some(utterly to My Country 'Tis Of and distinctly incomprehensible)thing:seriousness. Each speaks in turn,softly,then listens attentively to his neighbour. (Those voices seem firm,those eyes seem eager). To those eyes I do not exist—I never shall exist,I never have existed. Those eyes,which do not see the absurd fountain,cannot have not and shall never see my

dream

Spring:and unwe go out(cringing through what And How luxurious portal)into night(unwe step into dark warm air;a moving,swarming,of appearances;green leaves,softlyful sounds,mystery;warm bodies,strolling cajoling,squirming-whistling gigg ling,muttermurmuring)dive unwe through a seem of dim forms to the-sudden-cool-pavement. . . . Beneath,very fiercely,a paralysed port glitters:unvisibly beyond,its ocean chorneeyeh(nicht Blau)moryeh . . . Unwe turn. Past unus human float semblances drift through night,shapes throng through Spring

shapes alike,childish,all legs and awkwardness,shyly talking all tittering clumsily

the merciless and motley proletarian parade. Some of these are girls;many of these girls are pretty,most of these prettinesses cannot help themunselves. Elsewhere being whatever makes life beautiful or exuberant,here merely life seems. Merely and ghostfully here seems Seem. Not actual,nor beauty:ghostfully sprawled spawning flesh;merely desiring opened nerves. Beauty nyet,Love nyet—but flat,but dense(but craving)ghostlife. It is how graceless,this ghostthingless! How predetermined! How considered obstinate allpremeditated joyless(it seems to say Hello;you—look at unme,alias the future,alias zahftrah—do not wonder,you;every question has its answer—here is unme(here is the answer of a species and the answer is Take This Face Multiply By Any Number And Subtract Death)). . . . Meanwhileless a wind moves the moves in the leaves a,helpless glares paralysed glitters. & spectres wander. Are they hopeless? Not at all;they have never felt what hope is. Are they hopeful? Never;they merely can seem. Merely they seemingly cry(Hello;you—a phenomenon has occurred—do not attempt to formulate it—& if lightning strikes a barn and exterminates the pig who lives in the barn do not measure the lightning by the pig or the pig by the lightning & goodbye). . . . Are these infantile ghosts or shadows clumsy? Yes. And How. They float and swirl clumsily upon skilful night. Efficiently they wear just enough to attract each other. Now they seem how only a little less—the merely how little!—as they splash clumsily through this darkness which unwe breathe,clumsy than when strolling nakedly those nonbeaches which unwe have wan-dered.

—Factoryfodder all,all machines' meat,efficiently disporting itselfless necessarily itselfless seeking automatically finding itselfless. Directed flesh,managed vitality,conditioned purpose. Movement sans precision illusion or collision,delusion painless exact joyless;clumsiness incapable of ecstasy or of agony:moveunmovingunmovemoving. Linear and logical religion of Of. Predicted,futile,necessary And How cult alias the because. . . . But—ecco!—even these ghostbreasts are firm,even these ghostgirls walk with high bosoms;under their very foolishness lives health (Young!)from whose utter silliness radiates very dignity. Night stinks of foolishness but reeks of dignity. Staggers with silliness but with health struts

Spring

(for Lachaise makes manprouderect

and Rodin could make a statue of man-à-la-chaise

and a sculptor disguised as(please)a man did make a statue of a(please do)man disguised as a sculptor and who is(please do not)in the act of making(please do not believe)a statue of a man disguised as a(please do not believe me)gladiator,sic

page Mr. Santakarl Marxclaus)

"excusez!" . . . I'd supposed he was long ago jolly well tucked in the upper . . . respectful blushing who dons pyj(hastily)ama(dis

appear

ing)murmurs

". . . j'étais dans le costume de monsieur Adam"

(a moving slowly through sunlight WorldWoman struggling with(gently
in sun snowil(struGGling)ylight)worlds A world-voice crying to great
eyes plucking for small hands her)worlds.

Créateur du ciel et de la terre,
et les bat(collid)(entangl)eaux(dis)(ing)&(crisp tini(now)-ly howfleet—
Leap;stoopsailsing:veerbrighthulls!&1(a.the caught un,der al?ways
wwaatteerrffaallll))young childdreams old

comment aurait-il des enfants,
& p lo ddi ng l yd onk ey s nowflic(which,ear)urgedonby shY-cries &
p:hi:los:ophi(pullings olemnl yaliv edollsi ncars)cally astaregoats disd.
ainful o & merRygOrounD Especially The Trees The Avenues And
gui("atten-tion")Gardens(",monsieur!")gnols

lui qui n'a pas de compagne?

(and such of ocean there will an immeasurable distance be)balancing
will there what immensity be the of sky(will hurlthrob of against night
riding there be suddenly mountains)

ago week A,a Week
ago;Ago week a:
a week ago.
AGO WEEK A

—

"comment?"
lypect(toandfroing heatedly in heat And How in pyj)points
Flatness

(what was that American bathroom station?when mustachios)
I "douane?" query;vaguest
nod
(flat unnoise. A platform without human. Formless. Deathful-
empty)

They Have Shut It AGAIN said pointing WHILSTward jolres Dirty
Foul Disgusting Filthy FEMALES
grunt(I &

—

oga

Monsieur Adam staggers as they splash clumsily through shapes like children subtract All Aboard nipples Puff. Engines means wink darkness STOPPAGE The Greater Miss Turkey for ruins,they make all their rugs by fireflies among little white guy(with blue glasses)Rings: lingadinga. In such very gush gaily like petals made of ONE MEAT paper Round swings the Ford cars are golden anemones Toys only distance rush bargained for cages are moving birds eyes,death;freckles and apple hugE w-a-i-l mom aboil,O sir this is a street called Breathes new Nowhere suspenders pound?civilization It's All Aboard!the ark & Eddie's cherub's night's;a match's pulLpulL AND BE QUICK par ici,dude not,sorrow spherically remembering each contradiction surely and of no thing conscious except And Trees THANKS. !YES. (1 by 1)caviar w-a-i-t-i-n-g;own toilet!encourages Initiative?chainstores the man with the patent mistake horse's face forgot to;I mean a picture of a Hallelujah was given two years and,by;god:We're;back,in(not French)but everybody here seems to play the gumorning:Wait. There should be blankets without whom agony will not a fineness(s a f)rail shrIEking frANZ esquire,and(ree-ling)lurch-es to sell their bodies I've never been so prophylactic veev 3 dozen moans imperson & A Dream GET MEE?Any Roubles?Ordnance!!!1 package of—TRAVAILLER!Hah;rah;shoh and Uh POUND Uv BUTTUR the Last?comes-on & comes-off drunk etceteras,child seizes shadow:a real coon not probably earth's Two Good equals Morale it's so funny laugh—REEAY!BOOVAY!MONJAY! Up comes dignity turnstile syehvohdnyah)

   ago

(. . . day I was . . . which doesn't . . .)today;& whisperfully dark bozo a very terrifying haven't killed her yet she died a raving atom of completely squashed TRUE!!!Everything is loosening. Freedom is what matters,because I was just wondering if you haven't yet scratched the Bon voyage:I want to buy dollars! I must autograph you cannot turn the train will go she shoots that unstructure with eagles. And you'll need all those dismal little things a thumping screaming band! preposterous:Nature,always,same—For all,comrade I write pinkeyed rabbits windmills drunkening kindness to animals 2 phibetas are you carrying man's my father of my children I Kiev!—jerk-hideous -exlovenest air:SPACE—The churches are drowning in comrades & shadows dear god Geld zahlen cherchez la equals:when in doubt,buy a giftstore(BRGONXFH!)foghorns baby dim mess of legarms welter of

finhooves Kommen American corres- NYET!! & a gate but why Kiev?why
pipe-elf-blacksmith-brakemanish-ghost-and ½ . . . —Bleiben Sie shoes on
impossible!Ocean ist Blau!a bidet in a small oldmiddleaged good,huh?fair
uhnuf Ringer young shine?les siddown HAY j'étais fou shine?we're here
because ain so turrible,pausing near where those great stairs begin their
steep Electricity?kindness. Rain & the worm What like shot deer;Head
flowers!people feel freer. Mee?says thih genurul that next god damned
why not?everything's forever simply lousy Futile She is living for the future
SAMEness!—choochoo kookoo poopoo googoo Nut wun bee-utsh,yis
a nook pouting advancing coyly essays now & & & Down. dowN.
—Arcadia?downupdown hardest thing,it's nicht vergessen and mentor
tore up sheets,buzzjoo mushyoo was a musician bad news Kumon Sun
a barbedwire Dante,O baw poor luh drooling female vast naked unfirm
enormous sob ma maison serait la yunno Sun a(gentlest)Salute!(day which
doesn't exist)because of tomorrow(NYET zahftrah—TOMORROW)

alias demain S.V.P.
   for oggi:alias caldo;equals Italia,alias
   Hot.
            dolce country here & now fa niente people swarm smile gape
sprawl bubble silprettyliness no more the sterile starving pastures no
more the barren shaggy language. Only
   hOt
            -ter than . . . Exactly. His country. . . . Ah,but how pleasant a
luscious a positively agreeable a sweet and lovely and absolutely habitable
inferno was my distinguished predecessor's;yea,& is(for that matter)even
this Simplon this even Orient even this even Express this—compared with
a certainly uncertain realm I've impossibly And How recently explored!
Terrors of the pit?tortures of the flesh?merde! What's,after all,merely
   hoT
   ?compared(enter white;by child pridefully escorted and proudly
bearing
   Unless
            that next god damned word?
                                             Reason?)with
   —now—
   (or am I dead)
   hot

ecco Venezia:alias Venise;equals Venice & memories . . . San Marco
we knew,first street I lost in . . . alias

merely a miraculous(a prodigious)ly wickedly unbreathable railway-
station. Si. DEJEUNER we gahlstookless(pour qu'elle peut respirer)in-
Orient-in-station(à la doll within a doll within a)we within Within(miles
aeons)alias heatsquared

. . . alias plusorminus glimpse of(leant.wist Sunroa-sting)dreammen
proimpelling(across si si burning this piece-of-spaceless not air)that;
a:sandola(I dream)

if only something happens if only
this agony will not if
something will
not this
if only if
Alive

    (Rain making alive)ness uttered comes(all marvellous
transforming magical all being Rain)newly,arrives hugely(& swooping
the)merciful;now(amazingly)with how alive gifts laden:beautifully the
sharp the great wish;the,Now(falling from when immeasurable where
with a forever cry)!

nyet
imposs
can't

    (wake to find myself spelling it to)myself,the;god:damned
HOT
I
who(clutching unsudden life
smile)—I like everything
I

don't care it doesn't matter because 1(angular squats)(droops hugging
a)gently a(& I supposed that I had known . . . of a than any universe
older faceless;and such eyes,flowers of complete . . .

)
a
m
e
n

Dinner:sweat,runs(not drips)rolls continuously purls & uninter-
ruptedly pours rains yes(Lugete,)rains down all me over my throughout
self who just a god damned blooming sits who can you babbling brook
who imagine no really who no if who anything

—directly opposite the remains of poor once-jolly(of still,if melting
steadily-&-fragrantly,respectful)1 absolutely contained(positively
comprised And How)signora inglese(1 not more sweatless than perhaps
Mont Blanc where is it or don't we)toys(and we shall come home)with 1:
Greater,Hotel;Saint then irredescentishfulously orders(in the And How
language not to mention patois of so to speak the country or environs
or soi-disant district or if you like locale or whathaveyou(I have only
amazement)a,1,one,glass of acqua minerale . . . meanwhile touchable
almost through openness ecco(—an islandvillagio:just so picturesque
it kindof sortof hurts—)lake. & mountains downdashing mountains
skybumping rocketing crazily mountains)&

a-n-d
it
would
take
HAHRAHSHOH
—aria
     suddenly!
now & everything.changes.pass gray villages.alias.snug as a bug.
little.smug in a rug.little.nestling acme of.priggery.Suisse(& what
skies!)
softer;softest O
Now,we are,saved cool I,can feel air you,may breathe soon will
be,night and then no,more Sunday sUnday,suNday sunday,SUN(day
. . . lurch;:.)
oui la machine feels ja der Zug responds It leans il treno toward night
toward breathe toward cool(mightily & through mountains leaping
is)into tomorrow . . .
si,si
gnor
toward
demain
ogA

447

(. . . day I was . . . which doesn't . . .)today;& I'm only happy in the Poles are more they go into a conference. Have you seen naked bee-essers who hand out a huge gorillaface recalls Hello air,Air,AIR so very many better was not made of climb & climbing leave The & a reddish beard(rightturn)old ghost old skull I did not move as when a man whose eyelids moveunmove 3 comrades move;unshaven bearded,all toward Un-moveunmove,hoof foot- claw fin- hand- Our-not-his:face Face move-do-not-move—eachotherish numberlessly Smilingless.(stooping in their deathskins)dirt dirt's father was killed by the Darksmoothlyestishful (yellow whirls on)intolerance isn't an everything's a question of trust-worthy saw the American certainly dresses at Gogol's statue I-want-you do-me a lit-tle fa-vor . . . an—suddenly are words Are you happy give Rose(that universal language!)have a purpose:he says he means unrooms nasty with fearhush.in August allow me Noone can dare to grow(she was tall)doll and 2 real communist schoolbooks for 4 34full Don't worry . . . Russia's miraculous . . . really electric personified(micro- smiles sadly,studying carefully atrocity)out of the un- . . . going you—are not . . . a cap- knough . . . & appear letters,words;skilfully and we shall hoo-weye doo-yoo goe-too 1 soft grouch is nyet Bang!Crabs hellish tomorrow?a poet little kitten He wasn't an idea. He wasn't a person who takes so long to the world is Probably Russians Good painters on voudrait the bottom of the sea. Now comrade who,not I(my life?)P flopstruts luck lies a what,what do you pistol,of all more less,more simply darling & bolshoy means upstairs egocentrically Vive I like I Am a little I said many threelegged Queen Mab Wood's head redhot forms horseshoelike hole— Are you married(eyes)little like a goldfish — including Chinesey(O Paris!I dream)Feed an American all my toes and what's sexual about Nat is honest And who wins the all -ists are tasteless Come in!a three rouble boy!(black grandmother)fier I bow,white ample A child opens knock. Folk you lost in the gulf of(stolsintheirbreeches) askew bangs robin cricket we Russians are blonde nonlooks my mother collected stray(simply) goatee too elongated gruesomely(especially candlesticks)Charlie! There won't be elephants The Last Decisive Laughter a Gay-Pay I grin STAND UP!(And How)staggerstuttering machinegunfire . . . blunder and I'm speaking as a friend of No Diner. of whom=Phi pawnshop motif a different Will live with millionaire soul was his military Yahvas je crois. Out of do not pity pity only those who sorry and very this little engineer came to the earthly u— u— u—u

u–u u– u–u u–   eyes of the world,relax;open Or any man with
roots ye dead Xmas tree dog?tough I(feel=a word)& unbelievably
Matisse!incredible—Picasso . . . oasis a sacred in Disappointment I see
you with two children publicity!Tverskaya:1 claps while 2 wobble—
never is,or will be(and what eyes!)They don't ring sleeping Turk's wife,
delighted,& climb. CREAM an His Master's wig(exile)tovarich curtain
descends intermission a large cloth rock but am lost. Something's,née
Sunshine,the Ay Pee man the person to change it is locked out 2
unknown 1 carrotheaded Revolutionary ogress's day

ago

1 omelet bellyward.day which the day I was barberpolemiracle- opium
H meaning anywhere bourgeois Lack marble-and-really the best looking
pinwheelish O no. Your name arrived in perfect cringecurltwitch—Crash—
quietly Out;We:DeeDum The Big Heart can kiss my Interim,shall we
say,life?pas payer,I feel. It is no longer. Tell him I'm afraid to be on top of
all Moscow go by on the architect's ça sent la boyhat and piescout it can't
be turned reelingly woman's touch bfghjklmnpqrstvwxyz SH:Moral:kopeks
waving a tower of slowly A world in the head is worth two unworlds in the
rab meaning Let's hope the child is not vashez poor Moscow hears Quiets
with—Dance!?!kwass is goldilocks Tips it's a she it's a lie!—speak. Demolish
the feathery crosses pyjamas mysterious theness of who this night dies.
Beautifully and who awakens,unearthly Meaning latchkey ½ of 1 Kem-
min-kz shall also look Under humanity's sloppail acreep with "art"(or
whatever actually is)SHCHOT 20 and riding unmeanings carved into
warm made us lie Garbo almighty to hell with that kitt'n dam chair
PEE-VOH!bellows:a church and some toctic il pleut Oxford DAwailing,
leisure is peuplier pickle split,skies into Dreambird!Friendship's boomjets
unvoice la lune Volks the Kremlin jail Grouch 2+2=(not;not butterfly?)
what?flyspecked hailstones Elsewhereish firm curling questions?
(kngaercgfkaeuqs)who are we?papierohsa,flockgush AND WILL
sterilization three cheers for the!world poster popping . . . he skips:Piscator
TairREEBLE 1 word. Yes sah. Mammy god Harold floorsoap and
roadapples Free Love. And lilacs red oh:boy & sope -among-men 83 blue
the nailpuller dishmop like kings HAS everything horsefat they're tired a
flowery,frail self inhabits 1 huge may relax between breasts.laughing will
there be elephants? . . . socialist reek smiting haven't any pants!—DUROV
a motheaten ALL EUROPEAN Superfinale of mashed bloody steak real
American breakfast locked out mutters,drowsily sucking god's

?FRANCE?

    & O my mon good bon they're robbing I'm help a victim disgraceful liars outrageous thieves cows camels the bandits "ils ont dévalisé ma malle

    !"

—dark

-ness

      "ils m'embêtent!"

unjollydisifspectreful dit

What's upstarting I whatshout—up?

(l-ightal-l:c-abindrenchedwit-h)

    . . . he's dragging & down valises tumbling & into pantalons ducking & through bretelles & ontwitching chausettes stamp&intoing chausures . . . meandeep radiowhilevoices I'm Going To Sleep la voix du mogul An American somebody Where du mogul Here:Diplomatic(sic)Passport . . . O nom de

    paraît

    que my

    coffinmate found himself

    unexpectedly confronted with 1

    formidable tax upon sunsunsundry artartarticles

by him imported(sans benefit of declaration)from where they lie and they steal from where they don't attack you from where they make rugs from where nobody changes from as it were kind of you know what in other pour ainsi dire Syria

    &(who returns)gnashing his

    (wringing)squirting oaths(reeling

    with indignation)woe

    (disenchantment)rage

    (disgust)

"!J'ai Payé Deux Cent Cinquante FRANCS!"

    —O

      G

      A

day I was born;also a day which doesn't exist,in the eau chaude of this diminutive teapot which roosts precariously atop an old man standing asleep beside Karl Santa Claus MARX SAID,if you can imagine a

cube,black and with a canopener—are you shy?if I hadn't been so
IMPERSONAL:It's like poker(That fate worse than death)& my trousers
fly on. Applause with the drowned man(but not a monosyllable)is
the terror of how do you do,Doctor,squatting in your dissimilar oo-
Bor-neye-ah we FEEL,1 new,1 old;both small and not too disappear
is Ta-de-de- dodger('tis himself not a picture)something moving is ten
years ago I you can't!nyeh hahchoo Something Fabulous L's M a filthy
big baby stealthily WHAT'S—a tension?that pill!Bolshoy means:
it's the cap—And time moans in(that serious disease)of marble-or-
something INTOURIST of wonderful one hoss;for both of us haven't
the train's. Deer in Sir Ladybug's world of Was hammer and a sickle and
sonofabitch—over nearly everything a mirror has been bandaged you
smoke mystic Thelike change,that's something in people are writing's as
funny . . . but life,life! Enlivened by si je me vous ne ça(lower of gent:
Verb The be to seems

    seems
    to be
    shutun)through which
    peering or(shut)myself
    (ness)partially which through I

am that unfeeling eachotherishly multitude of impotent timidities of
numerable items of guilty particles which
    are not dead are not alive are
    in time in space are in
    denying trying fearing of(which
    itfully And hatingly How possibly undreaming are that not shining
called real picture monotonously moveunmoving
    of seem)unseems to be
    through not which(or
    myselfless)beautifully into
    everywhere and
    always

leaning I am this hurling inexhaustibly from june huge rushing
    upon august until whirlingly with
    harvest huger happens bloodily prodigious october
    (golden supremely hugest daemon glittering with abundance

with fulfilment gleaming creature magnificent complete brutal intense
miraculously and)
    finally
    (and what
    stars)descendingly assuming
    only shutting gradually this
    perfection(and I am)becoming

silently
        made
               of
                    silent.
                          &

silence is made of
    (behind perfectly or
    final rising
    humbly
    more dark
    most luminous proudly
    whereless fragrant whenlessly erect
    a sudden the!entirely blossoming)

Voice
    (Who:
    Loves;
    Creates,
    Imagines)
    OPENS

Afterword

by

Norman Friedman

I.

Cummings's thirty-six-day journey to Russia and back during the spring of 1931 found the Soviet Union in its ninth year of existence and the Western world a year and a half into the Great Depression. Both areas of the world were in upheaval; the West trying to patch up its failed economic system, and the USSR engaging in a draconian effort to reconstruct its entire society from the ground up. Lenin died in 1924 and a power struggle ensued, centering ultimately on Stalin versus Trotsky, with Stalin emerging as the undisputed dictator in 1928. Agriculture was collectivized and industrialization sped up, but—what was not fully grasped until later—at great cost in human liberties and lives.

During the first decade of Stalin's reign, many artists and intellectuals of the West, distraught over the inequalities, poverty, and suffering endemic in capitalist society during the Depression, were impressed by the supposed idealism and egalitarianism professed by the Soviet state, and began to contrast the promise of socialism with the failure of our own culture and economy. These included such writers and critics as Edmund Wilson, Sherwood Anderson, James T. Farrell, Malcolm Cowley, and Alfred Kazin. Even Hemingway and Fitzgerald, almost wholly devoted to other concerns, felt the pull of this struggle in *To Have and Have Not* (1934, 7), *For Whom the Bell Tolls* (1940), and *The Last Tycoon* (1941). Some, such as Sidney Hook, John Dos Passos, and Theodore Dreiser, preceded Cummings in visiting the Soviet Union to see for themselves; others, such as Paul Robeson and Richard Wright, joined the Communist Party, only to become painfully disillusioned later.

Cummings too was interested in the Soviet experiment in the twelve years before his visit to Russia. There are half a dozen references in his

Selected Letters (edited by F. W. Dupree and George Stade; New York: Harcourt, Brace, 1969) to Russia and Communism between 1919 and 1923, and they are usually positive—although it should be noted that this was pre-Stalin. The conclusion of a letter to his father in 1923 states, after some remarks about international affairs, "As usual, I admire Russia" (104). He writes from Paris to his mother in April of 1931, "have applied for a Russian visa which, if am the lil lawd fongleroi they wish—should arrive in 2 weeks: intend to reach Moscow on or before May day (international celebrations): receive Russian lessons daily . . . " (121). His actual visit occurred during the third year of Stalin's long and brutal reign.

Curiously, Jack London, that proponent of the vigorous life and survival of the fittest, who had died in 1916, was still enormously popular in the Soviet Union during that time. He plays a significant role in *Eimi* because chief among Cummings's hosts during his stay in Russia were Jack London's daughter, Joan, and her husband Charles Malamuth, a Slavic languages professor from the University of California who was working as a journalist in Russia. In his diaristic way, Cummings refers to her as "Lack Dungeon's daughter," and also as Beatrice, alluding to Dante (a significant reference throughout *Eimi*), also Turkess or Harem, as her husband is called Turk or Assyrian.

In addition to making Cummings's stay in Moscow more comfortable, hosting and guiding him, the Malamuths provided an island of sanity for him in their prescient realization that the price of the Communist experiment was far greater than its rewards, Cummings recounts a number of conversations with them about that tragic disparity. This prescience was not shared by Cummings's other guide in Moscow, Henry Wadsworth Longfellow Dana, a Harvard theater professor and apologist for the regime, termed variously by Cummings as Virgil (via Dante), mentor, and benefactor.

It was not until the Nazi-Soviet Pact of 1939 that many previously sympathetic artists and intellectuals of the West began to suspect that the ostensible dictatorship of the proletariat in Russia was in fact the dictatorship of Stalin, as cruel and barbarous a despot as any Tartar chieftain or Mongol potentate. In 1953, the year of Stalin's death, Cummings wrote to his sister: "In 1931 I went to Russia, & what I found may be refound by anybody capable of reading a book called Eimi. Since (grâce à mass 'education'—the 'bread & circuses' of contemporary

Caesarhood) almost nobody can read practically anything, let me add that I wouldn't like 'communism' if 'communism' were good" (223).

From the perspective of the latter years of the twentieth century we can see with greater clarity not only the terrible price of the Russian experiment but also the historical fact of its utter failure.

II.

While *Eimi* is sometimes termed a "novel," often with the supposed consent of its author, it is in fact of a travel-journal or travel-diary, in which the life experience of the writer is the primary organizing principle, however artistically elaborated. In a novel, the life experience of the author, if such is being used for the purpose, is artistically subordinate to the story, plot, or action presented.

And *Eimi* is indeed elaborated from Cummings's on-the-spot jottings in his notebooks. It is loosely structured along the lines of Dante's *Divine Comedy*, which he pointedly refers to a number of times. Cummings even fashions a frame of sorts by covering a period of thirty-six consecutive days, beginning and ending on a Sunday. Yet its overall structure remains that of a chronological account of his doings, encounters, thoughts, and feelings on a day-to-day basis—almost hourly—as he negotiates through the difficulties and pleasures of his visit. So too is his other great prose work, *The Enormous Room*, not a "novel," though it also has an archetypal frame along the lines of Bunyan's *Pilgrim's Progress*.

Coming in at just short of 430 pages in 1933, *Eimi* is Cummings's longest published work, and into it he poured all of the art and vision he had achieved to date. Behind him were eight published volumes: *The Enormous Room* (1922), *Tulips & Chimneys* (1923), *XLI Poems* (1925), *is 5* (1926), *HIM* (1927), *No Title* (1930), *CIOPW* (1931), and *W* (*ViVa* [1931]). And as with those earlier works, *Eimi* is a stylistic tour de force, only more so. Although written mostly in prose, it is in a mélange of styles and tones, also accommodating a number of lyrical passages, some of them spaced on the page as verse—albeit in Cummings's distinctive kind of spacing. The prose itself is experimental, containing many abbreviations, typographical devices, compounds, grammatical-syntactical shifts, and word coinages—ways of fracturing the meaning in a Cubist manner in aiming to embody his sense of timelessness in the midst of time, a vision which may properly be seen as a form of transcendentalism.

Published eleven years before *Eimi*, *The Enormous Room* already contained the beginnings of Cummings's characteristic ways with prose in the service of his vision, his attempts to manifest "that precision which creates movement."[1] So did some of the speeches in *HIM* or the Dadaist prose in *No Title*. More specifically, the style in *Eimi* answers to the need to record more accurately the disruptions he experienced in the disjointed and incongruous Alice-in-Wonderland world of the Soviet Union, so shiny in its professed idealism, so shabby in its manifestations.

Echoing some of the ideas, words, and phrases of his 1920 essay on the sculptor Gaston Lachaise, Cummings peppers *Eimi* with repetitions of "is," "am," "the verb," the "actual" versus the merely "real," feeling versus thinking, "alive" versus "undead," "give" versus "keep," and art versus politics. Russia is the land of "un," "a world of Was," "the apotheosis of isn't," a "joyless experiment in force and fear." The clothes are shapeless, the food is tasteless, the women are "nonmen," even the circus is dreary. He feels he is in a gray landscape of somnambulists. Thus he is even more ready than usual to greet the blossoming spring flowers, the rain descending softly, and the occasional apparition of an alive human being.

Far from causing Cummings to develop his transcendental vision in reaction to his experiences in the descendental Soviet Union, as some have suggested, his encounter with the Russian subhuman superstate, to use his own lingo, served primarily to *confirm* his already established position, which he had put forth, not only in his Lachaise essay, but also in *The Enormous Room* of 1922 and *Tulips & Chimneys* of 1923. It confirmed Cummings's position so by exposing him to a form of society diametrically opposed to it. He had had, of course, ample opportunity to criticize the society of his own United States before this time—its commercialism, materialism, phony patriotism, and so on—but in Russia he saw all the faults of an industrial society magnified a hundredfold by virtue of the political dictatorship under which that unfortunate county was laboring. And in both cases the arrival of World War II provided some relief, however tragic and costly.

Let me quote three brief but revelatory passages to catch the true flavor

---

[1] From Cummings's Foreword to *is* 5 (1926).

of Cummings's basic theme. "Government's merely an exteriorization, isn't it?an outward symbol?a projection?" (117). "What a murderfully vast difference exists between 'standing up for an idea' (between combatting unvalues;for instance,American unvalues)and inhabiting the 'practice' 'of' an 'idea', inhabiting socalled socialist Russia!" (186–187). "Should unpoets [i.e., scientists] live their unlives,people would live lives,people would eat when hungry;people would unlearn how not to hunger without eating(that most redoubtable goal of progress life civilization whathaveyou etcetera)" (402). There is a Zen koan—"When I am hungry, I eat; when I am tired, I sleep"—whose meaning will become additionally relevant as we proceed.

III.

The journey and the book begin reaching for their climax, with "prophecy" and "revelation," during the last two days of their return trip to Paris. These terms are taken from Cummings's own interpretation in his "Sketch for a Preface," where he says, under the heading of June 13, the penultimate day of his journey homeward, "I stroll out to see our locomotive,& address it in terms of *prophecy*(436–437). And *revelation* (437)" The prophecy is Cummings's address at a station stop to the locomotive which is bringing him back: "metal steed,very treacherously wherefrom descending the promiscuous urbans plundered rus!through you I greet all itgods," against whom he counterposes "a totally adventuring Is Who breathes,not hope and not despair,but timeless deep unspace—" who is Poietes (himself, the poet), "for guilt may not cancel instinct and logic defeat wish . . . " In other words, organic transcendentalism will not be defeated by materialism and industrialism.

There follows the revelation, the concluding lines of the sixteenth poem of the *Tao Te Ching*, attributed to Lao Tzu, supposedly an older contemporary of Confucius (551–479 B.C.):

> he who knoweth the eternal is comprehensive;
> comprehensive, therefore just;
> just, therefore a king;
> a king, therefore celestial;
> celestial, therefore in Tao;
> in Tao, therefore enduring;
> without hurt he suffereth the loss of the body (438–39)

The essence of Taoism lies in the principle of "nonaction," which is not at all equivalent to "no-action." Rather, it refers to a way of acting consonant with the organic order of Nature and the Given. "Transcendence" for Cummings, then, means being alive in the ongoing flux of the present, the "actual," as we have seen, as opposed to settling for the static categories of habit in the merely "real" world, an issue Cummings characteristically expressed as "feeling" versus "thinking." To realize that this vision is not simply an exotic piece of Orientalism, consider Wordsworth's "wise passiveness," Keats's "negative capability," or Tolstoy's portrayal of General Kutuzov in *War and Peace* as one who "had only the capacity for the calm contemplation of the course of events," "instead of intellect grasping events and making plans." Thus, sixty years ahead of his time, Cummings condemns the self-contradictory experiment: you cannot "perfect" human life by killing thousands of human beings.

IV.

Upon its publication in 1933, nearly two years after the journey itself, *Eimi* was bound to kick up a storm among the reviewers and the reading public. Almost fifty reviews appeared during that same year, and they were, of course, mixed. Most obviously, the book ran counter to the mood of many at that time, that socialism offered a viable alternative to the evident failure of capitalism. Cummings's clear anti-Soviet position worked against him. In addition, the difficult experimental style of the book provoked the scorn of anti-modernists. But there were a few who understood what Cummings was doing and approved.

S. Foster Damon wrote in April 1933, "The people he encounters form a whole gallery of brilliant portraits: . . . they are allowed their right to exist in the universe, silly or dirty or cruel though they may be." In July, Paul Rosenfeld said, "*Eimi* of all his works alone expresses a self-consciousness, a clear intellectual possession and absolute certainty of the divinity which all along has been at work in him." Marianne Moore in August: "the typography . . . is not something superimposed on the meaning but the author's mental handwriting." In December of the following year, Ezra Pound instructed his British readers that to be a writer is "to take it in at the pores, and lay it out there pellucidly on the page in all its Slavic unfinishedness, in all of its Dostoievskian slobberyness, brought up to date . . . Does any man wish to know about Russia? 'EIMI'!"

The story of the book's career after the 1930s is, alas, spotty. Cummings returned to his poetry, publishing *No Thanks* in 1935—the title thumbing its nose at all the publishers who rejected it—and *Collected Poems* in 1938, which at last consolidated and extended his reputation as a poet. His only other prose works thereafter were *i: six nonlectures* (1953), *A Miscellany* (1958, 1965), and *Fairy Tales* (1965). But a few serious studies of *Eimi* were published during these years and thereafter, including chapters in my *Growth of a Writer* and Richard S. Kennedy's two books on Cummings. Several dissertations, completed or underway, are promising, and one hopes that a perspective of seventy years or more will stimulate, both regarding its politics and its experimental style, a broader and deeper interest in *Eimi*—a hope which this new edition will help fulfill.

V.

Eimi was first published on March 28, 1933, by Covici, Friede, Inc. This edition was limited to 1,381 copies, according to the number of orders received. A second printing was subsequently issued during that same year. Covici, Friede had also published *No Title* in 1930 and *CIOPW* in 1931. (Portions of *Eimi* had been previously published in *Hound & Horn* in 1932, which explains why Cummings referred to it in his 1932 Introduction to the 1934 Modern Library edition of *The Enormous Room*.)

A second edition of *Eimi* was issued sixteen years later by William Sloane Associates, Inc., consisting of 1,500 copies.

The Grove Press edition came out in 1958, 3,000 copies paperbound and 100 copies clothbound. A specially bound edition was limited to twenty-six numbered copies signed by the author. Cummings's title "Sketch for a Preface to the Fourth Edition of *Eimi*" is an error: the Grove Press edition is the *third*.

Thus the present edition is the fourth, after a gap of almost fifty years—the largest interval so far. George J. Firmage, Cummings's devoted editor and bibliographer, reset and corrected the whole so that the reading and scholarly public may more than ever before enjoy one of Cummings's most substantial accomplishments.

—Flushing, New York, 1997